Violet Jacob (1863–1946) was born Violet Kennedy-Erskine at the family home at Dun near Montrose on the north-east coast of Scotland. Erskines had lived at the House of Dun since the fifteenth century and Violet published the family history as *The Lairds of Dun* in 1931. Her father died when Violet was young and she lost a sister and a brother in later years, but her childhood was a happy one and she retained a close attachment to the countryside and the broad Scots spoken there. She was artistic with a penchant for flower illustration, and some of her early works and her diaries from India contained drawings and paintings.

In 1894 she married Arthur Jacob, an Irish officer serving in the British Army. After the birth of her son Harry in 1895, Violet joined her husband on service in India where she recorded her experiences for the next four years in letters and diaries (published by Canongate in 1990). It was during this time that she began her first novel *The Sheepstealers* (1902) a historical story of rural protest set in the Welsh borders – where her mother was born. *The Interloper* followed in 1904 with a tale of character conflict and small-town tensions in 'Kaims', a fictional version of Montrose.

Violet returned to England when Arthur's regiment took him to South Africa and the Boer War, and apart from a spell together in Egypt, their life was spent in garrison towns in England. After the success of *The Sheepstealers* Jacob continued to write novels and short stories, *The Golden Heart and Other Fairy Stories* (1905), *Irresolute Catherine* (1908), *The History of Aythan Waring* (1908), *The Fortune Hunters and Other Stories* (1910) and *Flemington* (1911), which used Montrose and some of her own family history for her finest historical novel about the turbulent times of the 1745 rising.

The Jacobs visited India again in the early 1920s, but Violet was haunted by memories of her son who had been killed at the Somme in 1916. Jacob had published some verses in her early years, but with *Songs of Angus* (1915) she started to write in a Scots vernacular which looked back to the Doric tradition of Charles Murray and forward to the Scots lyrics of MacDiarmid. *More Songs of Angus* followed in 1918, with *Bonnie Joann and Other Poems* (1921) and *The Northern Lights and Other Poems* (1927). The same desire to make contact with her early upbringing led to the short stories in *Tales of My Own Country* (1922), and those later collected in *The Lum Hat and Other Stories: Last Tales of Violet Jacob* (1982).

Violet Jacob was awarded an honorary LLD from Edinburgh in 1936. After her husband's death she retired to Kirriemuir where she spent the last ten years of her life.

Violet Jacob

FLEMINGTON

&

TALES FROM ANGUS

edited and introduced by

Carol Anderson

CANONGATE
CLASSICS
83

Flemington first published in 1911 in Great Britain by John Murray. This version first published in 1994 in Great Britain by the Association for Scottish Literary Studies. *Tales from Angus* first published in *Tales of My Own Country* (John Murray, 1922) and *The Lum Hat and Other Stories: Last Tales of Violet Jacob* (Aberdeen University Press, 1982) Aberdeen. This edition first published as a Canongate Classic in 1998 by Canongate Books, 14 High Street, Edinburgh EH1 1TE. Introductions copyright © Carol Anderson 1994, 1998.

Set in 10pt Plantin by Hewer Text Ltd, Edinburgh. Printed and bound by Caledonian International, Bishopbriggs.

The publishers gratefully acknowledge general subsidy from the Scottish Arts Council towards the Canongate Classics series and a specific grant towards the publication of this volume.

Canongate Classics
Series Editor: Roderick Watson
Editorial board: J.B. Pick and Cairns Craig

British Library Cataloguing-in-Publication Data
A catalogue record for this book is available on request from the British Library.

ISBN 0 86241 784 8

Contents

TALES
FROM ANGUS

Contents

Introduction

MANY OF the stories in this volume are drawn from *Tales of My Own Country*, first published in 1922, and except for a couple of tales which have been anthologised, long out of print. The title of that volume suggests the importance of location: Violet Jacob wants to map out her 'own country' – to record and give imaginative life to places she knew and loved. Other work included here is drawn from *The Lum Hat and Other Stories*; this was published posthumously (in 1982), but the stories date back to the 1920s and 30s, and are set in the same landscapes as those in the earlier volume.

Born at the House of Dun, near the east coast port of Montrose, in 1863, Violet Kennedy-Erskine played as a child on the family estate a few miles from the town, overlooking the stretch of tidal waters known as the Basin. In her family history, *The Lairds of Dun* (1931), Jacob presents an evocative thumbnail sketch of her home territory:

> The House of Dun stands in the county of Angus, at the far eastern end of Strathmore through which the South Esk runs to empty itself into the Basin of Montrose. Between the tidal marshes of the Basin and the North Sea there is a strip of land on which the town of Montrose is built, and the river washes its quays on its seaward way through a harbour which, within living memory, was full of fair-haired, ear-ringed sailors ashore from the vessels in the Baltic trade. In the back streets near the dock a touch of Scandinavia lingered until a couple of score years ago in spite of the deadly uniformity that was so soon to begin its creeping progress over the world. But a stranger may yet

look up at the pediment of the Town House and learn
from the mermaids supporting the arms of Montrose
the amphibious character of the place. The tall steeple
of the parish kirk, seen from far out at sea, throws
its shadow at low tide on the wet sands of the Basin;
and on winter nights the sound of the bar thundering
beyond it is carried far in across the fields.

The Grampians lie along the northern horizon,
distant enough to be a shadow-swept mystery and near
enough to be a rampart between Angus and Mearns
and the Highlands. The broad spaces of sky hang over
a land hampered by no fretful detail of close lane and
narrow field, steeped in a light that seems, to those who
have eyes for it, to belong to no other region.

A rich farming country of spacious arable land and
heavy woods slopes to the hills; the cottages and farms
with which it is sparsely sown catch the declining gleam
on their walls; and the self-contained look of the white
gable-ends, aloof against the background hill and tree,
strikes the heart of the home-coming son of Angus
with a charm as of some attractive trick of manner in a
familiar friend (pp. 1–2).

This is the world of Jacob's short fiction. Its landscapes and
towns are based on real places, many of them named or easily
identifiable, some lightly fictionalised. Several of the stories
here, including 'The Figurehead' and the novella 'The Lum
Hat', are clearly set in or near Montrose. Others portray little
inland parishes (key scenes often actually feature the church)
and farming communities, while 'The Watch-Tower' is set
in Glenesk. Angus is a varied region, both Lowland and
Highland, encompassing sea-scape and rich agricultural land.
Jacob's 'country', too, is varied. Its boundaries and borderlines
are both actual and symbolic; for of course, although based
on a physical reality, this 'country' is also fictional. In a note
to *Tales of My Own Country* Jacob states that it contains
'portraits of places', but any portrait involves selection and
interpretation. Jacob's 'country' is as much a landscape of
the mind, of imagination and memory as it is a real place.

Like Stevenson, Violet Jacob had a strong sense of the

suggestiveness of place. In a short essay, 'From the Corner Seat' (in *Country Life*, 14th May, 1910), echoing Stevenson's 'A Gossip on Romance', she remarks the powerful glimpses caught by the traveller on a train of 'that misty borderland of illusion lying just beyond our reach'; real places, briefly seen through a window, are evocative of mystery and of undeveloped narratives. Through the frames of Violet Jacob's short fiction, too, the reader catches sight of a real yet imaginary country whose complexity is economically suggested.

Violet Jacob's 'own country' has several dimensions in the temporal sense. Like Stevenson a long-term exile, she seemed driven to capture in her writing the well-loved landscapes and people of her youth. While spending much of her adult life in India and Egypt, England and Wales, Jacob wrote frequently of Angus in her fiction and poetry; she visited when she could, but drew constantly on memory and on oral and written history. She researched her own family, writing, at the end of *The Lairds of Dun*, with a sense of wonder and respect, of 'that partly discovered and partly undiscovered country, the world that was'. Imaginatively compelled by the past, Jacob locates many of her short stories in the eighteenth and nineteenth centuries, with others set closer to her own age; like many Scottish writers from Scott to Lewis Grassic Gibbon, desiring to record a world that was passing, Jacob vividly recreates societies just slipping from view. Sometimes there are references to real people and events, but this is art, not history, and these are carefully crafted stories. In some, like 'The Fiddler', there are tales within tales, where one time period provides the framework, enclosing memories of another, implying strong bonds between past and present. Elsewhere landscape suggests a sense of the deeper past, bringing intimations of mortality: 'on her left the sea lay cold and hidden by the dunes along the shore. Its voice, like the voice of a shell held to the ear, had the breath of a far away history reaching from childhood to death, from time to the end of time' ('The Lum Hat').

Violet Jacob delineates little-recognised places and their too easily-forgotten histories; but these stories are also, importantly, portraits of people. Jacob refers in one tale to those who have 'marginal sketches on the maps of their minds; unofficial scraps which give outside points of view' ('The Overthrow of Adam Pitcaithley'), and her own work might be seen in this light. Like James Joyce in *Dubliners* (1914), Jacob illustrates lives 'outside' the fashionable world; lives that might be seen as obscure, sometimes frustrated. Although the writer herself came from an ancient landed family, her work depicts characters of various social classes. Many are poor working people: farm-labourers and servants, quiet young men, solitary shepherds and strong-willed country-women such as the spirited, red-haired Euphemia in the story of that name, or Auntie Thompson with her 'large, determined pink face'. These people are given voice, and the splendid dialogue in the vernacular is cannily deployed, the minister in 'The Fiddler', for instance, lapsing into Scots only at moments of high emotion.

Jacob's characters are often 'marginal' figures within communities, like Phemie Moir in 'The Fiddler', or Annie Cargill, 'just a lassie' to the men who dismiss her memory, her grave bearing 'no date, no text, not the baldest record'. These women have sad fates, though others survive, like Jessie-Mary, the orphan in 'The Debatable Land', who escapes into the free 'no-man's land', departing at the end with a passing tinker. Such figures, anticipatory of Jessie Kesson's outsiders or 'ootlins', tend to be sympathetically represented, even if not all (Janet Robb in 'Thievie', for instance) are wholly likeable, and some, like the sheepstealer in 'The Watch-Tower', are lawbreakers. Their plight is human, and touching. 'A Middle-Aged Drama' is moving especially because the focus is on a couple whose lives – and love – are not the stuff of conventional romance. These small Angus communities themselves might seem odd or unimportant if viewed from a distant perspective, like that of the visiting Englishman in 'The Fiddler', but are rendered significant by a writer dwelling on their particularities.

There are reminders of a larger context, though any assumption of its superiority is undermined. In 'A Middle-Aged Drama', Hedderwick's son Robert 'who was apprenticed to a watch-maker in Dundee, came home at intervals to spend Sunday with his father and to impress the parish with that knowledge of men and matters which he believed to be the exclusive possession of dwellers in manufacturing towns'. But wealth, if not wisdom, does tend to exist elsewhere; like Lewis Grassic Gibbon writing a little later, Jacob notes the diaspora of poor rural folk to Canada and America. Fortunes earned by those who have lighted out for 'the colonies' are key to the plots of 'Auntie Thompson' and 'Thievie'. And those who lead wandering lives are contrasted in Jacob's fiction with narrower, staider folk, like Malvina Birse (in 'The Figurehead') or genteel Christina Mills, of whom we learn that the sea-captain and the gipsy woman 'touched some sleeping thing in her mind which feared to be awakened'. Freedom and constraint are recurring concerns.

The boundaries of human life themselves are not absolute. Just as Jacob's poetry hints at a liminal realm where the living and the dead meet, so does her short fiction allude to 'those fringes of spiritual life that surround humanity' ('A Middle-Aged Drama'). As in many ballads and folk tales, figures from beyond the grave visit the human world: Annie Cargill appears to an elderly man who once abandoned her; a yellow dog (unlike the faithful cur in *Flemington*) may be a supernatural being presaging, perhaps bringing, death. This concern with the supernatural links Jacob's short stories with those of Scott and Hogg, Margaret Oliphant, Stevenson and her contemporary, John Buchan. Like several of these Scottish writers she uses Scots powerfully, and is able to create a sense of ambiguity and the presence of something like evil.

There is a toughness and vigour to Jacob's shorter fiction, which is at its best both symbolic and realist. In 'Thievie' the stormy elements parallel a woman's desperation and growing anger, while the story also offers a sharp analysis of her social and economic entrapment. In a telling scene in 'A Middle-Aged Drama' a woman sees from the church window 'a shambling figure that moved among the graves'; it appears her past is returning to haunt her, 'a long-buried tragedy . . . being revived', but here death paradoxically brings new life. Although many of these stories deal with death, violence, sometimes madness, melodrama is counterbalanced by glimmers of hope and love, and by Jacob's characteristically understated prose.

Satirical observation especially of socially aspiring and snobbish characters runs throughout Jacob's work; the come-uppance of Isa MacAndrew and her family in 'The Disgracefulness of Auntie Thompson' is one enjoyable example. The reverse side of romance is exposed, too, attitudes to marriage revealed with dry irony; in 'The Lum Hat', we learn of Uncle Halket, who has remarried after his wife's death, that 'he had no ill-will at Isabella but he had liked her predecessor better', while the sea-captain Baird 'did not want a wife with a vivid personality who might be likely to get into mischief whilst he was at sea'. The portrait of Christina Mills is presented by a cool, detached narrator, but 'The Lum Hat' itself is not lacking in vigour. It is, like much of Jacob's fiction, notable for a relative frankness about sex. Women can be lusty: ' "Baird's the lad I'd take" ' declares 'a woman over eighty', though Christina, well-read in the 'decorous books of her day', shrinks from the advances of the strongly physical sea-captain. There are many memorable and suggestive visual images: a church tower Christina imagines falling on her when she meets Baird, a woman selling brooms, the brawny ship's figurehead of a ship called *Sirius* after the Greek-named 'hot and scorching' dog-star.

Christina receives from her other suitor, Aeneas, a picture of St Cecilia playing a musical instrument; it is unstated, yet significant, that St Cecilia is patron saint also of the blind:

> She [Christina] strolled between town and sea. On her right hand the tall, beautiful steeple of the parish kirk held its flying buttresses against the sky and over the roofs crowded below it. The sun was near the horizon and the smoke from many chimneys, the varied skyline with its slopes and steepnesses and angles, caught the smouldering sundown and became welded into one vision of romance like the embodiment of the soul of a town. Christina saw nothing of these things.

This strongly visual passage is brilliantly undercut by that last sentence, summing up Christina's fatal limitation. A sensitivity to the visual is often a mark of the imaginative or idealistic character in Jacob's work; Tom Falconer in 'The Figurehead', for instance, like Archie in *Flemington*, sees 'in pictures'. Poor Christina is found wanting. Yet we can feel compassion for her, for ironically – and chillingly – it is a visual image which finally turns her from making what might have been a happier second marriage: the sight of the tall man's hat worn by her father, so richly emblematic of the forces of class, convention and gender, which gives this remarkable tale its title.

Jacob's own fiction is strongly pictorial, as might be expected of a writer who was also a gifted painter (a few of her attractive paintings and sketches of Angus can be seen at the House of Dun and in Montrose Museum: cottages at Ferryden, a man resting in a cornfield, the steeples and roofs of Montrose against the sky). But description is spare and rarely present merely for its own sake; the colour and shadow at the opening of 'A Middle-Aged Drama', for example, foreshadow the story's dramatic concerns. Jacob's fiction has a range of effects; it is sometimes poignant, sometimes lyrical, often humorous. There is gusto in the creation of the marvellous Auntie Thompson, and a gentler touch in the handling of young Anderson and his kindly friend the horseman. Joy is granted to unlikely people, like the cantankerous old man who longs to see and hear the 'Fifty-eight wild swans'. Yet Jacob's portrayal of humanity is rarely mawkish, because of the narrative economy of her work, a tendency to avoid direct narrative comment or judgement, and her abrupt, sometimes ambiguous endings.

The short story has a long and robust history in Scotland, and one that looks increasingly interesting, as new writers emerge, and older ones are rediscovered. Now that Jacob's short fiction is again in print, we can begin to appreciate her distinctive contribution to the form and to Scottish tradition.

Acknowledgments

I WOULD like to thank Malcolm Hutton for his kind help and co-operation in publishing these stories. I must acknowledge, too, the invaluable work of the late Ronald Garden, who first brought the *Lum Hat* stories to light. Thank you also to Katy Gordon, Faith Hobbis and Margery Palmer McCulloch, and to librarians at Montrose Public Library, especially John Doherty and Fiona Sharlaw, and Kirsten Tomlinson at Montrose Museum, who were all very helpful.

'Thievie'

THE SIDE street of the Angus town was as grey a thing as could be seen even on this grey dripping day. The houses, thick-walled, small-windowed, sturdily uniform and old-fashioned, contemplated the soaking cobble-stones and the 'causeys' which ran like rivers on either side; the complacent eyes of their dark panes, made yet darker by the potted geraniums whose smouldering red gave no liveliness to a reeking world, stared out, endlessly aloof, upon the discomfort of the occasional passer-by. Under their breath they seemed to be chorusing unanimously the words of St. Paul and saying, 'None of these things move me.' The dried haddocks, which usually hung on their wooden 'hakes' nailed to the walls, had been brought in, as had the small children whose natural playground was the pavement; chalk-marks made by schoolboys in their various evening games had been obliterated from the flags. Newbiggin Street was a featureless place given over to the sulky elements.

All night it had rained steadily, for with evening the fitful drizzle of the day before had settled down to business. The woman who stood framed in the only open doorway of the street looked up and down, frowning. She was a thickset, bony woman, one of those who, unremarkable in feature, are yet remarkable in presence, and though in daily life she made no bid for attractiveness, it was because she did not happen to know where, or in what, attraction lay. Her eyes were steady, and full, at times, of a purposeful though not alluring light. Her hair was dark and thick, her skin sallow, and her head well carried. She was dressed tidily, in stout, ill-fitting clothes, in strong contrast to which she wore a cheap, new hat with a crude blue flower; this was a recognition of the occasion, for she had walked yesterday from her home, five miles away, with her bundle in her hand, to see an aunt whose voice could now be heard in conversation behind her. She was not paying the smallest attention to the old woman's talk; her return journey was before her and the prospect did not please her.

A lad came up the street with his hands in his pockets and his head ducked into his collar under the downpour.

'Bad weather,' she observed, as he passed the doorstep.

'Bad weather!' he exclaimed, with a half-contemptuous laugh; 'wumman, hae ye seen the river?'

Her face changed. She stood hesitating, staring; then, without a word to the unseen aunt within, she gathered up her bundle and stepped out.

Soon she was in the movement of the main street which declined in a steep hill to the lower levels; there were many others making in the same direction and as she went along she could hear, above the noise of wheels and footsteps, a steady roaring. Not a breath of wind was stirring to make the sound fluctuate, and the even relentlessness of it awed her a little. She crossed the way that lay at right angles to the bottom of the street and stood looking down over the iron-railed wall which held up the road at the riverside. The grey, moving mass that slipped by was almost up to the railings.

Beyond her and all along the row of houses, the people were gathered to watch the rising water. The doors of the one-storied dwellings were choked with furniture that was being lugged out and carried away. Chairs, tubs, tables, birds in cages appeared and disappeared up the hill; women screamed angrily to venturesome children whose curiosity had lured them from the maternal skirts, frightened infants cried, men pushed about laden with cooking-pots and bedding; boys shouted to each other, running about in the crowd, the thud of their bare feet lost in the changeless, covetous voice that rose from between the banks. A blind man was being led towards the rise of the hill; he too was playing his part, for he carried a 'wag-at-the-wa' ' clock with a gaudily-painted face clasped in his arms. She paused a few minutes to look up and down the torrent and then struck away from the crowd, seeking through the outlying streets for her straightest line home.

Janet Robb's life had been much concerned with the elements. The house for which she was making at her steady, uncompromising tramp was a waterside cottage just above the spot where the river wound into a lake-like estuary on its way to the North Sea. Here she was born, here she had lived out her thirty-four years, for her father had been ferryman until the building of a new bridge a short distance up-stream had shovelled his trade into the limbo of outworn necessities. She had kept house in it almost ever since she could remember; for her mother, who had been an invalid, died when her girl was thirteen, and the ferryman, in spite of the prophecies of his neighbours, did not marry again. Women had no attraction for him, and the need of a housekeeper, which, more than any other cause, drives middle-aged working men into matrimony, did not exist while he had a daughter like Janet, so well able and so well accustomed to grapple with domestic needs. She was a hardy woman now, close-fisted and shrewd. She had been an invaluable help, both in the house and out of it; the two had worked the ferry between them, for the river was not wide and the traffic was small. Carts and horses had to go round to a point about a mile westward, and only foot-passengers on their way to the town troubled that part of the shore; when her father was out, she could leave her house-work to put them across to the farther bank without much interruption to it.

The ferryman was not an inspiring acquaintance. Though he belonged, in company with publicans, barbers, and blacksmiths, to a trade eminently social in its opportunities, he cared nothing for that part of it. He could put over a boatful of people without addressing a word to any of them and with scarcely an answer to any man enterprising enough to attack his silence. He was not popular, and, as those who give nothing of their mind to the world must perforce submit to have the gaps they create filled up according to the taste of their neighbours, a whole crop of tales sprang up at the water-side like so much duckweed. He was a secret drinker; he was worth ten thousand pounds; he kept a woman in

the town whom he ill-treated – had she not been seen
with her head bandaged, crying ill names after him on
the public road? – he starved his daughter; she starved
him – all these whisperings surrounded his unconscious
head. He was a spare man, smaller in build than Janet,
lined and clean-shaven. Besides his recognised business he
had a cart and an old horse by means of which he did a
little carrying, going townwards three times a week, whilst
she took charge of the boat; and though nobody outside
the cottage knew anything about it, he received substantial
help from a son who had left home early and was making a
good income in Canada. While the neighbours went wide
of the mark in most of the rumours they set afloat about
him, one of these had a fragile foundation of truth. Davie
Robb kept no woman and cared as little for drink as he did
for company; there was only one thing that he cared about
at all, and that lay in a box under his bed. The contents
of this box did not amount to ten thousand pounds, but
they went into several hundreds. They were his soul, his
life. Waking, he thought of them; and sleeping, they were
not far from his dreams. When he opened the lid to add
to the hoard he counted and re-counted them, running up
the figures on paper. It mattered not to him that he knew
them by heart; he would roll them about in his brain as a
child rolls a sweet about in its mouth.

Not even Janet knew the amount of these savings, though
she made many guesses and was, perhaps, near enough to
the truth. The box was never spoken of between father
and daughter. It was the ferryman's god, and in one sense
it had the same place in their household as God has in
most others: it was never mentioned, even when taken
for granted. In another sense, its place was different: for
it was continually in the mind of both.

JANET THRUST ALONG the road, leaving the country town
quickly behind her, urged on by strong necessity. Her
father was now permanently disabled, for some years almost
crippled by rheumatism. He was an old man, shrunken and
very helpless. The cottage was two-storied, and its upper
floor was approached by an outside staircase running up

at the gable end. There was a stair inside, too, which had been added later because of the occasional spates in the river, to allow the inmates to move to the upper room without opening the door when water surrounded the walls. Old Robb slept upstairs and was just able to get down by himself, though he could never manage to get up again without assistance; and yesterday, before leaving home, Janet had arranged with a boy who lived upstream near the new bridge that he should come in the evening to convey the old man to his bedroom. The lad had consented reluctantly, for, to the young, there was something uncanny about 'Auld Thievie.' Scottish people are addicted, perhaps more than any others, to nicknames, and the ferryman's surname, combined with his late extortions as a carrier, had earned him the title by which he was known for some miles round. Nobody liked Thievie.

Not even Janet. It was scarcely affection that was hastening her. Perhaps it was duty, perhaps custom. Something was menaced for which she was responsible. That, with capable people, is generally all that is wanted in the way of a key to wind them up and set them going. The rain had stopped and she put down her dripping umbrella. The blue flower in her unsuitable hat had lost its backbone and flagged, a limp, large thing; there was a fine powdering of wet on her thick eyebrows and the harsh twist of hair at the back of her head. Mist was pouring in from the sea, the wind having sat in the south-east – the wet quarter on the east coast – for three days; and though it had dropped like lead with last night's tide, the 'haar' was coming miles inland as though some huge, unseen engine out seaward were puffing its damp breath across the fields. The cultivated slopes of the Sidlaws, a mile on her right, diminishing in height as they neared the estuary, were hidden. The Grampians, ten miles away on her left, were hidden too; that quarter of the horizon where, on ordinary days, they raised their blue and purple wall, being a mere blank. The river whose infancy they cradled had burst from them angrily, like a disobedient child from its parents, and was tearing along, mad with lust of destruction, to the sea.

When she was some way out of the town a figure emerged from the vapour ahead, growing familiar as the two wayfarers approached each other. Her expression lightened a little as she recognised the advancing man. He was smiling too.

'Hey, Janet!' he cried, 'I was wond'rin' what-like daft wife was oot on sic a day.'

His face was red and moist with the mist.

'I've been at Newbiggin Street. I'm just awa' hame,' said she.

He was a connection of the Robb family, so her words conveyed something to him.

'An' foo's auntie?' he inquired.

'Weel eneuch – but I maun awa' back. There's an awfae spate, ye ken.'

'Tuts, bide you a minute. I haena seen ye this twa weeks syne.'

She made no move to go on. Willie Black had a different place in her mind from anyone else. It was not easy to deflect Janet Robb from her way, but she would do more for this man, a little younger than herself and infinitely her inferior in will, than for any other person. He was the only male living being who approached her from the more easy and lighter standpoint from which such men as she knew approached girls, and their quasi-relationship had brought them into a familiarity which she enjoyed. He was one of those who looked upon women in a general way with a kind of jocose patronage, always implied and often expressed. He meant no harm by this manner; it was natural to him, and he was not nearly so bold a character as his attitude would suggest. Janet was so much unlike the other women he knew that he would have thought it right to assume superiority even had he, in her case, not felt it. She attracted him, not through his heart and certainly not through his senses, but as a curiosity to be explored in a mildly comic spirit. He knew, too, that Thievie was well off; for once, in a moment of confidence, Janet had hinted at her father's savings, and Black felt vaguely, but insistently, that in the fullness of time he would be wise in proposing to her. The day was distant yet, but meanwhile he sought opportunities of considering her and discovering how far she would be endurable as a wife.

Janet fidgeted from one foot to the other. By one half of herself she was urged to continue her way; the other half being impelled to stay by the invitation in his eyes. She did not know for how much this counted, so great was her ignorance of the amenities of men. Black was the only man who had ever come nearer to her life than the baker's cartman from whom she took the bread at her door or the cadger from whom she bought the fish. She had a great longing to be like other women, a factor in the male world. She was too busy to brood over the subject, and had inherited too much of her father's love of money-making to be deeply affected by any other idea. But when she was with Black she was conscious of all she lacked and was lured beyond measure by her perception of his attitude. It suggested that she took rank with the rest of her sex.

'I'll need awa',' she began, 'feyther's himsel' i' the hoose. There's an awfae water comin' doon an' he canna win up the stair his lane. I maun hae tae gang on.'

'I didna ken ye thocht sic a deal o' Thievie. Ye micht think o' me a bittie,' he added, with knowing reproachfulness.

She looked away from him into the blankness of the mist.

'Heuch! – you?' she exclaimed.

'He's an auld, dune crater. Ye could dae weel, wantin' him.'

'Haud yer tongue!' she cried, actuated purely by a sense of what was fitting.

'Weel, what's the advantage o' him sittin' yonder, an' a' that siller just nae use ava' till him – an' nae use tae ony ither body?'

She made no reply. There is something silencing in hearing another person voice an idea one believes to be one's own private property.

'Ye'd be a real fine lass wi' yon at yer back,' he continued; 'it's a fair shame ye should be dancin' after the like o' yon auld deil when ye micht be daein' sae muckle better.'

She withdrew her gaze from the mist and met his eyes.

'What would I be daein' better?' she inquired, rather fiercely.

He gave a sort of crowing laugh.

'What wad ye be daein'? Gie's a kiss, Janet, an' maybe I'll tell ye.'

Before she had time to think he had flung his arm about her and the roughness of his dripping moustache was on her lips.

She thrust him from her with all her very considerable strength. He laughed again.

It was the first time that a man had ever attempted such a thing and her heart almost stopped. She was torn between wrath and a thrilling, overmastering sense of something achieved. She stood panting, her bundle fallen into the mud. Then she snatched it and dashed into the greyness. It took but a moment to swallow up her figure, but he stayed where he was, staring, his coarse shoulders shaking with laughter. She could hear his jesting voice calling after her as she went. When she had gone a little distance she paused, listening to discover whether he was following; but there was no sound of footsteps.

She hurried on though she had ceased to think of her goal. Her thoughts drove her, rushing and tumbling like birds with beating wings, crowding and jostling and crying in her ears. Black's words had let them loose, stirring her as much as his action. Yes, it was quite true. She was tied, as she had been all her life, to her father and his box. She drudged for him, year in, year out, and got nothing by it, while he clung like an old dog in the manger to the thing he would neither use nor share. She would be a wife worth having for any man with the contents of that box to start housekeeping on! Willie Black would realise that. She remembered her years at the ferry in fair weather and foul, the picking and scraping she had done and suffered in the house, that the hoarding might go on that was no good to anyone. There had never been any love lost between herself and Thievie, and though he was her father she had long known that she hated him. Yes, she hated him. She had no fear of work and had taken it as a normal condition, but it had come between her and all that was worth having; the toil that had been a man's toil, not a woman's, had built a barrier round her to cut her off from a woman's life. All this had lurked, unrecognised, in her mind, but now it had leaped up, aroused by a man's careless, familiar horseplay.

Her breath came quick as she thought of her own meagre stake in the world. She knew herself for some kind of a power, and that was awaking the dormant realisation of her slavery, all the more bitter for its long sleep. She pushed back her hat and the drops came tumbling to her shoulder from the draggled blue flower, now a flower in name only, a sodden streak of blackened colour. She found herself shaking all over and she longed to sit down, but the milestone, which had often served her for a seat on her walks to and from the town, was a good way on.

The roadside landmarks were growing a little clearer. It was almost noon, and the flash of false brightness which that hour will often bring hovered somewhere in the veiled sky. She heard the ring of a hammer coming muffled from the smithy ahead, and pushed on, thinking to sit a little in some corner behind the ploughs and harrows. She was unnerved by the tumult in her; anger and self-pity were undermining her self-control; she was a self-controlled woman, and the agony of disorganised feeling was, in consequence, all the worse. It seemed that she had never been aware of the large injustices of life till now. Her difficulties had been small, physical ones and she had known how to scatter them with a high hand; but these new ones pressed round her like a troop of sturdy, truculent beggars, clamouring and menacing. Another woman might have wept but she only suffered.

She reached the smithy door and looked in. The smith was at his anvil, holding a red-hot horseshoe with the tongs. The blowing had ceased and in the dimness of the shed a pair of huge, patient Clydesdales were in process of being shod. A young 'horseman' was standing by, his hands in his pockets, watching the sputter of flaming sparks that rose with each blow and fell here and there. The hot scent of horses and leather and scorching hoof seemed one with the rich browns and warm shadows that hang about smithy fires. Behind the mysterious limbs of the bellows the elf-like

face of the smith's 'prentice-lad peered at Janet, though
both the men's interest in the matter in hand made them
unaware of the woman who slipped noiselessly in.

She laid her bundle down behind a cart that stood jacked
up with a wheel off, amid a medley of implements, and
sat down, concealed by the litter, in a cobwebby corner
of the long building. The hammering stopped and one
of the carthorses shifted its feet and blew a shattering
sigh into the rafters; the horseman gave one of those
sudden expostulatory cries that his profession addresses
to its charges, and all was still again. The smith threw
down his hammer and left the shoe to cool a little.

'They'll be haein' a bad time doon at the hooses yonder,'
said he, nodding his head backwards in the direction of the
low ground.

'Aye, coorse,' said the horseman.

'I wad believe that,' continued the smith, whose noisy
trade gave him less opportunity of hearing his own voice
than he liked. 'I mind weel eneuch when we got a
terrible-like spate – saxteen year syne, come Martinmas.
I was doon aboot Pairthshire way then, an' I wasna lang
merriet, an' the wife was that ta'en up aboot it. She was
fae the toon, ye understan', an' she didna like tae see the
swine an' the sheep jist rowin' past i' the water. Ah weel,
ye see, we'll jist hae tae dae oor best.'

'Aye,' said the horseman.

'There'll be big losses. Aye, weel, weel, we canna control
the weather, ye see.'

'Na,' said the horseman.

'An' I doot auld Thievie doon at the ferry'll be swampit.
Aye, ye see, ye canna tell when yer time's tae come.'

'The auld scabbit craw,' said the horseman.

The smith took up his tools, and approaching one of
the horses, laid hold of an enormous hind foot and began,
strenuously, to pare the hoof. The beast looked round with
an all-embracing toleration. The horseman spat.

Janet sat still, trying to quell the storm within her and
to think connectedly. There had been no need for the
blacksmith's words to bring her father's plight before
her. In all likelihood the riverside cottage was already

surrounded, and the fact that the few neighbours were well aware that none knew better than she how to handle oars might easily make them slow to bestir themselves on Thievie's behalf. The old ferry-boat, still seaworthy, lay in its shed some way up the bank, ready for the occasional use to which it was put; and no one but the little boy who had been in to help the old man on the preceding night knew that Janet was absent; and the boy was probably at school.

Even now her freedom might be coming to her on the rising spate! She shivered, chilled after her excitement and her transit from hot heart-burning to the cold horror upon which, with the inward eye, she looked. Thievie could not get up the ladder-like stair – not even with the gurgling water behind him – without a helping hand. It was years since he had even been willing to try. Perhaps she had only to stay where she was and to take what gift this day might bring! Her hands were shaking, though she had clasped them tightly on her lap, and she set her teeth, almost fearing that their chattering would betray her to the smith and his taciturn companion. Of what use was that old withering life by the riverside to itself or to any other living thing? It was as dead, already, as the dead money in the box below the bed. But the money would be dead no longer. Willie Black would not think it dead. She would wait where she was; the smith might go to his dinner when the shoeing was done, but the smithy door stood always open and she would sit, unmolested, till such time as she judged . . .

Her thoughts stopped there and she closed her eyes, leaning her head against the wall.

She could not hang about the road in such weather, waiting. She had not the courage to do that, for fear of drawing attention and making her neighbours ask inconvenient questions . . . afterwards. Though she assured herself that no one would guess, or be sufficiently interested to try to guess, what was causing her to loiter, her nerves would not allow her to face so much as an innocent stranger. She wished the lad behind the bellows had not peered at her in that way. Suppose he should tell the smith – but anything was better than the public road! She tried to force herself into composure.

All at once a loud voice sounded at the door. She opened her eyes and recognised a local carrier through her screen of lumber. He took off the sack which enveloped him and shook it till the drops flew.

'No muckle daein' the day,' he began.

'Dod aye, the water that's oot! Whiles I couldna get forrit.'

The smith looked up from the hairy foot gripped between his knees.

'Queer times, queer times,' he said. 'Weel, we canna change it, ye see.'

'How's a' wi' you, Ake?' said the carrier, turning to the horseman.

'Whoa. S-ss-ss!' cried the latter, for the horse, feeling the smith's movement, tried to release its foot.

'I was thinkin' Thievie wad be drooned,' continued the carrier, grinning from ear to ear and remembering the days when they had been rivals on the road.

'And is he no?' inquired the horseman, roused to interest at last.

'No him. I'm tae hae a word wi' some o' they folk by the brig. I saw the river-watcher's boat gaein' oot nae lang aifter it was licht, an' I cried on him, whaur was he gaein'? Dod, when he tell't me he was awa tae seek Thievie, I was fair angert. "Let him be," I says, "wad ye cast awa' the Lord's maircies yon way?" But there's the auld thrawn stock safe an' soond, and folk lossin' their guid cocks an' hens. Fie!'

The horseman gave a loud shout of laughter and relapsed immediately into gravity.

'Aye, the ways o' Providence,' observed the smith.

'Weel, I maun be movin',' said the carrier. 'Thievie'll be on the pairish yet. There's mair water tae come doon frae the hills afore it's finished. There'll be naething left o' the sma' hoosies on the bank. A'thing 'll just gang traivellin' tae the sea. There was naebody believed it wad be sae bad the morn, airly, when I was doon by the auld ferry, but lord! they tellt me an hour syne that there's no been

onything like it this aichty year past. An' the tide's comin'
in, ye ken.'

He called the last sentence over his shoulder as he turned
from the door.

Janet had all but cried out aloud during the carrier's
speech. Her father was gone – sitting safe now under some
sheltering roof above the reach of the insurgent river!

But it was not the thought of this which overwhelmed
her. She knew from long experience that there was hardly
anything he would not do to prevent anyone, even herself,
from seeing his precious box, and she could swear that
he would never consent to expose it to a strange human
eye while there was the smallest possibility of keeping
it hidden. At that hour, soon after daybreak, when the
carrier had seen the boat go for him, the torrential rain
which was to follow had not yet turned the ordinary spate
into something unknown for half a century. That being so,
it was plain to her that, sooner than disclose the box to
his rescuer, Thievie would leave it in what had been, at
other spate-times, the perfect security of the upper storey.
So completely was she convinced of this that she would
have staked everything she had on it. But she had nothing;
and all that she had a prospect of having was surely lying
in the rickety upper room waiting for the abnormal torrent
to wreck the little house and carry its precious contents to
the fathomless recesses of the sea.

She sprang up, the frantic idea banishing all else; and she
had dashed boldly out of the smithy under the astonished
gaze of the two men before it struck her with measureless
relief that she had now nothing to fear from the most
suspicious eye. Her father was safe; her secret design
thwarted by the river-watcher; the reason for anything
she did was of interest to no one. She saw now how
futile her fears had been; the outcome of disorganised
nerves. Conscience had almost made her believe that she
carried her thoughts outside her body like her clothes.

At last, breathless, the perspiration on her face mingled
with the wet, she reached the diverging road that led to the
river, and as she turned into it the mist began to lift. It grew
brighter behind the cloud-wrappings that veiled the world.

She stopped, listening for the river's voice. The noonday gleam had strengthened and she came out suddenly from a belt of vapour into comparative clearness and saw the submerged levels lying some little way before her. The broken water above them was all that told her where the banks were, and here and there she could recognise certain tall clumps of alder above the swirl. She redoubled her pace till, at the place in the road from which Thievie's cottage could be seen, she noted with rising hope that the flood had not yet reached the tops of the ground-floor windows. The outside stair was still practicable.

At the water's edge, at the nearest spot to the little house, she stood still. She had hung her bundle and her umbrella on a stout thorn-tree growing on a knoll by the wayside. She would need both hands for what she was going to do. The boat-shed was safe, but she would have to wade almost to the knees to reach it. She drew up her skirts and walked into the chilly water.

She felt its steady push against her legs, and her riverside knowledge told her that the tide at the estuary's mouth had turned and was coming in. It was thrusting the overflow out from the banks on either side and the area of dry fields was diminishing. She looked up apprehensively, for the gleam of brightness had paled in the last few minutes and she dreaded lest the mist should close in again before her task was done.

At last she reached the shed. The oars were afloat inside, kept from sailing away by the pressure of the incoming tide on the flood-water. She waded through the doorway and mounted, hampered by the weight of her soaking boots, on a projecting wooden ledge; then as she clung to an iron hook in the wall, she stretched out her foot and drawing the old craft towards her, stepped in. When she had secured the oars, she loosed the painter from its ring and guided herself out between the narrow walls.

It was easy work rowing, in spite of the slight current against her. The boat was not a heavy one, and only built to carry a few people at a time across fifty yards of water. She rowed as fast as she could, for the damp vapour was drifting in again, and the sun's face, which had looked like a new shilling above her, had now withdrawn itself, leaving a blurred, nebulous spot in its place. Pulling across the shallows on the skirts of the spate, she refused to picture what might happen should she find, on emerging from the cottage with the box, that all landmarks were lost in the mist. Her only guide would then be the sound of that menacing rush from which it would take all the strength of her arms to keep clear.

When the boat's nose bumped against the outside stair she made the painter fast to the railings and stood up, wringing the water from her petticoats. As she clambered out and ascended to the stairhead, small streams trickled down the stone steps from her boots. The door of the upper room was locked inside, but she was not much perturbed by this, having expected it, and moreover she knew the old crazy wood could not stand much ill-usage. Its thin boards were gaping inside and had been pasted up with brown paper by her own hands. She drew back to the outer edge of the stairhead and flung her whole weight against them. The door cracked loudly, and though the lock held, she saw that another couple of blows would split it at one of its many weak places. Again and again she barged into it, and at last the wood parted in a long, vertical break. She was down the steps in a moment and dragging one of the short, stout oars from the boat. She stood on the stairhead, looking round. She could still see the boathouse, a dark blur, no more, but from the south-east there came a splash of rain. She struck the door with the butt end of the oar, once, twice. It gave suddenly, almost precipitating her into the room. She recovered her balance, and then, with that boatman's prudence which never left her, carried her weapon down and threw it into its place.

In another minute she had thrust her way in and was face to face with her father.

Thievie was sitting crouched under the tiny window with his box in his arms. His nostrils were dilated, his eyes looked as though he would strike, though his hand was still. He had sat listening to the bumping of the boat below and to the blows that burst in the rotten door; humanity seemed to have gone from him, leaving in its place the fierce, agonised watchfulness of some helpless, murderous thing, some broken-backed viper. His eyes fixed Janet, unrecognising. Not a word came from his lips.

'What are ye daein' there?' cried Janet hoarsely.

Her knees were shaking, but not from her exertions at the door.

His tongue passed over his lips. He looked as though he would bite. She sickened, she knew not why, but revulsion passed shuddering through her.

'Foo is't ye're no awa'?' she exclaimed, mastering herself.

'I wadna gang.'

He smiled as he said this and held the box tighter. As she looked at it in his grasp, some inherited instinct rose in her, and though it had been mainly valuable to her for what it would bring, should it pass from his drowned hands into her living ones, it became, at that moment, a thing desired and desirable for itself. She did not know what sum was in it, but the rage for possession of it came to her.

He laughed quietly, his toothless mouth drawn into a long line. She pounced on him, shaking his arm.

'Weel, awa' ye come noo – the boat's waitin' on ye!'

He shook his head.

She had never laid rough hands on him before, but she gripped him now. She was strong and he was helpless; and he knew, in his helplessness, that she had come for the box. He had feared the river-watcher, and he now feared her. He did not know what she meant to do to him; his mind was obsessed by the box and the fear of its loss, and unhinged by the flood. He would have liked to resist her, but he could not, should he dare try. His concentrated hate shot at her like a serpent's tongue.

'I ken what's wrang we' ye!' she shouted. 'Ye're feared for yer box! Ye're feared yon man gets a sicht o' it! Aye, but he'll be here syne – he's aifter ye! I saw his boat i' the noo, an' him in it – ye'd best come.'

His face changed. On the dusty window-pane the drops beat smartly.

'Ach, ye auld fule!' she cried savagely, 'wad ye loss it a'? Div ye no see the rain? Div ye no ken the water's creepin' up? Muckle guid yer box'll dae ye when the spate's owre yer heid an' you tapsalterie amang the gear the water's washin' doon! Haste ye noo. We'll need awa' frae this.'

She dragged him to his feet and he leaned on her, clutching his burden and unable to resist her violence.

They struggled across the floor and through the broken-down door. It was raining pitilessly. Thievie took no notice of it. He, who had known the river in every phase of drought or flood, should have had small doubt of the danger in which they stood. The roaring of its voice was increasing and there were fewer stone steps to be seen than when Janet made her entrance. It was pouring in the hills and the tide had yet a few hours to rise before it turned. Thievie looked this way and that. What he feared most was to see the river-watcher slide out of the mist in his boat; for the elements, the world and all the men and women in it were, to his disordered imagination, intent on one thing – the box. He would never sleep peacefully again should a strange eye see it. He would be robbed. He had long since been the slave of this one thought, and now it overwhelmed his dim, senile mind, even as the resistless water was overwhelming the land about them.

It took all her force and resolution to get him into the boat; he was so crippled and his arms so much hampered by the burden he carried. Though he cursed her as they went down the stair, his thoughts were of the river-watcher. In the middle of their descent he laughed his mirthless laugh.

'God-aye, but he'll be comin'!' he said, 'but it'll no be there – he'll no get a sicht o't!'

At last she got him safely afloat, and having loosed the boat, rowed away from the stairs. The surrounding floods were peppered by the onslaught of heavy drops from the low sky, and then, as though a sluice-gate had been pulled up in the firmament, a very deluge was upon them. The little they could see was washed out and they were isolated from everything in a universe without form and void, at the inmost heart of the hissing downpour. The river's noise was lost in it and all sense of direction left Janet. She pulled blindly, believing that she was heading for the boathouse. Soon they bumped and scraped against some projection

and the stern swung round. She felt the boat move under
her, as though drawn by a rope. She tried to straighten
it, but the blinding descent of the rain bewildered her; a
branch of an alder suddenly loomed out of it, the lower
twigs sweeping her face. Thievie cried out and crouched,
clinging with frenzy to his box, and she guessed they had
drifted above the deep, wide drain whose mouth was in
the river. Her blood ran cold, for its swollen waters must
inevitably carry them into the very midst of the tumult.

The drain was running hard under the flood-water and
she despaired of being able to struggle against it. They
were broadside on; besides which she dreaded to be swept
out of her seat by another branch, for there were several
alder trees by the edge of the channel. The rain began to
slacken.

As its fall abated, the river grew louder and the sky
lifted a little and she could see the large alders, gaunt and
threatening as spectres, blurred and towering over them.
With that strange observance of detail, often so sharp in
moments of desperate peril, she noticed a turnip, washed
out of the ground and carried by the torrent, sticking
in a cleft between two straggling branches, just below
water-level. She made a tremendous effort and slewed the
boat straight; and working with might and main at her oars,
got it out of the under-tow that urged it riverwards.

All at once the river-watcher's voice rang out from the
direction of the boathouse, calling the old man's name.
She answered with all the breath she had left.

'Yon's him! Yon's the river-watcher!' shrieked Thievie,
from where he still crouched in the bottom of the boat.

She ignored him, tugging at her oars and pulling with
renewed strength towards the sound.

He raised himself, and clinging to one of them, tried to
drag it from her. She wasted no breath but set her teeth,
thrusting out at him with her foot. He clung with all his
weight, the very helplessness of his legs adding to it. She
dared not let go an oar to strike at him. She could not have
believed him able to hamper her so – but then, neither had
she believed he could get himself up the inside stair of the
cottage unaided; and yet he had done it. It was as though

the senseless god of his worship, lying in the box, gave him
the unhallowed tenacity by which he was delivering them
over to the roaring enemy they could not see, but could
hear, plain and yet plainer.

She was growing weary and Thievie's weight seemed to
increase. Could she spare a hand to stun him she would
have done so for dear life. She had heard of the many-armed
octopus of the southern seas, and she remembered it now in
this struggle that was no active struggle because one would
not, and one dared not, lose grip.

The boat, with one oar rendered useless, swung round
and drifted anew into the channel between the trees. Again
the river-watcher was heard calling and again Janet tried to
answer, but her breath was gone and her strength spent.
The current had got them.

Thievie relaxed his grip as he felt the distance increase
between himself and the voice. A branch stayed their
progress for a moment, whipping the sodden hat from
Janet's head; her clothes were clinging to her limbs, her
hair had fallen from its ungainly twist and hung about
her neck. They went faster as they neared the racing
river. Then the swirl caught them and they spun in its
grip and were carried headlong through the mist. Janet
shut her eyes and waited for the end.

Time seemed to be lost in the noise, like everything else.
They sped on. At last they were not far from the estuary
and the river had widened. Once they were all but turned
over by a couple of sheaves, the spoil of the late harvest,
which came driving alongside; once they passed within a
foot of a tree which rode the torrent, plunging, its roots
sticking up like gaunt arms supplicating mercy from the
shrouded sky.

Finally they found themselves drifting in the comparative
quiet of the broad sheet of tidal water, among the bits of
seaweed carried inland above the deeps of the river-bed.
The terrors of death had blinded Janet as they were swept
along, and she now awoke as from a nightmare. An oar
had been reft from her grasp in the stress of their anguished
journey. Thievie was staring at her like an animal; his
sufferings, as they were battered between one death and

another on the boiling river, were nothing compared to hers. His god had upheld him. He had crawled back to his seat in the stern.

'Aye, he micht cry on us,' he said. 'We're far awa' frae him noo – he'll no ken what I've got here!'

He began to rock about, laughing as he thought of the river-watcher's fruitless attempt to find him.

'Haud still,' said Janet sternly. 'God, hae ye no done eneuch mischieve the day? Gin yon mist doesna lift an' let them see us frae the shore we'll be oot tae sea when the tide gangs back.'

'Naebody'll see us, naebody'll see us!' he exclaimed, hugging the box and rocking himself again.

Janet rose to her feet, fury in her eyes; she could no longer keep her hands off him.

As he saw her movement, he snatched the box from where it lay at his feet.

'Stand still, or I'll tak' it frae ye!' she cried loudly, making towards him.

He gave one cry of horror and, with the box in his arms, hurled himself sideways into the waters that closed over him and his god.

THE TIDE WAS on the turn and the rain had ceased. A wind had sprung up in the west, driving the 'haar' before it back to the sea whence it came. Some men from the fishing village near the lighthouse were rowing smartly out into the tideway where a boat drifted carrying a solitary human being, a woman who sat dazed and frozen and who had not so much as turned her head as they hailed her.

As they brought her ashore one of them took off his coat and wrapped it round her. She seemed oblivious of his action.

'Hae,' said he, with clumsy kindness, 'pit it on, lass. What'll yer lad say gin ye stairve?'

Janet thrust the coat from her.

The Disgracefulness of Auntie Thompson

AUNTIE THOMPSON came round the corner of her whitewashed cottage with a heavy zinc pail in either hand. The sun beat hot upon her back and intensified the piercing scarlet and yellow of the climbing nasturtiums which swarmed up the window-sills and seemed likely to engulf the windows of her dwelling. The whole made a strident little picture in the violence of its white and scarlet and in the aggressive industry of its principal figure; and the squeaking of one of the pails, the handle of which fitted too tightly in its socket, seemed to be calling attention to Auntie Thompson all down the road. There lacked but one further touch to the loud homeliness of the scene, and that was added as the two immense pigs in the black-boarded sty for which Auntie Thompson was bound raised their voices to welcome their meal. There is no sound so unrelievedly low as the gross and ignoble outcry by which a pig marks his interest in the events which concern him.

Perhaps there was something appropriate about the unseemly noise with which Auntie Thompson was hailed, for in this quiet neighbourhood she was not far from being a public scandal. Her appearance, which was intensely plebeian; her tongue, which was very outspoken; and her circumstances, which were a deal better than her habits warranted – all these disagreed in some undefined way with the ideas of her small world. A woman who had laid by as much as she was reported to own had no business to keep no servant and to speak her mind on all subjects to those who did, as if she were on the same social level as themselves. She was unabashed and disgraceful; she did not deride convention, because she seemed to be unaware that it existed. She kept her fingers out of everyone else's

affairs, and though she expected other people to take the
same line, she met their interference without malice, for
she was perfectly good-tempered. But her disregard of them
being instinctive and complete, it was more effective than
mountains of insult. At this moment the censuring eyes of
several of the dwellers down the road were upon her as she
heaved the pails on to the top of the pigsty fence with her
strong red arms and tipped their gushing contents into the
troughs.

Auntie Thompson was no beauty. She had a large,
determined pink face and her tiny eyes looked out under
fierce, sandy eyebrows set close on either side of her rather
solemn-looking nose. Her hair was sandy too, and was
brushed tidily from her parting and given a twist just
over her ears before it was gathered into an old-fashioned,
black chenille net at the back of her head. She was of
moderate height and solid, with the bursting solidity of
a pincushion. On every conceivable occasion she wore a
grey wincey dress short enough to reveal her stout ankles.
Her hair was beginning to grizzle, and now, as the sun
struck on it, bits of it shone like spots of mica on a hillside.
She had only two feminine weaknesses; one was a tender
heart and the other was a consuming horror of bats.

Whilst she stood watching her pigs, a neighbour passed
up the road and sent a cold glance in at her over the low
wall, patched with stonecrop, which enclosed the garden.
Auntie Thompson turned her head and nodded with an
impersonal smile, as though in answer to a greeting; she
did not notice that there was none to answer. Had she
lived on a desert island, she might not have observed that
there was no one else present.

Only one being stood out against the background of thrift,
pigs, healthy work and placidity in which she revelled, and
that was her nephew, Alec, whom she had brought up since
his sixth year. Twenty years ago he had come to her as an
orphan and he was with her still. The pair lived together
in great peace by the roadside.

'The Muir Road,' as it was called, connected two
important highways and ran across the piece of heathy
land which had once been the muir of Pitairdrie, but

which was now enclosed and cultivated and cribbed in between fences and dykes. It had not lost all its attractions, for stretches of fir-wood broke its levels; and, as it stood high, with the distant Grampians on its northern side, the back of Auntie Thompson's cottage looked over a sloping piece of country across which the cloud-shadows sailed and flitted towards the purple of the hills.

Auntie Thompson turned from her swine and re-entered her house without looking up the road, or she would have seen Alec Soutar, who was stepping homeward with an expression of deep content on his face. No wonder he was contented; for on this Saturday afternoon he had seen the end of his long courting and was coming home with Isa's consent fresh in his mind.

It had been uphill work. Isa was the only daughter of William MacAndrew, and as everybody was well aware, MacAndrew, who had, by reason of a timely legacy, transformed himself from a cottager into a small farmer, was a man full of vainglory and the husband of a wife who matched himself. They were not a popular pair; and though they lived far enough from Auntie Thompson to be surrounded by a different community, their fame had spread to the cottage. It was rumoured that they drove their four miles to Pitairdrie kirk every Sunday so that the world might see that they could afford to arrive there on wheels. There was a church so near MacAndrew's farm that, when its door was open, a man could follow the sermon from the stackyard; but only chronic invalidism, or the fact of being overturned, can make it possible to ascend and descend from a vehicle within the same fifty yards. Isa had been to a boarding school in Aberdeen, and her dress and manners were the envy of every young lass who beheld her as she sat in her father's high-backed pew with her silk parasol beside her. It had taken Alec Soutar a long time to make himself acceptable to her and a longer one to get her parents to give the reluctant consent that he was carrying home.

'Pridefu' folk,' Auntie Thompson had said.

Alec, who worked on a farm half-way between his own home and that of his love, was very honest, rather stupid, and extremely good looking. He had Auntie Thompson's sandy hair, but his head was set finely on his broad shoulders, and the outline of his bony face had some suggestion of power that made observant people look at him with interest as he stood on the half-made stack against the sky or sat on the dashboard of a cart behind the gigantic farm-horses. He loved his aunt sincerely and without the slightest suspicion of the real originality of her character, for he had no eye for her quaintnesses and would have been immensely surprised had he been told that he lived with a really remarkable person. But he needed no one to tell him of the gratitude he owed her; and mere gratitude will carry some people a long way.

He was too happy even to whistle as he swung along the road, for he grudged anything that might take his thoughts from Isa. She had walked along the field with him as far as the road and had only turned back there because she said that she could not risk being seen by strangers in her working-clothes. Alec did not quite understand her reasons, but he had a vague feeling that they must be right, though they were of so little profit to himself. Her 'working-clothes' struck him as being very different from those of Auntie Thompson – as indeed they were – but then Isa's and Auntie Thompson's definitions of work were hardly identical. He thought she looked beautiful in them and he told her so.

'Mrs. Thompson is very thrifty,' she had observed, disengaging herself from his arms. (They were still in the field.)

'Aye, is she,' he replied heartily. 'There's no very mony like her.'

'No, indeed,' simpered Isa, with a sidelong look that he did not see; 'but, Alec, we'll no need to be a burden to her. I was thinking it would be better if we could go nearer to Aberdeen. There's plenty of work to be got thereabout. And it's no so far off but I could go back and see mama when I like,' she added, in the genteel accent she had cultivated so carefully.

She pronounced 'mama' as though it rhymed with 'awe.'

'Oh, we'll dae weel eneuch here,' said he. 'Ye'll niver need tae gang far frae yer mither, ye see, Isa.'

'No,' said Isa faintly.

It was her future distance from Auntie Thompson that she was considering.

But Alec did not suspect that, any more than he suspected that this aunt supplied the reasons both for and against his marriage. The MacAndrew family were fully alive to the disgracefulness of Auntie Thompson, but they did not forget that she had solid savings and that Alec was her adopted son.

When he turned into the cottage garden his aunt had gone out again and was wheeling a heavy barrow of manure from the pigsty to the midden at the back of the house. It was Saturday, and she liked to have everything clean for the morrow. Alec followed her retreating figure.

'Weel,' he said plainly, 'a'm tae get her.'

She sat down on a shaft of the empty barrow.

'Ye'll be fine an' pleased,' she said, looking up at him.

His own good fortune obliterated everything else from his mind. He did not ask what she thought about it and she gave no opinion. She looked neither glad nor sorry. At last she rose.

'A dinna think vera muckle o' MacAndrew,' she observed as she took up the shafts of the barrow again.

They sat very silent over their supper that evening. Experience had made the young man so well aware of her support on every occasion that he needed no outward sign of it. He, himself, was not given to talking.

Next morning he awoke to the prospect of a day of happiness, and everything he saw seemed to reflect his own spirit as he went out bare-headed to contemplate the world in the light of his good fortune. The warm mist of the morning lay like a veil of faint lilac colour in shady places and the sun sent its shafts slanting across the wide fields that dipped and rose again in their long slope to the hills; the fir-woods stood as though painted on the atmosphere in blurs of smoky green with patches of copper-red gleaming through where the light caught their stems; the dew that had fallen on the sprawling nasturtiums rolled in beads on their leaves. Through the open door of the cottage the sound of Auntie Thompson's preparations for breakfast made a cheerful clinking stir of cups and homeliness. Sunday, that day on which Isa revealed herself to an admiring world, was always the main point of Alec's week, yet it was not often that he looked forward to the church hour with the excitement that he felt to-day. He glanced continually at the 'wag-at-the-wa' ' whose sober pendulum swung to and fro, scanning its matter of fact dial and thinking that its hands had never moved so slowly. For the whole length of the service he would be able to gaze upon Isa, as she sat, like a beautiful flower among vegetables, between her father and mother.

Pitairdrie kirk was a small, box-like building squatting at the roadside a mile and a half away, with its back to the line of the fir-woods and its iron gate set in a privet hedge. The latter gave access to a decent little gravel sweep on which the congregation would stand talking until the minister was reported to be in the vestry and the elders entered to take their places. Inside, the church had no great pretensions to beauty, and even the gallery which ran round three sides of it was innocent of the least grandeur; for the laird, who was the chief heritor, being an Episcopalian, his family did not ornament it by their presence; and the 'breist o' the laft,' as the front gallery pew was called, was occupied by that portion of his tenants which dwelt on the Muir Road. In the very middle of it was the place sacred to Auntie Thompson and Alec sat at her right hand. It was a splendid point of vantage for the young man, who could look down and have an uninterrupted view of the MacAndrew family.

As time went on, Alec grew more restless. Never had he known his aunt so slow in her preparations; never had there seemed so many small jobs to be done before she was ready to lock up the hen-house and proceed to her toilette. There were not many concessions that she was prepared to make to Sunday, but at last she disappeared into her little room to make them. She divested herself of her apron and took from her box the Sunday bonnet that had served her faithfully for the last ten years. It had a high crown of rusty black net, and its trimmings, which consisted of a black feather, a band of jet and a purple rose, added to the height at which it towered over her shining face. Above the short wincey dress it looked amazing.

She had taken her corpulent umbrella from behind the door and was tying her bonnet-strings in a long-ended bow under her chin, when Alec, standing in the garden and cursing fate, saw a sight that made his blood run cold.

The pigsty door stood open and the two pigs, which had pushed through a hole in the hedge, were escaping at a surging canter into the field behind the cottage. In another moment Auntie Thompson would come out and summon her nephew to help in the chase. Alec knew pigs intimately and he foresaw that their capture might be a matter of half an hour. He stole one wary glance at the house, set his hand upon the low garden wall, and vaulting into the road, ran for quite a hundred yards before he fell into a brisk walk; for he dreaded to hear some sound of the chase borne on the warm breeze that followed him.

He had stepped guiltily along for a few minutes when he heard the sound of trotting hoofs behind him and turned to look back. His heart gave a bound when he realised that the MacAndrew family had reached the last stage of their four-mile drive and were overtaking him at the steady jog of the hairy farm pony whose duties extended over the Sabbath day.

He redoubled his pace, for he did not want to lose one fragment of Isa's company. Pitairdrie kirk was not three-quarters of a mile ahead.

As the MacAndrew conveyance passed him his eyes met those of his promised bride and she smiled at him with a kind of reserved approval. The tiny seat on which she sat with her back to the pony was hidden by the frothy flounces of her blue Sunday gown, and the feather in her Leghorn hat curled downwards towards her shoulder. She managed to look graceful even in her cramped position. Opposite to their daughter, Mr. and Mrs. MacAndrew sat stiff and large; they could not enjoy very great ease of body because the ancient basket carriage was extremely low at the back and hung so near the ground that the boots of its occupants were a bare half foot from the ground. MacAndrew and Mrs. MacAndrew knew in their hearts

how much discomfort they would be spared if they were
but stepping the road like other people, but they would
have perished where they sat sooner than admit it to each
other. The reins in MacAndrew's hands went up in a steep
incline to the fork-like contrivance above Isa's head before
beginning their even steeper descent to the pony's mouth
on the other side of it. Neither husband nor wife had any
idea of the oddity of their appearance. They were 'carriage
people,' and that was enough. Their response to Alec's
greeting was tempered by the view they had just had of
Auntie Thompson in her grey wincey and towering bonnet
in full cry after the pigs.

The bell had not yet begun to ring when Alec entered
the kirk gate and saw Isa standing a little apart by her
mother upon the gravel; MacAndrew was in conversation
with a knot of acquaintances by the vestry door. Quite by
himself was a pale young man in a black coat, who looked
rather out of place among the strictly countrified men of the
congregation; he had a gold watchchain and he wore gloves.
He was good-looking in a townish way and he seemed to
be scanning his surroundings with some interest. It was
evident that Isa's curiosity was aroused by him.

'I don't know who that gentleman can be,' she said
to her lover, almost in the same breath in which she
greeted him.

As she spoke she adjusted a ribbon she wore at her
throat.

'A'm no carin' vera muckle wha he is,' replied he. 'It's
yersel' a'm thinkin' about, Isa.'

'Everybody will hear you if you speak so loud.'

'And what for no? A'm fine an' pleased they should
ken. Isa, will ye no walk back wi' me aifter the kirk's
skailed?'

'Maybe,' said the girl.

'Isa'll be tae drive i' the carriage,' broke in Mrs.
MacAndrew, who stood by watching her daughter like
an overfed Providence.

Alec looked at her with a sudden misgiving. He had never
thought much about a mother-in-law. His experience of
elderly women began and ended with Auntie Thompson,

whom he had so shamefully deserted in her need this morning.

The bell began to ring over their heads, and MacAndrew left his friends and joined his belongings.

'D'ye see yon lad yonder?' said he, nodding his head backwards over his shoulder towards the stranger.

Both his wife and his daughter closed in on him eagerly.

'He's just newly back frae Ameriky wi' a braw bittie money; he's no been hame since he was a bairn an' syne he's come back tae buy a fairm. He's got fowk he's seekin' hereaboot, they tell me, but a dinna ken wha they'll be. James Petrie couldna tell me, nor ony ither body.'

Mrs. MacAndrew's eyes were running over the strange young man as though she were pricing every garment he wore.

'Aye, aye,' she murmured, twisting her mouth appreciatively, 'a'll no say but he looks weel aff.'

There was a general move into the kirk, and Mrs. MacAndrew pushed in and squeezed into her seat, which was on the ground floor at right angles to the pulpit. It gave a good view of 'the breist o' the laft,' from end to end. Isa was swept from her lover, who made his way up to his own place. The strange young man went in after everybody else and stood looking round to see where he should go. A genial-looking old labourer beckoned him to a place at his side.

The minister was ushered up the pulpit steps by the beadle, and the ensuing psalm brought the minds of the congregation together. The stranger shared a book with his companion and contributed to the singing in a correct tenor which drew general attention to him once more. Isa observed him from under the brim of her Leghorn hat, noticing his trim hair and the gold tie-pin which made a bright spot in the sunshine that streamed from a window near him. She did not once look up at Alec, who sat in the gallery with his eyes riveted on her. Mrs. MacAndrew's thoughts were flowing in the same direction as those of her daughter. She was wondering what farm the stranger might have in his mind; there was one to be sold shortly, not a mile from her own roof. If only he had returned a Sunday earlier! Still . . .

She lost herself in speculations during the prayer that followed, and was only roused from them by the opening of the kirk door and the tramp of heavy boots climbing the gallery stairs. Up they came, and step by step the head of Auntie Thompson rose in a succession of jerks and was revealed to the worshippers below. Her glistening face was scarlet, for she had been engaged in a grim chase before starting on her walk and the steep stairs were the culmination of the whole. She stood still, panting audibly, while Alec held open the door of their pew, her grey wincey shoulders heaving and the monstrous erection, with its nodding feather and purple rose, pushed to one side. Most of those who looked up and saw her grinned. Mrs. MacAndrew turned her head away.

When the temporary distraction was over, quiet fell on the kirk again and the service went on decorously. The sun shifted from the window near the stranger and the gleam of his tie-pin transferred itself to the spectacles that lay beside his neighbour; the sermon began and one or two settled themselves for covert sleep. The rustling of the Bible leaves which followed the giving out of the text was over when a tiny black shadow darted across the ceiling of the kirk and dived with incredible swiftness down to the floor, across to a corner below the gallery, out and up again, whisking past the sounding-board of the pulpit. Finally it flew up and disappeared into one of the gaping ventilators overhead. Only Alec and a few occupants of the side galleries noticed the awful change that had come over Auntie Thompson's countenance.

She was looking at the ventilator that had swallowed the bat with an expression of concentrated dismay. Her red face had lost its colour and her eyes stared. Her breath came in gasps. Alec, who knew her weakness, stared at the ventilator too, for he did not know what might happen if the creature should come out. For one moment she seemed petrified, and he was too slow at grasping an emergency to whisper to her the suggestion that she should leave the kirk. Some girls in the gallery who were watching the situation stuffed their handkerchiefs into their mouths as they looked at Auntie Thompson. The minister, who, though exactly opposite and on the gallery level, was short-sighted, preached on undisturbed.

The bat shot out of the ventilator again like a flash of black lightning, and this time circled round the upper part of the building. Sometimes its circles were narrow and sometimes wide; once the angular wings almost brushed Alec's face; the wind of them lifted a stray lock of his hair, and Auntie Thompson leaned back with a convulsive noise, like a sob, in her throat. It was loud enough to attract the people below and many looked round. MacAndrew, who was asleep, awoke. His wife and Isa were looking up at Auntie Thompson like a couple of cats watching a nest of young birds.

The bat gave one of those faint, fretful chirrups peculiar to its kind and shot straight at the spot where the purple rose bloomed over Auntie Thompson's agonised face. As an armed man draws his revolver in defence of his life, she snatched her umbrella and put it up.

A smothered giggle burst from the gallery. Downstairs, the congregation, with a few exceptions, gazed up in horrified surprise; but the young stranger's friendly neighbour, having put on his spectacles, sat wearing a delighted grin that displayed his one remaining front tooth. The minister paused in his sermon; he did not know what had happened, but he could see clearly enough that the rigid image in the middle of the gallery which weekly experience told him was Auntie Thompson had changed its shape, and that a dark blur enveloped the spot where a face had been. He went on manfully, raising his voice.

Then the bat, in one of its wide sweeps, struck against the open umbrella. Auntie Thompson sprang up, and holding it slanting before her face, made stiffly, blindly, for the door. Her nephew opened it, and she passed out and disappeared from the public eye. Her heavy tread descended the stairs, and the tension which bound the assembly, as the plod of her boots marked each step of her descent, was only broken by the slam of the kirk door as she drew it to behind her. The sweat broke out on Alec's forehead.

At last the congregation got back its composure. The old man shut his mouth and the young suppressed their mirth. The faces of the MacAndrew family were set like stone; their sense of the outrage committed radiated from every feature and laid its chilly shadow on poor Alec across the whole space of the kirk.

When the last paraphrase was sung he hurried downstairs. Not a look had Isa given him. She hurried out with her father and mother, and by the time the young man had reached the gate MacAndrew had grasped the reins from the boy in charge of the pony and the carriage with its load was starting homewards. The girl turned away her head, so that he saw nothing but the outline of her cheek and the drooping feather as they drove away. Mr. and Mrs. MacAndrew looked steadily at the horizon in front of them. Alec's heart was hot with grief and wrath as he watched the absurd conveyance grow smaller and smaller in the distance.

He did not wait to speak to anyone. His pride was bitterly hurt and his sense of injury was forcing him to action of some kind; he was not clever, but his instinct told him that matters could not stay as they were. They must either go forward or back. It was lucky for him that the insolence of his future family-in-law was so marked that it helped him to act and to forget the ache in his heart in healthy anger. A mean-minded man might have blamed Auntie Thompson for her innocent share in the catastrophe, but Alec had no meanness in him.

He went past his own door without turning in, and on, up the Muir Road, until at the end of the four miles MacAndrew's little farm, with its varnished gate and perky laurel bushes, came into sight. The house was like a child's drawing in a copy-book; it had one window on either side of the door and three above. He approached boldly and knocked with his fist instead of pulling out the brass handle. He was not accustomed to bell-handles. Isa and Mrs. MacAndrew were watching him from behind a blind.

'The impidence o' him!' exclaimed the latter, 'aifter this mornin'—!'

'If it was not for Mrs. Thompson, I'd like him well enough,' sighed Isa, whose resolution was beginning to be a little affected by the sight of her lover.

'He'll need tae be done wi' yon auld limmer afore he can hae vera muckle tae say tae *us*,' rejoined her mother. 'Isa, ye'll no—'

But she was cut short by the servant, who opened the door and thrust Alec forward.

'Robina-Ann, a seat for Mr. Soutar,' said Mrs. MacAndrew, determined to put all possible distance between herself and the visitor by her knowledge of worldly customs.

The maid was bewildered. The room was full of chairs. There was a whole 'suite' of them in walnut.

'Wull a be tae hurl yer ain chair in-by frae the kitchen?' she inquired loudly.

Confusion smote the party, only missing Alec, who took no notice of any chair, but stood in the middle of the room.

Robina-Ann retreated before the eye of her mistress. The latter turned upon the young man. She meant to avenge the discomfiture dealt her by her servant on somebody.

But he forestalled her.

'Isa, what way would ye no speak tae me at the kirk? What ails ye at me?'

'A'll tell ye just now!' exclaimed Mrs. MacAndrew, her gentility forsaking her. 'A'll warrant ye it'll no tak' me lang! A'm seekin' tae ken what-like impidence brings ye here aifter the affront that Mrs. Thompson put upon the hale congregation!'

'A've come tae see Isa,' said Alec, the angry blood rising to his face.

'Weel, yonder's Isa!' cried Mrs. MacAndrew, pointing a finger that shook with rage, 'but ye'll no get vera muckle guid o' Isa! A'm no tae let a lassie o'mine waste hersel' on a plough-laddie – a fushionless loon that maybe hasna twa coats till his back – a lad a'd be fair ashamed o'—'

'O mamawe—!' began Isa.

'I'll mamawe ye!' shouted Mrs. MacAndrew, gathering rage from the sound of her own voice, 'hey! gang awa' oot o' this, you that's got nae richt tae speak till a lassie like mine! Gang awa' back tae yer auld besom o' an aunt that's nae mair nor a disgrace tae the parish!'

He stood looking at the coarse-grained, furious creature, astonished. Then he turned to Isa, prim and aloof, in her flounces.

'Isa—'

Mrs. MacAndrew opened her mouth again, but Alec stepped towards her. His eyes were so fierce that she drew back.

'Haud yer whisht, woman,' he said hoarsely, 'dinna get in my road. Isa, what are ye tae say? Ye wasna this way, yesterday.'

The girl looked rather frightened, and the corners of her small mouth drooped. She liked Alec, but she liked other things better. She was weak, but she was obstinate, and she had never overcome the feeling that she was throwing herself away. Before her mind's eye rose the vision of the stranger in church.

'What's wrang wi' me that wasna wrang yesterday?' he demanded.

Isa's vision, the vision with the trim hair, a gold tie-pin and a prospective farm, was making her feel rather guilty. It was so real to her that she felt she must hide it.

'It's – it's Mrs. Thompson,' faltered she.

'*What?*'

'Ye'll need to have no more to do with Mrs. Thompson if you're to marry me,' said she, plucking up courage.

An angry exclamation broke from him.

'Awa' ye gang!' cried Mrs. MacAndrew.

'Isa,' said Alec, 'd'ye mean that ye're seeking tae gar me turn ma back on m' Auntie Thompson?'

'Aye,' said the girl, nodding stubbornly.

He turned and went. On the threshold he looked back.

'Ye can bide whaur ye are,' said he. '*A'm* no wantin' ye.'

NOT MANY DAYS afterwards Isa walked down the Muir Road with a little packet in her hand. The hairy pony was at work on the farm, or she would have had herself driven in the basket carriage. But although she was on foot, she

wore her best hat with the drooping feather and her blue
flounced dress.

She had two excellent reasons for this extravagance. She
was going to the very door of the white cottage, and she
was anxious that Auntie Thompson's neighbours should
have a good chance of observing how superior she was to
Alec; also, she hoped that some happy stroke of fortune
might throw her against the interesting stranger. She had
heard nothing about him since the last eventful Sunday,
when he and Auntie Thompson respectively had produced
so much effect. Though she and her mother would have
maintained with their last breaths that it was the woman
who had brought about the change in Isa's situation, each
knew in her secret heart that it was the man. As she stepped
along the girl told herself that he must surely be somewhere
in the neighbourhood. Why had he come to Pitairdrie kirk
if he had no connection with Pitairdrie parish?

The parcel she carried contained some little presents her
lover had given her – a silk handkerchief, some strings of
beads, a pair of earrings.

She could not forgive him for his last words to her; her
vanity smarted and she longed to repay him for them.
There was something of her mother in her, for all her
elegant looks and refined aspirations. The pair had agreed
that the returning of the gifts by her own hand would be
an effective means of showing how little the parting from
Alec troubled her. If he should come to the door she
would hand him the packet with a few scornful words,
and if Auntie Thompson came, she would know how to
crush her by her manners and appearance. She had never
spoken to Auntie Thompson.

She turned into the little garden path. The tangle
of nasturtiums by the kitchen window prevented her
from seeing the two people who were observing her
approach from the hearth at which they sat. She knocked
at the door.

Words almost forsook her a moment later when it was
opened by the stranger, the object of all her day-dreams
and speculations. This time he was not dressed for Sunday.
But he had lost little by the change.

She was absolutely bewildered. He made no offer to admit her; he did not even ask her business. She gathered her wits as quickly as she could and addressed him, smiling and gracious. Her heart was beating.

'Does Mrs. Thompson live here?' she inquired, snatching, by the unnecessary question, at the chance of conversation.

'Yes.'

He had a strange accent.

'Perhaps you will kindly give this to Mr. Soutar?'

She held out the little packet.

'Thanks.'

He took it and shut the door in her face. The blood rushed to her cheeks. He had looked at her as though she were a puddle to be avoided in the road. There was nothing to do but to walk away with what dignity she could command.

Just as she went through the little gate an elderly woman passed. She was presumably a neighbour, for she had come from a house close by.

She overtook her in a few paces.

'What is the name of the gentleman who lives there?' she asked her, pointing back to the nasturtium-covered walls.

'Alec Soutar,' said the woman.

'I don't mean *him*,' said Isa, whose wits were coming back. 'I mean the *gentleman* I was speaking to.'

'Have ye no heard? Yon man's newly come frae Ameriky wi' a fortune. He's seekin' a wife, they tell me,' added the other, with a twinkle in her eye.

'But who is he? What is his name?'

'Dod, that's just Mistress Thompson's ither nephew, John MacQueen, that gaed awa' when he was a sma' laddie,' said the woman.

The Debatable Land

OF THE birth and origin of Jessie-Mary no one in the parish knew anything definite. Those who passed up the unfrequented cart-road by her grandmother's thatched hovel used to see the shock-headed child among the gooseberry bushes of the old woman's garden, peering at them, like an animal, over the fence.

Whether she were really the granddaughter of the old beldame inside the mud walls no one knew, neither, for that matter, did anybody care. The hovel was the last remaining house of a little settlement which had disappeared from the side of the burn. Just where it stood, a shallow stream ran across the way and plunged into a wood in which Jessie-Mary had many a time feasted on the plentiful wild raspberries, and run, like a little squirrel, among the trees.

It was not until she was left alone in the world that much attention was paid to her existence, and then she presented herself to the parish as a problem; for her life was lived a full half-century before the all-powerful Board School arose to direct rustic parents and guardians, and she had received little education. She had grown into a sturdy girl of twenty, with brown hair which the sun had bleached to a dull yellow, twisted up at the back of her head and hanging heavily over her brows. She was a fierce-looking lass, with her hot grey eyes. The parish turned its mind to the question of how she might earn a living and was presently relieved when Mrs. Muirhead, who was looking for an able-bodied servant, hired her in that capacity. She was to have a somewhat meagre wage and her clothes, and was to help her mistress in house and yard. When the matter was settled she packed her few possessions into a bundle and sauntered up the green loaning which ran between the hovel and Mrs. Muirhead's decent roof, marking where one fir-wood ended and another began.

Mrs. Muirhead was the widow of a joiner, and she inhabited a cottage standing just where the woods and the mouth of the loaning touched the high road that ran north to the hills. She was well to do, for a cottager, and her little yard, besides being stacked with planks which her son, Peter, sawed and planed as his father had done before him, contained a row of hen-coops and a sty enclosing a pig whose proportions waxed as autumn waned. When the laird trotted by, he cast a favourable eye on the place, which was as neat as it befitted the last house on a man's property to be. When he had passed on and was trotting alongside the farther wood he was no longer on his own ground, for the green, whin-choked loaning was debatable land lying between him and his neighbour.

As Jessie-Mary, with her bundle, came through the whins and opened the gate, Peter Muirhead, who was in the yard, heard the latch click and looked up from his work. At sight of the yellow head by the holly bushes he laid down the spokeshave he was using and came round to the front. The girl was looking at him with eyes whose directness a youth of his type is liable to misunderstand. He began to smile.

'Will Mistress Muirhead be ben?' said Jessie-Mary tentatively.

Peter did not answer, but approached, his smile taking meaning.

'Will Mistress Muirhead be ben the hoose?' she inquired, more loudly.

It occurred to her that he might not be in his right senses, for the mile or two of debatable track which separated her old home from her future one might as well have been ten, for all she had seen of the world at the other end of it. She knew very well that Muirhead the joiner had lived where she now stood, and she had seen the old man, but the shambling figure before her was entirely strange. Once, at the edge of the wood, she had listened to the whirr of sawing in the vicinity of the road and had gathered that the work went on, though Muirhead himself had departed.

'She's no here. Ye'll just hae to put up wi' me,' said Peter jocosely. His mother was in the house, but he saw no reason for divulging the fact.

Jessie-Mary stood silent, scarcely knowing what to say.

'Ye're a fine lassie,' observed Peter, still smiling alluringly.

She eyed him with distrust and her heavy brows lowered over her eyes; she began to walk towards the cottage. He sprang forward, as though to intercept her, and, as she knocked, he laid hold of her free hand. Mrs. Muirhead, from within, opened the door just in time to see him drop it. She was a short, hard-featured woman, presenting an expanse of white apron to the world; a bunch of turkeys' feathers, in which to stick knitting needles, was secured between her person and the band of this garment, the points of the quills uppermost. She looked from one to the other, then drawing Jessie-Mary over the threshold, she slammed the door.

'Dinna think a didna see ye, ye limmer!' she exclaimed, taking the girl roughly by the shoulder.

And so Jessie-Mary's working life began.

The little room allotted to her, looking over the yard, was no smaller than the corner she had inhabited in the mud cottage, yet it had a stifling effect; and its paper, which bore a small lilac flower on a buff ground, dazzled her eyes and seemed to press on her from all sides. In the cracked looking-glass which hung on it she could see the disturbing background behind her head as she combed and flattened her thick hair in accordance with Mrs. Muirhead's ideas. In leisure moments she hemmed at an apron which she was to wear when completed. Mrs. Muirhead was annoyed at finding she could hardly use a needle; she was far from being an unkind woman, but her understanding stopped at the limits of her own requirements. Jessie-Mary's equally marked limitations struck her as the result of natural wickedness.

Wherever the yard was unoccupied by the planks or the pigsty, it was set about with hencoops, whose inmates strayed at will from the enclosure to pervade the nearer parts of the wood in those eternal perambulations which occupy fowls. Just outside, where the trees began, was a pleasant strip of sandy soil in which the hens would settle themselves with much clucking and tail-shaking, to sit blinking, like so many vindictive dowagers, at their kind. Through this, the Dorking cock, self-conscious and gallant, would conduct the ladies of his family to scratch among the tree-roots; and the wood for about twenty yards from the house wore that peculiar scraped and befeathered look which announces the proximity of a hen-roost. At night the lower branches were alive with dark forms and the suppressed gurgling that would escape from them. It was part of Jessie-Mary's duty to attend to the wants of this rabble.

There were times when a longing for flight took the half-civilised girl. Life, for her, had always been a sort of inevitable accident, a state in whose ordering she had no part as a whole, however much choice she might have had in its details. But now there was little choice in these; Mrs. Muirhead ordered her day and she tolerated it as best she could. She hardly knew what to do with her small wage when she got it, for the finery dear to the heart of the modern country lass was a thing of which she had no knowledge, and there was no dependent relative who might demand it of her.

The principal trouble of her life was Peter, whose occupations kept him of necessity at home, and whose presence grew more hateful as time went on. There was no peace for her within sight of his leering smile. There was only one day of the week that she was free of him; and on these Sunday afternoons, as he went up the road to join the loitering knot of horsemen from the nearest farm, she would thankfully watch him out of sight from the shelter of the loaning. She hated him with all her heart.

He would lurk about in the evenings, trying to waylay her amongst the trees as she went to gather in the fowls, and once, coming suddenly on her as she turned the corner of the house, he had put his arm about her neck. She had felt his hot breath on her ear, and, in her fury, pushed him

from her with such violence that he staggered back against
a weak place in the yard fence and fell through, cutting
his elbow on a piece of broken glass. She stood staring
at him, half terrified at what she had done, but rejoicing
to see the blood trickle down his sleeve. She would have
liked to kill him. The dreadful combination of his instincts
and his shamblingness was what physically revolted her,
though she did not realise it; and his meanness had, more
than once, got her into trouble with his mother. She had
no consideration to expect from Mrs. Muirhead, as she
knew well. To a more complicated nature the position
would have been unendurable, but Jessie-Mary endured
stubbornly, vindictively, as an animal endures. She was in
a cruel position and her only safeguard lay in the fact that
Peter Muirhead was repulsive to her. But neither morality
nor expediency nor the armed panoply of all the cardinal
virtues have yet succeeded in inventing for a woman a
safeguard so strong as her own taste.

It was on a Sunday afternoon towards the end of September that Peter emerged from the garden and strolled up
the road. The sun was high above the woods, his rim as yet
clear of the tree-tops, and the long shadow from the young
man's feet lay in a dark strip between himself and the fence
at his side. He wore his black Sunday suit and a tie bought
from a travelling salesman who had visited Montrose fair
the year before. In his best clothes he looked more ungainly
than usual, and even the group of friends who watched his
approach allowed themselves a joke at his expense as he
neared them. He could hear their rough laughter, though
he was far from guessing its cause. Nature had given him
a good conceit of himself.

Jessie-Mary drew a breath of relief as his steps died
away and she hailed the blessed time, granted to her
but weekly, in which she might go about without risk of
meeting him. Everything was quiet. Mrs. Muirhead was
sitting in the kitchen with her Bible; the door was ajar
and the girl could just see a section of her skirt and the
self-contained face of the cat which blinked on the hearth
beside her. She had accompanied her mistress to the kirk
that morning and had thought, as they returned decorously

together, that she would go down the loaning again to see
the thatched cottage by the burn – perhaps stray a little
in the wood among the familiar raspberry-stalks. She had
not seen these old haunts since she left them for Mrs.
Muirhead's service.

She took off her apron and went out bareheaded. On the
outskirts of the trees the hens were rustling and fluttering in
the dust; as she passed, they all arose and followed her. She
had not remembered that their feeding-time was due in half
an hour and for a moment she stood irresolute. If she were
to go on her intended way there would be no one to give
them their food. She determined to make and administer
it at once; there would be plenty of time afterwards to do
what she wished to do.

She was so little delayed that, when the pail was put away
and the water poured into the tin dishes, there was still a
long afternoon before her. She threaded her way slowly
through the fir-stems, stopping to look at the rabbit-runs
or to listen to the cooing of wood pigeons, her path fragrant
with the scent of pine. After walking some way she struck
across the far end of the loaning into the road which led
to the mud hovel.

Autumn was approaching its very zenith, and the debatable land offered gorgeous tribute to the season. Like some
outlandish savage ruler, it brought treasures unnumbered
in the wealth of the more civilised earth. Here and there
a branch of broom stood, like a sceptre, among the black
jewels of its hanging pods, and brambles, pushing through
the whin-thickets like flames, hung in ragged splashes
of carmine and orange and acid yellow. Bushes of that
sweetbrier whose little ardent-coloured rose is one of the
glories of eastern Scotland were dressed in the scarlet hips
succeeding their bloom, and between them and the whin
the thrifty spider had woven her net. Underfoot, bracken,
escaping from the ditches, had invaded the loaning to clothe
it in lemon and russet. Where the ground was marshy,
patches of fine rush mixed with the small purple scabious
which has its home in the vagabond corners of the land.
As Jessie-Mary emerged from the trees her sun-bleached
hair seemed the right culmination to this scale of natural

colour; had it not been for the dark blue of her cotton gown she might as easily have become absorbed into her surroundings as the roe-deer, which is lost, a brown streak, in the labyrinth of trunks.

The air had the faint scent of coming decay which haunts even the earliest of autumn days, and the pale, high sky wore a blue suggestive of tears; the exhalations of earth were touched with the bitterness of lichen and fungus. Far away under the slope of the fields, and so hidden from sight, Montrose lay between the ocean and the estuary of the South Esk, with, beyond its spire, the sweep of the North Sea.

A few minutes later she found herself standing on the large, flat stone which bridged the burn where the footpath crossed it by her grandmother's hovel. She remained gazing at the walls rising from the unkempt tangle to which months of neglect were reducing the garden. The fence was broken in many places, and clumps of phlox, growing in a corner, had been trodden by the feet of strayed animals. Beneath her, the water sang with the same irresponsible babble which had once been the accompaniment to her life; she turned to follow it with her eyes as it dived under the matted grasses and disappeared into the wood.

All at once, from beyond the cottage, there rose a shout that made her heart jump, and she started to see two figures approaching through the field by the side of the burn; the blood left her face as she recognised one of them as Peter Muirhead. She sprang quickly from the stone and over the rail dividing the wood from the path; it was a foolish action and it produced its natural result. As she did so, a yell came from the field and she saw that Peter and his companion had begun to run.

Through the trees she fled, the derisive voices whooping behind her. She was terrified of her tormentor and the unreasoning animal fear of pursuit was upon her. As she heard the rail crack she knew that he had entered the wood, and instinct turned her towards the loaning, where the cover was thick and where she might turn aside in the tangle and be lost in some hidden nook while they passed her by. It was her best chance.

She plunged out from among the firs into the open track. For a hundred yards ahead the bushes were sparse and there was no obstacle to hinder her flight. She was swift of foot, and the damp earth flew beneath her. Through the whins beyond she went, scratching her hands on protruding brambles and stumbling among the roots. Once her dress caught on a stiff branch and she rent it away, tearing it from knee to hem. The voices behind her rose again and her breath was giving out.

Emerging from the thicket, she almost bounded into a little circle of fire, the smoke of which she had been too much excited to notice, though it was rising, blue and fine, from the clearing she had reached. A small tent was before her, made of tattered sail-cloth stretched over some dry branches, and beside it a light cart reposed, empty, upon its tailboard, the shafts to the sky.

In front of the tent stood a tall, lean man. His look was fixed upon her as she appeared and he had evidently been listening to the sound of her approaching feet. His face was as brown as the fir-stems that closed him in on either side of the loaning, and his eyes, brown also, had a peculiar, watchful light that was almost startling. He stood as still as though he were an image, and he wore a gold ring in either ear.

To Jessie-Mary, a living creature at this moment represented salvation, and before the man had time to turn his head she had leaped into the tent. Inside, by a little heap of brushwood, lay a tarpaulin, evidently used in wet weather to supplement its shelter, and she flung herself down on the ground and dragged the thing over her. The man stood immovable, looking fixedly at the bushes, from the other side of which came the noise of jeering voices.

As Peter Muirhead and his friend pushed into the open space, red and panting, they came upon the unexpected apparition with some astonishment. Tinkers and gipsies were far from uncommon in the debatable land, but the tall, still figure, with its intent eyes, brought them to a standstill. Peter mopped his forehead.

'Did ye see a lassie gae by yon way?' he inquired, halting

dishevelled from his race through the undergrowth, the sensational tie under one ear.

The brown man nodded, and, without a word, pointed his thumb over his shoulder in the direction in which they were going.

Peter and his companion glanced at each other; the former was rather blown, for he was not naturally active.

'Huts! a've had eneuch o' yon damned tawpie!' he exclaimed, throwing his cap on the ground.

The brown man looked him carefully over and smiled; there was a kind of primitive subtlety in his face.

Like many ill-favoured persons, Peter was vain and the look displeased him, for its faint ridicule was sharpened by the silence that accompanied it.

'A'll awa' to Montrose an' get the pollis tae ye the nicht,' he said, with as much superiority as he could muster; 'the like o' you's better oot o' this.'

'Ye'll no can rin sae far,' replied the other.

The answer was a mere burst of abuse.

'Come awa' noo, come awa',' said Peter's friend, scenting difficulties and unwilling to embroil himself.

But Peter was in a quarrelsome humour, and it was some time before the two young men disappeared down the track and Jessie-Mary could crawl from her hiding-place. She came out from under the sail-cloth, holding together the rent in her gown. The brown man smiled a different smile from the one with which he had regarded Peter; then he stepped up on a high tussock of rush to look after the pursuers.

'Are they awa'?' she asked, her eyes still dilated.

'Aye,' he replied. 'A didna tell on ye, ye see.'

'A'd like fine tae bide a bit,' said the girl nervously, 'they michtna be far yet.'

'Just sit ye doon there,' said he, pointing to his tattered apology for a dwelling.

She re-entered the tent and he seated himself before her on the threshold. For some minutes neither spoke and he considered her from head to foot. It was plain he was one chary of words. He took a short pipe from his pocket and, stuffing in some tobacco, lit it deliberately.

'A saw yon lad last time a was this way,' he said, jerking his head in the direction in which Peter had disappeared.

As she opened her mouth to reply the snort of a horse came through the bushes a few yards from where they sat. She started violently. There was a sudden gleam in his face which seemed to be his nearest approach to a laugh. 'Dod, ye needna be feared,' he said. 'Naebody'll touch ye wi' me.'

'A was fine an' glad tae see ye,' broke out the girl. 'Yon Muirhead's an ill lad tae hae i' the hoose – a bide wi' his mither, ye ken.'

As she spoke the tears welled up in her eyes and rolled over. She was by no means given to weeping, but she was a good deal shaken by her flight, and it was months since she had spoken to anyone whose point of view could approach her own. Not that she had any conscious point of view, but in common with us all she had a subconscious one. She brushed her sleeve across her eyes.

He sat silent, pulling at his pipe. From the trees came the long-drawn note of a wood-pigeon.

'A'll need tae be awa' hame and see tae the hens,' said the girl, at last.

The man sat still as she rose, watching her till the whins closed behind her; then he got up slowly and went to water the pony which was hobbled a few yards off. When evening fell on the debatable land, it found him sitting at his transitory threshold, smoking as he mended the rabbit-snare in his hand.

For Jessie-Mary, the days that followed these events were troublous enough. The tear in her gown was badly mended, and Mrs. Muirhead, who had provided the clothes her servant wore, scolded her angrily. Peter was sulky, and, though he left her alone, he vented his anger in small ways which made domestic life intolerable to the women. Added to this, the young Black Spanish hen was missing.

The search ranged far and near over the wood. The bird, an incorrigible strayer, had repaid previous effort by being found in some outlying tangle with a 'stolen nest' and an air of irritated surprise at interruption. But hens were not clucking at this season, and Mrs. Muirhead, in the dusk of one evening, announced her certainty that some cat or trap had removed the truant from her reach for ever.

'There's mony wad put a lazy cutty like you oot o' the place for this!' she exclaimed, as she and Jessie-Mary met outside the yard after their fruitless search. 'A'm fair disgustit wi' ye. Awa' ye gang ben the hoose an' get the kitchen reddit up – just awa in-by wi' ye, d'ye hear?'

Jessie-Mary obeyed sullenly. The kitchen window was half open and she paused beside it before beginning to clear the table and set out the evening meal. A cupboard close to her hand held the cheese and bannocks but she did not turn its key. Her listless look fell upon the planet that was coming out of the approaching twilight and taking definiteness above a mass of dark tree-tops framed in by the window sash. She had small conscious joy in such sights, for the pleasures given by these are the outcome of a higher civilisation than she had yet attained. But even to her, the point of serene silver, hung in the translucent field of sky, had a remote, wordless peace. She stood staring, her arms dropped at her sides.

The shrill tones of her mistress came to her ear; she was telling Peter, who stood outside, the history of her loss. Lamentation for the Black Spanish hen mingled with the recital of Jessie-Mary's carelessness, the villainy of serving-lasses as a body, the height in price of young poultry stock. Like many more valuable beings, the froward bird was assuming after death an importance she had never known in life.

A high-pitched exclamation came from Peter's lips.

'Ye needna speir owre muckle for her,' he said, 'she's roastit by this time. There's a lad doon the loan kens mair aboot her nor ony ither body!'

'Michty-me!' cried Mrs. Muirhead.

'Aye, a'm tellin' ye,' continued he, 'the warst-lookin' great deevil that iver ye saw yet. He gie'd me impidence, aye did he, but a didna tak' muckle o' that. "Anither word," says I, "an' ye'll get the best thrashin' that iver ye got." He hadna vera muckle tae say after that, I warrant ye!'

Seldom had Mrs. Muirhead been so much disturbed. Her voice rose to unusual heights as she discussed the matter; the local policeman must be fetched at once, she declared; and, as she adjured her son to start for his house without delay, Jessie-Mary could hear the young man's refusal to move a step before he had had his tea. She was recalled to her work by this and began hurriedly to set out the meal.

As she sat, a few minutes later, taking her own share at the farther end of the table, the subject was still uppermost, and by the time she rose mother and son were fiercely divided; for Peter, who had taken off his boots and was comfortable, refused to stir till the following morning. The hen had been missing three days, he said, and the thief was still in his place; it was not likely he would run that night. And the constable's cottage was over a mile off. The household dispersed in wrath.

In the hour when midnight grew into morning, Jessie-Mary closed the cottage door behind her and stole out among the silent trees. The pine-scent came up from under her feet as she trod and down from the blackness overhead. The moon, which had risen late, was near her setting, and the light of the little sickle just showed her the direction in which she should go. In and out of the shadows she went, her goal the clearing among the whins in the debatable land. As the steeple of distant Montrose, slumbering calmly between the marshes and the sea, rang one, she slipped out of the bushes and, going into the tent, awakened the sleeping man.

IT WAS SOME time before the two came out of the shelter, and the first cock was crowing as the pony was roused and led from his tether under the tilted shafts. The sail-cloth was taken down and a medley of pots and pans and odd-looking implements thrown into the cart; the wheels were noiseless on the soft sod of the loaning as, by twists and turns, they thrust their way along the overgrown path.

Day broke on the figures of a man and woman who descended the slope of the fields towards the road. The man walked first.

And, in the debatable land among the brambles, a few black feathers blew on the morning wind.

The Fiddler

DALMAIN VILLAGE lies a few miles from Forfar town
in that part of western Angus where the land runs up in great
undulations from Strathmore towards the Grampians; and
it is tucked away, deep down in a trough between a couple
of these solid waves. A narrow burn slips westward to the
Isla through this particular trough with the roughest of
rough country roads alongside it. The two together pass
in front of a small collection of low cottages which forms
the village. There is just room, and no more, for the little
hamlet, and from their southern windows the dwellers in
the kirkton of Dalmain can see their kirk perched on the
bank above them where the shoulder of the next wave rises
in their faces. In the dusky evenings of late autumn it looks
like a resident ghost with its dead white sides glimmering
through the trees that surround it. It is the quietest place
imaginable, and no doubt it was quieter still in the days
of which I am writing; for the 'forty-five', with its agonies
and anxieties, had passed by nearly forty years back; and
though the beadle was still lame from a sword-cut, the old
man's limp was all that was left to show any trace of that
convulsion of Scotland to the outward eye.

It was on one of these October afternoons of 1784 that two
men sat talking in Dalmain manse; one was the minister,
Mr. Laidlaw, and the other was an Englishman who had
arrived a few hours earlier. The latter had never seen his
host before, and had crossed the Tweed a few days before,
for the first time. He had just started upon the business
which had brought him from Northumberland and the
stir of Newcastle into this – to him – remotest of all
possible places.

The minister was a plain, elderly man with pursed lips

which gave him the look of being a duller person than he actually was, and his companion, a good many years the younger of the two, alarmed him by his unfamiliar accent. The Englishman had a pleasant, alert expression. He was leaning over the table at which both were sitting, one on either side.

'I know that his name was Moir,' he was saying, 'and that is all I know, except that they were seen together in Glen Aird soon after Culloden, and that my cousin Musgrave was badly wounded in the side. I have discovered from the records of his regiment that there was a Moir in it, a native of Dalmain. I can only guess that this man is the same. No doubt I have set out on a wild-goose chase, sir, but I thought it might be worth while to make the experiment of coming here.'

'It is a matter of an inheritance, you say,' said Mr. Laidlaw, pursing his lips more than ever and raising his eyebrows, 'I got that from your letter, I think?'

'It is. We are a Jacobite family, though we are not Scots – there are many such in the north of England – and this officer in the Prince's army, whom, of course, I never saw, made my father his heir. He had nothing to leave, as a matter of fact,' he added, smiling.

'Then, sir, I would remark that it is not very easy to see your difficulty,' observed Laidlaw drily.

'There's an answer to that. It has only lately been discovered that he had an interest in a foreign business which has never paid until now. His share of the profits should come to me, as my father is dead and I am his only surviving child. But it appears that I cannot claim the money until my cousin Musgrave's death is legally proven. It is barely possible that he is still alive, for it is about forty years since he disappeared, and he has made no sign, though his wife was living until six months ago.'

'He would be an old man too, no doubt?'

'He would be nearing eighty by this time.'

There was a pause.

'You tell me there are still some of the Moir family left in this parish,' continued the Englishman.

Laidlaw cleared his throat. 'I doubt you may not find

much to help you,' he said. 'It is curious that you should choose this time for your search. It is not just a fortunate one; for though, as I have said, I shall be happy to serve your interests, I fear it is little I can do. There are two persons of the name of Moir in the parish, two elderly bodies. One is at this moment dying – indeed she may be dead by now. She has been unconscious these few days, and it is for that reason that I am not beside her; my ministrations are useless.'

'I see,' said the Englishman, his face falling; 'of course I could not trouble her sister in the circumstances.'

'It is not that, sir, for I should be glad to give you what hospitality I can till she was able to see you; but she is a strange creature – both are strange. The dying one has been slightly deranged in her mind since she was a young lass – for the last twelve-month she has been completely so – and the younger sister, Phemie, is a very extraordinary character. The bairns are feared of her, and some of the more foolish of my congregation take her for a witch, though I tell them such things are just havers. She seems to have no ill-will at anybody.'

'But what is wrong with her, then?'

'She will speak to nobody. Months at a time she will keep the house. I have only been a short while in this place, just three years past, and in that time she has been twice at the kirk on the Lord's Day, no more.'

'There must be madness in the family, sir, I should think.'

'I believe not,' replied the minister. 'She is thrawn, that's all – twisted, I suppose you might say in England.'

'And are there no male relations?'

'I understand there was an older brother, but he left Dalmain long ago. I have heard no more than that.'

'If my cousin and the man Moir fled together after the battle of Culloden, the same fate may have overtaken them both. I admit that my chances of discovering the truth are not promising.'

'That is true enough,' said Laidlaw, 'but we should wait awhile before we despair.'

'But I cannot trespass indefinitely on you, Mr. Laidlaw—'

'You'll need to bide a day or two, sir; I shall be happy if you will. I am not much company for you, I know,' he added diffidently.

'You are only too kind!' exclaimed the other. 'I have heard many a time that Scotland is a hospitable country and now I see it. I am very fortunate to be here with you instead of hunting a dead man by myself.'

Laidlaw coloured a little. He was a shy man and a humble one.

'And now,' said his companion, rising, 'I will not waste your time with my affairs. You are probably busy at this hour. I will go for a stroll and see something of this place before dark sets in.'

He walked to the window, which was open to the still October air.

'Surely that is someone tuning a violin,' he said, turning round to the minister. His face was bright. 'I am something of a musician myself,' he added.

'Oh!' exclaimed Laidlaw, jumping up, 'I had forgotten! You have come at a good time, sir – the great Neil Gow is here!'

'And who is he?'

'Presairv's!' cried Laidlaw, growing, as he always did, more Scottish under astonishment, 'did ye never hear o' Neil Gow?'

'I have not had that advantage,' replied his guest, becoming correspondingly English.

'He is the greatest fiddler in Scotland!'

'Indeed.'

The minister was oblivious of any humour but his own. 'This is a chance an English body might not get in a lifetime! It's many a long day since he was here. It was the year of Culloden, they tell me, before they had put the plough on thae fields west o' the kirkton. There was a green yonder, below the braes o' broom, that was a fine place for dancing. The English soldiers were about these parts then at the foot of the glens, waiting for the poor lads that were seeking their homes after the battle, but they danced for all that. Neil was a young lad himsel' then. There's nobody here but the beadle minds of it.

But he'll never forget yon days till they take him to the
kirkyard.'

'Indeed,' said the Englishman again.

'Aye, he was lying in his bed in a house that looked
on the green with a wound in his leg, though his wife
tellt everybody it was typhus, to keep folks from going
in. It was June-month, and the broom was out on the
brae. They said Neil was daft; the beadle could hear him
from where he lay, skirling and laying on the bow. He kept
them dancing till it was too late for a man to see the lass he
danced with, and Neil's arm was that stiff he had it tied
up next day when he left Dalmain; and a callant had to
go with him to carry the fiddle. But time flies, sir. Likely
there'll no be a lad dancing to it the night that ever heard
him play before. I am a Dunkeld man mysel', so I am well
acquaint with him. He's playing at a dance at the Knowes'
farm. Knowes' wife is a niece o' Neil's.'

'Then you do not disapprove of dancing?'

'Toots, no! And suppose I did, what would it avail me
in Perth or Angus?'

'Are they great dancers here?'

Laidlaw gave an impatient snort. There seemed to be so
many things his travelled-looking guest had not heard of.

'I will certainly go and hear your fiddler,' said the
Englishman. 'But sir, you must come with me.'

Laidlaw sighed. His sermon lay heavy on his mind. 'I
must follow you later – but it's a pity,' said he.

While this conversation was going on in the manse,
a little group was assembled in the kitchen of Phemie
Moir's cottage, where the beadle of Dalmain kirk stood
with open psalm-book in the middle of the room. He was
a lean, lame old man with aquiline features set in a fringe
of white whisker, and he was sending his stentorian voice
into the faces of the men before him. The place was full
of rough figures, roughly clothed. Two women were in the
kitchen, but only one was visible, and she sat by the hearth.
The other lay behind the drawn curtain of the box-bed let
into the wall; for she was dying, and had nearly got to the
end of what was proving to be a very easy business. The
elders had gathered together this evening to give point to

Margaret Moir's passage into the next world, and were well embarked on the psalm that was following the prayer they had offered. A shadow of officialdom impelled the singers to hold their books breast-high and to keep their eyes fixed upon the page, though the dimness of the cruisie at the wall turned their action into a pure piece of romance. It was romance and officialdom mixed that made those who had no books look over the shoulders of those who had; for none could see and all had the metrical psalms by heart. They went about their work with a disinterested unanimity that levelled them all into a mere setting for the beadle, Phemie, and the unseen figure behind the curtain.

No stir nor sign came from the drawn hangings of the box-bed, and though the most tremendous event of human life was enacting itself in that hidden space sunk in the wall, the assembly seemed to be entirely concerned with keeping up the gale of psalmody. Even Phemie, who neither sang nor prayed, and to whom the approaching loss must convey some personal significance, remained detached and impassive, with the tortoiseshell cat at her feet. The animal alone appeared to be conscious that anything unusual was going forward, for it sat bolt upright, looking with uneasy, unblinking eyes to the bed.

In the middle of the fourteenth verse, the last but one of the dragging psalm, the cat rose and walked with slow, tentative feet towards the wall. It sprang up on the seat of a chair at the bedside and disappeared behind the short curtain; whilst the singers, aroused from their preoccupation by the movement of the stealthy creature across the flags, wavered a moment in their tune.

Before a man had time to do more than nudge his neighbour the cat had leaped back into view and made frantically for the door, where it crouched, miaowing and scraping at the threshold.

The verse faltered and fell and a faint breath of disquiet went over the singers; they were dumb as the beadle limped across the kitchen and, drawing back the wisp of hanging stuff, peered into the dark, square space that opened behind it like a mouth. There was a moment's silence; then he turned to them again!

'Sing on, lads,' he said, 'anither verse'll land her!'

The elders struck up once more. They sang steadily to the end and then stood back with closed books and shuffling feet. The beadle released the terrified cat. The company filed solemnly out, leaving him and Phemie in the kitchen – only two now; that hidden, third presence was gone.

The woman stood by the bed.

'Aye, she's awa',' she said.

Her sister had been practically dead for the last twelve months, a mere mindless puppet to be fed a little less regularly than the cat, a little more regularly than the hens.

The beadle looked on, silent, as his companion drew the sheet over the dead woman's face. His legitimate part in the event was to come later. Then he also went out, crossing the small, rapid burn which divided Phemie's cottage from the road. Under the overhanging weeds it was gurgling loud, for it had rained in the hills and the streams were swelling.

He stood looking up and down the way. Voices were floating to him from the Knowes' farm. He had done what he considered was required of him as an official and relaxation was his due. Also it was unthinkable that anything, from a kirk meeting to a pig-killing, should go on without him at Dalmain. He clapped his psalm-book into his pocket and turned towards the Knowes', for, like the Englishman, he heard the fiddle tuning. He had worn a completely suitable expression at the scene he had just left, and as he drew nearer to the steading it changed with every step; by the time he had kicked the mud from his feet at the threshold of the big barn, which was filling with people from all corners of this and neighbouring parishes, he wore a look of consistent joviality. His long mouth was drawn across his hatchet face and grinned like that of a sly old collie dog.

The barn was roughly decorated with branches of rowan nailed here and there against the walls, and the scarlet berries of the autumn-stricken leaves were like outbreaks of flame. The floor was swept clean and a few stable lanterns were hung from rafters, or set on boxes in the angles of the building; the light from these being so much dispersed that it only served to illuminate such groups as came into the individual radius of each. The greater part of those who stood about waiting for the dancing to begin were dark figures with undistinguishable faces. There was a hum of talk and an occasional burst of laughter and horseplay. At the further end of the place a heavy wooden chair was set upon a stout table. Knowes, the giver of the entertainment, loitered rather sheepishly in the background; he was of no account, though he was a recent bridegroom; for it was his wife's relationship to the great fiddler who was to preside this evening which shed a glory on his household and turned their house-warming into an event. He was an honest fellow and popular, but the merrymakers had no thought for anyone but Neil.

The position that Neil Gow had made for himself was a remarkable one. There was no community in Perthshire, Angus, or the Mearns, that did not look on him with possessive affection. He played alike at farmhouse dances, at public balls, in villages and bothies, at the houses of lairds and dukes; he met every class and was on terms of friendship with the members of each. He had humour and spirit; and though he was entirely outspoken and used a merry tongue on every rank and denomination among his friends, his wit and good sense and the glamour of a fine personality allowed him to do so without offence. He was accustomed to speak his mind to his great friend and patron, the Duke of Atholl, as well as to his guests. 'Gang doon to yer suppers, ye daft limmers,' he had once cried to the dancers at Atholl House, 'an' dinna haud me here reelin' as if hunger an' drouth were unkent i' the land!' Many a poor man knew Neil's generosity and many a richer one in difficulties; out of his own good fortune he liked to help those less happy than himself. He had an answer for everybody, a hand for all. He was a self-made king whose sceptre was his bow and whose crown was his upright soul and overflowing humanity.

At last the group inside the barn-door dispersed, and Neil, who had been the centre of it, shook himself free and went over, his fiddle under his arm, to the table

beside which a long bench was set that he might step
up to his place. He would begin to play alone to-night,
for his brother Donald, who was his violoncello, had been
detained upon their way.

'Aye, sit doon, twa-three o' ye, on the tither end o't,'
he exclaimed to a knot of girls who were watching him
with expectant eyes; 'ye'd nane o' ye get yer fling wi' yer
lads the nicht, gin a was tae turn tapsalterie!'

They threw themselves simultaneously upon the bench,
tittering, and he stepped up on the table, a tall, broad
figure in tartan breeches and hose. His hair was parted
in the middle and hung straight and iron grey, almost to
his great shoulders, and his cheekbones looked even higher
than they already were from the shadows cast under them
by the lantern swinging above. There was no need for the
light, for he carried no music and would have scorned
to depend upon it. His marked eyebrows rose from his
nose to the line that drew them level along the temples
above his bright and fearless eyes. His large, finely cut
mouth was shut, his shoulders back, as he surveyed the
crowd below him. A subdued murmur rose from it. The
company began to arrange itself in pairs. He smiled and
stood with his bow hand raised; he was just going to drop
it to the strings when Donald Gow came in.

WHEN THE ENGLISHMAN had left the minister to his sermon
he made his way slowly to the village. He was in no hurry,
for though Laidlaw had stirred a slight curiosity in him
about the fiddler, he was principally interested in seeing
what it was that this unsophisticated little world, of which
he knew nothing, had magnified into a marvel. The thought
of it amused him. It was a kindly amusement, for he was
a good-hearted man who liked his fellow-creatures as a
whole. The rotting leaves were half fallen and their moist
scent rose from underfoot, a little acrid, but so much mixed
with earth's composite breath that it was not disagreeable. A
robin hopped along at a few yards' distance with the trustful
inquisitiveness of its kind. The fiddle had begun, but he was

too far from it to hear plainly, and it sounded muffled, as though from the interior of some enclosed place. One or two faint lights were showing in cottage windows across the burn. The gurgling voice of the water made him feel drowsy. He was in the humour which makes people lean their folded arms on gates, but he could not do that, for there were no gates here; rough bars thrust across the gaps in unpointed walls were the nearest approach to gates that he could see. How much poorer it all looked than England, and how different! He knew that it was a wilder place over which his cousin had fought, and he thought of the wounded fugitive tramping this comfortless country with the vanished and problematical Moir. He feared, as he had said to Laidlaw, that he was on a wild-goose chase. He felt a stirring of pity in him for the dwellers in this lost, strange backwater; and it seemed no wonder to him that a common fiddler should arouse so much delight, even in a moderately educated man, such as he took Laidlaw to be. As the dusk fell it grew chilly, so he went to the Knowes' farm and found his way among the stacks to the barn-door. The dancing was now in full swing, so he stood unnoticed by the threshold, looking in.

The lights were flickering in the draught created by the whirl of the reel which was in progress, and men and women of all ages between sixteen and sixty seemed lost to everything but the ecstasy of recurrent rhythm that swayed them. The extraordinary elaboration of steps and the dexterity of feet shod in heavy brogues amazed the Englishman. He could not follow any single pair long enough to disentangle their intricacies of movement, for no sooner did he think he was on the way to it than the whole body of dancers was swallowed up in collective loops of motion, and then were spinning anew in couples till the fiddle put them back in their places and the maze of steps began again. The rhythmic stamping went on like the smothered footfall of a gigantic approaching host; not so much a host of humanity as of some elemental force gathering power behind it. It gripped him as he listened and felt the rocking of the wooden floor. His eyes were drawn across the swinging crowd, the confused shadows and the dust of the thickening atmosphere, to what was the live heart of it all.

The largest lantern, high above, hung direct from its rafter over the head of Donald Gow as he sat on his chair with the dark, dim-looking violoncello between his knees. Before him on the broad table stood Neil, the light at his back magnifying his size. His cheek was laid against his violin, his right foot, a little advanced, tapped the solid boards, as, pivoted on his left one, he turned to and fro, swaying now this way, now that, his eye roving over the mass that responded, as though hypnotised, to the spur of his moving bow. It was as if he saw each individual dancer and was playing to him or to her alone; as if his very being was urging each one to answer to his own abounding force and compelling the whole gathering to reflect every impulse of his mind. The stream of the reel poured on, throbbing and racing, leaping above the sonorous undertone of the violoncello, but never, for all the ardent crying of the string, leaving the measured beat of the matchless time. Now and again, at some point of tension, he would throw a short, exultant yell across the barn, and the tumult of ordered movement would quicken to the sharp inspiration of the sound.

The Englishman stood, with beating pulses and every nerve and muscle taut, gazing at Neil. He loved music and had toiled patiently, and with a measure of success, at the violin. He knew enough to recognise his technical skill, yet the pleasure of that recognition, so great even to one with less knowledge than he possessed, was forgotten in the pure rush of feeling, the illumination cast upon his mind by which intangible things became clear. He seemed to understand – perhaps only for a moment – the spirit of the land he was in, and the heart of the kinsman whose track he was trying to follow, whose body lay, perchance, somewhere among those hills he had seen before him guarding the northern horizon, as he neared Dalmain. For a moment he could have envied him his participation in the forlorn cause he had espoused. The love of country, which was a passion in the race around him, which, unexpressed in mere words, poured out of the violin in this master-hand, was revealed to him, though he could only grasp it vicariously. As he stood, thrilled, on the brink of the whirlpool, its outer circles were rising about his feet. The music stopped suddenly and Neil threw down his bow.

The Englishman awoke as from a dream and drew back. One or two people, aware for the first time of a stranger's presence, looked at him curiously, but most of the dancers were crowding round the table where Neil was now sitting in his brother's place.

'Na, na,' he was saying, 'a'll no win doon till a hae a drink. Man Donal', awa' wi' ye an' get a dram till us baith.'

The Englishman went back to the stackyard; he wished Mr. Laidlaw had not stayed behind, for he did not mean to return to the manse till he had heard Neil play again. He was an intruder, which was a little embarrassing to him, and he felt his position would be bettered if he had someone to speak to. But the scraps of talk he heard did not encourage him to address anyone, because he was not sure of understanding any reply he might get. Soon a small boy came out of the barn and paused in surprise to look at him; he was apparently of an inquisitive turn of mind, for he hung about examining every detail of the stranger's appearance. He bore the scrutiny for a few minutes.

'What is your name, my lad?' he inquired at last, reflecting that it would not matter if he *did* look like a fool before this child.

The boy made no answer but backed a step, open-mouthed. The question was repeated, and this time produced an effect, for he turned and ran, as though accosted by an ogre.

He did not stop till he was clear of the stackyard, but when he reached the road he stood still. He had been told by his mother to come home before dark, and when he had first caught sight of the Englishman he was debating whether or no he should obey her. He was now put out at finding himself on the way there, and stood undecided, pouting and kicking his heels in the mud. Looking back, he saw a figure moving among the stacks, and the sight decided him. He set off resentfully, cheated into virtue; a situation that was hateful.

He had no mind to hurry. If he was diddled by an unfair chance into respecting his mother's orders, he was not going to interpret them literally. Everything was close together in the kirkton of Dalmain, and though he was not a dozen yards from the farm-gate he was abreast of the first cottage in the row. The fiddle had begun again and he could hear it very plainly and the shouts and thudding of feet. It was almost as good as being in the barn, if only there was something to look at. He began to amuse himself by building a little promontory out into the burn with the biggest stones he could collect. He had often been forbidden to do this, and he was glad of the opportunity of being even with fate. When he had been at it for some time, and even disobedience began to pall, he noticed that a bar of light was lying on the water, falling on it from the window of a cottage down stream. Bands of shadow were crossing and recrossing this in a strange way, as if some movement were going on behind the window panes. He jumped over the burn, crept along by the harled wall and, crouching by the sill, peered in.

WHEN THE ELDERS had left the Moirs' house and the beadle had betaken himself to the Knowes', Phemie sat on by the fire, like some commonplace image of endurance, seemingly stupefied. Another woman might have been aroused by the entrance of neighbours drawn by the news of what had happened and ready to help in those duties necessitated by a death that the poor share so faithfully with one another. But she had no neighbours in the fuller sense of the word, and the few with whom she had even the slightest communication were enjoying themselves not a furlong from her door. Her thoughts had gone back – far back; years and years back – to the turning-point of her obscure life. She saw it dimly, across the everlasting monotony that had closed down on her and hers at that last time upon which she had taken her place among her kind. Secrecy and servitude to the stricken creature who now lay rigid upon the box-bed; these had been her lot. Servitude was over, but her tardy freedom conveyed little to her, and secrecy – long since unnecessary, though she had never grasped the fact that it was so – clung to her as a useless, threadbare garment. Her solitariness would be no greater. The doors of her prison had opened, but she could not go free because of the fetters she wore.

She got up at last and threw some fuel into the grate. The flame rose and she tried to collect herself. There were things she must do. She went to the outhouse that opened from the back of the kitchen and got a bucket to fill at the burn. This she carried out to the water, but as she stooped with it, it dropped from her hands. The sound of leaping, compelling reel-music cut its way from the Knowes' farm to her ears. A blind fiddler had once said that he could tell the stroke of Neil Gow's bow among a hundred others, and Phemie Moir knew who was playing. She clasped her hands over her face and fled indoors.

The lethargy that had enveloped her was gone, snatched away as a wayfarer's cloak is snatched from him by the wind. She began to run to and fro, crying out, now lifting her arms over her head, now thrusting them forward; her sobs filled the kitchen though her eyes were tearless. She had slammed the door behind her that she might not hear the fiddle. Once she paused by it, not daring to open it, but laying her ear to the edge of the jamb, in the hope of finding that it had ceased. It was going on steadily, and she turned the little shawl she wore up over her head and ran back into the outhouse to get farther from the sound. But a broken plank in the thin wooden walls brought it to her afresh, and she rushed back again and sank upon the chair she had left by the hearth.

When she was a little quieter she returned to the door to listen, the tension of fear upon her. It was at this moment that the urchin, creeping along outside, stumbled over the fallen pail. The sudden noise shattered the temporary quiet of her strained nerves and let loose the unreasoning demon of her terror again. She ran up and down between the walls like a frenzied thing.

The boy crept nearer. It was now dark enough to conceal him from the inmate of the house so long as he did not approach his face to the deep-set panes. He was having his fill of wonders to-night and he watched her, fascinated.

He had heard no word of Margaret Moir's death. Phemie was a person he had seldom seen at close quarters, because his home was at some distance from the kirkton, and the garden of her cottage, beyond which she rarely ventured, lay behind it, out of sight of passers along the road. But he knew from the children he played with that there was something disquieting about her, and that the minister had rebuked a friend of his mother's for saying that she was a witch. What he now saw woke the horrid suspicion that it was the minister who was in the wrong. His sense of adventure in gazing at her thus was great; only the wall between them gave him the courage to indulge it. The cat, which, since the beadle had let it out, had been skulking restlessly about the roadside, came, a parti-coloured shadow, out of the darkness and thrust itself between his feet. He was not sorry to have a familiar living creature so near him. He was about to touch its warm head with his fingers when his eye fell upon the bed. There was no more to see on it than the square space revealed, but that was enough. There is something about the lines of a dead figure not to be mistaken, even by a child, particularly by a child bred up among the plain-spoken inhabitants of a countryside. Panic-struck, he plunged through the burn and made as hard as he could for the cheerful commotion of the Knowes'. The cat stood looking after him, its back arched, recoiling a little, like a gently bred dame from some unforeseen vulgarity.

The fiddle had stopped and Neil had gone out to get a breath of fresh air and to gossip with his niece, whom he had not seen since her wedding. Several of the guests were in the stackyard cooling themselves, but the hostess and the fiddler sauntered out to the roadside where it sloped to the kirkton. The boy almost ran into them, weeping loudly; blaring, after the fashion of unsophisticated childhood.

'Maircy, laddie! What ails ye?' exclaimed the young woman.

'Phemie's daft! Ragin' daft – the wifie's deid!'

His words came out with an incoherent burst of blubbering, and to Knowes' bride, who had been a bare ten days in the place, the name conveyed nothing.

'Lord's sake!' she cried, 'what is't? wha is't?'

He pointed down the road.

'Ragin' – roarin' daft doon yonder – whaur the licht is – gang doon the brae an' ye'll see't yonder!'

'But wha's deid?' cried the woman. 'Is't a murder?'

'Aye, aye – she's deid! Phemie's ragin' mad!' bawled the boy, gathering excitement from his companion's trembling voice, and only concerned for someone to share his emotions.

She poured out a string of questions, and as she grew more insistent, his tale grew more difficult to follow. She looked round for her uncle, but by this time he had started for the village to investigate for himself.

'Oh, Uncle Neil! dinna gang!' she wailed; 'like as no ye'll be murder't yersel' – come awa back, Uncle Neil!'

Hearing his steps die away in the darkness, she rushed through the stackyard with the headlong run of a startled fowl. 'There's a puir body murdert i' the kirkton!' she shouted as she went.

The words ran from mouth to mouth. In a few minutes the main part of the company was on its way down the brae, leaving behind it a handful of nervous women, some men who had discovered the fountain-head of the whisky, and Donald Gow, whose instinct, probably from years of attendance on a bigger man than himself, was always for the background.

Neil strode into the kirkton, making for the light pointed out by the boy. Most of the cottages were darkened, but Phemie's uncurtained window shone like a beacon. He did not stop to look through it, fearing that he might be seen and the house barred against him. He pushed open the door and stood still, completely taken aback. There was no sign of disorder, nothing to suggest a struggle. Phemie, exhausted by her own violence, was sitting at the hearth, her body turned from the fire; her elbows were on the chair-back, her hands clasped over her bowed head. At the click of the latch she looked up and saw him in the doorway. She gave a terrible cry and ran towards him.

'Neil Gow! Neil Gow! Div ye no mind o' me?'

His amazement deepened. Death, whose presence he

realised as he looked about him, had come quietly here, as he comes to most houses; but he supposed that bereavement must have turned the brain of the desperate creature who clung to him.

'Whisht, wumman, whisht!' he exclaimed, 'whisht noo, puir thing.'

'Hae maircy on me, Neil Gow!'

'Whisht, whisht – a'll awa' an' get the minister tae ye.'

But she only held him tighter; he had not believed a woman's hands could be so strong. He did not like to force them open.

'Ye mauna seek tae tell him – ye winna! Ye winna hae me ta'en awa'?'

'Na, na, na. Wumman, what ill wad a dae ye?' he cried, bewildered; 'a dinna ken ye – a'm no seekin' tae hurt ye.'

'Oh, Neil Gow, div ye no mind o' playin' on the auld green o' Dalmain? It's me – it's Phemie Moir!'

The name 'Moir' arrested him. He turned her round to the firelight, gazing into her face.

'Moir?' he said. 'Is it yersel'?' He could hardly trace in it the features of the girl he remembered.

'Moir,' she said. 'Jimmy Moir was the lad ye saved frae the sodgers – him an' the ither ane – ma bonnie brither. Neil Gow, ye'll save me – ye winna speak o't – ye winna let them tak' me noo?'

'Hoots!' he exclaimed. Then looking into her anguished eyes, he realised the depths of her simplicity; the cruelty of that ignorance whose burden she had borne these two score of years. He was silent, seeking for words with which to bring conviction to her warped understanding, to overthrow the tyranny of a fixed idea. There was a sound of feet outside, and both he and she looked towards the window. Beyond the narrow panes a crowd of faces were gathered, pressing against them. She tore herself from him and ran to the door. She turned the key just as a hand outside was about to lift the latch.

Neil drew the curtain across the casement, and, taking her by the arm, led her to the hearth.

'See noo,' said he, 'sit ye doon. There's naebody'll touch ye. They're a' freends. Will ye no believe me?'

'A hae nae freends, Neil Gow – man, ye dinna understand.'

The tears came at last and she rocked herself to and fro.

'Ye fule!' he exclaimed, 'is there no me? Was a no a freend tae ye, yon time ye mind?'

'Ye was that – ye was that,' she murmured.

'An' wad a tell ye a lee?'

The latch rattled again.

He went to the door and opened it. Someone pressed up against him and would have entered. He was flung back.

'Awa'!' he cried, 'awa' wi' ye a'! There's nane murdert here. There's just a done body that's deed in her bed. There's nane o' ye'll hear the sound o' my fiddle the nicht gin ye dinna leave the puir cratur' that's greetin' in-by in peace. There's just the minister'll win in, an' nae mair!'

There was an irresolute collective movement, but the beadle pushed himself forward.

'Na, na,' said Neil simply, filling the doorway with his bulk. The beadle was pulled back by several hands. The sensation was dying down, and a dance without music was a chill prospect.

'We'll see an' get Donal' tae play,' said the beadle angrily.

'No him,' replied Neil.

'Here's the minister,' said a voice.

Phemie's dread seemed to have left her. She sat quietly listening to what was going on round the doorstep; an unformulated hope was glimmering in her mind like dawn on a stretch of devastated country. She could hear the people dispersing and returning to the Knowes' and the minister's subdued murmur of talk with the fiddler outside. It went on till the two men came in together. She was dumb and still.

'Ye've naething to fear i' this warld,' said Laidlaw, dropping into the vernacular. 'I'd tell ye the same, if I was to tell ye frae the pulpit.'

And he put his hand on her shoulder. She laid her head against his arm, like a child.

IT WAS A full hour later that Laidlaw returned to the manse. He had stayed some little time at the cottage after Gow went back to the Knowes' to finish his evening's work. One half of his mind was full of the story he had heard pieced together by Phemie and the fiddler. He was a thoughtful man, with sympathies stronger than many who knew him were inclined to suspect, and he was deeply stirred by the obscure tragedy which had dragged on, unrealised by himself, ever since he had been called to Dalmain. He blamed himself. His sense of his own limitations, a healthy quality in most people, had been a stumbling-block to him; for he had taken the discouragements received in his timid efforts to know more of Phemie as proofs of how little he was fitted to deal with her. He envied people like Neil Gow; people whose masterful humanity carried them full sail into those waters where their fellow-men were drowning for want of a rope. The other half of his mind was amazed by the prank of a coincidence that had brought the Englishman here to meet the one man necessary to him in his quest.

He hurried home, hoping that his guest would soon return; in the crowd at the farm he had noticed his presence, but lost him in the sudden scare which dispersed the party. He entered the little living-room to find him.

'You look perturbed,' said the Englishman. 'Certainly you have no lack of incident in Dalmain. I'm truly glad it was a false alarm.'

'I have much to say to you,' began Laidlaw, sitting down.

'Well, before you begin, let me have my turn. Perhaps you thought me sceptical when you spoke of Neil Gow, and I will not deny that I was. I was a fool – since I have heard him I know how great a fool. And now, sir, go on, and I will listen. My mind has been lightened of a little of its conceit.'

His frankness struck some sensitive chord in Laidlaw. Perhaps the minister's reserve was shaken by the sharp contact with realities tonight, perhaps stirred by sympathies he saw in others.

'I am glad you came here,' he stammered. 'I should be

glad to think – to hope – I have got some information for you, sir. Your cousin was lost sight of here; he reached Dalmain.'

'You have got news of him?'

'Something. Little enough; but I have heard a strange tale from Neil Gow.'

'From Neil Gow?'

Laidlaw nodded.

'Margaret Moir died this evening, and a little laddie saw her through the window and came crying some havers to the Knowes'. Her sister was nearly wild, poor soul, and the bairn got a fright – but you were there, no doubt?'

'I saw there was a disturbance, but I stayed where I was.'

'The door was locked when I arrived,' went on Laidlaw, 'and Gow was with her. But he got her quiet and I went in-by. You'll mind that I told you he was here the year of Culloden, playing on the old green? It was three nights before that dance that Jimmy Moir, who was the brother of these two lasses – as they were then – Margaret and Phemie, came to Dalmain with a wounded officer – likely the man you are seeking – and they hid themselves on the brae in a cave that is there, in amongst the broom. You can see it still; the bairns play at the mouth of it often enough, though I do not think they go far in. I have never been to it myself, but they say it runs a long way into the hillside. Moir got into the kirkton, without being seen, to tell his sisters, and Phemie and Margaret went out in the dark to bring them food and water; but there was no one in the place knew they were there, not even the beadle, that had been fighting himself, for he was lying ill in his house. The English soldiers were all about the country. The officer was so bad with his wound they could not get forward to the coast, and the day Neil came he was shouting and raving in a fever. You could hear him at the foot of the brae, Phemie says, just where the dancing was to be, and the lasses made sure the poor fellows would be discovered. They got short shrift in those times, you see, sir.'

'But would anyone have given them up?' asked the other.

'Aye, well,' said the minister, 'whiles a man's foes are they of his own household, and they said there were some in the kirkton that favoured King George. But Phemie was bold and went to seek Neil Gow. He was a young lad then, but she told him the truth and he said he would play till he had no arms left before anyone should hear aucht but his fiddle. When I spoke to you of that dance, not a couple of hours syne, little I thought how much it concerned you.'

'Nor I, indeed.'

'Margaret was a puir, timid thing and Jimmy was all the world to her. She stopped at home her lane, but Phemie went out and danced till the most o' them were fou with whisky and Neil had played them off their legs. She waited till the last were gone. There was no crying from the broom when she went home. It was an awesome night for her, but it was the ruin of Margaret. She lay ill a long while, and when she rose from her bed her mind was never the same again.'

'But the men – what became of them?' asked the Englishman, getting impatient to reach what was, for him, the main point.

'The days were long in June-month and Phemie had to wait for dark to go back. She found the place empty.'

'And did no news ever come? Was nothing more heard?'

'Nothing, sir. Nothing.'

The other made a sharp exclamation of disappointment.

'It has been a wild-goose chase after all,' he said at last.

The progress of Laidlaw's detailed history had raised his expectations and he was half resentful at finding it end, for all the difference it would make to him, where it had begun. But he was too just a man to let the other see it.

'I am greatly to blame!' cried the minister, with sudden vehemence. 'Here am I, a servant of men's souls, and it was left for Neil Gow to loose Phemie Moir from her martyrdom while I went by on the other side! Aye! but I am an unprofitable servant!' he exclaimed, seeing the other man's astonished face; 'that poor creature shut herself up

with her sister and would thole nobody near them for fear
some word should slip from the daft body and Moir be
traced. Then, as time went by, her heart failed her and
concealment grew in her mind like some poisonous weed,
and she took the notion that, if word got out, the two of
them would have to suffer for what they had done. Fear sat
down with her to her meat and fear lay down with her in her
bed. The years passed on, but she was too ignorant to ken
that the world changes with them and old things go out of
mind. People wonder that she's not like other folk; they
wouldna wonder if they knew! She was feared that Gow,
who had stood friend to her, would let out what he kent,
and fail her. Poor foolish wife to think such a thing of Gow!
And the man had forgotten her till he saw her, and then she
had need to tell him before he remembered! But when she
heard his playing again she was fairly demented.'

His face changed and he turned away. '*Mea culpa,*' he faltered. He had little Latin, but he understood that much.

'I fear the burden has shifted to you, my poor friend,'
said the Englishman gently.

IT WAS ON the forenoon of the morrow that Laidlaw, the
beadle and the Englishman stood up to their middles in
the broom. The pods were black in the green mist of stems.
About their feet rabbits had riddled the earth. The outcrop
of rock had broken open in the hill-side, to be roofed with
the turf of the overhanging brae and swallowed by the sea
of broom and whin and the ash-coloured blur of seeding
thistles. Interlacing whin-roots lurked about the burrows,
traps for human steps. When they had climbed to their goal
the three men stopped to get breath, and turned to look at
the kirkton below them. Westward, through the creek cut by
the burn to the Isla, they could see the indigo-blue Sidlaws
with such lights as seem only to fall on Angus bathing their
undulating shoulders.

Each man carried a lantern, and when all were lighted
they went crouching, one after another, into the cave.
In a few paces they were able to stand up and look
about them.

Both Laidlaw and the Englishman had gone late to sleep

on the preceding night, and the latter, lying thinking in the dark hours, turning over in his mind all he had heard, had come to a definite conclusion. He told himself that no man with a serious body-wound, exhausted by days of wandering and ill enough to be shouting in delirium, could escape on foot from a place in which he had once lain down. A man may go till he drops, but when he falls he will not rise again in circumstances like these, far less escape unseen. But Moir could accomplish what was impossible to his companion.

'I believe Musgrave to be lying up there in the hill-side,' he had said to Laidlaw that morning.

'But—' began the minister.

'Yes, sir, I know what you would say; I know that the village children play there, in the cave, at times. For all that, Moir left him there. But he left a dead man.'

The minister stared at him, incredulous.

'But Phemie went next night. She would have lit a light there,' said he.

'She saw no one *above ground*. You said that when Neil Gow had stopped playing and she went home to her sister, all was quiet. Depend upon it, Musgrave died in the small hours, as sick men will; Moir buried him next day and escaped at dusk.'

'But he had no tools,' objected Laidlaw, unconvinced.

'If the rock is hollowed deep and there is sand and loose earth choking much of it, he did it. A man in his case makes shift to use anything.'

'He maybe had his dirk,' suggested the minister, his doubts a little shaken.

'He is there, sir; believe me, he is there.'

And now Laidlaw was sitting at a short distance from the cave on a bare patch in the tangle. He had come out of its heavy atmosphere to leave room for the Englishman and the beadle, who were working inside with the pick and shovel the latter had brought up from the kirkyard. The opening tunnelled some way into the hill, narrowing as it went, but in one place at which the rock fell back in an irregular recess they had resolved to make their experiment.

The shine from the lanterns had cast up the faint outline of a mound. This decided them, this and the belief that a

man engaged in a work like Moir's would get as far from
the entrance as he might.

The minister looked a little less harassed. His shyness of
the Englishman's accent was gone. Like many people whose
days are spent in remote places, he was intensely surprised
at seeing the human side of a stranger, and he still doubted
that the outer world contained others of a similar sort. His
face grew a little wistful as he remembered that they would
go down the hill to part at its foot. The Englishman would
ride to Stirling to meet the Edinburgh coach. He fell to
musing. The early autumn sunshine, warm and very clear,
and the healing quiet of the braes were pleasant to him.
He could see his small world lying below like a plaything
on the floor. In his vigil last night he had burnt his tallow
till within a short time of daylight, for his sermon had been
interrupted by the clamour that had arisen and he was fain
to finish it. He was not much of a preacher and the task of
writing it was a weekly load upon him. He had got up early
too, and gone to Phemie's cottage; for there was something
he wanted to say to her and his self-distrust made him eager
to put this also behind him, lest he should lose courage. But
his visit was accomplished and he was now more at ease.
His eyes closed wearily; they ached this morning from his
midnight labours as his heart had ached last night from
his own shortcomings. But now he forgot all these as he
dozed among the broom and the fluffy thistledown . . .

He awoke to a touch on his shoulder. The Englishman
was beside him. For a moment, bewildered, he could not
recollect where he was, nor how he had come to such
a place.

'Look,' said the other, who was holding out a little
discoloured silver snuff-box, 'his name is on it. We have
found him.'

IN THE KIRKTON of Dalmain the two men bade each other
good-bye, but said it as those do who are to meet again.
The Englishman wished Musgrave to lie under the wall of
its spectral kirk; and when the necessary steps should be
taken to establish the dead man's identity in the eyes of
the law, his skeleton, clothed in the rags of his tattered

uniform, would be carried from the bosom of the hill that had sheltered it for so long and committed by Laidlaw to the earth.

'I believe you are less troubled than you were last night,' said the Englishman, leaning from his horse as they parted. 'I should be happy to know it.'

The minister's plain face brightened.

'I have seen Phemie already,' he replied; 'she is to come to me to take care of the manse – my serving lass is just a silly tawpie—'

The rider pulled up a little later upon the southern brae and turned to look back. On the northern one, two dark figures were doing the like. The taller of these, seeing him, took off his bonnet and stood holding it high in air. It was Neil Gow.

A Middle-Aged Drama

THE HOUSE of Hedderwick the grieve was a furlong east of the kirk, divided from it by a country road and a couple of ploughed fields. From its windows the sunset could be seen spreading, like a fire, behind the building, of which only the belfry was visible as it rose above the young larch plantation pressing up to the kirkyard gate. The belfry itself was a mere shelter, like a little bridge standing on the kirk roof, and the dark shape of its occupant showed strong against the sky, dead black when the flame of colour ran beyond the ascending skyline to the farm on the hill. This farm with its stacks and byres would then share importance with the bell, the two becoming the most marked objects against the light.

Hedderwick's house was grey and square, with an upper storey and a way of staring impartially on the world. At the death of his wife, three years before the date of this history, it began to give signs, both within and without, of the demoralisation that sets in on a widower's possessions.

Mrs. Hedderwick had been a shrew and there were many who pitied the grieve more during her life than after her death. It was experience that made the bereaved man turn an ear as deaf as that of the traditional adder to the voices of those who urged on him the necessity of a housekeeper. But discomfort is a potent reasoner and the day came when a tall woman with a black bonnet and a corded wooden box descended from the carrier's cart at his door.

Hedderwick was a lean, heavy-boned man of fifty-two, decent with the decency of the well-to-do lowland Scot, sparing of words, just of mind, and only moderately devout – so the minister said – for a man who lived so near the church. In his youth he had been a hard swearer, and a bedrock of determination lay below the surface of his infrequent speech, to be struck by those who crossed him. He had no daughters; his son Robert, who was apprenticed to a watchmaker in Dundee, came home at intervals to spend Sunday with his father and to impress the parish with that knowledge of men and matters which he believed to be the exclusive possession of dwellers in manufacturing towns.

In spite of his just mind, Hedderwick's manner to his housekeeper, during the first year, showed the light in which he saw her. She was a necessary evil, but an evil nevertheless, and he did not allow her to forget the fact. He wasted fewer words on her than he did on any other person; when she came into the room he looked resentful; and though he had never before known such comfort as she had brought with her into the house, he would have died sooner than let her suspect it. If obliged to mention her, he spoke of 'yon woman,' and while so doing gave the impression that, but for his age and position, he would have used a less decorous noun.

'Margaret Burness, a single woman' – so she had described herself when applying for the place – was a pale, quiet person, as silent as the grieve, with the look of one who has suffered in spirit without suffering in character. Her eyes were still soft and had once been beautiful, and her dark, plainly parted hair was turning grey. Though the sharp angles of jaw and cheekbone gave her face a certain austere pathos, it was easy, when looking at her, to suppose that her smile would be pleasant. But she rarely smiled.

When another six months had gone by, Hedderwick's obstinacy, though dying hard, began to give way in details. 'Yon woman' had become 'she,' and her place at the fireside commanded, not his side aspect, but his full face; for he sat no longer in the middle of the hearth, but with his chair opposite to hers. Occasionally he would read her bits from the newspaper. Robert, who had always treated her as though she did not exist, returned one Sunday, and, remarking sourly on her cooking, perceived a new state of things.

'If yer meat disna please ye, Rob, ye can seek it some other gait,' observed Hedderwick.

Margaret smiled a little more in these days; she was as
quiet as ever, but her eyes, when they rested upon the
grieve, seemed to have taken back something of their
youth. She was experiencing the first taste of security she
had ever known, and, with his dawning consideration, a
tenderness she scarcely realised was growing up for him
in her heart.

Nothing had prepared Hedderwick to find peace and
a woman's society compatible. He began to look on the
evening as a pleasant time, and on one occasion, when
chance delayed her return from marketing by a couple
of hours, he went down the road to meet her, swearing
as each turn of the way revealed a new piece of empty
track and foreseeing the most unlikely mishaps. He waited
for her now on Sundays instead of letting her follow him
to the kirk, and her Bible made the journey there in his
pocket with his own. No stranger who saw them sitting
in the pew below the gallery would have doubted that the
grim-looking grieve and the pale woman beside him were
man and wife. By the time a few more months had gone
by she had become 'Marget.'

It was early November. Hedderwick, who had business
in Dundee, had returned there with his son, leaving her in
charge of the house. She was expecting him home, and, her
work being over and the tea set in the kitchen, she stood at
an upper window looking at the sky which flamed behind
the belfry. The four small pinnacles at its corners were
inky black, and the bell below them was turned, by the
majesty of the heavens, from the commonplace instrument
of the beadle's weekly summons into a fateful object. It
hung there, dark and still, the spokes of its wheel and
the corners and angles of the ironwork standing out into
unfamiliar distinctness, and suggesting some appurtenance
of mediaeval magic. Behind it, the west had dissolved into
a molten sea of gold that seemed to stretch beyond the
bounds of this present world, and to be lying, at a point
far outrunning human sight, upon the shores of the one
to come. The farm, with its steadings, was like the last
outpost of this earth. The plain darkness of the ploughed
fields before the house made the glory more isolated, more

remote, more a revelation of the unattainable – a region between which and humanity stood the narrow portal of death. The tops of the larches by the kirk were so fine that in the great effulgence the smaller twigs disappeared like little, fretted souls, swallowed into eternal peace. And above them hung the bell whose sound would one day proclaim for each and all within range of its voice that the time had come to rise up and go out into the remoteness.

As she watched, the figure of Hedderwick turned off the road and came up the muddy way skirting the fields. She went down quickly to make the tea and put the slices of bread she had cut into the toaster. As she bent over the fire she heard him kicking the mud off his boots against the doorstep and hanging up his hat on the peg.

He said little during the meal, but when it was over he went out and returned with a parcel which he laid before her on the table.

'A bocht this tae ye in Dundee, Marget,' said he.

She opened the paper shyly. It held a Paisley shawl of the sort worn at that time by nearly every woman of her class who could afford the luxury. The possession of such a thing was, in itself, a badge of settled position. The colour ran to her face.

'Oh, but yon's pretty!' she exclaimed, as the folds fell from her hands to the floor in the subdued reds and yellows of the intricate Oriental pattern. She put it round her and it hung with a certain grace from her thin shoulders to her knees.

'Ye set it fine,' observed Hedderwick, from his chair.

Her heart sang in her all the evening. No woman, no matter of what age, can be quite cold to the charm of a new garment; and this one, though it did not differ from those she saw, on good occasions, on the backs of most well-to-do working-men's wives, was, perhaps, the more acceptable for that. It seemed to give her a place among them. As she imagined the grieve entering the Dundee shop with the intention of buying such a thing for her, her cheek kindled again. He had chosen well, too; the fine softness of the gift told her that. She laid her treasure away in her box, glad that it was only the middle of the week, that she might have the more time to realise its beauty before wearing it. But its overwhelming worth, to her, was neither in its texture nor its cost.

She sat in her place on Sunday in the midst of a great spiritual peace. Love, as love, was a thing outside her reckoning, and she would have checked the bare thought that she loved the grieve. But there was on her the beatitude of a woman who finds herself valued by the being most precious to her. She had come into such a haven as she had never hoped to see in the days of her hard, troubled existence, and there was only one point on which she was not quite easy. It stood out now before her, its shadow deepened by the light shining in her heart.

There was a secret in Margaret's life which she had kept from everyone, which lay so far back in the years that its memory was almost like the memory of a dream; and she wished now that she had told Hedderwick the truth. But, sinless as that secret was, she had recoiled from sharing it with all but the few who had known her in youth, fearing, in her sore need of work by which to keep herself, that it would go against her in her quest. And, as the good opinion of the grieve grew, she hid it the more closely, for she had so little to cling to that she could not bear to jeopardise what consideration she had earned. There was not one cloud upon her content and the peace which enfolded her; but that small concealment, a concealment advised by those who had concerned themselves for her after the storm burst, and by whose suggestion she had taken back her maiden name, would rise, at times, to her mind and make her sigh. She wished, as she sat with her eyes on her book and the clean pocket-handkerchief folded beside it, that she had told Hedderwick. She was so much preoccupied that she never looked up, nor settled herself against the pewback, as did her neighbours, when the sermon began. It was a few minutes before she shook herself from her abstraction and composed herself to listen to the minister's voice.

The kirk was a plain square place with a gallery, supported on thin pillars, running round all but its western side where the tall pulpit stood between high windows. The minister, under the umbrella-like sounding-board poised over him, was far above the heads of the congregation and on a level with the occupants of the upstair pews, looking across the intervening chasm into the faces of the laird and his family. The north wall, by which Hedderwick sat, was unbroken, but on the farther side of the kirk two small windows under the gallery floor looked out upon the little kirkyard surrounding the building. There were not many tombstones on that side of it, and the light, chilly autumn wind rippled the long grass till it looked like grey waves.

Margaret never knew what made her turn her head sharply and glance across to the diamond-shaped panes. Between her and one of the windows the seats were almost empty, and there was nothing to interrupt her view of a shambling figure that moved among the graves. While she watched, the leaded panes darkened, as a man approached and looked through; the sill was cut so deep in the wall that few of the congregation could see him, and the two or three whose positions would allow them to do so had their attention fixed upon the pulpit. The man's eyes searched as much of the interior of the kirk as he could command, and, stopping at Margaret, became centred upon her.

She looked down at her knee, faint with the suggestion shot into her terror-struck heart by the face staring in at her from outside. Hedderwick, who could have seen what she saw, was drowsy, and his closed lids shut out from him the new act of that long-buried tragedy that was being revived for the woman at his side. When she raised her head again the figure had retreated a few paces from the pane, and its outlines turned her apprehension into certainty.

The preacher's voice ran on through the silence, but it seemed to Margaret as though her heartbeats drowned it; she forced herself to overcome the mental dizziness that wrapped her like the shawl whose fringes lay spread on the slippery wood of the pew. Its warmth was turned to a chill mockery. She closed her eyes that she might shut out the familiar things about her; the accustomed faces, the high pulpit, the red cushion on its ledge, the long, pendent tassels swinging into space; the grieve's bulky shoulders and Sunday clothes, his brown leather Bible with its corners frayed by its weekly sojourns in his pocket. All these things had become immeasurably dear; and now, this Sunday morning might be – probably would be – the last time she should ever see them.

When the congregation dispersed she sat still. Hedderwick would have waited for her, but she motioned him dumbly to go on. After the last shuffle of feet had retreated over the threshold and the beadle came in to shut the doors, she rose and went out.

The man was waiting there for her among the gravestones as she rounded the angle of the wall. Though he was a few years younger than herself he looked much older; there was white on his unshaven chin, and she saw, as she approached, that he was almost in rags. Whether he were a beggar or not, he had the unmistakable shifting look of mendicancy. But his features were unchanged and she would have known the set of his eyebrows anywhere. She opened her lips to speak, but the pounding of her heart choked her breath.

'A've been seekin' ye,' he said, in the thick voice that told of long drinking. 'A speired at Netherside an' they tellt me ye was here.'

Netherside was Margaret's old home; a village over the county border.

'We got word ye was deid after ye cam' oot o' jail,' said she, 'but a didna ken whether tae believe it. But when sic a time gaed by—'

'Heuch!' rejoined he, with a flicker of grim humour, 'a was fine an' pleased tae be deid; a grave's a bonnie safe place. They canna catch ye there, ye ken.'

'And what way was it ye didna send me word? A micht hae gi'ed ye a hand, Tam.'

'A tell ye a was deid. An' a wasna needin' ye in Ameriky.'

A throb of pity came to her as she saw his shaking hands, and the way he drew his ragged coat together as the wind played in gusts over the grass. It is terrible to see the professional attitudes of the beggar in one we have once loved, no matter how far life may have drifted him from us. Margaret had not a spark of affection left for the wretched creature before her, but she had a long memory.

'Ye're gey an' braw,' he said, with a sidelong glance at her tidy clothes and the rich colouring of her fine shawl. 'Ye bide wi' the grieve, a'm tellt. Maybe ye've pit by a bittie.'

Margaret's lips shook, and, for a moment, her eyes looked on beyond him into space.

'Tam, we'll need to do oor best,' she began tremulously, brought back to the present by the mention of Hedderwick. 'A've a bit saved. Maybe we micht gang to Dundee an' get work i' the mills—'

'An' wha tellt ye a was seekin' work? A'm no needin' work an' a'm no needin' you. Bide you wi' the grieve – I'll no tak' ye frae him; but a'll be here-about till the new year an' a'll come tae the hoose the nicht. Ye can gie me a piece an' a wheen siller tae gang on wi'.'

'A'll no let ye near the hoose,' said Margaret firmly.

'An' a'm no askin' ye. A'm tae come.'

'But Hedderwick'll see ye, Tam.'

'Dod, a'm no carin' for Hedderwick.'

'But a'll come oot-by an' bring ye a piece!' she exclaimed in terror. 'Ye'll no need tae come then.'

They parted a few minutes later and she returned home. Her world had indeed grown complicated in the last hour, and the light of duty, for which, in all her troubled life, she had been wont to look, seemed to have gone out, extinguished by some diabolical hand. It was plain that her husband would have none of her, and had no desire that she should throw in her lot with his; he feared respectability as she feared sin, and, while she was in a position to minister to his wants, his present way of living would suit him well. She had promised, before leaving him, to bring him a little money, if he would wait after dusk, where the larch-wood hid the road from the kirk. She refused to bring him food, for though her small savings were her own, every crumb in the house was the grieve's and she would sooner have died than take so much as a crust. Whosoever might suffer for what had happened that day, it should not be Hedderwick.

It was almost dark that evening as she slipped out of the house and went towards the larches; she had a little money in her hand, taken out of the box in which she

kept her savings. The owls were beginning to call and
hoot from the wood by the manse, and she hurried along
among the eerie voices floating in shrill mockery over the
plough-land. Tom Weir was lurking like a shadow at the
appointed place, and when she had given him her dole he
departed towards the farm on the hill; a deserted cottage
which stood in a field over the crest would shelter him
that night, he said, and be a place to which he could
come back in the intervals of tramping. He was going
off on the morrow and would expect her to meet him on
his return with a further pittance. Her hesitation brought
down a shower of abuse.

Margaret knew well to what slavery she was condemning
herself when she put the money into his dirty palm; but she
dared not tell Hedderwick, for, besides her dismay at the
thought of confessing what she had kept from him so long,
she had a vague dread that the law, were her case known,
would force her to return to Weir. Weir did not want her,
but she had known of old that his spite was a thing to be
reckoned with, and it might be gratified by her downfall,
when her savings came to an end. That knowledge and
the fear that he might make a public claim on her, were
she to refuse him help, bound her hand and foot. She had
not the courage to turn her back on all she had grown to
love, and she quieted her scruples by vowing that, while
keeping the grieve in ignorance, she would not bestow on
her tormentor one crust that she had not paid for herself;
but she was prepared, were it necessary, to threaten her
own departure from her employment and the consequent
stoppage of her means of supply, should he approach the
grey house. She was prepared, also, to keep her word. It
should be her last resource.

And so the final, dying month of autumn went by and
winter fell on the land, crisping the edges of the long
furrows and setting a tracery of bare boughs against the
diminished light. Weir came and went, haunting the towns
within reach, and coming back every seven days to take
his tithe of her dwindling purse; and winter fell, too, upon
Margaret's heart. Saturday brought a sinister end to her
week; and her troubles, as dusk set in, were intensified by

the presence of Rob Hedderwick, who now returned by the midday train on that day to spend Sunday at his father's house. It was difficult to escape his sharp eye and restless mind – made, perhaps, more intrusive by perpetual prying into the workings of complicated things. It did not take the young man long to notice her absences. In the evenings by the fireside he would look covertly at her from behind his paper, or over the top of his book, as she sat at her knitting; his thoughts were busy with the mystery he scented. Once or twice he had left the kitchen before dark, and, from the shadow of the wash-house door, watched her go silently towards the road with something in her apron. He did not like Margaret. Once, too, he had mentioned his suspicions to the grieve, bidding him look to his money-box; and, angered by the scant encouragement that he got, and by the scathing definitions of the limits of his own business, he determined to justify himself; for his growing suspicion that his father's housekeeper sold the food, or disposed of it in some way profitable to herself, could, he believed, be proved. He was bent upon proving it, for, in addition to his dislike, he had the thirsty rabidness of the would-be detective.

There was a cessation of his visits through January and February, as the master watchmaker was called away and his assistant left for a two months' charge of the shop; therefore it was on a moonless March evening that Rob Hedderwick hid himself in the manse wood. It touched the road just where the path to the grieve's house joined it, and in its shelter he waited till he heard a woman's step come down the track. Margaret passed within a few yards of him, her head muffled in a woollen wrapper and her apron gathered into a bag and bulging with what she carried in it. He had never yet followed her, but he meant to do so now, for there was just enough of hidden starlight behind the thin clouds to enable him to keep her in sight from a little distance.

Her figure disappeared among the larches by the kirk; he almost came upon her, for the road between them made a bend, and she had stopped, apparently expecting to be joined by someone. Her back was to him and he retreated softly. The cold was considerable and Rob had forgotten to put on his greatcoat; so when, after what seemed to him nearer to half an hour than a quarter, she went swiftly up the hill towards the farm on its summit, he followed again, thankful to be moving.

She never slackened her pace till she had reached the top. Led more by sound than by sight, he trod in her wake; the desolation of night was wide around them, and from the ridge the land was as though falling away into nothingness before and behind. The farm was quiet as they passed it and began to descend, he taking advantage of a scanty cover of hedge to get closer to her. As the ground grew level again, he could hear the gurgle of a small burn crossing their road at a place where a hamlet of thatched mud houses had once stood. There was but one ruin of a cottage left, a little way from the country road, and he was near enough to see Margaret strike off towards it. He went round the roofless hovel till he came to its door, which was still standing. She had entered and closed it after her.

There was a gleam of light inside, and, putting his eye to a gaping crack in the wood, he could see what took place within the walls. A man was sitting on a bundle of straw covered with sacking and a battered lantern beside him shed its light on him and on the woman. As it flickered in the draught, the shadows, ghastly and fantastic, played among the broken beams and the tufts of dried vegetation, springing up where rain had fallen in upon the floor.

Rob held his breath as Margaret unfolded her apron and laid a loaf with a large piece of cheese upon the straw. It was just such a loaf as he had seen her buy from the baker's cart at his father's doorstep. The idea that she might have paid for it herself did not enter his mind, for it was of a type to which such ideas are foreign. It was not easy to distinguish what they said. He pressed nearer in his eagerness, and a brick on which he trod turning under his foot, he slipped, lurching heavily against the rotten panel. The immediate silence which followed told him that the blow had startled Margaret and her companion, so, regaining his balance, he fled towards the road and made his way home in the darkness. He had seen all that he needed for his purpose.

The grieve was out when he reached the house and his disappointment was keen; he had hoped, his tale once told, to make his father confront the ill-doer as she entered fresh from her errand. But he had to keep his discovery till the morrow, for it was nearing ten o'clock when Hedderwick came home and went to bed in silence with the uncommunicativeness of a weary man. Rob followed his example sulkily. The next day as the two men strolled down the road after their midday dinner, he embarked on the story of what he had seen and done overnight.

Rob Hedderwick drove his words home with the straight precision of a man assured of the convincing power of his case. He could reason well, and the education which the grieve lacked, but had given to his son, clothed his opinions with a certain force. Hedderwick's mind was turned up as by a ploughshare. His anger at the long chain of petty thefts, which seemed to have been effectively proved before the young man's eyes, lay on him like a weight of lead; and that the one who had been forging that chain these many months sat at his hearth and ate of his food made it all the heavier. Treachery was what he could not bear. He was honest himself and dishonesty was a fault to which he was pitiless. The thing, unendurable in an enemy, was doubly so in the woman who had come to be, to him, indispensable. But, as he pictured the house without Margaret, his heart sank. Now, and only now, was he to realise what she had been – what she was – to him. He stood leaning his arms on a gate; Rob, having done his duty, had gone off to spend the afternoon with some neighbours; and he remained, sore at heart, where he was – looking towards his own house and drawn this way and that by resentment, disillusion and another feeling which was perhaps more painful than either. Rob had been right, no doubt, but that did not prevent his father from hating him because he had destroyed his peace, and he was glad that he would be leaving early next morning. What steps he might take in consequence of his hateful discovery should be taken after he had gone; for he suspected a touch of malicious satisfaction in his son that he would be careful not to gratify. He turned grimly from the gate and went home.

The two following days went by and he remained silent. At times he had almost made up his mind to ignore everything he had heard, so great was his dread of parting with Margaret. On the evening after Rob left he opened his mouth to speak, but it was as though an unseen hand closed his lips. He could not do it. He desired and yet feared to be alone with her; and when, on the second day of his torment, he saw her start for the farm on some business of domestic supply, he stood in the patch of garden and watched her go with a feeling of relief.

The days were lengthening now, and the wistful notes of blackbirds told their perpetual spring story of the fragility of youth and the pathos of coming pain; but Margaret took time to do her business and the light was beginning to fall as she came out of the farm-gate. Somehow, the heavy load she had carried for so many months seemed to press less cruelly in the alluring quiet of the outdoor world. Instead of going back to the house she turned into a rough way that circled westward and would bring her home by the manse.

She wandered on; behind her, at a little distance, a boy was carrying a milk-can, whistling as he went. The road took her past a disused quarry, a place where steep angles of ragged stone struck out, like headlands, into the garment of weed and bush with which the years were clothing it. It was deep, and, through the dusk, she could just see its bottom and a dark object which lay among the pieces of fallen rock. She peered down – for the remnant of a crazy rail was all that protected unwary passengers from the chasm – and then held up her hand to stop the boy's whistle. From the heap below came a sound like a human voice.

Margaret was an active woman. At the point where she stood the earth had slipped in an outward incline, and a few young ashes that had seeded themselves in the thick tangle of wood offered a comparatively easy descent. She began to go down, waist-deep in the dried thistle-fluff, keeping her foothold in the sliding soil by clinging to the undergrowth.

Among the roots and boulders lay a man, face downwards. From the helpless huddle in which he lay, and the moans which struck her ear as she scrambled towards him, she knew that he must be desperately hurt. At sight of the blood on the surrounding stones she paused and cried to the boy who watched her from above to run for help. Then she sat down and raised the unhappy creature to lie with his head on her knee, and saw, through the growing dusk, that she was looking into the face of her husband.

How long she sat with her half-conscious burden she never knew; but the moments till the return of her messenger were double their length to her. The shadow fell deeper about them and bats began to come out of their fastnesses in the creeks and holes of the stone. It was chilly cold. A tuft of thistle, half-way up the slope she had descended, was catching the remaining light, and the cluster of its blurred, sere head stared on her like a face, with the fantastic attraction that irrelevant things will take on for humanity in its hours of horror.

Weir stirred a little and his eyes opened for a moment. 'It's me,' she whispered, bending lower; but she could not tell whether he knew her or not, for he had slipped back into unconsciousness.

Just before the boy came back he looked up once more; this time with comprehension; it seemed to her that he had grown heavier in her arms.

'Ye'll no gang?' he asked feebly.

'No; a'll no gang,' replied Margaret.

A minute later the voices of the boy and the men he had brought came to her from above. Her arms tightened protectingly, for the thought of the transport made her shudder. Then she gazed down at Weir and saw that she need fear pain for him no more.

IT WAS THE DAY of the inquiry. Parish details were not so complete forty years ago as they are now and communication with towns was more difficult; so Tom Weir's body lay in an outhouse of the farm. The 'fiscal' was summoned, and

Margaret, the whistling boy, and the handful of men who had carried the vagrant from his rough deathbed were on their way to attend at the place appointed.

Margaret Weir walked alone, her face set in the hard-won peace of a resolution long dreaded, but accomplished at last. The time spent in the quarry had merged her dumb patience, her rebellion against the wreck of her content and growing love, into a vast, steadfast pity. The dead man had been thief, jail-bird, destroyer of her youth; but the old, broken bond had been drawn together again by his appeal as he died in her arms among the nettles. 'Ye'll no gang?' he had said. 'No, a'll no gang,' she had replied, And she was not going now; not till all was done. She was on her way to identify his body and to declare herself his widow; and what money he had not taken from her was to buy him the decent 'burying' which, with her kind, stands for so much.

The shadow of disrespectability lying on Hedderwick's household was a thing she would not contemplate, and she was sure that the answer to all difficulties lay in her own departure. She could not, in justice to him, reveal herself for what she had been – the wife of a tramp – and keep her place. So she reasoned. She was a simple person, in spite of her concealments, and at this crisis she saw her way simply. She had mended all his clothes, put the house in order and packed her box, which would be fetched by the carrier and sent after her. She had written two letters; one to the minister about Weir's funeral, the money for which she gave into his charge, and the other to Hedderwick. In the latter she explained her position as fully as her small scholarship permitted and bade him good-bye. The balance of the sum he had given her for domestic expenses last market day would, she told him, be in a packet under her pillow. The letter was placed on the kitchen table to await him, for she did not expect him in till evening.

It was past noon when she came out of the room where the 'fiscal' sat and went down the hill. She looked neither to right nor left, for she was afraid. She needed all her great courage to reach the station; all her strength to sail steadfastly out of her late-found haven into the heavy weather. Had she raised her eyes she would have seen the tall figure of Hedderwick emerge from his house and come striding towards her across the fields.

They met in the larch plantation, just where she had so often met Weir. He walked up to her and took her by the wrist.

'Marget,' said he, 'come awa' hame.'

She began to tremble. Her strength of purpose was ebbing in this new trial. Was she to be spared nothing? The tears she believed she had left behind with her youth rose and choked her utterance.

'But a wrote ye, Hedderwick,' she faltered. Her eyes were too much blinded to see the corner of her envelope sticking out of his pocket.

'Ye'll just come hame wi' me,' said the grieve.

'Marget, there's naethin' can part you and me, for a canna live wantin' ye.'

Annie Cargill

YOUNG BOB Davidson had an odd assortment of tastes. He combined the average out-of-door sporting tendencies with a curious love of straying down intellectual byways. He was not clever and he had been very idle at school; he knew no Greek, had forgotten such Latin as had been hammered into him, was innocent of modern languages, and abhorred mathematics. The more amusing passages of history gave him true pleasure and heraldry was a thing that he really knew something about. He was twenty, and in mortal combat with his father over the choice of a profession. Old Mr. Davidson favoured the law and his son's mind was for a land agency. In the midst of the strife Bob's godfather, Colonel Alexander Lindsay of Pitriven, invited him to spend a fortnight with him and to shoot the dregs of the Pitriven coverts. Bob hesitated, for he had never seen Sandy Lindsay and had at that moment some private interests in Edinburgh; but Mr. Davidson, a Writer to the Signet, had no idea of offending a godfather who was also a well-to-do bachelor. So Bob, grumbling, packed his portmanteau and a copy of Douglas Whittingham's *Armorial Bearings of the Lowland Families* and departed for Pitriven. The young lady who represented the private interests cried a little and desired the housemaid to abstract her early letters, daily, from the hall table.

Pitriven was a small, shabby house with an unlived-in atmosphere that laid hold upon the young man as he entered; a long-disused billiard-table almost choked the hall, and only the comforting smell of tobacco cheered him as the butler led him into his godfather's presence. At any rate, he reflected, he would be allowed to smoke. Somehow, the place had suggested restrictions.

'Sandy Lindsay,' as he was always called, astonished Bob more than anyone he had seen for some time. He was so immensely tall that his head nearly touched the ceiling of the low smoking-room, and in the dusk of the December afternoon his gigantic outline practically blocked up the window in front of which he stood. He had stiff, white whiskers which curled inwards; his brassy voice had the harshness of a blow as it broke the silence. His features were not ill-favoured, but they looked as though carved out of wood with a blunt knife. Bob found him civil, almost cordial, but there was a hint of potential roughness lurking behind voice, words and manner that had a disturbing effect and gave the young man the sensation of knowing neither what to speak of, nor what to do, nor what to think.

But by the time he had been a few days at Pitriven Bob had begun to like Sandy Lindsay, though he would wonder sometimes, as they sat at the hearth in the evening, what quality in the man beside him had attracted the friendship of his father. He could not quite get over his first impressions but he told himself that it was childish to blame his godfather for having a dreadful personality; he had not chosen it for himself. But it was quite clear to Bob that it was a dreadful one. He found himself noting with surprise that Lindsay's dog was not afraid of him. Somehow he had taken it for granted that the red setter which lived in the house and slept at night in the smoking-room would feel what he felt, perhaps more strongly.

He could not fathom his godfather. There was a rude detachment about him that he could not penetrate; he was alien, out-of-date, barbarous. He decided that he was 'a survival,' for he was fond of making definitions in his careless way, and so he put it. He looked him up in a *Landed Gentry* that he found lying about and was mightily astonished to see that he was seventy-one. Certainly he did not look it.

Though Pitriven house had little attraction for Bob, its surroundings held much that he liked. The timber was beautiful and the great limbs of the trees, with their

spreading network of branches etched upon the winter
skies, dwarfed the mansion and gave it an insignificance
that had something mean. The windows were like malignant
eyes staring out into the grandeur of trunk and bough.

The parks round Pitriven were cut by a deep 'den' beyond
which the ground rose, steeply, to old Pitriven Kirk. Trees
choked the cleft and clothed the ground about the building,
but now that the leaves were fallen its walls could be seen
from the windows of the house, perched above the den and
rising from among the gravestones. Bob had passed near it
when shooting with his godfather; his eye had fallen upon
the armorial bearings which decorated much of the older
stonework, and he promised himself a good time spent in
the researches dear to his heraldic soul.

One afternoon he set forth with his notebook in his
pocket and a veteran scrubbing-brush in his hand that he
had begged from the housemaid; for he had seen that the
mosses were thick upon the gravestones. When he went
in at the kirkyard gates he stood a while looking round
upon the place and contrasting the semi-modern stones
with the ancient table-topped ones set thick in that corner
of the enclosure where the older graves clustered by the
low boundary wall. The kirk was in ruins and stood, like
a derelict among the masts of a harbour, in the midst of
the upright stones; for the modern kirk which sheltered the
devotions of Pitriven parish was some little way off. Bob
Davidson, considering the prospect and listening to the soft
rush of water in the den below, took in the expression of the
place with an interested eye. It was so near to humanity, yet
so remote. The kitchen-garden wall flanked it on one side,
but its air of desertion and finality set it miles away, in spirit,
from living things. The afternoon was heavy and thick, like
many another near the year's end. It was as though nature,
wearied out, could struggle no more and was letting time
run by without the effort to live.

He was not long in choosing a table-topped monument
whose square mass had sunk from its proper level, and he set
to with his scrubbing-brush upon the layer of moss which, to
judge from a piece of mantling that stuck through its green
woof, must hide some elaborate design. He foresaw a long

task, for the growth was not of that spongy sort which can be ripped back like a carpet, but a close and detestable conglomeration of pincushion-like stuff that defied the power of bristles. He fell to with a blunt stick and worked on and on until his back ached, and he straightened himself, stretching his arms. His eyes were tired and he had bent forward so long that he was quite giddy. He sat down on the stone and looked round again.

The place had been closed for burials for about thirty years and there were no distressingly new monstrosities to spoil its quiet effect. Opposite, on the farther side of the kirk, the local dead of the last half-century were gathered together, herded in a flock according to their generations as they had been herded whilst living. Where Bob sat, the environment was historic, but yonder it was merely dull.

His eye lingered upon the most prominent of those gathered graves, or rather upon its appurtenances, for the headstone was invisible, being surrounded by a rusty iron railing made of chains that hung in a double row, festooned between the uprights. Inside the enclosure there stood up such a nest of Irish yews that nothing could be seen but their close blackness; some leaned on their neighbours, thrust sideways by the east-coast wind, but all were cheek by jowl, a conspiracy of heavy shadows in the dull light of the pulseless afternoon.

Bob disliked their look, suddenly, and for no reason; they were too much dilapidated to be imposing, and the stone which, presumably, they sheltered could not have the dignity of the one on which he was working, for the battered chains of the railing made a futile attempt at pomp that went ill with everything near it. Yet the atmosphere hanging about that enclosed place was not commonplace; it had some other and worse quality. A wave of repulsion, half spiritual, half physical, came over him, so that he was near to shuddering and he turned to go on with his cleaning; at least the scrubbing-brush was prosaic and therefore comfortable.

While he worked he found that a small, fresh-faced, rather sly-looking old man with a rake over his shoulder was contemplating him from the other side of the low wall. He was smiling too, with a slightly interested and wholly curious smile that uncovered four teeth divided by enormous gaps.

'Guid wurk,' said he, with the amused patronage that he might have given to a child at play.

'It's harder than you think,' said Bob.

The old man clambered over the wall with deliberation, his heavy boots knocking against it, and stood by Bob. The brush had uncovered a coat of arms, several skulls and crossbones and a long Latin inscription.

'Yon's dandy,' observed the new-comer, looking at him with approval, as though he were responsible for the whole.

'It's a pity they're so smothered up in moss,' said Bob. 'I've no doubt there are plenty better than this one.'

But the other was more interested in Bob than in antiquities.

'Ye'll be a scholar?' he inquired, with the same suggestion of suppressed comedy.

'Well – no; but I like these things.'

The old man laughed soundlessly.

'Graves doesna pleasure mony fowk owre muckle,' said he.

'There's one over there that doesn't pleasure *me* very much,' returned Bob, pointing to the huddled company of Irish yews.

His friend's eye followed the direction of his finger; then his smile widened and his eyebrows went up. He seemed to take a persistently but sardonically jocose view of everything in this world.

'Yon?' said he, wagging his head, 'fegs, there's them that'll agree fine wi' ye there!'

'Why, what do you think of it?' asked Bob.

'Heuch! what wad a' be thinkin'?' exclaimed the other, putting his rake over his shoulder again; 'a'm just thinkin' it's fell near time a' was awa' hame.'

He moved away with a nod which conveyed to Bob that he still took him for a semi-comic character.

'But who's buried there?' cried the latter after him.

'Just a lassie!' called the old man as he went.

When he had disappeared Bob went over to the yews. He would have laughed at the idea of being nervous, but there was that in him which made him keep his eye steadily on the enclosure as he approached it. He found that it was not, as he imagined, quite surrounded by trees, for the foot of the grave was clear and from it he could see into the darkness to where the plain, square stone sat, as though in hiding, like the inmate of a cave. He stepped over the chains and stood above the 'lassie' to read her name. There was no date, no text, not the baldest, barest record; only 'ANNIE CARGILL.'

The name lingered in his brain as he went home. It conveyed nothing, but he could not get it out of his head all that evening. The odd feeling that the surroundings of these two carved words had given him stamped them into his mind. Once or twice, as he sat after dinner with Sandy Lindsay and the red setter, he had almost opened his mouth to ask some question about them, but he did not do so. His godfather was the last man to whom he could speak of anything not perfectly obvious, and he guessed that he would not only think him a fool for the way in which he had spent his afternoon but call him one too. Bob always steered clear of conversational cross currents. It was one of the reasons that he was genuinely popular.

He did not go back to the kirkyard for several days, but when the next opportunity came he departed secretly, for Sandy Lindsay had gone to a sale of cattle and the coast was clear for him to do as he would. He had come to accept his godfather's disapproval of these excursions of his as certain – why he could not tell. Also, he hoped he should not meet the old man with the rake, for the subtle mixture of reticence and derisive patronage with which he had been treated did not promise much. He was beginning to be glad that he was leaving Pitriven in a few days, for he was a little tired of being out of real sympathy with anybody and he had not exchanged a word with a creature of his own age since he left Edinburgh.

'I am pleased that you have managed to get on well with Lindsay,' his father had written. 'He is an odd being and I can understand something of your surprise at our friendship. As a matter of fact, I have seen very little of him for a number of years, but your mother's people were under some obligation to him and she never forgot it, and since her death I have not let him quite slip out of my life. There were strange stories about him in his youth, I believe, but they were none of my business, nor did I ever hear what they were . . .'

His father's want of curiosity was tiresome, Bob thought.

He hurried along, for he needed all the light he could get and he had started later than he intended. There were two stones close to the first one which he wanted to uncover and he stuck manfully to them till both were laid bare. He was interrupted by nobody, but when at last he took out his notebook to make a rough sketch of the complicated armorial bearings which made one of them a treasure, the light was beginning to fail. He scrawled and scribbled, then shut up the book with a sigh of relief. His fingers were chilly and he could hear the wheels of Lindsay's dog-cart grinding up the avenue on the further side of the den. He would have one more look at Annie Cargill, and go. He had almost forgotten her sinister fascination as he worked.

As he approached across the grass a small bird skimmed swiftly out of a tree, as though to light in one of the Irish yews, but turned within a yard of its goal, with a violent flutter of wings, and flew almost into Bob's face. Another step took him to the foot of the grave, and there he stepped back as though he had been struck.

A figure was sitting crouched in the very middle of the dank closeness inside the chains, and he knew that it was this that had made the bird change its course. He would have liked to do the same but he stood there petrified, his heart smiting against his ribs and a cold horror settling about him. He could not move for the swift dread that took him lest he should see the creature's face; he could not make out whether the huddled shape was male or female, for the head was averted and it seemed to him in this desperate moment that, if it turned, his eyes would meet something so horrible that he could never get over it, never be the same again. He felt the drops break out under his hair as he stood, not daring to move for his insane fear of attracting attention.

The dusk was not far advanced, but between the closed-in walls of the yews the outline of the figure was indefinite, muffled in some wrapping drawn about its head and shoulders. It might be an old woman – he thought it was – it might be a mere huddled lump of clothes, though why they should be in that place was beyond his struggling wits to imagine. He tried to take his eyes from the thing – for it had no other name to him – and as he did so, the head turned as quietly and as independently of the rest of the body as the head of an owl turns when some intruder peers into the hollow in which it is lodged. The young man saw a wisp of long hair and a mouth and chin; the upper part of the face was covered by the hood or cloak, or whatsoever garment was held close about the bodily part of the lurking presence between the yews. It *was* a woman.

The discovery of something tangible, something definite, brought back a little of his banished courage and gave power to his limbs. He walked away swiftly, his face set resolutely to the kirkyard gates, not looking behind. As he trod on a stick that cracked under his boot he nearly leaped into the air, but he went on, stiff and holding himself rigidly together. His notebook and scrubbing-brush lay on the table-topped stone; he had forgotten them, nor, had he remembered them, would he have gone back to fetch them for all the kingdoms of the world.

He hurried out of the kirkyard and through the door of the walled kitchen garden. His heart was beating and the sight of a gardener, a healthy-looking, upstanding young man who was coming out of a tool-shed, was of infinite comfort to him. Here was a human being, young and stirring like himself, a normal creature, and his presence brought him back into the everyday, reasonable world which had receded from him in the last few minutes. As they passed each other he stopped.

'I say,' he began.

The other touched his cap.

'Look here,' said Bob, rather breathlessly, 'there's something so odd in the kirkyard – there!'

He threw out his arm towards the place where the gable of the ruin showed above the garden wall.

The gardener stared at him, astonished.

'What like is it?' he asked, setting down the basket he carried.

'It's – a person,' said Bob.

Visions of accidents, poachers, trespassers, swept across the gardener's practical mind. He moved forward quickly, and a chill ran over Bob again at the thought of going back into the kirkyard. But the human personality beside him put a different aspect on everything and he was immediately ashamed of his childishness.

They went out of the garden together and made their way among the stones to Annie Cargill's grave. At the head they paused and Bob went softly round the trees to the gap at its foot, the other following; and here he stopped in blank astonishment.

The place was empty

He turned to the gardener, speechless, feeling like a fool.

'It's gone!' he exclaimed at last.

The other pushed back his cap and stood looking at him with a half smile.

'I suppose you think I'm mad,' said Bob, throwing out his hands, 'but I tell you it was there – not a minute ago – just before I met you!'

'But wha was it?' said the gardener.

'That's what I want to know!' cried Bob. 'It was a woman – an old, old woman – I am certain it was a woman. It was there, sitting huddled up in front of the stone.'

'There's no auld body comes in hereabouts that a can mind of.'

'It looked mad – extraordinary,' continued Bob, 'not like anyone I've ever seen.'

'Well, it's awa now, anyhow,' said the gardener.

'But *who* was Annie Cargill?' burst out Bob. 'There's something strange about this place – I know there is! An old man I met here told me so – but I knew it myself. He said other people besides me don't like the look of those trees and that chained-in place. He couldn't have been lying – why should he tell me that?'

His companion seemed as non-communicative as the man with the rake, but Bob felt that he would be put off no longer. It was too annoying; also he had a passionate desire to justify himself, to force some admission that he was not altogether childish in his excitement.

'Well, maybe a've heard tell o' things,' said the other cautiously; 'a'll not say that a havena'. But a've been here just twa year – it's fowk aulder nor me that ye should speir at.'

'But *who* was Annie Cargill?' cried Bob again. 'That's what I want to know! The old man said she was "a lassie".'

'She was a lassie, and she wasna very weel used, they say. There was them that made owre muckle o' her, that set her up aboon her place. She was just a gipsy lassie.'

'A gipsy?'

'Well, a dinna ken the rights o't, but they say she was left to dee her lane, some way aboot the loan yonder.'

'And who left her to die?'

A look came over the gardener's face that made Bob think of the closing of a door.

'A canna just mind about that,' he replied. 'A ken nae mair nor what a'm telling ye. An' they buried her in here.'

'Was she pretty?' asked Bob.

'Aye was she,' said the other. 'But she'll no be bonnie now,' he added grimly. 'She's been lyin' here owre lang.'

'And the trees? Who planted the trees?'

'Well, they were plantit to hide the stane,' said the gardener. 'It's an ugly thing and ye can see it frae the windows o' the house.'

'But they *don't* hide it,' rejoined Bob; 'you can see it quite well, even across the den.'

'Aye, but there's twa trees wantin' at the fit o't. They were plantit, but the wind wadna let them stand. They got them in three times, they say, but the wind was aye owre muckle for them.'

'There's no mark of them now.'

'Na. They wadna stand, ye see, and the roots was howkit out. It's forty year syne that they did that.'

'Well, it's an extraordinary place,' said Bob, as they turned to go, 'and it's a more extraordinary creature that I saw in there. Come outside and let us look if we can find any trace of her.'

They walked through the wood, then ran down to the den, they searched about in the neighbouring byroad and in the fields. No one was to be seen and the gathering dusk soon sent the gardener to lock the garden doors. He was anxious to get back to his tea. Bob bade him good night and they parted.

When the dinner-bell brought Bob downstairs that evening, Lyall, the butler, was waiting for him in the hall. He was to dine alone, it seemed, for his godfather was not going to leave his room. He had got a chill at the cattle-fair, said the butler, for he had refused to take his greatcoat with him, although it had been put in the dogcart. He had thrown it out angrily – so Bob gathered – and the butler had been angry too. He was grim to-night and wore the tense and self-righteous face of one who is justified of his words. Bob ate in silence and then betook himself to the smoking-room with the setter and installed himself with a book.

It was ten o'clock when Lyall came in and asked him to go up to Lindsay's room; he had been having great trouble with his master, and, though from the old servant's customary manner Bob believed himself to hold a mean place in his estimation, it was evident that he wished for his support now.

'Hadn't you better send for the doctor?' he asked as they went out together.

The other snorted.

'A doctor?' he exclaimed. 'I've done my best, but it's neither you nor me that can make him see a doctor! There's no doctor been in this house since *I* cam' to it, and that's twenty-five years syne.'

Lindsay was lying in his solid fourposter with his angry eyes fixed on the door; he looked desperately ill and as Bob approached he sat up.

'What are you doing here?' he cried. 'Who told you to come up?'

The butler went quietly out. He had no mind for another scene.

'I came to see how you were, sir,' said Bob. 'I am sorry you are not well.'

'Now look here!' said Lindsay, 'let me have none of your nonsense here. That damned old fool outside has been telling me I ought to send for a doctor. I'll have none of *that*! If you have come to say the same thing, out you go, and be quick about it too. I'll see no doctors, I tell you! I'm not going to have one near me. I hate the whole lot! A set of . . .'

His abuse was searching. He shouted so loudly that the dog below in the smoking-room began to bark.

'I'm not going to ask you to do anything,' said Bob quietly, 'only I wish you would lie down and get some sleep. I can sit here and if you want anything I can get it for you. Then you need not have Lyall up here to bother you.'

Lindsay looked at him suspiciously but he seemed not ill-pleased. He lay down again and turned over with his back to the young man.

The shutters were not closed nor the blinds pulled down and Bob was afraid of rousing Lindsay by moving about, so he sat quite still till the breathing in the bed told him that his godfather was asleep. The hands of the clock ticking on the mantelpiece were hard on eleven when he rose and went downstairs, priding himself a little on the success of his methods. He had just time to find his place in his book when a violent bell-ringing woke the house.

He heard Lyall run upstairs and he sat still, waiting. In another moment the man was down again.

'You'll need to go back, sir,' said he. 'The Colonel wants ye.'

Bob ran up.

'Why did you go?' cried Lindsay. 'Stay here. You said you would stay! That damned fellow, Lyall, will drive me mad with his doctors. Don't let him in!'

Bob looked at the harsh face and white whiskers of the

solitary, uncouth old man in the bed. He pitied him, not so much because he was ill, but because of his rough, forlorn detachment from the humanities.

'It's late, you know, sir,' said he, 'but I'll get my mattress and sleep on the floor. I will stay, certainly.'

The idea seemed to quiet Lindsay and he fell asleep; now and then he tossed his heavy body from one side to another, but Bob made up his shakedown bed and got into it without interruption and was soon lost in the healthy slumber of youth. He was roused from it a short time later by something which was not a noise but which had made appeal to some suspended sense of his own. He sat up.

There was no moon, but the starless night had not the solidity of deep darkness. The unshuttered window gave him his bearings when he looked round wondering, as the sleeper in a strange bed so often wonders, where he could possibly be, though its grey square was almost blocked out by a figure before it. Lindsay had got out of bed and was standing, just as he stood when his godson first entered Pitriven, colossal and still, against the pane.

Bob struck a match quickly and Lindsay turned as the candle-flame rose up.

'Put it out!' he said fiercely. 'I tell you, put it out! Do you want the whole parish to see in?'

'Come back,' begged Bob, 'for heaven's sake go back into your bed – why, you will perish with cold standing there.'

He was on his feet and half-way to the window.

'Do you hear me?' roared Lindsay. 'Put out that damned candle!'

Bob obeyed and then went and laid his hand on Lindsay's sleeve. Though the old man was not cold his teeth were chattering.

He shook him off.

'Look at that,' he said, pointing into the night outside.

'Go to bed, sir – please go to bed,' said Bob again.

'But look!' cried Lindsay, taking him by the shoulder.

The young man strained his eyes. The windows looked straight across the cleft of the den towards the spot where the kirk stood high upon the farther bank. The indication of a dark mass was just visible, like a pyramid thrusting into the sky, which Bob knew must be the crowded yews round Annie Cargill's grave.

'Do you see the light?' asked Lindsay.

'Where?' said Bob, peering out, 'I can't see anything.'

'Are you blind, boy?' cried Lindsay – 'it's there by the foot of the trees, and *she's* there too! She's old now – old – old. Not like she was then!'

Bob turned colder. The young gardener's words came back to him. 'She's no bonnie noo,' he had said, 'she's been lyin' there owre lang.' It had seemed to him a grim speech, but its suggestion then had been of mere physical horror. His godfather's words conveyed a spiritual one.

'By the trees,' he said. 'Which trees?'

'Good God, can't you see it, you young fool?

There's a little dim light – at the foot – in the gap.'

Bob was silent. He knew exactly which place Lindsay meant.

'It's there!' cried the other again – 'beside her – round her!'

He seemed to be terribly excited, and Bob, who felt the burning fever of the hand gripping his shoulder, longed to get him back between his sheets. He was quite certain that he was delirious.

'Yes, I see it now,' he said, lying, but hoping to quiet him, 'perhaps it is a bit of glass or a shining stone.'

He knew how senseless his words were, but they were the first that came into his head.

'The stone's in there,' said Lindsay, 'in among the trees. But they won't hide it – they won't hide her!'

'I know,' said Bob; 'come, sir, you must rest.'

'Rest? I can't rest. She knows that. She has known it for years. Ah, she's old now, you see, and bitter. Older – every year older—'

Bob tried to draw him away. To his surprise the other made no resistance. Lindsay lay down and he covered him carefully. He put on a coat that was hanging in the room and sat down by the bed; he wondered dismally if this miserable night would ever end. It was past one o'clock and he resolved that he would send for a doctor the moment the house was stirring. He dared not leave Lindsay and he dared not ring the bell for Lyall, lest he should upset him further. In about half an hour he rose and crept into his shakedown to sleep, for the old man was quiet.

All the rest of his days Bob wondered what would have happened if he had kept awake. How far might he have seen into the mysteries of those fringes of spiritual life that surround humanity, and how far listened to the echoes that come floating in broken notes from the hidden conflict of good and evil?

A faint light was breaking outside when consciousness came to him with the knowledge that he was half frozen. His limbs were aching from the way in which he had huddled himself together. A strong draught was sweeping into the room and when he lit the candle he found that the door was wide open. He leaped up and shut it, and then went softly to see whether Lindsay slept.

The bedclothes were thrown back and the bed was empty.

He dressed hurriedly and ran out into the passage. Lindsay's clothes, which had been lying on a chair at the foot of the fourposter, had disappeared with their owner. When he reached the hall the air blew strong against his face, for the front door stood wide and a chill wind that was rising with morning was heaving the boughs outside. No wonder that he had shivered on the floor. On the inner side of the smoking-room door the setter was whining and snuffling. He turned the handle and looked in, vainly hoping that he might find Lindsay, and the dog rushed out past him, through the house door and into the December morning, with his nose on the ground. He watched him as he shot away towards the den of Pitriven, and followed, running.

A wooden gate led to the bridge that spanned the den, and here the setter paused, crying, till Bob came up with him. As the gate swung behind them the dog rushed on before, up the flight of steps that ascended to the kitchen garden.

Bob knew quite well where he and his dumb comrade were going, and his heart sank with each step that took them nearer to their goal. But he was a courageous youth, in spite of his spiritual misgivings, and it would have been impossible to him to leave anyone in the lurch. Nevertheless, he remembered, with instinctive thankfulness, that the outer door of the garden would be locked and that he must rouse the gardener in the bothy if he wished to get through it.

The bothy was built against the outer side of the wall, but one of its windows looked in over the beds and raspberry canes. He took a handful of earth and flung it against the pane. The window was thrown up and the face of the young man he had met that afternoon looked out, dim in the widening daylight.

'It's Colonel Lindsay!' shouted Bob, 'he is ill – he is somewhere *there*! Come down quick for God's sake, and bring the key of the door, for we must find him!'

He pointed to the kirkyard, and as he did so he noticed that the dog had not followed him across the garden. He could hear him barking among the gravestones. As he waited for the gardener, Bob remembered, what he had forgotten before, that there was a short cut to the place through a thicket. The trail the setter followed must have turned off there.

The head above disappeared. The gardener was half dressed, for he was rising to go to his hothouse fires. He was inclined to think that Bob Davidson was wrong in the head, but he came down with the key in his hand.

They took the same way that they had taken in the afternoon, and passed through the kirkyard gate into a world of shadows and stones. The great black mass above Annie Cargill's head was a landmark in the indefinite greys.

The two young men approached and it seemed to them as though a swift movement ran through the yew trees, as though something they could not define stirred amongst them. They advanced, heartened each by the other's presence, and paused where they had stood in the falling light of the winter evening. Sandy Lindsay was lying dead on Annie Cargill's grave.

*   *   *

A FEW MINUTES later they went to fetch a hurdle on which to carry him to the house. Neither was anxious to remain alone till the other returned, so they went side by side. Bob was asking himself, what was that light, invisible to his own eyes, which Lindsay had seen? God only knew; he could not tell.

The setter stayed behind, but not to watch by his master's body, after the traditional habit of dogs. He crouched by the gap made by the missing trees, staring into the gloom of the enclosure, his feet planted stiffly before him – snarling at something to which the two young men had been blind, but which was evidently plain to him.

The Watch-Tower

FINLAYSON THE shepherd came slowly down the glen behind his flock. The sun of a late autumn day had long since disappeared, even from the topmost peaks, and the cold greenness of twilight was settling on Glen Esk; at his left hand the barren hill-sides were beginning to soften into fields lately shorn of their crop, for he was within a couple of miles of the glen's mouth. On his right the land ran down to the North Esk, which was narrowing itself for a rush between high rocks a little farther on; and, across the water, the hills rose again, a barrier between Angus and the west. He could hear the purring kiss of stream and pebble and see the clear, cold glimmer between the alder roots; to his professionally wayfaring mind the growing softness of outlook spoke comfortable words, prophetic of the valley and cultivation.

Though he had been afoot since early morning the distance he had covered was not great; for he had sacrificed a little time that the flock might straggle forward on the wayside turf instead of keeping directly to the road. He did not want to deliver them footsore to their new owner; for they were black-faced, mountain-bred sheep, and road travel was new to them.

As he went he thought pleasantly of his last night's lodging, for he had been well housed by the owner of one of the few hill-farms that lay in his way, and the sheep were penned in an empty yard. A seat at the kitchen hearth had been his portion and a share in the contents of the black, three-legged pot swinging over the blaze.

Like nearly all shepherds, he had a love of books and narrative, born of a solitary life and of hours when the mind, free of effort, longs for food. Books, in those days, were a rarity, reserved for the few; and though he could read well enough, Finlayson seldom had the chance of doing so. But the tongue was as mighty as the pen, in his time and in his walk of life, and his head was full, just now, of last night's fire-side talk.

It had run principally on the sheep-stealer whose doings were agitating farmers, and who was even now hiding from the law in the upper fastnesses of Glen Esk. It was scarcely a couple of weeks since 'Muckle Johnnie,' as he was called, had contrived to escape from the prison in which he lay awaiting his execution; for in those early days of eighteen hundred, sheep-stealing was still a capital offence. Finlayson, listening to the details of his bid for life, had not known what to feel; for he was torn by a constitutional hankering for adventure and adventurers and the grim resentment natural to a man of his calling. He now looked at the foolish crowd moving before him and his hand tightened on his crook; he loved all sheep, and, as in his mind he grappled with the thief, the radical savagery that lies in every man worth the name rose and made his breath come short.

Though he would so soon emerge from the glen, he could see no dwelling in front of him; but he cared little whether he spent the night under a roof or not, as the air was soft, despite the chill purity of the heavens. As the gold and silver of the birches and their stems began to lose colour in the dusk, he made his way down the slope towards the water, near which he saw one of those walled, circular folds that dot the more accessible parts of the Grampians.

The sheep, with their tacit acceptance of another animal's dominion, poured through the bracken as the dog, trotting now on one side, now on the other, kept them heading for the rude enclosure; and when the last straggler was chivied in and the gate shut, the young shepherd stood looking about with a view to his own shelter. Tay, the dog, turned up a lean face and brilliant eyes tentatively; his mind still lingered on duty, though, at the moment, he did not quite know where it lay.

'Come awa', min,' said Finlayson.

The two mounted a knoll which rose a little farther on

than the fold. This was the beginning of the steep rocks
through the gorge of which the river ran for over a quarter
of a mile. A dark mass that the shepherd could not define
crowned its summit, and a few stunted trees made a black
tracery against a patch of chrysophrase green which lay,
like an inland lake, in a bar of smoky cloud.

On reaching the top of the rising ground he was surprised
to find himself close to the unknown object, which, like most
things seen in the half dark, had lost its perspective and
seemed to have leaped suddenly from the distance to the
foreground. He saw that this was a ruinous tower-shaped
building between twenty and thirty feet high, ragged with
clinging brier and clothed by a shock of ivy. There was
enough light to show him the windows, which stared one
towards each point of the compass; all were widened
from their original size by the falling away of stones,
and their respective aspects suggested that the tower was
less a defensive erection than a vantage-point from which
one watcher might command the whole of the glen. To
Finlayson it promised very excellent shelter.

It was about an hour later when he looked over the wall
at his flock and turned again towards the tower. The stars
were out now, and the moon, a night over her full, was
sailing into mid-sky, leaving the eastern horizon blurred
behind her. The entrance to the building faced towards
the little sheepfold, and the young man reflected, as he
stood just inside it and looked out on the country growing
each moment plainer in the moonlight, that he could watch
every movement of his creatures without leaving his shelter.
He had cut a bundle of heather at the brae's foot and he
threw it on the floor of the tower for a bed. The purr of
the water below was, in itself, an invitation to sleep, and
he gave Tay's head a slap, for the dog's uneasy sniffing
annoyed him. He was weary and glad to stretch his long
legs in peace.

But though his master slept, Tay's eyes never closed; and
when at last his nose went down between his paws, they
were still fixed upon a spot in the surrounding darkness;
now and then a growl escaped him, chocked in his throat
for fear of Finlayson's hand.

It was almost ten o'clock when the shepherd turned and sat up. It had grown much colder and a touch of frost had crept into the air. His limbs were stiff, so, telling the dog to stay where he was, he went out to collect a few sticks for a fire. But for the running river, the night was as still as death, and the ripple of white wool in the fold below him was like a spot of foam moored in a backwater. He tore up the dry bracken and filled his arms with spoil from a tree, dead and fallen on the slope. Then he heaped it just below a yawning gap in the roof, and kneeling down, set the pile alight. As the spark caught the brittle stuff, man and dog stood illuminated as though by magnesium wire. The flare turned the walls from indefinite black to light brick-colour. Every stone and crevice sprang into importance, and Tay's teeth showed white as he remained standing like the wooden image of a dog, his whole being concentrated on a battered stairway which Finlayson now saw for the first time. The steps ran upwards from the farthest angle of darkness to a staging which had, apparently, been the floor of an upper room. It was now hardly more than a ledge, some six feet deep, which skirted the west side of the wall under one of the windows and supported a few pieces of broken masonry. Behind one of these, the firelight revealed to the young man the outline of a foot.

Tay's loud snarling filled the place and Finlayson, thrusting him back, began to climb the stair. A figure was standing among the heaped-up fragments of flooring – a figure ragged and unshorn. The bare ends of the steps jutted rudely into the glow, for their outer rail had fallen, and the shepherd saw how perilous a road they might be for one who should meet a resolute defender at the top. What suggested this to him was the attitude of the man above.

He paused, and his eyes met another pair – savage, watchful. All at once Finlayson drew back.

'Lord presairv's!' he exclaimed.

An expression ran over as much of the stranger's face as was uncovered by beard. It might have been a wave of relief.

'Nichol!' exclaimed Finlayson again; 'gude sakes, Nichol!'

As he spoke there flashed on his brain the memory of a

spring morning a couple of years back. He saw a lowland farm set on a slope and the wet road running down from it. Two men were walking side by side, himself and another; and that other stood above him now, haggard and menacing. At the foot of the hill they had parted and he had gone back to his work, heavy-spirited for the loss of the companion who had been his fellow-servant for months. The bothy was dull afterwards and he had soon changed the plough for the crook, drifting away, like Nichol, to find employment beyond the Grampians, farther north.

'Whisht, whisht, lad!' whispered the strange figure, coming a step downwards; 'man, haud doon yer dog. Finlayson, there'll no be anither man wi' ye?'

As he spoke he stretched out his hand, and the young man could see, in the light that filled the tower, how emaciated he was. The arm, left bare in many places by the tattered shirt, was so thin that it surprised him. He remembered Nichol a heavy man, for all his uncommon activity.

'Na, na,' replied he. 'Come awa doon, – Nichol, doon the stair wi' ye tae the fire.'

The sight of the stranger approaching his master sent Tay into a frenzy of barking, and it took the roughest side of Finlayson's hand and tongue to quiet him. By nature the shepherd was a merciful man, and the beast was his friend as well as servant, but he cuffed him remorselessly into peace, for he knew that the price of his noise might be a man's life. He guessed that Nichol and the sheep-stealer, the story of whose escape had held him spellbound last night, were the same.

He had always known him bearded, and, standing below in the light, he perceived that he was little changed, but for his emaciation and the restlessness of the hunted creature, which looked from his eyes.

The first burst of flame was dying down and Finlayson added nothing to the fuel; after a careful scrutiny of every approach to the tower, he sat down to hear the history of Nichol's wanderings.

'Weel,' he commented, as his friend's voice ceased, 'ye'll dae best tae bide up yonder whaur a found ye; ye maun bide aff the road wi' the mune glowerin' on a'thing, the way she is the nicht. An' a'll gin ye the bit bannock that's in ma poke. A canna gie ye ma breeks, but ye'll get the plaid, an' gin ye tak' yon crook i' yer hand, there's nane'll speir but ye're the same's mysel', an' awa' south, seekin' work.'

They sat still as the night went by, the younger man reviewing in his mind the desperate runs by night, the suspense, the hunger, the slow days in wet ditches, the scraps of food snatched in the dark hours from hill-side cots or begged in the dusk.

'Man, but it's an ill job,' he said at last.

'It'll be a' that till a'm south o' Edinburgh,' rejoined Nichol. 'A'body kens me i' they glens, ye see, Finlayson.'

The dregs of the short-lived embers were cool, and long silence fell upon the two. They sat side by side, their backs against the wall. Tay, finally satisfied of the stranger's happy relations with his master, had crept close, and slept; sighing, now and then, from the depths of his free lungs and untrammelled conscience. Nichol's elbows were on his knees and he leaned his head on his hands; there are times when there is no such effort as relaxation.

'Tak' a rest,' said the shepherd; 'the mune'll no be muckle doon or after twa o'clock. Ye needna be fear'd – a'll no sleep, mysel'. Tak' the plaid, an' a'll wauken ye syne it's time for ye tae be awa'.'

He gathered it from where it lay and thrust it into his companion's hand.

'Ye micht gie a look round about, Finlayson,' said Nichol, fingering the stuff; 'a canna lie doon sae easy-like as yersel'.'

The young man rose and went to the door. No movement, far or near, troubled the blank serenity of the moonlight. There was nothing within sight to suggest life. As the other drew the plaid over his rags the shepherd felt his way cautiously over the broken steps and stood on the floor above, leaning from the wide gap that had once been a window. Tay stirred below, but, with a mind now at rest, lay undisquieted by the sheep-stealer's feet.

Finlayson would have been glad enough to stretch himself alongside his friend; but in case he should fall incontinently

asleep, he resolved to stay on his feet. When the moon
should set over the high ground he would rouse Nichol.
From the yawning windows above he could see the whole
countryside and could warn him of the approach of any
human being. But for the fact that he was drowsy, he
was content to watch. That was his profession, and
great silences were the background of his working life.
His education was small, his mind very simple; he had
no consciousness of the possibilities crowding on those
who, for days at a stretch, need never open their lips. The
influences that may touch the solitary inhabitant of great
spaces are outside the suspicions of the western man.

He had been some time at his post when he became
aware of a dim figure, a mere moving spot of darkness,
which approached the tower and which had come out
from the trees, where the rocks overhung the river. It was
coming cautiously, dodging among odd bits of bush and
stone. He turned to go down the steps, but, in the one
stride that it took to reach the top of them, Tay's voice
burst on the stillness. He stopped, for two men, who must
have advanced on the eastern side of the tower whilst he,
intent on the third one, was watching from the western
window, were standing in the doorway.

A curse dropped from one of them.

'Ye doited fule, it's a shepherd!' he exclaimed, giving
his companion a shove with his shoulder that sent him
barging into the wall.

Finlayson heard Nichol spring up.

With relief he remembered the inference that must be
drawn from the presence of the dog and the crook lying
near the plaided figure below. He crouched quickly down
on the flooring, holding his breath.

'What's ado?' said Nichol's voice.

'Div ye no ken, an' you a shepherd?' said one of the
intruders with a laugh. 'Mind yer beasts, or ye'll ken owre
sune! Yon lad they ca' Muckle Johnnie's awa' again – ye
canna haud the like o' they folk but wi' the rope. The man
that gets him's tae get fifty poond frae the croun' – but a'm
feared it'll no be me.'

'*Him*!' exclaimed Nichol – and Finlayson could hear no

tremor in his voice – 'ye'll need tae rin, then; a cam across
frae Aberdeen way a puckle o' days syne, an' it's weel kent
there that he's no far awa'. A' wouldna wonder gin he was
ca' in' nets, a mile or twa oot tae sea.'

At this moment the person whom the shepherd had seen
from the window came into the tower. It was evident that the
three man-hunters had had some method in their approach.
The newcomer stood on the threshold, as though to bar
the way.

'Come ben,' cried one of his companions; 'we've ta'en
naethin' waur nor a shepherd! Cry on the dog, man or
he'll hae us a' murder't!'

Nichol's voice rose in a string of abuse at the excited
animal, but Tay cared nothing for him, and one of the
men, whose eyes had grown accustomed to the dimness
of the building, picked up the crook. Finlayson heard a
heavy blow and a yelp; in a moment a wet nose was thrust
against his hand. The sweat broke out on his forehead as
he threw his arms around the collie's neck and dragged
him down behind the stones and rubbish.

Nichol had always been a man of ready wits, but the
listener overhead wondered afresh at them and at the
boldness with which he turned his position to account.
Two of the intruders sat down on the heather couch; their
jests and gossip rose with sinister suggestion to the upper
floor as time went by. Only the last comer remained silent,
standing in the white patch that then moon had laid inside
the doorway.

Suddenly he turned towards the dim group, holding out
his pipe. 'A'm needin' a licht, Jock,' he said.

Finlayson had dragged himself near the edge, and, still
smothering the dog's head against his breast, was peering
through a chink.

The click of flint and steel followed, and, hard upon
it, a violent flame – as bright, almost, as the flame of the
bracken now lying in ashes. The man stood holding the
frayed and lighted end of a piece of rope which protruded
in a loop from his pocket, and he stepped forward and
held the burning thing before Nichol's face.

Then came a shout, a scuffle of hands and feet against the

wall, and the sheep-stealer struck his enemy to the ground. The light went out under the fall of a heavy body.

There was a moment of confusion, of groping hands, of inarticulate words; the darkness below the shepherd was alive with blind struggle and the hard-drawn breaths of those whose primitive instincts had risen above all others. It lasted scarcely a minute, but, to him, it seemed as though he were looking down into a pit of wolves. Tay burst from him and bounded down the steps, leaping and snapping indiscriminately. Before he could feel his way after him, Nichol had dashed past the man who was now gathering himself up from the ground, and his gaunt figure crossed the threshold into the moonlight and was gone.

By the time Finlayson reached the bottom the place was empty, but for the collie who darted back to him, whining and springing. He ran out on to the bareness of the hill-side. To follow was useless, for Nichol had doubled round the tower, making for the trees above the river. In their talk that night he had spoken of a crossing which he knew among the boulders, and his friend suspected that his goal must be that hidden spot. If his pursuers did not know of the place, and were to lose sight of their quarry, they might take some time in finding shallow water for wading, as the current ran deep and strong, boiling below the height on either side of it. The shepherd turned and climbed again to the window. By leaning out, he could see the whole loop of the Esk, as a man watches from the stand of a racecourse. He was in time to see Nichol disappear among the trunks. Two of the men were hard on his track; the third, still giddy from his fall upon the stony floor, staggered along far behind his comrades.

All had vanished out of sight, but Finlayson stood fixed at his post. His eyes, trained to long scrutiny of the crevices of the hills, scoured the ground across the river, for, on this side and on that, the scrub left the lips of the heights unclothed and the sailing moon was white on them.

All at once the figure of the sheep-stealer emerged from the trees and turned back up the bank towards the tower; he had, apparently, either been headed off or had overshot the exact spot which offered him escape; in his haste he did not see what was plain to Finlayson from his point of vantage – namely, that he was running straight towards the third man, who, finding himself left so far behind, had sat down on a piece of protruding stone among the bushes, and now rose stealthily, waiting, ready to spring, behind a tree-trunk.

Nichol dodged, as though he had caught sight of his enemy, and would have turned; but, behind him, the two others were gaining hard. Finlayson threw out his arms, raving and crying to him to make for the open country, but his shouts were unheard by either hunters or hunted; and he could not see that Nichol, worn with prison fare, hardship, and hunger, was beginning to flag.

The sheep-stealer dashed a second time into the shadow of the trees, his face to the Esk. The men closed in behind him. Between wood and water the rock jutted out, a rugged white promontory, with, beyond and below it, the river swirling nearly a hundred feet down. The shepherd saw him clear the fringe of wood and run out upon the bald triangle that cut into the dark mystery of ravine. The pursuers were pressing close, almost upon him. As they reached the edge, the nearer to him of the two flung out his hand and grasped Nichol.

For a moment the sheep-stealer was checked; then Finlayson saw him spring forward – outward – dragging his captor's weight with him.

The cry that came back along the night seemed to the watcher in the tower as though it had risen from his own lips.

'He saved himself from the rope, at any rate,' said the young shepherd to himself, as he stood below and felt his foot touch the plaid that his friend had dropped.

When he laid himself again by the wall he could not sleep; the place echoed in his ears with that cry. He rose and went down the hill to the little fold, and stretched himself there, thankful for the company of the foolish, untroubled sheep.

The Figurehead

THE BRIG *William and Joann* of Montrose lay beside
the quay at the Old Shore. She had come in very early
from the Baltic and was to sail again at the beginning
of November for Galatz, and her crew looked forward,
each man according to his taste, to such distractions as
the east-coast seaport could offer. From the bridge and
along the Old Shore to Ferry Street there were fifty-seven
public-houses, and the little steep wynds running down
from the Sea-Gate to the water that lapped the quay-side
were loud with the roaring company that frequented them.
Swedes, Norwegians, Danes and Scots and the tow-headed,
loud-voiced girls who shared their lighter moments, made
the place ring from dusk onwards; and the sedate part of
the townsfolk in the reputable streets, so near the thievish
corners of the disreputable ones, would hurry along with
their mouths drawn down as the gales of song and oaths
and laughter assailed their ears.

It was a well-built, rather solemn-looking town which
stood on a narrow stretch of land between the Basin of
Montrose and the North Sea. Smoke and blue mist and
cloud would brood over its long line of roofs, and, soaring
through the vapours, rose the slim beauty of the high steeple
that reared its grace of flying buttress and weather-vaned
summit to be a mark to its homing sons as they rolled
in from the Baltic. It was a place of wide thorough-fares,
and in the days when the *William and Joann* came in and
out over the bar at varying intervals there was a deal of
trade and herring-fishing, and wind-jammers of every kind
would ride in past the lighthouse to lie up in the harbour.
A lovable town and one towards which a native might look
with a warming of the heart, as he saw, from far out, the

steeple come up over the horizon. At least, so thought
Tom Falconer, mate of the *William and Joann*.

Falconer had been at sea since he was a lad of fifteen,
and now, after more than a dozen years of it, he knew he
had made the right choice. Not that he was aware of having
any great passion for it, or of formulating such a sentiment
in his mind; he was only sure that he was more contented
in a ship than in any other place. He was a quiet fellow,
unaggressive and rather gently-spoken for the traditional
mate. Sometimes he was called 'soft' by men who had never
sailed with him before, but that word would drop out of their
talk, never to reappear, by the time they were a day or two
out and the crew had had time to settle down together. He
was an excellent seaman too, and the unassuming reserve,
a puzzle to his shipmates, which was always a bar between
himself and them till they had learned to take it for granted,
did not make him unpopular. Skippers thought well of him,
though perhaps they understood him less well than did the
crews. In port he was usually as quiet as at sea, but not
always. Hard-working men do not analyse one another
much; they either do or do not accept one another, and
that is all. He had a serious, tanned face and seafaring
eyes – eyes, that is, whose focus appears to be on an exact
level with the horizon, neither above nor below it; and
preserving that level through every movement and every
conversation. His short hair turned up crisply under the
dark cloth of his peaked cap; his hands were brown and
sinewy. The signs of strength that he carried about him
seemed to be dormant behind his personality, like sleeping
dogs behind a kennel door.

Books said little to Falconer, and most of his leisure was
spent in placid smoking. The men would wonder what
their quiet-mannered mate thought about as he looked
over into the water or out across the general vastness,
alone with his pipe. Some people – and he was one of
them – see their thoughts in very definite pictures, and
the images he sometimes saw mentally were odd chunks
of his childhood, of days at the little school in one of the
wynds at the Old Shore, or strange people that he could
recollect in the moving kaleidoscope of a seaport; things

that had fascinated him. He remembered one, a gaudy fan of stiff, papery white feathers, speckled and painted in garish green and scarlet, that his father had brought from the China Seas. It had been a wonder to him, a kind of signpost pointing to those outlandish, desirable places that he got reflected glimpses of from foreign shells and from careful paintings of sailing vessels by heathen hands which he had admired in the houses of his father's friends. He loved his town in a steady, unemotional way and still had a home in it; for though both his parents were dead long since, an ancient bachelor uncle who lived on that side of Montrose farthest from the harbour, had an empty room in his cottage that Tom was free to go and come to as he liked.

He stepped ashore one October day, his bundle in his hand and a very small box on his shoulder; but he laid both of these down on the cobble-stones of the quay and stood staring at the bows of the *William and Joann*. Then he picked up his baggage and went off to the town between the piles of lumber lying about the wharf. As he reached the point where the streets began he turned to look back again at the brig. He could just distinguish the form of her figurehead sharp and clear against the wide background of shining water.

This figurehead was a thing that fascinated Falconer. It might be said that, while he was on board the *William and Joann*, he was never wholly unconscious of it. It had come to represent certain ideas in his mind. Often, lying in his bunk on a starlight night, he would fancy the white creature he could not see, her still face half turned up to the glittering, pathless spaces, her fixed eyes set on her course, her hands drawn up, folded together and pointing forward, as those of a swimmer, under her lifted chin. He could see nothing as he lay there but the small, swinging oil-lamp and the crowding sides of the cabin, but she, outside, in the forefront of their enterprise, her calm, sightless eyes gazing ahead, was pressing forward, self-contained and alone, into the night, with her ship's company behind her. To-night he would sleep on shore, and should he awake in the dark hours he would remember that she was not near him. He was thinking of that as he went up Baltic Street and along the familiar ways to his uncle, old Geordie Falconer's house.

The old man lived in a long, harled cottage, an old-fashioned place in an old-fashioned neighbourhood; here, off the smaller streets running down from the North Port to the links, there were many of these half-countrified cottages left with open ground around them. Triangular 'hakes' hung on the walls with drying haddocks, and hardy flowers stood in bushes below the window-sills; pink and white rocket – relic of the fag-end of summer – and the purple and pink asters of autumn. Clothes flew bravely in the wind on washing days; currant and gooseberry bushes, like chapels of ease accommodating superfluous congregations of garments; in many places, little home-made wooden whirligigs stood up on poles varied by odd figures of marionettes waving their arms. Old Falconer had a drying-green of his own, a stretch of coarse grass enclosed in a paling, with a fair-sized sycamore, now faintly tinged with brown. His female neighbours said it was a waste for a single man to have such a thing, but Falconer, who was the owner of this tiny property, took their remarks, as he took everything else of the sort, with that look, peculiar to himself, of knowing something ridiculous about the person who spoke.

Tom and his uncle got on excellently. The latter had been a ship's chandler in a small way upon the Old Shore, but he had done well enough with his business to retire from it before age set in and had bought his house and its drying-green with a view – so gossip said – of taking a wife. But the gossips were wrong, though he did not contradict them and though he was secretly inclined to encourage the idea for joy of the fraudulent pleasure he got from their mystification; the ministrations of the woman who came in daily to clean his house and wash for him were his nearest approach to the advantages of domesticity. He was wonderfully adroit in looking after himself, and, till rheumatism compelled him to walk with a stout stick in either hand, he had done his own cooking and marketing, the latter with all the sagacity of one who had spent years behind a counter. When the mate came home with his sailor's handiness, the two were very comfortable together.

The old man was standing looking at a retreating fish-cadger's cart when Tom reached his door, and the derisive expression that his conversation with the cadger had left on his face remained there like the afterglow of a sunset. When he turned round and saw his nephew it intensified, as though he would include him in the gibe he had arrived too late to hear. The mate knew that there had been a gibe, because old Falconer always opened his mouth wide after such an event. It was his manner of laughing, and though he kept perfectly silent and did not so much as shake, his upraised eyebrows and penetrating stare into the countenance of his victim were as expressive and sensational as if he had thrown up his arms and crowed. No formal greeting passed between the two and they entered the cottage together.

It was a soft, fresh day as they came out again on the following morning. The figurehead had not obtruded herself on the mate, for he slept like a child in his stationary bed and there were no waking moments in which to think whether she were near or far. He had dressed himself with care, for, after clearing the board at which they breakfasted and putting aside the crockery for the woman to wash, he meant to look up some friends in the town. As he would have gone out, his uncle called to him to wait and they emerged together into the sunshine.

Though, to a stranger, the pair might have represented two generations of seafaring men, old Falconer was a landsman and perhaps had caught something of his air from his former customers, for the square white beard below his lean face and the cut of his clothes would make most people suppose that he had 'followed the sea.' He might be said to have followed it from a safe distance, not only because he had lived by making his bread from the requirements of its followers, but because, in the dark ages of his youth, he had been a ship's boy for a couple of years. He was a slow walker and Tom found plenty of time to look about him as he went. There was hardly a

breeze. The sky out over the sea lay in long lines, pearly
and soft. The morning shadows on the stone-work of walls
and chimneys was pearly too. As they entered the streets
and passed along the pavements the young man looked
down the closes at glimpses of green vegetables, scarlet
runners growing a little dusty and weary, and the thick
wreaths of the white bindweed that Angus people love to
train about their doors. He thought that strangers coming
casually to Montrose might never see the real town. You
had but to dive down one of these closes to come out
into a different Montrose. Behind the frontage of the
old-fashioned streets was a whole world of little dwellings,
one and two-storied, sitting snug in their tiny gardens, some
ordered and set neatly, like small residential squares, some
in rows and double rows, some solitary. The stairheads
of their outside stairs, vantage-grounds for conversations
with neighbours, would have pot-plants hanging through
the railings as though to join hands with the geraniums and
bushes of 'apple-ringie' by the low green palings, no higher
than a man's knee, which divided plot from plot. There
were houses with spiky sea-shells sitting decorously on the
window-sills; older houses with circular stone staircases
inside rounded towers built against the wall; houses with
doorsteps washed pale blue. Tom always liked to see these
things; it was some time since he had been home, and he
strolled down one or two of these closes to look in, old
Falconer waiting patiently for him outside, tolerant of his
whims; for he, as well as Tom's shipmates, felt the necessity
of accepting them as part of the man. But at one close's
mouth his patience gave way and he pursued his road. He
was getting bored and he turned the first corner he came
to with alacrity, glancing behind him like an old dog-fox
and hoping that his nephew would pass it and continue
his loitering alone.

The mate had forgotten his existence. He was standing in
the shadow of the close's mouth gazing up at the stairhead
of a house. It was one of the newer ones and the green door
above the flight had a brass knocker. A young woman was
leaning her elbows on the railing at the top, very still, her
hands under her chin, her head, as he saw it from below,

silhouetted against the sky. Her arms were bare, firm and symmetrical under her rolled-up sleeves. Perhaps she had been washing and had come out for a moment's rest into the fresh air. She was a pale girl with regular, rather thick features, but the outline of her head had some nobility and the outward curve of her throat was beautiful. Her abundant, heavy hair was gathered into a loose knot, which, from her attitude and the forward position of her arms, almost rested upon her back. He was not very near her, in fact there was another stairhead between them, but she may have felt, as people will, that there were eyes upon her, for she raised herself and stood up straight and then turned and looked him in the face. He grew rather red. A smile was on her mouth, as though she hesitated whether to say something to him. He drew back quickly and was gone. She stretched herself, laughing, and went through the door behind her.

He found that old Falconer had disappeared, and so continued his way cursing, for the old man knew all about every living creature in that quarter of the town and could have told him the name of the family in the brass-knockered house. He would not ask him anything about the girl. These questions he would lay by to discover the answers for himself. He did not know why her appearance had produced such an effect on him, but he was filled with an intense wish to see her again. He had seen hundreds of better-looking girls about the town than this lass with the rolled-up sleeves and dull, light hair. He might just as well have spoken to her, for she had looked as if she expected it. Something that was not shyness – for he was not shy – had prevented it; something of diffidence. He debated whether he should go back and just call out to her, as most men would have done. He returned and went softly up the close but the stairhead was empty. What a fool he had been! When he had arrived at being interested in a woman he had never dawdled over preliminaries. He would set to and discover all about her as soon as possible. All at once he knew that what had attracted and what had restrained him were one and the same thing. Perhaps it was her attitude and its stillness, perhaps her sharpness of outline, placed as she was, above him, perhaps a certain colourlessness – but she reminded him of the figurehead of the *William and Joann*.

After their midday meal the two Falconers strolled out into the drying-green and sat down, each with his pipe, on the rough seat which the mate had knocked together under the sycamore. The old man had not commented on his own disappearance; he was one who neither asked nor gave explanations. His part in life was that of a passively interested and faintly malicious spectator; he wished no one any real harm, but he preferred his entertainers to be foolish because he got better value out of their antics. He suffered fools not only gladly, but delightedly. It was characteristic of him that, though he had wondered what was keeping Tom so long, he had not gone to find out; but this was because he knew perfectly well that it would be revealed to him. Everything was revealed to old Falconer sooner or later.

'Wha bides in yon house wi' the brass chapper awa' doon Bailie Craig's close?' asked Tom.

The other removed his pipe and opened his mouth wide. He said nothing, but his eyes lit up like those of a child who sees a desirable toy in a shop-window.

'Ye'll ken the place, Uncle Geordie?'

Falconer's mouth closed a little, but what it lost in height it gained in width.

'Birse's lassie,' said he.

His eyes pierced the mate's self-consciousness like gimlets.

'And wha's Birse?' inquired Tom, as casually as he could.

'He's deid.'

Uncle Geordie shook with silent mirth, but whether at the thought of Birse's death or of his own entire comprehension of Tom's mind, it is impossible to say.

'She's a widdie,' he added. 'Yon hizzy's her eldest.'

The mate had something of his uncle in him, so he knew that pretences were superfluous. Also he did not care. He had shown a little embarrassment, but that was because he was surprised, not because he minded. Uncle

Geordie would be put off by no pretence that he had not seen Mrs. Birse's 'eldest.' He was not quite pleased with the word 'hizzy,' but he had sense to conceal that.

It did not take him long to make further discoveries, though not from his uncle. The old man vouchsafed no more, perhaps expecting to be questioned. But the mate, having found out the name he wanted, preferred to push his way into the girl's acquaintance without providing more amusement for him than he could help. He soon learned that the widowed Mrs. Birse made her living by taking in sewing and that she had two other children besides the eldest, Malvina, who worked daily as assistant to Miss Wiseman of the greengrocer's shop in the New Wynd.

Next day the shops closed early. Before ten struck from the steeple he was standing outside, gazing in cautiously between the early chrysanthemums, cabbages and spinach which formed the foreground of Miss Wiseman's window. Through these he could see Malvina Birse sitting in the corner behind the counter. It was too soon yet for much custom, he supposed; anyhow, the moment was fortunate. He opened the door boldly.

She recognised him immediately, but it took her a moment to decide whether she would receive him with smiles or with disdain. She was not astonished, for at the moment he appeared she was speculating about him. She decided for coldness.

'What can I do for you?' she inquired in her best genteel accent.

Her outward composure brought the figurehead to his mind again. Her clear, dead-white skin, her heavy hair and the pale pink of her full lips all looked paler against the background of greenstuff and ruddy fruit.

'What can I do for you?' she asked again.

'Maybe ye'd come out wi' me,' he replied.

She eyed him curiously, adding him up, as it were. The situation was not new to her, though it had never presented itself quite in this way.

'I dinna ken yer name.'

'Falconer.'

'But I'm not acquaint wi' ye. Ye'll be a fisher-fella?' she added, tossing her head.

'Na, I'm no that. But I bide intill a ship. I'm frae the *William an' Joann.*'

'Ye'll no be the captain, I'se warrant!'

'I'm the mate,' said he.

She eyed him with more interest. She had not really supposed he was a 'fisher-fella.' A mate is somebody.

'I'll think o't,' she said.

'Dinna think owre lang, then. I'll be at the heid o' the Kirk Walk three o'clock the day.'

He looked at his watch. She did too, and saw it was a good one.

'Ye'll no suffer frae want o' impidence!' she exclaimed. But she giggled as she said it.

He left the shop, well pleased.

That afternoon he turned into the Kirk Walk from Baltic Street. The minute hand of the steeple clock neared the hour and he strolled up towards the Town Hall. He did not know from which direction she would come, and he had almost reached the top when round the corner came a knot of three girls, arm-in-arm, laughing shrilly and looking back over their shoulders. He knew that the benches on the Town Hall pavement were generally full of idlers, and he smiled at the well-known elements of the scene. One of the girls detached herself and came towards him. The others turned back, tittering.

Malvina Birse's eyes sparkled as they met. She carried herself well and the mate felt a pleased thrill as he looked at her. Certainly she was a fine-looking creature and the poise of her head was magnificent. There was no cinema to take a girl to in those days. Tea-shops were unknown; a walk was the only form of entertainment to be had. By tacit consent they turned towards the links and sauntered towards the sandhills covered with bent-grass that bordered the shore. There was not a sail on the sea but the brown patches of canvas of a few herring-smacks some way out. They roamed about for an hour or so and finally sat down on a hillock. They had not talked intimately enough to find out much about each other, but Malvina had taken in enough

about the man beside her to find that he was unlike most
of the men she knew. She had a hazy idea that he was
creditable to her as a companion. He said things that she
did not understand, but she was little impressed by that,
though she realised a certain simplicity in him and disliked
it. There were many things she wished to know about him,
but it seemed that they were not those about which he
was willing to tell. She was completely uninterested in the
seafaring part of him, for, unlike most of her neighbours in
the town, she had no connection with salt water. He had at
his command none of the boisterous chaff to which she was
accustomed in her admirers. He lay on the hillock looking
up at her and thinking of the figurehead. So far, he had
paid her no court.

'I was fair amazed when I saw ye come ben the shop
the day,' she began, hoping to get nearer to the personal
note. 'My! but ye hae a cheek! Was ye no feared I'd be
affronted?'

He shook his head.

'I'se warrant ye it's no the first time ye've done that.'

'Aweel,' said he, 'it is.'

'Haud yer tongue!' exclaimed Malvina, giving him a
smart tap on the arm.

'It's the truth.'

'Maybe ye'll tell me ye're no carin' for the lassies?'

'I wadna tell ye that. I'd be leein'.'

She did not know how to take this. There was no challenge
in his words. She glanced down at the figure lying at her
feet with the peculiar passivity of the seaman ashore. He
was smoking and his teeth were closed upon his pipe. The
tide was coming in; his crisp hair was just stirred by the
breeze blowing faintly from the encroaching waves.

All at once she was exasperated. She snatched up his
peaked cap that lay beside him and flung it out towards
the water. He rose as easily and lightly as an animal and
bounded down the sandhill after it. Malvina jumped up
too and fled back over the bents. He came up with her,
the cap on his head. His colour had risen. He threw his
arm round her waist.

'Ye're due me ane for that,' he said, and kissed her.

They went back to the town, a barrier broken down
between them by the touch of his lips on hers, and he left
her at the foot of Mrs. Birse's outside stair. In Bailie Craig's
Close he had kissed her again and she had promised to meet
him again on the morrow.

Their acquaintance ripened; it seemed that the figurehead faded from Tom Falconer's thoughts in proportion as
his relations with Malvina grew more ordinary and familiar.
He had admitted to himself that he was in love with her,
though he had not admitted it to her; but he did not think
of marriage as the consequence, and he was kept from
thinking of anything less regular by the figurehead – or
rather, by something which the figurehead had represented
to his mind. Malvina had been sought out by him because
of that likeness whose reality was growing fainter, though
it thrust itself like a spectre between him and any deed of
his that could detract from her.

The girl herself was falling in love too in her own fashion.
He was still a puzzle to her with his lack of pretence,
which she despised, his absolute self-possession, which she
resentfully respected, and his personality, which continued
to attract her. She felt a suspicion of her own inferiority,
and this led her to assume a veneer of pert disdain to
hide the ruffling of her vanity. But she was impressed,
completely, and her mother was impressed too. She had
brought him home to tea on the Sunday after their walk
to the shore, and this visit had been the first of many, for a
light had broken in on Mrs. Birse. To Malvina, he was the
mate of the *William and Joann*, a young man difficult to
understand but puzzlingly attractive; to her mother he was
Geordie Falconer's nephew. She had almost embraced her
daughter when she discovered whom she was entertaining
unawares. As a Montrose woman she knew the old man by
sight, for rumour had made him rich and settled that the
person who was to profit by his good fortune and inherit
the house with the drying-green was that vague shadow
that haunts so many speculations about inheritances, 'a
nephew.' And now the shadow had taken substance as
Malvina's admirer. Malvina, looking through Mrs. Birse's
eyes, began to see herself as mistress of a house larger than

her mother's, with a husband who, though not a captain, was on his way to becoming one. A captain's lady! With her gaze on this vision, she must respect herself accordingly. She was protected by her own ambition as well as by that influence unknown to her, the figurehead.

Inch by inch Tom was stepping into the net of domesticity spread in his sight. He would rather have enjoyed all of Malvina's company out-of-doors, but she would insist upon his coming to fetch her when her work was over, not to the shop, but to her home, and Mrs. Birse seldom let him go without an invitation to supper. Sometimes he would refuse, only to be persuaded by Malvina in the end. He did not care for the evenings spent under the patronage of the square, stout woman. Mrs. Birse showed her gums when she talked, and her bodice, tight across a solid bust, was stuck with pins, signs of her vocation.

The weather had broken; storms of rain and gales swept Montrose and retarded the 'tattie-lifting' which, though the Fast Day was some little time past, was still in full swing. Outside the town the roads were lively with wheels. Long brakes, carrying men and women whom the farmers had hired for the lifting, were going to and fro and families were abroad on the same errand; for the humbler townsfolk would buy a couple of drills as they stood in the field and would join with friends and neighbours in the business of getting the potatoes home. Sometimes they would band together and go out in small parties, and the girls of a family were expected by their parents to get a day's work out of their young men when the time came round.

Malvina had done her share. Tom had willingly promised to lend a hand, and besides this she had contrived to get the loan of Miss Wiseman's cart and driver as soon as her employer could spare it. Falconer looked forward to the expedition, for he was becoming tired of sitting in the house with Malvina, and when he could persuade her to come out between the onslaughts of the wet she was generally cross. They had gone near to several small quarrels. In the parlour there was little to say, and outside it her goal was always the shops and her talk of them and of the private affairs of the people who passed. He would not tell himself how the latter

wearied him nor how much the former lightened his purse.
The sea had not the remotest interest for her, and he, who
would so joyfully have shared the pictures and scenes of his
travels with the right woman, knew better than to make the
attempt. Once there had been a wreck, and he had left her
and gone down to where the lifeboat was being launched.
She had been furious at this, and because he would not
promise to take himself out of the way, should there be
a call for extra hands. He had not gone near her for two
days after this, yet he had come back on the third.

During all this time Geordie Falconer had kept his own
counsel, and while he was perfectly aware of what was going
on, both from his own observations and from those of other
people, he had not said a word to the mate. No one knew
what he thought about the matter. Mrs. Birse, for one,
would have given a good deal to know and had made
many attempts on his acquaintance; but though she had
invited him over and over again to accompany Tom when
he came to spend an evening, she had not yet succeeded in
getting him to the house. It was all the more surprising that,
when she suggested he should come to the supper by which
she meant to celebrate their return from tattie-lifting, he
accepted the invitation.

Tom had given it rather sheepishly as they sat together
with their pipes one afternoon. Falconer was deep in a
newspaper column on Arctic discovery, his face hidden
by the printed sheet, and the mate brought out his words
with a certain constraint.

'Aye, Tam. Ye can tell Mistress Birse I'd like it fine.'

The young man looked with puzzled earnestness at the
all-concealing expanse of *The People's Journal*, and while
he was doing so it was suddenly dropped.

He was a little disconcerted.

'Oh, what a lives an' money's been wastit seekin' for
they poles,' observed Uncle Geordie, with fervent gravity,
'an' likely though they were tae find them they wadna ken
them when they saw them!'

The paper went up again immediately, leaving Tom's
dignity intact; but this was because he could not see what
was going on on the other side of it.

The party which set out next day to lift the potatoes were the three young Birses, their mother and Tom. They were to walk back in the evening, for the cart would be loaded and there would be no choice for them but their feet. It was a light, open, four-wheeled cart, only just heavy enough for their purpose; and while the little boy and the younger of his two sisters squeezed themselves together on the plank beside the driver, Tom and Malvina had to be contented to share with Mrs. Birse that part of it usually occupied by the vegetables in their transit to and from Miss Wiseman's shop. Straw had been laid in the bottom of it to make it more comfortable. Mrs. Birse's jokes about her own part as gooseberry had begun to pall upon the mate by the time they arrived at their destination, and he was glad when he found himself at work in the field side by side with Malvina, while the rest of her family were busy at the other drill.

They had piled a good heap of potatoes, Tom working with the fork and Malvina following with the basket, when the girl paused, pushing back the hair that had fallen over her hot face.

'I didna do sae badly, gettin' the loan o' yon machine frae the auld witch,' she remarked, as her eyes roved to the cart standing at the headrig of the field. 'I'd a sair job, I can tell ye. She said she was need'n't to gang oot an' see her sister that's ill at Marykirk.'

Tom paused too. 'It was richt guid o' her,' said he.

'Heuch! I just tellt her I'd a freend comin' tae help's that couldna come ony other time – that's you, ye ken. Yon auld fule believes onything!'

'Ye needna hae done that. A' days wad hae suited me.'

'Fie! wha's carin' for the likes o' her?'

The mate was vexed. He bent down again to his work in silence. His shirt-sleeves were rolled above his elbows and the ship tattooed on his forearm showed blue against his skin. She came nearer to look at it. He worked on without heeding her.

'What ails ye?' she said sharply.

'Naething.'

'That's a lee,' said Malvina, gazing angrily at his averted head.

He raised himself and faced her. There was something in her that jarred, and a wave of rebellion against it surged up in him, drowning all else.

'It's no you that should speak o' lees,' he said steadily.

Her eyes seemed to grow smaller and her lips were set in a thick, hard line.

'Maybe ye think a'body's sinners but yersel'!'

He had never seen her in a real rage before. She was shaking.

'Gowk that ye are!' she cried, as he made no reply.

Some women look well when they are angry, but she was not one of these; there was an underlying meanness in her face and it repelled him, though he scarcely knew what it was. All the same, he was sorry to have spoken so bluntly. He would have told her so had not a dumb misgiving dropped down and lain like a suffocating weight on him. She left him and went off to where the others were working. In a few minutes her sister came over to him and, taking Malvina's place, began to shake the potatoes from the shaws as he forked them up. She chattered away and he answered absently now and again, sticking with dogged industry to his task. At midday they ate the food they had brought with them; Malvina sat near her mother, whilst her young brother, delighted by such an opportunity, devoted himself to the mate, whom he admired, but of whom he had seen little at home, being still young enough to go to bed early and to be hurried there even earlier than usual when there was company.

Malvina said nothing to her mother of what had passed, though Mrs. Birse was aware of something wrong. She was not a discreet woman, but she had learned from experience that it was impossible to coax her daughter to do anything that she did not want to do, so she asked no questions. The day wore on till dark set in and the loaded cart emerged upon the road and, followed by them, began its homeward way. All were physically weary, except Tom, and he was weary at heart. Malvina made no effort, as she would have done at another time, to separate herself and him from the others, and all trudged on in a group. The little boy, who was very tired, tried to hang on to her arm, but she shook him off, and Tom would have set him on his shoulder but that, by so doing, he would have lost any chance he had of being alone with her. He was blaming himself for his rough words.

It was a still evening and sound carried far. Stars were coming out and the long fields that border the Montrose road lay quiet and dim. A few peewits cried from beyond the stone dykes. About half-way to the town they heard a jingling coming up behind them and the slow trotting of hoofs mixed with noisy voices. Soon the brake with returning tattie-lifters went past them in the dusk, filled with shadowy figures, some with shawls on their heads, in two long rows behind the plodding horses. Men and women cried boisterous good nights and were swallowed in the gathering darkness ahead. Then the long-drawn notes of 'Annie Laurie' floated back to them as the tattie-lifters broke into singing. They were too far off for the words to be distinguishable, but the voices, strident, some of them, were mellowed by distance and came with an appealing cadence through the evening. As they died away, the mate thrust his arm through Malvina's and drew her back behind the others. She resisted for a moment, but finally gave in and they followed their companions more slowly.

By the time the whole party reached home it was almost as if there had been no disturbance of their harmony. Though it had ended in reconciliation, the outing had not been much of a success from Tom's point of view, and that unformulated misgiving lurked in his heart yet. But Malvina, sitting next him at the supper-table, her cheek flushed with the long day's exertion in the air and her eyes shining under her thick brows, seemed very alluring. She was a woman of fine gestures in spite of her hoydenishnesses, and she had changed the rough clothes she had worn all day and tied a blue snood round her heavy hair. She stood out in the crowded little room like a symbol of something freer and wider than the tame daily round suggested by its commonplace appurtenances. He thought again of the figurehead.

Uncle Geordie sat at the board steeped in his usual philosophic content. Mrs. Birse's assiduous hospitality was bringing to his face an expression which she interpreted in a very favourable manner; and certainly she was not wrong in thinking that he was enjoying himself. When the meal was over and her two younger children were sent into the scullery to wash up the tea-things, the mate and Malvina went out to the stairhead.

'We ha'na seen the new moon yet,' Mrs. Birse remarked, by way of legalising the retreat of the two.

'An' if she's no better nor the auld ane we needna mind though we never see her,' replied Uncle Geordie.

'Draw in-by tae the fire, Mr. Falconer,' said Mrs. Birse. 'Guid folk's scarce, ye ken.'

'They'll be scarcer sune. A doot it's near time a was awa'.'

His mouth widened. He was one of the many old men in Scotland who always allude to death as a joke.

'Think shame o' yersel', speakin' that way, Mr. Falconer!'

'O weel, ye see, we've got tae think o' thae things.'

'Fie, there's time yet, wi' you.'

'Mebbe, mebbe, but a'm no like them that leaves a'thing tae chance. A've been a business body a' ma life. Aye, ye'd wonder, Mistress Birse, tae see the money a've haun'lt i' ma time – aye, aye—'

He looked into the grate as though losing himself in a reverie of gold and merchandise.

'Aye, times – times—' he said again.

Her eyes stared like glass marbles.

'I mind ye had a business doon aboot the Auld Shore,' she began.

'Ye should hae seen the folk that cam' in-by yonder,' he continued, 'a' sorts an' kinds – lads that couldna speak a word o' Christianity—'

'Aw, terrible swearers, nae doot!' she exclaimed, wagging her head.

'Na, na. Black craturs aff the Indian Ocean that when they saw the sun gang doon wad be oot-by turnin' tapsalterie wi' their heids amangst the stanes an' their doups in folks' faces; an' lads frae the tea-clippers an' Baltic men. They cam' a' ben tae me. Skippers an' mates an' powerfu' traders. The shoppie lookit sma' eneuch, but it wasna i' the shoppie ye saw the things a dealt wi' – muckle profits, grand days—'

He broke off. She felt unable to speak. Few people were aware of the luxuriance of old Falconer's imagination; it was a thing he kept so closely to himself.

'It'll be a sad thocht to think o' leavin' it a' to strangers,' she hazarded, at last, trembling to feel she was at the very heart of the great subject of his legacies.

'A've been guidit. Providence has lairned me that a can be awa' contentit when the time comes, an' ken a's for the best. Ye see there's Tam—'

She was almost choking.

'Aye, Tam's a guid lad. "Uncle Geordie," says he tae me when a spoke aboot ma hoose an' a' ma savin's, "a ken what yer intentions is. Ye hae aye been a kind uncle tae me," says he, "but the sea's a' a care for. There's mony," says he, "that has mair use for the money nor a chap like me. Lot them hae it that needs it." '

'There's no sic a thing as gratitude i' this warld!' almost shouted Mrs. Birse.

'Aye, but a respec'it the lad! Mistress Birse, a couldna but admir't. "*Hae yer wull,*" says I. And noo the hoose an' the bittie green, an' a' that's sittin' i' the bank's tae gang tae Dorward's Hoose o' Refuge. A's for the best, ye see.'

He smiled widely. To Mrs. Birse it was the smile of misplaced righteousness, the smile of a fool. She little knew that her own face was its sole cause.

The old man went home that night in high good humour. No notion of liberating Tom from the toils he was in had prompted his highly coloured disclosures; he had only acted as a small boy acts when he throws a stone into a pool to hear the splash and to see the widening circles in the water. If the mate wished to marry Malvina he did not desire to prevent him, for he had no further animosity against her than was expressed in the word 'hizzy' which he had used. No doubt she *was* a hizzy, but many women were that. It was Tom's affair.

October was three parts through and November would see Tom afloat again. He was moderately happy; that is, as happy as a man can be who does not quite know what he wants. He saw that he must either lose Malvina altogether or pledge himself to her for good. Often it had been on his lips to do this; on the night of the tattie-picking, his feelings stirred by their quarrel and reconciliation, he had all but spoken, and yet he had refrained. He would not allow himself to believe that he was gradually becoming disillusioned. The things that offended him were often trifles, but the worst of it was that there were so many of them. But he disliked Mrs. Birse and had drifted into putting down her daughter's every fault to her influence.

But the real victim of disillusion was Mrs. Birse; and in the first heat of her feelings she had forbidden Malvina to have anything more to do with the mate. There was an angry scene between the two women which made the girl more resolved than ever to see as much of him as she could. Though the vision of old Falconer's house and money was gone, Tom was still a man to be considered; the potential captain of a ship; and at least she meant to get all the advantages and the excitement of his attentions whether she threw him over or not. She was quite determined that he should propose to her before he went to sea again, and this made her strain every nerve to please him. Also, because with human beings the value of a thing goes up in proportion to what they have to pay for it, the fact that Malvina had a good deal to endure from her mother on the mate's account was making her fonder of him. It seemed to him, as the days went on, that she was growing softer, and that, after all, she really was the woman for him.

It was Sunday – two days before the *William and Joann* was to sail – and they were still unengaged. But his mind was made up and he would speak. He had no doubt about the answer he would get or that this would be his last voyage of freedom. She was good-looking and he believed that she loved him, and he knew that he was looked upon by their acquaintances as an accepted lover. He might do worse. The evenings were drawing in now and the sun set at half-past four. To-morrow he would be busy the whole day, for they would go out early on Tuesday with the tide. In an expansive moment and with the prospect of the parting before her, Malvina had said that she would like to see the brig. He had proposed this many times, but she had always put him off on one pretext or another, and at last, rather chagrined, he had given up the idea. She would not be able to go over her now, he told her, for the cargo was still coming on board. He wished that she had not developed her interest so late.

He was more silent than usual. He had chosen finally, but still he was oppressed; in that part of his mind into which he would not look he knew that on the first idle morning ashore his imagination had been set alight by something fantastic; he had seen with his bodily eyes what he had misread with the eyes of his soul. He did not put it in this way, but he knew the truth. If he married Malvina he would not even then have the possession he longed for, which was no physical one, but a thing imagined, a thing that did not exist. And yet, even now, the shadow of that likeness – or rather, the remembrance of its lure – clung round her. On this, their last day, she was in a quiet mood that he had only seen of late. Her laments over his departure had ceased and the shallow chatter of trivialities that had so often irked him; her face and speech were softer, and it touched him and made him ashamed of his hesitations. She looked on him as hers; that was evident and had been evident for some time, but long courtships were the usual thing, and from keeping company to being 'cried in the kirk' was a far step. He reflected that he would still have the same sea-life of his own, and that a man with a 'master's ticket' and fourteen years' experience need not be longer ashore than he liked. It was no vanity that assured him he would never be out of a job. He wondered if she would wait for him. He thought she would, but he could not be sure . . . Here he left off thinking, because he could not tell whether, if she did not, he would be glad or sorry . . . Anyhow, he would speak before he said good-bye.

There was a long stretch of pale, rainy yellow in the west, and sky and water were growing colder as they approached the quay and came in sight of the *William and Joann*. There was little doing on this Sunday afternoon, and with the threat of rain the Sunday idlers from the town were not many. A few figures were moving about the brig, and bales and sacking and sea-chests were strewn at her side. The sun had set, but the light was still good. Malvina stared at the ship with the absolute lack of interest of her strictly feminine point of view. It was the same to her as any other inanimate object that she could neither eat nor wear; as a thing that would take Tom away from her it was more disagreeable than most. Scores of Montrose girls would have looked at the *William and Joann* with comprehending eyes, but Malvina was a child not of the docks and the Old Shore, but of the High Street and the shop-windows. Had Tom been the captain of her dreams, it might have been a little different, but not very different. The mate, watching her, saw her listless eye and the petulance about her mouth. She moved away impatiently and walked on a few steps. Stopping level with the bows, she looked up and noticed the figurehead. Something in the sightless yet rapt face must have struck her as an oddity, for she pointed at it with her forefinger and burst into a loud peal of boisterous laughter.

THE WILLIAM AND JOANN sailed with the tide on Tuesday morning; the sky was high and the horizon very clear. A fresh breeze was blowing, and outside the bar, where the waves were breaking into thin white caps, the bows of the brig were beginning to lift and sink. The mate was on deck. He had come on board with his traps on Sunday night after leaving Malvina at her mother's door, where he had seen her first. He had scarcely opened his lips on the way home.

He did not look back at the receding town. There was nobody waving to him from the quay, for old Falconer's rheumatism was bad and he did not come down to watch them go. But in front of him, where he could not see her, the still, white woman with her uplifted face rose and fell with the brig's motion, the little whips of spray striking her breast and her joined hands pointing out to the wideness of the sea.

Euphemia

IT WAS nearing evening. The corn was cut and stood in stooks on the fields. Overhead, the sky glowed with the faint primrose and saffron which is a foretaste of splendour to come, and in its midst, hanging above the west, a little thread of a new moon, almost transparent, was becoming visible in the delicateness of its pearly immaturity.

Where the road climbed a short hill stood a farm-house whose walls made a bold angle upon the sky. Its gable-end showed a plain face of stone in which, high up, one small window was cut below the slope of the roof. A red-haired girl leaned from it, her arms on the sill, looking out into the light. At the wall's foot was a round, thick bush of white Stuart roses, and, at the bottom of the hill, a stream ran under a low bridge to wind away between the fields and to dribble through the marshes into the Basin of Montrose.

The stream was swollen, and where, by the bridge, it widened into the farm pond, the weeds at its edge were sodden and matted; only now the earth was drying itself after the steady downpour that had fallen on that rich crop, still ungarnered as far as eye could see. There was none of the fine, white crispness which is the last stage of a cut harvest; and the loads which had been brought into Braes of Aird stackyard wore the dark, suspicious gold of imperfectly dried stuff.

Anderson (or 'Braes,' as the farmer was generally called) had been leading[1] since noon and his gaunt face had an anxious look as he went into his house. He was weather-wise, as befitted a man of his calling, and it seemed to him that this clear spell might not last. Soon the grain would

1. *Anglice* – carrying.

begin to sprout where it stood. He had met the minister
a few hours since and had been emphatically told that it
would be justifiable to load on the morrow, Sabbath day
though it was, should the weather hold.

'D'ye think Noah waited till Monday to get into the ark
when he felt the first spot of rain?' asked the minister, as
Braes approached the subject with unnecessary caution.

He was a man of very practical opinions. And now, as
the red-haired girl leaned from her window, she could hear
one outcome of this interview which was taking place at
the corner of the stackyard; Braes had offered his hands a
double wage for the Sunday work and the young men of the
farm were discussing the situation with their fellows. The
voices came up to Euphemia in varying notes of strength;
she could not see the group, though occasionally the black
head of Lachland Henderson would appear above the wall
at the turn of the road. The predominant tones were those
of the 'head horseman,' Patrick Duthie.

Euphemia's temper was stirred just now, for she was a
woman of strong feelings and as practical minded as the
minister. In Angus, women do much field-work, and she
had been a well-known figure in the Braes of Aird fields
for a couple of years or more. She had the high cheekbones
and square jaws of her race, and her decided good looks
were of that fundamental sort which outlasts youth. Hers
was a face of possibilities. The fact that she had done well
at school was either admired or cast in her teeth, according
to the respective temperaments of her acquaintances.

She knew well what was going on up the road. Wherever
Patrick Duthie was there would be strife of some kind, for
the red-whiskered, spare young man was a stormy petrel
indeed. Euphemia could hear the flow of his talk, though
only a word, now and again, was distinguishable; but it
needed nothing to tell her that, if Duthie could prevent his
hearers from accepting the terms held out for the morrow,
he would do so, not from the Sabbatarian point of view,
but from the economic one. He was not satisfied with the
offer – so he said; but had he been so, she knew that he
would neither accept himself nor allow anyone else to do
so, because he hated Braes. Euphemia, who did not like

the head horseman, could never understand the influence
he had in the bothy. It was a subject on which she and
Lachland Henderson differed. Lachland was a silent youth
and Duthie's flow of words seemed to hypnotise him. And
he was easily led, too.

The girl's own opinion was decided, as most of her
opinions were. She had no particular sympathy for Braes,
but the sight of those stooks waiting to be saved from their
fate was too much for her sane and thrifty soul. They were
dry enough to load now, but, with another wet day their
chances of salvation might be gone. There was a strong
dash of public-spiritedness in Euphemia, which made the
notion of their loss for want of a little goodwill hateful.

When fractions of the dispersing group began to dot the
rickyard she left the window and went out through the patch
of garden into the road. A long-legged, very dark-headed
young man was coming to meet her. He made as though
he would pass by, but she called to him derisively across
the way.

'Well, have ye speired permission at Duthie? Is he to let
ye gang?'

Lachland Henderson looked annoyed and a little foolish,
but he stopped.

'Braes is gie'in' us owre little,' said he sullenly.

'Duthie tellt ye that, did he? Well,' she went on, 'if he'll
no let ye work, he'll mebbe let ye gang to the kirk the morn's
morn; but ye'll need to ask him canny, Lachland.'

'Tuts!' exclaimed Lachland, with as much scorn as he
could muster. It was not a brilliant reply, but he did not
know what else to say.

'It'll be a grand thing to be a man,' observed Euphemia,
'but ye'd hae done better to be a lassie, I'm thinkin'. Ye'd
hae been fine and biddable. I wonder ye dinna think shame
to see a' yon guid stuff standin' to be wastit, an' you that
feared o' Duthie ye daurna put a hand to it.'

'Haud yer tongue, lassie,' growled Henderson. A few of
the men were coming towards them and he was getting
angry. He was a steady and rather obstinate young
fellow and slow to take offence. But she was plying the
goad well.

She tossed her head. Patrick Duthie was approaching with his hands deep in his trousers pockets.

A studied unconsciousness of his approach fell upon Euphemia, and Duthie, seeing it and knowing her attitude of mind by instinct, made the mistake of addressing her; for he was one of those who could never leave well alone. Though he had prevailed with his audience, the sight of this one rebel, a girl who had no voice in the question at issue, was too much for him.

'Lachland'll no be to mind the likes o' you. He's got mair sense than fash himself for a haverin' lassie,' he began, with that lack of dignity which will challenge unexpressed opposition.

She turned her back upon him and disappeared between the ricks.

She marched along towards the stone dwelling-house from whose windows Braes and his family could see across the fields to the other side of that sheet of tidal water, the Basin of Montrose. At low tide, the river which ran into its western end would lie like a silver snake upon the uncovered sands and the gulls scream on the salt marshes full of thrift and mauve sea-aster. Between the foot of the hill and the water the stooks were ranked like an army waiting for someone to lead the forlorn hope of the morrow.

Euphemia knocked boldly at the dwelling-house door, kicking her muddy boots against the step. The door was answered by a tidy maid, who opened her mouth as she saw the visitor and then smiled broadly. The two were good friends.

'It's Braes a'm wanting,' observed Euphemia shortly.

'Losh!' exclaimed the other.

'Away ye go,' continued Euphemia, jerking her head sideways towards the closed door of the farmer's business room.

Before the maid could obey, it opened and Braes looked out.

'A'm seekin' a word wi' ye, Mr. Anderson,' said Euphemia, advancing; and the astonished servant found herself alone in the little hall.

When Euphemia came out again she made for her own

lodging. Five of the farm women were waiting for her in the garden by the rose-bush and she hastened to tell them the result of her mission; for it had been determined by them that, should the men refuse to work on the morrow, they would offer their own services and demand the rejected wage.

All were well accustomed to harvest work, and the six who had come forward to Braes's rescue professed themselves able and willing to keep two of the carts going all day. They consisted of Euphemia, the woman who looked after the men's bothy, three girls, and the young wife of a horseman who had, at the time, no domestic complication on hand to keep her from the fields. Euphemia, as the originator of the scheme, had been unanimously chosen to approach the farmer upon the matter.

Her colour was high and her eye gleamed as she sought her comrades. Braes had accepted their proposal, though he had been inclined to haggle over the sum he had offered, which, he said, he had intended as a man's wage; but in the end he had given in. Perhaps the sight, from his windows, of the acres of imperilled grain standing under the uncertain sky decided him; perhaps the finger of the fluctuating barometer; perhaps the not unwelcome thought of making his men look foolish. In any case, he agreed to the proposal and announced that he would be at the farm stables early in the morning to superintend the harnessing of the two carts. Not a word was to be said of the projected plan. The men would take their Sunday 'long lie' next day, and Euphemia and the women meant to get a load or two home before the bothy stirred. The horseman's wife determined to put her working clothes in the scullery overnight that she might dress before sunrise without disturbing her man. The little company of petticoats dispersed to their respective homes in the dusk.

It was getting light next morning when Braes opened the stable door with his master key. The men were asleep in the bothy and the horseman's wife had left her husband sound in one of those cottages at the foot of the hill where the married workmen lived; the six women went down to the fields, six shadows in the dimness.

The clover had sprouted high among the sheaves. They had stood so long that there had been ample time for its greenness to swamp the stubble. The sun was heaving himself up from behind the steeple of Montrose, and Braes, as he followed his volunteers down the road, told himself that the price of this Sabbath day's work might be well-spent money.

Euphemia, bare-headed, walked beside the foremost cart, her pitchfork over her shoulder. She was a dexterous loader – as good as Lachland Henderson, allowing for their difference in strength. In her mind's eye she saw the stack, left half finished yesterday, ready for thatching by the time the kirk bell should ring. She had got a new hat which she had meant to wear today. She was smiling ironically at the thought of it lying on the rough deal chest of drawers in her little room under the roof.

BY THE TIME the beadle's hand sent the first clang of the bell ringing over the country, the girl was sitting in her empty cart looking at her handiwork before starting again down the hill. Yesterday's stack was finished and a new one begun. As she turned the horse's head towards the fields there passed her a handful of the farm men.

The black coat of maturer respectability and the grey suit by which the young farm labourer of Angus honoured the first day of the week made a combination that smote Euphemia for a moment with some inherited feeling of wrong-doing. But it was only for a moment. Had she not the minister's sanction at her back as she toiled to save the Lord's bounty to His creatures? She sent a look of defiance at the group which stood aside with jeers to let the stringless farm cart rumble past. Patrick Duthie burst into a loud laugh; he had a pink geranium in his button-hole that went ill with his ginger-coloured whiskers. She did not care for his laughter while the new stack was rising steadily in the yard.

Duthie had made himself more than usually smart; every touch of sanctification that he could apply to himself was especially appropriate to-day. Neither he nor his admirers had pretended to found their action on any Sabbatarian feeling, but they realised at the same time the extreme suitability of the strong muster they were making as churchgoers. They stood, after the custom of their kind, loitering about the kirk door till the last of the congregation had entered.

The sun came slanting brightly through the windows as Lachland Henderson sat not far from the precentor. Most of the young men from Braes of Aird farm liked hearing their own voices, and the minister liked it too, for they made a considerable difference to the psalms and paraphrases. But, for once in his life, he would sooner have seen their places empty. He looked grimly down upon them to-day and upon Henderson's sleek head, as he laid his hand on the Bible and the usual rustle of opening books which heralded the giving-out of the text came up to the pulpit. There were several gaps in the assembly which pleased him better than the sight of those Sunday coats which had confronted Euphemia by the stackyard corner half an hour ago. The places where sat the men from Windy Edge and Mains of Balmanno were vacant. His feelings were as robust as his opinions; and, as he noticed Duthie's pink geranium and consciously church-going look, his frame of mind was, perhaps, not the ideal one for a man of his age and calling. And another thing which he noted as he looked down on the familiar up-turned faces, was the great advantage there may occasionally be in extempore preaching.

He had chosen his text from the nineteenth chapter of Matthew, intending to base his sermon upon its last verse. But, during the singing of the preceding psalm, his eye had fallen upon the chapter which followed. He adjusted his black gown on his shoulders, with a gesture which came to him sometimes, and cleared his throat; and as Patrick Duthie settled himself in a convenient attitude for surreptitious slumber, the words '*Why stand ye here idle?*' rolled out over his head.

News flew as fast in the parish of Aird as it does in most country places, and it was not only the minister who had heard of the action of the Braes of Aird men, though these had, for various reasons, kept their own counsel about the women. There were many who listened that day in the kirk and few who slept. The mistress of Windy Edge sat upright in her pew, her piercing eyes fixed on the young horsemen. The sole member of her own establishment present was the old hen-wife, who had passed her seventieth birthday; the place beside her was empty, and her thoughts went to her husband, toiling with every available hand on his sloping acres a couple of miles away. She sniffed complacently.

'*Why stand ye here idle?*' thundered the minister, finally, when he had applied the text in its wider meaning to human life and character. There was a pause in which the congregation almost expected him to address certain of his hearers by name, and the back of Duthie's neck was seen by the occupants of the pews behind him to grow crimson as he fingered the metrical version of the Psalms lying on his knee.

'I have no message to the shirker,' added the minister, 'no word of encouragement for those who will stand by and see the Lord's good gifts perish when they might be saved; no feelings but those of contempt – I say *contempt* advisedly – for the man who will withhold his help when his fellow-creature is struggling in the stress of this adversity for what is his living and his daily bread. I miss many here to-day; but of those absent ones I can say that the vacant seats wherein I am wont to look for them do them as much honour as their presence in this church does in less anxious times, when we may meet together to praise the Lord of harvest with quiet minds . . .'

Not a sound stirred in the kirk but the noise of fidgeting feet that came from a small child which sat by its mother and was conscious of nothing but its own desire for release.

The sermon went on and drew to its close; and, with the opening of the door, Lachland Henderson and his companions made their way out of the kirk. There was no loitering now. They sheered off together in a little knot, and when they had put a short distance between themselves and the building the wrath of Patrick Duthie was let loose; for this advocate of plain speaking was deaf to the suggestion that he should wait in the kirkyard and have his say out with the minister. The sharp voice of the mistress of Windy Edge could be heard as they went their way up the Manse hill. There was not much doubt about her opinions. Lachland Henderson walked a little apart. Certain misgivings that had come to him before the kirk went in knocked at his conscience more loudly. The others were too much occupied with their own comments to notice him as he slipped away from them and let them disappear down the road. He did not want to go back to Braes of Aird, for he had not quite enough courage to get home, to pull off his coat like a man, and to go into the fields.

He stood, half-hearted, at a turn of the way; had he met one living soul who would have given him a word of persuasion or sympathy, he might have repented yet, and gone, like the servants in the parable from which the accusing words had been taken, to work at the eleventh hour. But no one spoke to him; the world was hurrying back to its dinner; and he turned on his tracks and went off northwards. He decided to ask for a piece of bread-and-cheese at the house of a woman he knew and to keep out of the way till evening; for the present he was sick of Duthie and the rest of them, and he promised himself fervently that, should there be leading on the morrow, he would work like ten men.

He hated Euphemia with a jealous hatred for what she was doing and he would have liked to drag her home from the work and to shut her up while he wrought in her stead. She was a reproach, a living, taunting, maddening reproach. He put his hand into his waistcoat pocket for his watch, and in his absence of mind and perturbation of spirit drew out a copper instead. Britannia holding the trident reminded him of Euphemia sitting in the farm cart and holding her pitchfork. She had barely looked at him in passing by.

The shadows were lying eastward of the trees when he turned, after some hours of purposeless loafing, and sauntered homewards. His pipe had been no solace to him, and, though he avoided the more frequented ways, he would have welcomed even the company of the cross farm dog which often followed him in his leisure moments. He was out of step with every man and everything, including himself; most of all he was angry with Duthie, though his anger would have been more suitably turned upon his own weakness. Almost within sight of Braes of Aird, he was suddenly confronted with the beadle.

The beadle had a face like a full moon, but he had the eye that properly belongs to the more active part of mankind. Besides being a public functionary he was 'the minister's man,' and, in opinion, he took his colour from his master; grave-digging had robbed him of none of his cheerfulness and he played the fiddle. He was the sharpest-tongued man in the parish, and the precentor, who was sensitive, hated him. He contemplated Lachland with the leisurely interest he might have given to some odd but harmless beast.

There was more humour in him than in the minister.

'He was a bittie sair on ye i' the poupit,' he observed, as though continuing a conversation.

'He was that,' replied the young horseman, moved to the admission by his need of human intercourse.

'It'll no hairm ye,' said the beadle. 'A tellt him that when a ca'ed off his gown till him.'

'It'll no hairm ye,' he resumed, as Lachland was silent, 'but a'm thinkin' it'll na dae ony guid to Duthie (a tellt him that, forbye). Says I to the minister, "Them that's fond o' their ain blethers doesna like other folks' blethers." (Dod, he wasna owre pleased at that, though he kent weel eneuch a liket fine tae hear him sort the lot o' ye.) Man, ye need it.'

Lachland writhed.

'Duthie was fair rantin',' continued the old man, smiling unregenerately, 'what way did ye no gang hame wi' him?'

'A couldna just say—' began Lachland.

'Weel, a'll tell ye then,' interrupted the beadle, now absolutely in his element. 'Ye was feared tae meet the lasses.'

Lachland swore heartily and with some originality.

'Whisht, whisht!' cried the other, drawing in his mouth with an effort that was a mere sop to convention, 'lad, a'll gang down the hill wi' ye.'

He had been dying to get to the farm all day, but had not found a pretext. Lachland could have dispensed with his company, but there was no help for it.

They walked on together; and the young man, though

he would not admit it to his companion, was much out of conceit with himself. He had done shabbily and he was sorry in his heart. The beadle's caustic comments made his vanity smart, but what had gripped him and stung him all day was that sentence of the minister's about withholding help from a hard-pressed fellow-creature; though, to men like the one he had listened to in his folly, employers were a breed apart. And Braes, though not specially free-handed, had offered a fair price.

The beadle's talk ceased because they were nearing the farm and he was enjoying himself in anticipation. He was listening, with a hand over his ear, to unusual sounds that were coming up from the bottom of the hill, and, as the two got within sight of it, they saw a small mass of people contending in the road.

The beadle's jaw dropped and he came to a standstill. Euphemia was struggling with a handful of men who seemed to be forcing her towards the bridge. Her hair had come loose and fell down her back in a long tail, and her field apron was hanging by one string. Duthie had hold of her wrists and was dragging her along, while a ploughman, whose arm was about her, was doing his best to lift her from her feet. One or two women who had apparently come to her rescue were being held off by the remaining men. Cries and loud laughter were mixed with the sound of trampling boots.

'Rin, Lachland, man!' cried the beadle.

Patrick Duthie had come back from the kirk in a frenzy of resentment. His tongue had never rested on the homeward road, but the minister had now taken the place of Braes as a theme for his eloquence. No one could get in a word. As a rule he was quick to apply to his neighbours any home truths that came from the pulpit, but he liked to reserve the choice of culprits for himself. He did not notice the absence of Lachland from his audience.

The women were having their dinner in the fields when he had finished his own meal, and he went out with his comrades to spend the afternoon in hanging about under the great sycamore by the stable door. It was a convenient place from which to let them hear what he thought of them as they passed and repassed with their two carts, especially as Braes, who remained in the field, was out of earshot.

When evening came his state of mind was not improved by the complete lack of interest with which they heard him, and it was the culminating effect of the day's events that Henderson and the beadle were looking at now.

Lachland ran down the hill and came up with the strugglers as they reached the bridge. Braes had stopped work and gone home to his house, for the light was beginning to fail, and the clear western heavens and a keen bite in the air were giving promise of a fair morrow.

'Come awa', man! come awa'!' cried one of the ploughmen as the young man dashed in among them; 'we're to gie her a drookin' that'll be fine for her aifter sic a day's work!'

'Gie's a hand, Lachland!' shouted another.

Some were laughing and some were merely urging their friends on, but the expression of Duthie's face as he haled Euphemia towards the water suggested more than horseplay. He had found a way of making an impression on these women at last.

Euphemia was a strong woman, but her strength was availing her little against the men, and the grasp on her wrists seemed to her to be breaking them. Someone had got hold of her long tail of hair too. Her breath came short and she was so much exhausted that she had ceased to fight when she turned her desperate eyes and saw Lachland Henderson strike Duthie full upon the cheekbone.

The head horseman staggered, but his hold on her kept him on his feet and he recovered his balance in a moment. Before the young man could attack him again he was overpowered by three of the others.

'Haud him ticht!' cried Euphemia's second assailant, loosing his grip upon her; 'Man! we're no to hurt her! We're just to gie her a fleg! Losh, Patrick! but he's gar'd ye look bonnie!'

The blood was trickling down Duthie's face. He would have liked to turn on Henderson, but he had not done with Euphemia yet. They had come to the water's edge, and he suddenly let her wrists go, pushing her from him into the shallow pool. She sprang away, slipped on the muddy weeds and fell with one arm bent under her.

At the sound of the splash Lachland made a tremendous effort and wrenched himself free, hatless and with his coat torn half-way down his back. Euphemia's pale face and her hair dripping in the pool horrified him as he rushed in to her help. The stones were so slimy that he could hardly keep on his legs and his plungings in the shallow water raised a roar of laughter from the men at the brink; a clod of mud flew after him through the air and hit him on his white Sunday collar, then another and another. They came in such a storm that one of them missed Euphemia by an inch. She had raised herself painfully and stood beside him.

'Get ahint me, lassie,' said Lachland, thrusting himself between her and the shower. 'A'll no let them touch ye. Just you wait, Duthie,' he shouted, 'you and me's got to settle for this job—!'

He broke off as he felt a hand clutch at him and looked round. He was barely in time to catch Euphemia as she fell against him.

He stood in the middle of the pond with his arms round her. The sight of the fainting girl had somewhat subdued Duthie, and he turned away and began to push through the increasing number of men and women which had been attracted to the place by the noise. He looked up to see Braes and the beadle standing together on the bridge. The latter was proclaiming his opinion of everyone present with extraordinary freedom, but Braes was silent. Nevertheless, as Duthie met his eyes it was borne in upon him that he had better be looking for a new place.

The weather mended with the last week of September and the equinox came in with a dry wind. All over the country the leading went on undisturbed and the agricultural part of the world began to hold up its head and make concessions to Providence. It was admitted that things might be worse. Duthie, who had departed summarily, was busy preparing to sue James Anderson of Braes of Aird farm for wrongful dismissal. But, unluckily, when the case came before the Sheriff, he stated that the dismissal was due to his own feeling against Sunday work,

while the farmer based his action on the circumstance
that the head horseman had mishandled a woman in his
employment and broken her arm. Euphemia appeared in
court wearing a sling; the Sheriff dismissed the case, and
the plaintiff paid the costs.

At last the fields sloping to the Basin of Montrose were
bare and the stackyards dotted the landscape like so many
tall yellow villages. The plough-horses had resumed their
normal occupation, and, at Aird kirk, a Sunday came round
on which the minister conceived it time to give thanks for
what had, after all, proved to be a not indifferent harvest.
Then, when the last words of the psalm which followed
died away, he took up a little paper from between the
leaves of his book and read:

'There is a purpose of marriage between Lachland
Henderson, bachelor, and Euphemia Mary Maclaren,
spinster, both of this parish.'

And the beadle, looking across the pews, grinned, as he
saw a black head whose owner seemed anxious that the
earth should open and swallow him.

The Overthrow of Adam Pitcaithley

PEOPLE WHO have a taste for byways and are not too much overdriven by the clock to frequent them are free of certain byways of memory too; marginal sketches on the maps of their minds; unofficial scraps which give outside points of view. Unaccustomed crops of knowledge hang on brier and whin, ungarnered as the bramble fruit, pungent as the wild raspberry hiding in its green shelter in still hours, to stand forth, a coral spark, when the wind blows and turns up the white undersides of its leaves. It was in one of these byways that Jimmy's loon was revealed to me.

But first of Jimmy, the youthful flippancy of whose name belied him; for he could not have been less than seventy when I knew him nor have travelled the east coast of Scotland with his wife and his 'hurley' for anything short of forty years.

The smithy stood at the end of the loan haunted by him in his passings to and fro; and sitting one day, ben the house, with the blacksmith's wife, I saw a light-coloured streak of swiftness flash by the window.

'That'll be Jimmy's loon,' said she, as our heads turned simultaneously.

I hurried away. My friend was, apparently, in his old quarters and I made haste to find him; as I came out upon the grass track I could see the ripple which was the trail of the vanishing 'loon' running along the sea of green. He must be pretty small, I argued, if the broom could submerge him like that.

Jimmy was sitting on a log beside his very simple residence when I reached the accustomed spot; a large weather-stained piece of sacking was tied round the trimmed and inverted head of a fir which stood like a half-opened umbrella, resting its points on the ground. In the space within its area a fire burned and smoke rose straight into the air. The blaze was being fed with sticks by Jimmy's wife, whose figure I could see through the shortage of sacking that formed the doorway. It shone upon her wedding ring and on a few odds and ends of pots. I did not greet her, for I knew her of old for a woman of no hostilities, but few words. My acquaintance with the couple was of that restful kind in which all things are taken for granted. I sat down beside the old man; we had not met for two years and there were gaps of experience to be filled up.

'And what about *him*?' I inquired, as a small boy came round the apology for a tent and halted before us.

Jimmy took his pipe from his mouth in silence and paused, as he had a habit of doing, before making the most ordinary reply.

'Bell's lad,' said he.

(Bell was his daughter, the wife of a prosperous tinker.)

'She's awa' north to Inverness,' he explained.

It was not easy to tell how old the boy was, for his eyes and stature suggested different ages. His hair was like the roofing of a haystack. His bare feet were tan-coloured, as was every visible inch of his skin, and a pair of aggressively new red braces upheld tattered trousers which had certainly come to him from someone three times his size. The back buttons were on a level with his shoulder-blades. His features were angelic in type, his chin delicately pointed. But it was not of angels that I thought as I surveyed him.

'He's very small for tramping,' I remarked.

'Aw, he does fine,' replied Jimmy, 'an' whiles, maybe, he gets a lift i' the hurley.'

The boy did not give us much of his company; after a long look at me he probably put me down as insignificant, and departed, leaving me to finish my talk with his grandparent.

I went home, a little later, by way of Pitcaithley's farm which stood in the fields near where the loan debouched upon the cart road. I waited a moment behind an alder

which had sprung up unmolested in the path, for, with
a tramping of hoofs, a pair of plough-horses were coming
down to the pond hard by. The first was ridden by one
of Pitcaithley's horsemen, and the second, an enormous
bay with mealy coloured muzzle and belly, by the farmer's
youngest boy, Adam, who, with a look of pride and some
oaths unsuitable to his years, urged the horse forward with
fists and heels. The gigantic creature took as much notice
of him as if he were a splash of mud on its back.

'Ca' awa', man, ca' awa'; ye're dae'in brawly!'

The voice came from a broom-bush in which showed
something red. Young Adam Pitcaithley stared round, and
seeing nobody, rode solemnly on into the water. From the
green growth Jimmy's loon emerged and stood, hands on
hips and legs apart, watching the rider with an expression
so comprehensive that it staggered me. Admiration was in
it and contempt; the first was for the oaths and the second
for the person who emitted them.

'Come doon, till a' sort ye!' he cried, at last.

It was not a genial invitation; but it did not seem to
move young Pitcaithley one way or another. He sat on the
swilling carthorse, his body dragged forward by the pull
on the rein and his smug nose and puffy cheeks in strong
contrast with those of the little vagabond who eyed him.
The latter changed his tune.

'What's yer name, man?' he inquired in a milder voice
as he approached the pool.

'Awdam,' replied the other, probably from habit.

'Come awa' doon, Awdam, an' a'll gie ye a ride i' the
hurley.'

'No me,' replied the other.

The ploughman had left the water and was disappearing
towards the farm with his horse as the boys gazed defiantly
one upon the other.

'It's no for the likes o' me to play wi' the likes o' you,'
said Adam.

Jimmy's loon surveyed him sharply.

'*You're* no gentry,' he observed.

'A'm fell near it,' replied Adam portentously.

If Jimmy's loon were awed, he made no sign; and I

knew enough about boys to see that the hostile attitude of
these two was as conventional as the stiff walk with which
one dog seeks to impress another at a first meeting. Soon
they might be playing together among the bushes. All the
same it struck me that Adam Pitcaithley was safer where
he was.

'What like's yer hurley?' said he, after a silence.

'Braw.'

'Will there be a shelt?'

'Gran'pa' hurls it himsel'.'

A cold consideration entered into the rider's face; then
hesitation, then interest. After all, a hand-cart has more
original possibilities and can be treated more fancifully
than the everyday vehicle drawn by a horse. Besides which,
driving was no novelty to a farmer's son.

His haughtiness began to give way.

'Ye'll gie me a hurl?' said he.

'Fegs will I.'

The immense beast under him had finished its drink
and raised a dripping muzzle. Its ears were cocked and
its clear eye focused on the spot where its yoke-fellow
was growing smaller. With one of those thunderous
sighs heaved by Clydesdales it turned from the pool.
The movement decided Adam.

'S – ss – ss!' he cried; and, as the obedient leviathan
stopped, he embedded his fingers in the mane and
lowered himself to the ground. The act was not that
of a really practised horseman, for half-way to earth a
convulsiveness came into it which I thought was not lost
on Jimmy's loon.

The next moment the two boys had vanished in the
direction of Jimmy's tent, and I was left watching the
horse pursuing its way home with human good sense.
Before I followed its example I heard shouts and laughter
in the loan, and I hoped that Jimmy's hurley was pretty
strong.

Next day was Sunday. The very skies seemed to look
down with added benignity as I took my way to the kirk
in the little company of the godly. In the distance a swarm
of black figures was gathering round the door, and, in the

church-going stream around me, my eye caught a familiar form. I recognised Mrs. Pitcaithley's black beaded mantle and the splendour of her Sunday bonnet.

Beside her walked her son, Adam, the same as yesterday and yet how changed! He had not passed the age for frilled collars – at least his mother thought he had not – and the starched white stuff stood out below his conspicuous ears. A dark-blue velvet blouse with mother-of-pearl buttons and a pair of tight knickerbockers proclaimed the occasion. He carried a gilt-clasped Bible; and he appeared to be as proud of it and his clothes to-day as he had been of his oaths and his horsemanship yesterday. His scrubbed cheeks shone. Pride was evidently his besetting sin.

The clangour of the bell had not roused the congregation to a brisker pace when, over the roadside dyke, uprose a shock head with angelic features and eyes fixed – whether or no in admiration I could not tell – upon the glorious figure marching beside Mrs. Pitcaithley.

'Hey, Awdam!' cried the apparition.

A stir went through the church-going ranks and Adam stopped for one moment. Then he went forward, his mouth drawn down and his Bible clasped to him as though to ward off Satan.

'Man, Awdam!' shouted Jimmy's loon, more loudly.

Mrs. Pitcaithley turned in outraged dignity and threw a glance of rebuke towards the dyke.

We tramped on in silence.

The footsteps in the field kept up with our advance.

'What ails ye?' cried Jimmy's loon. 'Man, ye warna sweer to speak i' the hurley!'

Adam was deaf; he turned neither to right nor left.

'I'st yer ma ye're feared at?' yelled the other; 'maybe she'll gie ye yer wheeps when the kirk's skailed!'

Even this taunt was fruitless, and the situation grew plain to Jimmy's loon, as well as the trend of public opinion. Pitcaithley himself approached the dyke shaking his stick. The enemy dodged behind some thorn bushes and was seen no more.

*   *   *

THAT EVENING I walked again to the loan's end by the pond. That grassy bit by the alder was a favourite place of mine, and I sat where I had sat yesterday. My thoughts were far from Jimmy's loon and his time-serving acquaintance as I heard the approach of horses and realised that these animals must be watered even on Sunday. It was the same pair and the same riders, but Adam, resplendent still in his Sunday clothes, was this time behind his companion. The latter had entered the water and left it before the young hero rode in, velvet blouse, knickerbockers, frilled collar and all. The only thing missing was the Bible.

Not a leaf stirred, not a sound; nothing but the gurgling draughts of the horse, when the bushes parted. Adam was facing the other way and the tail and quarters of the carthorse were presented full to the undergrowth from which crawled Jimmy's loon. I saw the boy drop on his knee and draw his hand back to his ear. Something whizzed through the air. The horse flung up its head and plunged round, churning the pond into waves. There was a cry, a falling splash of dark blue, and in another moment Adam Pitcaithley, crowned with weeds and mire, stood up to his arm-pits in the deepest part of the pool.

THERE WAS WRATH in Pitcaithley's farm the next morning. Adam, fearful of his mother's eye, had slunk home after dark, but when the truth was out a ploughman was sent down to the loan with a whip to search for Jimmy's loon.

But Jimmy, his wife, his hurley, and his loon had all disappeared.

The Lum Hat

I

CHRISTINA MILL is so hard a person to portray, both physically and mentally, that there is no help but to describe the small photograph – taken in the very early days of the art – which is the only record of her looks. She was almost twenty-seven when it was done though she looks much younger. It is set in an absurd little leather case with a clasp. She is not beautiful, scarcely even good-looking; she wears a turnover collar like a schoolboy's, but soft and scallop-edged, and a dark velvet spencer. Short, hanging curls cover her ears, no ringlets, but the solid sausage sort; her parted hair lies smooth till it joins them. Her face is a longish oval and her lips, more heavy than thin, are a little parted.

This is a mere inventory of clothes and feature. Expression is what matters and here the difficulty begins. It is self-contained and innocent, reserved, yet immature. The smooth, stolid face seems scarcely grown-up and the grace of velvet and silk belies it. Her shapely long fingers with their rings and her braceleted wrists might belong to the placid hands of a far older woman. They look so settled.

The house she lived in, in the east coast Scottish seaport still stands, a trifle back from the street, in the Bow Butts, just where it joins Ferry Street on the way to the quays. In her day, if you walked fifty yards down Ferry Street you could see the windjammers lying alongside with the glittering water beyond them. It is a plain three-storied house with tall narrow windows. The flagged enclosure along its frontage is so much straitened by the low wall dividing it from the street that it has an air of being on tip-toe in order to get above its adjuncts and to be demanding, in the name of gentility, to be allowed more space. A couple of slim-stemmed ornamental trees are close to the windows.

Four people lived in it: Christina, her father, a maid-servant and Ann Wishart, the cook; for William Mill, who was manager of the local Bank of Angus, had some means and his daughter had no need to spoil her refined hands with housework. She kept them for the naive bits of fancy work that slaked the artistic thirst of her contemporaries. Sometimes she would pretend to help the cook when preserving was going on, but Ann, who had been of the household years before Christina grew up, discouraged this, because of her passionate belief that the gentry should keep the pose thrust upon them by God.

The banker's wife was a pale myth to her child. The recollection of ourselves at four years old are only flashes of unoutlined scenes. She remembered the figure of someone sitting by a downstairs window with a red curtain – still in its place – behind her and a thin face on the pillow of the four-poster to which her father still repaired nightly, and that was all. The solid female presence which had once been her aunt Isabella Mill and was now her aunt Isabella Halket had obliterated the other one. Isabella Mill had come to the rescue of her bereaved brother, a stout resourceful woman with whom Ann Wishart had never contrived to quarrel openly, probably because of the indolence which inclined the lady to leave the major troubles of housekeeping to somebody else; she would have liked to be upside with Ann but her robust, everday perceptions told her that Ann was best left alone. For all her assured demeanour, caution lurked in her. Christina, whose attitude from childhood had been a contemplative one, would look at her aunt with the half-smile that sat so often on her parted lips. She watched everything, seeing nothing but the outside and contented with that. Yet there was something faintly curious in her mind, a semi-conscious fingering at the doorkey of life. But nothing that disturbed her.

Many people, though they may be happy, never let themselves formulate the idea. Christina had been saved from that misfortune by reason of her conception of what happiness was; she mistook contentment for it. She would put down her fancy work complacently, thinking of her advantages, of her good clothes, of her father's uniform kindness – nothing positive or emotional, but something to be counted on. Then there was the consideration of friends and neighbours, and even of those who were neither; who lived in mean streets and smaller houses and who knew her only by seeing her on the pavements, a figure set apart, creditable and established. It would have astonished her very much had she known that, to a large part of the town, she was Miss 'Lummie' Mill and she would not have liked it. She shared the homely word with her father whose unusually tall 'chimney-pot' hat had caused him to be known as 'Lummie Mill' to a population devoted (as all Scottish towns are) to nicknames. That hat was as much a part of the community as the wooden Highlander who had stood for some generations at a tobacconist's door in the Seagate, or the spire of the parish kirk. Lummie was a thin man with a nervous jocular manner much mimicked by his clerks. People continually said they were surprised at the success in life of such a fool, forgetting that, though he was no genius, he had two valuable qualities, a dislike of giving offence and a habit of leaving things he did not understand to those who did.

The family sat in the first pew under the gallery in the parish church where they could be clearly observed by their fellow worshippers; Christina passive and aloof in her silks and velvet spencer, her father with pursed lips, bald and attentive to his Bible, with the lum hat, like a third presence, occupying the end of the long red cushion. Girls would look with awe on Christina's dress, loitering about the church door to get a nearer view of it when the kirk 'came out'. She was aware of this and it pleased a vanity not personal enough to be offensive. It was not herself that she was so satisfied with but her circumstances and had it been her own beauty that impressed the girls she would have found it less interesting. She thought little about beauty; she did not possess it and it had never occurred to her to desire it.

It was only of late years that father and daughter had
sat alone with the lum hat. Christina was twenty when
her aunt was courted by a well-to-do insurance agent who
transported her to Gayfield Square, Edinburgh. Uncle
Halket, as Christina called him, came little into her life
and died suddenly five years after his marriage. The widow
moved into a smaller house for she was not left as well off
as she had expected to be and her visits to her brother
grew longer. She would have liked to come back to her
old place permanently but Christina showed no desire to
give up the reins to which she had grown accustomed and
Ann Wishart was determined she should not do so; Mrs
Halket knew that as well as if she had been told it.

The reason for her disappointing circumstances as the
relict of a comparatively rich man was that much, including
the Gayfield Square house, had been left to Aeneas, his son
by his first wife. He had no ill-will at Isabella but he had
liked her predecessor better and he was extremely fond of
his son; for Aeneas had an excellent position with a firm
of glove manufacturers in France, and while little more
than a boy had shown such industry and capabilities that
his father had been given to understand his future to be
assured, should he go on as he had begun. He was sent
to the Edinburgh branch of the business though his duties
often took him abroad.

Christina had never had a lover nor a ghost of a love affair
– the only sign of a man's interest in her had come from
Aeneas Halket. They had met at her aunt's house on one
of her visits there and the young man, whose profession had
made him notice woman's hands, had told his stepmother
that he had never seen more beautiful ones than those of
her niece. Once, he had said to Christina that a cast ought
to be taken of them and she had blushed; but the idea
seemed to her so odd that she had taken little pleasure in
it. But she looked at them carefully in her room that night
when she was undressing and wondered if they were really
so beautiful. Faces were beautiful, she knew, but she had
never thought about hands.

Not long after this Aeneas spent a fortnight in France
and brought her back a little coloured picture of St Cecilia

sitting at a musical instrument with her long tapered fingers touching the keys. It was very pretty and French and affected with lilies in the background and she kept it on her bedroom mantelpiece. Sometimes she thought of Aeneas and wondered how much he liked her. She had no girl friends with whom to discuss the point; for they were all mere acquaintances, but Ann Wishart, whose long service had made her one of the family, discovered from whom the picture had come and commented on it.

'A'm thinkin' the young gentleman should hae kent better nor send a Popish thing the like o' yon till a young leddy,' she remarked.

'But it was very kind of him,' replied Christina.

'It was an attention, surely.'

'Oh, do you think so, Ann?'

Ann was an avowed expert of custom and deportment. The girl waited, open-eyed, for a reply. Getting none, she repeated her words.

'Heuch! – they Halkets!' exclaimed Ann, enigmatically.

Perhaps Ann was the only one of the household who looked beyond the daily round; Lummie Mill glided along on a path of ledgers from one year's end to another, satisfied to return to a long evening and the snug company of some casually dropping-in neighbour. He liked Christina to preside at the eight o'clock tea tray, silent and well-attired. The neighbour, from civility, would address her now and again with that mixture of sprightly yet deferential patronage which people often use to the children of rich men, though she had, as the French say, 'coiffé Sainte Caterine' and her flounces went ill with his attempt to adjust himself.

Aeneas was not inclined to forget Christina. She occupied his thoughts often. He did not know what it was that attracted him besides her hands. She had little to say and the half-smile she seemed to use to supplement her want of words would have irritated some people. He admitted that, but he was not irritated. He was dark himself, and her shining pale hair pleased his eye. He liked her effortlessness to please by any of the accepted charms of girlhood. It struck him as an original thing, for he had not learnt yet exactly how to estimate the obvious.

[When the manuscript for this story was rediscovered in 1977, five pages were missing. This is one point in the text where a passage is incomplete; no attempt has been made here editorially to add to the text, since the abrupt ending is in any case not uncharacteristic of Jacob's prose. Later, where missing pages leave more of a gap (at page 174), a passage in brackets is inserted to provide a brief link to the next part of the text.]

II

MARTINMAS FAIR CAME. It had no interest for Christina but Ann liked it and persuaded her to go.

'It may be a little coarse,' said Ann, 'but we winna bide lang and ye haena been out these three-fower days.'

So they started. The Fair was in full swing and they were engulfed. Whistles blew, men roared, women roared too; children ran between grown-up people's legs, dodging the cuffs of their elders. Penny trumpets brayed in falsetto.

Christina stood and looked round on the crowd. Many were drunk and more were on the way to it. A dog-fight had started and a knot of women, under whose feet the savage din had arisen as suddenly as a gale of wind, flew asunder screaming. The girl had little mind for the rough business of returning by the way she came. Ann had some domestic errand on hand so she left her and turned down a quiet street leading to the links.

There was no golf course in those days. Along the grassy spaces she would walk home away from the pandemonium of the town. She strolled along between town and sea. On her right hand the tall, beautiful steeple of the parish kirk held its flying buttresses against the sky and over the roofs crowded below it. The sun was near the horizon and the smoke from many chimneys, the varied skyline with its slopes and steepnesses and angles, caught the smouldering sundown and became welded into one vision of romance like the embodiment of the soul of a town. Christina saw nothing of these things.

On her left the sea lay cold and hidden by the dunes along the shore. Its voice, like the voice of a shell held to the ear, had the breath of a far away history reaching from childhood to death, from time to the end of time. The white finger of the lighthouse stood up where the river, having passed the shipping, ran out to the bar.

Not far from her was moored one of those vehicles that everybody except those who own them call 'caravans'. A woman sat on the step.

What interested Christina was the basket hanging above her head full of small red and green feather brooms. She had seen some like them in the High Street but the crowd had prevented her from getting near to buy one. She stopped, hesitating, and would have pulled out her purse had she been sure of the propriety of speaking to a person between whom and herself was so great a gulf. It was no vulgar pride which impeded her but a distrust of the unknown and the shadow of Ann Wishart.

The woman, as a citizen of the world, had the advantage of her and stepping down, came forward.

'What is't ye're seekin?' she enquired.

She seemed a few years older than Christina and she had all the weight of a human being whose position – whatever it may be – is so well defined that there is no need to insist upon it. There was nothing of the apology of the vagrant in her voice and the girl saw that the waggon was freshly painted; the horse – though Christina did not notice this – was well rugged up with a piece of sacking. The woman was unlike anyone she had ever spoken to before; she was definitely good-looking with hair of the corn-coloured yellow never seen but on the heads of the hatless; it was dressed with a resolute neatness that in itself amounted to beauty. It looked as if a hairdresser had done it and as if nobody, not a hairdresser, could ever undo it again. Her eyes were light hazel and she was wrapped in a green plaid.

'I want a little broom,' said Christina. 'Like those,' she added, pointing to the basket.

'Come awa' an' ye'll get ane,' said the other.

Christina followed her with a fluttering sense of risk. She did not know whether she would be sorry or glad just now to see Ann Wishart. Sorry, she thought, perhaps.

The woman unhooked the basket and took out a brush of each colour; the western light made a crimson blur and a green one as she held them up.

'The reid's bonnie,' she said, gravely. Though she was friendly she seemed as little likely to smile as an animal.

Christina bought and paid for the red one.

'I saw a man in the fair with some like that,' she said.

'Aye. Yon's ma man. He's there.'

'Do you always come to it?' asked the girl, prolonging her adventuresomeness now that it seemed so harmless.

'Na. We hae na been this road afore. We gang doon aboot Pairth and Edinburgh.'

'That's a long way,' observed Christina with a little sententious air.

The other smiled for the first time.

'It's nae sae far as England.'

'But do you ever go there?'

'Aye, div we.'

'To England in that cart?'

'And what for no? Maybe ye've never seen London.'

Christina shook her head.

'Aweel, we gang nae far oot-by it.'

'And have you been in it and seen the streets?'

'Aye, have I. We got a lad tae mind the horse and we ga'ed in and got a sight o't, ma man and me.'

Christina's amazed face stirred something in her companion's vanity and loosened her tongue.

'Ye'll see a' thing in London,' she went on. 'Sic-like shops ye wadna believe't and muckle hooses for the gentry. And them that rides i' their twa-horse machines has twa men tae drive them – ane sitting up aside the ither. And gin ye stand still ye'll see mair grand folk ganging past ye in a meenit than ye'd see here in a towmont. Ye should gang an' tak a sicht o't yersel'!'

'Oh, but I could not do that,' said Christina.

'And what for no? You that has plenty siller.'

'My father never leaves here. We are always here.'

'Weel,' rejoined the woman, reflectively. 'I couldna thole tae bide in ae place yon gait. I dinna ken what I wad dae. But ye'll weary, na doubt. Fegs, I shouldna like tae be you though I'll no say but ye hae a bonnie goon on ye and ye'll likely be gettin' meat till yer denner ilka day.'

Christina was silent. It was difficult to know what to say to such a strange person: nor was she accustomed to be pitied, certainly not by a woman who sold brooms by the wayside.

She was turning away.

'Ye should get a man,' said the other. 'Get you a man that'll tak' ye awa and gie ye a sicht of the world.'

Christina had almost opened her mouth to reply that there was no man she knew who was likely to do that, but some inherent feminine instinct stopped her. She bade her acquaintance good evening, a little ruffled, and went homewards.

As she went, she thought of Aeneas Halket and wished again that she knew his real feelings for her. She had read about love in the decorous books of her day, and reading, had stood aloof looking on at the story from the detached standpoint of one watching the life of a street through the cold window pane. She supposed, from what she read, that gentlemen made their proposals on one knee, expressing themselves well as they did so and she gathered from Ann's criticisms of such things that sometimes they wrote letters expressing themselves even better. She considered the paraphernalia of weddings, the satin and flowers and excitement, delightful. One day they might be her lot and she knew there was generally 'a wedding journey'. That would be the time for seeing the world and that was what the woman had meant in her case. She decided to tell no one about her. Ann would not approve of her stopping to talk to strangers of that kind.

★   ★   ★

III

THE WOMAN WITH the brooms had begun to fade a little from Christina's mind. There was rather more stir in the seafaring world that winter and this had its effect upon the town and even upon the household of Lummie Mill; for a four-masted barque came in in December to load timber for Adelaide and the carpenters were soon busy in her; for now, at the end of a long cruise she was to be refitted to sail in the spring.

It so happened that the captain of the *Sirius* was related to the manager of another branch of the Bank of Angus and he carried a letter of introduction to Lummie from his colleague. He was described in it as one of the best captains in his line and one considered by his owners as a rising sun. 'You will find Andrew Baird good company,' said the writer. 'He has seen a deal of the world and should be something of a variety to you and Miss.'

But the captain had little need of his cousin's good offices. He had soon found himself a suitable lodging and a footing among the principal people of the town. He had no family to claim his attention on shore and he was anxious to be near his ship while the workmen were in her. His owners, willing to do things handsomely for one of their best seamen, had given him what was almost a free hand in some improvements he had asked for in his cabin accommodation and he meant to avail himself of this to the full. He was a young man to have a ship like the *Sirius*, which was reckoned the pick of her line. He was aware of that and was sensible that behoved him to make others aware of it too.

On the second Sunday after the *Sirius* came in he was to be seen in the parish kirk having determined to run his eye over the townspeople before becoming acquainted with any of them. He took the seat shown him and having disposed of his hat, he watched the entrance of the congregation, his arms folded across his broad chest. He was dressed well and with care and he thought that, though he had spent most of his thirty-six years in ships, he looked just the same as his neighbours. In this he made a vast mistake for he was as much like the town-bred men about him as a bull terrier is like a spaniel. But he had not a rough appearance and on this Sunday morning he was rather sleek though his dark clipped beard was coarse and his face tanned.

In a small town a stranger in church is a godsend. People surveyed Baird openly over their bibles and covertly between their fingers and those fortunate enough to be able to see him without moving anything but their eyes behaved with a plainness that did not become them. Straight opposite, under the gallery, Christina and her father were compelled to see him whether they wished it or not and he was compelled to see them. As something unusual, arresting, he riveted Christina and gave her an indefinite feeling that he ought not to be there; his unusualness seemed to disturb the decorum of a church. He did not exactly attract her although she took her customary passive pleasure in anything she had not seen before; and when her father hurried out at the end of the service, whispering to her that this was evidently the captain of the big ship and that he must introduce himself to him without delay, dumbness of both tongue and spirit came over her.

As they waited outside on the kirk pavement – that meeting place of all and sundry – with the tall steeple above it, she stood back alone. To avoid setting her eyes on Baird as he came through the church door, she looked upwards at the great mass of stonework towering pointed above them to its weather vane and received from the moving clouds beyond it the sensation of being under something that was falling on her. Turning abruptly to earth, she met a direct look from Captain Baird who was replacing his hat.

It was not from 'Lummie' Mill that his daughter got her placidity. In some things the banker was very active. Minor hospitalities, inquiries after health and trivial exchanges of civility were dear to him. Baird, who had not known of his kinsman's letter, was astonished at being accosted and shewed it; but he was not displeased, for Christina's shining hair and detached look gave his generally robust fancy a new and curious pleasure. She represented an unknown craft on his horizon.

'A fine, easy fellow – a very pleasant way with him,' said Lummie after they parted. 'He mustn't think himself altogether a stranger after all Dixon wrote to me about him. 'You'll have to look out your best fal-lals when he comes to drink tea.'

'His beard is very black,' said the girl, accustomed to the incurved, silky whiskers of her contemporaries.

'He's a sailor, you see, my dear,' replied Lummie, who was a loose reasoner.

'And does that make them black?'

She spoke without a touch of sarcasm.

'No, no, nonsense – I mean sailors are different.'

It was strange that Baird made her think of the woman with the brooms; both were things whose purpose seemed obscure – almost like forbidden things. She was faintly uncomfortable in their presence. They touched some sleeping thing in her mind which feared to be awakened. Perhaps, after all there was some imagination in her, inherited from some sources beyond her memory, buried below the mountain of small satisfactions that made up her easy life. She had only exchanged a few unmeaning words with Baird and he had appeared to be much more aware of her father's talk than of herself; yet, in spite of her uncomfortableness, she was glad he was coming to the house. She told Ann of the meeting.

There had been a great deal of exaggerated talk in the town about the *Sirius*. It was said the Baird was part owner of her and that his cabin was to have silver fittings; that this was to be his last voyage and that he was going to retire, some way on the right side of forty, to an opulent leisure when it was over; but Baird's age was the only point that was right. Ann had heard it, with even more exaggeration and she announced that he meant to settle in the place and live in great style in one of the new turreted houses with Venetian blinds that were springing up the landward side. But though she was impressed she would not have been herself if she had not asserted some superiority, even over such a dazzling person.

'You'd wonder that Mr Mill would ask the like o'they sailor-folk intill his hoose,' she said.

'But he is Mr Dixon's cousin,' replied Christina, with the least hint of reproof in her voice.

Ann made no answer. She saw the force of this, but she and her household had got to be superior to something. She turned away to her oven.

It was scarcely a week later that the skipper, having dined at the house in the Bow Butts, followed his host up to the drawing-room. Late dinner was then a rare enough institution to confer a breath of distinction on those who consumed it, but the after-dinner tea table lingered, though coffee was never thought of. Baird could be both genial and morose. Mill had not diverted him much, yet he felt that he was at least surrounded by a refinement not to be matched at sea. Isabella Halket had, on her visits, grafted into the household some of the ornamental details of life to which she had grown accustomed in Edinburgh and her niece had accepted them with her usual unquestioning docility.

The girl sat very silent during their meal. She was feeling the guest to be less of a responsibility than she had expected and she sat serene in her voluminous silk dress, a little too rich for her years; her hair shone and she looked up with her dimly expectant half-smile as the two men came in. She made such a picture of feminine suitability as she paused in her tatting that Baird, responsive to the good wine he had drunk, took in the spectacle of the room of which she was the culminating point, with facile pleasure.

He did not sit down by her with the directness of social assurance but stood on the hearth with Lummie before nerving himself to do so. He would accomplish it in the end; whilst any action that suited him seemed simple enough on deck he felt it to be rather different in a house, though he concealed the fact very well. The atmosphere of this place attracted him. He liked its suggestion of solid worldly advantage, though he could hardly have found anything further from the world than this decorous, monotonous drawing room. As he took his teacup from Christina's hand he drew a chair nearer to her table. She might have linked him to it by some commonplace remark but she said nothing. He did not know how to speak to a girl like the one before him, she was so utterly different from the women he had come across; but he was not really embarrassed because he had not the habit of being so and he knew that she was

just a chit whose circumstances were all that was to blame
for her divergence from type.

'I wish I could get as good a cup of tea as this on board,'
he said.

'I hear your ship is to have a very fine cabin,' she
observed, timidly.

'I'll see to *that*,' he laughed. 'We poor fellows have
a right to some comforts and I mean to have the best
accommodation in the line. She's the biggest ship they've
got – but I suppose a young lady has little interest in
a ship.'

'It is a schooner, I suppose?' asked Christina, who had
heard the word and supposed all seagoing vessels to be
alike except in size. He laughed a little louder.

'No, no, she's a barque – a four-masted barque. I doubt
you don't go often to the harbour, Miss Mill.'

'I never go there.' She was quite complacent, though
she had coloured.

'Well, when they've finished her you should step down
with Mr Mill and look at her. There will be something to
show you then.'

She turned, pleased, to her father.

'Yes, indeed we will come,' said Lummie, 'I've never
been on anything bigger than the ferry. But you'll not need
to sail off with us, Captain. They would never do without
me here, you know,' he added, with his high-pitched laugh
which always doubled him up a little.

'I won't do that. At any rate I'll put *your father* ashore,'
rejoined Baird, looking hard at Christina.

'I should be very much frightened on a ship,' she said.

'And why, Miss?'

'There might be a storm.'

'And, if there were, you'd be as safe as you are
ashore.'

'Oh – surely not—'

'And why, surely not? You might get a slate off a roof
on your head, or be blown against the wall of a house.'

'Very true, very true, indeed,' said Lummie with the
sudden gravity of one who bows to resistless logic.

'And of course I know there is the lifeboat,' said Christina, willing to show that she understood at least something of what was being talked about.

Baird checked the smile on his lips.

'You'd never need that.'

She was silent, a little reassured. He had been many voyages, round the world, perhaps, and had great experience.

'And where will you go, when you sail away from here?'

'Adelaide, next voyage. A fine place, too.'

'It is the capital of South Australia, is it not? Just as Edinburgh is the capital of Scotland?'

He nodded.

'A fine city, Miss Mill. Everything a man can want when he comes off the sea. Good company – the best.'

He cast a sophisticated glance at his host and got the acquiescent laugh from him that he would have got for any statement not definitely funereal.

'Fine shops, fine streets, fine houses, fine living. I remember being at a great banquet there. The owners of another line were entertaining their own skippers and ours. Their ladies were there too, fine women, some of them and they knew how to show themselves off. There was one of them a real beauty. We dined off silver plate – everything of the best.'

'Is it a very gay place then?' asked Christina.

'We thought so, all the time we were there. It may be a lonely life at sea, Miss Mill, but you can make up for that in these foreign places.'

'Yes, no doubt,' exclaimed Mill with his mild knowingness, 'if you are captain of a big ship like the *Serious*. Why did they call her the *Serious*, by the way?'

'*Sirius*, Sir – the dog-star.'

'To be sure, to be sure.'

Baird did not know what to make of his host. In general, men looked on Mill as a fool. The skipper only knew him in one aspect and his social judgements were of a rough order. He was feeling an amused contempt for Mill which did not extend itself to his daughter. She was even more simple, he considered; but simplicity, which sat ill on a bank manager sat well enough on a girl. It would soon pass, given the right experiences, and he rather admired a sheltered delicacy, in theory. He had enjoyed his dinner, for Ann Wishart, though she might affect to look down on seafarers, was ready to pamper the whole race sooner than abate a farthing's worth of credit from her particular household.

Christina woke up a little that evening. The guest was ready to talk about his voyages and though the seamanship that set him so high in his profession conveyed absolutely nothing to his hearers, his accounts of that rich merchant life existing in the great seaports of the world fascinated the banker and was also fascinating Christina. He made a sequel – a grand sequel to the humble volume opened for her by the woman on the links. She was almost bewildered when, Baird having gone and her father's cackling laugh ceased with the shutting of the house door, she had heard the chain being put up.

She dawdled over her undressing and stood some time in front of Saint Cecilia simpering among her lilies. But she did not so much as give a thought to her.

Winter wore slowly into Spring and the town went through its changes of aspect. Grey 'haar' sweeping in from the sea, obliterating it so that, inland, there seemed nothing to tell of its presence but the voice of the steeple clock. Cold sunlight at times laid a hand on it that had nothing to do with friendship but rather suggested distant patronage; snow fell softly, like forgetfulness, and sharply, like ill-luck; . . .

IV[1]

'YOU SEE THEY didn't forget her figurehead when they were building her,' he said.

His companions followed him obediently to the bows and, looking up, were silent. Lummie, because he did not know what to say. He was most willing to take Baird's word for its fineness though it appeared to him mainly

[1] Baird invited Christina and her father to visit the ship *Sirius*, now refitted and loaded with timber for departure to Australia.

as a mass of extraordinary huge and unfamiliar contours;
size, always likely to appal Christina, appalled her here, for
the great torso that reared itself high above the horizontal
line of the quay was awe-inspiring because of its human
shape, because of a terrific solidity which held suggestion
of latent violence in the sharp, arresting outline; it made
her shudder. Perhaps she had never before realised the
importance of Baird. That he was in absolute command
of living men on errands involving great profits and losses,
and carried out between the snarling teeth of the powers of
nature for weeks and months at a stretch, had never come
home to her. Life, death, risk, a responsibility, more direct
and pressing than almost any other in the world; she had
realised none of these. She did not realise them now but her
awe of the inanimate presence towering above her extended
itself in some measure to her suitor – for she now believed
him to be that – and gave him a more important place in
her mind.

The man who designed the figurehead of the *Sirius* had
been proud of his work. He had set the ruler of the dog-star
with his arms folded across his broad breast that would meet
the forefront onslaught of the seas, his head thrown back
into a crown of stars. Below the scroll work from which
his loins rose was a couchant greyhound.

They went up the gangway and stood on deck. Father
and daughter looked round rather shyly.

'Come below,' said Baird, leading the way down the
companion from which the smell of new paint was mingling
with the salt air.

There had been a great scrub-out on the foregoing day
and all traces of workmen had vanished. They descended
into the mellow darkness and Christina, who had not
dreamed that a ship could feel so solid underfoot, let
her wondering eyes roam over the new red Utrecht velvet
and rich brown teak of the saloon. No detail of comfort
was lacking; an ornamental clock presented to Baird in
Australia was screwed above the moulded sideboard and
a gold embroidered Indian shawl had been laid as a cloth
over the polished dining-table. The skipper had put a few
of his possessions about the opulent upholstery of his own

cabin to add to the effect he desired. Christina looked
curiously at the bunk covered with a fur rug. She had
supposed that all sailors slept in hammocks.

There were a couple of bottles of good sherry awaiting
the guests and a cake for Christina. She admired the neat
way he had cut it and set it out with the glasses on the
costly Oriental fabric.

'You must come back again when I'm living on board
and have a steward to wait on you,' said he, as he poured
out the wine, 'I shall be here a while before we sail.'

'No use paying for lodgings when you've such a place
as this,' observed Mill.

'And what do *you* think of it, Miss?'

'It's not very like what I expected.'

'Better or worse – eh?'

'Oh, far better!' said Christina, growing a little pink.

Baird leaned back in his chair and looked at her from
under his thick, short eyelashes. He laughed loudly.
Her timidity pleased him and he was gratified by her
approval.

'Did you think I berthed in the fo'c'sle?' he exclaimed.
She turned scarlet, embarrassed by his laugh and the
unfamiliar words.

'Oh, no offence meant,' he said quickly, alarmed lest
he should have estranged her. 'I've no business to use
sailors' talk to a lady. I'm forgetting my manners and I
expect I've got too proud to remember them because I've
superintended all this myself. I've had a free hand and no
expense spared.'

The excellent sherry had stirred up Lummie's natural
infelicity of speech.

'You're a silly girl, Christina,' said he, leaning across
the table. 'Here we are, entertained by the Captain and
favoured with a sight of his ship. You should know better
than to be so silly.'

Though he did not speak with real harshness, her lips
trembled. Baird was a past master, when he liked, in
representing himself agreeably.

'I like a lady to *be* a lady,' he said, looking very straight
at Mill, 'and I'm all with Miss Christina, and that's the

truth, Sir. My uncle was at sea and my aunt often went with him but I've heard him say that he never allowed a nautical word at table so long as she was there. You'll excuse my freedom, but I'd take Miss Christina's taste before anyone else's, if I may say so.'

It was Lummie's turn to be out of countenance and he was much impressed. He had not known in the least what he was blaming his daughter for; he had only gathered that the skipper was apologising for something and he had taken for granted that it was unnecessary. He murmured in a propitiating way. Christina's heart beat. He was a wonderful man, their host. For all her set ways, she had no conceit and she was astonished to find that he could value her opinion so highly. She thought of it a good deal and after she got home she stayed some time in her room in the dusk considering the little incident as if it had happened to somebody else.

When Baird had seen his guests home he returned to the ship and he also sat thinking in the saloon. Lummie had not drunk much sherry and the captain poured out and emptied glass after glass. He was no drinker, as drinkers went in those days, but the wine helped to develop the satisfaction in him.

He now believed that Christina would accept him and he was pleased with the way he had turned her little embarrassment to account; it was one of those lucky strokes that he made sometimes. He twirled the wineglass in his fingers and remembered how Mill's jaw had dropped as he rounded on him and the honest freedom of his own words – just what was wanted to take the fancy of a bread and butter Miss. How could she know that any man might deal anyhow with the like of her father? Some of his own dealing with those who got in his way – or who thought they were going to – came back to him pleasantly. How well he went down with his fellow creatures! He was by no means the sea-bully dear to fiction, yet those to whom he was most acceptable were apt to be landsmen. There was little need on land for the rough side of himself to compel the attention he wished to have in the world, for he realised very well that his virile appeal disposed it in his favour.

That evening Ann Wishart had a description of the visit to the *Sirius* with its main points left out. Though Christina had been wont to discuss every word spoken by Aeneas Halket with her, she said little about Baird. Nor could Ann, who was well versed in the gossip of the place and had been asked when the wedding at Lummie Mill's was to be, get anything from her. It was this silence on Christina's part which led to the opening of her father's eyes.

Lummie had seen nothing in the skipper but a desirable acquaintance with whom to interchange the small amenities he loved. He was really sorry the time was coming when Baird would go to sea again and be no more at hand to stroll with him on the links when the Bank of Angus was shut. He had never considered him in relation to his daughter.

Ann had long burned with curiosity. Her contempt for sailors had abated where Baird was concerned. He had cut a great figure in the town and the firm of Torrie, Gibson and Hunter, whose man he was, took a high place in the world of commercial shipping. Whether he went to sea again after his next voyage or whether, as rumour had it, he would retire, she could imagine Christina installed in one of those new houses – some of which had even carriage drives – and taking a position to match her setting.

It was Ann's habit to attend, personally, to the hearth of Mill's study. The evening had grown chilly at sundown and she found him with his slippered feet on the fender. The fire lacked nothing but she began to use the poker.

Mill was always ready for a word with anybody.

'We've had a visit to Captain Baird's ship,' he began.

'Aye, I kent ye was there. I could believe it was a grand ship.'

'Cake and wine for us. Nothing spared.'

She tossed her head.

'I wid believe that too. He'd be thinkin' naething guid eneuch for Miss Christina.'

'Yes, Oh yes,' said Lummie with his little gratified squeak. 'He's a very polite man, the Captain.'

She could almost have choked him for his innocence.

'He's lucky', she observed, grimly.

'Quite, quite. He had all the money he required for the

furnishing. A fine rug on his bed too; I forget the name of
the fur though he told me he'd got it in a present when he
was in America.'

Ann saw that a bombshell was needed, but she was a
woman of action.

'And ye'll be no sparin' expense yersel', I doot, for the
weddin'.'

'The wedding—?'

He looked up at the tight spare figure and at length her
meaning dawned on him.

'Oh dear me,' he exclaimed, 'dear, dear me! But
surely—'

'Aw—' breathed Ann, slowly, closing her eyes and
drawing her lips back from her prominent gums in a
smile of ineffable knowledge, 'it's easy seen—'

'But—' He began again.

'I'll need tae be gangin',' she broke in. 'The roast's on
the jack and Eliza's awa' oot.'

It was two days after this that Baird formally asked Mill
for permission to pay his addresses to Christina and that
Mill replied, 'Of course, of course,' with the responsiveness
of a door bell to the hand of a caller. A small seizure of
politeness had ripped the words from him; also there was
an idea at the back of his mind that should he wish to do
so, he could still direct Christina to refuse before there
was time for a proposal. But Baird, thanking him warmly
for his consent departed, leaving him a good deal fussed.
As the skipper walked upstairs without further ado and
asked Christina to marry him there was no opportunity
for parental advice.

Mill stood bewildered below. He had expected to hear
the front door shut; what he did hear was the sound of
Baird's voice in the drawingroom above. He had not realised
enough to go up and protest against this unauthorised haste,
nor was he really certain of which way he wished the matter
to turn.

While Baird declared his love, Christina was standing
with her back to the window almost as much disturbed as
her father, but getting over it as the scene she had been
led to look on as a possibility enacted itself. Andrew Baird

had never made an honourable proposal to a woman in his life, and to anyone understanding the whole truth about the situation, there might have been a lurking humour in the fact that the skipper, knowing as little about it as the girl did, conceived the same procedure to be necessary. He went down on one knee and the sight hypnotised the spectator that was in Christina. Her vision was coming true and it was a wonderful thing to realise that she was, indeed, playing a part in the romantic drama, suspected, shadowed, that lay outside her placid life. It was a sense of the fitness of things which made her turn away and say in her quiet voice, 'It is very kind of you but I must take a day or two to think about it.'

She had turned it over in her mind a good deal in the last week. She had not liked to speak of it to her father, feeling that it was not her place to suggest such a thing as a love affair. Only to Ann, had she ever hinted the possibility of marriage and that in a remote disembodied manner.

'Mr Mill has given me his word he will consent. All I need now is for you to say you'll take me,' said Baird.

A wave of relief went over her to think there was no necessity to broach the subject to her father.

'You mustn't say "no",' said Baird. 'You won't do that.'

She had stepped back and he caught her hand. It lay in his like something inanimate. She was a little flustered by the strong grip but the sensation of his taking her into the more important half of womankind obsessed her. He made as though to draw her to him but the startled look that came into her eyes caused him to refrain. He must risk nothing, and he imagined that all honest women saw fit to behave in the same way at first whatever they might do afterwards. Of course she was acting a comedy. In a measure he was quite right, for she was absorbed in the part that circumstances had given her; yet he had never been further from understanding her than at that moment.

'You'll make up your mind the right way tomorrow,' said he. 'I shall come back the next day and you won't refuse. Mind, I have your father's word that he'll consent.'

'Oh, I am quite pleased,' faltered she.

Lummie, who had recovered his wits, opened the door and stood looking at them.

Baird was at a loss for a minute. There was a flat silence. At times, the most simple people do the right thing from sheer simplicity and it was Christina who gave the death-blow to the uncomfortable moment.

'Goodbye, Captain Baird,' she said, putting out her hand again. Baird laid hold of it as though it had been a tow-rope and then left the room.

'I'll be back the day after tomorrow,' he said again as he went.

'What's that he was saying about the day after tomorrow?' enquired Mill, after he had gone.

'He said he was coming back, Papa.'

'I suppose he was telling you some nonsense about being in love with you?'

Though he had no real objection to the engagement and though, since his enlightenment by Ann, he was inclined to think well of it, this seemed to him the legitimate way of approaching the subject. It was the custom of his time.

'He was asking me to marry him.'

'And what did you say to it, Christina?'

'I said I would think about it.'

Her calm lack of enthusiasm at once revealed his true wishes to him.

'You might be throwing away a good chance. D'ye like him, Christina?'

'Yes, I like him well enough.'

'You might do worse. My bit of money – it's more than you might think too – will go to you and with what he makes, you'll be well set up. Torrie, Gibson and Hunter are not likely to let him go.'

There was no word about love from either of them. To Mill, love meant the bygone shadow of a slight thing and Christina took it to be identical with marriage. But she was proud to be chosen by Baird and the remembrance of his championship on board the *Sirius* was a secret pleasure, something like the picture of St Cecilia had once been. She was happy and two thoughts were mixed in her mind in an

agreeable manner; that of Baird on one knee and the words
of her acquaintance with the red and green brushes. She
had said, 'Ye should get a man that'll gie ye a sicht o' the
world.'

The engagement rolled over the house like an incoming
tide. Mill talked about nothing else, Christina said little,
but Ann made up for her lack of words with the plenitude
of her own. The girl was lost in the effort of realising
her new circumstances. She had no misgivings about
the changes which must come to all her ways of life.
Having taken prosperity for granted in the placidity of
home, lacking nothing, disturbed by nothing, at ease
and contented for nearly twenty-seven years, she could
not imagine that fortune could play her false; anything
so outrageous could never happen. She did not reassure
herself, having no need of reassurance. She was so young
in some ways, so old in others, having nothing of the high
spirits of youth, none of its rebellions or aspirations but
all and more than its inexperience. The only progressive
stir that had ever touched her had been set going by the
woman with the brooms.

And now, she enjoyed her added importance. Ann, once
the engagement was a fact, went over to the captain, horse
and foot, for she admired him as an adjunct to the family.
To Christina, he was mainly a guarantee of security and
consideration from whose protection she would look tran-
quilly on the novelties of a world she did not know.

The town could hardly believe its ears when it heard that
Baird was to take his bride with him on the approaching
voyage and that they were to be married on the day they
sailed. It had cost him a deal of talking to get this decided
but he was a good talker and Mill gave in after a half-hearted
resistance. Time was getting on, there were settlements to be
made and the wedding outfit to be completed. There would
be little space for a honeymoon. Baird put it to Mill that it
would be a hard case for a man to leave his new-made wife
and go off at once on an Australian voyage. There was every
comfort on board the *Sirius* and his last steward, who was
signing on again, had a daughter who could be engaged and
taken with them to wait on the captain's wife. At Adelaide,

where he had a large acquaintance, Christina would be a
woman of standing. How often she had listened to his
big accounts of the fine town and gay company and the
hospitable houses of the shipowners and their friends. She
told herself that she would see all this from her vantage point
behind her travelled husband. And, before all, was she not
herself – Christina – safe and hedged by the consideration of
those around her from the rough things that might happen
to the less favoured? And now that she had been inside
a ship, and felt how big and solid it was, she could well
believe what Baird had said about its safety.

Lummie did not write the news to his sister Isabella until
the matter was settled in detail; he did not know how far
she would approve the notion of Christina being whisked
off to such a distance. But he had no mind to be in the
line of fire between Isabella and the skipper so he waited
till the wedding day was settled and the matter clinched by
publicity before writing to her himself or letting Christina do
so. Things went quickly where Andrew Baird was concerned
so it was a week after that 'day after tomorrow' when he
returned for his answer that Mrs Halket learned of the
engagement. Had Lummie seen her lay down his letter
he would have been reassured. She looked out of her
window on to the unpretentious street – so sad a contrast
to Gayfield Square – and a slow smile crept to her lips. She
saw herself presiding over the house in the Bow Butts; even,
at last, with Ann Wishart. It was for the best for everybody.
Christina was nearly twenty-seven and though Isabella had
once fancied that her stepson was attracted by her, she had
evidently been mistaken, for Aeneas, whose business was
now keeping him a good deal abroad, had made no special
effort to see the girl when he came home. She wrote to
congratulate her niece and suggested that she should help
her to get her wedding clothes. The stars in their courses
fought for Baird, as they do for most thrusters.

Though the skipper's courtship had been begun for a
variety of reasons, many of which had little to do with love,
his fancy, in some measure, had been caught. He did not
want a wife with a vivid personality who might be likely to
get into mischief whilst he was at sea; he wanted a woman

a little superior to himself socially. He came of a family whose members were no rovers at heart, and who, though they had one seaman among them, were far from pleased by the production of a second. He had flown in their faces by his choice of a profession but there was enough of the hereditary smug instinct of worldly advancement in him to make him desire a wife who dressed richly and had the air of being apart from the herd of everyday. Christina was an only child, daughter of a man who had something to leave. And, beyond that, her intense femininity pleased him, the rustle of her silk skirt, the thin shoe on her pointed foot; he admired her white fingers too as Aeneas had done, but not with the same knowledge. He liked them to be white because they looked as if they did not work but the unusual beauty of their shape was a subtlety beyond him. She was not clever or accomplished but men married their wives for convenience mainly, and were lucky if they got any attraction thrown in. He found enough of that in Christina to make a voyage with her pleasant while the novelty lasted; and when he brought her home and settled her in a handsome house he would not be likely to take her to sea again and he would be able to live his own life, unmolested on one side of the world and a very reputable one on the other. And there would be a good deal less of the latter than of the former.

He had had a universal success with the women he had admired and he would have been much surprised if Christina had rejected him. No doubt she was glad enough to get away from her old ninny of a father, he told himself, though to see her stiff ways with a lover she did not wish you to suppose it. He smiled, thinking of her pretences; he would soon knock them out of her and she would like him all the better for it. In any case he would weary of her sooner or later but the advantages which had influenced him would still be left. And meantime he liked her well enough.

Spring is late in Scotland, but this year it arrived unusually early, and, on Christina's wedding day, it was bright and the sun warm. The town was hugely interested in the event and Lummie's guests were dressed in their best. The ceremony would take place in the drawing room and in the dining room below the table was laid for wedding 'breakfast'.

A crowd of the humbler townsfolk were gathered in the Bow Butts, agog to see the company arriving, though the real sight would be when Captain Baird and his bride drove down to the harbour from which the *Sirius* – now covered with bunting – would be tugged out to sea. Inside the house Mrs Halket and Ann, united for once, attired Christina in the white finery and bridal wreath which had cost them so much thought.

Christina herself was calm and smiling. As the couple stood before the minister she thought again of the woman on the links; she would have liked to be able to tell her that she was taking her advice. She sat through the wedding feast listening to the speeches and healths and congratulations and heard her husband assuring his friends that this was the happiest day of his life. Baird liked wine as much as anyone but he knew that he had to keep his head clear and get out to sea triumphantly in the face of half the town and he drank little; the two distant relations of the bride, an elderly brother and sister, were very favourably impressed by him.

'You have got a fine man,' said the old lady. 'See that you value him, my dear. Such a chance never came my way.'

Christina wondered if this was the happiest day of her life and she supposed it was. She was sorry to leave home and her father and she wished Ann were coming with her. For one minute fear of the unknown sprang up in her – only for one minute. Surely she had got the strongest protector anyone could desire and he loved her. Some day, when he was away at sea she would come home again and stay in the familiar house. She could not feel she was leaving for good and all.

By four o'clock the Bow Butts was crowded again, for the open carriage, hired for the occasion, was at the gate; the bridegroom had insisted that grey horses were to be got somehow, and a very creditable pair were produced. There was a bunch of white ribbons on the whip, and the boy who came in to clean the knives had tied an old shoe to the axle above which they sat. When they started the crowd hurried after them to the harbour.

Ferry Street was thick with people: the ships' chandlers

and other small provision merchants left their shops to take care of themselves whilst they made for the quay. Half way down the street, where the model of a sailing ship projected from the upper storey a knot of sailors and fishermen raised a shout as the carriage passed which was taken up further on. Women stood in their doors looking after it, keeping their mouths open and their eyes screwed up as all inhabitants of east coast Scottish towns seem to do at the passage of anything arresting. The younger women followed their neighbours to see the end of the show and the old ones peeping round the sides of their doorways enchange comments with each other.

'Aye, Miss Lummie Mill,' said one. 'She's a denty thing tae be awa' till Austrailly wi' a caird like yon.'

'Ah, I mind her when she was a wee thing wi' a tow-heid,' said another.

'What'll Lummie dae the noo, puir stock? He'll hae tae get a wife, himsel'!'

'Fie! – *him*? Wha'd hae Lummie?'

'No me!' exclaimed a woman over eighty. 'Baird's the lad I'd tak.'

Meanwhile the couple stood on the quay. The *Sirius* lay in the strait with the tug in attendance.

To the new-made wife of the Captain the ship looked smaller than when she had stared up at her bows a few weeks ago. Mill and his sister and the guests who were arriving in twos and threes, pressed round them and spectators from the town grew in number every minute. One of the *Sirius*'s boats was rising and falling almost imperceptibly with the scarcely moving water at the foot of the landing steps; now and then a ripple from nowhere made little licking sounds about the steps fringed with fine pieces of weed. Across the watermouth below the fishing village and divided from there by the River Esk merging itself in the salt water estuary, the reflections of the stone houses and whitewashed walls with the little kirk up the rising ground were mirrored upside down.

Ann Wishart was sniffling and Lummie's nervous hilarity had stopped. Baird took off his hat and held out his hand to his father-in-law; people crowded about him, wishing him prosperity and health and wealth and everything they could think of.

Christina bade goodbye to Mrs Halket and Ann and, almost for the first time in her life, put her arms around her father's neck. The tears were in her eyes. She could hardly see as Baird handed her down the steps and into the boat where a red cushion awaited her. Then they were sliding along the surface of the oily water.

The party ashore watched them reach the ship and stand on deck together, a dark figure and a light one with a floating veil. The boat ran up the davits.

The sound of voices and a shouted order or two came across and in a few minutes the tug drew into line ahead of the ship and the centre of the half submerged tow-rope rose to form a taut line with the ends; there was a churning of water and they were moving. Baird had disappeared and the cheer from the quay came to Christina over the sound of thrashing paddles. Looking back, she could distinguish for a long time above the waving handkerchiefs her father's tall hat held high over his head.

She had no suspicion of its celebrity.

V

IT WAS ON the second afternoon since they had sailed that Christina Baird sat in the shelter of the midshiphouse, her eyes on the sullen horizon of grey water between which and herself there burst out an occasional bar of ragged white; morning had dawned to a falling glass that by midday had dropped and was dropping lower and lower. She was very cold in spite of her thick cloak; but though they were beginning to roll a good deal she had not felt seasick. Like many tenderly nurtured people she was proving a good sailor. But the growing instability of the deck and the sudden periodical shocks that were going through the *Sirius* in answer to some unseen force were but one of her troubles. A loneliness and a lostness such as she had never dreamed of in her sheltered life were on her. She would catch her breath and tears would rise at the thought of the house she had left only the day before yesterday; of Ann in her safe, warm kitchen and her father with his newspaper in the evenings.

She had seen nothing of Baird all day and she knew him to be busied with the mysteries of his profession. For this she was deeply grateful. It had been one of his favourite theories that all women were alike and Christina's terrified recoil from his love-making was proving him to be wrong. He was exasperated by her and had sworn at her in his contemptuous wrath and to the girl, who had never heard a word of profanity nearer than a distant corner of a street, the mildest oath seemed a branding crime. He had never supposed such a woman to exist and today he had not so much as inquired whether she were sick or well, dry or drenched, or whether she had found a corner to protect her from the seas that were getting up in the chill of the shifting grey world around them. He knew by the barometer and the look of things that he might soon have his hands full. He would be glad to forget her; idiot that she was. He had come to no meal and she had tried to eat the food the steward brought her as she sat alone with Baird's empty chair screwed to the floor at the other side of the saloon table. The steward had found her a cloak and a sheltered corner. He was a kind man and had told her that the Captain would soon be along to look after her and that the first days out were always busy ones with him. She had thanked him faintly, understanding his desire to be kind; but Baird's absence was welcome; she found his anger and his love-making equally dreadful. The girl who was her maid watched her, wondering, from the head of the companion. She had been born by the sea and lived among its followers and the voyage was much to her taste. She pitied the young lady down whose cheek she had more than once seen the homesick tears drip in the forty-eight hours they had been out. Both she and her father had asked her if she would not be better in her cabin and had been answered by a shake of the head.

At sunset, a bank of cloud low in the south-east was feeling its way along the horizon and the sun's vanishing presence could be guessed rather than seen through the thickness that invaded the west. They had begun to pitch and the shocks under Christina's feet were coming at shorter intervals; each one brought a dull, thudding bang that spent itself in the white line of stinging foam that drove, hissing, to starboard from under the ship. Suddenly a splash of water leaped over the side, spouting like a fountain, and in spite of her preoccupation an acute start of dismay took her. There was another bang and a seething hiss; a scream of wind flew somewhere overhead. She was aware that her feet were drenched. She gripped the arms of her chair and tried to get up. But the deck rose in front of her and she sat down, her eyes staring. It was getting dark and through the livid colour that had fallen on the world Baird came tramping round on her. He was in oilskins and looked unfamiliar and uncouth with the wet shining on him. Before she could speak he had snatched her arm and was dragging her from her seat. She clung to him frantically as the deck rose again.

'What are you doing here?' he shouted. 'Do you think I'm going to put down a boat for every fool that's whipped overboard? Get down, I tell you! You'll be glad enough to be in your bunk in an hour or two.'

There was a whirling rose in the rigging as he held her at the top of the companion and shouted for the steward. The man came up and he thrust her into his arms, cursing both him and his daughter for leaving her so long on deck. The girl and her father, holding to everything they could reach, supported Christina till they got her below and into her cabin. The glass was still dropping.

'See and get her beddit, Maggie, and I'll awa' and seek a drappie whisky till her,' said the steward.

Maggie took off Christina's dress and her soaked stockings and covered her with blankets in her berth. Her arm ached from Baird's grip and she was frightened and dazed by his rough grasp and angry words; but now the physical fear that grew on her as they went into the weather that came to meet them was obliterating everything else.

March had come in and gone out like a lamb and April had worn a face that was falsely bright. That lying spring month was to be paid for her lies and the North Sea was going to help to pay her.

As the hours went by the gale increased and in the lulls of its unholy yelling, Christina could hear the scudding of bare feet above and a stir that made her heart sink. She did not know what was happening – perhaps they were going down – perhaps they were getting out the boats; she lay cowering, using all her strength not to be thrown on the floor. She had told Maggie to leave her, but since Maggie had gone, every moment was laden with greater dread. She could distinguish occasional wafts of men's shouting and once she heard Baird's voice of brass above the bewilderment of banging and swinging. One or two crashes of crockery came to her ears. The cabin was a large one, as the cabins of sailing ships went, but they were battened down now, and closed ports let in little air. The rocking and plunging grew more and more violent and every moveable object began to slide across the drugget, to be shot back again and merged with others till a fresh pitch scattered the wedge anew. She lay clinging to the bracket of a little shelf beside her. Had she been seasick she would have suffered less, mentally, but she had not even a headache to take her thoughts from the anguish of fear.

At eight o'clock Maggie wormed and thrust her way through the door and stood precariously over her with a metal bowl containing a piece of toast.

'A was bringing ye a puckle soup,' she was saying into her ear, 'but it wadna bide intill the bowl. It was awa' afore A could win till ye.'

'Stay with me,' begged Christina, 'Don't go away and leave me.'

The girl sat down on the floor holding onto the edge of the bunk, for she could hardly stand, but she managed to secure Christina's little trunk in a corner so that it should not roll on the top of them. She wondered what was the matter with the lady who seemed in no danger of seasickness.

'Ye're no feared are ye, Mistress Baird?' she enquired at last.

'Oh, I am, I am.'

'But ye'll no need to fleg yersel'.' The sea's a bittie coorse, whiles, but ye need na mak' ado about that. A'm no feared, ye see.'

'Is that true? Are you not?' whispered Christina.

'Na, na.'

Maggie spoke stoutly but she was not really happy; she had never been on a long voyage, though she had spent some hours at a time on fishing smacks. She had hailed the notion of going all the way to Australia with the Captain's lady. But such noise of wind and water awed her and all the medley of sounds that go on in a windjammer in bad weather were increasing with every plunge. To Christina there was no awe; the imminent heartbreaking fear of death was with her and nothing else. She could scarcely distinguish one thing from another. All was merged into the blackness of terror. Cries like the voices of dying fiends, twanged and battled in the rigging. The ship groaned and creaked. Sometimes she seemed to sink as though she must long since have left the surface of the ocean under the thuds and blows that assailed her. The scudding of feet above Christina's head would be swallowed by the roar that enveloped everything.

The two young women spoke no more as the hours dragged by. They could not have heard each other's voices. In one of their dizzying plunges their lamp went out and the dark closed in on them. Towards the small hours of the morning at a turn of the wind, the seas began to strike the ship's bell and spasms of ringing were sharp above the pandemonium of the storm and the pounding and rattling as the water thrashed the deck. Then, in the midst of it all the malign elements pounced on them, a hundred and a thousandfold strong, and side by side, they clung together in what seemed to them to be the very breaking up of the universe. What they had gone through was as nothing compared to what swooped upon them before dawn of that chill April morning; now they were tossed as to the skies, now cast down to bottomlessness. In the dark they were blind and their hearing grew more acute for the different sounds contending together. It seemed to their quickened ears that nothing could survive and no plank hold. The *Sirius* was thrown, bashed, hurled in the trough

of the seas. There were no more scudding feet. Only the
ship's bell punctuating chaos with its crazy and tormented
tongue.

Just before sunrise the wind dropped and the sea began
to go down.

In the pale light Maggie went out to see what remained
to be seen after such a night; she was able to stand now and
she made her way to the saloon where she found her father
setting out coffee for Captain Baird. She took a cupful for
Christina and having coaxed her to swallow it, she set to
work to clear the cabin of the things strewn about it, for
the slow swell that the sea's fury had left behind did not
hinder her movements much.

When she came back from her own meal she brought
news of the night's damage. They had lost two boats; the
side of the galley was stove in and the second mate had
been dashed against the angle of a locker and his leg was
broken. They were going to put in to Leith that night.

'Aye, the Captain's no very pleased tae be gangin' in,'
said Maggie, 'but ye ken yon lad's mither – she's a widdy
that was married upon Maister Torrie, Martinmas last –
wad gar her man skirl gin aucht gae'd wrang wi' him. Syne
it wadna dae tae let him want the doctor.'

There was no persuading her mistress to go on deck now.
Christina lay, thankful to be quiet. She had washed her
tearstained face and Maggie had brushed her hair. Too
tired to give way to grief, she asked nothing of the girl
but that she would stay beside her.

A drizzling rain had come on that was sprinkling the
face of the quieted sea and in the watery light showing
through the port she fell into the dreamless dead sleep of
exhaustion. At last her maid stole quietly to her side and,
after listening to her regular breathing, went on tiptoe out
of the cabin. When she looked in again all was still. In the
afternoon she returned with food and laid her hand on her
to wake her; Christina waved her away.

'Let me sleep,' she murmured.

'I'd no let onybody disturb ye till ye cry on me,'
said Maggie who was longing for repose on her own
account.

'Oh yes – thank you,' sighed Christina, turning over into the oblivion from which she had scarcely emerged.

It was almost dark when the fathomless sleep of utter fatigue began to wear thin, like a garment, and Christina awoke with a start. She could not imagine where she was. Then, drop by drop, realisation came back in such a tumult that it was a few moments before she became aware that they were not moving. The cabin floor was as still as pavement. What new terror was this? She sat up, her hands pressed together. There was a sound of hammering that echoed in a curious way as though flung across a wide space of silence. Everything else was quiet except for an occasional casual voice. There was that blank dumb suggestion of suspended animation round her which pervades the cabin of a stationary ship. Her heart leaped in her and she sprang to the port hole. They were lying in Leith Dock.

Baird had decided that the second mate must be landed and for the better accomplishment of this they lay alongside the wharf where Torrie Gibson and Hunter had their warehouses and offices. He had gone ashore to find the firm's Edinburgh agent and send word to Torrie of his stepson's mishap; also he meant to get extra help and work all night on the repairing begun already on board so as to get out, if possible, on the next afternoon's tide. He would have to see the young fellow disposed where he could be attended to and that might take time. There was a black look on Baird's face. He was exasperated by the delay, by the damage to the ship, by the clumsiness of Torrie's stepson who had been ass enough to get himself injured at the very start of the voyage and must be replaced; by the woman he had neither seen nor heard of since he had thrust her into the steward's arms at the head of the companion.

What kind of life was he going to have with such a bargain as he had saddled himself with? He had imagined that he had done well for himself and her money was all right of course but now he had to sail all the way to Australia and back with a woman who seemed to be no more than a useless encumbrance, who had repulsed his every advance to her with sulks and tears. Thank God, he could leave her ashore once they were at home again. She was not worth troubling about and there were plenty of women where they were going who were. Let her stay in her cabin and sulk to her heart's content. He thrust her out of his mind; he had other things to do than bother about her. He would have a square meal ashore that would do him good after the strain and racket of the last twenty-four hours.

Christina stole to the door and opened it. All was quiet. She had lain down half-dressed that morning but she went back for her cloak and, wrapping herself in it, crept up the companion steps and peered round. A steady rain was falling and making pools of mud on the wharf. In the dim, lowering light she could see that the gangway was down. She stood holding her breath. Supposing—!

She turned and went down to her cabin, shaking all over and trying to calm herself – here – now – was a chance! She did not know how soon Maggie might come back. Maggie was a good, kind girl—

She dressed herself as quickly as she could with her trembling fingers. For the first time in her life she was nerving herself for an effort. Terror can do strange things. Her fears sprang upon her like leaping dogs but she held them down with all her force. Anything that could happen to her must be better than those desperate experiences and she might have to live through others of the same sort. The idea nerved her. She put all her money in her pocket and drew her cloak more closely around her.

She could never afterwards remember how she got on deck. That shutting of the door behind her began a blank of sickening apprehension, but she knew that her husband would be away, from something Maggie had said, and she saw that though there were men moving about the fore part of the ship, the short distance between them and her goal was empty. She would have waited till it was quite dark but for Maggie's possible appearance at any minute. There were a few scattered figures a little way along the quay and she had sense to know that she must not run while they were anywhere in sight. If she kept her head and went slowly casual loiterers might pay her nothing but a passing heed; the terror that had been able to rouse her to action made her take any risk sooner than delay for a moment; there was not only the voyage across the world but its return journey on that frightful sea.

She slipped like a shadow to the gangway and crossed it, too terrified to send a glance towards the fo'c'sle where the hammering was going on.

In the darkness of a shed she stood to regain her dazed wits. She was prepared to run if she was observed till she fell dead. But hammering went on and the voices in the fo'c'sle. She was crying from the reaction of her effort but she checked her tears and began to slip like a hunted cat among the shanties and wood piles and varied buildings in the direction of the lighted houses. She did not know where she was going except that it was inland, away from the ship.

When she emerged into a wide cobble-stoned place her fears, dulled for a space by her success, beset her again. But the sparse oil lamps, blurred by the wet, threw so little light that she was swallowed up by the grey of the east-coast evening. Fear of the sea and fear of discovery abating, she began to fear her own lostness in this world of dark, grimy little streets and rough-looking strangers.

She knew that she must speak to somebody if she was to find her way to Edinburgh, for it was her Aunt Halket's house that she was counting on for a refuge. It was a desperate policy for she was ignorant of whether Baird knew Mrs Halket's address. She thought he did not. But, once behind its walls, no power should drag her to the ship again. Surely, surely there would be someone who would pity her and get her home. And Andrew Baird would be gone – far on the other side of the world.

The rain came down, increasing from a steady fall to a deluge. The causeys ran like rivers and the onslaught of drops beat up from the cobbles and chilled her feet through her thin boots. Her cloak was sopped and her ankles icy cold; her voluminous skirt, which she tried to hold up, grew heavy with the leaden wet. She stopped, dismayed, by a little house at whose firelit window, about the height of her elbow from the ground, there was the dark outline of a figure staring at her from the inner side

of the pane. Then it was gone and the window all light.
Some one opened the door, beckoning. There was a step
down from its threshold and she nearly stumbled in as a
kindly hand drew her in.

'Lordsakes!' a small, square woman was saying. 'Sic a
night for a leddy to be oot! Come in-by to the fire. Aw
dear – aye, sic a nicht!'

The exclamations were due to the sight of Christina's
fine poplin skirt bordered with grimy mud.

She led her to the fire and a man in a deal chair in front
of it pulled aside to give her room, looking at her with
astonishment, pipe in hand.

She started back. It seemed to her distracted mind and
overstrained nerves that she must have reached the end of
her journey and landed amongst savages. The man was
quite black.

The square woman laughed.

'Na, na, ye need'na be feared!' she exclaimed, clapping
her protectingly on the shoulder, 'He'll no hurt ye. He's
the sweep, ye ken. Sit doon, puir thing, and I'll mak' ye
a cuppie tea.'

'You're so kind,' said Christina, faintly, 'and I've lost
my way.'

She sat down and warmed her feet, water dripping from
her on to the hearthstone. The woman took a kettle and
went into the scullery. A clock ticked steadily and after a
little it wheezed and struck eight.

'And whaur are ye for?' asked the sweep, who had not
yet spoken.

'I want to go to Edinburgh. My aunt lives there,' replied
Christina, her eyes filling again.

'Dod, ye'll no can walk.'

'No, I can't. If I could only hire a carriage! Do you think
I could get one anywhere? I've got a lot of money?' she
added, naively.

At such an unusual statement the woman came out of
the scullery. Husband and wife considered her from head
to foot.

'Ye'd maybe get a machine from the Black Horse,' said
the wife, recovering first.

The sweep remained speechless. Never had he met anybody who made such a claim.

'I will give you ten shillings if you will get me a carriage that I can go to Edinburgh in.'

There was another awed silence. The woman's kind heart had made her take in this dripping bird of passage but her thrifty mind must have its turn now.

'Awa wi' ye, Geordie, to the Black Horse!' she exclaimed, briskly.

He hesitated, got up and took his hat from a peg. As he opened the door the rain drove in. A gleam of humour came into his eye.

'Aweel, A'm needin' a wash,' said he as he stepped out.

Christina sipped her tea nervously, for now that the prospect had improved, she was in an agony to get on. She was determined not to say she had come from the ship, lest some rumour of her flight should reach the dock and it was not easy to evade the woman's questions. She did not know how far inland she had come. It seemed like miles. The rain had almost stopped when the immense shadow of a rickety hood darkened the window and the sweep, whose face was beginning to look like the map of a hilly country, came back with it.

She thanked the couple profusely and, having produced a ten-shilling bit from her purse, climbed in and shrank back as far as she could into the recesses of her new-found shelter.

'Whaur'll she be gangin' till?' asked the driver of the sweep, as Christina did not speak.

'Oh, please tell him 41 Niven Street,' she said, collecting her wits.

'I dinna ken whaur that'll be,' said the driver, 'Will't be i' the Auld Toon?'

'It's by Barbados Place, aside the Kirk,' said the sweep. 'Noo then, awa ye go.' They trotted slowly away.

Christina was very cold in spite of the hot tea she had swallowed and by the time they had traversed interminally through the wretched evening and were getting into the Edinburgh streets she was aching from the jolting over

ill-kept roads. At the end of the journey she got out feasting
her eyes on the sanctuary of a familiar place and rang the
bell. The door opened, but where she had expected to
meet her aunt's maid-servant she found Aeneas Halket.

The overwhelming surprise upset what composure she
had gained in her solitary drive and she almost thrust
herself against him, crying, 'Let me in! Let me in!'

Aeneas was staggered. He drew her into the little hall
and she sat down on a bench, a dishevelled, muddied
figure. Her boots made damp marks on the stone.

'Where have you come from? What's the matter?' he
exclaimed. 'What has happened?'

The driver had left his perch. He was hammering at the
door. He wanted to be paid. Christina sought her purse
and gave it to Aeneas.

'I daren't go out – pay him, please! Give him anything
he asks, only tell him to say nothing about me. Be sure
you tell him to say nothing!' she sobbed.

When the man had gone Aeneas brought her into the
room he had been sitting in. It was warm and lighted.

'Why are you here?' she asked him.

He smiled, thinking the question might have come more
fittingly from himself.

'I came from France yesterday. My stepmother is
away.'

Then he stopped, remembering that Mrs Halket had
gone to Christina's wedding.

'But what is the matter? Where is Captain Baird?'

She turned a shade paler.

'Promise me that you will let nobody know I am here
– *promise!*' She began to cry hysterically.

He was so dumbfounded that no word of pity for her
plight had come from him.

'Don't cry, don't cry like that,' he said at last, putting his
hand on her shoulder. She wept on, but more quietly.

'Tell me,' he said again. 'You *must* tell me what's the
matter. I heard you were to sail with Captain Baird, but
what can have happened? Have they left you behind?'

A step sounded on the pavement outside and she clasped
her hands, her eyes wide, listening. It passed.

'You won't give me up?' she cried, seizing his hand.

'I will not,' he said, 'don't be frightened. Here, I'll take off your wet boots. Mrs Halket's servant will be back directly and she will take care of you. But what has happened? Tell me.'

She had little skill in description at any time but she tried to calm herself and to give an account of the black hours she and Maggie had gone through and how she had fled from the ship, panic-stricken and wild with terror of the sea. He could imagine something of it for the morning news sheets had been full of disasters on the coast.

'And you will not let me send word to your husband?' said Aeneas, when she had stopped. 'He must be in a terrible state of anxiety. He would surely never wish you to go on when he sees how you have suffered.'

'No, no! she cried, hiding her face in her hands, 'he doesn't mind – he is angry with me, and you *promised* you'd let no one take me away—'

'But what can we do?' cried Aeneas, desperately, 'you'll make yourself ill. As soon as she comes back the maid shall light the fire in your aunt's room and you must go to bed and try to sleep. Your hands are like ice. Tomorrow—'

'Help me to get home,' she broke in. 'Tomorrow, as soon as I can, I must go. Say you will help me – oh, I pray you to help me. You don't know what dreadful things I've been through to get away! You will – you will—'

Sobbing shook her from head to foot.

'Yes,' said Aeneas, slowly, after a pause, 'I will.'

He was thankful to hear movement in the house, as the maid returned. Never had he been in such a difficult position.

Afterwards when Christina was between the warmed sheets in Mrs Halket's bed, he sat up long by the burnt-out fire. He had promised Christina to get her away and he had learned from her that the *Sirius* would have repairs done before she could sail; he could only hope fervently that Baird might not get on his wife's track that night. Certainly the only thing he could do was to get her home to her father. Poor Christina, with her sodden hair and her lovely hands – he could not understand how she had come to adventure herself out of her calm environment. What had old Lummie Mill been about to let her take a step that a more experienced woman might have shrunk from and walk out of her trim feminine world into the thunderously male one of a ship? He knew nothing about Baird but that he was a first rate seaman and that Mrs Halket had described him as prosperous and popular. As he looked at her, Aeneas told himself that he had never actually been in love with her; yet she attracted him.

Red-eyed and with her draggled garments limp about her, she still appealed to him. He had heard of her engagement with a dim regret – nothing more; and the state of mind described as 'feeling out of it' had kept him from going to her wedding, though he would be in Scotland about the time it was to take place.

He lay awake, thinking what he should do in the morning and determining to take her to the earliest train and send her off to her father. He would not go with her for he knew that her return in the company of a young man would set the tongues of her neighbours loose. But he could not fail Christina to whom he had promised protection before she would consent to go to rest and if Baird should appear while she was in the house, his own position might be dreadful.

The railway service of those days gave no great choice of north-going trains but there was one leaving Edinburgh at nine o'clock; and as soon as she was dressed and, compelled by him, had eaten some breakfast, he hurried her away. She had never travelled alone in her life and he commended her to the guard who made himself responsible for her on the strength of what Aeneas gave him.

He watched the train depart with relief. Christina thanked him, her lips quivering. He had held her hand at the carriage door till they started – her pretty hand. She had fled from the ship ungloved, which indecorum distressed her, and the servant had found a pair of gloves belonging to Mrs Halket, gloves whose make and texture shocked Aeneas. As the train disappeared he turned back to Niven Street; he had let his own house in Gayfield Square and because his stepmother liked him and bore him no malice for its possession she always gave him a bed in his short visits to Edinburgh.

He walked along rather ruefully for his embarrassments were not yet at an end. He felt himself bound to go to Leith and tell the Captain of the *Sirius* of his wife's safety. There must be a hue and cry on the ship by now. He had promised Christina not to give her up to anyone and had been mercifully spared from all difficulty in keeping his word. The security of her father's house would be hers in a few hours and his responsibility was over; but if Baird were ever to hear of the part he had taken he must hear it from no lips but his own. He wished he had not been dragged into it, but what could he have done? Poor little thing! It was dreadful that such a gentle creature should have escaped like a thief through the rough purlieus of Leith docks. She had a dignity, he thought, which had survived her piteous situation that even the drenching and battering of the elements had left intact. Her face, looking trustfully at him from the railway carriage window followed him as, with a resigned sigh, he let himself out of the door of 41 Niven Street and set off for Leith.

Baird, meanwhile, had lost no time; he had raked up a second mate and a couple of journeymen to help the carpenter. The first mate had orders to see that the work went on with all speed and all night. He himself had not returned till daylight. He was quite sober though he had drunk a good deal and his anger, stirred by his ill-luck, burst out when he heard that Christina was missing. Everyone but the carpenter and the men from the shore was gathered round him as he questioned the crew. Nobody had a word to put forward nor a glimmer of light to throw on how or where Mrs Baird had disappeared till the cook raised his voice.

'Aye,' said he, 'I mind when I was in the *Mary Ann Macginister* lyin' alangside at Greenock, we had a leddy wi's and i' the nicht she just poupit owre the side o—.'

As the torrent with which Baird cut him short abated, the ship's boy was put forward. He had seen a woman on the gangway in the dusk.

'A was settin' down yonder wi' ma piece ahint yon,'

said he, pointing to the fo'c'sle door, 'an' a saw a wifie gang frae the ship. She didna bide lang. She was awa' in a meenit.'

'And why didn't you tell anybody, you damned young limb?'

'A thocht it was Maggie. A didna spier whaur she was gaein'. A thoucht she maybe had a lad waitin' for her.' There was a laugh.

Baird dismissed the crew and went below. He did not for a moment believe that his wife had gone overboard like the lady in the cook's reminiscences, but he was perturbed by the idea of being delayed by the enquiry that would result should anything untoward have befallen her. Maggie had not left the ship last night, her father said. She had looked at Mrs Baird asleep, but seeing that, she had gone to her own bed.

'She was fair done, after sic a nicht,' he said.

Baird sent the steward ashore to find out if any of the customary dock labourers had seen anything of Christina and as he ate a hurried breakfast he listened to the hammering overhead and cursed his luck, thinking of how he might be ready to go to sea that night and yet be held back. He did not want the police to get at the matter but, was the steward unsuccessful, he would have to go to them. He certainly had something to complain of.

Eleven o'clock struck as the man came back. He brought word that a stevedore in the Black Horse bar had picked up a tale of a lady wandering near the dock; a sweep had come to the inn asking for some vehicle to take her to Edinburgh. The steward had seen the driver who spoke of a fair young lady and gave the address at which he had set her down.

It was while Baird was taking it down in his pocket book that a young man came along the quay and stopping by the gangway of the *Sirius* called across to know if Captain Baird was on board.

The skipper was in no mood for strangers; the mention of Niven Street had relieved his mind. He had heard that Mrs Halket lived there. The fool of a girl must have forgotten that her aunt was not to return there at once. He looked with impatience at the youth who was stepping on to his deck without so much as a by-your-leave. He was pale and slim and Baird despised his looks as effeminate.

'What's your business?' he asked.

'My name is Halket,' replied the other without embarrassment, 'and my business is more yours than mine. If we can go where we may speak privately, I can tell it to you.'

Baird was not entirely pleased with his companion's imperturbability but he turned without a word and led the way below. They sat down at the table from which the remains of breakfast had not been cleared.

'I thought you must be anxious about Mrs Baird,' Halket said, 'and I have come to relieve your mind.'

He spoke so simply that the skipper's irritation lessened.

'I am obliged to you,' he said. 'I understand that you know where she is.'

'I do. She is on her way home.'

'Are you sure of that, Mr Halket?'

'I took her to the train myself.'

Baird stared. He had never heard of Aeneas.

'Indeed. And what business had you to do it?'

'I am coming to that, Sir, if you will allow me. And I imagine you will say I did right.'

'We'll see about that.'

'Mrs Baird arrived at my stepmother's door last night. I was never so astonished to see anyone. She was soaked from head to foot and in a terrible state of distress and I brought her in. I could hardly get her calm enough to explain what was wrong. She was nearly mad with terror of the sea and what she had suffered in the storm. The slates had been flying about in Edinburgh and I knew it had been very bad.'

'Pshaw!' exclaimed Baird, drumming his fingers on the table.

'She was almost too exhausted to eat and I could only persuade her to let the maidservant put her to bed by promising I would let nobody know where she was. She was in terror lest she should be compelled to go back to sea – so much so that I feared she would make herself ill.

But I assured her that no man with the least humanity in
him would force her to go back if the sea could bring her
to such a state.'

'You took a good deal on yourself.'

'I did. And I would do it again.'

'And so you shipped her back to her father and now
you come and tell me about it.'

'Exactly,' said Aeneas.

Baird did not move but sat considering him. He had the
makings of wrath in him for the young man's composure
struck him as unsuitable.

'I thought it unfair to you not to let you know that she
is safe,' said Aeneas. 'I have nothing more to say, Sir, and
I must be going.'

He rose as he spoke. Baird sat still, feeling that Halket
should make some apology for what he had done and
realising that there was nothing further from the young
man's thoughts. What really had kept Baird quiet was the
dawning conviction that this meddling fellow had played
into his hands. He was now rid of his bad bargain for two
voyages.

'I must wish you a good morning,' continued Aeneas.
'I have business I must go back to.'

Baird rose.

'Thanks,' he said briskly. 'I see you have meant well;
and I am obliged to you.'

The shock of the amazing apparition of Christina on
her father's doorstep was a couple of days old when
Baird's letter reached Lummie Mill. The fact that his
daughter received none slipped over the bank manager's
unperceptive mind like the even flow of water over a stone.
The skipper wrote at some length, for he was a man who
could use his pen easily; he was sorry, he said, that he
had not been able to bring Christina home himself, but
duty was duty, as Mr Mill would understand without his
telling him, and he had no right to leave his ship on any
other business than that of his owner, once the voyage was
begun. Christina was quite unfit to endure the sea. The bad
weather they had met with had produced a worse effect on
her than he had believed possible and he blamed himself

because he had not realised how greatly a delicate woman might suffer in the circumstances. He had felt – and here Aeneas' words had come in usefully – that no man with the least humanity would wish her to continue a voyage that could inflict such misery on her. It was very hard on himself, he added but there were times when a man had to think of others, however hard it might be, and he was cheered by the knowledge that his wife had a home in which he knew her to be safe and happy. There followed more in the same suitable strain. There was no possibility of an answer as the *Sirius* was ready to sail as he wrote.

Mill was quite pleased to have his daughter back and after the surprise had worn off everything settled down into the old ways. It was only Mrs Halket who was at all put out. Christina never spoke much and was even more silent. She seemed rather to avoid her aunt and Mrs Halket retired quietly to Niven Street, not wishing to miss her stepson who had been nearer to the centre of upheaval than anybody else.

The town was earnest in its commiseration of its favourite, who had been robbed of his bride in not more than forty-eight hours. Everybody claimed to have foreseen what would happen but as Aeneas Halket kept his own counsel no rumour of her frantic escape reached Christina's neighbours. The terrible weather had upset her health so much that her husband had shirked the responsibility of taking her further and to everyone the flying slates and blown-in windows, the toll of wrecks on the coast spoke for themselves.

'Aw! fulishness!' said Ann Wishart. 'It was na recht! A young leddy brocht up in a hoose the like o' Mr Mill's! It was na for the like o' her. But the Captain's tae be hame in a towmont. He'll be tae buy a hoose till her and she'll have her own kerrage.'

Ann was torn between anger that the elements had not respected Mr Mill's daughter and pleasure at being able to vaunt a refinement too great to face them; when Christina's trunks, sent ashore by Baird before sailing, arrived and were unpacked, she insisted on her decking herself in what she would have worn in the antipodes. Maggie had been sent ashore with them, but as her home was in Broughty Ferry no account of her mistress's flight reached the house in the Bow Butts through her. It was as though the whole episode from the day of the *Sirius* first coming and the day when she sailed with Baird and his bride were a dream from which the town had awakened. Lummie Mill, his daughter and the tall hat were in their places in the kirk. None of them had even missed being there, Christina's departure and return having taken place between two Sundays.

It was on one of the calmest and brightest long-lingering summer days when Christina, returned from shopping contentedly in the town, got the news that the *Sirius* had gone down with all hands on that death-trap for Australia-bound ships, King's Island.

VI

THE KNOWLEDGE THAT she was a widow kept Christina exceedingly thoughtful during the days in which she sat in deep black, behind the drawn-down blinds. Across the world, Baird had been long buried under the seas he had navigated so successfully for more than half of his thirty-six years, but Ann had rigidly closed the eyes of the house till the right time should elapse between a death and a funeral. It would have been an indecency for Christina to go out to order her mourning, so Ann, with Mill's purse at her disposal, swathed her in crape from head to foot. The girl could not see to do her needlework, nor to read had she wished to in the dim light that entered, as she sat in the drawing-room on the spot where she had been proposed to by the dead man. She was awed by her thoughts. The sudden news of his fate had shaken her and brought the startled tears, but she had not really wept though she carried her black-bordered handkerchief in her hand all day. What awed her was the idea of the wrecked ship and she shuddered, remembering that night in the dark cabin with Maggie and the intolerable ringing of the ship's bell as they were flung about in the jaws of the seas. She was glad to think Maggie was safe and not drowned with the others. Had it been like that night – the hour when they were lost? Perhaps they had gone down to the ringing of that bell and its voice had clanged on till the waters swallowed them. She had not the imagination that will picture distant events in an ordinary way but she had never been able to look back on her short voyage without hearing its crying tongue. Her eyes went over the familiar furniture surrounding her father's footstool to his place on the hearth; the stiff portrait of him as a young man over the mantelpiece, and she was grateful for their reassuring sameness. She was at home – back with them – and yet she was that definite thing, a widow. She felt even more conscious of taking her place in life than when she had stood up in this room to be married. The thought of Baird drowning came upon her and she sobbed, not from grief but from the horror of his end. Perhaps the same end had been near that night when the bell was ringing.

She got up and went down to the kitchen where she could be near Ann and away from the dim light. Ann's kingdom looked on the back of the house and the blinds would be up there. She was a widow. She would have to do as widows did and she had never heard of a new made widow sitting in the kitchen. She paused. Perhaps she ought not to do it but she could not help thinking of the bell when she was alone. She went downstairs in her rustling silk and crape. Ann was stirring something on the fire and looked up.

'Eh, Mistress Baird, this is no place for you!' she cried. 'Dinna sit there by the window! Maybe the flesher's laddie'll gae by wi' the meat an' it would be an awfae thing if he saw ye there i' the noo! Bide you aside the door whaur ye can win oot easy.'

'It's so dark upstairs, Ann, and I've nothing to do. Couldn't I do something to help you?'

'Na, na, ye mauna. Did anybody ever hear the like! Just compose yersel', Mistress Baird.'

'But I am not *very* unhappy, Ann.'

'Whisht! Whisht! ye dinna ken what ye're sayin'.'

'But it's true. Oh, I'm so thankful I was not drowned – I'm so thankful to be home.'

'Ye'll dae better yet,' rejoined Ann 'Ye'll be gettin' a grand hoose o' yer ain. Ye'll be weel left, I'll warrant. Aye, we'll be seein' ye established.'

Christina had given no thought to the future. Some little time must elapse before her husband's business affairs could be settled and her prospects of money made clear; she sat wishing Ann would not force her up against details she was unprepared to face. She was at home and that was all that mattered.

'I don't know anything about that. I am quite happy here.'

'Maybe,' said Ann. 'Ye'll hae tae be estaiblished, for a' that.'

The more Ann struck forward to the future, the more Christina drew back to the past. Only now, when she had been cut free from the life in which she had entangled herself, like some timid creature strayed into a gamekeeper's snare, could she venture to look behind her; and she liked doing it because it made the darkened house seem light by contrast.

'It is dreadful to be on a ship,' she said. 'I was so frightened. The light went out in the night and there was only Maggie, the girl, beside me.'

Ann was cooking. 'And whaur was the Captain?' she enquired, over her shoulder.

'I didn't see him at all in the storm.'

In grim silence, Ann turned around.

'He should hae ken't better,' she said at last.

'He was too busy. He had no time.'

'He should na hae left ye.'

'But he had to mind the ship, Ann.'

'*He should na hae left ye*,' said Ann, firmly.

'Ann, you don't understand.'

But Ann had turned back to her fire again.

'I understand what's due till a young leddy like you,' she replied in a repressed voice. 'Dinna haver tae me – and you a bride! Ye mauna speak ill o' deid folk, but lord! A wouldna hae believed it! and you Miss Mill! But ye'll dae better yet; aye, will ye!'

Christina sat twisting her black-bordered handkerchief.

She wondered which was the worst, the kitchen or the lugubrious drawingroom, as the step of the butcher's lad fell on the flagged court outside.

'Awa' wi ye, Mistress Baird!' cried Ann. Christina fled.

Ann threw open the back door.

'It's a sad hoose we hae here,' she said, as she received the meat he brought.

'It will be,' replied he.

'But she's bearin' up.'

The boy was hardly thirteen and unused to dealing single-handed with solemn topics, so he said nothing.

'Aw the *expense*!' exclaimed Ann. 'Ye wouldna believe what the gentry has tae tak' frae their pocket when there's a death!'

He was bewildered. The costly pomps of funerals was all he could think of.

'Was he washed up?' he asked, almost in a whisper.

'Ye haverin' trash!' cried Ann.

But he was a practical child.

'Ye canna hae a bur'al wantin', the corp,' he observed doggedly.

'Div' ye think there's nae mair tae't nor that? Corp or nae corp, A tell ye Mistress Baird's blacks' had tae be the best. Haud awa' wi ye, now – what div the like o' you ken aboot the gentry? See now, here's the basket.'

She pushed him off. She was satisfied, in spite of her contempt, for she hoped he would repeat every word she had said to him to his mother.

It was a sad surprise to her when Baird's money affairs were wound up and Christina's prospects made known; she had built on the assumption that he would come back a rich man from this voyage or another. But he would never come back from any voyage and his widow had no more than a modest income and asked no better than to live with her father in the house in the Bow Butts; the only difference that Ann could see in her importance was the matronly title on her few letters and the billowing majesty of her 'blacks'. And even the latter would be modified in time.

Ann's opinion of Baird was modifying too. He had had no right to presume to Christina's hand and she began to

obliterate his memory in a sea of silence as deep as the sea
that lay upon his body. His widow was silent too and when
the first anniversary of her wedding passed and that of her
widowhood followed, it was marked by a faint abatement in
the rigour of her mourning. The captain's masterful shadow
had left the house; there were none of his small possessions
about nor letters to destroy, for the former had been lost
with him and the latter, owing to his presence in the town
during the whole of his courtship, had no existence.

Before the last trace of her weeds had disappeared
Christina sat on a morning of early Autumn under one
of the trees by the house reading a letter the post had
just brought her. Its torn wrapper lay on the ground at
her feet. She had changed a little in the two years since
her marriage for her face had lost a trifle of its youth and
gained something in confidence. She was thirty and the
fact gave her the mild astonishment that comes to most
people on starting a new decade.

She knew the writing that lay on her knee.

My dear Mrs Baird [Aeneas Halket wrote],
I have long intended to write to you and an event has
occurred that has taken away my last hesitation in doing
so. I have been made a partner in my business and with
this good fortune at my back, I feel I have a better right
to tell you what I have had in my heart for some time.
You may not know – how should you – that you have
always held a particular place in my mind. In the couple
of years before your marriage I had almost told you of
those feelings of regard but my not having a definite
home to offer you kept me silent. I was just beginning
to see my way when I heard of your approaching
marriage, and almost before I could adjust my mind to
the misfortune of having delayed too long, you arrived
at my stepmother's house on the memorable evening
when I had the chance of serving you in your difficulty.
When I heard you were a widow, respect for custom
kept me again silent during the term of your deeper
mourning. But it is two years since the wreck of the
Sirius and I think I may be justified in declaring myself.

If you will be my wife I will try to make you happy. I
am in a position to give you a home in which I hope
you will have everything to which you are accustomed
as well as a husband who will love you sincerely. I trust
you will give me the answer I hope for . . .

As she laid the letter down just below Aeneas Halket's
signature she saw a pencilled line. 'I like to think that
this paper will be held in your beautiful hands.'

It was not exactly an ardent letter but its steady kindness
was perhaps the thing to commend it most to her and the
few words at the end gave her a shy pleasure. She held out
her hands with her luckless wedding ring on one of them
and examined them. She was glad Aeneas admired them
still. She got up and went in, leaving the envelope lying
by her chair.

Up in her room, she put the letter in her workbox and
turned the key; then she went to a drawer and took out
the picture of the modish St Cecilia and set it in its old
place on the mantelpiece, considering it. It had almost been
forgotten but she liked it and its presence there committed
her to nothing, she told herself. The question of marriage
could be deferred for a short time. He could not expect
her to make up her mind without consideration.

That evening Ann Wishart went out to fetch in Christina's
chair and picking up the envelope, saw the French script.
She had often seen that writing on letters to Mrs Halket
and she knew very well whence it came.

There was only one post daily yet Christina who had
been looking over house linen with Ann, that afternoon,
had not said a word about what was probably lying in
her pocket all the time. Ann drew down her mouth and
reflected that marriage made people 'very close'.

It was some time before the hoped opportunity came.
Christina was in her bedroom when Ann knocked and,
going up to her with a wooden face, held out the
envelope.

'Ye left that i' the garden, Mistress Baird. I've been tae
gie't ye this while. Maister Halket'll be weel?'

'Oh yes. He has been made partner in his business. He

knew we should be pleased to hear that. He will be quite rich,' added Christina, leaving the room lest she should be further questioned.

It was all but a fortnight before she could make up her mind to answer Aeneas; she liked the idea of his affection, but though the chain of habit that bound her so long had been violently cut it had not been severed long enough to prevent the ends from joining anew. She was still luxuriating in the unruffled peace to which she had been miraculously restored and Aeneas' constancy was like some pleasant book in the shelf whose back recalls its contents without the trouble of opening it. The town was beginning to forget she had ever been away.

She had written to Aeneas, asking for time to consider. Lummie remained ignorant for she was loth to utter a word that seemed to crystallise what she hoped at present to keep vague. Meantime in Ann's mind, Aeneas' star was rising.

'Aye, she'll hae tae be estaiblished,' she would say to herself as she watched the clicking jack turn in front of the bars with its load of meat. The great weights like millstones hung at the corner of the kitchen and the ropes that worked them ran like a narrow frieze round the walls. She imagined Christina's kitchen, her chandeliered dining-room and the noble joints that would travel from one to the other to steam on a rich man's table at the head of which Christina would preside; the green venetian blinds behind the silk-clad figure were almost visible to her gaze and the carriage drive outside them. She would stand still contemplating her vision with the eye of faith.

Christina had not told Aeneas whether she required a week or a month or a year for consideration. But some day the letters would have to be answered and the simpering face of St Cecilia would remind her of it. And there was not a day when Ann did not set her personal view of her duty before her; she had long ago guessed the contents of Aeneas' letter.

'Ye'll see,' she said to Christina, 'that Maister Mill'll no be left langer than ony other body. He just wants a year o' saxty-four. Him and ma brither James is ages. Saxty-three,

the pair o' them. Ye're young yet but ye'll hae tae see and
be estaiblished afore ye're left yer lane. It's no muckle the
Captain did for ye – he was ane o' they folk that doesna
keep what they get. Mind you, A'm no sayin' ye hae the
need tae better yersel' for ye'll be weel left when Maister
Mill's awa'; but I'd like fine tae see ye in yer carriage. And
a man's a man; gin I'd had a lad like Halket seekin' me
I'd no hae been sic a fule as let him gang. No me.'

'Ann, why did you never marry?' asked Christina,
suddenly. 'Did you ever – like anyone?'

'Aye, did I.'

'But are you sorry? Do you mind now?' continued
Christina stupidly.

'Am I mindin'?' cried Ann, turning on her. 'Div ye
think that there's onybody pleased that has naethin' o'
their ain? Are ye thinkin' it's a grand thing tae gang intae
the kirkyard and niver hae gotten a man or a wean?'

At sight of her quivering face a measure of comprehension
came to Christina – a small measure.

'I'm so sorry, Ann,' she exclaimed, kindly, standing still
and staring. 'But you've got me, you know,' she added
after a moment.

For reply, the other flung from her, banging the door.
She had looked at her as if she hated her.

Christina had never known her as anything but masterful,
certain, invulnerable; a mainstay. The young widow was
not naturally selfish but she had not been forced by life to
think much of anyone but herself. Her father, wrapped up
like a packet in the padding of his own small affairs, was
independent of her sympathies; her aunt had no need of
them. Though she was truly grieved to find that Ann had
lacked anything to make her happy, Christina's feeling was
one of absolute astonishment.

There seemed to be so much round her that she had
never imagined. She began to guess how much mistaken
it is possible to be in things taken for granted. Would she
ever feel as Ann – the unfailing Ann – felt? She remained
planted on the spot, wondering.

There was nothing, next day, to remind her of the depths
opened before her, yesterday. Ann was as decided and

trenchant as ever, but Christina felt shaken. In the scheme
of things that could so unnerve Ann what chance of security
was there for herself? All at once the coming years looked
forlorn. Might she have to go through an unknown dimness
crowded with unrevealed experiences lying in wait for her?
Why should she be at the mercy of chances and changes
when those she knew – placid neighbours and accepted
acquaintances – seemed to have nothing to disturb their
equanimity? In her innocent egotism she thought of herself
as the sole sufferer from the hazards of what should be
stable things – not exactly the sole sufferer, perhaps, but
the one who would feel them most. It was through these
troubled pools of thought that there swam up the thought
that Aeneas Halket had been her shield in the extremity
of her need, had listened to her and stood between her
and her terror. She did not want to marry anybody but
she trusted Aeneas, though she was too unsophisticated to
gauge the position he had faced on her account. Men will
face artillery, bulls, epidemics, the duties of steeplejacks,
savages and fire – all the licensed dangers that inhabit this
tormented earth – but not one in a hundred will stand up
to the risk of ridicule or misconstruction where there is the
shadow of a petticoat in the matter. It was part of Aeneas'
misfortune that Christina was the last woman alive who
would understand the cold-blooded courage of what he
had done. She was grateful to him but not more so than
if she had slipped and hurt herself in the street and he had
given her his arm home.

Before long another letter came.

Dear Christina,
I am not trying to press you for an answer though
I am hoping for one every day. It is on a matter of
business that I have to write now. The lease of my
house in Gayfield Square will run out at the term and
the tenant is asking me to renew it. I should be willing
to do so, had I not another prospect at heart. I am
hoping to require it for myself and to see you mistress
of it. As I have said, I am not trying to hurry you and
you will admit that I am patient, but I cannot keep my

tenant waiting. It is not fair to him. I could not live in
that house alone. It is too large for a single man and
there is no use in letting it stand empty. I am waiting
for you to tell me what I should do. There is no need
for me to repeat what I said in my last letter, for it all
stands the same. I shall hope for your answer soon . . .

Christina looked up from her reading. She was almost
glad that something tangible and important like the lease
of a house had sprung up to make her decision necessary.
Vacillation is one of the most painful things in the world
and yet there are some people that can never have enough
of it and she was beginning to suffer a mental giddiness
from its see-saw. She knew that Ann had no hesitations
on the subject; and that now she was indisputably at
the turning-point, brought there by the lease, she was
almost more afraid to speak to her father. To him she
had never mentioned the subject of the future because
its discussion had always been shut off behind the same
curtain of mysterious delicacy that shrouded any serious
allusion to love, religion or money; but this was a reality
– a lease!

'Papa,' she began, 'Mr Halket has written me a letter—'
she stopped; it was not easy.

'It'll be a proposal!' he exclaimed with a giggle.

'But it is about his house,' she said, growing confused.
'He wants to know if he should let it – I mean, he will
let it if I do not marry him. What shall I do?'

'What do you mean?' said he, bewildered too. 'I don't
understand.'

'He wants me to marry him and live in the house – I
don't know—'

Lummie slapped his leg and crowed, as if he had found
out a conjuring trick.

'I knew it was an offer!' he cried.

'But had I better say "yes", Papa?'

'Why not, my dear? He's a nice lad. I always liked
Aeneas.'

'I really don't know what is best.'

'Take him, my dear, of course. I could believe you'll do

better this time.' He pursed his lips with elaborate wisdom
and repeated his words.

'You'll likely be better suited this time.'

She would have spoken again but he was looking with
a sort of prim joviality into space.

'There'll be another wedding breakfast!' he cried.

She awoke next morning to the necessity of writing her
letter. She had delayed too long and her conscience smote
her. Her father had been acquiescent though he seemed to
give his consideration more to the details of the wedding
than to the desirability of its taking place; and when she had
parted from him last night, the engagement was understood
to be settled. She now sat at the little walnut writing table in
the drawing room; her handwriting was rather pretty and she
expressed herself better on paper than in speaking. When the
letter was addressed she put on her hat with its long feather
that swept over the brim just behind her ear for she meant
to carry it to the post office and then to return to tell Ann
what she had done.

In the September sunshine, an attractive and decorous
figure in her billowing lavender-coloured skirt and drooping
plume, she had some grace of movement and as she passed
along the stony greyness of the street a couple of passers-by
looked after her and wondered whether Captain Baird's
widow would marry again.

The remembrance came to her of another walk through
grey streets; but then, they had been dark and soaking and
she was lost and terrified as she fled from that nightmare
in which the bell's desolate clanging had rung crazily out
among the thrashing seas. She rejoiced that Aeneas was
no longer employed in France and that she need never
set foot in a ship again.

This letter of acceptance that she carried must be the
beginning of a far safer venture than the last one and she was
doing a wise thing for herself and an apparently satisfactory
one to her relations. Mrs Halket had been away in England
for some weeks but she would be pleased when she heard
the news. Christina wished that her aunt were with her
now, because, though she was convinced of the wisdom
of her action, she would have liked someone beside Ann

Wishart to uphold her definitely. But that was a foolish feeling, no doubt.

She walked on in her voluminous folds of lavender. The post office was a small place tucked away below the town hall, a stone's throw from the steeple under whose shadow she had first met Baird.

The long High Street was rather hazy at its further end in the mistiness of light that comes to the East Coast before the full poignancy of autumn. A good many figures were moving about because it was market day, but the place was not thronged, the main thoroughfare being so spacious.

Some way off on the pavement Lummie Mill was coming towards her and she could see the movement of his hat among the heads of the people. She was at the entrance to the post office, just about to cross the threshold, when, as she paused with her hand on the door, the vision of the well-known shape that had always been one with her father's existence and inseparable from him, brought, in a staggering rush to her heart, an assaulting realisation of the surroundings that had been her life and without which she could not live; childhood, her placid existence, her home; the chain of Sundays stretching back into vacancy on which she had sat in the pew under the gallery; that background into which her soul, as well as her body, had fitted so smoothly and safely. In the very jaws of her decision, the sight of the tall hat intensified her consciousness of these things a thousand fold. Here had been security, shelter, all that was best. And they were about to go from her by her own act.

She turned quickly and in a few minutes had let herself in at the door of the house in the Bow Butts.

Like a thief she hurried noiselessly upstairs and tore up her letter, thrusting its fragments into the drawing-room fire.

The Fifty-Eight Wild Swans

THE ONLY person who had any control over old Jimmy Strachan was Maria Mitchell, his niece, who lived in the cottage adjoining his own. He was seventy-six, and when he retired from work, much crippled by rheumatism and with a bad heart, he had gone into this particular dwelling so that Maria, a widow woman, would be able to do his cooking. He was a bachelor who had no hobbies, despised gardening, and read nothing but the newspaper, which he could do without spectacles, for his sight was wonderful. His mouth was twisted with years of ill temper and his powerful hands with rheumatism; this had now become worse, and made walking a dreadful exertion, very bad for his heart. He was not without pleasures, because he was greedy, and Maria was a splendid cook. She saw to it that he was comfortable, for she was a hard, confident woman and liked doing things thoroughly, tall and stout, with the black, thick watchful eye of a gander. Strachan's fits of temper produced no more effect upon Maria than if they had taken place in the moon, instead of next door; and it was not in his power to do anything to annoy her but abuse the food she set before him, which he was far too wise to do. He was comfortably off, with his savings and his old-age pension. He had all he wanted and could keep himself handsomely in tobacco.

In good weather Strachan would sit in his garden, for while he despised the place as an ornament, he liked it as a point from which he could talk to passers-by when he was in the humour for it, though they were little inclined to loiter for the pleasure of his company. It was a fairly frequented road down which an occasional motor car sped or a motor cyclist rushed by to disappear between the hedges like an escaping goblin. His underhung jaw and startling white eyebrows made children uncomfortable, and some of them were afraid when they saw him looking out with his pipe between the teeth. Alister MacHugh, an inquisitive, solemn, cautious child of twelve who lived farther up the road, was not afraid, because he reasoned very sensibly that, Strachan being almost crippled, could not reach him if he wanted to, and that hard words, if they come over a thorn hedge, lose much of their menace. He liked staring at the old man and was attracted in the same way that some people are attracted by such horrors as they can contemplate in safety.

An acquaintance had begun between these two which approached toleration, though it went no further. Strachan disliked the bold children, who were often rude, but the timid ones, who would run by looking back at him as if he were a buffalo in a cage, were those he could least endure, perhaps because the beast-in-the-cage idea came home to him too much; for he had been a very active man and the stultified and superintended comfort in which Maria kept him grated on some fierce thing in him, though he would have resented its absence.

The acquaintance had begun one day when Alister passed and came to a standstill before Strachan's house. The old man hobbled as far as the garden gate and leaned upon its rail, smoking. The boy was used to seeing the upper part of him, but the lower half had always been concealed by the hedge, and he was now interested in the revelation of the whole through the bars. It was a chance not to be missed. His eyes were fixed on the thick, cramped figure which scowled with lowered head at the leggy one in the road. Neither spoke, but a wordless growl came over the gate. Many another brat would have run, but Alister MacHugh's ponderous interest and plain good sense kept him still.

Presently there was not a growl, but a shout, and in its accomplishment Strachan's pipe fell and, striking the rail, rebounded on to the road. It was a good briar pipe and was none the worse, but it lay well out of reach of the stick. In his heart he was dismayed, because of the hostility taken for granted between himself and the young. One kind of

child would make off with the pipe and hide it, and the
other kind would not approach him with it.

But Alister MacHugh belonged to neither sort. When
a thing falls you pick it up, if only to see what it feels
like to have it in your hand. Strachan was so much
astounded to get his treasure returned that he did not
so much as say thank you; in fact, he was rather angry
at losing a fraction of his general grievance against the
youth of his parish. Alister MacHugh went on his way
wrapped in the impersonal placidity which attended him.
Strachan watched him out of sight, and it dawned on his
cross-grained mind that here was a being curiously unlike
anyone else.

The infinitesimal tinge of approval which the episode
left with the old man had been imperilled by their next
meeting.

'Dinna cowp yer pipe,' Alister had said, pausing as he
passed. Strachan drew in his breath and his brows lowered.
But there was no shade of impudence in the words, merely
an obvious plainness of thought, and the occasion sailed by
safely, like a leaf on a running stream that has been almost
side-tracked by a rock.

Nobody who knew Strachan had the faintest notion that
any gleam of romance had ever illuminated his mind. He
had never been known to look at a woman nor listen to
a song nor go to any place of entertainment, but the
public house, and there he drank little and talked less;
he had never shown a preference for anybody. But the
neighbours did not know everything about him. He had
come from another part of Scotland, a lad of nineteen,
and nobody had troubled to ask how he had spent his
earlier life; he slipped into farm work like other people,
and his companions were unaware that he had been in the
employ of a wildfowler somewhere on the border.

Those had been the halcyon days of Strachan's life, and
their remembrance stayed with him; the flighting duck; the
skein of wild geese lacing the skies in rhythmic loops of
pulsating wings; the sound of their remote voices; the flap
of a heron beating up out of the rushes to disappear with the
long curve of his neck laid back till his breast-bone looked

like the prow of a Viking ship against the atmosphere. At that time his own 'thrawnness' had obscured from him the knowledge of how happy he was. Now he admitted to himself his crass unawareness of his luck. A gull flying inland or the cry of any large bird would stir him, no matter what he was doing. He spoke of these things to nobody.

Less than a mile from his cottage there was a sheet of water lying solitary in a stretch of flat land. A traveller, knowing where to look for it, might, from the road, see its gleam through the alders beyond the fields. On its northern side the ground sloped gently to a farm whose steading was the only thing to suggest human occupation, and, beyond this, lay the Grampians on the horizon. On the western end of the water was a narrow belt of green shore on the confines of which stood high fir woods. Though the place was so near cultivation, it had an aloofness that seemed to remove it miles away; lying idly on its eastern side and looking across, you might expect to see some tall befeathered Indian step out from between the fir-stems and launch his noiseless canoe. There were duck there and coot, and once or twice in living memory a wild swan or two had come down from the Findhorn and made a transitory sojourn in the quiet spot.

The cold set in early that year; by the beginning of November the winds were bitter and there was a good deal of rain. The east coast was dark with stormy twilights; the late leaves came whirling to the ground to be chased and harried to death in damp corners. Tattie-lifting was over and Alister MacHugh, who had been assisting at it, was back at school again when suddenly the wind went into the north and the sopping earth began to harden. The nights were black, for the moon had just gone out of her last quarter, but they were still. It was between one and two in the morning when Jimmy Strachan, lying wakeful, heard a sound that made him drag himself painfully up in bed. He sat with clenched hands pressed against his chest and eyes turned towards the window. Like most of his kind, he slept with it shut, and though the curtain was not drawn, there was no gleam of starlight to reveal its sunken square. His heart beat against his ribs, but he held his breath. Through the dead stillness came the long cry of the whooper swan.

Again – again. From the direction of that sleeping water beyond the fields the voices flowed out of the air. He rose, hobbling and groping, till his hand was on the matchbox. As he lit the candle and the flame caught, the cry rang out afresh. He pressed his face to the window pane, but he could not so much as see where the garden hedge ended and the sky began, and after shivering a few minutes he went back to bed, pinching out the flame with his broad fingers. Though he drew his blankets close, the moisture broke out on his forehead at the thought that, even should morning find the stranger birds lying like anchored ships not a mile away, he would not be able to see them. His disabilities leaned over him and knocked upon his heart, stifling his breath. The dark hours were bitter to him till he slept.

When he awoke the candle was lit again and Maria, who had come in from next door with her head muffled in a shawl, was raking the ash from the fire. The cup of tea she had brought steamed beside him and the clock-hands pointed to seven.

'Tak' yer tea when it's het,' she said.

He did not move.

'Tak' yer tea, I tell ye – what ails ye? Are ye no weel?'

He sat up and took a tentative sip, noisy and prolonged.

'I'm weel eneuch. Did ye no hear onything i' the nicht?'

'Was ye cryin' on me?'

He made a contemptuous sound.

'There'll be swans upo' the water out yonder,' he said. 'I heard the skelloch o' them.'

'Maybe,' she said.

'An' there'll be mair nor ane.'

'Haste-ye noo. I'm needin' the cup.'

'But ye did no hear them?' he persisted, sticking out his under lip.

'Dod! What wad I dae list'nin' on the like o' yon?'

'I heard them,' said he, doggedly.

'Tuts! Ye heard the swine at the back o' the hoose.'

'A *swine*?' he exclaimed, with wrath.

But she had gone out. He dragged himself out of bed. There was nothing to be got from Maria and he must find some better source of news.

As soon as he had dressed he went out, in spite of the cold, and established himself in the garden. It was Monday; and on Mondays the farmer north of the water sent his grieve to the town. Every Monday he passed on his way to the station. The old man went to the gate as he saw the familiar figure approach.

'Ony news?' he asked.

'Na, fegs!' said the other. 'Naethin' tae dae onybody ony guid. But they tell me the water out yonder's just fair fu' o' birds. Swans, they say. Auld Tibbie Mowatt that bides oot yon way was sayin' she couldna get sleepit the streen for their noise – dirty brutes. Fufty-aicht o' them.'

'Maybe they're awa' by this,' said Strachan, his words almost sticking in his throat.

'I dinna think it. They're sittin' as canny as sheep intill a field, Tibbie said.'

Strachan was speechless. Fifty-eight! He felt as if he were suffocating. He knew that, impossible though it must be for him to see them, a part of him could not give up the hope. He went into the house and sat down and the whole anguish of his helplessness came over him. The desire of his eyes was so near, and yet he could never see it. Fifty-eight! He put his hand over his surly face. His lids were wet.

Then began a very torment of unrest. He tried to read his newspaper, but he could take in nothing. He left it and went out again to see whether anyone was coming by who could tell him more of the sight that would be so much to him, so little to anyone else. And all the time he knew that, were he to talk of it to the whole parish, he would be brought no nearer to what he longed for, ached for. He was like a little schoolboy, piteous over some promised delight refused at the last moment.

The day went heavily by, and at night he turned his face to the wall and tried to forget those white phantoms that came

between him and his rest. But again he awoke in the stillness
and heard the voices calling across the darkened fields.

Next day the baker's van stopped at Maria's door. He
could hear the driver telling her of the swans. He had seen
them from that bit of his road from which the water was
visible.

'Ye should awa' an' see them,' said he as he handed
out her two loaves.

'Heuch!' she cried, snorting, 'muckle time I hae for
rinnin' after birds!'

The driver looked round and saw Strachan in his
garden.

'Aweel,' said he, with eyes sociably including the old
man in the converstion, 'there's mony wad like fine tae
get a sicht o' them, nae doot.'

'Fine, fine wad I like it!' burst out Strachan, his hide of
surliness penetrated by the mere shadow of a sympathetic
outlook, 'an' maybe, gin I could get a ride—'

Maria's gander eye was upon him.

'Ye needna think tae try that,' she exclaimed, 'you that
canna sae muckle as win tae the kirk!'

'Wha askit ye?' shouted Strachan, losing his temper, 'I
wasna speakin' tae ye – haud yer wisht, ye bizzar!'

'Ye needna seek tae win out o' this, gin *I'm* here,' she
said, as she went in with her loaves.

The van drove on and Strachan, with a bursting heart,
made for his fireside.

He sat down, breathing hard from exertion and wrath
and humiliation, and the tears, whose compelling rush
age and the sense of his helplessness alone could force
from his stubborn soul, welled up and ran down his nose,
dropping on the back of Maria's cat, which sometimes
came in to enjoy a quiet not always available at home.
He knew by experience that Maria always attained her
objects somehow.

Time went by; the clock struck more than once and he
did not move; he had often heard it said that there is a way
out of everything, if you can only find it, and he stared at
the fire as though, by glaring long enough, he might see
in its depths some path of relief in his passionate need.

When he rose at last a step on the road made him look out. Beyond the bars of the garden gate he saw Alister MacHugh returning from school to his dinner. A great light entered into his mind.

When his own meal was brought in he could hardly touch it. He had fetched a shilling from the cupboard and was squeezing it in his hand as Alister came back on his return journey, and the boy was surprised to see him in his doorway, beckoning him in with wordless signs. He stood still, considering whether he should respond, but reflecting that he had never seen the inside of Strachan's dwelling, he opened the gate. At the threshold he was haled in.

As he left, ten minutes later, Strachan shook him by the arm.

'Ye'll no tell onybody what ye're tae dae,' he said, gripping him fiercely.

'Dinna roog me. I ken fine.'

'And ye'll no let on tae the dominie,' continued Strachan, shaking him.

'Na. He's an auld gowk.'

When the boy got home that evening he stowed his coin away in some corner known to himself. He had left Strachan's door with the prospect of another shilling if he carried out the plan that the old man had unfolded. There were some risks attending it and a great deal of secrecy: the former did not seem to him so very startling (as he did not know Maria), and the latter he loved.

Strachan was going to try to reach his goal on his own feet and he had chosen Alister as an accomplice for excellent reasons. The scheme was so wild that only a child would consent to take part in it, and he also knew in an undefined way that Alister's qualities were not all childish ones. Saturday was the school holiday and Maria was going to Arbroath for the day, and these coinciding events would make the scheme possible; but he hated the delay, fearing that the swans should take flight before the week was out. It was two years since he had been more than a stone's throw from home for the mere crossing of his garden was an effort; it took so much force to move his bent body and stiff joints. He had long made up his mind, with what was more like callousness than resignation, to the restraints of age and fate, but now his callousness had broken down. He was going to see the wild swans, cost what it might, if only Maria did not hear of it and terrorise Alister into withholding his help. Then, indeed, he would be undone.

It was the first part of the journey that made him anxious. Once across the road and into the stubble field opposite, he might be unseen by any officious neighbour. At the farther side of it there was a gate into the green loaning choked with broom, and along this he would reach a strip of wood that ended on the waste ground by the water. He neither cared nor considered how he was to get back. He could see no further than the swans. All the week he watched the heavens, dreading that, in their wrath with his madness, they might pour with sufficient malice to keep Maria at home.

But Saturday dawned, one of the strangest and most beautiful days that had befallen this autumn. The week had ended as though bewitched. Frost had set in and, with it, a clear whiteness and stillness in which all nature seemed to hold its breath. The tall trees by the loan stood drawn up like an array waiting motionless for some word of awe that was to come through the spellbound air. The atmosphere was steely, ecstatic; the sun was faint in it. The larger lines of the landscape were sharp and full of meaning, like divine truths. You might feel that your faculties were interchangeable – that you saw with your mind, understood with your eyes; or, rather, that you needed no faculties, because everything was resolved into its essence.

Maria brought his food for the day and departed. She expected to be home by three. Alister, conveniently ambushed, watched her round the turn of the road before betaking himself to Strachan's cottage. The old man was sitting gripping the arm of his chair; the moment was come, and his hand shook as he signed to the boy to fetch his warm coat from the peg.

The door key lay in his pocket as they crossed the garden painfully, but a kind of false strength had come to him and his spirits rose. The highway was clear, and Alister got him

across it and between the gaping gateposts into the field.
They proceded slowly, neither speaking, for both had need
of breath as they struggled along. Every ridge hardened by
the frost, every declivity was a jar to the old man, but his
lips were set, and with his arm laid on Alister's immature
shoulder, he pushed doggedly forward. The boy felt his
weight so much that he had to revive his courage with the
thought of the shilling in Strachan's pocket, which would
be transferred to his own when they reached the waterside.
Four times in their crawling progress through the stubble
they stopped to rest; Strachan's pale face and deep breaths
told of the torture of his efforts. Once he almost fell. They
reached the loan, and behind an ambuscade of broom halted
so that he could lean against a stake. Alister's shoulder
was numb and his legs felt as if they were misfits. The
ditches beside them were full of ice. Their breath rose in
hot vapour.

In a little while they began their *via dolorosa* again.

'I should hae gotten a drappie whuskey wi' me,' said
Strachan, stopping and panting when they had gone a few
yards; 'sic a dawmed fule I was no tae tak' ma boattle
alang wi's.'

The MacHughs were a teetotal family.

'It's pushon,' said Alister, solemnly.

Strachan's ready anger flamed up, but he dared not give
vent to it. It would take more energy than he could spare
to say what he thought, but he ground his arm viciously
down on Alister's collar bone. The boy wriggled.

'I'm no for gangin' on,' he exclaimed, wavering.

'Twa shillin's – twa—,' gasped Strachan.

They moved forward.

All things come to an end at last, and they were
approaching the wood. It was terrible ground for such as
Strachan to travel. Tussocks, coming against his stumbling
feet, were like lumps of cement and the frozen ruts
like stone coping; as the sides of his boots grated on
them shocks of fire ran up his knee joints. In spite
of the cold, sweat stood upon his forehead. He was
past recking of anything but his goal and the conflict
he waged against weakness and suffering. In the beech

wood giddiness attacked him and he swayed against the boy.

'I canna haud ye up,' whimpered Alister.

'Twa shillin's – twa shillin's,' groaned Strachan between his teeth.

He leaned against a young tree and clung with convulsive hands to its lower boughs, while the earth seemed to rock and gravitation to be at an end. Through his reeling senses a swan's cry floated, half submerged, as sea tangle on Atlantic waves.

'They're no awa',' he whispered when he came out of the grip of the disintegrating terror.

Slowly they added another hundred yards to the tale of their grievous progress; their task was growing short and the path was near its turn into the open. Horizontal gleams beyond the stems told of the water.

The sun was beginning to dominate the upper air as they set foot on the boggy turf, now firm with frost. Beside them a row of thin rowans displayed the yellowing leaves on their shiny dark branches; the berries had long gone down the throat of the greedy missel thrush. Here the labouring figures stopped and Strachan lifted his eyes.

They were there – the creatures of his desire, of his troubled sleep, his bitter wakings, his long thoughts. He put up the ancient field glass that had hung for years behind his door and saw the snowy line laid along the ice, showing here and there a ripple of movement. Now that he had accomplished his end he was hardly able to bear it.

'They're owre mony tae coont,' he said, thickly; 'coont you, laddie.'

He held out the glass.

'Whaur's ma boab?' said Alister MacHugh.

'Coont you and ye'll get it. Can ye see?'

'Aye, div I, ane, twa—' began Alister.

When he had passed fifty Strachan grew impatient and took the glass away. 'Here's tae ye,' he said. But his hand trembled so that the shilling fell at their feet. Alister picked it up.

'It was tae be twa.'

But Strachan's pockets were empty. He had forgotten when he made his lavish promises, that he had only one coin. His truculence seemed to have left him.

'I haena got anither,' he replied, rather shakily, 'but ye'll get it when we win hame.'

The boy contemplated him with still disapproval. He did not doubt the words, but he felt defrauded.

'A'm tae bide a bit,' said the other. 'Give me a haund till I sit doon.'

When this had been done, Strachan devoured the spectacle before him with sunken yet piercing eyes. Alister went off towards the wood, dragging his feet; his shoulder was stiff and he dragged them in protest as boys will. The deferred shilling rankled and the less satisfactory aspects of the adventure took more importance in his mind. The day had passed noon. He began to think about his dinner, less because he was hungry than because his absence would have to be accounted for, and he guessed that, should any harm come to Strachan, and he were known to have abetted his exploit, he might get into trouble. He loitered, irresolute. Should he stay here, awaiting Strachan's pleasure or should he run home, escape privily after dinner and come back to finish his task? The absence of the second shilling turned the scale. He departed quickly.

Strachan's head began to clear and his senses to take in the sight before him. A more indifferent beholder than the one who now looked on it might well be overpowered by its wonder. It was like a vision isolated from the clamorous earth, a glory cast from something remote and set, for a space, within the cognisance of men. The air was as still as though time had stopped; but carried over the frozen water came that indefinable stir which hardly amounts to a sound, that muffled vibration emanating from collective creatures. Over the sharp clarity of ice, turned to metallic indigo with the sun's strengthening, it travelled like a breath. Beyond, across the polished surface, the wall of firwood rose in dense and sombre mass, its foot lost in the grey blueness of mist that had not yet withdrawn from the farther shore. The crowded line of swans stretched in a thick bar against it, and now from one part of the line, now from another, a white, sinuous neck would raise itself and cut into the blur of tree-stems and vapour.

Strachan gazed on; weary with holding the glass, he leaned back against a rowan. His sight was still so keen that not a movement of that snow-coloured company was lost on him, not the uplifting of a curved neck, not the extended arch of a shifting wing. The dark blue ice under the birds flung up their white beauty against the austere mystery of the woods. He had never beheld the like, not in his young days, not in the careless times when he had been free to go about in the strength of his powerful manhood. He lay back, swallowed and lost in the rapture of attainment. It was cold, bitter cold, but he did not know it. A shiver or two went through him. He had forgotten Alister, or the fact that Alister lived. Though weariness was on him, it was not the dismayed agony of giddiness. He was exhausted, but he could rest, looking at the swans. Farther and farther he leaned back upon his rowan. He weakened, but his weakness did not trouble him. Darkness came over his sight, but as it blotted out his physical vision there rose somewhere in his consciousness an exhilarating rush – though he was blinded, with some unknown faculty he could see . . . He was among the swans, and yet he knew dimly that he was still lying on the ground. They were over him, around him, so that he saw the soft yellow shadows under their down, the silver light on their strong feathers . . . yet they were there, over the water, out on the blue ice . . .

The chill glory that enwrapped both him and them pressed upon his heart. How had he never known before what strange things there were in the world? . . . How had he ever believed that he was old and crippled? . . . How had he never felt what it was to be sucked into the very core of life? With a sudden, ardent effort he sat up, throwing his arms forward, and then fell back.

When Alister neared home he saw his mother standing in the road with Maria. She had returned from Arbroath, having got there to discover that the shops were shut: and now she had made a worse discovery; for Strachan's door was locked and the place empty. She was terribly put about, and the boy could hear the anger in her raised voice. He was in a dreadful position. If he went back to fetch the old man now, he would prove his own guilt; if he stayed away, he would certainly never see the remaining half of its price. In any case the secret must come out, and Strachan, himself discovered, would inevitably reveal his help. The sooner Strachan was got home the better, and he would go and apply for the shilling to-morrow.

'Hae ye seen Maister Strachan, callant?' Maria shouted as he came up.

'Aye, he's awa' tae get a sicht o' yon birds.'

They were soon pushing through the whins of the loan, Maria and a couple of men who had come up. Alister followed some way after; instinct told him to keep clear of Maria. When they passed through the beech wood he saw her rush forward and, hearing her loud outcry, he almost turned and fled.

But he did not flee. Cowering among the trees he realised that the part he had played would lie for ever hidden.

With awed curiosity he stole up to the little group. The four stood looking down at Strachan. At last the silence was broken.

'He looks fine an' pleased,' said Alister MacHugh.

The Yellow Dog

'AYE, A doag's grand company.'

The platitude floated out on the murky air of the smiddy in which three men were smoking; it hung for a minute, unanswered, and the shepherd took his pipe out of his mouth and emitted a solemn 'aye'.

Outside, the late October afternoon dwindled to evening; work being over, the smith sat on his anvil facing the shepherd and old Robert Spence.

'Grand, grand company,' said Spence again.

The blacksmith pushed his cap back. He was very much younger than his companions and perhaps had not outgrown the taste for disagreeing with his elders.

'Weel,' he said slowly, 'I kent a man – I didna exactly ken him weel, though I kent plenty about him – that wasna just benefited by the company o' a doag.'

'It isna ilka body that understands doags,' said Spence.

'The man I'm tellin' ye o' was a lang time or he understood ane o' them.'

The shepherd made no comment, but the quality of contempt in his silence was a challenge to the smith.

'It was ma wife's uncle,' he began, 'that had a fairm oot yonder at the fit o' the Sidlaws – a cantankered-like carle that hadna very muckle tae say till onybody. He'd naethin' tae say tae me, at ony rate, for I was coortin' at the time, and the lassie had an awfae wark tae get ootby tae meet me. I daur'd na come near the hoose. Ye see, he was that set against me, but whiles we'd hae a word thegither, her an' me, ahint a dyke, when it was possible. Weel, there was a nicht we was there and we could hear the tried o' a man runnin' an pechin' up the brae and we were fair fleggit, Bell an' me, but the auld deevil gae'd by

an' never saw naethin'. He was that pit aboot. Ye could
see the heid o'm against the sma' licht there was i' the sky
and his hair was tousled an' his bonnet lost.'

'Was't a doag chasin' him?' asked Spence.

'Na, na – but listen you till I tell ye – it had been him
chasin' a doag—'

'The fule,' broke in the shepherd.

'Ye micht think that, perhaps. But I mind when Bell got
the chance tae tell me the richts o' it, I was whiles fear'd
tae gang oot i' the dairk ma lane – aye was I.'

'Feech!' exclaimed the shepherd, 'ye were owre young
tae be oot late – coortin' tae! Ye're no muckle mair nor
a laddie the noo.'

'I'm a married man this twa year,' rejoined the smith,
'and there's a wean at hame and anither comin'. But that's
nae matter. Mind you what I'm tae tell ye. It'll gar ye think.
Yon man, Bell's uncle, had got sheep awa' up upo' the hill
and he'd been oot seekin' a yowe that was missin' frae
the flock.'

At the mention of a flock the shepherd's humour began
to change and the two old men fixed their eyes on the
smith's face.

'Aye, he was up amang the hills an' he couldna get word
o' the yowe and he was fair done, what wi' traiv'lin' the
bogs he didna ken, an' trampin' a' kind o' places an'
duntin' himsel' amang the stanes. It was i' the autumn, a
day like this; the afternoon was gettin' on an' he couldna
see whaur he was, for he was newly come tae the fairm
and he wasna accustomed tae the hills. He was a Fife
body. I'se warrant ye he said some queer things, for he
was an ill-tongued man, and at last he thocht he wadna
fash himsel' ony mair wi' the yowe an' just leave the bizzer
tae dee in her sins. Forbye there was a pucklie mist, and it
was takin' him a' his time tae win doon tae ceevilisation
or sunset.

'At last he got his feet on the flat ground and he cam'
upon a warld o' whins; there wasna a hoose nor a beast
tae be seen, an' when he was through the whins it was
the same; naethin' but a muckle green place wi' clumps
o' rashes and ne'er a peewee nor a whaup tae cry owre his

heid. He was standin' like a fule when a dairk-like thing
cam' oot frae ahint a tree-stump aboot as far aheid as he
micht see, an' it had the appearance o' a doag. It cam'
towards him wi' its heid doon an' he could tell through
the gloamin' that it was a kind o' a yella colour; its tail was
hangin' atween its legs. It lookit queer, he thocht. (Man, I
dinna like thae things!)'

He paused for breath; the old men said nothing, for the
smith was transporting them into places whose like they
had seen many a time.

'It cam' and stoppit a wee bittie in front o' him; syne it
startit rinnin' roond him. Whiles it ran in a muckle circle,
whiles in sma' anes. But aye it ran; roond an' roond wi'
its heid hangin', and whiles it lookit up at him wi' its yella
een, whiles no. He couldna say what tae mak' o' it, but it
seemed as if the cratur kent somethin' that gar'd it behave
yon way. His he'rt was like tae dee, he said, yon thing had
that ill look aboot it; he tried strikin' oot wi' his stick, but
he couldna reach it, and at last he just steppit forrit though
he didna ken the road he was takin'; a' he thocht was tae get
rid o' the brute. But it was nae use, for it gae'd on afore him,
turnin' its heid an' lookin' back tae see if he was comin'. He
stude still when he saw that and the doag commenced tae
rin roond him the same as before. Whatever he tried, he
couldna get quit o'm.'

'I dinna believe ye,' said Spence.

'I'm no' carin',' replied the smith, 'but I can haud ma
tongue gin ye like. Am I tae gang on?'

Spence and the shepherd put their pride in their pockets,
and the smith continued.

'Weel, it cam' intill the man's mind that the beast micht
be makin' for its hame, and gin he was to folla it he'd maybe
land at some hoose whaur he'd get put on his road, so he
began to think shame o' himsel' for no seein' that it was
just a nat'ral thing, and awa' they went, him an' the doag.
There was bogs an' ditches, broom an' tracks rinnin' in
and oot o' the lang grass, amangst the black shaws o' the
weepies that was deein' i' the autumn. He didna ken foo
lang they'd traivelt, and gin he stude tae tak's breith the
thing afore him wad stap an' turn back, and though he tell't

himsel' that a doag was a doag and nae mair, he couldna thole the notion o' it comin' near an' maybe rinnin' roond him again. There wasna a body tae be seen nor a man's voice tae hear as they gaed ane ahint the ither, but at last the doag loupit through a broken place whaur the stanes had whummled oot o' a dyke on till a road. It was a narra road and there was a bittie green grass at the side o' it, and he was fine an' pleased when he saw it, for he kent it, and yonder no' far aheid was the muckle grey stane that stickit up like the figure o' a man, by the arn trees i' the weet ditch. He wasna mair nor a mile frae hame and the kent, nat'ral look o't made him bauld, the same as a suppie whusky micht hae done, and anger't him aye the mair at the doag though it had brocht him sae far on his journey. As I tell't ye, he was a thrawn cratur and he up an' hurled his stick and struck the beast i' the side. It didna cry nor rin; it just cam' back till him and ran a great circle roond him. He didna like that and he saw he'd get nae peace till he was at his ain door and could clap it i' the doag's face; sae he gaed on again, an' it rinnin' afore him, and as they passed the stane amang the arn trees the beast stoppit that quick he was near steppin' on it. He lookit doon tae his feet, and it was gone. There was nae doag there.'

'Nae doag there?' cried the shepherd.

'Aye, naethin'. There was naethin'. The road was toom but for himsel', and he was that terrified that he started awa' wi' the cauld sweit drippin' on his cheeks and ran till his breith was done. That was the nicht Bell an' me saw him come hame.'

The smith stopped and looked at his companions.

'Noo, what div ye mak' o' that?' he asked, as neither of them spoke.

'I wad say that yon man had been a leear,' replied the shepherd judicially; 'and, ony way, it's time I was awa'. Come on, min.'

The collie rose at the summons and followed his master to the door.

The smith turned to Spence.

'Ah weel, ye see,' said the old man. 'I wasna there mysel', and I couldna exactly say . . .'

He began to bestir himself too.

'But will ye no bide and hear the end o' it?' called the smith to the shepherd's back, which, square and heavy, filled the doorway.

'An' is that no' the end?'

'Na, there's mair.'

The young man had not moved from the anvil; but the shepherd, though he turned round, stayed in the doorway; to have approached would have been a concession to folly, to youth, to all sorts of officially negligible things.

'It was a while after when I got this job here an' was married,' began the smith again. 'I was acquaint wi' yon business o' the doag and we'd speak aboot it at times, her an' me. But the man himsel' couldna thole tae hear aboot it, for there was some that made a joke o't an' wad cry oot when he passed, '*Whaur's yer doag, Fifie? Hae ye gi'en him a holiday?*' But there wasna very muckle use for him tae be pretendin' wi' us that had seen him yon nicht comin' hame dementit-like, and Bell had been i' the hoose and got the tale frae his ain lips. But we said naethin' tae upset him, and noo that the lassie an' me was man an' wife, and the smiddy daein' weel, he didna tak sae ill at me, and we'd gang tae the fairm, noo and again, o' Sawbaths, for her auntie likit Bell.

'It was on ane o' thae days that we was there. There was just the auntie at hame, for her man had gane awa' aifter the kirk was oot and tell't her he wad be hame for tea time. A braw November day it was, saft and freish, and I mind we went oot i' the yaird when dinner was done, for Bell had wrocht wi' the turkey when she was at fairm and was seekin' tae see what like birds her auntie had gotten this year. The turkey-hens were steppin' aboot an' the bubblyjock scrapin' his wings alang the ground because I was whustlin' at him tae gar him rage; we was lauchin' at him when a little lassie lookit ower the palin' an' cried on us.

'Mistress Donal'! Mistress Donal'! Yer man tell't me tae come for ye, for he's no verra weel – he's got a sair pain in his he'rt an' he canna stand. He bad me mak' haste. He's doon this way!'

'We a' set aff, and the lassie brocht us tae the same road that he'd traiv'led wi' the doag mair nor a year syne. Puir Mistress Donald was no' that quick on her feet for she was stoot and no just young, and I left Bell wi' her an' ran. When I got roond a turn I could see the arn trees that were bare but for a wheen broun leaves, wi' the muckle stane stickin' up below them frae the rank grass, an' there was a dark heap lyin' terrible still at the stane's fit.

'It was him, deid. It took me a while tae mak' sure, and when I raised mysel' tae see whether Bell and the puir body was comin', I heard a kind o' movin' an' lookit roond.

'Aboot a stane's thraw frae's, there was a yella doag standin' lookin' at me.'

Anderson

'COME AWA' an' get yer wheeps!'

Anderson Craig MacNichol, who was thus summoned, sat in the yard rubbing down a wooden hobbyhorse, a creature with legs like the handles of hearth-brooms and a strip of fur mane nailed on its flat, semi-circular neck.

Anderson put out his tongue till it almost covered his chin. There was nothing odd in that; children have done the same from time immemorial, but he did it automatically and without so much as raising his eyes to the figure standing at the kitchen door. It was a sufficiently intimidating one too; for Mrs Craig, Anderson's maternal grandmother, was a tall spare beldame and wore a high black cap tied with purple ribbons. It was from her that he had got his middle name; the first one had been given him in honour of an uncle in America. Another thing that had come to him from his grandmother was his long nose, and though his pointed chin and pink and white complexion had a girlish look, it was a misleading one, for, in character, he was Napoleonic and his small blue eyes should have been warning to all who stood in his way.

'Come awa'!' cried the old woman again.

'No me,' replied Anderson.

'Did I no tell ye no tae mairter yer guid claes 'yont i' the dirt? Ye'll get the tawse for that. Div ye no hear me?'

'Aye, fine', said he.

She took a step towards him, but only one; for she had felt shoes on and there was an extensive puddle before the door.

He did not move. It was not worth his while.

She turned and went in. Prudence had its place in Anderson's character and he did not know whether his father was about, for it was Sunday. He looked down at the splashes of mud on his nether garments that had been spotless in the morning when his mother had driven him kirkwards before her. Mrs MacNichol was proud of the smug little figure in front, scrubbed and brushed as became the child of a man who farmed seventy acres and kept a horseman for his pair.

Anderson put his hands in his pockets as he had seen the horseman do and was soon out of the yard and on his way down the side road that led to the river. It had rained a good deal and he could hear the South Esk, growling and swollen, pushing its course through the rocks below the bridge. Home was unsuitable to him at the moment and his mind open to anything that should be less so, therefore he saw with pleasure that a group of boys of his own age was gathered a little way on. Here was company and something to put his mind to. He advanced on them with interest; they were coming towards him and they laughed and shouted as they surrounded one of their number. As he neared them one of the crowd ran forward holding up something that writhed and wriggled.

'Hae!' he shouted. 'See what we've gotten!'

Anderson stopped as he saw a wretched draggled kitten that miaued and struggled in the boy's grip. The others came pressing round.

'We're tae pit it into yon!' cried one, pointing to a pond that the rain had swollen till it encroached on the wayside, 'and we've gaithered stanes tae see wha'll git it the first crack!'

The sight of the little creature held up aloft made Anderson's small eyes grow as hard as marbles. His one weakness was for animals. Even the wooden hobby-horse, that his parents said was a shame for anyone of seven years old to play with, was dear to him because it had its very remote likeness to a beast on four legs. Without further ado he rushed at the boy with his head down and butted him in the stomach. The victim was the taller of the two, so the blow landed in the right place, and before there was time to recover from it Anderson had seized the kitten; the others shouted with delight, for it did not occur to them that his sudden act was anything but a bid to be the executioner himself; but when the truth became clear to them and they saw their prey slipping from them, they made for Anderson whose practical mind was aware now that home was no longer a danger but a haven. He set off for it with the whole lot at his heels and the kitten, now the only creature that misunderstood his motives, clawed his hands.

It was unlucky for him that his road lay uphill and that he was rather blown from the violence of his onslaught, but the surprise it had created and the fact that his enemy had sat violently down among the feet of his companions delayed matters a little. They started after him, leaving their shaken leader to pick himself up. Anderson ran on, but a glance over his shoulder showed him he had no time to lose. He made all the speed he could but the hill was against him and, with blind instinct, he fled to a tree standing near; it was not big enough to be a protection but it was the one solid thing by the empty road; to the cat it was everything, for as he put his back to it and turned to face his pursuers the little beast sprung from his shoulder and clawed its way up into the lower branches.

'We'll hae't yet!' shouted a boy. But Anderson's face was not reassuring and one of the smaller ones began to cry.

The effect on the company was bad and they stood in a little malicious knot, turning the situation over in their minds. Anderson must be got the better of, but they did not know how to do it. The cat, high up among the boughs, looked down, round-eyed, as though it thought little of its champion's chances. Its mouth opened soundlessly, now and again, in a pink spot. The boys drew together, a mob in miniature.

'What'll ye gie's the poosie for?' cried one, coming a little forward – not far, but a pace or two, 'ye'll get a sweetie frae wee Charlie's bag – or mebbe them a'.'

Wee Charlie, to whom this juggling with other people's possessions was not pleasant, turned round and would have retreated, had he not been laid hold of.

'Wull ye gie's the poosie?' cried the other again.

'Na,' said Anderson.

'But, we'll get it, aye wull we!'

There was a rush and two of them made a dive at him, but his Sunday boots were new and had thick soles. There was a howl of pain as the attackers fell back.

'Bide you, bide you yet and we'll sort ye!' cried a voice from the enemy's rear, 'here's the stanes we've gotten for the poosie!'

One whizzed through the air and missed its mark, striking harmlessly against the tree trunk above Anderson's head. As others followed he ducked again and again and at last a shot caught him on the cheek and a little line of blood began to trickle down. He rubbed it off, rather shaken in spite of his valour, but he stood his ground though his heart began to beat harder and the tears were not far from his eyes. It was happy for him that the person he most admired in the world was taking a leisurely Sunday stroll through the fields which brought him at this moment within fifty yards of the conflict.

'Hey!' he shouted at the top of very powerful lungs, and Anderson saw Willie Keith, his father's horseman, throw his long leg over the gate. The assailants fled as one man, leaving wee Charlie toiling in their wake with his sweetie bag and crying on them to stop.

'What's wrang, laddie?' enquired Keith, as Anderson, now less of a champion and more of a little boy with a fast swelling face, seized him by the sleeve.

'I wadna gie them the cat.'

'The cat – what-like cat?'

Anderson pointed up into the tree from which the kitten was looking down upon the astonished horseman. As the story came out he dabbed the cut cheek with his brightly patterned handkerchief. The enemy had stopped his flight and was sending shouts of defiance from a safe distance.

'Rin awa' hame noo, ma mannie,' said Keith, 'and get a drappie water tae yer face.'

'Will ye no gang after them and sort them, Wullie?'

'Fie, let them be – but I'm thinkin' ye'll get yer licks when ye win hame.'

'I'm no carin',' replied Anderson.

'Sic a lad! Come awa' noo and I'll gang back wi' ye.'

'But I'll no leave the poosie.' His voice shook a little.

'It'll dae fine whaur it is.'

'But they ken it's there an' they'll be back tae get it!' cried Anderson, desperately.

Willie Keith was a humane young man. He pushed back his cap and stood regarding the forlorn little image. Anderson's hair hung down limp on his swollen face and the wet mud that the stones had spirted up as they landed round him had plastered his clothes; he certainly needed someone to speak for him.

'See now, Anderson,' said Keith, 'dinna greet. I'll awa' up an' get the cattie tae ye.'

'I'm no greetin',' he replied, a large tear rolling down and trickling on his coat.

The horseman swung himself into the tree.

'Come awa' noo, I'm tae gang hame wi' ye,' he said when he had returned to earth and delivered the kitten into Anderson's arms. 'I'd no like ye tae get yer licks.'

But Anderson paid little heed, for he had attained his end and that was what mattered to him. Physical consequences were a detail, in spite of everything.

They set off up the road, a strange contrast, for Willie Keith was something of a dandy on Sundays. The handkerchief he had applied to Anderson's dirty cheek was a silk one; he brushed bits of lichen off himself as they went. The boy hugged the cat and stepped out; the horseman – that great man – would see him through, he believed, if there should be any question of parting him from his treasure. Much had been gained while the long lad strode at his side. All the same, as they neared the farm he was very silent. He knew that the large, slothful tabby which snored, day in, day out, by the kitchen range was the only animal allowed inside the house; the dog, when not on the chain, did not dare to violate the floors with its dirty footprints. He confided these anxieties to his companion as they went.

'Ye'll gie't tae me and I'll keep it,' said the horseman as they parted at the farm gate.

'But ye'll no be tae droun it, Wullie?'

'Na, na. Ye're nae better nor a fule, Anderson, awa' ye gang. Ye'll hae it back the morn's morn.'

It said much for the boy's belief in his friend that he handed him the cat without another word and went to meet his fate.

It was early next morning when the farmer went out and passed the bothie adjoining the farm buildings in which his horseman and the odd man had their habitation. Willie Keith was coming out of it with his coat over his arm.

'There's a terrible mice i' the stable,' he said, solemnly.

'There's plenty traps about the place and ye ken whaur tae get them as weel as me,' said the farmer, dryly. He was in a hurry and it was not like Keith to worry him about trifles.

'Aye, but they're that wise-like they winna gang in. Ye wadna credit the common sense o' thae brutes when they're aifter the oats.'

'Tak' the cat frae the hoose,' said the master.

'She's owre fond o' the fire. She wadna bide. We'd be the better o' anither ane.'

'Get it then, an' dinna bother me.'

'I've got it,' said the horseman, pulling the kitten from under his coat.

'Lord sake, man, what's the use o' a thing that size?'

But Keith did nothing by halves.

'They're best young,' he said, pontifically. 'THEY LAIRN THE PLACE.'

MacNichol looked at him to see if he was joking, but the young man's grave face told him nothing.

'But it's sic a helpless thing. Wha's tae gie't its meat? The mistress'll no thole it i' the hoose.'

'I was thinkin' Anderson micht tak' it,' said Keith, meditatively. 'He's got sic a grand way wi' beasts.'

'Weel, gie't him then an' awa' wi' ye!'

Notes

AMONG WORKS consulted, are: Ian Carter *Farm Life in Northeast Scotland* 1840–1914: The Poor Man's Country (Edinburgh: John Donald, 1979; 1997 edn); Sydney and Olive Checkland *Industry and Ethos: Scotland* 1832–1914 (London: Edward Arnold, 1984); Francis Collinson *The Traditional and National Music of Scotland* (London: Routledge, 1976); Mairi Robinson (ed.) *The Concise Scots Dictionary* (Aberdeen: Aberdeen University Press, 1985); Paul H. Scott (ed.) *Scotland: A Concise Cultural History* (Edinburgh and London: Mainstream, 1993); T.C. Smout *A Century of the Scottish People* 1830–1950 (London: William Collins, 1986); Alex J. Warden *Angus or Forfarshire: The Land and the People* 3 vols (Dundee: Charles Alexander, 1880–82).

TALES OF MY OWN COUNTRY
The collection of this name was published by John Murray, London, in 1922.

`THIEVIE´
The unnamed town at the opening is probably based on Brechin ('Newbigging' is a local area). The river is almost certainly the South Esk, flowing into the Basin of Montrose ('lake-like estuary'). Floods here were not uncommon in the nineteenth century.

p.1   *the words of St Paul:* 'None of these things move me.' St Paul, the apostle and missionary of Christianity, and author of the principal *Epistles* of the New Testament, was, before his conversion on the road to Damascus, a bitter persecutor of the Christians. The reference is possibly to 2 Corinthians, 4, 8–18.

The adjoining image of the haddocks in this context might echo George Douglas Brown's *The House with the Green Shutters* (1901):

> For many reasons intimate to the Scots character, envious scandal is rampant in petty towns such as Barbie. To go back to the beginning, the Scot, as pundits will tell you, is an individualist. His religion alone is enough to make him so. For it is a scheme of personal salvation significantly described once by the Reverend Mr Struthers of Barbie. 'At the Day of Judgment, my frehnds,' said Mr Struthers; 'at the Day of Judgment every herring must hang by his own tail!' Self-dependence was never more luridly expressed. (Chapter 5)

THE DISGRACEFULNESS OF AUNTIE THOMPSON

The character of Auntie Thompson foreshadows Lewis Grassic Gibbon's Meg Menzies in the short story 'Smeddum', first published 1933.

p.26   This seems to be a fictional parish, though the church described here ('Pitairdrie kirk') sounds like Dun Kirk.

THE DEBATABLE LAND

'The debatable land' was traditionally known to be that on the border between Scotland and England, in the area of Liddesdale. However, Warden also describes the 'maritime region' of Angus as 'debatable land' (vol. 1, pp. 96–7).

p.37   *the Board School:* the Education Act (Scotland) of 1872 ('Young's Act') introduced board schools. The Act made education compulsory for children between the ages of five and thirteen.

THE FIDDLER

p.49   *Dalmain village:* the location here seems to be a fictitious hamlet in the Braes of Angus.

p.52   *Neil Gow:* this historical personage (1727–1807), whose name is more correctly spelled Niel Gow, was a famous fiddler and composer of airs and dance-tunes whose works live on today. He was born the son of a plaid weaver, at Inver, Perthshire, where he lived all his life. His son, Nathaniel Gow, was also a musician and composer.

p.53   *I am a Dunkeld man mysel'.* The town of Dunkeld is near Inver.

p.55   *branches of rowan:* the rowan is traditionally thought to provide protection against evil.

p.56   *the Duke of Atholl.* Niel Gow enjoyed the patronage of three Dukes of Atholl during his lifetime.

p.57   The description of the fiddler here echoes the portrait of Niel Gow by Henry Raeburn, painted in 1806.

p.69   *some . . . favoured King George:* Angus was predominantly Jacobite in its sympathies in the eighteenth century; those referred to here were supporters of King George II (reigned 1727–1760), of the Hanoverian line.

p.70   *'mea culpa':* Latin, meaning 'my fault or blame'. Form of words formerly used in the Roman Catholic confession.

A MIDDLE-AGED DRAMA

p.74   *Hedderwick the grieve:* Hedderwick is the ancient name of an area near Dun. A grieve is a farm bailiff or over-seer.

p.77   *paisley shawl:* from around 1790–1840 the town of Paisley was a major centre of handloom-weaving. Shawls with the distinctive 'paisley pattern' were popular.

p.80   *a grave's a bonnie safe place:* this echoes lines by Andrew Marvell: 'The grave's a fine and private place/But none I think do there embrace' (1650).

p.81   *get work i' the mills:* throughout much of the nineteenth century, thousands of people, including many women, worked in the Dundee jute mills.

p.89   *a canna live wantin' ye:* the Scots word 'wantin' ' means 'lacking, without'; but obviously the English sense also enriches the meaning here.

ANNIE CARGILL

p.90   *A Writer to the Signet:* someone who prepared writs and other legal written work, rather than speaking before the courts.

    At one time the Lindsays were a family of renown in the area around Edzell, and built Edzell Castle in the sixteenth and seventeenth centuries, but their lands passed into other hands. The name Lyall is local as well.

pp.90–1   The references to Armorial Bearings and the Landed Gentry are a reminder that Jacob's own family, the Kennedy-Erskines, were aristocrats with a long lineage; the Erskines of Dun and the Kennedy family with whom they were joined by marriage both appear in such volumes. Interestingly, the story does not paint a flattering picture of the gentry.

pp.92–3   The graveyard and settings described here sound like those at the House of Dun. Violet Jacob herself is buried not in her family's private graveyard, but with her husband, in the public kirkyard nearby.

The story bears some resemblance to certain of John Buchan's supernatural short fictions.

THE WATCH-TOWER

The 'watchtower' itself may be modelled on a tower which actually stands in Glenesk. The figure of the sheepstealer appears again in Jacob's first novel *The Sheepstealers* (1902).

p.108   *Tay, the dog:* there was a working dog of this name at one time in the Kennedy-Erskine household at the House of Dun.

p.109   *chrysophrase green:* a bright apple-green.

THE FIGUREHEAD

p.117   The setting here is Montrose; many of the names of streets (e.g. Ferry Street) remain unchanged today.

the Baltic: Montrose was once a major port trading with the Baltic. There are references to the Baltic in Jacob's poetry, where it acquires symbolic force.

Galatz: a city on the Danube, inland from the Black Sea.

p.119   A female figurehead is symbolically suggestive in Stevenson's 'The Ebb Tide' (1894). A male figurehead is also significant in Jacob's own 'The Lum Hat'.

p.121   *fish-cadger's cart:* a fish-cadger is a fish-hawker.

p.130   *The People's Journal:* popular journal.

p.137   *'cried in the kirk':* to have marriage banns read out in church.

EUPHEMIA

The location, Braes of Aird, again seems fictitious, although obviously based on landscapes near Dun.

p.140   *in Angus, women do much field-work:* according to Ian Carter, around the middle of the nineteenth century, many farms in north-east Scotland had female 'outworkers', or employed day-labourers (Carter, pp.101–2).

p.144   *beadle:* person in the service of an ecclesiastical organisation; a kirk officer; a gravedigger.

p.145   *precentor:* person who leads or directs the singing of a choir etc; specifically in Presbyterian churches, an official appointed by the Kirk Session to lead the singing.

THE OVERTHROW OF ADAM PITCAITHLEY

p.154 *He's very small for tramping:* Ian Carter's research shows that children were working on farms in considerable numbers, even into the twentieth century (see Carter, p.99).

THE LUM HAT

In 1944 Violet Jacob offered Oliver & Boyd a collection of stories; a couple of these had appeared in magazines, but most, including the novella *The Lum Hat,* had never been published. The publishers, who had issued *The Scottish Poems of Violet Jacob,* replied that they could not print the stories at that time because of paper rationing, although they might publish them later. These stories were brought to light by Ronald Garden, and appeared in *The Lum Hat and Other Stories: Last Tales of Violet Jacob* (Aberdeen: Aberdeen University Press, 1982). The manuscripts are in the National Library of Scotland, Edinburgh. The stories are not, in fact, necessarily all that 'late', as some of them date to the 1920s.

Title: a kind of hat worn in nineteenth century Scotland, taking its name from its resemblance to a 'lum' or chimney.

p.159 *photograph – taken in the very early days of the art:* this dates the period of the story to the 1840s at the very earliest.

her . . . fingers: Cecilia's hands are important in this story; Aeneas works for a firm of glove-manufacturers, perhaps hinting at the idea that these two would be well-suited, to fit each other 'like hand in glove'.

east coast Scottish seaport: this is certainly Montrose; again, real place-names in the town are used.

p.159 *velvet spencer:* short jacket.

p.160 *Ann Wishart:* plays a role slightly akin to that of Nanny in Nancy Brysson Morrison's *The Gowk Storm,* enforcing convention.

p.162 *Aeneas:* the name of a figure in Greek mythology, and the voyaging hero of Virgil's *Aeneid.*

The character in this story also bears some resemblance to Archie Flemington, in that he is associated with France, often represented in nineteenth century British literature as a location of the erotic and dangerous. Like Archie he is also dark, and contrasted with a more aggressively and traditionally 'masculine' man; he is 'pale and slim and Baird despised his looks as effeminate'.

St Cecilia: patron saint of music, especially of church music, and patron also of the blind.

p.163   'coifféd Sainte Caterine': used of a woman, meaning to have reached one's twenty-fifth birthday without marrying. St Catherine was a virgin and martyr of noble birth in Alexandria, who was put to death on a wheel (hence Catherine wheel). 'To braid St Catherine's tresses' is to die a virgin.

p.164   Martinmas Fair: the feast of St Martin, 11th November (also the day of a pagan feast). St Martin is the patron saint of innkeepers and reformed drunkards.

p.167   she had read about love . . . through the cold window pane: various metaphors represent Christina's attitude to life as if it is something fictional, throughout the novella. See also, for instance, p.212: 'Aeneas' constancy was like some pleasant book in the shelf'.

p.168   the woman with the brooms: gipsies and tinkers recur in Jacob's work, linked to themes of freedom from ownership and constriction.

timber for Adelaide: the ships of Montrose did ply to Australia in the nineteenth century, with loads of timber, often Canadian.

p.169   an unknown craft on his horizon: the nautical metaphor is especially apt for the sea-captain Baird, but the story is shot through with sea and water imagery.

p.170   one of the new turreted houses: presumably Scots Neo-Baronial architecture was just coming into fashion, as a trend of the Victorian period, following the rebuilding of Balmoral Castle by William Smith for Queen Victoria and Prince Albert in the 1850s.

p.173   Sirius . . . the dog-star: so-called by the Greeks from the adjective seirios, hot and scorching.

p.179   the roast's on the jack: the jack was a machine for turning a spit in roasting meat.

p.206   King's Island: this is probably King Island, which lies between the south coast of Victoria, Australia, and Tasmania.

p.217   the full poignancy of autumn: the novella early on features the more celebratory aspect of Autumn, with the Martinmas fair; it ends with the more melancholic aspect of the season.

THE FIFTY-EIGHT WILD SWANS
First published in *Country Life*, August 1926.
This echoes Y.B. Yeats' poem, 'The Wild Swans at Coole', from his collection of the same name

(1919), in which the speaker dwells on the 'nine-and-fifty swans'.

The association of wild birds with memory and spiritual longing is present also in Jacob's poem, 'The Wild Geese', from her collection *Songs of Angus* (1915). The Montrose basin is a wintering place for many wildfowl, and now a nature reserve.

p.220   The old man is not local; like many of Jacob's other characters he is an outsider.

p.221   *the Findhorn:* a river flowing into the Moray Firth, east of Inverness.

p.224   *ye bizzar:* Violet Jacob exchanged letters with her friend James Christison, librarian at Montrose Public Library, about the precise derivation and meaning of this word. Jacob had received a letter from the Scottish National Dictionary Association inquiring about the word, which she had used in a poem, as they were interested in incorporating it. Jacob says in her (undated) letter: 'I heard it about fifteen years ago, and used it because I liked it so much.' She asks Christison 'Will you tell me whether you think it is authentic, or a corruption of "besom" and whether, in that case, it is, in your opinion, obsolete?' Christison replies (in a letter also undated): 'I see in the copy of your poem "Kirrie" in "Bonnie Joann" you put the meaning of the word as "jade". Now I think the form "bizzar" is a Scottish form of the word "buzzar" similar to what you hear sounding as a call to mill workers to return to their work. It is quite a suitable expression for a loud-tongued, boastful, or as we would say in Scotland, a person given to making a "blaw". I think this is quite a feasible theory about the word, but I do not think it is a corruption of the word "Besom". I would not say that the word is obsolete, but it is not in common use.' (The correspondence is held in Montrose Public Library.)

p.227   *'via dolorosa':* the route Jesus Christ Our Lord went from the place of judgment to Calvary, now marked by the fourteen Stations of the Cross.

THE YELLOW DOG

First published in *Scottish Literary Journal*, May 1979. In medieval art, the dog symbolises fidelity; yellow tends to indicate inconstancy or jealousy, although in Christian symbolism, like gold, it emblematises faith, so there are ambiguities here. Hounds of various kinds feature in Celtic legend, and according to superstition, dogs howl at death. Warden remarks: 'The people dwelling in the landward part of Angus were, in the olden time, extremely superstitious' (vol. 1, p.214). The 'yellow dog' in this story is very different from the one in *Flemington*.

p.233   *He was a Fife body:* another incomer.

p.235   *arn trees:* alder trees. The alder tree in George Macdonald's *Phantastes* (1858) is associated with danger.

ANDERSON
First published in *Scottish Literary Journal*, May 1979. The protagonist's forename, Anderson, is more usually a surname, and extremely common in north-east Scotland. Here, the name has been given 'in honour of an uncle in America', one of several reminders of emigration from this part of rural Scotland, a trend which continued into the early twentieth century.

FLEMINGTON

Contents

Introduction

VIOLET JACOB'S *Flemington*, first published in 1911, and long out of print, is a gripping historical novel; it is also a tragic drama, tightly written, poetic in its symbolic intensity, leavened by flashes of dry humour.

Flemington opens in 1727, giving us a glimpse of Archie Flemington's childhood. The larger part of the novel deals with Archie's young adulthood in the period around and following the Jacobite Rebellion of 1745, when Archie, ostensibly a humble portrait painter, is working as a spy for the Whig government. A commission to paint the portrait of a leading Jacobite leads Archie to a terrible inner conflict.

The plot components, commented a contemporary reviewer, are not fresh, but the treatment of them is:

> Many are the gallant romances which have been woven out of the grim tragedy of the rising under Bonnie Prince Charlie; the dilemma, too, of the secret service agent or, in the plain language of desperate men, the spy whose finer feelings are awakened by being trusted by those who were meant to be watched and betrayed by him is by no means original. These scenes and situations have been made familiar to us by great and favourite novelists alike, but even so, whosoever begins to read *Flemington* by Violet Jacob, in the expectation that he is about to traverse a well-worn path will surely be disappointed, and that very quickly . . . In truth, though the characters perform in an old theatre, there is nothing old about their play. There is an element of the unexpected and yet the inevitable running throughout the whole story which lifts it high above the ordinary level of the historical novel.[1]

Flemington, then, was well-received when it first appeared, and soon found some notable admirers. John Buchan wrote to Violet Jacob: 'My wife and I are overcome with admiration for it and we both agree that it is years since we read so satisfying a book. I think it the best Scots romance since *The Master of Ballantrae*. The art of it is outstanding'.[2] Violet Jacob also received letters from members of the public who were moved by her work. Madge Robertson of Paisley wrote to her about *Flemington* a few years after it first appeared: 'There were tears on my cheeks as I finished it – the emotion of it is so very genuine and it is expressed with so much restraint.'[3]

Violet Jacob was not a novice at the art of fiction. When *Flemington* appeared, its author was forty-four, and had already published four novels, and three volumes of short stories (two of these for children), as well as some volumes of poetry, both for adults and children. She had also written extensive diaries and letters while in India with her husband in the latter years of the nineteenth century.[4]

Flemington is therefore the work of a practised writer, although Violet Jacob's prose shows from the beginning considerable poise. Her first sustained work of fiction, *The Sheepstealers* (1902), is a vivid and entertaining work set against the so-called 'Rebecca riots' which took place in the 1830s and 1840s in south-west Wales.[5] The rioters in this protest movement, mainly the rural poor, outraged at having to pay tolls to travel along roads once free of passage, were led by men with blackened faces, dressed in women's clothing and claiming to act in the name of 'Rebecca'. Violet Jacob, who lived in the Anglo-Welsh borderlands for some years, and whose mother was Welsh, obviously had personal reasons for her concern with this episode in Welsh history, but the novel is interesting for its concern with social protest, and its exploration of character and psychology are striking too. Another early novel, *The Interloper* (1904), is a tautly-written, absorbing and moving romance, that also shows some engagement with themes Jacob would later develop. It has as its setting the scenes of her early life in Scotland, and it is to this world that *Flemington* returns.

A sense of place, and of the connections between people and place, seems to have been important to Violet Jacob, as they were to many writers in a period when 'regional' literature flourished, and not only in Scotland.[6] Before her marriage, Jacob had been Violet Kennedy-Erskine, belonging to a family that had held lands in the area of Dun, near Montrose, for many centuries. Violet herself lived furth of Scotland for much of her life, after her marriage to Arthur Jacob, an army officer of Irish origin, in 1894. Along with their son, Harry, who was born in 1895, they lived in, variously, India, Egypt, parts of England and the Anglo-Welsh borders. Violet Jacob's imagination, though, seems to have been most deeply stirred by the places she knew best. Chief among these was her 'Own Country'[7] – Scotland and especially Angus, which provides the landscapes of *Flemington*, and to which Violet Jacob returned for the last ten years of her life after Arthur's death. Unlike Willa Muir, for instance,[8] one of several writers who grew up in this area, Violet Jacob loved Montrose and the countryside around it. It would be wrong to limit her significance to the merely local; nevertheless, much of the matter of the novel draws on her experience and knowledge of this area.

Montrose was, in the eighteenth century, an important port, doing trade primarily with the Baltic countries, Holland, Flanders and France, all of which play a part either real or symbolic in Jacob's poetry and prose (her poetry, for instance, is full of references to the Baltic).[9] Like the north east of Scotland generally, Montrose and the area around the town were strongly Episcopalian and Jacobite; indeed, the 1715 Jacobite Rebellion ended here, when the defeated James (the 'Old Pretender') set sail for France from Montrose. Although traditionally a Presbyterian family (John Knox visited Dun), some of Jacob's ancestors, the Erskines of Dun, had played a part in the Jacobite movement. The House of Dun itself, the family home, now owned by the National Trust for Scotland and open to the public, was built to plans by William Adam, but original plans had been drawn up by 'Bobbing Johnnie' Erskine, the Earl of Mar, an ambiguous and changeable figure politically, and a leader of the 1715 rising. Another Erskine, David Erskine, Lord Dun (1670–1758), a judge in Edinburgh alongside such well-known figures as Lord Grange, was responsible for having the house built. He was an opponent of the Act of Union that linked Scotland and England politically in 1707, and a covert Jacobite.

Violet Jacob knew her family history well and wrote it up in *The Lairds of Dun*, which appeared in 1931; evidently, though, she knew the family stories long before this, for she puts them to good imaginative use in her novels, especially *Flemington*, just as Naomi Mitchison was to do in her later 'family history' novel, *The Bull Calves* (1947).[10] The character of David Logie of Balnillo in *Flemington* is obviously based on that of David Erskine, the Jacobite judge, and Dun is almost certainly the prototype for the House of Balnillo in the novel. The character of her real-life ancestor is described by John Ramsay of Ochtertyre, who knew the old judge, and comments that he was:

> . . . accounted a man of honour and integrity, both
> on and off the bench. His piety and zeal for religion
> were conspicuous, even in times when all men prided
> themselves upon being decent in these matters. The
> pedantry of his talk and the starchiness of his manners
> made him the subject of ridicule among people who had
> neither his worth nor innocence of heart and life. He
> was likewise overrun with prejudice, which sometimes
> warps the judgment of able, well-intentioned men;
> but for that, one would be at a loss to account for his
> Toryism which approached very near to Jacobitism.
> How this could be reconciled to the oaths he had taken,
> is not the question here; but sometimes we see people
> wonderfully ingenious in grossly deceiving themselves.[11]

Violet Jacob herself remarks his apparently somewhat humourless, prim nature, but notes shrewdly: 'But under all this must have lain some sharp contradictory streak like the crack of light through a split panel which had made him the first Laird of Dun since the days of the Superintendant to venture to rebel against the overwhelming Presbyterian tradition that had held the family'.[12] There is here, perhaps, one clue as to the possible derivation of some of the numerous conflicts and dualities that haunt the novel.

The character of James Logie, David's brother in the novel, also seems inspired by the character of David Erskine's real-life elder brother, James (not younger as in the novel), a man of action, who fought all over Europe, not only with the Jacobites, but with Marlborough at Blenheim (and thus on different sides). Jacob had to use more imagination here than with David, for only a few bare facts are known of James, that suggest an adventurous, reckless character: he was always short of money and was disinherited by his family.[13] Portraits of both men hang in the House of Dun, and Violet Jacob must have grown up with these images. Perhaps it is from seeing these and other family portraits that she conceived also the idea of making Flemington himself a portrait painter; but then again, she herself was a gifted artist, and there is, arguably, much of Violet Jacob herself in the young protagonist of the novel.

Other elements in *Flemington* are based on historical events. The taking of the Government sloop in the novel, as Violet Jacob remarks in her prefatory note, is drawn from a true incident, which she recounts in *The Lairds of Dun*;[14] only a few details have been altered. The original vessel was called 'The Hazard', not 'The Venture', as it becomes in the novel, and although James Erskine was one of the protagonists along with a man called David Ferrier, the real-life James was at the time of the events actually seventy-four and not thirty-seven, illustrating how much imaginative transformation has taken place.

Violet Jacob denies that the novel is 'historical', 'none of the principal people in it being historic characters',[15] and it is true that she is not *primarily* interested in recreating past incidents or characters. Her *TLS* reviewer commented that *Flemington* is 'in fact little concerned with history, save as the background to the action'. In this sense she is unlike novelists such as Galt or Scott, who revelled, amongst other things, in the minutiae of the past for their own sake. But clearly the novel does make use of history, and it is perhaps Jacob's deep knowledge of, and involvement

with, places, events and people that lends the novel some
of its emotional power and air of veracity.

Yet if *Flemington* draws on the Scottish past, it is equally
rooted in literature. Among the most important influences
is that of Walter Scott, whose poetic works still line the
shelves at the House of Dun. Several of the characters in
Jacob's novels echo figures from Scott's fiction. A character
called 'Mad Moll' in *The History of Aythan Waring* (1908),
for example, recalls Madge Wildfire from *The Heart of
Midlothian*, a novel which may also have fed into *The
Sheepstealers*. Grannie Stirk in *The Interloper* seems to draw
on Scott's vigorous older peasant women characters, and
the strong aristocratic women in Jacob's fiction are remi-
niscent of Scott too, though more sympathetically drawn.
In *Flemington* itself, Skirling Wattie, the main speaker of
Scots in the novel, whose lyrics form a significant part
of the text, and whose sweet singing voice has in it 'the
whole distinctive spirit of the national poetry of Scotland'
(p.404), is a debased version of Scott's folk characters such
as Wandering Willie in *Redgauntlet* and Edie Ochiltree in
The Antiquary.[16] As in *Waverley*, the young protagonist
gives the novel its title, and Flemington himself recalls
Edward Waverley in certain respects:

> The youth and apparent frankness of Waverley stood
> in strong contrast to the shades of suspicion which
> darkened around him, and he had a sort of naivete and
> openness of demeanour that seemed to belong to one
> unhackneyed in the ways of intrigue, and which pleaded
> highly in his favour.[17]

Besides such local similarities, there are broad resem-
blances. Like Scott – and after him, Stevenson, another
writer whose influence can be discerned in her work –
Jacob takes a period in Scottish history in which warring
factions clash, and the central conflict of the novel generates
themes both specifically national (as Douglas Gifford, for
instance, argues)[18] and also more general. The opening
section of *Flemington* illustrates the way in which events
and characters are rooted in, and formed by, the past,
and the novel goes on to develop these themes and to show

how the personal history of individuals is inseparable from larger events.

Focussed on two families, *Flemington* is based on a central structural opposition: that between Whig and Jacobite, opposing political and religious factions. On each side there is deeply-held conviction, indeed, dogmatism. Madam Flemington, one of the most ruthless characters in the novel, whose personal name, Christian, seems ironic, tells her grandson, 'I will have no half-measures as I have no half-sentiments' (p.357), and even more chillingly, when Archie protests that he cannot betray James Logie, 'We have to do with principles, not men' (p.356). Even James, a more sympathetic character, is nevertheless limited in vision; he has a 'generous and rather bigoted heart. For him, there were only two kinds of men, those who were for the Stuarts and those who were not' (p.336).

Thus, like Scott and Stevenson before her, Jacob explores such themes as the nature of loyalty, the effects of rigid devotion to political ends, and the allied concepts of treachery and betrayal. Madam Flemington has felt betrayed in the past at St Germain, and she in turn accuses Archie of betraying the Whig cause and herself. James, who is to feel betrayed by Archie too, has a stern view: 'when God calls us all to judgment, there will be no mercy for treachery' (p.341).

In the society of *Flemington*, it would seem, there is no room for humane compromise; and because of this, members of both the opposed families, which are themselves internally divided by differences of age and personality, face a series of dilemmas. *Flemington* explores the moral options for characters – and for readers – in a world where corruption co-exists with bigotry to destructive ends.

Between the warring factions, Archie, essentially principled but flexible, is caught. Like Scott's Edward Waverley, Jacob's hero comes from a politically divided background, his own parents being Jacobite; but unlike Waverley he is far from 'passive', and desperately embroiled in the situation. Although of firm Whig convictions like his grandmother, he can see beyond politics to common humanity and finds himself in an intolerable situation when required to betray

James Logie, for the men are drawn to one another like brothers (p.343, p.349); the appalling alternative is to cut himself off from his grandmother.

Jacob explores the problems of choice elsewhere in her fiction: a difficult conflict is faced by Cecilia Raeburn in *The Interloper*, for instance, but the issues are more seriously developed here than in Jacob's earlier, lighter novel, with its more conventional 'happy ending', and the outcome of inflexible devotion to political ends and to moral stances is tragically illustrated. The boyish Archie has much in common with Stevenson's David Balfour, who faces a corrupt society and says near the end of *Catriona* 'till the end of time young folk (who are not yet used with the duplicity of life and men) will struggle as I did, and make heroical resolves . . . and the course of events will push them upon one side'.[19]

It should be noted, of course, that while Archie is by comparison with others in the novel a humane figure, he is in some ways an unlikely 'hero'; he not only belongs to the 'unromantic', unpopular Whig side, he is not straightforwardly 'in the right'. He is a government spy who sets out to betray a man offering him generous hospitality. Yet the reader is likely to be caught up in Archie's dilemma, and moved by it. Although the novel is related in the third person, the use of point of view establishes our sympathy for Archie; we share his perspective at key moments in the action, such as during the tense scenes at 'The Happy Land', and in the following chapter. With his 'feminine' refinement (p.313) he is vulnerable in a brutish society, although he appeals, paradoxically, to the soldier James (who has little time for 'this womanish trade' of painting, p.310), and to his betrayer, Skirling Wattie. Both, like the reader, respond to Archie's 'sensuous joy in the world, his love of life and its hazards and energies' (p.330), thus suggesting the problematic issues involved in forming judgments.

As in an earlier fictional tradition, appearance is shown to be no true guide to value in this morally treacherous universe. Of Archie, we read that 'his looks were the only really unreliable part of him' (p.360). James, too, is not altogether what he appears; he has a 'crooked mouth' (p.289), but he is an honest speaker, and his memories of the past, directly related by him, are touching for the reader as well as Archie. What is more, this man of war with his 'look of virility' (p.289) nevertheless reveals vulnerability 'like the defencelessness of a child looking upon the dark' (p.338). Strangely emblematic of many of the key concerns in the novel is the yellow dog. Outwardly the colour of cowardice, the ugly cur is nevertheless both brave and loyal.

Skirling Wattie, on the other hand, is described at one point as having a 'jovial face' (p.371), and yet, as the novel reveals, he is, at the same time, corrupt and unreliable. But then again, like other charcters, Skirling Wattie is a complex figure. He may betray Archie, but he fights for survival in a cruel world, and it is difficult not to respect his tenacious love of life and his spirit. David Balnillo, pompous and self-interested, both Jacobite and judge, treads the moral borderlands and survives where others more courageous are destroyed, but he is not, in the last analysis, evil.

Among the more challenging figures in the novel, Christian Flemington is a particularly interesting creation. Manipulative and in many ways destructive – her fan tellingly bears a picture of a bull-fight (p.439), and she brings war into her personal relationships (p.355) – she is at the same time a passionate and spirited woman: like other Scottish women writers such as Margaret Oliphant before her, and Willa Muir later, Violet Jacob created some very powerful female characters.[20] Christian Flemington seems all the more remarkable when seen beside such weak men as the judge, or the minister in the opening scene, to whom she seems dangerously sexual and 'foreign'. Yet she is an isolated figure, one of the few female characters in the novel, and the reader may feel some pity for her errors, too, at the awful moment when she faces Cumberland and understands Archie's sure fate, especially when, after her exit the 'Butcher' cruelly remarks, 'Damn me, but I hate old women! They should have their tongues cut out' (p.507). His words suggest the nature of a

society that despises women as well as 'feminine' qualities.

While Christian and other characters may not attract
our fullest sympathy, the shifting perspective of the narrative voice, illuminating their experience and setting
their attitudes in the context of this place and time,
suggests they are not wholly to be condemned. In fact,
with the exception of the Duke of Cumberland, there
is no character one could describe as wholly bad or
unsympathetic.

Flemington, then, sets out to undermine moral rigidity,
and present a more complex vision than is held by
many of the characters within its pages. Avoiding the
'moral certainties' of Scottish 'kailyard' fiction,[21] this
novel offers a challenge to its readers, too; refusing to
elicit clear or simple judgments, it implies that toler-
ance and compassion are qualities to be prized over
all.

Morally challenging, this early twentieth century novel
is, somewhat like Stevenson's fiction a little earlier, also
both intensely realist and powerfully symbolic in its effects.
Jacob presents Scotland at a deeply difficult period in its
history. As James Logie tells Archie: 'I know how hard
life can be and how anxious, nowadays. There is so much
loss and trouble – God knows what may happen to this
tormented country' (p.335). The troubled nature of the
land and times is suggested in various ways. The name of
the brothel, 'The Happy Land', is ironic, especially in the
face of Jacob's descriptions of Scotland after Culloden.[22]
Skirling Wattie, too, ironically seeming 'like the sovereign
of some jovial and misgoverned kingdom' (p.364), may
symbolically suggest the truncated and enfeebled state
of Scottish culture, and its corruption; his soul is dark,
his vanity about his singing 'the one piece of romance
belonging to him; it hung over his muddy soul as a
weaving of honeysuckle may hang over a dank pond'
(p.427).

The 'muddy', barren nature of Scotland is suggested in
the landscape, which is metaphorically suggestive throughout:

> [Archie] sat down on the scrubby waste land by a
> broom-bush, whose dry, burst pods hung like tattered
> black flags in the brush of green; their acrid smell was
> coming out as the sun mounted higher. Below him the
> marshy ground ran out to meet the water; and eastward
> the uncovered mud and wet sand, bared by the tide
> ebbing beyond Montrose, stretched along its shores to
> the town. (p.333)

The 'tattered black flags' seem to prefigure war; and the
sea imagery that permeates the novel is disturbing. Archie
is 'Adrift' (Chapter 10), a solitary figure in a sea of troubles
(see p.401); the North Sea is 'a formless void in the night'
(p.373), and James, on Inchbrayock, thinks how its only
dwellers now are the dead:

> . . . those who were lying under his feet – seamen, for
> the most part, and fisher-folk, who had known the fury
> of the North Sea that was now beginning to crawl in
> and to surround them in their little township with its
> insidious arms, encircling in death the bodies that had
> escaped it in life. (p.385)

The people in this death-touched land are described as
being like animals, emphasising the struggle for survival
and, at times, the savagery of human nature. Logie's eyes
'shone in the dim room like the eyes of some animal
watching in a cave' (p.324), Balnillo 'threw out his chest
like a pouter pigeon' (p.443), Captain Hall is like a rabbit
(p.375), Skirling Wattie a wild boar (p.403), Christian a
cat (p.496). Some of these similes and metaphors are
sustained and developed, such as the comparison of
Archie with a dog; Christian Flemington 'had smiled at
his devotion to her as she would have smiled with gratified
comprehension at the fidelity of a favourite dog' (p.356).
Archie 'was like a stray dog in a market place' (p.386);
later, Lord Balnillo is like a dog in relation to Christian
(p.457).

Many scenes take place in the darkness that is a creeping
force 'drawing itself like an insidious net' (p.486), but light
gleams through from time to time: 'the sun heaved up from

beyond the bar' (p.386), so that the novel takes place 'In Darkness and in Light' (the title given to Chapter 6). There are flashes of brilliant colour: the crimson of tulips in Holland (p.340), the jewels that dangle from Christian Flemington's ears, 'the ruby earrings which shot blood-red sparks around her when she moved' (p.439), the 'rowan tree, whose berries were already beginning to colour for autumn' (p.486), and the 'red and gold' of the gean trees (p.297) on the Balnillo estate, which 'glowed carmine and orange, touches of quickening fire shot through the interstices of their branches' (p.331). It is a very visual book, a novel about a painter written with the eye of a painter.

The autumn scenes and colours and other seasonal references contribute to the creation of mood as well as the development of themes. Archie himself is associated, in James's mind, with Spring (p.315), but even the 'Prologue', set in the spring of Archie's life, takes place in autumn: Archie watches Mr Duthie depart 'between the yellowing leaves of the tree which autumn was turning into the clear-tinted ghost of itself' (p.286). Much of the action is set in a landscape of fallen leaves (p.301) and October light (p.330), and the 'Epilogue' closes with a sad autumnal scene. The chapter 'Winter' foreshadows the poem by Edwin Muir, 'Scotland's Winter',[23] that links that season with the times.

Flemington is not all dark: the narrative is compelling, with the qualities of a good adventure story, and there is a strain of wry humour, present in the narrative voice and suggested through the handling of David, for instance, and of Skirling Wattie and Christian Flemington. But unlike some of the many historical romances which appeared in this period, *Flemington* also has claims to be called a genuinely tragic novel.[24] Interesting, as its early *TLS* reviewer noted, for its sharp and effective depiction of character,[25] it works within a tight framework: events and characters move with seeming inevitability towards their fated ends.

The key figure is a young man with some of the characteristic qualities of the young Romantic hero. Archie is sensitive and artistic with a 'roving imagination' (p.292), one of those 'who live their lives with every nerve and fibre' (p.351), and pay the price for it. Like Archie Weir in *Weir of Hermiston*, Archie Flemington is a young idealist (see p.331 for instance), and like his namesake he has a Rousseauist perception of nature and of the essential goodness of creation; he longs to 'cast his body down upon the light-pervaded earth' (p.331), and to 'fling his soul' upwards into the sun. The reference to the sun here is significant later, as is the depiction of Archie's soul as a bird (p.331).

The choices and pressures that build up around Archie are finely explored; from the beginning when the roots of the tragedy are exposed, to the bitter end, the forces that drive individual personalities interact relentlessly with circumstance. Jacob was compared in her own time to Hardy,[26] and like him she alludes throughout the novel to the work of 'Fate': 'To most people who are haunted by a particular dread, Fate plays one of the tricks she loves so much. She is an expert boxer . . .' (p.461); but the references to 'Chance' and 'luck' leave the ultimate question – how much is really 'predestined'? – an open one.

The question of whether Archie's fate is a just one is, I think, more conclusively answered. There is little sense that justice has been done. Archie's death seems a tragic waste, and the reader's sense of injustice is heightened by the proximity of the scene in which Madam Flemington has her interview with Cumberland. The man's brutal inhumanity is in sharp contrast with the condemned youth's compassion and moral seriousness.

Tragic irony is omnipresent. It is ironic that Skirling Wattie should so misunderstand Archie's nature. It is ironic that Christian could have saved him in ways she did not understand. It is ironic that Archie is finally executed by one of the few men of honour, Callander, 'steadfast' (p.466) like the yellow cur, comparable to Archie himself in his integrity, yet 'the most repressed person' (p.464) Archie had met, inflexible in his devotion to duty. Although Archie understands and forgives, the reader may feel frustration.

There is some relief, however. Archie is, at least, released from an intolerable situation. The image, at his death, is of a solitary bird: 'this one was going into the sunrise' (p.514), recalling the scene when Archie longed for union with nature, with the sun; his birdsoul has finally been set free. His end in this way can be seen as modestly Christian, cathartic and affirmative. There is even, quite early on in the novel, an unusually explicit hint at an austere yet 'positive' view of suffering, foreshadowing later events:

> He did not think, any more than any of us think, that perhaps when we come to lie on our death-beds we shall know that, of all the privileges of the life behind us, the greatest has been the privilege of having suffered and fought. (p.370)

With his death the tormented Archie is released from suffering, and from the prison of the mere human flesh, having indeed 'suffered and fought', and the sunrise is a sign of hope for the future.

Nevertheless, the novel is shot through with events that reverberate long after they are over. This tragedy ends not with a death, but with those left behind. Early on in the novel, James remarks that 'the old beech tree by the stables wants a limb' (p.289), and this image recurs at the end, when we see him, alone in a dark autumnal room in Holland, with, outside, 'the jealous shadows of the beech-tree's mutilated arms' (p.515). James, in lonely exile, has returned to the scenes of his early love – and loss. It is significant that James has rescued the yellow dog, but the dead, mutilated beggar's bonnet is a reminder of what has gone before. We have been told 'love and loss are things that lay their shadows everywhere, and Madam Flemington had lost much' (p.427), and the sense of loss that has been frequently evoked is stronger here at the end than ever. We may remember James' words to Archie much earlier: 'We outlive trouble in time, Flemington; we outlive it, though we cannot outlive memory. We outlast it – that is a better word' (p.343).

James has told Archie that fighting can be, for some soldiers like himself, a means of escaping private pain; James himself at one time turned to war 'for consolation as a man may turn to his religion' (p.338). By the end war surely offers little consolation; certainly, we have seen Archie's honourable sacrifice, and the compassionate gestures of James and Callander; but the way in which personal and public destruction and pain are interwoven is all the clearer.

Jacob's novel recreates the past in ways that seem, with hindsight, uncannily relevant not only to her own time, but her own life. *Flemington* was published in 1911: in Scotland it was the year of the big Glasgow Exhibition, when nationalism was on the agenda, a time of political uncertainty and growing industrial unrest. Above all, though, this was the period of build-up to war. Jacob's powerful images of wasteland and warfare, and of private grief, anticipate the outbreak of World War I in 1914 a mere three years after the publication of *Flemington*.

There is a grim irony in this, for Jacob's moving depiction of the young artist Archie Flemington surely owes much to her knowledge of, and love for, her own son, Harry Jacob, who died at the age of twenty in 1916, at the Battle of the Somme, five years after the novel appeared. This was the great, real tragedy of Violet Jacob's life, and according to Susan Tweedsmuir who knew her, it was a blow from which she never recovered:

> Violet Jacob had one son, whom she loved with
> all the depth of an imaginative and passionate
> nature. When he was killed in the 1914 War a
> spring in her broke. She never wrote a long book
> again, and turned to writing poems in the Scottish
> vernacular.[27]

NOTES

1 *Times Literary Supplement*, Thursday 30 November 1911, p.493, unsigned review of *Flemington* titled 'A Tale of the '45'.
2 Letter, 31 December 1911; National Library of Scotland, Acc. 6686.

3 Letter, 7 September 1915; National Library of Scotland, Acc. 6686.

4 Published for the first time in 1990. For full details of this and other publications by Violet Jacob see Bibliography.

5 This historical episode is documented by David J.V. Jones in *Rebecca's Children: A study of rural society, crime and protest* (Oxford: Clarendon Press, 1990).

6 Peter Keating discusses the 'new self-conscious regionalism' in British literature in chapter 6 of *The Haunted Study: A Social History of the English Novel 1875–1914* (first published London: Martin Secker and Warburg, 1989; reference here to the paperback edition, London: Fontana, 1991). He gives a good account of the Scottish dimension.

7 A reference to Jacob's volume of short stories, *Tales of My Own Country*, of 1922.

8 Muir's fictional town Calderwick is based on her experience of Montrose. In *Imagined Corners* (1935), for instance, the town is not flatteringly presented.

9 Jacob's poems include, for example, 'Baltic Street' (the name of a real street in Montrose) and 'The Wind Frae the Baltic', in the collection *Bonnie Joann*.

10 *The Bull Calves* (London: Jonathan Cape, 1947; reprinted Glasgow: Richard Drew Publishing, 1985).

11 *Scotland and Scotsmen in the Eighteenth Century* from the MSS of John Ramsay Esq of Ochtertyre, edited by Alexander Allardyce (Edinburgh and London: William Blackwood and Sons, 1888), 2 vols; vol 1, p.85.

12 *The Lairds of Dun* (London: John Murray, 1931), p.234.

13 For more details see *The Lairds of Dun*, pp.232–3.

14 *The Lairds of Dun*, pp.249–57.

15 'Author's Note to *Flemington*', p.275. Further references to the novel are to this edition, and will be given in brackets after quotations.

16 Scott himself wrote in an Advertisement to the 1829 edition of *The Antiquary*: 'Many of the old Scottish mendicants were by no means to be confounded with the utterly degraded class of beings who now practise that wandering trade.'

17 Walter Scott, *Waverley* (first published 1814; see the recent edition ed. Claire Lamont (Oxford: Oxford University Press, 1986), Vol. II, Ch. IX, p.161).

18 See 'Myth, Parody and Dissociation: Scottish Fiction 1814–1914', in Douglas Gifford (ed.), *The History of Scottish Literature, vol* 3: Nineteenth Century (Aberdeen: Aberdeen University Press, 1988), pp.217–259, esp. pp.242–3.

19 *Catriona*, first published 1893; see the recent edition ed.

Emma Letley (Oxford: Oxford University Press, 1986), Ch. XX, p.382.

20 Among Oliphant's many novels, mention might be made of *Miss Marjoriebanks* (Edinburgh and London: Blackwood & Sons; reprinted London: Virago, 1988), *Hester* (London: Macmillan, 1883; reprinted London: Virago, 1984), *Kirsteen* (London: Macmillan, 1890; reprinted London: Dent, 1984). See also Willa Muir's *Mrs Ritchie* (London: Secker, 1933).

21 See Keating, *The Haunted Study*, p.338.

22 Apparently this was a real place, as suggested in *Montrose Standard and Mearns Register* 26 January 1912, p.12. See also note to pp.318–19 of this novel.

23 First published in *One Foot in Eden* (London: Faber and Faber, 1956).

24 Keating (pp.348–56) discusses the great quantity and variety of historical fiction by British writers in this period, arguing that it was ultimately largely a 'literary disappointment' (p.351).

25 The reviewer comments that 'there is abundance of incident, vividly told, in the book, but the main interest is that of character. Every one who has any part to play, whether essential or supernumerary, is drawn with a sure and skilful hand, most powerful when it is most restrained; every one is given a definite individuality and no one is in any degree commonplace . . .' (p.493).

26 For instance by contemporary reviewers of *The Sheepstealers* (1902), as in *The Spectator*, 13 September 1902, p.368: 'it is free from the crushing pessimism of the novels of Mr Hardy, the writer to whom on his best and most poetic side Miss Jacob is more closely related'.

27 *The Lilac and the Rose* (London: Gerald Duckworth, 1952), p.55.

Acknowledgments

I WOULD like to thank the following people in particular for their interest, encouragement and generous help of various kinds: Margaret and Nigel Anderson, Sarah Bing, Tom Crawford, Joris and Jo Duytschaever, Emma Letley, Christopher MacLachlan, Douglas Mack and Isobel Murray. In addition I appreciate the assistance of librarians at Montrose Public Library and the National Library of Scotland, and representatives of the National Trust at the House of Dun. I am also indebted to numerous friends and colleagues in Scotland, especially in Glasgow, and in Italy and Japan, for their support.

Note on the Text

The text is based on the first edition of 1911. The following corrections have been made in the present edition.

MINOR CORRECTIONS (page references are to the present edition, with references to the 1911 edition in brackets)

p.292, l.28: 'carrin' amended to 'carrying' (p.22).
p.298, l.20: space inserted between 'when you' (p.32).
p.318, l.6: word 'incessantly' split between lines has been restored (p.60).
p.352, l.19: 'over' corrected to 'ever' (p.111).
p.384, l.7: 'shiping' corrected to 'shipping' (p.157).
p.395, l.22: 'grapling' corrected to 'grappling' (p.175).
p.407, l.1: 'ruuning' corrected to 'running' (p.190).
p.434, l.26: 'seearch' corrected to 'search' (p.229).
p.471, l.8: 'began' corrected to 'begun' (p.280).
p.477, l.2: correct spacing inserted between 'which the' (p.288).
p.479, l.2: correct spacing inserted between 'him the' (p.291).
p.485, l.36: word 'in' inserted (p.297).
p.491, l.37: letter 'c' lowered to usual level of case (p.311).

OTHER AMENDMENTS

The Scots Brigade: pages 289, 339, 343, 347; 520 (note to p. 289) (1911 edition pages 17–18, 92, 97, 104). This was printed both with and without an apostrophe. In the present edition the apostrophe has been dropped.

Bergen-op-Zoom: pages 342, 347, 385; 525 (note to p.342) (1911 edition pages 96, 104, 161). This name was spelled both with and without hyphens in the 1911 edition. In the present edition the hyphens have been used in all instances (following the majority of cases in Jacob's text, and given that both forms appear to be in modern usage).

p.290 (1911 edition, p.19). ' "He is cursin', ma lord" ': the 1911 edition omits 'is' (or 's). It is not clear whether this is deliberate or not.

p.363 (1991 edition, p.128) East Neuk. The 1911 edition spells
the second word 'Nauk', a variant on the more usual 'Neuk',
perhaps to suggest a particular pronunciation.

p.503 (1911 edition, p.327) Canongate. The 1911 edition uses
the spelling 'Cannongate'.

Author's Note

This book has no claim to be considered an historical
novel, none of the principal people in it being historic
characters; but the taking of the ship, as also the manner
of its accomplishment, is true.

V.J.

BOOK I

ONE

Prologue

MR. DUTHIE walked up the hill with the gurgle of the burn he had just crossed purring in his ears. The road was narrow and muddy, and the house of Ardguys, for which he was making, stood a little way in front of him, looking across the dip threaded by the water. The tall white walls, discoloured by damp and crowned by their steep roof, glimmered through the ash-trees on the bank at his right hand. There was something distasteful to the reverend man's decent mind in this homely approach to the mansion inhabited by the lady he was on his way to visit, and he found the remoteness of this byway among the grazing lands of Angus oppressive.

The Kilpie burn, travelling to the river Isla, farther west, had pushed its way through the undulations of pasture that gave this particular tract, lying north of the Sidlaws, a definite character; and the formation of the land seemed to suggest that some vast groundswell had taken place in the earth, to be arrested, suddenly, in its heaving, for all time. Thus it was that a stranger, wandering about, might come unwarily upon little outlying farms and cottages hidden in the trough of these terrestrial waves, and find himself, when he least awaited it, with his feet on a level with some humble roof, snug in a fold of the braes. It was in one of the largest of these miniature valleys that the house of Ardguys stood, with the Kilpie burn running at the bottom of its sloping garden.

Mr. Duthie was not a stranger, but he did not admire the unexpected; he disliked the approach to Ardguys, for his sense of suitability was great; indeed, it was its greatness which was driving him on his present errand. He had no gifts except the quality of decency, which is a gift like any other;

and he was apt, in the company of Madam Flemington,
to whose presence he was now hastening, to be made
aware of the great inconvenience of his shortcomings,
and the still greater inconvenience of his advantage. He
crossed the piece of uneven turf dividing the house from
the road, and ascended the short flight of stone steps, a
spare, black figure in a three-cornered hat, to knock with
no uncertain hand upon the door. His one great quality
was staying him up.

Like the rest of his compeers in the first half of the
seventeen hundreds, Mr. Duthie wore garments of rusty
blue or grey during the week, but for this occasion he had
plunged his ungainly arms and legs into the black which he
generally kept for the Sabbath-day, though the change gave
him little distinction. He was a homely and very uncultured
person; and while the approaching middle of the century
was bringing a marked improvement to country ministers
as a class, mentally and socially, he had stood still.

He was ushered into a small panelled room in which
he waited alone for a few minutes, his hat on his knee.
Then there was a movement outside, and a lady came in,
whose appearance let loose upon him all those devils of
apprehension which had hovered about him as he made
his way from his manse to the chair on which he sat. He
rose, stricken yet resolute, with the cold forlorn courage
which is the bravest thing in the world.

As Madam Flemington entered, she took possession of
the room to the exclusion of everything else, and the
minister felt as if he had no right to exist. Her eyes,
meeting his, reflected the idea.

Christian Flemington carried with her that atmosphere
which enwraps a woman who has been much courted
by men, and, though she was just over forty-two, and
a grandmother, the most inexperienced observer might
know how strongly the fires of life were burning in her
still. An experienced one would be led to think of all
kinds of disturbing subjects by her mere presence; intrigue,
love, power – a thousand abstract yet stirring things, far,
far remote from the weather-beaten house which was the
incongruous shell of this compelling personality. Dignity

was hers in an almost appalling degree, but it was a quality unlike the vulgar conception of it; a dignity which could be all things besides distant; unscrupulous in its uses, at times rather brutal, outspoken, even jovial; born of absolute fearlessness, and conveying the certainty that its possessor would speak and act as she chose, because she regarded encroachment as impossible and had the power of cutting the bridge between herself and humanity at will. That power was hers to use and to abuse, and she was accustomed to do both. In speech she could have a plain coarseness which has nothing to do with vulgarity, and is, indeed, scarcely compatible with it; a coarseness which is disappearing from the world in company with many better and worse things.

She moved slowly, for she was a large woman and had never been an active one; but the bold and steady brilliance of her eyes, which the years had not faded, suggested swift and sudden action in a way that was disconcerting. She had the short, straight nose common to feline types, and time, which had spared her eyes, was duplicating her chin. Her eyebrows, even and black, accentuated the heavy silver of her abundant unpowered hair, which had turned colour early, and an immense ruby hung from each of her tiny ears in a setting of small diamonds. Mr. Duthie, who noticed none of these things particularly, was, nevertheless, crushed by their general combination.

It was nine years before this story opens that Christian Flemington had left France to take up her abode on the small estate of Ardguys, which had been left to her by a distant relation. Whilst still almost a child, she had married a man much older than herself, and her whole wedded life had been spent at the Court of James II of England at St. Germain, whither her husband, a Scottish gentleman of good birth in the exiled King's suite, had followed his master, remaining after his death in attendance upon his widow, Mary Beatrice of Modena.

Flemington did not long survive the King. He left his wife with one son, who, on reaching manhood, estranged himself from his mother by an undesirable marriage; indeed, it was immediately after this latter event that Christian quitted her post at Court, retiring to Rouen, where she lived until the possession of Ardguys, which she inherited a few months later, gave her a home of her own.

Different stories were afloat concerning her departure. Many people said that she had gambled away the greater part of her small fortune and was forced to retrench in some quiet place; others, that she had quarrelled with, and been dismissed by, Mary Beatrice. Others, again, declared that she had been paid too much attention by the young Chevalier de St. George and had found it discreet to take herself out of his way; but the believers in this last theory were laughed to scorn; not because the world saw anything strange in the Chevalier's alleged infatuation, but because it was quite sure that Christian Flemington would have acted very differently in the circumstances. But no one could be certain of the truth: the one certain thing was that she was gone and that since her retreat to Rouen she had openly professed Whig sympathies. She had been settled at Ardguys, where she kept her political leanings strictly to herself, for some little time, when news came that smallpox had carried off her son and his undesirable wife, and, as a consequence, their little boy was sent home to the care of his Whig grandmother, much against the will of those Jacobites at the Court of St. Germain who were still interested in the family. But as nobody's objection was strong enough to affect his pocket, the child departed.

'Madam' Flemington, as she was called by her few neighbours, was in correspondence with none of her old friends, and none of these had the least idea what she felt about her loss or about the prospect of the child's arrival. She was his natural guardian, and, though so many shook their heads at the notion of his being brought up by a rank Whig, no one was prepared to relieve her of her responsibility. Only Mary Beatrice, mindful of the elder Flemington's faithful services to James, granted a small pension for the boy's upbringing from her meagre private purse; but as this was refused by Christian, the matter ended. And now, in the year of grace 1727, young Archie Flemington was a boy of eight, and the living cause of the Rev. William Duthie's present predicament.

Madam Flemington and the minister sat opposite to each other, silent. He was evidently trying to make a beginning of his business, but his companion was not in a mood to help him. He was a person who wearied her, and she hated red hair; besides which, she was an Episcopalian and out of sympathy with himself and his community. She found him common and limited, and at the present moment, intrusive.

'It's sma' pleasure I have in coming to Ardguys the day,' he began, and then stopped, because her eyes paralysed his tongue.

'You are no flatterer,' said she.

But the contempt in her voice braced him.

'Indeed, that I am not, madam,' he replied; 'neither shall it be said of me that I gang back from my duty. Nane shall assail nor make a mock of the Kirk while I am its minister.'

'Who has made a mock of the Kirk, my good man?'

'Airchie.'

The vision of her eight-year-old grandson going forth, like a young David, to war against the Presbyterian stronghold, brought back Madam Flemington's good-humour.

'Ye may smile, madam,' said Duthie, plunged deeper into the vernacular by agitation, 'ay, ye may lauch. But it ill beseems the grey hair on yer pow.'

Irony always pleased her and she laughed outright, showing her strong white teeth. It was not only Archie and the Kirk that amused her, but the whimsical turn of her own fate which had made her hear such an argument from a man. It was not thus that men had approached her in the old days.

'You are no flatterer, Mr. Duthie, as I said before.'

He looked at her with uncomprehending eyes.

A shout, as of a boy playing outside, came through the window, and a bunch of cattle upon the slope cantered by with their tails in the air. Evidently somebody was chasing them.

'Let me hear about Archie,' said the lady, recalled to the main point by the sight.

'Madam, I would wish that ye could step west to the

manse wi' me and see the evil abomination at my gate. It would gar ye blush.'

'I am obliged to you, sir. I had not thought to be put to that necessity by one of your cloth.'

'Madam—'

'Go on, Mr. Duthie. I can blush without going to the manse for it.'

'An evil image has been set up upon my gate,' he continued, raising his voice as though to cry down her levity, 'an idolatrous picture. I think shame that the weans ganging by to the schule should see it. But I rejoice that there's mony o' them doesna' ken wha it is.'

'Fie, Mr. Duthie! Is it Venus?'

'It has idolatrous garments,' continued he, with the loud monotony of one shouting against a tempest, 'and a muckle crown on its head—'

'Then it is not Venus,' observed she. 'Venus goes stripped.'

'It is the Pope of Rome,' went on Mr. Duthie; 'I kent him when I saw the gaudy claes o' him and the heathen vanities on his pow. I kent it was himsel'! And it was written at the foot o' him, forbye that. Ay, madam, there was writing too. There was a muckle bag out frae his mou' wi' wicked words on it! "Come awa' to Babylon wi' me, Mr. Duthie." I gar'd the beadle run for water and a clout, for I could not thole that sic' a thing should be seen.'

'And you left the Pope?' said Madam Flemington.

'I did,' replied the minister. 'I would wish to let ye see to whatlike misuse Airchie has put his talents.'

'And how do you know it was Archie's work?'

'There's naebody hereabouts but Airchie could have made sic' a thing. The beadle tell't me that he saw him sitting ahint the whins wi' his box of paint as he gae'd down the manse road, and syne when he came back the image was there.'

As he finished his sentence the door opened and a small figure was arrested on the threshold by the sight of him. The little boy paused, disconcerted and staring, and a faint colour rose in his olive face. Then his glum look changed to a smile in which roguery, misgiving, and an intense malicious joy were blended. He looked from one to the other.

'Archie, come in and make your reverence to Mr. Duthie,' said Madam Flemington, who had all at once relapsed into punctiliousness.

Archie obeyed. His skin and his dark eyes hinted at his mother's French blood, but his bow made it a certainty.

The minister offered no acknowledgment.

If Archie had any doubt about the reason of Mr. Duthie's visit, it did not last long. The minister was not a very stern man in daily life, but now the Pope and Madam Flemington between them had goaded him off his normal peaceable path, and his expression bade the little boy prepare for the inevitable. Archie reflected that his grandmother was a disciplinarian, and his mind went to a cupboard in the attics where she kept a cane. But the strain of childish philosophy which ran through his volatile nature was of a practical kind, and it reminded him that he must pay for his pleasures, and that sometimes they were worth the expense. Even in the grip of Nemesis he was not altogether sorry that he had drawn that picture.

Madam Flemington said nothing, and Mr. Duthie beckoned to him to come nearer.

'Child,' said he, 'you have put an affront upon the whole o' the folk of this parish. You have raised up an image to be a scandal to the passers-by. You have set up a notorious thing in our midst, and you have caused words to issue from its mouth that the very kirk-officer, when he dichted it out wi' his clout, thought shame to look upon. I have jaloused it right to complain to your grandmother and to warn her, that she may check you before you bring disgrace and dismay upon her and upon her house.'

Archie's eyes had grown rounder as he listened, for the pomp of the high-sounding words impressed him with a sense of importance, and he was rather astonished to find that any deed of his own could produce such an effect. He contemplated the minister with a curious detachment that belonged to himself. Then he turned to look at his grandmother, and, though her face betrayed no encouragement, the subtle smile he had worn when he stood at the door appeared for a moment upon his lips.

Mr. Duthie saw it. Madam Flemington had not urged one word in defence of the culprit, but, rightly or wrongly, he scented lack of sympathy with his errand. He turned upon her.

'I charge you – nay, I demand it of you,' he exclaimed – 'that you root out the evil in yon bairn's nature! Tak' awa' from him the foolish toy that he has put to sic' a vile use. I will require of you—'

'Sir,' said Madam Flemington, rising, 'I have need of nobody to teach me how to correct my grandson. I am obliged to you for your visit, but I will not detain you longer.'

And almost before he realised what had happened, Mr. Duthie found himself once more upon the stone steps of Ardguys.

Archie and his grandmother were left together in the panelled room. Perhaps the boy's hopes were raised by the abrupt departure of his accuser. He glanced tentatively at her.

'You will not take away my box?' he inquired.

'No.'

'Mr. Duthie has a face like this,' he said airily, drawing his small features into a really brilliant imitation of the minister.

The answer was hardly what he expected.

'Go up to the cupboard and fetch me the cane,' said Madam Flemington.

It was a short time later when Archie, rather sore, but still comforted by his philosophy, sat among the boughs of a tree farther up the hill. It was a favourite spot of his, for he could look down through the light foliage over the roof of Ardguys and the Kilpie burn to the rough road ascending beyond them. The figure of the retreating Mr. Duthie had almost reached the top and was about to be lost in the whin-patch across the strath. The little boy's eyes followed him between the yellowing leaves of the tree which autumn was turning into the clear-tinted ghost of itself. He had not escaped justice, and the marks of tears were on his face; but they were not rancorous tears, whose traces live in the heart long after the outward sign of their fall has gone. They were tears forced from him by passing stress, and their sources were shallow. Madam Flemington could deal out punishment thoroughly, but she was not one of those who burn its raw wounds with sour words, and her grandson had not that woeful sense of estrangement which is the lot of many children when disciplined by those they love. Archie adored his grandmother, and the gap of years between them was bridged for him by his instinctive and deep admiration. She was no companion to him, but she was a deity, and he had never dreamed of investing her with those dull attributes which the young will tack on to those who are much their seniors, whether they possess them or not. Mr. Duthie, who had just reached middle life, seemed a much older person to Archie.

He felt in his pocket for the dilapidated box which held his chief treasures – those dirty lumps of paint with which he could do such surprising things. No, there was not very much black left, and he must contrive to get some more, for the adornment of the other manse gatepost was in his mind. He would need a great deal of black, because this time his subject would be the devil; and there should be the same – or very nearly the same – invitation to the minister.

TWO

Jetsam

EIGHTEEN YEARS after the last vestige of Archie's handiwork had vanished under the beadle's 'clout' two gentlemen were sitting in the library of a square stone mansion at the eastern end of the county of Angus. It was evening, and they had drawn their chairs up to a fireplace in which the flames danced between great hobs of polished brass, shooting the light from their thrusting tongues into a lofty room with drawn curtains and shelves of leather-bound books. Though the shutters were closed, the two men could hear, in the pauses of talk, a continuous distant roaring, which was the sound of surf breaking upon the bar outside the harbour of Montrose, three miles away. A small mahogany table with glasses and a decanter stood at Lord Balnillo's elbow, and he looked across at his brother James (whose life, as a soldier, had kept him much in foreign countries until the previous year) with an expression of mingled good-will and patronage.

David Logie was one of the many Scottish gentlemen of good birth who had made the law his profession, and he had just retired from the Edinburgh bench, on which, as Lord Balnillo, he had sat for hard upon a quarter of a century. His face was fresh-coloured and healthy, and, though he had not put on so much flesh as a man of sedentary ways who has reached the age of sixty-two might expect to carry, his main reason for retiring had been the long journeys on horseback over frightful roads, which a judge's duties forced him to take. Another reason was his estate of Balnillo, which was far enough from Edinburgh to make personal attention to it impossible. His wife Margaret, whose portrait hung in the dining-room, had done all the business for many years; but Margaret was dead, and perhaps David, who had been a devoted husband, felt the need of something besides the law to fill up his life. He was a lonely man, for he had no children, and his brother James, who sat opposite to him, was his junior by twenty-five years. For one who had attained to his position, he was slow and curiously dependent on others; there was a turn about the lines of his countenance which suggested fretfulness, and his eyes, which had looked upon so many criminals, could be anxious. He was a considerate landlord, and, in spite of the times in which he lived and the bottle at his elbow, a person of very sober habits.

James Logie, who had started his career in Lord Orkney's regiment of foot with the Scots Brigade in Holland, had the same fresh complexion as his brother and the same dark blue eyes; but they were eyes that had a different expression, and that seemed to see one thing at a time. He was a squarer, shorter man than Lord Balnillo, quicker of speech and movement. His mouth was a little crooked, for the centre of his lower lip did not come exactly under the centre of the upper one, and this slight mistake on the part of Nature had given his face a not unpleasant look of virility. Most people who passed James gave him a second glance. Both men were carefully dressed and wore fine cambric cravats and laced coats; and the shoes of the judge, which rested on the fender, were adorned by gilt buckles.

They had been silent for some time, as people are who have come to the same conclusion and find that there is no more to say, and in the quietness the heavy undercurrent of sound from the coast seemed to grow more insistent.

'The bar is very loud to-night, Jamie,' said Lord Balnillo. 'I doubt but there's bad weather coming, and I am loth to lose more trees.'

'I see that the old beech by the stables wants a limb,' observed the other. 'That's the only change about the place that I notice.'

'There'll be more yet,' said the judge.

'You've grown weather-wise since you left Edinburgh, David.'

'I had other matters to think upon there,' answered Balnillo, with some pomp.

James smiled faintly, making the little twist in his lip more apparent.

'Come out to the steps and look at the night,' said he, snatching, like most restless men, at the chance of movement.

They went out through the hall. James unbarred the front door and the two stood at the top of the flight of stone steps.

The entrance to Balnillo House faced northward, and a wet wind from the east, slight still, but rising, struck upon their right cheeks and carried the heavy muffled booming in through the trees. Balnillo looked frowning at their tops, which had begun to sway; but his brother's attention was fixed upon a man's figure, which was emerging from the darkness of the grass park in front of them.

'Who is that?' cried the judge, as the footsteps grew audible.

'It's a coach at the ford, ma lord – a muckle coach that's couped i' the water! Wully an' Tam an' Andrew Robieson are seekin' to ca' it oot, but it's fast, ma lord—'

'Is there anyone in it?' interrupted James.

'Ay, there was. But he's oot noo.'

'Where is he?'

'He'll na' get forward the night,' continued the man. 'Ane of the horse is lame. He is cursin', ma lord, an' nae wonder – he can curse bonnie! Robieson's got his wee laddie wi' him, and he gar'd the loonie put his hands to his lugs. He's an elder, ye see.'

The judge turned to his brother. It was not the first time that the ford in the Den of Balnillo had been the scene of disaster, for there was an unlucky hole in it, and the state of the roads made storm-bound and bedraggled visitors common apparitions in the lives of country gentlemen.

'If ye'll come wi' me, ma lord, ye'll hear him,' said the labourer, to whom the profane victim of the ford was evidently an object of admiration.

Balnillo looked down at his silk stockings and buck-led shoes.

'I should be telling the lasses to get a bed ready,' he remarked hurriedly, as he re-entered the house.

James was already throwing his leg across the fence, though it was scarcely the cursing which attracted him, for he had heard oaths to suit every taste in his time. He hurried across the grass after the labourer. The night was not very dark, and they made straight for the ford.

The Den of Balnillo ran from north to south, not a quarter of a mile from the house, and the long chain of miry hollows and cart-ruts which did duty for a high road from Perth to Aberdeen plunged through it at the point for which the men were heading. It was a steep ravine filled with trees and stones, through which the Balnillo burn flowed and fell and scrambled at different levels on its way to join the Basin of Montrose, as the great estuary of the river Esk was called. The ford lay just above one of the falls by which the water leaped downwards, and the dense darkness of the surrounding trees made it difficult for Captain Logie to see what was happening as he descended into the black well of the Den. He could distinguish a confusion of objects by the light of the lantern which his brother's men had brought and set upon a stone; the ford itself reflected nothing, for it was churned up into a sea of mud, in which, as Logie approached, the outline of a good-sized carriage, lying upon its side, became visible.

'Yonder's the captain coming,' said a voice.

Someone lifted the lantern, and he found himself confronted by a tall young man, whose features he could not see, but who was, no doubt, the expert in language.

'Sir,' he said, 'I fear you have had a bad accident. I am come from Lord Balnillo to find out what he can do for you.'

'His lordship is mighty good,' replied the young man, 'and if he could force this mud-hole – which, I am told, belongs to him – to yield up my conveyance, I should be his servant for life.'

There was a charm and softness in his voice which nullified the brisk impertinence of his words.

'I hope you are not hurt,' said James.

'Not at all, sir. Providence has spared me. But He has had no mercy upon one of my poor nags, which has broken its knees, nor on my stock-in-trade, which is in the water.

I am a travelling painter,' he added quickly, 'and had best introduce myself. My name is Archibald Flemington.'

The stranger had a difficulty in pronouncing his *r*'s; he spoke them like a Frenchman, with a purring roll.

The other was rather taken aback. Painters in those days had not the standing in society that they have now, but the voice and manner were unmistakably those of a man of breeding. Even his freedom was not the upstart licence of one trying to assert himself, but the easy expression of a roving imagination.

'I should introduce myself too,' said Logie. 'I am Captain James Logie, Lord Balnillo's brother. But we must rescue your – your – baggage. Where is your postilion?'

Flemington held up the lantern again, and its rays fell upon a man holding the two horses which were standing together under a tree. James went towards them.

'Poor beast,' said he, as he saw the knees of one of the pair, 'he would be better in a stall. Andrew Robieson, send your boy to the house for a light, and then you can guide them to the stables.'

Meanwhile, the two other men had almost succeeded in getting the carriage once more upon its wheels, and with the help of Flemington and Logie, it was soon righted. They decided to leave it where it was for the night, and it was dragged a little aside, lest it should prove a pitfall to any chance traveller who might pass before morning.

The two gentlemen went towards the house together, and the men followed, carrying Flemington's possessions and the great square package containing his canvases.

When they entered the Library Lord Balnillo was standing with his back to the fire.

'I have brought Mr. Flemington, brother,' said Logie, 'his coach has come to grief in the Den.'

Archie stopped short, and putting his heels together, made much the same bow as he had made to Mr. Duthie eighteen years before.

A feeling of admiration went through James as the warm light of the house revealed the person of his companion, and something in the shrewd wrinkles round his brother's unimpressive eyes irritated him. He felt a vivid interest in

the stranger, and the cautious old man's demeanour seemed
to have raised the atmosphere of a lawcourt round himself.
He was surveying the newcomer with stiff urbanity.

But Archie made small account of it.

'Sir,' said Balnillo, with condescension, 'if you will oblige
me by making yourself at home until you can continue your
road, I shall take myself for fortunate.'

'My lord,' replied Archie, 'if you knew how like heaven
this house appears to me after the bottomless pit in your
den, you might take yourself for the Almighty.'

Balnillo gave his guest a critical look, and was met by
all the soft darkness of a pair of liquid brown eyes which
drooped at the outer corners, and were set under thick
brows following their downward lines. Gentleness, inquiry,
appeal, were in them, and a quality which the judge, like
other observers, could not define – a quality that sat far,
far back from the surface. In spite of the eyes, there was
no suggestion of weakness in the slight young man, and
his long chin gave his olive face gravity. Speech and looks
corresponded so little in him that Balnillo was bewildered;
but he was a hospitable man, and he moved aside to make
room for Archie on the hearth. The latter was a sorry sight,
as far as mud went; for his coat was splashed, and his legs,
from the knee down, were of the colour of clay. He held
his hands out to the blaze, stretching his fingers as a cat
stretches her claws under a caressing touch.

'Sit down and put your feet to the fire,' said the judge,
drawing forward one of the large armchairs, 'and James,
do you call for another glass. When did you dine, Mr.
Flemington?'

'I did not dine at all, my lord. I was anxious to push on
to Montrose, and I pushed on to destruction instead.'

He looked up with such a whimsical smile at his
own mishaps that Balnillo found his mouth widening in
sympathy.

'I will go and tell them to make some food ready,' said
the captain, in answer to a sign from his brother.

Balnillo stood contemplating the young man; the lines
round his eyes were relaxing a little; he was fundamentally
inquisitive, and his companion matched no type he had

ever seen. He was a little disturbed by his assurance, yet his instinct of patronage was tickled by the situation.

'I am infinitely grateful to you,' said Archie. 'I know all the inns in Brechin, and am very sensible how much better I am likely to dine here than there. You are too kind.'

'Then you know these parts?'

'My home is at the other end of the county – at Ardguys.'

'I am familiar with the name,' said Balnillo, 'but until lately, I have been so much in Edinburgh that I am out of touch with other places. I am not even aware to whom it belongs.'

'It is a little property, my lord – nothing but a few fields and a battered old house. But it belongs to my grandmother Flemington, who brought me up. She lives very quietly.'

'Indeed, indeed,' said the judge, his mind making a cast for a clue as a hound does for the scent.

He was not successful.

'I had not taken you for a Scot,' he said, after a moment.

'I have been told that,' said Archie; 'and that reminds me that it would be proper to tell your lordship what I am. I am a painter, and at this moment your hall is full of my paraphernalia.'

Lord Balnillo did not usually show his feelings, but the look which, in spite of himself, flitted across his face, sent a gleam of entertainment through Archie.

'You are surprised,' he observed, sighing. 'But when a man has to mend his fortunes he must mend them with what tools he can. Nor am I ashamed of my trade.'

'There is no need, Mr. Flemington,' replied the other, with the measured benevolence he had sometimes used upon the bench; 'what you tell me does you honour – much honour, sir.'

'Then you did not take me for a painter any more than for a Scot?' said Archie, smiling at his host.

'I did not, sir,' said the judge shortly. He was not accustomed to be questioned by his witnesses and he had the uncomfortable sensation of being impelled, in spite of a certain prejudice, to think moderately well of his guest.

'I have heard tell of your lordship very often,' said the latter, suddenly, 'and I know very well into what good hands I have fallen. I could wish that all the world was more like yourself.'

He turned his head and stared wistfully at the coals.

Balnillo could not make out whether this young fellow's assurance or his humility was the real key-note to the man. But he liked some of his sentiments well enough. Archie wore his own hair, and the old man noticed how silky and fine the brown waves were in the firelight. They were so near his hand as their owner leaned forward that he could almost have stroked them.

'Are you going further than Montrose?' he inquired.

'I had hoped to cozen a little employment out of Aberdeen,' replied Flemington; 'but it is a mere speculation. I have a gallery of the most attractive canvases with me – women, divines, children, magistrates, provosts – all headless and all waiting to see what faces chance and I may fit on to their necks. I have one lady – an angel, I assure you, my lord! – a vision of green silk and white roses – shoulders like satin – the hands of Venus!'

Balnillo was further bewildered. He knew little about the arts and nothing about artists. He had looked at many a contemporary portrait without suspecting that the original had chosen, as sitters often did, an agreeable ready-made figure from a selection brought forward by a painter, on which to display his or her countenance. It was a custom which saved the trouble of many sittings and rectified much of the niggardliness or over-generosity of Nature.

'I puzzle you, I see,' added Archie, laughing, 'and no doubt the hair of Van Dyck would stand on end at some of our modern doings. But I am not Van Dyck, unhappily, and in common with some others I do half my business before my sitters ever see me. A client has only to choose a suitable body for his own head, and I can tell you that many are thankful to have the opportunity.'

'I had no idea that portraits were done like that,' said Lord Balnillo; 'I never heard of such an arrangement before.'

'But you do not think it wrong, I hope?' exclaimed

Flemington, the gaiety dying out of his face. 'There is no fraud about it! It is not as if a man deceived his sitter.'

The half-petulant distress in his voice struck Balnillo, and almost touched him; there was something so simple and confiding in it.

'It might have entertained your lordship to see them,' continued Archie ruefully. 'I should have liked to show you the strange company I travel with.'

'So you shall, Mr. Flemington,' said the old man. 'It would entertain me very greatly. I only fear that the lady with the white roses may enslave me,' he added, with rather obvious jocosity.

'Indeed, now is the time for that,' replied Archie, his face lighting up again, 'for I hope she may soon wear the head of some fat town councillor's wife of Aberdeen.'

As he spoke Captain Logie returned with the news that dinner was prepared.

'I have been out to the stable to see what we could do for your horses,' said he.

'Thank you a thousand times, sir,' exclaimed Archie.

Lord Balnillo watched his brother as he led the painter to the door.

'I think I will come, too, and sit with Mr. Flemington while he eats,' he said, after a moment's hesitation.

A couple of hours later Archie found himself in a comfortable bedroom. His valise had been soaked in the ford, and a nightshirt of Lord Balnillo's was warming at the fire. When he had put it on he went and looked at himself in an old-fashioned mirror which hung on the wall. He was a good deal taller than the judge, but it was not his own image that caused the indescribable expression on his face.

THREE

A Coach-and-Five

ARCHIE SAT in his bedroom at a table. The window was open, for it was a soft October afternoon, and he looked out meditatively at the prospect before him.

The wind that had howled in the night had spent itself towards morning, and by midday the tormented sky had cleared and the curtain of cloud rolled away, leaving a mellow sun smiling over the Basin of Montrose. He had never been within some miles of Balnillo, and the aspect of this piece of the country being new to him, his painter's eye rested appreciatively on what he saw.

Two avenues of ancient trees ran southward, one on either side of the house, and a succession of grass fields sloped away before him between these bands of timber to the tidal estuary, where the water lay blue and quiet with the ribbon of the South Esk winding into it from the west. Beyond it the low hills with their gentle rise touched the horizon; nearer at hand the beeches and gean-trees, so dear to Lord Balnillo's heart, were red and gold. Here and there, where the gale had thinned the leaves, the bareness of stem and bough let in glimpses of the distant purple which was the veil of the farther atmosphere. To the east, shut out from his sight by all this wood, was the town of Montrose, set, with its pointed steeple, like the blue silhouette of some Dutch town, between the Basin and the North Sea.

A pen was in Flemington's hand, and the very long letter he had just written was before him.

BALNILLO HOUSE.

MADAM, MY DEAR GRANDMOTHER,

I beg you to look upon the address at the head of this
letter, and to judge whether fortune has favoured your
devoted grandson.

I am *on the very spot*, and, what is more, seem like
to remain there indefinitely. Could anything in this
untoward world have fallen out better? Montrose is
a bare three miles from where I sit, and I can betake
myself there on business when necessary, while I live
as secluded as I please; cheek by jowl with the very
persons whose acquaintance I had laid so many plots
to compass. My dear grandmother, could you but have
seen me last night, when I lay down after my labours,
tricked out in my worshipful host's nightshirt! Though
the honest man is something of a fop in his attire, his
arms are not so long as mine, and the fine ruffles on
the sleeves did little more than adorn my elbows, which
made me feel like a lady till I looked at my skirts. Then
I felt more like a highlandman. But I am telling you
only effects when you are wanting causes.

I changed horses at Brechin, having got so far in
safety just after dark, and went on towards Montrose,
with the wind rising and never a star to look comfort at
me through the coach window. Though I knew we must
be on the right road, I asked my way at every hovel we
passed, and was much interested when I was told that
I was at the edge of my Lord Balnillo's estate, and not
far from his house.

The road soon afterwards took a plunge into the very
vilest place I ever saw – a steep way scarcely fit for a
cattle-road, between a mass of trees. I put out my head
and heard the rushing of water. Oh, what a fine thing
memory is! I remembered having heard of the Den of
Balnillo and being told that it was near Balnillo house and
I judged we must be there. Another minute and we were
clattering among stones; the water was up to the axle
and we rocked like a ship. One wheel was higher than
the other, and we leaned over so that I could scarcely sit.

Then I was inspired. I threw myself with all my weight against the side, and dragged so much of my cargo of canvases as I could lay hold of with me. There was a great splash and over we went. It was mighty hard work getting out, for the devil caused the door to stick fast, and I had to crawl through the window at that side of the coach which was turned to the sky, like a roof. I hope I may never be colder. We turned to and got the horses out and on to dry ground, and the postilion, a very frog for slime and mud, began to shout, which soon produced a couple of men with a lantern. I shouted too, and did my poor best in the way of oaths to give the affair all the colour of reality I could, and I believe I was successful. The noise brought more people about us, and with them my lord's brother, Captain Logie, hurrying to the rescue with a fellow who had run to the house with news of our trouble. The result was that we ended our night, the coach with a cracked axle and a hole in the panel, the postilion in the servants' hall with half a bottle of good Scots whisky inside him, the horses – one with a broken knee – in the stable, and myself, as I tell you, in his lordship's nightshirt.

I promise you that I thought myself happy when I got inside the mansion – a solemn block, with a grand manner of its own and Corinthian pillars in the dining-room. His lordship was on the hearthrug, as solemn as his house, but with a pinched, precise look which it has not got. He was no easy nut to crack, and it took me a little time to establish myself with him, but the good James, his brother, left us a little while alone, and I made all the way I could in his favour. I may have trouble with the old man, and, at any rate, must be always at my best with him, for he seems to me to be silly, virtuous and cunning all at once. He is vain, too, and suspicious, and has seen so many wicked people in his judicial career that I must not let him confound me with them. I could see that he had difficulty in making my occupation and appearance match to his satisfaction. He wears a mouse-coloured velvet coat, and is very nice in

the details of his dress. I should like you to see him
– not because he would amuse you, but because
it would entertain me so completely to see you
together.

James, his brother, is cut to a very different pattern.
He is many years younger than his lordship – not
a dozen years older than myself, I imagine – and
he has spent much of his life with Lord Orkney's
regiment in Holland. There is something mighty
attractive in his face, though I cannot make out
what it is. It is strange that, though he seems to be
a much simpler person than the old man, I feel less
able to describe him. I have had much talk with him
this morning, and I don't know when I have liked
anyone better.

And now comes the triumph of well-doing –
the climax to which all this faithful record leads. I
am to paint his lordship's portrait (in his Judge's
robes), and am installed here definitely for that
purpose! I shall be grateful if you will send me
my chestnut-brown suit and a couple of fine
shirts, also the silk stockings which are in the
top shelf of my cupboard, and all you can lay
hands on in the matter of cravats. My valise was
soaked through and through, and, though the
clothes I am wearing were dried in the night, I
am rather short of good coats, for I expected
to end in an inn at Montrose rather than in a
gentleman's house. Though I am within reach
of Ardguys, and might ride to fetch them in
person, I do not want to be absent unnecessarily.
Any *important* letters that I may send you will
go by a hand I know of. I shall go shortly to
Montrose by way of procuring myself some small
necessity, and shall search for that hand. Its
owner should not be difficult to recognise, by all
accounts. And now, my dear grandmother, I shall
write myself

Your dutiful and devoted grandson,

ARCHIBALD FLEMINGTON

Archie sealed his letter, and then rose and leaned far out of the window. The sun still bathed the land, but it was getting low; the treetops were thrusting their heads into a light which had already left the grass-parks slanting away from the house. The latter part of his morning had been taken up by his host's slow inspection of his canvases, and he longed for a sight of his surroundings. He knew that the brothers had gone out together, and he took his hat and stood irresolute, with his letter in his hand, before a humble-looking little locked case, which he had himself rescued the night before from among his submerged belongings in the coach, hesitating whether he should commit the paper to it or keep it upon his own person. It seemed to be a matter for some consideration. Finally, he put it into his pocket and went out.

He set forth down one of the avenues, walking on a gorgeous carpet of fallen leaves, and came out on a road running east and west, evidently another connecting Brechin with Montrose. He smiled as he considered it, realising that, had he taken it last night, he would have escaped the Den of Balnillo and many more desirable things at the same time.

As he stood looking up and down, he heard a liquid rush, and saw to his right a mill-dam glimmering through the trees, evidently the goal of the waters which had soused him so lately. He strolled towards it, attracted by the forest of stems and golden foliage reflected in the pool, and by the slide down which the stream poured into a field, to wind, like a little serpent, through the grass. Just where it disappeared stood a stone mill-house abutting on the highway, from which came the clacking of a wheel. The miller was at his door. Archie could see that he was watching something with interest, for the man stood out, a distinct white figure, on the steps running up from the road to the gaping doorway in the mill-wall.

Flemington was one of those blessed people for whom common sights do not glide by, a mere meaningless procession of alien things. Humanity's smallest actions had an interest for him, for he had that love of seeing effect follow cause, which is at once priceless and childish

– priceless because anything that lifts from us the irritating burden of ourselves for so much as a moment is priceless; and childish because it is a survival of the years when all the universe was new. Priceless yet again, because it will often lead us down unexpected side-tracks of knowledge in a world in which knowledge is power.

He sat down on the low wall bounding the mill-field, for he was determined to know what the miller was staring at. Whatever it was, it was on the farther side of a cottage built just across the road from the mill.

He was suddenly conscious that a bare-footed little girl with tow-coloured hair had appeared from nowhere, and was standing beside him. She also was staring at the house by the mill, but with occasional furtive glances at himself. All at once the heavy drone of a bagpipe came towards them, then the shrill notes of the chanter began to meander up and down on the blare of sonorous sound like a light pattern running over a dark background. The little girl removed her eyes from the stranger and cut a caper with her bare feet, as though she would like to dance.

It was evident that the sounds had affected Flemington, too, but not in the same way. He made a sharp exclamation under his breath, and turned to the child.

'Who is that playing?' he cried, putting out his hand.

She jumped back and stood staring.

'Who is that playing?' he repeated.

She was still dumb, scrubbing one foot against her bare ankle after the manner of the shoeless when embarrassed.

Archie was exasperated. He rose, without further noticing the child, and hurried towards the mill. When he had reached the place where the stream dived through a stone arch under the road he found she was following him. He heard the pad, pad, of her naked soles in the mud.

All at once she was moved to answer his question.

'Yon's Skirlin' Wattie!' she yelled after him.

But he strode on, taking no notice; fortune was playing into his hand so wonderfully that he was ceasing to be surprised. In the little yard of the cottage he found a small crowd of children, two women, and the miller's man, collected round the strangest assortment of living creatures he had ever seen. The name 'Skirlin' Wattie' had conveyed something to him, and he was prepared for the extraordinary, but his breath was almost taken away by the oddness of what he saw.

In the middle of the group was a stout wooden box, which, mounted on very low wheels, was transformed into the likeness of a rough go-cart, and to this were yoked five dogs of differing breeds and sizes. A half-bred mastiff in the wheel of the team was taking advantage of the halt and lay dozing, his jowl on his paws, undisturbed by the blast of sound which poured over his head, whilst his companion, a large, smooth-haired yellow cur, stood alert with an almost proprietary interest in what was going on awake in his amber eyes. The couple of collies in front of them sniffed furtively at the bystanders, and the wire-haired terrier, which, as leader, was harnessed singly in advance of the lot, was sharing a bannock with a newly-breeched man-child, the sinister nature of whose squint almost made the dog's confidence seem misplaced.

The occupant of the cart was an elderly man, whom accident had deprived of the lower part of his legs, both of which had been amputated just below the knee. He had the head of Falstaff, the shoulders of Hercules, and lack of exercise had made his thighs and back bulge out over the sides of his carriage, even as the bag of his pipes bulged under his elbow. He was dressed in tartan breeches and doublet, and he wore a huge Kilmarnock bonnet with a red knob on the top. The lower half of his face was distended by his occupation, and at the appearance of Flemington by the gate, he turned on him, above the billows of crimson cheek and grizzled whisker, the boldest pair of eyes that the young man had ever met. He was a masterly piper, and as the tune stopped a murmur of applause went through the audience.

'Man, ye're the most mountaineous player in Scotland!' said the miller's man, who was a coiner of words.

'Aye, dod, am I!' replied the piper.

'Hae?' continued the miller's man, holding out an apple.

The beggar took it with that silent wag of the back of the

head which seems peculiar to the east coast of Scotland, and dropped it into the cart.

Archie handed him a sixpence.

'Ye'll hae to gie us mair noo!' cried the squinting child, whose eyes had seen straight enough, and who seemed to have a keen sense of values.

'Aye, a sang this time,' added its mother.

'Ye'll get a pucklie meal an' a bawbee gin' ye sing "The Tod",'[1] chimed in an old woman, who had suddenly put her head out of the upper story of the cottage.

The beggar laid down his pipes and spat on earth. Then he opened his mouth and gave forth a voice whose volume, flexibility, and extreme sweetness seemed incredible, considering the being from whom it emanated.

There's a tod aye blinkin' when the nicht comes doon,
Blinkin' wi' his lang een, and keekin' round an' roun',
Creepin' by the farm-yaird when gloamin' is to fa',
And syne there'll be a chicken or a deuk awa'.
    Aye, when the guidwife rises there's a deuk awa'!

There's a lass sits greetin' ben the hoose at hame,
For when the guidwife's cankered she gie's her aye the
    blame,
And sair the lassie's sabbin', and fast the tears fa',
For the guidwife's tynt a bonnie hen, and it's awa'.
    Aye, she's no sae easy dealt wi' when her gear's awa'!

There's a lad aye roamin' when the day gets late,
A lang-leggit deevil wi' his hand upon the gate
And aye the guidwife cries to him to gar the toddie fa',
For she canna thole to let her chicks an' deuks awa'.
    Aye, the muckle bubbly-jock himsel' is ca'ed awa'!

The laddie saw the tod gae by, an' killed him wi' a stane,
And the bonnie lass wha grat sae sair she sits nae mair
    her lane
But the guidwife's no contented yet – her like ye never saw,
Cries she, 'This time it is the lass, an' she's awa'!'
    Aye, yon laddie's waur nor ony tod, for Jean's awa'!

1. Fox

Archie beat the top rail of the paling with so much enthusiasm that the yellow cur began to bark. The beggar quieted him with a storm of abuse.

The beldame disappeared from the window, and her steps could be heard descending the wooden stair of the cottage. She approached the cart with a handful of meal on a platter which Skirling Wattie tilted into an old leather bag that hung on his carriage.

'Whaur's the bawbee?' cried the squinting child.

A shout of laughter went up, led by Archie.

'He kens there's nae muckle weicht o' meal, and wha' should ken it better?' said the beggar, balancing the bag on his palm and winking at the miller's man.

The latter, who happened to be the child's unacknowledged parent, disappeared behind the house.

'One more song, and I will supply the bawbee,' said Archie, throwing another coin into the cart. Skirling Wattie sent a considering glance at his patron; though he might not understand refinement, he could recognize it; and much of his local success had come from his nice appraisement of audiences.

'I'll gie ye Logie Kirk,' said he.

> O Logie Kirk, among the braes
> I'm thinkin' o' the merry days
> Afore I trod the weary ways
>   That led me far frae Logie.
>
> Fine do I mind when I was young,
> Abune thy graves the mavis sung,
> And ilka birdie had a tongue
>   To ca' me back to Logie.
>
> O Logie Kirk, tho' aye the same,
> The burn sings ae remembered name,
> There's ne'er a voice to cry 'Come hame
>   To bonnie Bess at Logie!'
>
> Far, far awa' the years decline
> That took the lassie wha was mine
> And laid her sleepin' lang, lang syne
>   Among the braes at Logie.

His voice, and the wonderful pathos of his phrasing,
fascinated Archie, but as the last cadences fell from his
mouth, the beggar snatched up the long switch with which
he drove his team and began to roar.

'A'm awa'!' he shouted, making every wall and corner
echo. 'Open the gate an' let me through, ye misbegotten
bairns o' Auld Nick! Stand back, ye clortie-faced weans,
an' let me out! Round about an' up the road! Just round
about an' up the road, a' tell ye!'

The last sentences were addressed to the dogs who were
now all on their legs and mindful of the stick whirling in
the air above them.

Archie could see that he was not included in the beggar's
general address, but, being nearest to the gate, he swung
it open and the whole equipage dashed through, the dogs
guided with amazing dexterity between the posts by their
master's switch. The rapid circle they described on the
road as they were turned up the hill towards Brechin
seemed likely to upset the cart, but the beggar leaned
outwards so adroitly that none of the four wheels left the
ground. As they went up the incline he took up his pipes,
and leaving the team to its own guidance, tuned up and
disappeared round the next bend in a blast of sound.

Flemington would have given a great deal to run after
him, and could easily have overtaken the cart, for its
pace was not very formidable. But the whole community,
including the tow-headed little girl, was watching Skirling
Wattie out of sight and speculating, he knew, upon his own
identity. So he walked leisurely on till the road turned at
the top of the hill, and he was rewarded at the other side
of its bend by the sight of the beggar halting his team by
a pond at which the dogs were drinking. He threw a look
around and behind him; then, as no human creature was
to be seen, he gave a loud whistle, holding up his arm,
and began to run.

Skirling Wattie awaited him at the pond-side, and as
Archie approached, he could almost feel his bold eyes
searching him from top to toe. He stopped by the cart.

'My name is Flemington,' said he.

'A've heard worse,' replied the other calmly.

'And I have a description of you in my pocket,' continued Archie. 'Perhaps you would like to see it.'

The beggar looked up at him from under his bushy eyebrows, with a smile of the most robust and genial effrontery that he had ever seen on a human face.

'A'd need to,' said he.

Archie took a folded paper from his pocket.

'You see that signature,' he said, putting his forefinger on it.

The other reached up to take the paper.

'No, no,' said Flemington, 'this never goes out of my hand.'

'That's you!' exclaimed the beggar, with some admiration. 'Put it back. A' ken it.'

He unhooked his leather bag, which hung inside the cart on its front board. This Archie perceived to be made, apparently for additional strength, of two thicknesses of wood. Skirling Wattie slid the inner plank upwards, and the young man saw a couple of sealed letters hidden behind it, one of which was addressed to himself

'Tak' yon,' said the beggar, as the sound of a horse's tread was heard not far off, 'tak' it quick an' syne awa' ye gang! Mind ye, a gang ilka twa days frae Montrose to Brechin, an a'm aye skirlin' as a gang.'

'And do you take this one and have it sent on from Brechin,' said Archie hurriedly, handing him the letter he had written to Madam Flemington.

The other wagged the back of his head, and laid a finger against the rim of his bonnet.

Archie struck into the fields by the pond, and had time to drop down behind a whin-bush before an inoffensive-looking farmer went by on his way between the two towns.

The beggar continued his progress, singing to himself, and Flemington, who did not care to face the mill and the curious eyes of the tow-headed little girl again, took a line across country back to Balnillo.

He hated the tow-headed little girl.

FOUR

Business

EVENTS SEEMED to Flemington to be moving fast.

Lord Balnillo dined soon after five, and during the meal the young man tried to detach his mind from the contents of the letter lying in his pocket and to listen to his host's talk, which ran on the portrait to be begun next morning,

The judge had ordered his robes to be taken out and aired carefully, and a little room with a north aspect had been prepared for the first sitting. The details of Archie's trade had excited the household below stairs, and the servant who waited appeared to look upon him with the curious mixture of awe and contempt accorded to charlatans and to those connected with the arts. Only James seemed to remain outside the circle of interest, like a wayfarer who pauses to watch the progress of some wayside bargain with which he has no concern. Yet, though Archie's occupations did not move Logie, the young man felt intuitively that he was anything but a hostile presence.

'With your permission I shall go early to bed to-night,' said Flemington to his host, as the three sat over their wine by the dining-room fire and the clock's hands pointed to eight.

'Fie!' said the judge; 'you are a young man to be thinking of such things at this hour.'

'My bones have not forgotten yesterday—' began Archie.

'And what would you do if you had to ride the circuit, sir?' exclaimed Balnillo, looking sideways at him like a sly old crow. 'Man, James, you and I have had other things to consider besides our bones! And here's Mr. Flemington, who might be your son and my grandson, havering about his bed!'

Archie laughed aloud.

'Captain Logie would need to have married young for that!' he cried. 'And I cannot picture your lordship as anybody's grandfather.'

'Come, Jamie, how old are you?' inquired his brother in a tone that had a light touch of gratification.

'I lose count nowadays,' said James, sighing. 'I must be near upon eight-and-thirty, I suppose. Life's a long business, after all.'

'Yours has scarcely been long enough to have begotten me, unless you had done so at twelve years old,' observed Archie.

'When I had to ride the circuit,' began Balnillo, setting down his glass and joining his hands across his waistcoat, 'I had many a time to stick fast in worse places than the Den yonder – ay, and to leave my horse where he was and get forward on my clerk's nag. I've been forced to sit the bench in another man's wig because my own had rolled in the water in my luggage, and was a plaster of dirt – maybe never fit to be seen again upon a Lord of Session's head.'

Logie smiled with his crooked mouth. He remembered, though he did not mention, the vernacular rhyme written on that occasion by some impudent member of the junior bar:

> Auld David Balnillo gangs wantin' his wig,
> And he's seekin' the loan of anither as big.
> A modest request, an' there's naething agin' it,
> But he'd better hae soucht a new head to put in it!

'It was only last year,' continued his brother, 'that I gave up the saddle and the bench together.'

'That was more from choice than from necessity – at least, so I have heard,' said Archie.

'You heard that, Mr. Flemington?'

'My lord, do you think that we obscure country-folk know nothing? or that reputations don't fly farther than Edinburgh? The truth is that we of the younger generation are not made of the same stuff. That is what my grandmother tells me so often – so often that, from force of habit, I don't listen. But I have begun to believe it at last.'

'She is a wise woman,' said Balnillo.

'She has been a mighty attractive one,' observed Archie meditatively; 'at least, so she was thought at St. Germain.'

'At St. Germain?' exclaimed the judge.

'My grandfather died in exile with his master, and my father too,' replied Flemington quietly.

There was a silence, and then James Logie opened his mouth to speak, but Archie had risen.

'Let me go, Lord Balnillo,' he said. 'The truth is, my work needs a steady hand, and I mean to have it when I begin your portrait to-morrow.'

When he had gone James took the empty seat by his brother.

'His grandfather with the King, and he following this womanish trade!' he exclaimed.

'I should like to have asked him more about his father,' said Balnillo; 'but—'

'He did not wish to speak; I could see that,' said James. 'I like the fellow, David, in spite of his paint-pots. I would like him much if I had time to like anything.'

'I have been asking myself: am I a fool to be keeping him here?' said the other. 'Was I right to let a strange man into the house at such a time? I am relieved, James. He is on the right side.'

'He keeps his ears open, brother.'

'He seems to know all about *me*,' observed Balnillo. 'He's a fine lad, Jamie – a lad of fine taste; and his free tongue hasn't interfered with his good sense. And I am relieved, as I said.'

Logie smiled again. The affection he had for his brother was of that solid quality which accepts a character in the lump, and loves it for its best parts. David's little vanities and vacillations, his meticulous love of small things, were plain enough to the soldier, and he knew well that the bench and the bar alike had found plenty to make merry over in Balnillo. He had all the loyal feeling which the Scot of his time bore to the head of his family, and, as his sentiments towards him sprang from the heart rather than from the brain, it is possible that he undervalued the sudden fits of shrewdness which would attack his brother as headache or ague might attack another man. The fact that David's colleagues had never made this mistake was responsible for a career the success of which surprised many who knew the judge by hearsay alone. Drink, detail and indecision have probably ruined more characters than any three other influences in the world; but the two latter had not quite succeeded with Lord Balnillo, and the former had passed him over.

'I wonder—' said James – 'I wonder is it a good chance that has sent him here? Could we make anything of him, David?'

'Whisht, James!' said the other, turning his face away quickly. 'You go too fast. And, mind you, if a man has only one notion in his head, there are times when his skull is scarce thick enough to stand between his thoughts and the world.'

'That is true. But I doubt Flemington's mind is too much taken up with his pictures to think what is in other men's heads.'

'Maybe,' replied Balnillo; 'but we'll know that better a few days hence. I am not sorry he has gone to bed.'

'I will give him an hour to get between his blankets,' said Logie, drawing out his watch. 'That should make him safe.'

Meanwhile Flemington had reached his room and was pulling his great package of spare canvases from under his sombre four-poster. He undid the straps which secured them and drew from between two of them a long dark riding-coat, thrusting back the bundle into its place. He changed his clothes and threw those he had taken off on a chair. Then he took the little locked box he had saved so carefully from the catastrophe of the previous night, and, standing on the bed, he laid it on the top of the tester, which was near enough to the ceiling to prevent any object placed upon it from being seen. He gathered a couple of cushions from a couch, and, beating them up, arranged them between the bedclothes, patting them into a human-looking shape. Though he meant to lock his door and to keep the key in his pocket during the absence he contemplated, and though he had desired the servants

not to disturb him until an hour before breakfast, he had
the good habit of preparing for the worst.

He slipped out with the coat over his arm, turned the
key and walked softly but boldly down into the hall. He
paused outside the dining-room, listening to the hum of
the brothers' voices, then disappeared down the back-stairs.
If he found the door into the stable-yard secured he meant
to call someone from the kitchen regions to open it and
to announce that he was going out to look at his disabled
horse. He would say that he intended to return through
the front door, by which Captain Logie had promised to
admit him.

Everything was quiet. The only sign of life was the shrill
voice of a maid singing in the scullery as she washed the
dishes, and the house was not shut up for the night.
Through the yard he went and out unmolested, under
the great arch which supported the stable clock, and then
ran swiftly round to the front. He passed under the still
lighted windows and plunged into a mass of trees and
undergrowth which headed the eastern approach.

Once among the friendly shadows, he put on the coat,
buttoning it closely about his neck, and took a small grey
wig from one of its deep pockets. When he had adjusted
this under his hat he emerged, crossed the avenue, dropped
over the sunk wall dividing it from the fields, and made
down them till he reached the Montrose road. Through
the still darkness the sound of the Balnillo stable clock
floated after him, striking nine.

There was not enough light to show him anything but his
nearest surroundings. The wall which bounded the great
Balnillo grassparks was at his left hand, and by it he guided
his steps, keeping a perpetual look out to avoid stumbling
over the inequalities and loose stones, for there were no
side-paths to the roads in those days. He knew that the
town was only three miles off, and that the dark stretch
which extended on his right was the Basin of Montrose. A
cold snap played in the air, reminding him that autumn,
which in Scotland keeps its mellowness late, was some way
forward, and this sting in the breath of night was indicated
by a trembling of the stars in the dark vault overhead.

He hastened on, for time was precious. The paper which he had taken from Skirling Wattie's hands had bid him prepare to follow Logie into the town when dark set in, but it had been able to tell him neither at what hour the soldier would start nor whether he would walk or ride.

His chance in meeting the beggar so soon had put him in possession of James's usual movements immediately, but it had given him little time to think out many details, and the gaps in his plans had been filled in by guesswork. He did not think James would ride, for there had been no sound of preparation in the stable. His intention was to reach the town first, to conceal himself by its entrance, and when James should pass, to follow him to his destination. He had a rough map of Montrose in his possession, and with its help he had been able to locate the house for which he suspected him to be bound – a house known by the party he served to be one of the meeting-places of the adherents of Charles Edward Stuart.

Archie's buoyancy of spirit was sufficient to keep at arm's length a regret he could not quite banish; for he had the happy carelessness that carries a man easily on any errand which has possibilities of development, more from the cheerful love of chance than from responsible feeling. His light-hearted courage and tenacity were buried so deep under a luxuriance of effrontery, grace, and mother-wit, and the glamour of a manner difficult to resist, that hardly anyone but Madam Flemington, who had brought him up, suspected the toughness of their quality. He had the refinement of a woman, yet he had extorted the wonder of an east-coast Scotsman by his comprehensive profanity; the expression, at times, of a timid girl, yet he would plunge into a flood of difficulties, whose further shore he did not trouble to contemplate; but these contrasts in him spoke of no repression, no conscious effort. He merely rode every quality in his character with a loose rein, and while he attempted to puzzle nobody, he had the acuteness to know that his audience would puzzle itself by its own conception of him. The regret which he ignored was the regret that he was obliged to shadow a man who pleased him as much as did James Logie. He realized how much more satisfaction

he would have got out of his present business had its object
been Lord Balnillo. He liked James's voice, his bearing,
his crooked mouth, and something intangible about him
which he neither understood nor tried to understand. The
iron hand of Madam Flemington had brought him up so
consistently to his occupation that he accepted it as a part
of life. His painting he used as a means, not as an end, and
the changes and chances of his main employment were
congenial to a temperament at once boyish and capable.

The Pleiades rode high above Taurus, and Orion's hands
were coming up over the eastern horizon as he reached the
narrow street which was the beginning of Montrose. The
place was dark and ill-lit, like every country town of those
days; and here, by the North Port, as it was called, the
irregularities of the low houses, with their outside stairs,
offered a choice of odd corners in which he might wait
unseen.

He chose the narrowest part of the street, that he might
see across it the more readily, and drew back into the cavity,
roofed in by the 'stairhead' of a projecting flight of steps
which ran sideways up a wall. Few people would leave the
town at that hour, and those who were still abroad were
likely to keep within its limits. A wretched lamp, stuck
in a niche of an opposite building, made his position all
the more desirable, for the flicker which it cast would be
sufficient to throw up the figure of Logie should he pass
beneath it. He watched a stealthy cat cross its shine with
an air of suppressed melodrama that would have befitted
a man-eating tiger, and the genial bellowing of a couple
of drunken men came down the High Street as he settled
his shoulders against the masonry at his back and resigned
himself to a probable hour of tedium.

NOT A MILE distant, James Logie was coming along the
Montrose road. He had trodden it many times in the
darkness during the past weeks, and his mind was roving
far from his steps, far even from the errand on which he
was bent. He was thinking of Archie whom he believed to
be snug in bed at Balnillo.

He had gone out last night and landed this fantastic piece

of young humanity from the Den, as a man may land a salmon, and he had contemplated him ever since with a kind of fascination. Flemington was so much unlike any young man he had known that the difference half shocked him, and though he had told his brother that he liked the fellow, he had done so in spite of one side of himself. It was hard to believe that but a dozen years divided them, for he had imagined Archie much younger, and the appeal of his boyishness was a strong one to Logie, who had had so little time for boyishness himself. His life since he was fifteen had been merged in his profession, and the restoration of the Stuarts had been for many years the thing nearest to his heart. There had been one exception to this, and that had long gone out of his life, taking his youth with it. He was scarcely a sad man, but he had the habit of sadness, which is as hard a one to combat as any other, and the burst of youth and buoyancy that had come in suddenly with Archie had blown on James like a spring wind. Archie's father and grandfather had died in exile, too, with Charles Edward's parents. And his eyes reminded him of other eyes.

The events that had taken place since the landing of the Prince in July had made themselves felt all up the east coast, and the country was Jacobite almost to a man. Charles Edward had raised his standard at Glenfinnan, had marched on Edinburgh in the early part of September, and had established himself in Holyrood on the surrender of the town. After his victory over Cope at Preston Pans, he had collected his forces on Portobello sands – thirteen regiments composed of the Highland clans, five regiments of Lowlanders, two troops of horse commanded by Lords Elcho and Balmerino, with two others under Lord Kilmarnock and Lord Pitsligo. The command of the latter consisted of Angus men armed with such weapons as they owned or could gather.

The insurgent army had entered England in two portions: one of these led by Lord George Murray, and one by the Prince himself, who marched at the head of his men, sharing the fatigues of the road with them, and fascinating the imagination of the Scots by his hopeful good-humour and his keen desire to identify himself with his soldiers. The two bodies had concentrated on Carlisle, investing the city, and after a few days of defiance, the mayor displayed the white flag on the ramparts and surrendered the town keys. After this, the Prince and his father had been proclaimed at the market cross, in presence of the municipality.

But in spite of this success the signs of the times were not consistently cheering to the Jacobite party. There had been many desertions during the march across the border, and no sooner had the Prince's troops left Edinburgh than the city had gone back to the Whig dominion. At Perth and Dundee the wind seemed to be changing too, and only the country places stuck steadily to the Prince and went on recruiting for the Stuarts.

Although he was aching to go south with the invaders, now that the English were advancing in force, Logie was kept in the neighbourhood of Montrose by the business he had undertaken. His own instincts and inclinations were ever those of a fighter, and he groaned in spirit over the fate which had made it his duty to remain in Angus, concerned with recruiting and the raising of money and arms. He had not yet openly joined the Stuarts, in spite of his ardent devotion to their cause, because it had been represented to him that he was, for the moment, a more valuable asset to his party whilst he worked secretly than he could be in the field. The question that perplexed the coast of Angus was the landing of those French supplies so sorely needed by the half-fed, half-clothed, half-paid troops, in the face of the English cruisers that haunted the coast; and it was these matters that kept Logie busy.

James knew the harbour of Montrose as men know the places which are the scenes of the forbidden exploits of their youth. This younger son, who was so far removed in years from the rest of his family as to be almost like an only child, was running wild in the town among the fisher-folk, and taking surreptitious trips across the bar when the staid David was pursuing his respectable career at a very different kind of bar in Edinburgh. He was the man that Montrose needed in this emergency, and to-night he was on his way to the town; for he would come there a couple of times in the week, as secretly as he could, to meet one David Ferrier, a country gentleman who had joined the regiment of six hundred men raised by Lord Ogilvie, and had been made deputy-governor of Brechin for the Prince.

Ferrier also was a man well calculated to serve the cause. He owned a small property and a farm not far from the village of Edzell, situated at the foot of a glen running up into the Grampians, and his perfect knowledge of the country and its inhabitants of all degrees gave him an insight into every turn of feeling that swept through it in those troubled days. The business of his farm had brought him continually into both Brechin and Montrose, and the shepherds, travelling incessantly with their flocks from hill to strath, formed one of his many chains of intelligence. He had joined Lord Ogilvie a couple of months earlier, and, though he was now stationed at Brechin with a hundred men of his corps, he would absent himself for a night at a time, staying quietly at Montrose in the house of a former dependent of his own, that he might keep an eye upon the movements of an English ship.

The Government sloop-of-war *Venture* had come into the harbour, carrying sixteen guns and about eighty men, and had anchored south of the town, in the strait made by the passage of the River Esk into the sea. Montrose, apparently, was to suffer for the work she had done as a port for Stuart supplies, for the *Venture*, lying at a convenient distance just under the fishing village of Ferryden, had fired heavily on the town, though no Jacobite troops were there. The commander had unrigged the shipping and burned two trading barques whose owners were townsmen, and he had landed a force at the fort, which had captured the town guns and had carried them on board a vessel lying at the quay.

Ferrier looked with complete trust to James Logie and his brother Balnillo. The old man, during his judicial career, had made some parade of keeping himself aloof from politics; and as his retirement had taken place previous to the landing of the Prince, he had sunk the public servant in the country gentleman before the world of politicians began to divide the sheep from the goats. For

some time few troubled their heads about the peaceable
and cautious old Lord of Session, whose inconspicuous
talents were vegetating among the trees and grass-parks
that the late Lady Balnillo had husbanded so carefully for
him. As to his very much younger brother, who had been
incessantly absent from his native land, his existence was
practically forgotten. But because the Government's Secret
Intelligence Department on the east coast had remembered
it at last with some suspicion, Flemington had been sent to
Montrose with directions to send his reports to its agent in
Perth. And Flemington had bettered his orders in landing
himself at Balnillo.

As Archie heard a steady tread approaching, he shrank
farther back under the stair. He could only distinguish a
middle-sized male figure which might belong to anyone,
and he followed it with straining eyes to within a few feet
of the lamp. Here it paused, and, skirting the light patch,
stepped out into the middle of the way.

He scarcely breathed. He was not sure yet, though the
man had come nearer by half the street; but the height
matched his expectation, and the avoidance of the solitary
light proved the desire for secrecy in the person before
him. As the man moved on he slipped from his shelter
and followed him, keeping just enough distance between
them to allow him to see the way he went.

The two figures passed up the High Street, one behind
the other, Flemington shrinking close to the walls and
drawing a little nearer. Before they had gone a hundred
yards, his unconscious guide turned suddenly into one of
those narrow covered-in alleys, or closes, as they are called,
which started at right angles from the main street.

Archie dived in after him as unconcernedly as he would
have dived into the mouth of hell, had his interests taken
him that way. These closes, characteristic of Scottish
towns to this day, were so long, and burrowed under so
many sightless-looking windows and doors, to emerge in
unexpected places, that he admired James's knowledge of
the short cuts of Montrose, though it seemed to him no
more than natural. The place for which he conceived him
to be making was a house in the New Wynd nicknamed

the 'Happy Land', and kept by a well-known widow for purposes which made its insignificance an advantage. It was used, as he had heard, by the Jacobite community, because the frequent visitors who entered after dusk passed in without more comment from the townspeople than could be expressed in a lifted eyebrow or a sly nudge. It was a disconcerting moment, even to him, when the man in front of him stopped, and what he had taken for the distant glimmer of an open space revealed itself as a patch of whitewash with a door in it. The close was a cul-de-sac.

Flemington stood motionless as the other knocked at the door. Flight was undesirable, for James might give chase, and capture would mean the end of a piece of work of which he was justly proud. He guessed himself to be the fleeter-footed of the two, but he knew nothing of the town's byways, and other night-birds besides Logie might join in. But his bold wit did not desert him, for he gave a loud drunken shout, as like those he had heard at the North Port as he could make it, and lurched across the close. Its other inmate turned towards him, and as he did so Archie shouted again, and, stumbling against him, subsided upon the paved floor.

The door beyond them opened a little, showing a portion of a scared face and a hand which held a light.

'Guid sakes! what'll be wrang?' inquired a tremulous female voice.

The man was standing over Archie, pushing him with his foot. His answer may have reassured the questioner, but it had a different effect upon the heap on the ground.

'Hoot, woman! don't be a fool! It's me – Ferrier!'

FIVE

'The Happy Land'

THE DOOR opened a little further.

'Here,' said Ferrier to the woman, 'go up and bring me the roll of unwritten paper from the table.'

'You'll no be coming in?'

'Not now. Maybe in another hour or more.'

'But wha's yon?' said she.

'Lord! woman, have you lived all these years in Montrose and never seen a drunken man?' exclaimed he impatiently. 'Shut the door, I'm telling you, and get what I want. He will not trouble you. He's past troubling anybody.'

She obeyed, and Archie heard a bolt shot on the inside.

Though he had been startled on discovering his mistake, he now felt comforted by it, for, being unknown to Ferrier, he was much safer with him than he would have been with James. He raised his head and tried to get an idea of his companion's face, but the darkness of the close was too great to let him distinguish his features. He had discovered where he lived by accident, but though a description of the man was in the little box now reposing on the tester of his bed at Balnillo, he did not know him by sight. These things were going through his mind as the woman returned from her lodger's errand, and the door had just been made fast again when there was a step at the close's mouth and another man came quickly in, stopping short as he found it occupied.

Ferrier coughed.

'Ferrier?' said James's voice softly. 'What is this?' he asked as his foot came in contact with Archie.

'It's a drunken brute who came roaring in here a minute syne and fell head over heels at my door,' replied the other. 'The town is full of them to-night.'

He stooped down and took Flemington by the shoulder.

'Up you get!' he cried, shaking him.

Archie breathed heavily and let his whole weight hang on Ferrier's hand.

'Haud awa' frae me, lassie!' he expostulated thickly.

Logie laughed.

'He must be far gone indeed to take you for a lass,' he observed.

Ferrier gave Archie a stronger shake.

'A'll no gang hame wantin' Annie!' continued Flemington, whose humour was beginning to find some pleasure in the situation.

The raw vernacular that he had mastered with absolute success in childhood was at his tongue's end still.

'Come, come,' said James.

Ferrier moved forward, but Archie had reached out a limp hand and taken him by the ankle.

'Annie!' he muttered, 'ma bonnie, bonnie Annie!'

Ferrier, who had nearly fallen forward, tried to strike out with his foot, but Archie's grip, nerveless yet clinging as a limpet, held him fast.

'A' tell ye, a'll nae gang hame wantin' Annie!' he repeated more loudly.

'He has me by the foot, damn him!' said Ferrier.

James swore quietly but distinctly.

'Annie! *Annie!*' roared Archie, making the silent close echo again.

'Great heavens!' exclaimed the exasperated James, 'we shall have the whole town out of bed if this goes on! Shake him off, man, and let us be going.'

He bent down as he spoke and groping in the darkness, found Flemington's heels. He seized them and began to drag him backwards as a man drags a fighting dog. He had a grip of iron.

The effect of the sudden pull on Ferrier was to make him lose his balance. He staggered against the side of the close, calling to Logie to desist.

Archie still held on with back-boneless tenacity; but as the scrape of flint and steel cut the darkness he knew that he had carried his superfluous pleasantries too far. He dared not loose Ferrier's ankle and roll to the wall, lest the action should prove him to be more wideawake and less intoxicated than he seemed. He could only bury his face in his sleeve.

His next sensation was a violent stab of burning pain in his wrist that made him draw it back with a groan.

'I knew that would mend matters,' said James grimly, as he blew out the tiny twist of ignited tow and replaced it and the steel box in his pocket. 'Come away – this sot has wasted our time long enough. He can sleep off his liquor as well here as anywhere else.'

'You've helped to sober him,' said Ferrier, as the two men went out of the close.

Flemington sat up. The burn stung him dreadfully, for the saltpetre in which the tow had been dipped added to the smart. But there was no time to be lost, so he rose and followed again.

Ferrier and Logie went off up the High Street, and turned down an offshoot of it which Archie guessed to be the New Wynd, because it answered to its position in his map of the town. He dashed to the corner and watched them by the one light which illuminated the narrow street till he could see them no longer. Then he flitted after them, a soft-footed shadow, and withdrew under a friendly 'stairhead,' as he had done at the North Port. A little farther on he could distinguish the two ascending an outside stair to a squat building, and he heard the sound of their knuckles on wood. Another minute and they were admitted.

The two captains were let into a small room in the back premises of 'The Happy Land' by a slatternly-looking woman, who disappeared when she had given them a light. Pens and ink lay upon the table and the smoke of lamps had blackened the ceiling. It was a wretched place, and the sound of rough voices came now and again from other parts of the house. James drew up a chair, and Ferrier also sat down, tossing the roll of paper to his companion.

'A young man called Flemington is at Balnillo painting my brother's portrait,' said Logie. 'It's a pity that I have not something of his gift for drawing.'

'Flemington—?' said the other. 'There is a widow Flemington who lives a mile or so this side of the Perthshire border; but that is the only part of the country I do not know.'

'This is her grandson. She lived at St. Germain, and her husband was with King James. He is a strange lad – a fine lad too. My brother seems mightily taken up with him.'

'Where is your plan?' asked Ferrier.

James took out a small pocket-book and laid it on the table; then he smoothed out the roll of paper, drew the points of the compass on it, and began to copy from the rough sketches and signs which covered the leaf of his little book.

Ferrier watched him in silence,

'I could not do that were it to save my life,' he said at last.

'I learned something, campaigning by the walls of Dantzig,' replied James.

Ferrier watched the growing of the hasty map with admiration. His own talents for organization and tactics had given this obscure landowner the position he held in the Prince's haphazard army, but the professional soldier was invaluable to him. He sat wondering how he could have got on without James.

'See,' said Logie, pushing the paper to him, 'here lies the *Venture* off Ferryden, at the south side of the river, and here is Inchbrayock Island. That English captain is a fool, or he would have landed some men there. You and I will land on it, Ferrier. And now,' he went on, 'the man is twice a fool, for, though he has taken the guns from the fort and put them on board one of the unrigged ships, he has left her beside the quay. This point that I have marked with a cross is where she is moored. It would be idle not to make use of such folly! Why, man, if we can carry through the work I have in my mind, we shall blow the *Venture* out of the water! Three nights I have skulked round the harbour, and now I think that every close and every kennel that opens its mouth upon it is in my head. And the island is the key to everything.'

Logie's eyes shone in the dim room like the eyes of some animal watching in a cave.

'We must get possession of the ship at the quay-side,' continued he. 'Then we will take a couple of the town guns and land them on Inchbrayock. A hundred men from Brechin should be sufficient.'

'It must be done at night,' said the other.

'At night,' said James, getting up and putting his hands on the back of his chair. 'And now, as soon as possible, we must go down to the harbour and look carefully at the position of everything.'

Ferrier stood up and stretched himself, as men so often will when they are turning over some unacknowledged intention.

James took up the roll of paper, glanced at it and threw it down again.

'I see it as though it had come by inspiration!' he cried. 'I see that we have a blockhead to deal with, and when heaven sends such an advantage to His Highness, it is not you nor I, Ferrier, who will balk its design. You will not hang back?'

He looked at his friend as though he were ready to spring at him. But Ferrier went on with his own train of thought. He was a slower man than Logie, but if he lacked his fire, he lacked none of his resolution.

'You are right,' he said. 'A man is a fool who leaves what he has captured on the farther side of the river, who thinks, having taken his enemy's guns from a fort, that he can let it stand empty. He has done these follies because he knows that there are no troops in Montrose.'

'Ay, but there are troops in Brechin!' burst out James.

'There are troops in Brechin,' repeated Ferrier slowly, 'and they must be got quietly into the town. I wish there were not eight miles of road between the two.'

'I have not forgotten that,' said James, 'and to-night I mean to remain here till daylight and then return home by the side of the Basin. I will make my way along its shore and judge whether it be possible for you to bring your men by that route. If you can get them out of Brechin by the river-bank and so on along the side of the Esk, you will avoid the road and I will be waiting for you at the fort.'

Logie had come round the little table and stood by his friend, waiting for him to speak.

'I will go with you,' said Ferrier. 'We can part below Balnillo, and I, too, will go back to Brechin by the river. I must know every step before I attempt to bring them in the dark. There must be no delays when the time comes.'

James drew a long sigh of relief. He had never doubted his companion's zeal, but his heart had been on fire with the project he carried in it, and Ferrier's complete acceptance of it was balm to his spirit. He was a man who spared himself nothing, mentally or physically.

He folded the roll of paper and gave it to Ferrier.

'Keep it,' said he. 'Now we must go to the harbour.'

SIX

In Darkness and in Light

WHEN THE men had disappeared into the house, Archie remained under his stairhead considering. He had been told in his instructions to discover two things – whether Logie was in touch with Ferrier, and whether 'The Happy Land' was frequented by the pair. Though Ferrier was in command of the small Jacobite force in Brechin, it was suspected that he spent an unknown quantity of his time in Montrose.

To the first of these questions he had already mastered the answer; it only remained for him to be absolutely certain that the house in front of him was 'The Happy Land.' He could not swear that he was in the New Wynd, though he was morally certain of it, but there were marks upon the house which would be proof of its identity. There would be a little hole, covered by an inside sliding panel, in the door of 'The Happy Land,' through which its inmates could see anyone who ascended the stair without being seen themselves, and there would be the remains of an ancient 'risp,' or tirling-pin, at one side of it.

Archie ran lightly across the street, crept up the staircase, and passed his palm over the wood. Yes, there was the hole, two inches deep in the solid door. He put in his finger and felt the panel in the farther side. Then he searched along the wall till his hand came in contact with the jagged edge of the ancient risp. There was no ring on it, for it had long been disused, but it hung there still – a useless and maimed veteran, put out of action.

He returned to his post satisfied. His discoveries had earned him the right to go home, but he did not mean to do so. How he was going to get back into Balnillo House, unseen, he did not know, and had not, so far, troubled himself to imagine. Perhaps he might have to stop out all night. He hoped not, but he was not going to meet trouble half-way. The house would be locked, the household – with the exception of the errant James – abed, and his own room was not upon the ground-floor. However, these were matters for later consideration, and he would remain where he was for a time. For all he knew, Ferrier and Logie might combine business with pleasure by staying in 'The Happy Land' till morning; but they were just as likely to come out within measurable time, and then he could see where they went. He was quite happy, as he was everywhere.

He fell to thinking of other things: of his host; with his thin, neat legs and velvet coat; of that 'riding the circuit' upon which the old man valued himself so much. In his mind's eye he figured him astride of his floundering nag at the edge of some uninviting bog in an access of precise dismay. That was how he would have wished to paint him. His powers of detachment were such that he became fascinated by the idea, and awoke from it with a start to hear the footsteps of Logie and Ferrier coming down the stairway opposite.

They did not retrace their way up the Wynd, but went on to its end and turned into a street leading southwards, whilst Archie slipped along in their wake. At last they reached a wilderness of sheds and lumber, above which stood a windmill on a little eminence, and the strong smell of sea and tar proclaimed the region of the harbour. A light shone clear and large across the dark space of water, touching the moving ripples, and this Archie guessed to be the riding-light of the *Venture*, which lay like a sullen watch-dog under Ferryden village.

He had to go very warily, for the pair in front stopped often and stood talking in low voices, but the bales and coils of rope and heaps of timber with which the quays were strewn gave him cover. He could not get close enough to them to hear what they said, but their figures were much plainer against the background of water than they had been in the streets, and he noted how often Logie would stretch out his arm, pointing to the solitary light across the straight.

There was scarcely any illumination on this side of it, and the unrigged shipping lay in darkness as Ferrier and his friend went along the quay and seated themselves on a windlass. Archie, drawing closer, could hear the rustle as the former unrolled James's map. The soldier took out his flint and steel and struck a light, covering it with his hand, and both men bent their heads over the paper. Archie's wrist smarted afresh as he saw it; his sleeve had rubbed the burn, and he could feel the oozing blood.

He crouched behind them, peering through the medley of ropes and tackle which hung on the windlass. By standing up he could have touched the two men. He had no idea what it was that they were studying, but his sharp wits told him that it must be a map of some kind, something which might concern the English ship across the waterway. He longed to get it. His confidence in his own luck was one of the qualities that had served him best, and his confidence in his own speed was great and, moreover, well-placed. He knew that he had twelve years of advantage over James, and, from the sound of Ferrier's voice, he judged that he had the same, or more, over him.

The temptation of chance overmastered him. He raised himself noiselessly, leaned over the intervening tackle, and made a bold snatch at the map, which Ferrier held whilst James was occupied with the lighted twist of tow.

But his luck was to fail him this time. Logie moved his hand, knocking it against Flemington's, and the light caught the paper's edge. A soft puff of sea-wind was coming in from over the strait, and in one moment the sheet was ablaze. Archie snatched back his hand and fled; but the glare of the burning paper had been bright enough to show Logie a man's wrist, on which there was a fresh, bleeding mark.

The bright flare of the paper only intensified the darkness for the two astounded men, and though each was instantly on his feet and running in the direction of the retreating footsteps, Archie had threaded the maze of amphibious obstacles and was plunging between the sheds into the street before either of them could get clear of the pitfalls of the quay.

He tore on, not knowing whither he went. His start had

been a good one, but as he paused to listen, which he did when he had gone some way, he could hear them following. The town was so quiet that he met nobody, and he pressed on, trusting to luck for his direction.

Through the empty streets he went at the top of his speed, launched on the flood of chance, and steering as best he could for the north end of the town. Finally, an unexpected turning brought him within a few yards of the North Port. He waited close to the spot where he had first taken shelter, and listened; then, hearing nothing, he struck out at a brisk walk for the country, and was soon clear of Montrose.

He sat down by the wayside to rest. He had had a more sensational night than he expected, and though his spirits were still good, his ill-luck in missing the paper he had risked so much to obtain had cooled them a little, and by the light of this disappointment he looked rather ruefully on his poor prospects of getting to bed. It was past midnight, and there seemed nothing to do but to return to Balnillo and to make himself as comfortable as he could in one of the many out-buildings which the yard by its back-door contained. The household rose early, and at the unlocking of that door he must manage to slip in and gain his bedroom.

He rose, plodded home, and stole into the courtyard, where, searching in an outhouse, he found an endurable couch on a heap of straw. On this he spread his coat like a blanket, crawling under it, and, with a calmness born of perfect health and perfect nerves, was soon asleep.

When dawn broke it found him wakeful. He had not rested well, for his burnt wrist was very sore, and the straw seemed to find it out and to prick the wound, no matter how he might dispose his hand. He propped himself against the wall by the open outhouse-window, whence he could see the back door of Balnillo and watch for the moment of its first opening. It would be neck or nothing then, for he must enter boldly, trusting to hit on a lucky moment.

At last the growing light began to define details of the house, tracing them out on its great mass with an invisible pencil, and he thought he heard a movement

within. The stable-clock struck six, and high above he
could see the sun touching the slates and the stone angles
of the chimney-stacks with the first fresh ethereal beam of
a pure October morning. He inhaled its breath lovingly,
and with it there fell from him the heaviness of his uneasy
night. All was well, he told himself. His sensuous joy in
the world, his love of life and its hazards and energies
came back upon him, strong, clean, and ecstatic, and the
sounds of a bolt withdrawn made him rise to his feet.

A maidservant came out carrying a lantern, whose beam
burned with feeble pretentiousness in the coming sunlight.
She set it down by the threshold and went past his retreat to
the stable. No doubt she was going to call the men. When
she had gone by he slipped out, and in a dozen paces was
inside the house.

Another minute and he was in his room.

He looked with some amusement at the rough effigy
of himself which he had made in the bed overnight, and
when he had flung the cushion back to its place he got
out of his clothes and lay down, sinking into the cool
luxury of the sheets with a sigh of pleasure. But he had
no desire to sleep, and when a servant came to wake him
half an hour later he was ready to get up. He rose, dressed,
wrote out the detailed description of his night's discoveries,
and put the document in his pocket to await its chance of
transmission.

A message was brought to him from Lord Balnillo as he
left his room, which begged his guest to excuse his company
at breakfast. He had been long astir, and busy with his
correspondence; at eleven o'clock he would be ready for
his sitting, if that were agreeable to Mr. Flemington.

As Mr. Flemington realized how easily he might have
met the judge as he ran through the shuttered passage, his
belief in the luck that had used him so scurvily last night
returned.

There was no sign of James as Archie sat down to his meal,
though a second place was set at the table, and as he did not
want to ask embarrassing questions, he made no inquiry
about him. Besides which, being immoderately hungry, he
was too well occupied to trouble about anyone.

He went out upon the terrace when he had finished. The warm greyness of the autumn morning was lifting from the earth and it was still early enough for long shadows to lie cool on the westward side of the timber. As they shortened, the crystal of the dew was catching shafts from the sun, and the parks seemed to lie waiting till the energy of the young day should let loose the forces of life from under the mystery of its spangled veil. Where the gean-trees glowed carmine and orange, touches of quickening fire shot through the interstices of their branches, and coloured like a tress of trailing forget-me-not, the South Esk wound into the Basin of Montrose, where the tide, ebbing beyond the town, was leaving its wet sands as a feasting-ground for all sorts of roving birds whose crying voices came faintly to Archie, mellowed by distance.

Truly this was a fascinating place, with its changing element of distant water, its great plain lines of pasture, its ordered vistas of foliage! The passion for beauty lay deep below the tossing, driving impulses of Flemington's nature, and it rose up now as he stood on the yew-edged terraces of Balnillo and gazed before him. For the moment everything in his mind was swallowed up but the abstract, fundamental desire for perfection, which is, when all is said and done, humanity's mainspring, its incessant though often erring guide, whose perverted behests we call sin, whose legitimate ones we call virtue; whose very existence is a guarantee of immortality.

The world, this crystalline morning, was so beautiful to Archie that he ached with the uncomprehended longing to identify himself with perfection; to cast his body down upon the light-pervaded earth and to be one with it, to fling his soul into the heights and depths of the limitless encompassing ether, to be drawn into the heart of God's material manifestation on earth – the sun. He understood nothing of what he felt, neither the discomfort of his imprisonment of flesh, nor the rapturous, tentative, wing-sweeps of the spirit within it. He left the garden terrace and went off towards the Basin, with the touch of that elemental flood of truth into which he had been plunged for a moment fresh on his soul. The whole universe and its contents seemed to him good – and not only good, but of consummate interest – humanity was fascinating. His failure to snatch the map from Ferrier's hand last night only made him smile. In the perfection of this transcendent creation all was, and must be, well!

His thoughts, woven of the same radiant appreciation, flew to James, whose personality appealed to him so strongly. The gentle blood which ran in the veins of the pair of brothers ran closer to the surface in the younger one; and a steadfast, unostentatious gallantry of heart seemed to be the atmosphere in which he breathed. He was one of those whose presence in a room would always be the strongest force in it, whether he spoke or was silent, and his voice had the tone of something sounding over great and hidden depths. It was not necessary to talk to him to know that he had lived a life of vicissitude, and Archie, all unsuspected, in the watches of last night had seen a side of him which did not show at Balnillo. His grim resourcefulness in small things was illustrated by the raw spot on the young man's wrist. That episode pleased Flemington's imagination – though it might have pleased him even better had the victim been someone else; but he bore James no malice for it, and the picture of the man haunting the dark quays, strewn with romantic, sea-going lumber, and scheming for the cause at his heart, whilst the light from the hostile ship trailed the water beside him, charmed his active fancy.

But it was not only his fancy that was at work. He knew that the compelling atmosphere of Logie had not been created by mere fancy, because there was something larger than himself, and larger than anything he could understand, about the soldier. And feeling, as he was apt to do, every little change in the mental climate surrounding him he had guessed that Logie liked him. The thought added to the exultation produced in him by the glory of the pure morning; and he suddenly fell from his height as he remembered afresh that he was here to cheat him.

It was with a shock that he heard Skirling Wattie's pipes as he reached the Montrose road, and saw the beggar's outlandish cart approaching, evidently on its return journey to Montrose. His heart beat against the report that lay in his pocket awaiting the opportunity that Fate was bringing nearer every moment. There was nobody to be seen as the beggar drew up beside him. The insolent joviality that pervaded the man, his almost indecent oddness – things which had pleased Archie yesterday struck cold on him now. He had no wish to stay talking to him, and he gave him the paper without a word more than the injunction to have it despatched.

He left him, hurrying across the Montrose road and making for the place where the ground began to fall away to the Basin. He sat down on the scrubby waste land by a broom-bush, whose dry, burst pods hung like tattered black flags in the brush of green; their acrid smell was coming out as the sun mounted higher. Below him the marshy ground ran out to meet the water; and eastward the uncovered mud and wet sand, bared by the tide ebbing beyond Montrose, stretched along its shores to the town.

The fall of the broom-covered bank was steep enough to hide anyone coming up from the lower levels, and he listened to the movements of somebody who was approaching, and to the crackling noise of the bushes as they were thrust apart.

The sound stopped; and Archie, leaning forward, saw James standing half-way up the ascent, with his back turned towards him, looking out across the flats. He knew what his thoughts were. He drew his right sleeve lower. So long as he did not stretch out his arm the mark could not be seen.

He did not want to appear as if he were watching Logie, so he made a slight sound, and the other turned quickly and faced him, hidden from the waist downwards in the broom. Then his crooked lip moved, and he came up the bank and threw himself down beside Flemington.

SEVEN

Treachery

JAMES DID not look as if he had been up all night, though he had spent the most part of it on foot with Ferrier. The refreshment of morning had bathed him too, but he was still harassed in mind by some of the occurrences of the last few hours. Last night he had seen the mark on the wrist stretched suddenly between himself and his friend, and had understood its significance. It was the mark that he had put there. As the two men listened to the flying footsteps that mystified them by their doublings in the darkness, it had dawned upon them that the intruder skulking behind the windlass and the tipsy reveller prone in the close were one and the same person. The drunkard was a very daring spy, as sober as themselves.

'You are out betimes,' said Archie, with friendly innocence.

'I often am,' replied James simply.

Archie pulled up a blade of grass and began to chew it meditatively.

'I see your long night has done you good,' began Logie. 'There were many things I should have liked to ask you, yesterday evening, but you went away so early that I could not.'

Silence dropped upon the two: upon Logie, because his companion's manner last night had hinted at remembrances buried in regret and painful to dig up; on Flemington, because he knew the value of that impression, and because he would fain put off the moment when the more complete deception of the man whose sympathetic attitude he divined and whose generosity of soul was so obvious, must begin. He did not want to come to close quarters with James. He had hunted him and been hunted by him, but he had not

yet been obliged to lie to him by word of mouth; and he
had no desire to do so, here and now, in cold blood and
in the face of all this beauty and peace.

'I could not but be interested in what you said,' continued
the other. 'You did not tell us whether you had been at St.
Germain yourself.'

'Never!' replied Archie. 'I was sent to Scotland at eight
years old, and I have been here ever since.'

He had taken the plunge now, for he had been backwards
and forwards to France several times in the last few years,
since he had begun to work for King George, employed
in watching the movements of suspicious persons between
one country and the other.

He looked down on the ground.

The more he hesitated to speak, the more he knew that
he would impress James. He understood the delicacy of
his companion's feeling by instinct. It was not only
dissimulation which bade him act thus, it was the real
embarrassment and discomfort which were creeping on
him under the eyes of the honourable soldier; all the same,
he hoped that his reluctant silence would save him.

'You think me impertinent,' said Logie, 'but do not be
afraid that I mean to pry. I know how hard life can be and
how anxious, nowadays. There is so much loss and trouble
– God knows what may happen to this tormented country!
But trouble does not seem natural when a man is young
and light-hearted, as you are.'

Archie was collecting materials wherewith to screen
himself from his companion's sympathy. It would be
easy to tell him some rigmarole of early suffering, of
want endured for the cause which had lain dormant,
yet living, since the unsuccessful rising of the '15, of the
devotion to it of the parents he had scarcely known, of the
bitterness of their exile, but somehow he could not force
himself to do it. He remembered those parents principally
as vague people who were ceaselessly playing cards, and
whose quarrels had terrified him when he was small. His
real interest in life had begun when he arrived at Ardguys
and made the acquaintance of his grandmother, whose
fascination he had felt, in common with most other male

creatures. He had had a joyous youth, and he knew it. He
had run the pastures, climbed the trees, fished the Kilpie
burn, and known every country pleasure dear to boyhood.
If he had been solitary, he had yet been perfectly happy.
He had gone to Edinburgh at seventeen, at his own ardent
wish, to learn painting, not as a profession, but as a pastime.
His prospects were comfortable, for Madam Flemington
had made him her heir, and she had relations settled in
England who were always ready to bid him welcome when
he crossed the border. Life had been consistently pleasant,
and had grown exciting since the beginning of his work for
Government. He wished to Heaven he had not met James
this morning.

But to Logie, Archie was merely a youth of undoubted
good breeding struggling bravely for his bread in an
almost menial profession, and he honoured him for what
he deemed his courage. There was no need to seek a reason
for his poverty after hearing his words last night. His voice,
when he spoke of his father's death in exile had implied all
that was necessary to establish a claim on James's generous
and rather bigoted heart. For him, there were only two kinds
of men, those who were for the Stuarts and those who were
not. People were very reticent about their political feelings
in those days; some from pure caution and some because
these lay so deep under mountains of personal loss and
misfortune.

'I dare not look back,' said Archie, at last, 'I have to live
by my trade and fight the world with my brush. You live
by sticking your sword into its entrails and I by painting
its face a better colour than Nature chose for it, and I
think yours is the pleasanter calling of the two. But I am
grateful to mine, all the same, and now it has procured
me the acquaintance of his lordship and the pleasure of
being where I am. I need not tell you that I find myself
in clover.'

'I am heartily glad of it,' said James.

'Indeed, so am I,' rejoined Archie, pleased at having
turned the conversation so deftly, 'for you cannot think
what strange things happen to a man who has no recognized
place in the minds of respectable people.'

James rolled over on his chest, leaning on his elbows, and looked up at his companion sitting just above him with his dark, silky head clear cut against the background of green bush. The young man's words seemed to trip out and pirouette with impudent jauntiness in their hearer's face. Logie did not know that Archie's management of these puppets was a part of his charm. His detached points of view were restful to a man like James, one continually preoccupied by large issues. It was difficult to think of responsibilities in Archie's presence.

'You might never imagine how much I am admired below stairs!' said the latter. 'While I painted a lady in the south, I was expected to eat with the servants, and the attentions of a kitchen-girl all but cost me my life. I found a challenge, offering me the choice of weapons in the most approved manner, under my dish of porridge. It came from a groom.'

'What did you do?' asked James, astounded.

'I chose warming-pans,' said Archie, 'and that ended the matter.'

James laughed aloud, but there was bitterness in his mirth. And this was a man born at St. Germain!

'We laugh,' said he, 'but such a life could have been no laughing matter to you.'

'But I assure you it was! What else could I do?'

'You could have left the place—' began James. Then he stopped short, remembering that beggars cannot be choosers.

His expression was not lost on Archie, who saw that the boat he had steered so carefully into the shallows was drawing out to deep water again, and that he had used his luxuriant imagination to small purpose. He had so little self-consciousness that to keep James's interest upon himself was no temptation to him, though it might have been to some men. He cast about for something wherewith to blot his own figure from the picture.

'And you,' he said, gravely, 'you who think so much of my discomforts, and who have actually wielded the sword while I have merely threatened to wield the warming-pan – you must have seen stranger things than the kitchen.'

'I?' said James, looking fixedly out to where the town steeple threw its reflection on the wet sand – 'yes. I have seen things that I hope you will never see. It is not for me to speak ill of war, I who have turned to it for consolation as a man may turn to his religion. But war is not waged against men alone in some countries. I have seen it when it is waged against women and little children, when it is slaughter, not war. I have seen mothers – young, beautiful women – fighting like wild beasts for the poor babes that cowered behind their skirts, and I have seen their bodies afterwards. It would be best to forget – but who can forget?'

Archie sat still, with eyes from which all levity had vanished. He had known vaguely that James had fought under Marshal Lacy in the War of the Polish Succession, in the bloody campaign against the Turks, and again in Finland. The ironic futility of things in general struck him, for it was absurd to think that this man, seared by war and wise in the realities of events whose rumours shook Europe, one who had looked upon death daily in company with men like Peter Lacy, should come home to be hunted down back streets by a travelling painter. He contemplated his companion with renewed interest; no wonder he was ruthless in small things. He was decidedly the most fascinating person he had known.

'And you went to these things *for consolation* – so you said?'

'For consolation. For a thing that does not exist,' said the other slowly.

He paused and turned to his companion with an expression that horrified the young man and paralysed his curiosity. The power in his face seemed to have given way, revealing, for a moment, a defencelessness like the defencelessness of a child looking upon the dark; and it told Archie that there was something that even Logie dreaded and that that something was memory.

The deep places he had guessed in James's soul were deep indeed, and again Flemington was struck with humility, for his own unimportance in contrast with this experienced man seemed little less than pitiful. The feeling closed his lips, and he looked round at the shortening shadows and into the stir of coming sunlight as a man looks round for a door through which to escape from impending stress. He, who was always ready to go forward, recoiled because of what he foresaw in himself. His self-confidence was ebbing, for he was afraid of how much he might be turned out of his way by the influence on him of Logie. He wished that he could force their talk into a different channel, but his ready wits for once would not answer the call.

Something not understood by him was moving James to expression, as reserved men are compelled towards it at times. Perhaps the bygone youth in him rose up in response to the youth at his side. The many years dividing him from his brother, the judge, had never consciously troubled him in their intercourse, but the tremendous divergence in their respective characters had thrown him back upon himself. Archie seemed to have the power of turning a key that Balnillo had never held.

'But I am putting you out of conceit with the world,' cried James abruptly; 'let no one do that. Take all you can, Flemington! I did – I took it all. Love, roystering, good company, good wine, good play – all came to me, and I had my bellyful! There were merry times in Holland with the Scots Brigade. It was the best part of my life, and I went to it young. I was sixteen the day I stood up on parade for the first time.'

'I have often had a mind to invade Holland,' observed Archie, grasping eagerly at the impersonal part of the subject; 'it would be paradise to one of my trade. The very thought of a windmill weaves a picture for me, and those strange, striped flowers the Dutchmen raise – I cannot think of their names now – I would give much to see them growing. You must have seen them in every variety and hue.'

'Ay, I saw the tulips,' said James, in a strange voice.

'The Dutchmen can paint them too,' said Archie hurriedly.

'What devil makes you talk of tulips?' cried James. 'Fate painted the tulips for me. Oh, Flemington, Flemington! In every country, in every march, in every fight, among dead and dying, and among dancers and the music they danced to, I have seen nothing but those gaudy flowers – beds of them growing like a woven carpet, and Diane among them!'

No feminine figure had come into the background against which stood Archie's conception of Logie.

'Diane?' he exclaimed involuntarily.

James did not seem to hear him.

'Her eyes were like yours,' he went on. 'When I saw you come into the light of the house two evenings since, I thought of her.'

Neither spoke for a few moments; then James went on again:

'Fourteen years since the day I saw her last! She looked out at me from the window with her eyes full of tears. The window was filled with flowers – she loved them. The tulips were there again – crimson tulips – with her white face behind them.'

Flemington listened with parted lips. His personal feelings, his shrinking dread of being drawn into the confidence of the man whom it was his business to betray, were swallowed by a wave of interest.

'I was no more than a boy, with my head full of cards and women and horses, and every devilry under heaven, when I went to the house among the canals. The Conte de Montdelys had built it, for he lived in Holland a part of the year to grow his tulips. He was a rich man – a hard, old, pinched Frenchman – but his passion was tulip-growing, and their cultivation was a new thing. It was a great sight to see the gardens he had planned at the water's edge, with every colour reflected from the beds, and the green-shuttered house in the middle. Even the young men of the Brigade were glad to spend an afternoon looking upon the show, and the Conte would invite now one, now another. He loved to strut about exhibiting his gardens. Diane was his daughter – my poor Diane! Flemington, do I weary you?'

'No, no, indeed!' cried Archie, who had been lost, wandering in an enchanted labyrinth of bloom and colour as he listened. The image of the house rising from among

its waterways was as vivid to him as if he had seen it with
bodily eyes.

'She was so young,' said the soldier, 'so gentle, so little
suited to such as I. But she loved me – God knows why
– and she was brave – brave to the end, as she lay dying
by the roadside . . . and sending me her love . . .'

He stopped and turned away; Archie could say nothing,
for his throat had grown thick. Logie's unconscious gift of
filling his words with drama – a gift which is most often
given to those who suspect it least – wrought on him.

James looked round, staring steadily and blindly over
his companion's shoulder.

'I took her away,' he went on, as though describing
another man's experiences; 'there was no choice, for the
Conte would not tolerate me. I was a Protestant, and I was
poor, and there was a rich Spaniard whom he favoured.
So we went. We were married in Breda, and for a year we
lived in peace. Such days – such days! The Conte made
no sign, and I thought, in my folly, he would let us alone.
It seemed as though we had gained paradise at last; but I
did not know him – Montdelys.'

'Then the boy was born. When he was two months old
I was obliged to come back to Scotland; it was a matter
concerning money which could not be delayed, for my
little fortune had to be made doubly secure now, and I
got leave from my regiment. I could not take Diane and
the child, and I left them at Breda – safe, as I thought.
At twenty-three we do not know men, not the endless
treachery of them. Flemington, when God calls us all to
judgment, there will be no mercy for treachery.'

Archie's eyes, fixed on the other pair, whose keen grey
light was blurred with pain, dropped. He breathed hard,
and his nostrils quivered. 'You seem to me as young as I
was then. May God preserve you from man's treachery.
He did not preserve me,' said James.

'I do not know how Montdelys knew that she was
defenceless,' continued he, 'but I think there must have
been some spy of his watching us. As soon as I had left
Holland he sent to her to say he was ill, probably dying,
and that he had forgiven all. He longed for the sight of

the boy, and he asked her to bring him that he might see his grandchild; she was to make her home with him while I was absent, and he would send word to me to join them on my return. Diane sent me the good news and went, fearing nothing, to find herself a prisoner.

'And all this time he had been working – he and the Spaniard – to get the Pope to annul our marriage, and they had succeeded. What they said to her, what they did, I know not, and never shall know, but they could not shake Diane. I was on my way back to Holland when she managed to escape with the boy. Storms in the North Sea delayed me, but I was not disturbed, knowing her to be safe. I did not know when I landed at last that she was dead . . . She swam the canal, Flemington, with the child tied on her shoulders, and the brother-officer of mine – a man in my own company, whom she had contrived to communicate with – was waiting for her with a carriage. My regiment had moved to Bergen-op-Zoom, and he meant to take her there. He had arranged it with the wife of my colonel, who was to give her shelter till I arrived, and could protect her myself. They had gone more than half-way to Bergen when they were overtaken, early in the morning. She was shot, Flemington. The bullet was meant for Carmichael, the man who was with her, but it struck Diane . . . They laid her on the grass at the roadside and she died, holding Carmichael's hand, and sending – sending—'

He stopped.

'And the child?' said Archie at last.

'Carmichael brought him to Bergen, with his mother. He did not live. The bullet had grazed his poor little body as he lay in her arms, and the exposure did the rest. They are buried at Bergen.'

Again Archie was speechless.

'I killed the Spaniard,' said James. 'I could not reach Montdelys; he was too old to be able to settle his differences in the world of men.'

Archie did not know what to do. He longed with a bitter longing to show his companion something of what he felt, to give him some sign of the passion of sympathy which had shaken him as he listened; but his tongue was tied fast by the blighting knowledge of his true position, and to approach, by so much as a step, seemed only to blacken his soul and to load it yet more heavily with a treachery as vile as that which had undone James.

'I could not endure Holland afterwards,' continued Logie; 'once I had looked on that Spanish hound's dead body my work was done. I left the Scots Brigade and took service with Russia, and I joined Peter Lacy, who was on his way to fight in Poland. Fighting was all I wanted, and God knows I had it. I did not want to be killed, but to kill. Then I grew weary of that, but I still stayed with Lacy, and followed him to fight the Turks. We outlive trouble in time, Flemington; we outlive it, though we cannot outlive memory. We outlast it – that is a better word. I have outlasted, perhaps outlived. I can turn and look back upon myself as though I were another being. It is only when some chance word or circumstance brings my youth back in detail that I can scarce bear it. You have brought it back, Flemington, and this morning I am face to face with it again.'

'It does not sound as if you had outlived it,' said the young man.

'Life is made of many things,' said James; 'whether we have lost our all or not, we have to plough on to the end, and it is best to plough on merrily. Lacy never complained of me as a companion in the long time we were together, for I was on his staff, and I took all that came to me, as I have done always. There were some mad fellows among us, and I was no saner than they! But life is quiet enough here in the year since I came home to my good brother.'

The mention of Lord Balnillo made Flemington start.

'Gad!' he exclaimed, rising, thankful for escape, 'and I am to begin the portrait this morning, and have set out none of my colours!'

'And I have gone breakfastless,' said Logie with a smile, 'and worse than that, I have spoilt the sunshine for you with my tongue, that should have been silent.'

'No, no!' burst out Flemington rather hoarsely. 'Don't think of that! If you only knew—'

He stood, unable to finish his sentence or to utter

one word of comfort without plunging deeper into self-abhorrence.

'I must go,' he stammered. 'I must leave you and run.'

James laid a detaining hand on him.

'Listen, Flemington,' he said. 'Listen before you go. We have learnt something of each other, you and I. Promise me that if ever you should find yourself in such a position as the one you spoke of – if you should come to such a strait as that – if a little help could make you free, you will come to me as if I were your brother. Your eyes are so like Diane's – you might well be hers.'

Archie stood before him, dumb, as James held out his hand.

He grasped it for a moment, and then turned from him in a tumult of horror and despair.

EIGHT

The Heavy Hand

IT WAS on the following day that Lord Balnillo stood in front of a three-quarter length canvas in the improvised studio; Archie had begun to put on the colour that morning, and the judge had come quietly upstairs to study the first dawnings of his own countenance alone. From the midst of a chaos of paint his features were beginning to appear, like the sun through a fog. He had brought a small hand-glass with him, tucked away under his velvet coat where it could not be seen, and he now produced it and began to compare his face with the one before him. Flemington was a quick worker, and though he had been given only two sittings, there was enough on the canvas to prompt the gratified smile on the old man's lips. He looked alternately at his reflection and at the judicial figure on the easel; Archie had a tactful brush. But though Balnillo was pleased, he could not help sighing, for he wished fervently that his ankles had been included in the picture. He stooped and ran his hand lovingly down his silk stockings. Then he took up the glass again and began to compose his expression into the rather more lofty one with which Flemington had supplied him.

In the full swing of his occupation he turned round to find the painter standing in the doorway, but he was just too late to catch the sudden flash of amusement that played across Archie's face as he saw what the judge was doing. Balnillo thrust the glass out of sight and confronted his guest.

'I thought you had gone for a stroll, sir,' he said rather stiffly.

'My lord,' exclaimed Flemington, 'I have been searching for you everywhere. I've come, with infinite regret, to tell you that I must return to Ardguys at once.'

Balnillo's jaw dropped.

'I have just met a messenger on the road,' said the other; 'he has brought news that my grandmother is taken ill, and I must hurry home. It is most unfortunate, most disappointing; but go I must.'

'Tut, tut, tut!' exclaimed the old man, clicking his tongue against his teeth and forgetting to hope, as politeness decreed he should, that the matter was not serious.

'It is a heart-attack,' said Archie.

'Tut, tut,' said Balnillo again. 'I am most distressed to hear it; I am indeed.'

'I *may* be able to come back and finish the picture later.'

'I hope so. I sincerely hope so. I was just studying the admirable likeness when you came in,' said Balnillo, who would have given a great deal to know how much of his posturing Flemington had seen.

'Ah, my lord!' cried Archie, 'a poor devil like me has no chance with you! I saw the mirror in your hand. We painters use a piece of looking-glass to correct our drawing, but it is few of our sitters who know that trick.'

Guilty dismay was chased by relief across Balnillo's countenance.

'You are too clever for me!' laughed Flemington. 'How did you learn it, may I ask?'

But Balnillo had got his presence of mind back.

'Casually, Mr. Flemington, casually – as one learns many things, if one keeps one's ears open,' said he.

A couple of hours later Archie was on his way home. He had left one horse, still disabled, in the judge's stable, and he was riding the other into Brechin, where he would get a fresh one to take him on. Balnillo had persuaded him to leave his belongings where they were until he knew what chance there was of an early return. He had parted from Archie with reluctance. Although the portrait was the old man's principal interest, its maker counted for much with him; for it was some time since his ideas had been made to move as they always moved in Flemington's presence. The judge got much pleasure out of his own curiosity; and the element of the unexpected – that fascinating factor which had been introduced into domestic life – was a continual joy. Balnillo had missed it more than he knew since he had become a completely rural character.

Archie saw the Basin of Montrose drop behind him as he rode away with a stir of mixed feelings. The net that Logie had, in all ignorance, spread for him had entangled his feet. He had never conceived a like situation, and it startled him to discover that a difficulty, nowhere touching the tangible, could be so potent, so disastrous. He felt like a man who has been tripped up and who suddenly finds himself on the ground. He had risen and fled.

The position had become intolerable. He told himself in his impetuous way that it was more than he could bear; and now, every bit of luck he had turned to account, every precaution he had taken, all the ingenuity he had used to land himself in the hostile camp, were to go for nothing, because some look in his face, some droop of the eyes, had reminded another man of his own past, and had let loose in him an overwhelming impulse to expression.

'Remember what I told you yesterday,' had been James's last words as Flemington put his foot in the stirrup. 'There must be no more challenges.'

It was that high-coloured flower of his own imagination, the picture of himself in the servants' hall, that had finally accomplished his defeat. How could he betray the man who was ready to share his purse with him?

And, putting the matter of the purse aside, his painter's imagination was set alight. The glow of the tulips and the strange house by the winding water, the slim vision of Diane de Montdelys, the gallant background of the Scots Brigade, the grave at Bergen-op-Zoom – these things were like a mirage behind the figure of James. The power of seeing things picturesquely is a gift that can turn into a curse, and that power worked on his emotional and imaginative side now. And furthermore, beyond what might be called the ornamental part of his difficulty, he realized that friendship with James, had he been free to offer or to accept it, would have been a lifelong prize.

They had spent the preceding day together after the sitting was over, and though Logie had opened his heart

no more, and their talk had been of the common interests
of men's lives, it had strengthened Archie's resolve to end
the situation and to save himself while there was yet time.
There was nothing for it but flight. He had told the judge
that he would try to return, but he did not mean to enter
the gates of Balnillo again, not while the country was
seething with Prince Charlie's plots; perhaps never. He
would remember James all his life, but he hoped that their
ways might never cross again. And, behind that, there was
regret; regret for the friend who might have been his, who,
in his secret heart, would be his always.

He could, even now, hardly realize that he had been
actually turned from his purpose. It seemed to him
incredible. But there was one thing more incredible still,
and that was that he could raise his hand to strike again at
the man who had been stricken so terribly, and with the same
weapon of betrayal. It would be as if James lay wounded on
a battle-field and he should come by to stab him anew. The
blow he should deal him would have nothing to do with
the past, but Archie felt that James had so connected him
in mind with the memory of the woman he resembled –
had, by that one burst of confidence, given him so much
part in the sacred kingdom of remembrance wherein she
dwelt – that it would be almost as if something from out
of the past had struck at him across her grave.

Archie sighed, weary and sick with Fate's ironic jests.
There were some things he could not do.

The two men had avoided politics. Though Flemington's
insinuations had conveyed to the brothers that he was
like-minded with themselves, the Prince's name was not
mentioned. There was so much brewing in James's brain
that the very birds of the air must not hear. Sorry as he was
when Flemington met him with the news of his unexpected
recall, he had decided that it was well the young man
should go. When this time of stress was over, when – and
if – the cause he served should prevail, he would seek out
Archie. The 'if' was very clear to James, for he had seen
enough of men and causes, of troops and campaigns and
the practical difficulties of great movements, to know that
he was spending himself in what might well be a forlorn

hope. But none the less was he determined to see it through, for his heart was deep in it, and besides that, he had the temperament that is attracted by forlorn hopes.

He was a reticent man, in spite of the opening of that page in his life which he had laid before Flemington; and reticent characters are often those most prone to rare and unexpected bouts of self-revelation. But when the impulse is past, and the load ever present with them has been lightened for a moment, they will thrust it yet farther back behind the door of their lips, and give the key a double turn. He had enjoined Flemington to come to him as he would come to a brother for assistance, and it had seemed to Archie that life would have little more to offer had it only given him a brother like James. A cloud was on his spirit as he neared Brechin.

When he left the inn and would have paid the landlord, he thrust his hand into his pocket to discover a thin sealed packet at the bottom of it; he drew it out, and found to his surprise that, though his name was on it, it was unopened, and that he had never seen it before. While he turned it over something told him that the unknown handwriting it bore was that of James Logie. The coat he wore had hung in the hall at Balnillo since the preceding night, and the packet must have been slipped into it before he started.

As he rode along he broke the seal. The paper it contained had neither beginning nor signature, yet he knew that his guess was right:

'You will be surprised at finding this,' he read, 'but I wish you to read it when there are some miles between us. In these disturbed days it is not possible to tell when we may meet again. Should you return, I may be here or I may be gone God knows where, and for reasons of which I need not speak, my brother may be the last man to know where I am. But for the sake of all I spoke of yesterday, I ask you to believe that I am your friend. Do not forget that, in any strait, I am at your back. Because it is true, I give you these two directions: a message carried to Rob Smith's Tavern in the Castle Wynd at Stirling will reach me eventually, wheresoever I am. Nearer home you may hear of me also.

There is a little house on the Muir of Pert, the only house on the north side of the Muir, a mile west of the fir-wood. The man who lives there is in constant touch with me. If you should find yourself in urgent need, I will send you the sum of one hundred pounds through him.

'Flemington, you will make no hesitation in the matter. You will take it for the sake of one I have spoken of to none but you, these years and years past.'

And now he had to go home and to tell Madam Flemington that he had wantonly thrown away all the advantages gained in the last three days, that he had tossed them to the wind for a mere sentimental scruple! So far he had never quarrelled with his occupation; but now, because it had brought him up against a soldier of fortune whose existence he had been unaware of a few weeks ago, he had sacrificed it and played a sorry trick on his own prospects at the same time. He was trusted and valued by his own party, and, in spite of his youth, had given it excellent service again and again. He could hardly expect the determined woman who had made him what he was to see eye to eye with him.

Christian Flemington had kept her supremacy over her grandson. Parental authority was a much stronger thing in the mid-eighteenth century than it is now, and she stood in the position of a parent to him. His French blood and her long residence in France had made their relationship something like that of a French mother and son, and she had all his confidence in his young man's scrapes, for she recognized phases of life that are apt to be ignored by English parents in dealing with their children. She had cut him loose from her apron-strings early, but she had moulded him with infinite care before she let him go. There was a touch of genius in Archie, a flicker of what she called the *feu sacré*, and she had kept it burning before her own shrine. The fine unscrupulousness that was her main characteristic, her manner of breasting the tide of circumstance full sail, awed and charmed him. For all his boldness and initiative, his devil-may-care independence of will, and his originality in the conduct of his affairs, he had never freed his inner self from her thrall, and she held him by the strong impression she had made on his imagination years and years ago. She had set her mark upon the plastic character of the little boy whom she had beaten for painting Mr. Duthie's gate-post. That was an episode which he had never forgotten, which he always thought of with a smile; and while he remembered the sting of her cane, he also remembered her masterly routing of his enemy before she applied it. She had punished him with the thoroughness that was hers, but she had never allowed the minister to know what she had done. Technically she had been on the side of the angels, but in reality she had stood by the culprit. In spirit they had resented Mr. Duthie together.

He slept at Forfar that night, and pushed on again next morning; and as he saw the old house across the dip, and heard the purl of the burn at the end of his journey, something in his heart failed him. The liquid whisper of the water through the fine, rushlike grass spoke to him of childhood and of the time when there was no world but Ardguys, no monarch but Madam Flemington. He seemed to feel her influence coming out to meet him at every step his horse took. How could he tell his news? How could he explain what he had done? They had never touched on ethical questions, he and she.

As he came up the muddy road between the ash-trees he felt the chilly throe, the intense spiritual discomfort, that attends our plunges from one atmosphere into another. It is the penalty of those who live their lives with every nerve and fibre, who take fervent part in the lives of other people, to suffer acutely in the struggle to loose themselves from an environment they have just quitted, and to meet an impending one without distress. But it is no disproportionate price to pay for learning life as a whole. Also, it is the only price accepted.

He put his horse into the stable and went to the garden, being told that Madam Flemington was there. The day was warm and bright, and as he swung the gate to behind him he saw her sitting on a seat at the angle of the farther wall. She rose at the click of the latch, and came up the grass path to meet him between a line of espalier apple-trees and a row of

phlox on which October had still left a few red and
white blossoms.

The eighteen years that had gone by since the episode
of the manse gate-post had not done much to change her
appearance. The shrinking and obliterating of personality
which comes with the passing of middle life had not begun
its work on her, and at sixty-one she was more imposing
than ever. She had grown a great deal stouter, but the
distribution of flesh had been even, and she carried her
bulk with a kind of self-conscious triumph, as a ship
carries her canvas. A brown silk mantle woven with a
pattern of flower-bouquets was round her shoulders, and
she held its thick folds together with one hand; in the other
she carried the book she had been reading. Her hair was
as abundant as ever, and had grown no whiter. The sun
struck on its silver, and red flashes came from the rubies
in her ears.

She said nothing as Archie approached, but her eyes
spoke inquiry and a shadow of softness flickered ever so
slightly round her broad lips. She was pleased to see him,
but the shadow was caused less by her affection for him than
by her appreciation of the charming figure he presented,
seen thus suddenly and advancing with so much grace of
movement in the sunlight. She stopped short when he was
within a few steps of her, and, dropping her book upon
the ground without troubling to see where it fell, held out
her hand for him to kiss. He touched it with his lips, and
then, thrusting his arm into the phlox-bushes, drew out
the volume that had landed among them. From between
the leaves dropped a folded paper, on which he recognized
his own handwriting.

'This is a surprise,' said Madam Flemington, looking
her grandson up and down.

'I have ridden. My baggage is left at Balnillo.'

The moment of explanation would have to come, but
his desire was to put it off as long as possible.

'There is your letter between the pages of my book,'
said she. 'It came to me this morning, and I was reading
it again. It gave me immense pleasure, Archie. I suppose
you have come to search for the clothes you mentioned. I

am glad to see you, my dear; but it is a long ride to take for a few pairs of stockings.'

'You should see Balnillo's hose!' exclaimed Flemington hurriedly. 'I'll be bound the old buck's spindle-shanks cost him as much as his estate. If he had as many legs as a centipede he would have them all in silk.'

'And not a petticoat about the place?'

'None nearer than the kitchen.'

'He should have stayed in Edinburgh,' said Madam Flemington, laughing.

She loved Archie's society.

'I hear that this Captain Logie is one of the most dangerous rebels in Scotland,' she went on. 'If you can lay him by the heels it is a service that will not be forgotten. So far you have done mighty well, Archie.'

They had reached the gate, and she laid her hand on his arm.

'Turn back,' she said. 'I must consult you. I suppose that now you will be kept for some time at Balnillo? That nest of treason, Montrose, will give you occupation, and you must stretch out the portrait to match your convenience. I am going to take advantage of it too. I shall go to Edinburgh while you are away.'

'To Edinburgh?' exclaimed Flemington.

'Why not, pray?'

'But you leave Ardguys so seldom. It is years—'

'The more reason I should go now,' interrupted she. 'Among other things, I must see my man of business, and I have decided to do it now. I shall be more useful to you in Edinburgh, too. I have been too long out of personal touch with those who can advance your interests. I had a letter from Edinburgh yesterday; you are better thought of there than you suspect, Archie. I did not realize how important a scoundrel this man Logie is, nor what your despatch to Montrose implied.'

He was silent, looking on the ground.

She knew every turn of Archie's manner, every inflection of his voice. There was a gathering sign of opposition on his face – the phantom of some mood that must not be allowed to gain an instant's strength. It flashed on her that he had not returned merely to fetch his clothes. There was something wrong. She knew that at this moment he was afraid of her, he who was afraid of nothing else.

She stopped in the path and drew herself up, considering where she should strike. Never, never had she failed to bring him to his bearings. There was only one fitting place for him, and that was in the hollow of her hand.

'Grandmother, I shall not go back to Balnillo,' said he vehemently.

If the earth had risen up under her feet Madam Flemington could not have been more astonished. She stood immovable, looking at him, whilst an inward voice, flying through her mind like a snatch of broken sound, told her that she must keep her head. She made no feeble mistake in that moment, for she saw the vital importance of the conflict impending between them with clear eyes. She knew her back to be nearer the wall than it had been yet. Her mind was as agile as her body was by nature indolent, and it was always ready to turn in any direction and look any foe squarely in the face. She was startled, but she could not be shaken.

'I've left Balnillo for good,' said he again. 'I cannot go back – I will not!'

'You – *will not?*' said Christian, half closing her eyes. The pupils had contracted, and looked like tiny black beads set in a narrow glitter of grey. 'Is that what you have come home to say to *me?*'

'It is impossible!' he cried, turning away and flinging out his arms. 'It is more than I can do! I will not go man-hunting after Logie. I will go anywhere else, do anything else, but not that!'

'There is nothing else for you to do.'

'Then I will come back here.'

'That you will not,' said Christian.

He drew in his breath as if he had been struck.

'What are you that you should betray me, and yet think to force yourself on me without my resenting it? What do you think I am that I should suffer it?'

She laughed.

'I have not betrayed you,' said he in a husky voice.

The loyal worship he had given her unquestioning through the long dependence and the small but poignant vicissitudes of childhood came back on him like a returning tide and doubled the cruelty of her words. She was the one person against whom he felt unable to defend himself. He loved her truly, and the thought of absolute separation from her came over him like a chill.

'I did not think you could speak to me in this way. It is terrible!' he said. His dark eyes were full of pain. He spoke as simply as a little boy.

Satisfaction stole back to her. She had not lost her hold on him, would not lose it. Another woman might have flung an affectionate word into the balance to give the final dip to the scale, but she never thought of doing that; neither impulse nor calculation suggested it, because affection was not the weapon she was accustomed to trust. Her faith was in the heavy hand. Her generalship was good enough to tell her the exact moment of wavering in the enemy in front, the magic instant for a fresh attack.

'You are a bitter disappointment,' she said. 'Life has brought me many, but you are the greatest. I have had to go without some necessities in my time, and I now shall have to go without you. But I can do it, and I will.'

'You mean that you will turn from me altogether?'

'Am I not plain enough? I can be plainer if you like. You shall go out of this house and go where you will. I do not care where you go. But you are forgetting that I have some curiosity. I wish to understand what has happened to you since you wrote your letter. That is excusable, surely.'

'It is Logie,' said he. 'He has made it impossible for me. I cannot cheat a man who has given me all his confidence.'

'He gave you his confidence?' cried Madam Flemington. 'Heavens! He is well served, that stage-puppet Prince, when his servants confide in the first stranger they meet! Captain Logie must be a man of honour!'

'He is,' said Archie. 'It was his own private confidence he gave me. I heard his own history from his own lips, and, knowing it, I cannot go on deceiving him. I like him too much.'

Madam Flemington was confounded. The difficulty seemed so strangely puerile. A whim, a fancy, was to ruin the work of years and turn everything upside down. On the top, she was exasperated with Archie, but underneath, it was worse. She found her influence and her power at stake, and her slave was being wrested from her, in spite of every interest which had bound them together. She loved him with a jealous, untender love that was dependent on outward circumstances, and she was proud of him. She had smiled at his devotion to her as she would have smiled with gratified comprehension at the fidelity of a favourite dog, understanding the creature's justifiable feeling, and knowing how creditable it was to its intelligence.

'What has all this to do with your duty?' she demanded.

'My duty is too hard,' he cried. 'I cannot do it, grandmother!'

'*Too hard!*' she exclaimed. 'Pah! you weary me – you disgust me. I am sick of you, Archie!'

His lip quivered, and he met her eyes with a mist of dazed trouble in his own. A black curtain seemed to be falling between them.

'I told him every absurdity I could imagine,' said he. 'I made him believe that I was dependent upon my work for my daily bread. I did not think he would take my lies as he did. His kindness was so great – so generous! Grandmother, he would have had me promise to go to him for help. How can I spy upon him and cheat him after that?'

He stopped. He could not tell her more, for he knew that the mention of the hundred pounds would but make her more angry; the details of what Logie had written could be given to no one. He was only waiting for an opportunity to destroy the paper he carried.

'We have to do with principles, not men,' said Madam Flemington. 'He is a rebel to his King. If I thought you were so much as dreaming of going over to those worthless Stuarts, I would never see you nor speak to you again. I would sooner see you dead. Is *that* what is in your mind?'

'There is nothing farther from my thoughts,' said he. 'I can have no part with rebels. I am a Whig, and I shall always be a Whig. I have told you the plain truth.'

'And now *I* will tell you the plain truth,' said Madam Flemington. 'While I am alive you will not enter Ardguys. When you cut yourself off from me you will do so finally. I will have no half-measures as I have no half-sentiments. I have bred you up to support King George's interests against the whole band of paupers at St. Germain, that you may pay a part of the debt of injury they laid upon me and mine. Mary Beatrice took my son from me. You do not know what you have to thank her for, Archie, but I will tell you now! You have to thank her that your mother was a girl of the people – of the streets – a slut taken into the palace out of charity. She was forced on my son by the Queen and her favourite, Lady Despard. That was how they rewarded us, my husband and me, for our fidelity! He was in his grave, and knew nothing, but I was there. I am here still, and I remember still!'

The little muscles round her strong lips were quivering.

Archie had never seen Madam Flemington so much disturbed, and it was something of a shock to him to find that the power he had known always as self-dependent, aloof, unruffled, could be at the mercy of so much feeling.

'Lady Despard was one of that Irish rabble that followed King James along with better people, a woman given over to prayers and confessions and priests. She is dead, thank God! It was she who took your mother out of the gutter, where she sang from door to door, meaning to make a nun of her, for her voice was remarkable, and she and her priests would have trained her for a convent choir. But the girl had no stomach for a nunnery; the backstairs of the palace pleased her better, and the Queen took her into her household, and would have her sing to her in her own chamber. She was handsome, too, and she hid the devil that was in her from the women. The men knew her better, and the Chevalier and your father knew her best of all. But at last Lady Despard got wind of it. They dared not turn her into the streets for fear of the priests, and to save her own son the Queen sacrificed mine.'

She stopped, looking to see the effect of her words.
Archie was very pale.

'Is my true name Flemington?' he asked abruptly.

'You are my own flesh and blood,' said she, 'or you would
not be standing here. Their fear was that the Chevalier
would marry her privately, but they got him out of the
way, and your father seduced the girl. Then, to make the
Chevalier doubly safe, they forced him to make her his
wife – he who was only nineteen! They did it secretly,
but when the marriage was known, I would not receive
her, and I left the court and went to Rouen. I have lived
ever since in the hope of seeing the Stuarts swept from the
earth. Your father is gone, and you are all I have left, but
you shall go too if you join yourself to them.'

'I shall not do that,' said he.

'Do you understand now what it costs me to see you
turn back?' said Madam Flemington.

The mantle had slipped from her shoulders, and her
white hands, crossed at the wrists, lay with the fingers
along her arms. She stood trying to dissect the component
parts of his trouble and to fashion something out of them
on which she might make a new attack. Forces outside
her own understanding were at work in him which were
strong enough to take the fine edge of humiliation off the
history she had just told him; she guessed their presence,
unseen though they were, and her acute practical mind
was searching for them. She was like an astronomer whose
telescope is turned on the tract of sky in which, as his science
tells him, some unknown body will arise.

She had always taken his pride of race for granted,
as she took her own. The influx of the base blood of
the 'slut' had been a mortification unspeakable, but to
Madam Flemington, the actual treachery practised on her
had not been the crowning insult. The thing was bad, but
the manner of its doing was worse, for the Queen and Lady
Despard had used young Flemington as though he had
been of no account. The Flemingtons had served James
Stuart whole-heartedly, taking his evil fortunes as though
they had been their own; they had done it of their own free
will, high-handedly. But Mary Beatrice and her favourite

had treated Christian and her son as slaves, chattels to be sacrificed to the needs of their owner. There was enough nobility in Christian to see that part of the business as its blackest spot.

She had kept the knowledge of it from Archie, because she had the instinct common to all savage creatures (and Christian's affinity with savage creatures was a close one) for the concealment of desperate wounds. Her silks, her ruby earrings, her physical indolence, her white hands, all the refinements that had accrued to her in her world-loving life, all that went to make the outward presentment of the woman, was the mere ornamental covering of the savage in her. That savage watched Archie now.

Madam Flemington was removed by two generations from Archie, and there was a gulf of evolution between them, unrealized by either. Their conscious ideals might be identical; but their unconscious ideals, those that count with nations and with individuals, were different. And the same trouble, one that might be accepted and acknowledged by each, must affect each differently. The old regard a tragedy through its influences on the past, and the young through its influences on the future. To Archie, Madam Flemington's revelation was an insignificant thing compared to the horror that was upon him now. It was done and it could not be undone, and he was himself, with his life before him, in spite of it. It was like the withered leaf of a poisonous plant, a thing rendered innocuous by the processes of nature. What process of nature could make his agony innocuous? The word 'treachery' had become a nightmare to him, and on every side he was fated to hear it.

Its full meaning had only been brought home to him two days ago, and now the hateful thing was being pressed on him by one who had suffered from it bitterly. What could he say to her? How was he to make her see as he saw? His difficulty was a sentimental one, and one that she would not recognize.

Archie was not logical. He had still not much feeling about having deceived Lord Balnillo, whose hospitality he had accepted and enjoyed, but, as he had said, he could not go 'man-hunting' after James, who had offered him a brother's help, whose heart he had seen, whose life had already been cut in two by the baneful thing. There was little room in Archie's soul for anything but the shadow of that nightmare of treachery, and the shadow was creeping towards him. Had his mother been a grand-duchess of spotless reputation, what could her virtue or her blue blood avail him in his present distress? She was nothing to him, that 'slut' who had brought him forth; he owed her no allegiance, bore her no grudge. The living woman to whom he owed all stood before him beloved, admired, cutting him to the heart.

He assented silently; but Christian understood that, though he looked as if she had carried her point, his looks were the only really unreliable part of him. She knew that he was that curious thing – a man who could keep his true self separate from his moods. It had taken her years to learn that, but she had learnt it at last.

For once she was, like other people, baffled by his naturalness. It was plain that he suffered, yet she could not tell how she was to mould the hard stuff hidden below his suffering. But she must work with the heavy hand.

'You will leave here to-morrow,' she said; 'you shall not stay here to shirk your duty'; and again the pupils of her eyes contracted as she said it.

'I will go now,' said he.

NINE

'Toujours de l'Audace'

'DOAG,' SAID the beggar, addressing the yellow cur, 'you an' me'll need to be speerin' aboot this. Whiles, it's no sae easy tellin' havers frae truth.'

Though Skirling Wattie was on good terms with the whole of his team, the member of it whom he singled out for complete confidence, whom he regarded as an employer might regard the foreman of a working gang, was the yellow cur. The abuse he poured over the heads of his servants was meant more as incentive than as rebuke, and he fed them well, sharing his substance honestly with them, and looking to them for arduous service in return. They were a faithful, intelligent lot, good-tempered, but for one of the collies, and the accepted predominance of the yellow cur was merely one more illustration of the triumph of personality. His golden eyes, clear, like unclouded amber, contrasted with the thick and vulgar yellow of his close coat, and the contrast was like that between spirit and flesh. He was a strong, untiring creature, with blunt jaws and legs that seemed to be made of steel, and it was characteristic of him that he seldom laid down but at night, and would stand turned in his traces as though waiting for orders, looking towards his master as the latter sang or piped, whilst his comrades, extended in the dust, took advantage of the halt.

The party was drawn up under the lee of a low wall by the grassy side of the Brechin road, and its grotesqueness seemed greater than ever because of its entirely unsuitable background.

The wall encircled the site of an ancient building called Magdalen Chapel, which had long been ruined, and now only survived in one detached fragment and in the half-obliterated traces of its foundations. Round it the tangled grass rose, and a forest of withered hemlock that had nearly choked out the nettles, stood up, traced like lacework against the line of hills beyond the Basin. In summer its powdery white threw an evanescent grace over the spot. The place was a haunt of Skirling Wattie's, for it was a convenient half-way house between Montrose and Brechin, and the trees about it gave a comforting shelter from both sun and rain.

The tailboard of the cart was turned to the wall so that the piper could lean his broad back against it, and there being not a dozen inches between the bottom of his cart and the ground, he was hidden from anyone who might chance to be in the chapel precincts. The projecting stone which made a stile for those who entered the enclosure was just level with his shoulder, and he had laid his pipes on it while he sat with folded arms and considered the situation. He had just been begging at a farm, and he had heard a rumour there that Archie Flemington was gone from Balnillo, and had been seen in Brechin, riding westwards, on the preceding morning. The beggar had got a letter for him behind his sliding boards which had to be delivered without delay.

'Doag,' said he again, 'we'll awa' to auld Davie's.'

Skirling Wattie distrusted rumour, for the inexactitudes of human observation and human tongues are better known to a man who lives by his wits than to anybody else. He was not going to accept this news without sifting it. To Balnillo he would go to find out whether the report was true. The only drawback was that 'auld Davie,' as he called the judge, abhorred and disapproved of beggars, and he did not know how he might stay in the place long enough to find out what he wanted. He was a privileged person at most houses, from the sea on the east to Forfar on the west, but Lord Balnillo would none of him. Nevertheless, he turned the wheels of his chariot in his direction.

He wondered, as he went along, why he had not seen Archie by the way; but Archie had not left Balnillo by the Brechin road, being anxious to avoid him. What was the use of receiving instructions that he could not bring himself to carry out? The last person he wished to meet was the beggar.

Wattie turned into the Balnillo gates and went up the avenue towards the stable. His pipes were silent, and the fallen leaves muffled the sound of his wheels. He knew about the mishap that had brought Flemington as a guest to the judge, and about the portrait he was painting, for tidings of all the happenings in the house reached the mill sooner or later. That source of gossip was invaluable to him. But, though the miller had confirmed the report that Flemington had gone, he had been unable to tell him his exact destination.

He drove into the stable yard and found it empty but for a man who was chopping wood. The latter paused between his strokes as he saw who had arrived.

'A'm seekin' his lordship,' began Wattie, by way of discovering how the land lay.

'Then ye'll no find him,' replied the woodman, who was none other than the elder, Andrew Robieson, and who, like his master, disapproved consistently of the beggar. He was a sly old man, and he did not think it necessary to tell the intruder that the judge, though not in the house, was within hearing of the pipes. It was his boast that he 'left a' to Providence,' but he was not above an occasional shaping of events to suit himself.

The beggar rolled up to the back-door at the brisk pace he reserved for public occasions. A shriek of delight came from the kitchen window as the blast of his pipes buzzed and droned across the yard. The tune of the 'East Neuk of Fife' filled the place. A couple of maidservants came out and stood giggling as Wattie acknowledged their presence by a wag of the head that spoke gallantry, patronage, ribaldry – anything that a privileged old rogue can convey to young womanhood blooming near the soil. A groom came out of the stable and joined the group.

The feet of the girls were tapping the ground. The beggar's expression grew more genially provocative, and his eyeballs rolled more recklessly as he blew and blew; his time was perfect. The groom, who was dancing, began to compose steps on his own account. Suddenly there was a whirl of petticoats, and he had seized one of the girls round the middle.

They spun and counter-spun; now loosing each other for the more serious business of each one's individual steps, now enlacing again, seeming flung together by some resistless elemental wind. The man's gaze, while he danced alone, was fixed on his own feet as though he were chiding them, admiring them, directing them through niceties which only himself could appreciate. His partner's hair came down and fell in a loop of dull copper-colour over her back. She was a finely-made girl, and each curve of her body seemed to be surging against the agitated sheath of her clothes. The odd-woman-out circled round the pair like a fragment thrown off by the spin of some travelling meteor. The passion for dancing that is even now part of the life of Angus had caught all three, let loose upon them by the piper's handling of sound and rhythm.

In the full tide of their intoxication, a door in the high wall of the yard opened and Lord Balnillo came through it. The fragment broke from its erratic orbit and fled into the house with a scream; the meteor, a whirling twin-star, rushed on, unseeing. The piper, who saw well enough, played strong and loud; not the king himself could have stopped him in the middle of a strathspey. The yellow dog, on his feet among his reposing companions, showed a narrow white line between his lips, and the hackles rose upon his plebeian neck.

'Silence!' cried Lord Balnillo. But the rest of his words were drowned by the yell of the pipes.

As the dancers drew asunder again, they saw him and stopped. His wrath was centred on the beggar, and man and maid slunk away unrebuked.

Wattie finished his tune conscientiously. To Balnillo, impotent in the hurricane of braying reeds, each note that kept him dumb was a new insult, and he could see the knowledge of that fact in the piper's face. As the music ceased, the beggar swept off his bonnet, displaying his disreputable bald head, and bowed like the sovereign of some jovial and misgoverned kingdom. The yellow dog's attitude forbade Balnillo's nearer approach.

'Go!' shouted the judge, pointing a shaking forefinger into space. 'Out with you instantly! Is my house to be turned into a house of call for every thief and vagabond in Scotland? Have I not forbidden you my gates? Begone from here immediately, or I will send for my men to cudgel you out!'

But he leaped back, for he had taken a step forward in his excitement, and the yellow cur's teeth were bare.

'A'm seekin' the painter-laddie,' said the beggar, giving the dog a good-humoured cuff.

'Away with you!' cried the other, unheeding. 'You are a plague to the neighbourhood. I will have you put in Montrose jail! Tomorrow, I promise you, you will find yourself where you cannot make gentlemen's houses into pandemoniums with your noise.'

'A'd like Brechin better,' rejoined the beggar; 'it's couthier in there.'

Balnillo was a humane man, and he prided himself, as all the world knew, on some improvements he had suggested in the Montrose prison. He was speechless.

'Ay,' continued Wattie, 'a'm thinkin' you've sent mony a better man than mysel' to the tolbooth. But, dod! a'm no mindin' that. A'm asking ye, *whaur's the painter-lad?*'

One of Balnillo's fatal qualities was his power of turning in mid-career of wrath or eloquence to dally with side-issues.

He swallowed the fury rising to his lips,

'What! Mr. Flemington?' he stammered. 'What do you want of Mr. Flemington?'

'Is yon what they ca' him? Well, a'm no seekin' onything o' him. It's him that's seekin' me.'

Astonishment put everything else out of Balnillo's mind. He glared at the intruder, his lips pursed, his fingers working.

'He tell't me to come in-by to the muckle hoose and speer for him,' said the other. 'There was a sang he was needin'. He was seekin' to lairn it, for he liket it fine, an' he tell't me to come awa' to the hoose and lairn him. Dod! maybe he's forgotten. Callants like him's whiles sweer to mind what they say, but auld stocks like you an' me's got mair sense.'

'I do not believe a word of it,' protested Balnillo.

'Hoots! ye'll have to try, or the puir lad'll no get his sang,' exclaimed Skirling Wattie, smiling broadly. 'Just you cry on him to come down the stair, an' we'll awa' ahint the back o' yon wa', an' a'll lairn him the music! It's this way.'

He unscrewed the chanter and blew a few piercing notes. The sound flew into the judge's face like the impact of a shower of pebbles. He clapped his hands to his ears.

'I tell you Mr. Flemington is not here!' he bawled, raising his voice above the din. 'He is gone. He is at Ardguys by this time.'

'Man, is yon true? Ye're no leein'?' exclaimed Wattie, dropping his weapon.

'Is yon the way to speak to his lordship?' said the deep voice of Andrew Robieson, who had come up silently, his arms full of wood, behind the beggar's cart.

'Turn this vagabond away!' exclaimed Balnillo, almost beside himself. 'Send for the men; bring a horsewhip from the stable! Impudent rogue! Go, Robieson – quick, man!'

But Wattie's switch was in his hand, and the dogs were already turning; before the elder had time to reach the stables, he had passed out under the clock and was disappearing between the trees of the avenue. He had learned what he wished to know, and the farther side of Brechin would be the best place for him for the next few days. He reflected that fortune had favoured him in keeping Captain Logie out of the way. There would have been no parleying with Captain Logie.

BOOK II

TEN

Adrift

ARCHIE RODE along in a dream. He had gone straight out of the garden, taken his horse from the stable, and ridden back to Forfar, following the blind resolution to escape from Ardguys before he should have time to realize what it was costing him. He had changed horses at the posting-house, and turned his face along the way he had come. Through his pain and perplexity the only thing that stood fast was his determination not to return to Balnillo. 'I will go now,' he had said to Madam Flemington, and he had gone without another word, keeping his very thoughts within the walled circle of his resolution, lest they should turn to look at familiar things that might thrust out hands full of old memories to hold him back.

In the middle of his careless life he found himself cut adrift without warning from those associations that he now began to feel he had valued too little, taken for granted too much.

Balnillo was impossible for him, and in consequence he was to be a stranger in his own home. Madam Flemington had made no concession and had put no term to his banishment, and though he could not believe that such a state of things could last, and that one sudden impulse of hers could hurl him out of her life for ever, she, who had lived for him, had told him that she would 'do without him.' Then, as he assured himself of this, from that dim recess wherein a latent truth hides until some outside light flashes upon its lair, came the realization that she had not lived for him alone. She had lived for him that she might make him into the instrument she desired, a weapon fashioned to her hand, wherewith she might return blow for blow.

All at once the thought made him spiritually sick, and

the glory and desirableness of life seemed to fade. He could not see through its dark places, dark where all had been sunshine. He had been a boy yesterday, a man only by virtue of his astounding courage and resource, but he was awakening from boyhood, and manhood was hard. His education had begun, and he could not value the education of pain – the soundest, the most costly one there is – any more than any of us do whilst it lasts. He did not think, any more than any of us think, that perhaps when we come to lie on our death-beds we shall know that, of all the privileges of the life behind us, the greatest has been the privilege of having suffered and fought.

All he knew was that his heart ached, that he had disappointed and estranged the person he loved best, and had lost, at any rate temporarily, the home that had been so dear. But hope would not desert him, in spite of everything. Madam Flemington had gone very wide of the mark in suspecting him of any leaning towards the Stuarts, and she would soon understand how little intention he had of turning rebel. There was still work for him to do. He had been given a free hand in details, and he would go to Brechin for the night; to-morrow he must decide what to do. Possibly he would ask to be transferred to some other place. But nothing that heaven or earth could offer him should make him betray Logie.

Madam Flemington had seen him go, in ignorance of whether he had gone in obedience or in revolt. Perhaps she imagined that her arguments and the hateful story she had laid bare to him had prevailed, and that he was returning to his unfinished portrait. In the excitement of his interview with her, he had not told her anything but that he refused definitely to spy upon James any more.

He had started for Ardguys so early, and had been there such a short time, that he was back in Forfar by noon. There he left his horse, and, mounting another, set off for Brechin. He was within sight of its ancient round tower, grey among the yellowing trees above the South Esk, when close to his left hand there rose the shrill screech of a pipe, cutting into his abstraction of mind like a sharp stab of pain. It was so loud and sudden that the horse leaped to the farther side of the road, snorting, and Flemington, sitting loosely, nearly lost his seat. He pulled up the astonished animal, and peered into a thicket of alder growing by the wayside. The ground was marshy, and the stunted trees were set close, but, dividing their branches, he saw behind their screen an open patch in the midst of which was Skirling Wattie's cart. His jovial face seemed to illuminate the spot.

'Dod!' exclaimed the piper, 'ye was near doon! A'd no seek to change wi' you. A'm safer wi' ma' doags than you wi' yon horse. What ailed ye that ye gae'd awa' frae Balnillo?'

'Private matters,' said Archie shortly.

'Aweel, they private matters was no far frae putting me i' the tolbooth. What gar'd ye no tell me ye was gaein'?'

'Have you got a letter for me?' said Flemington, as Wattie began to draw up his sliding-board.

'Ay, there's ane. But just wait you, ma lad, till a tell ye what a was sayin' to auld Davie——'

'Never mind what you said to Lord Balnillo,' broke in Flemington; 'I want my letter.'

He slipped from the saddle and looped the rein over his arm.

'Dinna bring yon brute near me!' cried Wattie, as horse and man began to crush through the alders. 'A'm fell feared o' they unchancy cattle.'

Archie made an impatient sound and threw the rein over a stump. He approached the cart, and the yellow dog, who was for once lying down, opened his wary golden eyes, watching each movement that brought the intruder nearer to his master without raising his head.

'You are not often on this side of Brechin,' said Archie, as the beggar handed him the packet.

'Fegs, na!' returned Wattie, 'but auld Davie an' his tolbooth's on the ither side o't an' it's no safe yonder. It's yersel' I hae to thank for that, Mr. Flemington. A didna ken whaur ye was, sae a gae'd up to the muckle hoose to speer for ye. The auld stock came doon himsel'. Dod! the doag gar'd him loup an' the pipes gar'd him skelloch. But he tell't me whaur ye was.'

'Plague take you! did you go there asking for me?' cried Archie.

'What was a to dae? A tell't Davie ye was needin' me to lairn ye a sang! "The painter-lad was seekin' me," says I, "an' he tell't me to come in-by." '

Flemington's annoyance deepened. He did not know what the zeal of this insufferable rascal had led him to say or do in his name, and he had the rueful sense that the tangle he had paid such a heavy price to escape from was complicating round him. The officious familiarity of the piper exasperated him, and he resented Government's choice of such a tool. He put the letter in his pocket, and began to back out of the thicket. He would read his instructions by himself.

'Hey! ye're no awa', man?' cried Wattie.

'I have no time to waste,' said Flemington, his foot in the stirrup.

'But ye've no tell't me whaur ye're gaein'!'

'Brechin!'

Archie called the word over his shoulder, and started off at a trot, which he kept up until he had left the alder-bushes some way behind him.

Then he broke the seal of his letter, and found that he was to convey the substance of each report that he sent in, not only to His Majesty's intelligence officer at Perth, but to Captain Hall, of the English ship *Venture*, that was lying under Ferryden. He was to proceed at once to the vessel, to which further instructions for him would be sent in a couple of days' time.

He pocketed the letter and drew a breath of relief, blessing the encounter that he had just cursed, for a road of escape from his present difficulty began to open before him. He must take to his own feet on the other side of Brechin, and go straight to the *Venture*. He would be close to Montrose, in communication with it, though not within the precincts of the town, and safe from the chance of running against Logie. Balnillo and his brother would not know what had become of him, and Christian Flemington would be cured of her suspicions by the simple testimony of his whereabouts.

He would treat the two days that he had spent at the

judge's house as if they had dropped out of his life, and merely report his late presence in Montrose to the captain of the sloop. He would describe his watching of the two men who came out of 'The Happy Land,' and how he had followed them to the harbour through the darkness; how he had seen them stop opposite the ship's light as they discussed their plans; how he had tried to secure the paper they held. He would tell the captain that he believed some design against the ship to be on foot, but he would not let Logie's name pass his lips; and he would deny any knowledge of the identity of either man, lest the mention of Ferrier should confirm the suspicions of those who guessed he was working with James. When he had reported himself to Perth from the ship, he would no longer be brought into contact with Skirling Wattie, which at that moment struck him as an advantage.

The evenings had begun to close in early. As he crossed the Esk bridge and walked out of Brechin, the dusk was enwrapping its parapet like a veil. He hurried on, and struck out along the road that would lead him to Ferryden by the southern shore of the Basin. His way ran up a long ascent, and when he stood at the top of the hill the outline of the moon's disc was rising, faint behind the thin cloudy bank that rested on the sea beyond Montrose. There was just enough daylight left to show him the Basin lying between him and the broken line of the town's twinkling lights under the muffled moon.

It was quite dark when he stood at last within hail of the *Venture*. As he went along the bank at the Esk's mouth, he could see before him the cluster of houses that formed Ferryden village, and the North Sea beyond it, a formless void in the night, with the tide far out. Though the moon was well up, the cloud-bank had risen with her, and taken all sharpness out of the atmosphere.

At his left hand the water crawled slithering at the foot of the sloping bank, like a dark, full-fed snake, and not thirty yards out, just where it broadened, stretching to the quays of Montrose, the vessel lay at anchor, a stationary blot on the slow movement. Upstream, between her and the Basin, the wedge-shaped island

of Inchbrayock split the mass of water into two portions.

Flemington halted, taking in the dark scene, which he
had contemplated from its reverse side only a few nights
ago. Then he went down to the water and put his hands
round his mouth.

'*Venture* ahoy!' he shouted.

There was no movement on the ship. He waited, and
then called again, with the same result. Through an open
porthole came a man's laugh, sudden, as though provoked
by some unexpected jest. The water was deep here, and
the ship lay so near that every word was carried across it
to the shore.

The laugh exasperated him. He threw all the power of
his lungs into another shout.

'Who goes there?' said a voice.

'Friend,' replied Archie; and, fearing to be asked for
a countersign, he called quickly, 'Despatches for Captain Hall.'

'Captain Hall is ashore,' announced a second voice, 'and
no one boards us till he returns.'

The *Venture* was near enough to the bank for Archie to
hear some derisive comment, the words of which he could
not completely distinguish. A suppressed laugh followed.

'Damn it!' he cried, 'am I to be kept here all night?'

'Like enough, if you mean to wait for the captain.'

This reply came from the open porthole, in which the
light was obliterated by the head of the man who spoke.

There was a sound as of someone pulling him back by
the heels, and the port was an eye of light again.

Flemington turned and went up the bank, and as he
reached the top and sprang on to the path he ran into a
short, stoutish figure which was beginning to descend. An
impatient expletive burst from it.

'You needn't hurry, sir,' said Archie, as the other
hailed the vessel querulously; 'you are not likely to get
on board!'

'What? what? Not board my own ship?'

Flemington was a good deal taken aback. He could
not see much in the clouded night, but no impression of

authority seemed to emanate from the indistinguishable person beside him.

'Ten thousand pardons, sir!' exclaimed the young man. 'You are Captain Hall? I have information for you, and am sent by His Majesty's intelligence officer in Perth to report myself to you. Flemington is my name.'

For a minute the little man said nothing, and Archie felt rather than saw his fidgety movements. He seemed to be hesitating.

A boat was being put off from the ship. She lay so near to them that a mere push from her side brought the craft almost into the bank.

'It is so dark that I must show you my credentials on board,' said Archie, taking Captain Hall's acquiescence for granted.

He heard his companion drawing in his breath nervously through his teeth. No opposition was made as he stepped into the boat.

When he stood on deck beside Hall the ship was quiet and the sounds of laughter were silent. He had the feeling that everyone on board had got out of the way on purpose as he followed the captain down the companion to his cabin. As the latter opened the door the light within revealed him plainly for the first time.

He was a small ginger-haired man, whose furtive eyes were set very close to a thin-bridged, aquiline nose; his gait was remarkable because he trotted rather than walked; his restless fingers rubbed one another as he spoke. He looked peevish and a little dissipated, and his manner conveyed the idea that he felt himself to have no business where he was. As Archie remarked that, he told himself that it was a characteristic he had never yet seen in a seaman. His dress was careless, and a winestain on his cravat caught his companion's eye. He had the personality of a rabbit.

Hall did not sit down, but stood at the farther side of the table looking with a kind of grudging intentness at his guest, and Flemington was inclined to laugh, in spite of the heavy heart he had carried all day. The other moved about with undecided steps. When at last he sat down, just under the swinging lamp, Archie was certain that, though he could be called sober, he had been drinking.

'Your business, sir,' he began, in a husky voice. 'I must tell you that I am fatigued. I had hoped to go to bed in peace.'

He paused, leaning back, and surveyed Flemington with injured distaste.

'There is no reason that you should not,' replied Archie boldly. 'I have had a devilish hard day myself. Give me a corner to lie in tonight, and I will give you the details of my report quickly.'

He saw that he would meet with no opposition from Hall, whose one idea was to spare himself effort, and that his own quarters on board the *Venture* were sure. No doubt long practice had enabled the man to look less muddled than he felt. He sat down opposite to him.

The other put out his hand, as though to ward him off.

'I have no leisure for business to-night,' he said. 'This is not the time for it.'

'All the same, I have orders from Perth to report myself to you, as I have told you already,' said Archie. 'If you will listen, I will try to make myself clear without troubling you to read anything. I have information to give which you should hear at once.'

'I tell you that I cannot attend to you,' said Hall.

'I shall not keep you long. You do not realize that it is important, sir.'

'Am I to be dictated to?' exclaimed the other, raising his voice. 'This is my own ship, Mr. Flem— Fling— Fl—'

The name presented so much difficulty to Hall that it died away in a tangled murmur, and Archie saw that to try to make him understand anything important in his present state would be labour lost.

'Well, sir,' said he, 'I will tell you at once that I suspect an attack on you is brewing in Montrose. I believe that it may happen at any moment. Having delivered myself of that, I had best leave you.'

The word 'attack' found its way to the captain's brain.

'It's impossible!' he exclaimed crossly. 'Why, plague on't,

I've got all the town guns! Nonsense, sir – no'sense! Come, I will call for a bottle of wine, 'n you can go. There's an empty bunk, I s'pose.'

The order was given and the wine was brought. Archie noticed that the man who set the bottle and the two glasses on the table threw a casual look at Hall's hand, which shook as he helped his guest. He had eaten little since morning, and drunk less. Now that he had attained his object, and found himself in temporary shelter and temporary peace, he realized how glad he was of the wine. When, after a single glassful, he rose to follow the sailor who came to show him his bunk, he turned to bid good-night to Hall. The light hanging above the captain's head revealed every line, every contour of his face with merciless candour; and Flemington could see that no lover, counting the minutes till he should be left with his mistress, had ever longed more eagerly to be alone with her than this man longed to be alone with the bottle before him.

Archie threw himself thankfully into his bunk. There was evidently room for him on the ship, for there was no trace of another occupant in the little cabin; nevertheless, it looked untidy and unswept. The port close to which he lay was on the starboard side of the vessel, and looked across the strait towards the town. The lamps were nearly all extinguished on the quays, and only here and there a yellow spot of light made a faint ladder in the water. The pleasant trickling sound outside was soothing, with its impersonal, monotonous whisper. He wondered how long Hall would sit bemusing himself at the table, and what the discipline of a ship commanded by this curiously ineffective personality could be. Tomorrow he must make out his story to the little man. He could not reproach himself with having postponed his report, for he knew that Hall's brain, which might possibly be clearer in the morning, was incapable of taking in any but the simplest impressions to-night.

Tired as he was, he did not sleep for a long time. The scenes of the past few days ran through his head one after another – now they appeared unreal, now almost visible to his eyes. Sometimes the space of time they covered seemed age-long, sometimes a passing flash. This was Saturday night, and all the events that had culminated in the disjointing of his life had been crowded into it since Monday. On Monday he had not suspected what lay in himself. He would have gibed had he been told that another man's personality, a page out of another man's history, could play such havoc with his own interests.

He wondered what James was doing. Was he – now – over there in the darkness, looking across the rolling, sea-bound water straight to the spot on which he lay? Would he – could space be obliterated and night illumined – look up to find his steady eyes upon him? He lay quiet, marvelling, speculating. Then Logie, the shadowy town, the burning autumn-trees of Balnillo, the tulips round the house in far-away Holland, fell away from his mind, and in their place was the familiar background of Ardguys, the Ardguys of his childhood, with the silver-haired figure of Madam Flemington confronting him; that terrible, unsparing presence wrapped about with something greater and more arresting than mere beauty; the quality that had wrought on him since he was a little lad. He turned about with a convulsive breath that was almost a sob.

Then, at last, he slept soundly, to be awakened just at dawn by the roar of a gun, followed by a rattle of small shot, and the frantic hurrying of feet overhead.

ELEVEN

The Guns of Montrose

WHEN ARCHIE lay and pictured James on the other side of the water his vision was a true one, but, while he saw him on the quay among the sheds and windlasses, he had set him in the wrong place.

James stood at the point of the bay formed by the Basin of Montrose, at the inner and landward side of the town, not far from the empty fort from which Hall had taken the guns. The sands at his feet were bare, for the tide was out, and the salt, wet smell of the oozing weed blew round him on the faint wind. He was waiting for Ferrier.

They had chosen this night, as at this hour the ebbing water would make it possible for the hundred men of Ferrier's regiment to keep clear of the roads, and to make their way from Brechin on the secluded shore of the Basin. Logie had not been there long when he heard the soft sound of coming feet, and the occasional knocking of shoes against stone. As an increasing shadow took shape, he struck his hand twice against his thigh, and the shadow grew still. He struck again and in another minute Ferrier was beside him; the soldiers who followed halted behind their leader. The two men said little to each other, but moved on side by side, and the small company wound up the rising slope of the shore to the deserted fort and gathered at its foot.

James and his friend went on a little way and stood looking east down the townward shore of the strait past the huddled houses massed together at this end of Montrose. The water slid to the sea, and halfway down the long quay in front of them was moored the unrigged barque that held the town guns – the four-pounders and six-pounders that had pointed their muzzles for so many years from the fort walls towards the thundering bar.

Hall had not concerned himself to bring the vessel into his own immediate neighbourhood, nor even to put a few dozen yards of water between her and the shore. He knew that no organized rebel force existed within nine miles of where she lay, and that the Jacobites among the townsmen could not attempt any hostile movement unaided. He had eighty men on board the *Venture* with him, and from them he had taken a small guard which was left in charge of the barque. Every two or three days he would send a party from the sloop to patrol the streets of Montrose, and to impress disloyally inclined people. His own investigations of the place had not been great, for, though he went ashore a good deal, it cannot be said that King George's interests were much furthered by his doings when he got there.

When Logie and Ferrier had posted a handful of men in the empty fort, they went on towards the barque's moorings followed by the rest, and leaving a few to guard the mouth of each street that opened on the quay. The whole world was abed behind the darkened windows and the grim stone walls that brooded like blind faces over the stealthy band passing below. When they reached the spot where the ferry-boat lay that plied between Montrose and the south shore of the strait, two men went down to the landing-stage, and, detaching her chains, got her ready to push off. Then, with no more delay, the friends pressed on to the main business of their expedition. As they neared the barque, a faint shine forward where her bows pointed seaward suggested that someone on board was waking, so, judging it best to make the attack before an alarm could be given, the two captains ran on with their men, and were climbing over the bulwarks and tumbling on to her deck before Captain Hall's guard, who were playing cards round a lantern, had time to collect their senses.

The three players sprang to their feet, and one of them sent a loud cry ringing into the darkness before he sprawled senseless, with his head laid open by the butt-end of Ferrier's pistol. In this unlooked-for onslaught, that had come upon them as suddenly as the swoop of a squall in a treacherous sea, they struck blindly about, stumbling into the arms of the swarming, unrecognized figures that had poured in on their security out of the peaceful night. James had kicked over the lantern, and the cards lay scattered about under foot, white spots in the dimness. The bank of cloud was thinning a little round the moon, and the angles of the objects on deck began to be more clearly blocked out. One of the three, who had contrived to wrench himself from his assailant's hold, sprang away and raced towards the after-part of the ship, where, with the carelessness of security, he had left his musket. Three successive shots was the signal for help from the *Venture* in case of emergency, and he made a gallant effort to get free to send this sign of distress across the strait. But he was headed back and overpowered before he could carry out his intention. One of his companions was lying as if dead on the deck, and the other, who had been cajoled to silence by the suggestive caress of a pistol at the back of his ear, was having his arms bound behind him with his own belt.

Not a shot had been fired. Except for that one cry from the man who lay so still at their feet, no sound but the scuffling and cursing on the barque disturbed the quiet. Ferrier's men hustled their prisoners below into the cabin, where they were gagged and secured and left under the charge of a couple of soldiers. No roving citizen troubled the neighbourhood at this hour, for the fly-by-nights of Montrose looked farther inland for their entertainment, and the fisher-folk, who were the principal dwellers in the poor houses skirting the quays, slept sound, and recked little of who might be quarrelling out of doors so long as they lay warm within them. The barque was some way upstream from the general throng of shipping – apart, and, as Hall had thought, the more safe for that, for his calculations had taken no count of an enemy who might come from anywhere but the town. He had never dreamed of the silent band which had been yielded up by the misty stretches of the Basin.

James leaned over the vessel's side towards the *Venture*, and thought of Captain Hall. He had seen him in a tavern of the town, and had been as little impressed by his looks as was Flemington. He had noticed the uncertain eye, the

restless fingers, the trotting gait, and had held him lightly
as a force; for he knew as well as most men know who have
knocked about this world that character – none other – is the
hammer that drives home every nail into the framework of
achievement.

But he had no time to spend in speculations, for
his interest was centred in the ferry-boat that was now
slipping noiselessly towards them on the current, guided
down-stream by the couple of soldiers who had unmoored
her. As she reached the barque a rope was tossed down to
her, and she was made fast. The stolen guns were hauled
from their storage, and a six-pounder lowered, with its
ammunition, into the great tub that scarcely heaved on the
slow swirl of the river; and whilst the work was going on,
Ferrier and James stepped ashore to the quay, and walked
each a short way along it, watching for any movement or
for the chance of surprise. There was nothing: only, from
far out beyond the shipping, a soft rush, so low that it
seemed to be part of the atmosphere itself, told that the
tide was on the turn.

In the enshrouding night the boat was loaded, and a
dozen or so of the little company pushed off with their
spoil. Ferrier went with them, and Logie, who was to
follow with the second gun, watched the craft making
her way into obscurity, like some slow black river monster
pushing blindly out into space.

The scheme he had been putting together since the arrival
of the *Venture* was taking reality at last, and though he could
stand with folded arms on the bulwark looking calmly at
the departing boat, the fire in his heart burned hot. Custom
had inured him to risks of every kind, and if his keenness
of enterprise was the same as it had been in youth, the
excitement of youth had evaporated. It was the depths
that stirred in Logie, seldom the surface. Like Archie
Flemington, he loved life, but he loved it differently.
Flemington loved it consciously, joyously, pictorially;
James loved it desperately – so desperately that his spirit
had survived the shock which had robbed it of its glory,
for him. He was like a faithful lover whose mistress has
been scarred by smallpox.

He could throw himself heart and soul into the Stuart cause, its details and necessities – all that his support of it entailed upon him, because it had, so to speak, given him his second wind in the race of life. Though he was an adventurer by nature, he differed from the average adventurer in that he sought nothing for himself. He did not conform to the average adventuring type. He was too overwhelmingly masculine to be a dangler about women, though since the shipwreck of his youth he had more than once followed in the train of some complaisant goddess, and had reaped all the benefits of her notice; he was no snatcher at casual advantages, but a man to whom service in any interest meant solid effort and unsparing sacrifice. Also he was one who seldom looked back. He had done so once lately, and the act had shaken him to the heart. Perhaps he would do so oftener when he had wrought out the permanent need of action that lay at the foundation of his nature.

When the boat had come back, silent on the outflowing river, and had taken her second load, he lowered himself into the stern as her head was pulled round again towards Inchbrayock.

The scheme fashioned by the two men for the capture of the vessel depended for its success on their possession of this island. As soon as they should land on it, they were to entrench the two guns, one on its south-eastern side, as near to the *Venture* as possible, and the other on its northern shore, facing the quays. By this means the small party would command, not only the ship, but the whole breadth of the river and its landing-places, and would be able to stop communication between Captain Hall and the town. Heavy undergrowth covered a fair portion of Inchbrayock, and the only buildings upon it – if buildings they could be called – were the walls of an old graveyard and the stones and crosses they encircled. Though the island lay at a convenient part of the strait, no bridge connected it with Montrose, and those who wished to cross the Esk at that point were obliged to use the ferry. The channel dividing its southern shore from the mainland being comparatively narrow, a row of gigantic stepping-stones carried wayfarers dry-shod across its bed, for at low tide there was a mere streak of water curling serpentwise through the mud.

When the guns were got safely into position on the island it was decided that Ferrier was to return to the barque and take the remaining four-pounders with all despatch to a piece of rising ground called Dial Hill, that overlooked the mass of shipping opposite Ferryden.

He did not expect to meet with much opposition, should news of his action be carried to the town, for its main sympathies were with his side, and the force on the Government vessel would be prevented from coming over the strait to oppose him until he was settled on his eminence by the powerful dissuaders he had left behind him on Inchbrayock. He was to begin firing from Dial Hill at dawn, and James, who was near enough to the *Venture* to see any movement that might take place on her, was to be ready with his fire and with his small party of marksmen to check any offensive force despatched from the ship to the quays. Hall would thus be cut off from the town by the fire from Inchbrayock, on the one hand, and, should he attempt a landing nearer to the watermouth, by the guns on Dial Hill, on the other.

James had placed himself advantageously. The thicket of elder and thorn which had engulfed one end of the burial-ground made excellent concealment, and in front of him was the solid wall, through a gap in which he had turned the muzzle of his six-pounder. He sat on the stump of a thorn-tree, his head in his hands, waiting, as he knew he would have to wait, for some time yet, till the first round from Dial Hill should be the signal for his own attack. The moon had made her journey by this hour, and while she had been caught in her course through the zenith in the web of cloud and mist that thickened the sky, she was now descending towards her rest through a clear stretch; she swung, as though suspended above the Basin, tilted on her back, and a little yellower as she neared the earth; a dying, witch-like thing, halfway through her second quarter. James, looking up, could see her between the arms of the crosses and the leaning stones.

The strangeness of the place arrested his thoughts and

turned them into unusual tracks, for, though far from being an unimaginative man, he was little given to deliberate contemplation. The distant inland water under the lighted half disc was pale, and a faintness seemed to lie upon the earth in this hour between night and morning. His thoughts went to the only dwellers on Inchbrayock, those who were lying under his feet – seamen, for the most part, and fisher folk, who had known the fury of the North Sea that was now beginning to crawl in and to surround them in their little township with its insidious arms, encircling in death the bodies that had escaped it in life. Some of them had been far afield, farther than he had ever been, in spite of all his campaigns, but they had come in over the bar to lie here in the jaws of the outflowing river by their native town. He wondered whether he should do the same; times were so uncertain now that he might well take the road into the world again. The question of where his bones should lie was a matter of no great interest to him, and though there was a vague restfulness in the notion of coming at last to the slopes and shadows of Balnillo, he knew that the wideness of the world was his natural home. Then he thought of Bergen-op-Zoom . . .

After a while he raised his head again, roused, not by the streak of light that was growing upon the east, but by a shot that shattered the silence and sent the echoes rolling out from Dial Hill.

TWELVE

Inchbrayock

ARCHIE SPRANG up, unable, for a moment, to remember where he was. He was almost in darkness, for the port looked northward, and the pale light barely glimmered through it, but he could just see a spurt of white leap into the air midway across the channel, where a second shot had struck the water. As he rushed on deck a puff of smoke was dispersing above Dial Hill. Then another cloud rolled from the bushes on the nearest point of Inchbrayock Island, and he felt the *Venture* shiver and move in her moorings. Captain Hall's voice was rising above the scuffling and running that was going on all over the ship, and the dragging about of heavy objects was making the decks shake.

He went below and began to hustle on his clothes, for the morning air struck chill and he felt the need of being ready for action of some kind. In a few minutes he came up warily and crept round to the port side, taking what cover he could. Then a roar burst from the side of the *Venture* as she opened fire.

He stood, not knowing what to do with himself. It was dreadful to him to have to be inactive whilst his blood rose with the excitement round him. No one on the vessel remembered his existence; he was like a stray dog in a marketplace, thrust aside by every passer brushing by on the business of life.

It was soon evident that, though the guns on the hill commanded the *Venture*, their shot was falling short of her. As the sun heaved up from beyond the bar, the quays over the water could be seen filling with people, and the town bells began to ring. An increasing crowd swarmed upon the landing-stage of the ferry, but the boat herself had been brought by James to the shore of Inchbrayock, and nobody was likely to cross the water whilst the island and the high ground seaward of the town was held by the invisible enemy which had come upon them from heaven knew where. Captain Hall was turning his attention exclusively on Inchbrayock, and Flemington, who had got nearer to the place where he stood, gathered from what he could hear that the man on Dial Hill was wasting his ammunition on a target that was out of range. A shot from the vessel had torn up a shower of earth in the bank that sloped from the thicket to the river-mud, and another had struck one of the gravestones on the island, splitting it in two; but the fire went on steadily from the dense tangle where the churchyard wall no doubt concealed earthworks that had risen behind it in the dark hours. This, then, was the outcome of James's night-wanderings with Ferrier.

Archie contemplated Captain Hall where he stood in a little group of men. He looked even less of a personage in the morning light than he had done in the cabin, and the young man suspected that he had gone to bed in his clothes. This reminded him that he himself was unwashed, unshaven, and very hungry. Whatsoever the issue of the attack might be, there was no use in remaining starved and dirty, and he determined to go below to forage and to find some means of washing. There was no one to gainsay him at this time of stress, and he walked into Hall's cabin reflecting that he might safely steal anything he could carry from the ship, if he were so minded, and slip overboard across the narrow arm to the bank with nothing worse than a wetting.

Whilst he was attending to his own necessities, the booming went on overhead, and at last a shout from above sent him racing up from the welcome food he had contrived to secure. The wall on Inchbrayock was shattered in two or three places and the unseen gun was silent. The cannonade from Dial Hill had stopped, but a train of figures was hurrying across from the northern shore of the island, taking shelter among the bushes and stones. A boat was being lowered from the *Venture*, for the tide, now sweeping in, had covered the mud, making a landing possible. Men were crowding into her, and as

Flemington got round to his former place of observation she was being pushed off.

Hall, who was standing alone, caught sight of him and came towards him; his face looked swollen and puffy, and his eyes were bloodshot.

'We have been attacked,' he began – 'attacked most unexpectedly!'

'I had the honour to report that possibility to you last night, sir,' replied Flemington, with a trifle of insolence in his manner.

An angry look shot out of Hall's rabbit eyes. 'What could you possibly have known about such a thing?' he cried. 'What reason had you for making such a statement?'

'I had a great many,' said Archie, 'but you informed me that you had no leisure to listen to any of them until this morning. Perhaps you are at leisure now?'

'You are a damned impudent scoundrel!' cried the other, noticing Flemington's expression, which amply justified these words, 'but you had better take care! There is nothing to prevent me from putting you under arrest.'

'Nothing but the orders I carry in my pocket,' replied Archie. 'They are likely enough to deter you.'

The other opened his mouth to speak, but before he could do so a shot crashed into the fore part of the ship, and a hail of bullets ripped out from the thicket on the island; the boat, which was halfway between the *Venture* and Inchbrayock, spun round, and two of the rowers fell forward over their oars. Hall left Archie standing where he was.

The gun that the ship's gunners believed themselves to have disabled had opened fire again, after a silence that had been, perhaps, but a lure to draw a sortie from her; and as it was mere destruction for the boat to attempt a landing in the face of the shot, she had orders to put back.

The position in which he was placed was now becoming clear to Hall. He was cut off from communication with the quays by the guns safely entrenched on the island, and those on Dial Hill, though out of range for the moment, would prevent him from moving nearer to the water-mouth or making an attempt to get out to sea. He could not tell

what was happening in the town opposite, and he had
no means of finding out, for the whole of the cannon
that he had been mad enough to leave by the shore was
in the enemy's possession, and would remain so unless
the townspeople should rise in the Government interest
for their recapture. This he was well aware they would
not do.

His resentment against his luck, and the tale-bearing
voice within, which told him that he had nothing to thank for
it but his own carelessness, grew more insistent as his head
grew clearer. He had been jerked out of sleep, heavy-headed,
and with a brain still dulled by drink, but the morning
freshness worked on him, and the sun warmed his senses
into activity. The sight of Flemington, clean, impertinent,
and entirely comprehensive of the circumstances, drove
him mad; and it drove him still madder to know that
Archie understood why he had been unwilling to see his
report last night.

Hall's abilities were a little superior to his looks. So far
he had served his country, not conspicuously, but without
disaster, and had he been able to keep himself as sober as
most people contrived to be in those intemperate days, he
might have gone on his course with the same tepid success.
He was one who liked the distractions of towns, and he
bemoaned the fate that had sent him to anchor in a dull
creek of the East Coast, where the taverns held nothing
but faces whose unconcealed dislike forbade conviviality,
and where even the light women looked upon his uniform
askance. He was not a lively comrade at the best of times,
and here, where he was thrown upon the sole society of his
officers, with whom he was not popular, he was growing
more morose and more careless as his habits of stealthy
excess grew upon him. Archie, with his quick judgment of
his fellow-men, had measured him accurately, and he knew
it. In the midst of the morning's disaster the presence of
the interloper, his flippant civility of word and insolence
of manner, made his sluggish blood boil.

It was plain that the party on the island must be dislodged
before anything could be done to save the situation, and Hall
now decided to land as large a force as he could spare upon

the mainland. By marching it along the road to Ferryden he would give the impression that some attempt was to be made to cross the strait nearer to the coast, and to land it between Dial Hill and the sea. Behind Ferryden village a rough track turned sharply southward up the bank, and this they were to take; they would be completely hidden from Inchbrayock once they had got over the crest of the land, and they were to double back with all speed along the mainland under shelter of the ridge, and to go for about a mile parallel with the Basin. When they had got well to the westward side of the island, they were to wheel down to the Basin's shore at a spot where a grove of trees edged the brink; for here, in a sheltering turn of backwater among the trunks and roots, a few boats were moored for the convenience of those who wished to cross straight to Montrose by water instead of taking the usual path by the stepping-stones over Inchbrayock Island.

They were to embark at this place, and, hugging the shore, under cover of its irregularities, to approach Inchbrayock from the west. If they should succeed in landing unseen, they would surprise the enemy at the further side of the graveyard whilst his attention was turned on the *Venture*. The officer to be sent in command of the party believed it could be done, because the length of the island would intervene to hide their manoeuvres from the town, where the citizens, crowding on the quays, would be only too ready to direct the notice of the rebels to their approach.

As the boat put off from the ship Archie slipped into it; he seemed to have lost his definite place in the scheme of things during the last twenty-four hours; he was nobody's servant, nobody's master, nobody's concern; and in spite of his bold reply to Hall's threat of arrest, he knew quite well that though the captain would stop short of such a measure, he might order him below at any moment; the only wonder was that he had not done so already. He did not know into what hands he might fall, should Hall be obliged to surrender, and this contingency appeared to be growing likely. By tacking himself on to the landing-party he would at least have the chance of action, and though, having been careful to keep out of Hall's sight, he had not

been able to discover their destination, he had determined
to land with the men.

After they had disembarked, he went boldly up to the
officer in charge of the party and asked for permission
to go with it, and when this was accorded with some
surprise, he fell into step. As they tramped along towards
Ferryden, he managed to pick up something of the work
in hand from the man next to him. His only fear was
of the chance of running against Logie; nevertheless, he
made up his mind to trust to luck to save him from that,
because he believed that Logie, as a professional soldier,
would be in command of the guns on the hill. It was from
Dial Hill that the tactical details of the attack could best
be directed, and if either of the conspirators were upon
the island, Archie was convinced it would be Ferrier.

They soon reached Ferryden. The sun was clear and brave
in the salt air over the sea, and a flock of gulls was screaming
out beyond the bar, dipping, hovering, swinging sideways
against the light breeze, now this way, now that way, their
wanton voices full of mockery, as though the derisive
spirits imprisoned in the ocean had become articulate,
and were crying out on the land. The village looked
distrustfully at the approach of the small company, and
some of the fisher-wives dragged their children indoors as
if they thought to see them kidnapped. Such men as were
hanging about watched them with sullen eyes as they turned
in between the houses and made for the higher ground.

The boom of the *Venture*'s guns came to them from
time to time, and once they heard a great shout rise
from the quays, but they could see nothing because of
the intervening swell of the land. They passed a farm
and a few scattered cottages; but these were empty, for
their inmates had gone to the likeliest places they could
find for a view of what was happening in the harbour.

Presently they went down to the Basin, straggling by
twos and threes. At the water's edge a colony of beeches
stood naked and leafless, their heads listed over westward
by the winds that swept up the river's mouth. They were
crowded thick about the creek down which Flemington
and his companions came and at their feet, tied to the

gnarled elbows of the great roots beneath which the water had eaten deep into the bank, lay three or four boats with their oars piled inside them. The beech-mast of years had sunk into the soil, giving a curious mixture of heaviness and elasticity to the earth as it was trodden; a water-rat drew a lead-coloured ripple along the transparency, below which the undulations of the bottom lay like a bird's-eye view of some miniature world. The quiet of this hidden landing-place echoed to the clank of the rowlocks as the heavy oars were shipped, and two boatloads slid out between the stems.

Archie, who was unarmed, had borrowed one of the officer's pistols, not so much with the intention of using it as from the wish for a plausible pretext for joining the party. At any time his love of adventure would welcome such an opportunity, and at this moment he did not care what might happen to him. He seemed to have no chance of being true to anybody, and it was being revealed to him that, in these circumstances, life was scarcely endurable. He had never thought about it before, and he could think of nothing else now. It was some small comfort to know that, should his last half-hour of life be spent on Inchbrayock, Madam Flemington would at least understand that she had wronged him in suspecting him of being a turncoat. If only James could know that he had not betrayed him – or, rather, that his report was in the hands of that accursed beggar before they met among the broom-bushes! Yet, what if he did know it? Would his loathing of the spy under the roof-tree of his brother's house be any the less? He would never understand – never know. And yet he had been true to him in his heart, and the fact that he had now no roof-tree of his own proved it.

They slipped in under the bank of the island and disembarked silently. The higher ground in the middle of it crossed their front like the line of an incoming wave, hiding all that was going on on its farther side. They were to advance straight over it, and to rush down upon the thicket where the gun was entrenched with its muzzle towards the *Venture*. There was to be no working round the north shore, lest the hundreds of eyes on the quays should catch sight of them, and a hundred tongues give the alarm to the rebels. They were to attack at once, only waiting for the sound of another shot to locate the exact place for which they were to make. They stood drawn up, waiting for the order.

Archie dropped behind the others. His heart had begun to sink. He had assured himself over and over again that Logie must be on Dial Hill; yet as each moment brought him nearer to contact with the enemy, he felt cold misgiving stealing on him. What if his guesses had been wrong? He knew that he had been a fool to run the risk he had taken. Chance is such a smiling, happy-go-lucky deity when we see her afar off; but when we are well on our steady plod towards her, and the distance lessens between us, it is often all that we can do to meet her eyes – their expression has changed. Archie's willingness to take risks was unfailing and temperamental, and he had taken this one in the usual spirit, but so much had happened lately to shake his confidence in life and in himself that his high heart was beating slower. Never had he dreaded anything as much as he dreaded James's knowledge of the truth; yet the most agonizing part of it all was that James could not know the whole truth, nor understand it, even if he knew it. Archie's reading of the other man's character was accurate enough to tell him that no knowledge of facts could make Logie understand the part he had played.

Sick at heart, he stood back from the party, watching it gather before the officer. He did not belong to it; no one troubled his head about him, and the men's backs were towards him. He stole away, sheltered by a little hillock, and ran, bent almost double, to the southern shore of the island. He would creep round it and get as near as possible to the thicket. If he could conceal himself, he might be able to see the enemy and the enemy's commander, and to discover the truth while there was yet time for flight. He glanced over his shoulder to see if the officer had noticed his absence, and being reassured, he pressed on. He knew that anyone who thought about him at all would take him for a coward, but he did not reckon that. The dread of meeting James possessed him.

Sheep were often brought over to graze the island, and their tracks ran like network among the bushes. He trod softly in and out, anxious to get forward before the next sound of the gun should let loose the invading-party upon the rebels. He passed the end of the stepping-stones which crossed the Esk's bed to the mainland; they were now nearly submerged by the tide rising in the river. He had not known of their existence, and as he noticed them with surprise, a shot shook the air, and though the thicket, now not far before him, blocked his view of the *Venture's* hull, he saw the tops of her masts tremble, and knew that she had been struck.

Before him, the track took a sharp turn round a bend of the shore, which cut the path like a little promontory, so that he could see nothing beyond it, and here he paused. In another few minutes the island would be in confusion from the attack, and he might discover nothing. He set his teeth and stepped round the corner.

The track widened out and then plunged into the fringe of the thicket. A man was kneeling on one knee with his back to Flemington; his hands were shading his eyes, and he was peering along a tunnel-shaped gap in the branches, through which could be seen a patch of river and the damaged bows of the *Venture*.

Archie's instinct was to retreat, but before he could do so, the man jumped up and faced him. His heart leaped to his mouth, for it was James.

LOGIE STOOD STARING at him. Then he made a great effort to pick up the connecting-link of recollection that he felt sure he must have dropped. He had been so much absorbed in the business in hand that he found it impossible for a moment to estimate the significance of any outside matter. Though he was confounded and disturbed by the unlooked-for apparition of the painter, the idea of hostility never entered his mind.

'Flemington?' he exclaimed, stepping towards him.

But the other man's expression was so strange that he stopped, conscious of vague disaster. What had the intruder come to tell him? As he stood, Flemington murmured something he could not distinguish, then turned quickly in his tracks.

Logie leaped after him, and seized him by the shoulder before he had time to double round the bend.

'Let me go!' cried Archie, his chest heaving; 'let me go, man!'

But James's grip tightened; he was a strong man, and he almost dragged him over. As he held him, he caught sight of the Government pistol in his belt. It was one that the officer who had lent it to Flemington had taken from the ship.

He jerked Archie violently round and made a snatch at the weapon, and the younger man, all but thrown off his balance, thrust his arm convulsively into the air. His sleeve shot back, laying bare a round, red spot outside the brown, sinewy wrist.

Then there flashed retrospectively before James's eye that same wound, bright in the blaze of the flaming paper; and with it there flashed comprehension.

His impulse was to draw his own pistol, and to shoot the spy dead, but Archie recovered his balance, and was grappling with him so that he could not get his arm free. The strength of the slim, light young man astonished him. He was as agile as a weasel, but James found in him, added to his activity, a force that nearly matched his own.

There was no possible doubt of Logie's complete enlightenment, though he kept his crooked mouth shut and uttered no word. His eyes wore an expression not solely due to the violent struggle going on; they were terrible, and they woke the frantic instinct of self-preservation in Flemington. He knew that James was straining to get out his own pistol, and he hung on him and gripped him for dear life. As they swayed and swung to and fro, trampling the bents, there rose from behind the graveyard a yell that gathered and broke over the sound of their own quick breaths like a submerging flood, and the bullets began to whistle over the rising ground.

Archie saw a change come into James's eyes; then he found himself staggering, hurled with swift and tremendous force from his antagonist. He was flung headlong against the jutting bend round which he had come, and his forehead struck it heavily; then, rolling down to the track at its foot, he lay stunned and still.

THIRTEEN

The Interested Spectator

AS JAMES Logie dashed back to his men to meet this unexpected attack, he left Flemington lying with his face to the bank and his back towards the river; he was so close to the edge of the island that his hair rested on the wet sand permeated by the returning tide coming up the Esk. James's whole mind had gone back like a released spring to its natural preoccupation, and he almost forgot him before he had time to join the brisk affray that was going on.

But though Archie lay where he fell, and was as still as a heap of driftwood, it was only a few minutes before he came to himself. Perhaps the chill of the damp sand under his head helped to revive him; perhaps the violence of the blow had been broken by the sod against which he had been hurled. He stirred and raised himself, dazed, but listening to the confused sounds of fighting that rang over Inchbrayock. His head hurt him, and instinctively he grubbed up a handful of the cold, wet sand and held it to his brow. His wits had not gone far, for there had been no long break in his consciousness, and he got on his feet and looked round for the best means of escape.

James knew all. That was plain enough; and on the issue of the skirmish his own liberty would depend if he did not get clear of the island at once. He went back round the bend, and looking up the shore he saw a couple of the stepping-stones which were only half covered by the tide. In the middle of the channel they had disappeared already, but at either edge they lay visible, like the two ends of a partly submerged chain. Blood was trickling down his face, but he washed it off, and made hastily for the crossing, wading in.

The Esk was not wide just there, though it was far deeper than he had fancied it, and he stumbled along, churning up the mud into an opaque swirl through which he could not see the bottom. He climbed the further bank, wasting no time in looking behind him, and never stopped until he stood, panting and dizzy, on the high ridge of land from which he could overlook Inchbrayock and the harbour and town. He was a good deal exhausted, for his head throbbed like a boiling pot, and his hands were shaking. He lay down in a patch of whins, remembering that he was on the sky-line. He meant to see which way the fortunes of war were going to turn before deciding what to do with himself. Thanks to chance, his business with Captain Hall was not finished, nor even begun; but as things seemed at present, Captain Hall might be a prisoner before the leisure which had been the subject of his own gibes that morning should arrive. The vessel's guns had roared out again as he struggled up the steep, but there had been silence on the island, and even the rattle of musketry had now stopped. Something decisive must have taken place, though he could not guess what it was, and he was too far away to distinguish more than the moving figures in the graveyard.

He was high enough to see the curve of the watery horizon, for Ferryden village was some way below him. His view was only interrupted by a group of firs that stood like an outpost between him and the land's end. He lay among his friendly whin-bushes, staring down on the strait. If James were victorious he knew that there would soon be a hue and cry on his own tracks; but though alive to the desirableness of a good start in these circumstances, he felt that he could not run while there remained any chance of laying the whole of his report before Captain Hall. He thought, from what he had seen of the man, that the less he was reckoned with by his superiors the better, but it was not his business to consider that. As he turned these things over in his mind his eyes were attracted to Dial Hill, upon which the sudden sign of a new turn of events could be read.

He could see the group of men with the guns below the flagstaff which crowned its summit, and what now attracted his attention was a dark object that had been run up the ropes, its irregular outline flapping and flying against the sky as it was drawn frantically up and down.

Flemington was blessed with long sight, and he was certain that the two sharp-cut ends that waved like streamers as the dark object dipped and rose, were the sleeves of a man's coat. He saw a figure detach itself from the rest and run towards the seaward edge of the eminence. Ferrier – for he supposed now that Ferrier was on the hill – must be signalling out to sea with this makeshift flag.

He half raised himself from his lair. The cold grey-green of the ocean spread along the world's edge, broken by tiny streaks of foam as the wind began to freshen, and beyond the fir-trees, seen through their stems, the reason of the activity on Dial Hill slid into sight.

A ship was coming up the coast not a couple of miles out, and as Flemington watched her she stood in landward, as though attracted out of her course by the signals and the sound of firing in Montrose harbour. She was too far off for him to distinguish her colours, but he knew enough about shipping to be certain that she was a French frigate.

He dropped back into his place; whilst these sensational matters were going forward he did not suppose that anyone would think of pursuing him. The fact that the rebels were signalling her in suggested that the stranger might not be unexpected, and in all probability she carried French supplies and Jacobite troops. The likelihood of an interview with Captain Hall grew more remote.

The frigate drew closer; soon she was hidden from him by the jutting out of the land. Another shot broke from the *Venture*, but the quick reply from the island took all doubt of the issue of the conflict from Archie's mind. James was in full possession of the place, and the surprise must have been a failure.

Archie watched eagerly to see the ship arrive in the river-mouth. It was evident that Hall, from his position under the south shore of the strait, had not seen her yet. Presently she rounded the land and appeared to the hundreds of eyes on the quays, a gallant, silent, winged creature, a vivid apparition against the band of sea beyond the opening channel of the Esk, swept towards the town as though by some unseen impulse of fate. The shout that went up as she came into view rose to where Archie lay on the hillside.

The tide was now running high, and she passed in under Dial Hill. Her deck was covered with troops, and the waving of hats and the cheers of the townspeople, who were pouring along the further side of the harbour, made the truth plain to the solitary watcher among the whins. The *Venture* sent a shot to meet her that fell just in front of her bows, but although it was followed by a second, that cut her rigging, no great harm was done, and she answered with a broadside that echoed off the walls of the town till the strait was in a roar. It had no time to subside before James's gun on Inchbrayock began again.

Flemington could see that Hall's surrender could only be a matter of time; the new-comer would soon be landing her troops out of his range, and, having done so, would be certain to attack the *Venture* from the Ferryden side of the river. Half of Hall's men were on the island, which was in possession of the rebels, his vessel was damaged and in no condition to escape to sea, even had there been no hostile craft in his way and no Dial Hill to stand threatening between him and the ocean.

The time had come for Archie to think of his own plight and of his own prospects. He was adrift again, cut off even from the disorderly ship that had sheltered him last night, and from the unlucky sot who commanded her. His best plan would be to take the news of Hall's capture to Edinburgh, for it would be madness for him to think of going to Perth, whilst his identity as a Government agent would be published by Ferrier and Logie all over that part of the country. He was cast down as he sat with his hand to his aching head, and now that it had resulted in that fatal meeting, his own folly in going to the island seemed incredible.

His luck had been so good all his life, and after the many years that he had trusted her, the jade had turned on him! He had been too high-handed with her, that was the explanation of it! He had asked too much. He had been over-confident in her, over-confident in himself. Flemington was neither vain nor conceited, being too heartily interested in outside things to take very personal points of view; he merely went straight on, with the joy of life lighting his progress. But now he had put the crown on his foolhardiness. He had had so many good things – strength, health, wits, charm; the stage of his stirring life whereon to use them, and behind that stage the peaceful background of the home he loved, filled with the presence of the being he most admired and revered on earth.

But new lights had broken in on him of late. Troublous lights, playing from behind a curtain that hid unknown things. Suddenly he had turned and followed them, impelled by uncomprehended forces in himself, and it seemed that in consequence all around him had shifted, disintegrated, leaving him stranded. Once more as he watched, his anxious eyes on the scene below him, his heart full of his own perplexities, a last roar of shot filled the harbour, and then, on the *Venture*, he saw the flag hauled down.

He rose and looked about him, telling himself that he must get as far from the neighbourhood of Montrose as he could in the shortest possible time. Sixty miles of land stretched between him and Edinburgh, and the only thing for him to do was to start by way of the nearest seaport from which he could sail for Leith. He was a very different figure from the well-appointed young man who had ridden away from Ardguys only yesterday, for he was soaked to above the knees from wading in the Esk; blood had dripped on his coat from the cut on his forehead, and his hair at the back was clogged with sand. Excitement had kept him from thinking how cold he was, and he had not known that he was shivering; but he knew it as he stood in the teeth of the fresh wind. He laughed in spite of his plight; it was so odd to think of starting for Edinburgh from a whin-bush.

He turned southwards, determining to go forward till he should strike the road leading to the seaport of Aberbrothock; by sticking to the high ground he would soon come to it at the inland end of the Basin, and by it he might reach Aberbrothock by nightfall, and thence take sail in the morning. This was the best plan he could devise, though he did not care to contemplate the miles he would have to trudge. He knew that the broken coast took a great inward curve, and that by this means he would be avoiding its ins and outs, and he wished that he did not feel so giddy and so little able to face his difficulties. He remembered that the money he had on him made a respectable sum, and realized that the less worth robbing he looked, the more likely he would be to get to his journey's end in safety. He stepped out with an effort; southward he must go, and for some time to come Angus must know him no more.

FOURTEEN

In Search of Sensation

WHEN SKIRLING Wattie had delivered his letter to
Flemington on the foregoing day, he watched the young
man out of sight with disgust, and cursed him for a
high-handed jackanapes. He was not used to be treated
in such a fashion. There was that about Archie which
took his fancy, for the suggestion of stir and movement
that went everywhere with Flemington pleased him, and
roused his unfailing curiosity. The beggar's most pleasant
characteristic was his interest in everybody and everything; his worst, the unseasonable brutality with which
he gratified it.

A livelihood gained by his own powers of cajolery and
persistence had left him without a spark of respect for his
kind. He would have been a man of prowess had his limbs
been intact – and destiny, in robbing his body of activity,
had transferred that quality to his brains. His huge shoulders
and broad fists, the arrogant male glare of his roving eye,
might well hint at the wisdom of providence in keeping his
sphere of action to the narrow limits of a go-cart. Those who
look for likenesses between people and animals would be
reminded by him of a wild boar; and it was almost shocking
to anyone with a sense of fitness to hear the mellow and
touching voice, rich with the indescribable quiver of pathos
and tragedy, that proceeded from his bristly jaws when he
sang. The world that it conjured up before imaginative
listeners was a world of twilight; of stars that drew a trail
of tear-dimmed lustre about the ancient haunted places
of the country; stars that had shone on battlefields and
on the partings of lovers; that had looked on the raids
of the border, and had stood over the dark border-towers
among the peat. It was a strange truth that, in the voice of

this coarse and humble vagabond, lay the whole distinctive spirit of the national poetry of Scotland.

In the last few months his employment had added new zest to his life, for it was not only the pay he received for his occasional carrying of letters that was welcome to him; his bold and guileful soul delighted in the occupation for its own sake. He was something of a student of human nature, as all those who live by their wits must be of necessity; and the small services he was called upon to give brought him into contact with new varieties of men. Archie was new to him, and, in the beggar's opinion, immeasurably more amusing than anyone he had seen yet. In modern parlance he would be called 'a sportsman', this low-bred old ruffian who had lost his legs, and who was left to the mercy of his own ingenuity and to the efforts of the five dumb animals which supplemented his loss. He had – all honour to him – kept his love of life and its chances through his misfortune; and though he did not know it himself, it was his recognition of the same spirit in Flemington that made him appreciate the young man.

His services to the state had not been important up to the present time. A few letters carried, a little information collected, had been the extent of his usefulness. But, though he was not in their regular employ, the authorities were keeping a favourable eye on him, for he had so far proved himself capable, close-mouthed, and a very miracle of local knowledge.

He sat in his cart looking resentfully after Flemington between the stems of the alders and the lattice of their golden-brown leaves, and, though the one word tossed over the rider's shoulders did not tell him much, he determined he would not lose sight of Archie if he could help it. 'Brechin' might mean anything from a night's lodging to a lengthened stay, but he would follow him as far as he dared and set about discovering his movements. Skirling Wattie had friends in Brechin, as he had in most places round about, and certain bolt-holes of his own wherein he could always find shelter for himself and his dogs; but he did not mean to trust himself nearer than these refuges to Lord Balnillo, at any rate, not for a few days. Chance had relieved him of the letter for which he was responsible sooner than he expected, and at present he was a free man. He roused his team, tucked his pipes into their corner of the cart, and, guiding himself carefully between the trees, issued from the thicket like some ribald vision of goblinry escaped from the world of folk-lore.

He turned towards Brechin, and set off for the town at a brisk trot, the yellow dog straining at his harness, and his comrades taking their pace from him. Every inch of the road was known to Wattie, every tree and tuft, every rut and hole; and as there were plenty of these last, he bumped and swung along in a way that would have dislocated the bones of a lighter person. The violent roughness of his progress was what served him for exercise and kept him in health. There were not many houses near the highway, but the children playing round the doors of the few he passed hailed him with shouts, and he answered them, as he answered everyone, with his familiar wag of the head.

When he entered Brechin and rolled past the high, circular shaft of its round tower, the world made way for him with a grin, and when it was not agile enough to please him, he heralded himself with a shrill note from the chanter, which he had unscrewed from his pipes. Business was business with him. He meant to lie in the town to-night, but he was anxious to get on to Flemington's tracks before the scent was cold.

He drove to the Swan inn and entered the yard, and there he had the satisfaction of seeing Archie's horse being rubbed down with a wisp of straw. Its rider, he made out, had left the inn on foot half an hour earlier, so, with this meagre clue, he sought the streets and the company of the idlers haunting their thievish corners, to whom the passing stranger and what might be made out of him were the best interests of the day. By the time the light was failing he had traced Flemington down to the river, where he had been last seen crossing the bridge. The beggar was a good deal surprised; he could not imagine what was carrying Archie away from the place.

In the dusk he descended the steep streets running down to the Esk, and, slackening his pace, took out a short, stout pair of crutches that he kept beside him, using them as brakes on either side of the cart. People who saw Wattie for the first time would stand, spell-bound, to watch the incredible spectacle of his passage through a town, but, to the inhabitants of Brechin, he was too familiar a sight for anything but the natural widening of the mouth that his advent would produce from pure force of habit.

The lights lit here and there were beginning to repeat themselves in the water, and men were returning to their houses after the day's work as he stopped his cart and sent out that surest of all attractions, the first notes of 'The Tod', into the gathering mists of the riverside. By ones and twos, the details of a sympathetic audience drew together round him as his voice rose over the sliding rush of the Esk. Idlers on the bridge leaned over the grey arches as the sound came to them above the tongue of the little rapid that babbled as it lost itself in the shadow of the woods downstream.

Then the pipes took up their tune. Jests and roars of laughter oiled the springs of generosity, and the good prospects of supper and a bed began to smile upon the beggar. When darkness set in, he turned his wheels towards a shed that a publican had put at his disposal for the night, and he and his dogs laid themselves down to rest in its comfortable straw. The yellow cur, relieved from his harness, stole closer and closer to his master and lay with his jowl against the pipes. Presently Wattie's dirty hand went out and sought the coarse head of his servant.

'Doag,' he was muttering, as he went to sleep.

Perhaps in all the grim, grey little Scottish town, no living creature closed its eyes more contentedly than the poor cur whose head was pillowed in paradise because of the touch that was on it.

Morning found man and dogs out betimes and migrating to the heart of the town. Wattie was one who liked to get an early draught from the fountain-head of news, to be beforehand, so to speak, with his day. The Swan inn was his goal, and he had not got up the hill towards it when his practised eye, wise in other men's movements, saw that the world was hurrying along, drawn by some magnet stronger

than its legitimate work. The women were running out of
their houses too. As he toiled up the steep incline, a figure
burst from the mouth of a wynd and came flying down
the middle of the narrow way.

'Hey! what ails ye, man? What's 'ahind ye?' he cried,
stopping his cart and spreading out his arms as though to
embrace the approaching man.

The other paused. He was a pale, foolish-looking youth,
whose progress seemed as little responsible as that of a
discharged missile.

'There's fechtin'!' he yelled, apparently addressing the
air in general.

'Fechtin'?'

'Ay, there's fechtin' at Montrose this hour syne! Div ye
no hear them, ye deef muckle swine?' continued the youth,
rendered abusive by excitement.

The two stared in each other's faces as those do who
listen. Dull and distant, a muffled boom drove in from
the coast. A second throb followed it.

The youth dropped his raised hands and fled on.

Wattie turned his dogs, and set off down the hill without
more delay. Here was the reason that Archie had left the
town! It was in expectation of this present disturbance on
the coast that he had slipped out of Brechin by the less
frequented road round the Basin.

He scurried down the hill, scattering the children playing
in the kennel with loud imprecations and threats. He sped
over the bridge, and was soon climbing the rise on the
farther side of the Esk. If there was fighting going on,
he would make shift to see it, and Montrose would be
visible from most of his road. Soon he would get a view of
the distant harbour, and would see the smoke of the guns
whose throats continued to trouble the air. Also, he would
get forward unmolested, for there would be the width of
the Basin between himself and Lord Balnillo.

He breathed his team when he reached the top of the
hill; for he was a scientific driver, and he had some way to
go. He cast a glance down at the place he had left, rejoicing
that no one had followed him out of it. When he was on
his own errands he did not like company, preferring, like

most independent characters, to develop his intentions in the perfect freedom of silence.

When he drew near enough to distinguish the *Venture*, a dark spot under the lee of Ferryden, he saw the white puffs of smoke bursting from her, and the answering clouds rising from the island. There had been no time to hear the rumours of the morning before he met the pale young man, or he would have learned that a body of Prince Charles's men under Ferrier had left Brechin last night whilst he lay sound asleep in the straw among his dogs. He could not imagine where the assailants had come from who were pounding at the ship from Inchbrayock.

The fields sloped away from him to the water, leaving an uninterrupted view. He pressed on to the cross-roads at which he must turn along the Basin's shore. From there on, the conformation of the land, and the frequent clumps of trees, would shut out both town and harbour from his sight until he came parallel with the island.

He halted at the turning for a last look at the town. The firing had ceased, which reconciled him a little to the eclipse of the distant spectacle; then he drove on again, unconscious of the sight he was to miss. For, unsuspected by him, as by the crowd thronging the quays of Montrose, the French frigate was creeping up the coast, and she made her appearance in the river-mouth just as Wattie began the tamer stage of his journey.

The yellow cur and his companions toiled along at their steady trot, their red tongues hanging. The broadside from the French ship rang inland, and the beggar groaned, urging them with curses and chosen abuse. His intimate knowledge of the neighbourhood led him to steer for the identical spot on which Flemington, crouched in his whin-bush, had looked down on the affray, and he hoped devoutly that he might reach that point of vantage while there was still something to be seen from it. Silence had settled on the strait once more.

Not far in front a man was coming into sight, the first creature Wattie had seen since leaving Brechin, whose face was turned from the coast. He seemed a person of irresolute mind, as well as of vacillating feet, for every few yards he would stop, hesitating, before resuming his way. The beggar cursed him heartily for a drunkard, for, though he had a lively sympathy with backsliders of that kind, he knew that accurate information was the last thing to be expected from them. Before the wayfarers had halved the distance between them the man stopped, and sitting down by the tumbledown stone dyke at the roadside, dropped his head in his hands. As the cart passed him a few minutes later, he raised a ghastly face, and Skirling Wattie pulled up astounded, with a loud and profane exclamation, as he recognized Flemington.

Though Archie had been glad to escape from the beggar yesterday, he was now thankful to see anyone who might pass for a friend. He tried to smile, but his eyes closed again, and he put out his hand towards the dyke.

'I'm so devilish giddy,' he said.

Wattie looked at the cut on his head and the stains of blood on his coat.

'Ye've gotten a rare dunt,' he observed.

Archie, who seemed to himself to be slipping off the rounded edge of the world, made no reply.

The other sat eyeing him with perplexity and some impatience. He did not know what he wanted most – to get to Montrose, or to get news out of Flemington. The dogs lay down in the mud. Flemington kept his hand to his eyes for a minute, and then lifted his head again.

'The ship has surrendered,' he said, speaking with difficulty; 'I have been on the high ground watching. She struck her flag. A French frigate—'

He stopped again. The road on which he sat was whirling down into illimitable space.

The other took in his plight. His coat, torn in his struggle with Logie, was full of whin-prickles, and the wet mud was caked on his legs. His soft, silky hair was flattened on his forehead.

'Ye've been fechtin' yersel', ma lad,' said Wattie. 'Whaur hae ye been?'

'There's rebel force on Inchbrayock,' said Archie, with another effort; 'I have been on the island. Yes, I've been fighting. A man recognized me – a man I saw at – on the road by Balnillo. They will be hunting me soon, and I have papers on me they must not find, and money – all the money I have. God knows how I am to get away! I must get to Aberbrothock.'

'What was ye sayin' aboot the French?'

In broken sentences, and between his fits of giddiness, Archie explained the situation in the harbour, and the beggar listened, his bristly brows knit, his bonnet thrust back on his bald head; and his own best course of action grew clear to him. Montrose would soon be full of rebel soldiers, and though these might be generous audiences when merry with wine and loose upon the streets, their presence would make him no safer from Lord Balnillo. Wattie knew that the judge's loyalty was beginning to be suspected, and that he might well have friends among the Prince's officers, whose arrival might attract him to the town. And to serve Archie would be a good recommendation for himself with his employers, to say nothing of any private gratitude that the young man might feel.

'Bide you whaur ye are!' he exclaimed, rousing his dogs. 'Lad, a'll hae to ca' ye oot o' this, an' dod! we'll need a' our time!'

Not far from them a spring was trickling from the fields, dropping in a spurt through the damp mosses between the unpointed stones of the dyke. The obedient dogs drew their master close to it, and he filled a battered pannikin that he took from among his small collection of necessities in the bottom of the cart. He returned with the water, and when Archie had bathed his head in its icy coldness, he drew a whisky-bottle from its snug lair under the bagpipes, and forced him to drink. It was half full, for the friendly publican had replenished his store before they parted on the foregoing night. As the liquid warmed his stomach, Archie raised his head slowly.

'I believe I can walk now,' he said at last.

'Ye'll need to try,' observed Wattie dryly. 'Ye'll no can ride wi' me. Come awa', Maister Flemington. Will a gi' ye a skelloch o' the pipes to help ye alang?'

'In God's name, no!' cried Archie, whose head was splitting.

He struggled on to his feet. The whisky was beginning to overcome the giddiness, and he knew that every minute spent on the highroad was a risk.

The beggar was determined to go to Aberbrothock with Archie; he did not consider him in a fit state to be left alone, and he counselled him to leave the road at once, and to cut diagonally across the high ground, whilst he himself, debarred by his wheels from going across country, drove back to the cross roads, and took the one to the coast. By doing this the pair would meet, Flemington having taken one side of the triangle, while Wattie had traversed the other two. They were to await each other at a spot indicated by the latter, where a bit of moor encroached on the way.

As Wattie turned again to retrace his road, he watched his friend toiling painfully up the slanting ground among the uneven tussocks of grass with some anxiety. Archie laboured along, pausing now and again to rest, but he managed to gain the summit of the ridge. Wattie saw his figure shorten from the feet up as he crossed the sky-line, till his head and shoulders dropped out of sight like the topsails of a ship over a clear horizon; he was disappointed at having missed the sight of so much good fighting. Archie's account had been rather incoherent, but he gathered that the rebels were in possession of the harbour, and that a French ship had come in in the middle of the affray full of rebel troops. He shouted the information to the few people he met.

He turned southward at the cross roads. Behind him lay the panorama of the Basin and the spread of the rolling country; Brechin, the Esk, the woods of Monrummon Moor, stretching out to Forfar, and, northward, the Grampians, lying with their long shoulders in the autumn light. His beat for begging was down there across the water and round about the country between town and town; but though his activities were in that direction, he knew Aberbrothock and the coast well, for he had been born in a fishing-village in one of its creeks, and had spent his early years at sea. He would be able to put Archie in the way of a passage to Leith without much trouble and without unnecessary explanations; Archie had money on him, and could be trusted to pay his way.

He was the first to reach the trysting-place, and he drew up, glad to give his team a rest; at last he saw Archie coming along with the slow, careful gait of a man who is obliged to consider each step of his way separately in order to get on at all.

'Sit ye doon,' he exclaimed, as they met.

'If once I sit down I am lost,' said Archie. 'Come on.'

He started along the road with the same dogged step, the beggar keeping alongside. They had gone about half a mile when Flemington clutched at a wayside bush and then slid to the ground in a heap.

Wattie pulled up, dismayed, and scanned their surroundings. To let him lie there by the road was out of the question. He could not tell how much his head had been injured, but he knew enough to be sure that exposure and cold might bring a serious illness on a man in his state; he did not understand that the whisky he had given Archie was the worst possible thing for him. To the beggar, it was the sovereign remedy for all trouble of mind or body.

He cursed his own circumscribed energies; there was no one in sight. The nearest habitation was a little farmhouse on the skirts of the moor with one tiny window in its gable-end making a dark spot, high under the roof.

Wattie turned his wheels reluctantly towards it. Unwilling though he was to draw attention to his companion, there was no choice.

FIFTEEN

Wattie has Theories

THOUGH SKIRLING Wattie seldom occupied the same bed on many consecutive nights, his various resting-places had so great a family likeness that he could not always remember where he was when he chanced to wake in the small hours. Sheds, barns, stables harboured him in the cold months when luck was good; loanings, old quarries, whin-patches, the alder clump beyond Brechin, or the wall-side at Magdalen Chapel, in the summer.

To-night he lay in the barn abutting on the tiny farmhouse at which he had sought shelter for Archie. He had met with a half-hearted reception from the woman who came to the door. Her man was away, she told him, and she was unwilling to admit strangers in his absence. She had never seen Wattie before, and it was plain that she did not like his looks. He induced her at last, with the greatest difficulty, to give shelter in her barn to the comrade whom he described as lying in extremity at the roadside. Finally, she despatched her son, a youth of fifteen, to accompany the beggar, and to help to bring the sufferer back.

Cold water revived Archie again, and he reached the barn with the assistance of the lad, who, better disposed than his mother, cut a bundle of dry heather, which he spread in a corner for his comfort. The woman looked with silent surprise at her undesired guest; she had thought to see a fellow-traveller of different condition in company with the masterful old blackguard in the cart. Her glances and her expressive silence made Wattie uneasy, but there was no help for their plight whilst Flemington could scarcely stand.

The beggar had spent the rest of that day in the barn. He was not suffered to enter the farm, nor was he offered any food; but he had enough store by him from what he had collected in Brechin for his own needs and those of his team. Archie's only requirement was the bowl of water that his companion had obtained from the boy. He lay alternately dozing and tossing on his pile of heather. His body was chilled, for his high boots had been full of the Esk water, and Wattie had hesitated to draw them off, lest he should be unable to get them on again after their soaking.

Night fell on the barn at last. Wattie slept sound, with the yellow cur's muzzle against his shoulder; but he awoke towards midnight, for Archie's feverish voice was coming from the corner in which he lay. He inclined his ear, attracted by the recurrent name of Logie which ran through the disconnected babblings, rising again and again like some half-drowned object carried along a swift stream. The darkness made every word seem more distinct.

'Listen to me!' cried Flemington. 'Logie! Logie! you do not understand . . . it is safe . . . it is burnt! Nobody shall know it from me . . . I cannot take your money, Logie . . . I will tell you everything, but you will not understand . . .'

The beggar was holding his breath.

'I did not guess it was Inchbrayock . . . I thought it would not be Inchbrayock! Logie, I will say nothing . . . but I will tell you all. For God's sake, Logie, . . . I swear it is true! . . . Listen . . .'

Skirling Wattie could hear him struggling as though he were fighting for his life.

'Not to Ardguys . . . I cannot go back to Ardguys! I shall never tell . . . never, never tell . . . but I shall know where you are! They shall never know. *Ah!*' cried Archie, raising his voice like a man in distress calling for help, 'it is you, Logie! . . . My God, let me go!'

The beggar dragged himself nearer. The fragment of moon did no more than turn the chinks and cracks of the barn to a dull grey, and he could hardly see the outline of his companion.

The nightmares that were tormenting Archie pointed to something that must have happened before he came by his hurt, and the injury and the chill had produced these light-headed wanderings; there were troubles boiling in his mind that he had kept behind his teeth so long as his tongue was under control. Wattie wondered what was all this talk of Lord Balnillo's brother. It seemed as if there were some secret between this man, suspected, as he well knew, of being an active rebel, and Flemington. Had it been light, Wattie would have tried to get at the papers that Archie had spoken of as being on him when they met, for these might give him some clue to the mystery. He sat in the dark leaning against the wall of the barn, his arms tightly folded across his great chest, his lips pursed, his gaze bent on the restless figure that he could just distinguish.

All at once Archie sat up.

'Where are you?' he asked in a high, strained voice.

'A'm here,' replied the beggar.

'Is it you, Logie?' exclaimed Flemington.

'It's mysel'.'

Wattie smoothed the roughness out of his accent as best he could. The other seemed to be hovering on the brink of consciousness. He sank back.

'It is not Logie,' he said; 'but you can tell him—'

Wattie leaned forward and laid his broad palm firmly and very gently on his shoulder.

'What'll a' tell him?' said he.

Flemington turned towards him and groped about with his hot hand.

'Tell him from me that he can trust me,' he said in a hoarse, earnest whisper.

The beggar's touch seemed to quiet him. He lay still, murmuring indistinctly between snatches of silence. Once again he sat up, groping about.

'You will not forget?' he said.

'Na, na,' replied Wattie.

He pushed him gently back, patting him now and again as a nurse might pat a restless child, and Archie grew calmer. The hand quieted him. Rough, dirty, guileful, profane as he was, without scruple or conscience or anything but the desire to do the best for himself, Skirling Wattie had got, lodged in body or spirit, or in whatsoever part of man the uncomprehended force dwells, that personal magnetism which is independent alike of grace and of virtue, which can exist in a soil that is barren of either. It may have been that which the yellow cur, with the clear vision belonging to some animals, recognized and adored; seeing not only the coarse and jovial reprobate who was his master, but the shadow of the mysterious power that had touched him.

The dog, awakened by Archie's cry, found that the beggar had moved, and drew closer to his side. Flemington dozed off again, and Wattie sat thinking; he longed to stir him up, that he might have the chance of hearing more of his rambling talk. But he refrained, not from humane feeling, but from the fear that the talker, if he were tampered with, might be too ill to be moved on the morrow. Sleep was his best chance, and Wattie had made up his mind that if it were possible to move him, he would prevail on the boy to get a beast from the nearest place that boasted anything which could carry him to Aberbrothock. He knew that Flemington could pay for it, and he would direct him to a small inn in that place whose landlord, besides being a retired smuggler, was a distant kinsman of his own. The matter of a passage to Leith could be arranged through the same source for a consideration. Archie should take his chance by himself.

He realized with some bitterness the bright opportunities that can be lost upon a being who has no legs to speak of; for he could easily have relieved him of what money he carried had he been an able-bodied man. It was not that he lacked the force for such deeds, but that honesty was wantonly thrust upon him because his comings and goings were so conspicuous. Notoriety takes heavy toll; and he had about the same chance as the king of being conveniently mislaid. He would have given a good deal for a sight of the papers that Archie carried, and though the darkness interfered with him now, he promised himself that he would see them if the morning light should find him still delirious. He could not make out how ill he was; and in spite of his curiosity, he was not prepared to befriend him with the chance of his growing worse. To have him dying upon his hands would be a burden too great to endure, even should it lead to no awkward questionings.

He would get rid of him to-morrow, whether his curiosity were satisfied or not: he had heard enough to make him suspect very strongly that Flemington was in the pay of the rebels as well as in that of the King. It was a situation that he, personally, could very well understand. But the night turned, and Archie grew more peaceful as the hours went by. He had one or two bouts of talking, but they were incoherent and fitful, and his mind appeared now to be straying among different phantoms. There was no more about Logie, and Wattie could only make out the word 'Ardguys', which he knew as the name of a place beyond Forfar; and as he had discovered in Brechin that Flemington lived somewhere in those parts, he guessed that his thoughts were roving about his home. His breathing grew less laboured, and the watcher could hear at last that he slept. The moon dropped, and with her going the crevices lost their greyness and the barn grew black. The beggar, who was a healthy sleeper, laid himself down again, and in the middle of his cogitations passed into oblivion.

When he awoke the place was light, and Archie was looking at him with intelligent eyes; they were hollow, and there were dark shadows below them, but they were the eyes of a man in full possession of his wits.

'We must get out of this place,' he said. 'I have been standing up, but my knees seem so heavy I can hardly walk. My bones ache, Wattie; I believe there is fever in me, but I must get on. Damn it, man, we are a sorry pair to be cast on the world like this! I fear I took terrible liberties with your whisky yesterday.'

It was a still, misty morning when the beggar, having harnessed his dogs, went out to look for the boy. When he was gone, Flemington fumbled with his shaking fingers for the different packets that he carried. All were there safely – his letters, his money. He trusted nobody, and he did not like having to trust the beggar.

His feverish head and the ague in his bones told him that he could scarcely hope to get to Aberbrothock on foot. His boots were still wet, and a bruise on his hip that he had got in falling yesterday had begun to make itself felt. He propped himself against the wall and reached out for the water beside him.

Wattie had been some time away when the barn door opened and the farm-woman appeared on the threshold, considering him with suspicious disfavour.

He dragged himself to his feet and bowed as though he were standing upon an Aubusson carpet instead of upon a pallet of withered heather. The action seemed to confirm her distrust.

'Madam,' said he, 'I have to thank you for a night's shelter and for this excellent refreshment. You are too good. I drink to you.'

He raised the broken delf bowl with the drain of water that remained in it. Being conscious of inhospitality, she was not sure how much irony lay in his words, and his face told her nothing.

'It's the last ye'll get here,' said she.

The more she looked at Flemington the more she was impressed by his undesirability as a guest. She was one of those to whom anything uncommon seemed a menace.

'Madam, I notice that you dislike me – why?'

'Wha are ye?' she inquired after a pause, during which he faced her, smiling, his eyebrows raised.

'We are two noblemen, travelling for pleasure,' said he.

She crossed her arms, snorting.

'Heuch!' she exclaimed contemptuously. 'A' wish ma gudeman was hame. He'd sort the pair o' ye!'

'If you think we have any design on your virtue,' he continued, 'I beg you to dismiss the idea. I assure you, you are safe with us. We are persons of the greatest delicacy, and my friend is a musician of the first rank. I myself am what you see – your humble servant and admirer.'

'Ye're a leear and a Frenchman!' cried she.

Her eyes blazed. A little more provocation, and she might have attacked him. At this moment Wattie's cart drove into the yard behind her, axle deep in the sea of mud and manure that filled the place. She turned upon the newcomer. She could not deal with Archie, but the beggar was a foe she could understand, and she advanced, a whirl of abuse, upon him. The yellow dog's growling rose, battling with her strident tones, and Archie, seeing the mischief his tongue had wrought, limped out, fearful of what might happen.

'Stand awa' frae the doag, wumman! He'll hae the legs o' ye roogit aff yer henches gin he get's a haud o' ye!' roared Wattie, as the yellow body leaped and bounded in the traces.

Amid a hurricane of snarling and shouts he contrived, by plying his stick, to turn the animals and to get them out of the yard.

Archie followed him, but before he did so he paused to turn to his enemy, who had taken shelter in the doorway of the barn. He could not take off his hat to her because he had no hat to take off, having lost it on Inchbrayock Island, but he blew a kiss from the points of his fingers with an air that almost made her choke. Wattie, looking back over his shoulder, called angrily to him. He could not understand what he had done to the woman to move her to such a tempest of wrath, but he told himself that, in undertaking to escort Archie, he had made a leap in the dark. He would direct him to his cousin's house of entertainment in Aberbrothock, and return to his own haunts without delay.

At the nearest point of road the boy was standing by a sorry-looking nag that he held by the ear.

A few minutes later they had parted, and the boy, made happy by the coin he had been given, was returning to the farm, while the beggar, who had also reaped some profit in the last twenty-four hours, watched his late companion disappearing down the road. When he was out of sight he turned his own wheels in the direction of Brechin, and set off at a sober pace for that friendly town. He was singing to himself as he went, first because he owned the price of another bottle of whisky; secondly, because he was delighted to be rid of Flemington; and thirdly, because an inspiring idea had come to him.

His dogs, by the time they drew him into Brechin, would have done two heavy days' work, and would deserve the comparative holiday he meant to give them. He would

spend to-morrow in the town with his pipes in the company
of that congenial circle always ready to spring from the
gutter on his appearance. Then, after a good night's rest,
and when he should have collected a trifle, he would go
on to Forfar and learn for certain whether Archie lived at
Ardguys and who might be found there in his absence.

His idea was to arrive at the house with the last tidings
of the young man; to give an account of the attack on the
Venture, its surrender, Flemington's injury, and his own
part in befriending him. It took some time, in those days
of slow communication, for public news to travel so much
as across a county, but even should the tale of the ship have
reached Ardguys, the news of Archie could scarcely have
preceded him. He hoped to find someone – for preference
an anxious mother, who would be sensible of how much he
had done for her son. There would be fresh profit there.

And not only profit. There was something else for which
the beggar hoped, though profit was his main object.
He pictured some tender, emotional lady from whose
unsuspicious heart he might draw scraps of information
that would fit into his own theories. He would try the
effect of Logie's name, and there would be no harm
in taking a general survey of Flemington's surroundings
and picking up any small facts about him that he could
collect.

His own belief in Archie's double dealing grew stronger
as he jogged along; no doubt that shrewd and unaccount-
able young man was driving a stiff trade. There was little
question in his mind that the contents of the letter he
had put into his hands by the alder clump had been
sold to Captain James Logie, and that its immediate
result had been the taking of the ship. He had learned
from Archie's ravings that there had been a question
of money between himself and Logie. The part that
he could make nothing of was the suggestion, conveyed
by Archie in the night, that he and the judge's brother
had been fighting. 'Let me go, Logie!' he had cried
out in the darkness, and the blow on his forehead,
which was bleeding when he found him, proved recent
violence.

But though he could not explain these puzzles, nor make them tally with his belief, his theory remained. Flemington was in league with Logie. For the present he determined to keep his suspicions to himself.

SIXTEEN

The Two Ends of the Line

THREE DAYS afterwards Wattie sat at the gates of Ardguys and looked between the pale yellow ashtrees at the house. There was nobody about at the moment to forbid his entrance, and he drove quietly in at a foot's pace and approached the door. The sun shone with the clear lightness of autumn, and the leaves, which had almost finished the fitful process of falling, lay gathered in heaps by the gate, for Madam Flemington liked order. On the steep pitch of the ancient slate roof a few pigeons, white and grey, sat in pairs or walked about with spasmodic dignity. The whole made a picture, high in tone, like a water-colour, and the clean etched lines of the stripped branches gave it a sharp delicacy and threw up the tall, light walls. All these things were lost upon the beggar.

He had informed himself in Forfar. He knew that the place was owned and lived in by a lady of the name of Flemington, who was the grandmother of the young man from whom he had lately parted. He had learned nothing of her character and politics because of the seclusion in which she lived, and he stared about him on every side and scanned the house for any small sign that might give him a clue to the tastes or occupations of its inhabitant. Whilst he was so engaged the front-door opened and the sound sent all the pigeons whirling from the roof into the air in flashes of grey-blue and white. Madam Flemington stood on the top step.

The beggar's hand went instinctively to his bonnet. He was a little taken aback – why, he did not know – and he instantly abandoned his plan of an emotional description of Archie's plight. She stood quite still looking down at him.

Her luxuriant silver hair was covered by a three-cornered piece of black lace that was tied in a knot under her chin, and she wore the 'calash,' or hood, with which the ladies of those days protected their headdresses when they went out. A short furred cloak was round her.

She considered Wattie with astonishment. Then she beckoned to him to approach.

'Who and what are you?' she asked, laying her hand on the railing that encircled the landing of the steps.

That question was so seldom put to him that it struck him unawares, like a stone from behind a hedge. He hesitated.

'A've got news for yer leddyship,' he began.

'I asked your name,' said Madam Flemington.

'Wattie Caird,' replied he. 'Skirling Wattie, they ca' me.'

The countryside and its inhabitants did not appeal to Christian, but this amazing intruder was like no one she had ever seen before. She guessed that he was a beggar, and she brushed aside his announcement of news as merely a method of attracting attention.

'You are one of the few persons in these parts who can afford to keep a coach,' she remarked.

A broad smile overspread his ribald countenance, like the sun irradiating a public-house.

'Dod, ma leddy, a'd think shame to visit ye on fut,' said he, with a wag of his head.

'You have better reasons than that,' she replied rather grimly.

'Aye, aye, they're baith awa',' said he, looking at the place where his legs should have been. 'A'm an ill sicht for the soutars!'

She threw back her head and laughed a little.

She had seen no one for months, with the exception of Archie, who was so quick in mind and speech, and the humour of this vagabond on wheels took her fancy. There was no whining servility about him, in spite of his obvious profession.

The horrified face of a maidservant appeared for one moment at a window, then vanished, struck back by the

unblessed sight of her mistress, that paralysing, unap-
proachable power, jesting, apparently, with Skirling Wattie,
the lowest of the low. The girl was a native of Forfar, the
westernmost point of the beggar's travels, and she had
often seen him in the streets.

'You face life boldly,' said Madam Flemington.

'An' what for no? Fegs, greetin' fills naebody's kyte.'[1]

She laughed again.

'You shall fill yours handsomely,' said she; 'go to the
other door and I will send orders to the women to attend
to you.'

'Aye, will I,' he exclaimed, 'but it wasna' just for a piece
that a' cam' a' the way frae the muir o' Rossie.'

'From where?' said she.

'The muir o' Rossie,' repeated he. 'Ma leddy, it was
awa' yonder at the tail o' the muir that a' tell't Maister
Flemington the road to Aberbrothock.'

'Mr. Flemington?'

'Aye, yon lad Flemington – an' a deevil o' a lad he is to
tak' the road wi'! Ma leddy, there's been a pucklie fechtin'
aboot Montrose, an' the Prince's men hae gotten a haud
o' King George's ship that's in by Ferryden. As a' gaed
doon to the toon, a' kaipit[2] wi' Flemington i' the road.
He'd gotten a clour on's heed. He was fechtin' doon aboot
Inchbrayock, he tell't me.'

'Fighting? With whom?' asked Madam Flemington,
fixing her tiger's eyes on him.

The beggar had watched her face narrowly while he spoke
for the slightest flicker of expression that might indicate the
way her feelings were turning.

'He was fechtin' wi' Captain Logie,' he continued boldly,
'a fell man yon – ye'll ken him, yer leddyship?'

'By name,' said Christian.

'A'm thinkin' it was frae him that he got the clour on's
heed. A' gie'd him ma guid whisky bottle, an' a' got water
to him frae a well. A' ca'd him awa' frae the roadside – he
didna ken wha would be aifter him ye see – an' a' gar'd

1. Stomach.
2. Met.

a clatterin' auld wife at the muir side gie's a shelter yon nicht. A' didna' leave the callant, ma' leddy, till a' got a shelt to him. He's to Edinburgh. A' tell't him wha'd get him a passage to Leith – a'm an Aberbrothock man, mysel', ye ken.'

'And did he send you to me?'

'Aye, did he,' said he, lying boldly.

There was no sign of emotion, none even of surprise, on her face. Her heart had beaten hard as the beggar talked, and the weight of wrath and pain that she had carried since she had parted with Archie began to lighten. He had listened to her – he had not gone against her. How deep her words had fallen into his heart she could not tell, but deep enough to bring him to grips with the man who had made the rift between them.

'Are you sure of what you say?' she asked quickly; 'did you see them fight?'

'Na, na, but 'twas the lad himsel' that tell't me. He was on the ship.'

'He was on the ship?'

'Aye, was he. And he gae'd oot wi' the sodgers to deave they rebels frae Inchbrayock. They got the ship, ma leddy, but they didna get him. He escapit.'

'Did you say he was much hurt?' said Madam Flemington.

'Hoots! ye needna' fash yersel', ma leddy! A' was feared for him i' the nicht, but there wasna' muckle wrang wi' him when he gae'd awa', or, dod, a' wouldna' hae left him!'

He had no mind to spoil his presentment of himself as Good Samaritan.

So far he had learnt nothing. He had spoken of the Prince's men as rebels without a sign of displeasure showing on Madam Flemington's face. Archie might be playing a double game and she might be doing the same, but there was nothing to suggest it. She was magnificently impersonal. She had not even shown the natural concern that he expected with regard to her own flesh and blood.

'Go now,' said she, waving her hand towards the back part of the house; 'you shall feed well, you and your dogs; and when you have finished you can come to these steps again, and I will give you some money. You have done well by me.'

She re-entered the house and he drove away to the kitchen-door, dismissed.

If Wattie hoped to discover anything more there about the lady and her household, he was disappointed. The servants raised their chins in refined disapproval of the vagrant upon whom their mistress had seen fit to waste words under the very front windows of Ardguys. They resolved that he should find the back-door, socially, a different place, and only the awe in which they stood of Christian compelled them to obey her to the letter. A crust or two would have interpreted her wishes, had they dared to please themselves. But Madam Flemington knew every resource of her larder and kitchen, for French housekeeping and the frugality of her exiled years had taught her thrift. She would measure precisely what had been given to her egregious guest, down to the bones laid, by her order, before his dogs.

The beggar ate in silence, amid the brisk cracking made by five pairs of busy jaws; the maids were in the stronghold of the kitchen, far from the ungenteel sight of his coarse enjoyment. When he had satisfied himself, he put the fragments into his leathern bag and went round once more to the front of the house.

A window was open on the ground-floor, and Madam Flemington's large white hand came over the sill holding a couple of crown pieces. She was sitting on the window-seat within. Her cloak and the calash had disappeared, and Wattie could see the fine poise of her head. She dropped the coin into the cart as he drove below.

As he looked up he thought that if she had been imposing in her outdoor garments she was a hundredfold more so without them. He was at his ease with her, but he wondered at it, though he was accustomed to being at his ease with everybody. A certain vanity rose in him, coarse remnant of humanity as he was, before this magnificent woman, and when he had received the silver, he turned about, facing her, and began to sing.

He was used to the plebeian admiration of his own public, but a touch of it from her would have a different flavour. He

was vain of his singing, and that vanity was the one piece
of romance belonging to him; it hung over his muddy
soul as a weaving of honeysuckle may hang over a dank
pond. Had he understood Madam Flemington perfectly,
he might have sung 'The Tod', but as he only understood
her superficially, he sang 'Logie Kirk'. He did not know
how nearly the extremities of the social scale can draw
together in the primitive humours of humanity. It is the
ends of a line that can best be bent to meet, not one end
and the middle.

Yet, as 'Logie Kirk' rang out among the spectral ash-trees,
she sat still, astonished, her head erect, like some royal
animal listening; it moved her, though its sentiment had
naught to do with her mood at present, nor with her cast
of mind at any time. But love and loss are things that lay
their shadows everywhere, and Madam Flemington had
lost much; moreover, she had been a woman framed for
love, and she had not wasted her gifts.

As his voice ceased, she rose and threw the window up
higher.

'Go on,' she said.

He paused, taking breath, for a couple of minutes. He
knew songs to suit all political creeds, but this time he would
try one of the Jacobite lays that were floating round the
country; if it should provoke some illuminating comment
from her, he would have learned something more about her,
and incidentally about Archie, though it struck him that he
was not so sure of the unanimity of interest between the
grandmother and grandson which he had taken for granted
before seeing Madam Flemington.

His cunning eyes were rooted on her as he sang again.

> My love stood at the loanin' side
>   And held me by the hand,
> The bonniest lad that e'er did bide
>   In a' this waefu' land;
> There's but ae bonnier to be seen
>   Frae Pentland to the sea,
> And for his sake but yestereen
>   I sent my love frae me.

I gie'd my love the white, white rose
  That's at my feyther's wa',
It is the bonniest flower that grows
  Where ilka flower is braw.
There's but ae brawer that I ken
  Frae Perth unto the main,
And that's the flower o' Scotland's men
  That's fechtin' for his ain.

If I had kept whate'er was mine,
  As I had gie'd my best,
My hairt were licht by day, and syne
  The nicht wad bring me rest;
There is nae heavier hairt to find
  Frae Forfar toon to Ayr,
As aye I sit me doon to mind
  On him I see nae mair.

Lad, gin ye fa' by Chairlie's side,
  To rid this land o' shame,
There will na be a prouder bride
  Than her ye left at hame;
But I will see ye whaur ye sleep
  Frae lowlands to the peat,
And ilka nicht at mirk I'll creep
  To lay me at yer feet.

'You sing well,' said Christian when he had stopped;
'now go.'

She inclined her head and turned from the window. As
his broad back, so grotesque in its strange nearness to the
ground, passed out between the gate-posts of Ardguys, she
went over to the mantelpiece.

Her face was set, and she stood with clasped hands
gazing into the fireplace. She was deeply moved, but not
by the song, which only stirred her to bitterness, but by
the searching tones of the beggar's voice, that had smitten
a way through which her feelings surged to and from her
heart. The thought that Archie had not utterly broken away
from her unnerved her by the very relief it brought. She
had not known till now how much she had suffered from

what had passed between them. Her power was not all gone. She was not quite alone. She would have scorned to admit that she could not stand in complete isolation, and she admitted nothing, even to herself. She only stood still, her nerves quivering, making no outward sign.

Presently she rang a little hand-bell that was on the table.

The genteel-minded maid appeared.

'Mysie,' said Madam Flemington, 'in three days I shall go to Edinburgh.'

SEVENTEEN

Society

LORD BALNILLO looked out of his sedan chair as it emerged from the darkness of a close on the northern slope of the Old Town of Edinburgh. Far down in front of him, where the long alley stopped, a light or two was seen reflected in the black water of the Nor' Loch that lay between the ancient city and the ground on which the new one was so soon to rise. The shuffling footfalls of his chairmen, echoing off the sides of the covered entry, were drowned in the noise that was going on a little way farther forward, where the close widened out into a square courtyard. One side of this place was taken up by the house of Lady Anne Maxwell, for which the judge was bound.

It had been raining, and Edinburgh was most noisomely dirty under foot, so Balnillo's regard for his silk-clad legs and the buckled shoes on his slim feet, had made him decide to be carried to his kinswoman's party. He wore his favourite mouse colour, but the waistcoat under his velvet coat was of primrose satin, and the lace under his chin had cost him more than he liked to remember.

The courtyard sent up a glow of light into the atmosphere of the damp evening, for the high houses towering round it rose black into the sky, limiting the shine and concentrating it into one patch. From above, it must have looked like a dimly illuminated well. It was full of sedan chairs, footmen, lantern-carriers and caddies, and the chattering, pushing, jesting, and oaths were keeping the inhabitants of the neighbouring 'lands' – such of them as were awake, for Edinburgh kept early hours in those days – from going to sleep.

The sedan chairs were set down at the door, for they could seldom be carried into the low and narrow entrances of even the best town houses, and here, at Lady Anne's, the staircase wound up inside a circular tower projecting from the wall.

The caddies, or street-messengers of Edinburgh, that strange brotherhood of useful, omniscient rascals, without whose services nothing could prosper, ran in and out among the crowd in search of odd jobs. Their eyes were everywhere, their ears heard everything, their tongues carried news of every event. The caddies knew all that happened in society, on the bench, in shops, in wynds, in churches, and no traveller could be an hour in the town before they had made his name and business common property. In an hour and a half his character would have gone the same way. Their home by day was at the Market Cross in the High Street, where they stood in gossiping groups until a call let one of them loose upon somebody else's business. It was the perpetual pursuit of other people's business that had made them what they were.

A knot of caddies pressed round the door of Lady Anne Maxwell's house as Lord Balnillo, sitting erect in order not to crease his clothes and looking rather like an image carried in a procession, was kept at a standstill whilst another guest was set down. Through the open window of his chair there pressed a couple of inquisitive faces.

'Hey, lads!' cried a caddie, 'it's Davie Balnillo back again!'

'Losh, it's himsel'! Aweel, ma lord, we're fine an' pleased to see ye! Grange is awa' in ben the hoose. I'se warrant he doesna' ken wha's ahint him!'

Balnillo nodded affably. The instant recognition pleased the old man, for he had only reached Edinburgh in time to dress for his cousin's party; also, Lord Grange was a friend of his, and he was glad to hear that he was in front. As he looked complacently upon the crowd, his chairmen suddenly stepped forward, almost throwing him out of his seat.

A cry rose round him.

'Canny! Canny! ye Hieland deevils! Ye'll hae the pouthered wiggie o' him swiggit aff his heed! Haud on, Davie; we'll no let ye cowp!'

Balnillo was rather annoyed, for he had been knocked smartly against the window-frame, and a little cloud of powder had been shaken on his velvet sleeve; but he knew that the one thing a man might not lose before the caddies was his temper, if he did not want his rage, his gestures, and all the humiliating details of his discomfiture to be the town talk next day. He looked as bland as he could while he resettled himself.

'It'll no be waur nor ridin' the circuit, ma lord?' inquired a voice.

A laugh went round the group, and the chair moved on and was set down at its destination. Though the caddies' knowledge of the judge went as far down as his foibles, the one thing that they did not happen to know was the motive that had brought him to Edinburgh.

The doings in the harbour had disturbed Balnillo mightily; for, though the success of Ferrier and James in taking the *Venture* rejoiced him, he was dismayed by what he had heard about Archie Flemington. His brother had told him everything. When Captain Hall and his men had been conveyed as prisoners to the town, and the ship had been taken possession of by Prince Charles' agent in Montrose, Logie had gone hastily to Balnillo to give the news to David, and to prepare for his own departure to join the Stuart army. There was no longer any need for secrecy on his part, and it had always been his intention to declare himself openly as soon as he had done his work in Montrose. The place was well protected, and, besides the town guns that he and Ferrier had taken from Hall, there were the two armed vessels – both now belonging to the Prince – lying in the harbour.

The arrival of the frigate with her supplies had turned Montrose from a rebelliously-inclined town into a declared Jacobite stronghold. The streets and taverns were full of Lord John Drummond's troops, the citizens had given vent to their feelings upon the town bells, bonfires blazed in the streets, and Prince Charlie's name was on every lip; girls wore white roses on their breasts, and dreamed at night of the fascinating young spark who had come to set Scotland alight. The intense Jacobitism of Angus seemed to have culminated in the quiet seaport.

In all this outburst of loyalty and excitement the cautious Balnillo did not know what to do. The risk of announcing his leanings publicly was a greater one than he cared to take, for his stake in the country and the land was considerable, and he was neither sanguine enough to feel certain of the ultimate triumph of the Stuarts like the Montrose people, nor generous enough to disregard all results like James. As he told himself, after much deliberation, he was 'best away.'

He had heard from James of Archie's sudden appearance upon the island, armed with a Government weapon and in company with the attacking force from the ship, and had listened to James's grim denunciation of him as a spy, his passionate regrets that he had not blown his brains out there and then. James's bitterness had been so great that David told himself he could scarcely recognize his quiet brother.

There was abundant reason for it, but Logie had seemed to be beside himself. He had scarcely eaten or slept during the short time that he had been with him, and his face had kept the judge's tongue still. After his account of what had happened, Balnillo had not returned to the subject again.

Step by step the judge had gone over all the circumstances of Flemington's sudden emergence from the Den on that windy night, and had seen how he had himself been cozened and flattered into the business of the portrait which stood unfinished, in solitary and very marked dignity, in the room with the north light. He was a man who suspected some of his own weaknesses, though his knowledge did not prevent him from giving way to them when he thought he could do so safely, and he remembered the adroit bits of flattery that his guest had strewn in his path, and how obligingly he had picked them up. He was shrewd enough to see all that. He thought of the sudden departure when Madam Flemington's mysterious illness had spirited Archie out of the house at a moment's notice, and he saw how he had contrived to imbue both himself and James with the idea that he shared their political interests, without saying one definite word; he thought of his sigh and the change in his voice as he spoke of his father's death 'in exile with his master.'

These things stood up in a row before Balnillo, and ranged themselves into a sinister whole. The plain truth of it was that he had entertained a devil unawares.

There had been a great search for Flemington when the skirmish on Inchbrayock was over. It was only ceasing when the French frigate swam into the river-mouth like a huge water-bird, and James, plunged in the struggle, was unable to spare a thought to the antagonist he had flung from him at the first sound of the attack.

But when the firing had stopped, and the appearance of the foreign ship made the issue of the conflict certain, he returned to the spot where he had left Archie, and found him gone. He examined the sand for some trace of the vanished man's feet, but the tide was now high in the river, and his footprints had been swallowed by the incoming rush. The stepping-stones were completely covered, and he knew that these – great fragments of rock as they were – would now be lying under enough water to drown a man who should miss his footing while the tide surged through this narrow stretch of the Esk's bed. He guessed that the spy had escaped by then, though a short time later the attempt would have been impossible. He made a hasty search of the island, and, finding no sign of Flemington, he returned with his men and the prisoners they had taken, leaving the dead to be carried over later to the town for burial. The boats were on the Montrose side of Inchbrayock, and, their progress being hampered by the wounded, some time was lost before he could spare a handful of followers to begin the search for Flemington. He picked up a few volunteers upon the quays, and despatched them immediately to cross the strait and to search the southern shores of both the river and the Basin; but they had barely started when Flemington and the beggar were nearing the little farm on Rossie moor. Archie had spent so little time on the open road, thanks to his companion's advice, that none of those whom the pursuers met and questioned had seen him. Before dusk came on, their zeal had flagged; and though one, quicker-witted than his comrades, had suggested the moor as a likely goal for their quarry, he had been overborne by their determination that the fugitive, a man who had been described to them as coming from the other side of the county, would make in that direction.

When James had gone to join the Stuart army on its march to England, his brother, waiting until the Prince had left Holyrood, set forth for Edinburgh. It would have been difficult for him to remain at home within sound of the noisy rejoicings of Montrose without either joining in the general exultation or holding himself conspicuously aloof. Prudence and convenience pointed to the taking of a little holiday, and his own inclination did not gainsay them.

He had not been in Edinburgh since his retirement, and the notion of going there, once formed, grew more and more to his taste. A hundred things in his old haunts drew him: gossip, the liberal tables of his former colleagues, the latest modes in coats and cravats, the musical assemblies at which he had himself performed upon the flute, the scandals and anecdotes of the Parliament House and the society of elegant women. He loved all these, though his trees and parks had taken their places of late. He loved James too, and the year they had spent together had been agreeable to him; but politics and family affection – the latter of the general rather than the individual kind – strong as their bonds were, could not bring the brothers into true touch with each other. James was preoccupied, silent, restless, and David had sometimes felt him to be inhuman in his lack of interest in small things, and in his carelessness of all but the great events of life. And now, as Balnillo stepped forth at Lady Anne Maxwell's door, he was hugging himself at the prospect of his return to the trimmings and embroideries of existence. He walked up the circular staircase, and emerged into the candle-light of the long, low room in which his cousin's guests were assembled.

Lady Anne was a youngish widow, with a good fortune and a devouring passion for cards. She had all the means of indulging her taste, for not only did she know every living being who went to the making of Edinburgh society, but, unlike most of her neighbours, she owned the whole of the house in which she lived, and, consequently, had space wherein to entertain them. While nearly all the Edinburgh world dwelt in its flat, and while many greater ladies than herself were contented to receive their guests in their bedchambers, and to dance and drink tea in rooms not much bigger than the boudoirs of their descendants, Lady Anne could have received Prince Charles Edward himself in suitable circumstances had she been so minded. But she was very far from having any such aspiration, and had not set foot in Holyrood while the Prince was there, for she was a staunch Whig. As she greeted her cousin Balnillo, she was wondering how far certain rumours that she had heard about him were true, and whether he also had been privy to the taking of the sloop-of-war in Montrose harbour, for it was just a week since the news of Logie's exploit had reached Edinburgh. One of David's many reasons for coming to her party was his desire to make his reappearance in the polite world in a markedly Whig house.

He stood talking to Lord Grange in the oak-panelled room half full of people; through an open door another smaller apartment could be seen crowded with tables and card-players. Lady Anne, all of whose guests were arrived, had vanished into it, and the two judges stood side by side. Lord Grange, who valued his reputation for sanctity above rubies, did not play cards – at least, not openly – and Balnillo, discovering new faces, as those must who have been over a year absent from any community, was glad to have him at his elbow to answer questions. Silks rustled, fans clicked, and the medley of noises in the court below came up, though the windows were shut.

The candles, dim enough to our modern standards of lighting, shone against the darkness of polished wood, and laughter and talk were escaping, like running water out of a thicket, from a knot of people gathered round a small, plump, aquiline-nosed woman. The group was at the end of the room, and now and again an individual would detach himself from it, to return, drawn by some jest that reached him ere he had crossed the floor.

'Mrs. Cockburn's wit has not rusted this twelvemonth,' observed Lord Grange.

'I marvel she has any left after nine years of housekeeping with her straitlaced father-in-law,' replied Balnillo in a preoccupied voice.

His eyes were elsewhere.

'Ah!' said Grange, pulling a righteous face.

The group round Mrs. Cockburn opened, and she caught sight of him for the first time. She bowed and smiled civilly, showing her rather prominent teeth, then, noticing Balnillo, she came over to the two men. Her friends stepped apart to let her pass, watching her go with that touch of proprietary pride which a small intimate society feels in its more original members. It was evident that her least acts were deemed worthy of observation.

As she greeted David, he turned round with a low bow.

'My lord, I thought you were buried!' she exclaimed.

'Dead and buried,' droned Grange, for the sake of saying something.

'Not dead,' exclaimed she, 'else I had been in mourning!'

Balnillo bowed again, bringing his attention back with a jerk from the direction in which it had been fixed.

'Come, my lord, what have you been doing all this long time?'

'I have been endeavouring to improve my estate, ma'am.'

'And meanwhile you have left us to deteriorate. For shame, sir!'

'Edinburgh morals are safe in Lord Grange's hands,' rejoined Balnillo, with a sudden flash of slyness.

Mrs. Cockburn smiled behind her fan. There were odd stories afloat about Grange. She looked appreciatively at Balnillo. He had not changed, in spite of his country life; he was as dapper, as ineffective, and as unexpected as ever. She preferred him infinitely to Grange.

'Fie, Davie!' broke in the latter, with a leer; 'you are an ungallant dog! Here is Mrs. Cockburn wasting her words on you, and you do nothing but ogle the lady yonder by the window.'

Three pairs of eyes – the bright ones of Mrs. Cockburn, the rather furtive ones of Balnillo, and the sanctimonious orbs of Lord Grange – turned in one direction.

'Mrs. Cockburn is all knowledge, as she is all goodness,' observed the last named, pompously. 'Pray, ma'am, tell us who is that lady?'

EIGHTEEN

Balnillo finds Perfection

A SCONCE of candles beside a window-recess shed a collective illumination from the wall, and Christian Flemington stood full in their light, contemplating the company with superb detachment, and pervaded by that air, which never left her, of facing the world, unaided and unabashed, with such advantages as God had given her. Her neck, still white and firm, was bare, for she wore no jewels but the ruby earrings which shot blood-red sparks around her when she moved. Long necks were in fashion in those days, and hers was rather short, but the carriage of her head added enough to its length to do more than equalize the difference. Her hair was like massed silver, and her flesh – of which a good deal could be seen – rose like ivory above the wine-colour of her silk gown, which flowed in spreading folds from her waist to the ground. A Spanish fan with carved tortoiseshell sticks, a thing of mellow browns and golds, was half closed between her fingers. When she opened it, it displayed the picture of a bull-fight.

'That is Mrs. Flemington – Madam Flemington, as I am told many people call her – I presume, because she came to Scotland from France. You should know her, my lord,' she added, addressing Balnillo; 'you are from Angus.'

But Balnillo was speechless.

Grange, who was transferring a pinch of snuff from his box to his nose, paused, his hand midway between the two.

'Is she the widow of Andrew Flemington, who was in France with King James?'

'The same,' replied Mrs. Cockburn, tossing her head. She had small sympathy with the Stuarts.

'I had not expected to see the lady here. Not that I know aught about her views. We have a bare acquaintance, and she is like yourself, Lord Balnillo – just arrived in Edinburgh when our young hero has left Holyrood.'

'She has been a fine woman,' said Lord Grange, his eye kindling.

'You may use the present tense, my lord,' said Mrs. Cockburn.

'Aha!' sniggered Grange, who adhered to the time-honoured beliefs of his sex, 'you dare to show yourself generous!'

'I dare to show myself what I am, and that is more than all the world can do,' said she, looking at him very hard.

He shifted from foot to foot. At this moment the gallows, to which he had condemned a few people in his time, struck him as a personal inconvenience.

'Ma'am,' said he, swallowing his rage, 'you must present Davie, or he will lose what senses he has.'

'Come, then, my lord, I will befriend you,' said she, glad of the chance to be rid of Grange.

Balnillo followed her, unable to escape had he wished to do so.

Christian was a woman who stood very still. She turned her head without turning her body as Mrs. Cockburn approached with her request, and Balnillo saw her calm acquiescence.

His breath had been almost taken away as he learned the identity of the stranger. Here was the woman who knew everything about that astounding young man, his late guest, whose alarming illness had recalled him, who had lived at St. Germain with the exiled queen, yet who was the grandmother of a most audacious Whig spy! There was no trace of recent ill-health here. He had pictured some faint, feeble shred of old womanhood, not the commanding creature whose grey eyes were considering him as he advanced under cover of her leisurely consent. She seemed to measure him carelessly as he stood before her. He was torn asunder in mind, awestruck, dragged this way by his surprised admiration, that way by his intense desire to wring from her something about Flemington. Here was a chance, indeed! But Balnillo felt his courage drown in the rising fear of being unable to profit by that chance. Admiring bewilderment overcame every other feeling. He no longer regretted the price he had paid for the lace on his cravat.

His name had roused Madam Flemington, though she gave no sign of the thrill that went through her as it fell from Mrs. Cockburn's lips. As David stood before her in the correct yet sober foppery of his primrose and mouse-colour, she regretted that she was quite ignorant of the pretext on which Archie had left his picture unfinished, nor upon what terms he had parted with the judge. She had no reason for supposing Balnillo to be aware of the young man's real character. He had been fighting with James Logie, according to Skirling Wattie, yet there seemed to be no enmity in the business, for here was his brother, Lord Balnillo, assiduous in getting himself presented to her. Mrs. Cockburn had put her request with a smiling hint at the effect she had produced on his lordship. Christian glanced at David's meticulous person and smiled, arrogantly civil, secretly anxious, and remained silent, ready to follow his lead with caution.

The shrewd side of Balnillo was uppermost to-night, stimulated perhaps by the sight of society and by the exhilarating sound of its voice. He recovered his momentarily scattered wits and determined to approach his new acquaintance with such direct and simple questions as might seem to her to be the natural inquiries of a man interested in Flemington, and innocent of any mystery concerning him. It was quite possible – so he reasoned – that she was unaware of the details of what had happened on Inchbrayock Island. Archie had fled, and the search for him had produced no result; he was unlikely to have made for his own home if he did not wish to be found, and he and Madam Flemington might not have met since the affair of the *Venture*. It should be his – Balnillo's – task to convince her of his ignorance.

His intense curiosity about Archie was almost stronger than his wrath against him. Unlike James, whose bitterness was too deep for words, whose soul was driven before the fury of his own feelings like a restless ghost, David still looked back with a certain pleasant excitement to Flemington's meteoric flash through the even atmosphere of his daily life. He would dearly have liked to bring him to justice, but he was anxious to hear a little more of him first.

He had a curious mixture of feelings about him. There was no vainer man in Scotland than Balnillo, and if the mental half of his vanity had suffered from the deception practised on it, the physical half was yet preening itself in the sunny remembrance of the portrait at home – the portrait of David Balnillo as he would fain have had the world see him – the portrait, alas and alas! unfinished. He could not feel quite as James felt, who had opened his purse, and, more – far more than that – had laid open the most sacred page of his life before Flemington. He had placed his personal safety in his hands, too, though he counted that as a matter of less moment.

'Madam,' said Balnillo, 'to see you is to rejoice that you have recovered from your serious illness.'

'You are very obliging, my lord. I am quite well,' replied Christian, concealing a slight surprise at this remark.

'I am most happy in being presented to you,' he continued. 'What news have you of my charming friend Mr. Flemington, may I ask?'

'When I heard your name, my lord, I determined to be acquainted with you, if only to thank you for your kindness to my boy. He could not say enough of yourself and your brother. I hope Captain Logie is well. Is he with you this evening?'

The mention of James acted on David as he had designed that the mention of Archie should act on Madam Flemington. These two people who were playing at innocence were using the names of their relations to scare the enemy as savage tribes use the terrific faces painted on their shields. Balnillo, in beginning the attack, had forgotten his own weak point, and he remembered that he could give no satisfactory account of his brother at the present moment. But his cunning was always at hand.

'I had half expected to see him here,' said he, peering

round the room; 'there was some talk of his coming. I arrived somewhat late, and I have hardly spoken to anyone but my Lord Grange and Mrs. Cockburn. The sight of yourself, ma'am, put other matters out of my head.'

'Ah, sir,' exclaimed Christian, 'I fear that your ardour was all on behalf of Archie! But I am accustomed to that.'

She cast a look of indolent raillery at him, drawing back her head and veiling her eyes, fiery and seductive still, with the momentary sweep of their thick lashes.

Balnillo threw out his chest like a pouter pigeon. He had not been so happy for a long time. As he did so, she remembered Archie's account of his silk legs, and his description of him as being 'silly, virtuous, and cunning all at once.' Silly she could well believe him to be; virtuous he might be; whether he was cunning or not, time would show her. She did not mean to let him go until she had at least attempted to hear more about James Logie.

'Madam,' said he, 'since seeing you I have forgotten Mr. Flemington. Can I say more?'

So far she was completely puzzled as to how much he knew about Archie, but it was beginning to enter her mind that her own illness, of which she had just learned from him, had been the young man's pretext for leaving his work when it was only begun. Why else had the judge mentioned it? And who but Flemington could have put the idea into his head?

She determined to make a bold attack on possibilities.

'Archie was distracted by my illness, poor boy, and I fear that your lordship's portrait suffered. But you will understand his anxiety when I tell you that I am the only living relation that he has, and that his devotion to me—'

'He needs no excuse!' cried David fervently.

She laid her hand upon his arm.

'I am still hardly myself,' she said. 'I cannot stand long. Fetch me a chair, my lord.'

He skipped across the floor and laid hold upon one just in time, for a gentleman was on the point of claiming it. He carried it back with the air of a conqueror.

'Apart – by the curtain, if you please,' said Christian,

waving her hand. 'We can speak more comfortably on the fringe of this rout of chattering people.'

He set the chair down in a quiet place by the wall, and she settled herself upon it, leaning back, her shoulder turned from the company. Balnillo's delight deepened.

'And the portrait, my lord. He did not tell me what arrangement had been made for finishing it,' said Christian, looking up at him as he stood beside her.

She seemed to be completely unconcerned, and she spoke with a leisurely dignity and ease that turned his ideas upside down. He could make nothing of it. She appeared to court the subject of Archie and the picture. He could only guess her to be innocent, and his warm admiration helped his belief. At no moment since he knew the truth from his brother's lips had Archie's character seemed so black as it did now. David's indignation waxed as he grew more certain that Flemington had deceived the noble woman to whom he owed so much, even as he had deceived him. He was becoming so sure of it that he had no desire to enlighten her. He longed to ask plainly where Archie was, but he hesitated. Even the all-wise Mrs. Cockburn was ignorant of this lady's political sympathies, and knew her only as the widow of a loyal exile. What might – what would be her feelings if she were to see her grandson in his real character?

Righteous anger smouldered under Balnillo's primrose waistcoat, and his spasmodic shrewdness began to doze in the increasing warmth of his chivalrous pity for this new and interesting victim of the engaging rogue.

'Mr. Flemington's concern was so great when he left my house that no arrangement was made,' said he. 'I had not the heart to trouble him with my unimportant affairs when so much was at stake.'

Of the two cautious people who were feeling their way in the dark, it was the judge who was the more mystified, for he had laid hold of a definite idea, and it was the wrong one. Christian was merely putting a bold face on a hazardous matter, and hoping to hear something of Logie. She had not sought the introduction. David would have been the butt of her amused scorn had she been free enough from anxiety to be entertained. But she could not imagine on what footing matters really stood, and she was becoming inclined to suspect the beggar's statement that Flemington had been fighting with James. Her longing to see Archie was great.

She loved him in her own way, though she had driven him from her in her mortification and her furious pride. She had not believed that he would really go there and then; that he, who had served her purposes so gallantly all his life, would take her at her word. What was he doing? Why had he gone to Edinburgh? Her own reason for coming had been the hope of seeing him. She had been four days in the town now, and she dared not make open inquiries for him, not knowing how far his defection had gone. She had accused him of turning to the Stuarts, and he had denied the accusation, not angrily, but with quiet firmness. Two horrible possibilities had occurred to her: one, that he was with the Prince, and might be already known to the Government as a rebel; the other, that he had never reached Edinburgh – that his hurt had been worse than the beggar supposed, and that he might be ill or dying, perhaps dead. But it was only when she lay awake at night that she imagined these things. In saner moments and by daylight she put them from her. She was so well accustomed to being parted from him, and to the knowledge that he was on risky business, that she would not allow herself to be really disturbed. She assured herself that she must wait and watch; and now she was glad to find herself acquainted with Balnillo, who seemed to be the only clue in her hand. Mercifully, he had all the appearance of being an old fool.

'I see that you are too modest to tell me anything of the picture,' she began. 'I hope it promised well. You should make a fine portrait, and I believe that Archie could do you justice. He is at his best with high types. Describe it to me.'

David espied a vacant chair, and, drawing it towards him, sat down to the subject with the same gusto that most men bring to their dinners. He cleared his throat.

'I should have wished it to be full length,' said he, 'but

Mr. Flemington had no suitable canvas with him. I wore my robes, and he was good enough to say that the crimson was appropriate and becoming to me. Personally, I favour quiet colours, as you see, ma'am.'

'I see that you have excellent taste.'

He bowed, delighted.

'I remarked you as you came in,' continued she, 'and I asked myself why these gentlemen looked so garish. Observe that one beside the door of the card-room, my lord. I am sure that he chose his finery with some care, yet he reminds me of a clown at a merrymaking.'

'True, true – excellently true!'

'In my youth it was the man of the world who set the fashions; now it is the tailor and the young sir fresh from his studies. What should these persons know of the subject?'

Balnillo was in heaven; from force of habit he ran his hand down the leg crossed upon his knee. The familiar inward curve of the slim silk ankle between his fingers was like the touch of a tried and creditable friend; it might almost be said that he turned to it for sympathy. He would have liked to tell his ankle that to-night he had found a perfection almost as great as its own.

Lord Grange, who had taken leave of his hostess and was departing, paused to look at him.

'See,' said he, taking an acquaintance by the elbow, 'look yonder at that doited Davie Balnillo.'

'He is telling her about his riding of the circuit,' said the other, grinning.

'The circuit never made him smile like that,' replied Grange sardonically.

An hour later Christian Flemington stood at the top of the circular staircase. Below it, Balnillo was at the entrance-door, sending everyone within reach of his voice in search of her sedan chair. When it was discovered, he escorted her down and handed her into it, then, according to the custom of the time, he prepared to attend its progress to her lodgings in Hyndford's Close. The streets were even dirtier and damper than before, but he was as anxious to walk from Lady Anne's party as he had been determined to be carried to it. He stepped along at the side of the chair, turning, when they passed a light, to see the dignified silhouette of Madam Flemington's head as it appeared in shadow against the farther window.

Speech was impossible as they went, for avoidance of the kennel and the worse obstacles that strewed the city at that hour, before the scavengers had gone their rounds, kept David busy. The only profit that a man got by seeing his admired one home in Edinburgh in 1745 was the honour and glory of it.

When she emerged from the chair in Hyndford's Close he insisted upon mounting the staircase with her, though its narrowness compelled them to go in single file; and when they stopped halfway up at the door in the towering 'land,' he bade her goodnight and descended again, consoled for the parting by her permission that he should wait upon her on the following day.

Christian was admitted and sailed into her little room. A light was in it and Archie was standing at the foot of the bed.

Surprises had been rolling up round Madam Flemington all the evening; surprise at meeting Balnillo, surprise at his attitude; and this crowning surprise of all. She was bewildered, but the blessing of unexpected relief fell on her. She went towards him, her hands outstretched, and Flemington, who was looking at her with a wistfulness she had never seen in him before, took them and held them fast.

'Oh, Archie!' she exclaimed.

She could say no more.

They sat down at the wide hearth together, the shadow of the great carved bed sprawling over the crowded space between the walls and over Christian's swelling silks. Then he told her the history of the time since they parted in Ardguys garden; of his boarding of the *Venture*; of the fight with the rebels at Inchbrayock; of his meeting with Wattie; of how he had reached Aberbrothock half dead, and had lain sick for two days in an obscure tavern by the shore; how he had finally sailed for Leith and had reached Edinburgh.

Christian heard him, her gaze fixed upon the fire. She

had elicited nothing about James Logie from Balnillo, and there was no word of him in Archie's story. She longed to speak of him, but would not; she longed to know if the beggar had told the truth in saying that the two men had actually fought, but she asked nothing, for she knew that her wisest part was to accept the essentials, considering them as the whole. She would ask no questions.

Archie had come back. She had forbidden Ardguys to him and he had evaded her ban by coming here. Yet he came, having proved himself loyal, and she would ignore the rest.

BOOK III

NINETEEN

The Winter

APRIL IS slow in Scotland, distrustful of her own identity, timid of her own powers. Half dazed from the long winter sleep, she is often bewildered, and cannot remember whether she belongs to winter or to spring.

After the struggles and perplexities of the months that had elapsed since Balnillo and Christian Flemington met in Edinburgh, she had come slowly to herself amid storms of sleet. Beyond the Grampians, in the North, her awakened eyes looked on a country whose heart had been broken at Culloden. The ragged company that gathered round its Prince on that Wednesday morning was dispersed among the fastnesses of the hills, or lying dead and dying among the rushes and heather, whilst Cumberland's soldiers finished their bloody business; the April snow that had blown in the faces of the clansmen as they hurled their unavailing valour on the Whig army had melted upon mounds of slain, and in the struggle of an hour the hopes of half a century had perished. Superior numbers, superior artillery, and superior generalship, had done their work; when the English dragoons had recovered themselves after the Highland charge, they pursued almost to the gates of Inverness, returning again to the battlefield before night should darken upon the carnage, to despatch the wounded wretches who still breathed among their dead comrades.

The country smelt of blood; reeked of it. For miles and miles round Inverness, where the search for fugitives was hottest, burnt hovels and blackened walls made blots upon the tardy green of spring. Women went about, white-faced and silent, trying to keep from their eyes the self-betraying consciousness of hidden terrors; each striving to forget the peat-stack on the moor where some hunted creature was lying, the scrub in the hollow that sheltered some wounded body, the cranny in the hill to which she must journey painfully after dark with the crusts in her apron.

The shot still rattled out over the countryside where the search was going on, and where, when it had been successful, a few maimed and haggard men stood along some shieling wall in front of a platoon of Cumberland's musketry. All down the shores of Loch Ness and among the hills above the Nairn water south-west of Culloden, the dark rocks raised their broken heads to the sky over God knows what agonies of suffering and hunger. The carrion-crow was busy in the land. One-fifth of Prince Charles's army was dead upon the battle-field, and the church and tolbooth of Inverness were full of wounded prisoners, to whom none – not even the surgeons of their own party – were suffered to attend.

And so April passed, and May was near her passing. Cumberland lay at Fort Augustus, to which place he had retired with Kingston's Horse and eleven battalions of foot. The victorious army was the richer by much spoil, and money was free; the Duke's camp was merry with festivities and races, and in the midst of it he enjoyed a well-earned leisure, enlivened by women and dice. He had performed his task of stamping out the danger that threatened his family with admirable thoroughness, and he had, besides, the comfortable prospect of a glorious return to London, where he would be the hero of the general rejoicing that was to follow. He was rooted at Fort Augustus, a rock of success and convivial self-satisfaction in the flood of tears and anguish and broken aspiration that had drowned half Scotland.

The Prince had begun his wanderings in the West, hiding among the hills and corries of the islands, followed by a few faithful souls, and with a price of thirty thousand pounds on his head, whilst Cumberland's emissaries, chief among whom was John Campbell of Mamore, Commandant of the West Highland garrisons, searched the country in every direction. The rank and file of his army – such of his men as were not dead or in prison – were scattered to the four winds; and those officers who had escaped after Culloden were in hiding, too, some despairing, some holding yet to the forlorn hope of raising his standard anew when the evil day should be over. Among these last was James Logie.

He had come unhurt through the battle. Complete indifference about personal issues had wrapped him round in a protecting atmosphere, as it seems to enwrap and protect the unconcerned among men. He had left the field in company with the Prince and a few friends, with whom he reached the Ford of Falie on the Nairn River. They had held a rapid council at this place, Prince Charles desiring that the remnant of his army should rendezvous at Ruthven, in Badenoch, whilst he made his way to France; for his hopes were living still, and he still looked for support and supplies from the French king. He had taken leave of his companions at the ford, and had set off with half a dozen followers for the coast.

Logie turned his face towards Angus. He had been a conspicuous figure in the Prince's immediate circle, and he knew that he had no time to lose if he was to cross the Grampians alive. He thirsted to get back, and to test the temper of the east coast after the news of the reverse; like his master, he was not beaten yet. He did not know what had become of Ferrier and the Angus men, for he had been on the Prince's staff; but the friends had met on the night before the battle, and it was a compact between them, that, should the day go against them, and should either or both survive the fight, they were to make for the neighbourhood of Forfar, where they would be ready, in case of necessity, to begin on their task of raising new levies for the cause.

He had reached the Spey, and had gained Deeside in safety by the shores of the Avon, crossing the Grampians near the sources of the Isla.

In the long winter that had passed since he joined the Prince in the field, James had not forgotten Flemington. His own labours in Angus and at the taking of the *Venture*, completely as they had filled his mind in the autumn, had sunk back into the limbo of insignificant things, but Archie was often in his thoughts, and some time before the advance on Inverness he had heard with indescribable feelings that he was intelligence officer to the Duke of Cumberland. The terrible thing to Logie was that Archie's treachery seemed to have poisoned the sacred places in his own past; when he turned back to it now, it was as though the figure of the young man stood blocking his view, looking at him with those eyes that were so like the eyes of Diane, and were yet the eyes of a traitor.

He could not bear to think of that October morning by the Basin of Montrose. Perhaps the story that a fatal impulse had made him lay bare to his companion had been tossed about – a subject of ridicule on Flemington's lips, its telling but one more proof to him of the folly of men. He could scarcely believe that Archie would treat the record of his anguish in such a way; but then, neither could he have believed that the sympathy in Archie's face, the break in his voice, the tension of his listening attitude, were only the stock-in-trade of a practised spy. And yet this horror had been true. In spite of the unhealed wound that he carried, in spite of the batterings of his thirty-eight years, Logie had continued to love life, but now he had begun to tell himself that he was sick of it.

And for another very practical reason his generous impulses and his belief in Flemington had undone him. Perhaps if the young painter had come to Balnillo announcing an ostentatious adherence to the Stuarts, he might have hesitated before taking him at his own value; but his apparent caution and his unwillingness to speak, and the words about his father at St. Germain, which he had let fall with all the quiet dignity of a man too upright to pass under false colours, had done more to put the brothers on the wrong track than the most violent protestations. Balnillo had been careful, in spite of his confidence in his guest; but in the sympathy of his soul James had given Flemington the means of future access to himself. Now the tavern in the Castle Wynd at Stirling could be of use to him no longer, and he knew that only the last extremity must find him in any of the secret haunts known to him in the Muir of Pert.

Madam Flemington had never reopened the subject of James Logie with Archie. In her wisdom she had left well alone. Installed in her little lodging in Hyndford's Close, with her woman Mysie, she had made up her mind to remain where she was. There was much to keep her in Edinburgh, and she could not bring herself to leave the centre of information and to bury herself again in the old white house among the ash-trees, whilst every post and every horseman brought word of some new turn in the country's fortunes.

News of the Highland army's retreat to Scotland, of the Battle of Falkirk, of the despatch of the Duke of Cumberland to the North, followed one another as the year went by, and still she stayed on. With her emergence from the seclusion of the country came her emergence from the seclusion she had made for herself; and on the Duke's thirty hours' occupation of Holyrood, she threw off all pretence of neutrality, and repaired with other Whig ladies to the palace to pay her respects to the stout, ill-mannered young General whose unbeguiling person followed so awkwardly upon the attractive figure of his predecessor.

Now that Archie was restored to her, Christian found herself with plenty of occupation. The contempt she had hitherto professed for Edinburgh society seemed to have melted away, and every card-party, every assembly and rout, knew her chair at its door, her arresting presence in its midst. Madam Flemington's name was on a good many tongues that winter. Many feared her, some maligned her, but no one overlooked her. The fact that she was the widow of an exiled Jacobite lent her an additional interest; and as the polite world set itself to invent a motley choice of reasons for her adherence to the House of Hanover – which it discovered before her reception by the Duke at Holyrood made it public – it ended by stumbling on the old story of a bygone liaison with Prince Charles's father. The idea was so much to its taste that it was generally accepted; and Christian, unknown to herself, became the cast-off and alienated mistress of that Prince whom her party had begun to call 'The Old Pretender.' It was scarcely a legend that would have conciliated her had it come to her ears, but, as rumour is seldom on speaking terms with its victims, she was ignorant of the interested whispers which followed her through the wynds and up the staircases of the Old Town.

But the reflected halo of royalty, while it casts deep shadows, reaches far. The character of royal light of love stood her in good stead, even among those to whom her supposed former lover was an abhorred spectre of Popery and political danger. The path that her own personality would surely open for her in any community was illumined and made smooth by the baleful interest that hangs about all kingly irregularities, and there was that in her bearing which made people think more of the royal and less of the irregular part of the business. Also, among the Whigs, she was a brand plucked from the burning, one who had turned from the wrong party to embrace the right. Edinburgh, Whig at heart, in spite of its backslidings, admired Madam Flemington.

And not only Edinburgh, but that curious fraction of it, David Balnillo.

The impression that Christian had made upon the judge had deepened as the weeks went by. By the time he discovered her true principles, and realized that she was no dupe of Archie's, but his partisan, he had advanced so far in his acquaintance with her, had become so much her servant, that he could not bring himself to draw back. She had dazzled his wits and played on his vanity, and that vanity was not only warmed and cosseted by her manner to him, not only was he delighted with herself and her notice, but he had begun to find in his position of favoured cavalier to one of the most prominent figures in society a distinction that it would go hard with him to miss.

He had begun their conversation at Lady Anne Maxwell's party by the mention of Archie Flemington, but his name had not come up between them again, and when his enlightenment about her was complete, and the talk which he heard in every house that he frequented revealed her in her real colours, he had no further wish to discuss the man into whose trap he had fallen.

David Balnillo's discoveries were extremely unpalatable to him. If Christian had cherished his vanity, she had made it smart, too. No man, least of all one like the self-appreciative judge, can find without resentment that he has been, even indirectly, the dupe of a person to whom he has attached himself; but when that person is a woman, determined not to let him escape from her influence, the case is not always desperate. For three unblessed days it was well nigh desperate with Balnillo, and he avoided her completely, but at the end of that time a summons from her was brought to him that his inclination for her company and the chance sight of Lord Grange holding open the door of her chair forbade him to disobey. She had worded her command as though she were conferring a favour; nevertheless, after an hour's hesitation, David had taken his hat and repaired to Hyndford's Close, dragging his dignity after him like a dog on a leash.

If she guessed the reason of his absence from her side she made no remark, receiving him as if she had just parted from him, with that omission of greeting which implies so much. She had sent for him, she said, because her man of business had given her a legal paper that she would not sign without his advice. She looked him in the face as fearlessly as ever, and her glance sparkled with its wonted fire. For some tormented minutes he could not decide whether or no to charge her with knowledge of the fraud that had been carried on under his roof, but he had not the courage to do so. Also, he was acute enough to see that she might well reply to his reproaches by reminding him that he had only himself to thank for their acquaintance. She had not made the advances; his own zeal had brought about their situation. He felt like a fool, but he saw that in speaking he might look like one, which some consider worse.

He left her, assuring himself that all was fair in love and politics; that he could not, in common good breeding, withhold his help from her in her legal difficulty; that, should wind of Archie's dealings with him get abroad in the town, he would be saving appearances in avoiding a rupture with the lady whose shadow he had been since he arrived in Edinburgh, and that it was his duty as a well-wisher of Prince Charles to keep open any channel that might yield information about Flemington's movements. Whatsoever may have been the quality of his reasons, their

quantity was remarkable. He did not like the little voice
that whispered to him that he would not have dared to
offer them to James.

There was no further risk of a meeting with Archie, for
within a few days of the latter's appearance in Hyndford's
Close he had been sent to the Border with instructions
to watch Jedburgh and the neighbourhood of Liddesdale,
through which the Prince's army had passed on its march to
England. Madam Flemington knew that the coast was clear,
and David had no suspicion that it had been otherwise.
Very few people in Edinburgh were aware of Flemington's
visit to it; it was an event of which even the caddies were
ignorant.

And so Balnillo lingered on, putting off his return to
Angus from week to week. His mouse-coloured velvet
began to show signs of wear and was replaced by a suit
of dark purple; his funds were dwindling a little, for he
was not a rich man, and a new set of verses about him
was going the round of the town. Then, with January,
came the battle of Falkirk and the siege of Stirling Castle,
and the end of the month brought Cumberland and the
mustering of loyal Whigs to wait upon him at Holyrood
Palace.

David departed quietly. He had come to Edinburgh to
avoid playing a marked part in Angus, and he now returned
to Angus to avoid playing a marked part in Edinburgh. He
was behaving like the last remaining king in a game of
draughts when he skips from square to square in the safe
corner of the board; but he did not know that Government
had kept its eye on all his doings during the time of his stay.
Perhaps it was on account of her usefulness in this and in
other delicate matters that Madam Flemington augured
well for her grandson, for when the Whig army crossed
the Forth, Archie went with it as intelligence officer to the
Duke of Cumberland.

TWENTY

The Parting of the Ways

JULY SPREAD a mantle of heather over the Grampians. In Glen Esk, the rough road into the Lowlands, little better than a sheep-track, ran down the shore of Loch Lee, to come out at last into the large spaces at the foot of the hills. The greyness of the summer haze lay over everything, and the short grass and the roots of bog-myrtle and thyme smelt warm and heady, for the wind was still. The sun seemed to have sucked up some of the heather-colour out of the earth; the lower atmosphere was suffused with a dusty lilac where, high overhead, it softened the contours of the scattered rocks. Amongst carpets of rush and deep moss, dappled with wet patches, the ruddy stems of the bog-asphodel raised slim, golden heads that drooped a little, as though for faintness, in the scented warmth. An occasional bumble-bee passed down wind, purposeful and ostentatious, like a respectable citizen zealous on the business of life.

No one looking along the windings of the Glen, and drawing in the ardent quietness of the summer warmth, would have supposed that fire and sword had been through it so lately. Its vastness of outline hid the ruined huts and black fragments of skeleton gable-ends that had smoked up into the mountain stillness. Homeless women and children had fled down its secret tracks; hunted men had given up their souls under its heights. The rich plainland of Angus had sent its sons to fight for the Prince in the North, and of those who survived to make their way back to their homes, many had been overtaken by the pursuit that had swept down behind them through the hills. No place had a darker record than Glen Esk.

Archie Flemington rode down the Glen with his companion some little way in front of the corporal and the
three men who followed them. His left arm was in a sling,
for he had received a sabre-cut at Culloden; also, he had
been rolled on by his horse, which was killed under him,
and had broken a rib. His wound, though not serious, had
taken a long time to heal, for the steel had cut into the arm
bone; he looked thin, too, for the winter had been a time
of strenuous work.

One of the three private soldiers, the last of the small
string of horsemen, had a rope knotted into his reins, the
other end of which was secured round the middle of a
short, thickset man who paced sullenly along beside the
horse. The prisoner's arms were bound at his back, his
reddish beard was unkempt, and his clothes ragged; he
made a sorry figure in the surrounding beauty.

Nearly two months had gone by since the Battle of
Culloden, and the search for fugitives was still going on in
remote places. Cumberland, who was on the point of leaving
Fort Augustus for Edinburgh on his way to London, had
given orders for a last scouring of Glen Esk. The party had
almost reached its mouth, and its efforts had resulted only
in the capture of this one rebel; but, as there was some slight
doubt of his identity, and as the officer who rode beside
Archie was one whose conscience ranked a great way above
his convenience, the red-bearded man had fared better than
many of those taken by Cumberland's man-hunters. If he
were the person they supposed him to be, he was an Angus
farmer distantly related to David Ferrier, and he was now
being brought to his own country for identification.

Captain Callandar, the officer in command, was a long,
lean, bony man with a dark face, a silent, hard-bitten fellow
from Ligonier's regiment. He and Archie had met very little
before they started south together, and they had scarcely
progressed in acquaintance in the few days during which
they had ridden side by side. They had shared their food on
the bare turf by day, lain down within a few yards of each
other at night; they had gone through many of the same
experiences in the North, and they belonged to the same
victorious army, yet they knew little more of each other

than when they started. But there was no dislike between them, certainly none on Archie's side, and if the other was a little critical of the foreign roll of his companion's *r*'s, he did not show it.

Archie's tongue had been quiet enough. He was riding listlessly along, and, though he looked from side to side, taking in the details of what he saw from force of habit, they seemed to give him no interest. He puzzled Callandar a good deal, for he had proved to be totally different from anything that he had expected. The soldier was apt to study his fellow-men, when not entirely swallowed up by his duty, and he had been rather pleased when he found that Cumberland's brilliant intelligence officer was to accompany him down Glen Esk. He had heard much about him. Archie's quick answers and racy talk had amused the Duke, who, uncompanionable himself, felt the awkward man's amazement at the readiness of others, and scraps of Flemington's sayings had gone from lip to lip, hall-marked by his approval. Callandar was taciturn and grave, but he was not stupid, and he had begun to wonder what was amiss with his companion. He decided that his own society must be uncongenial to him, and, being a very modest man, he did not marvel at it.

But the sources of Archie's discomfort lay far, far deeper than any passing irritation. It seemed to him now, as he reached the mouth of the Glen, that there was nothing left in life to fear, because the worst that could come upon him was looming ahead, waiting for him, counting his horse's steps as he left the hills behind.

An apprehension, a mere suggestion of what might be remotely possible, a skeleton that had shown its face to him in sleepless or overwrought moments since Cumberland's victory, had become real. To most people who are haunted by a particular dread, Fate plays one of the tricks she loves so much. She is an expert boxer, and whilst each man stands up to her in his long, defensive fight, his eye upon hers, guarding himself from the blow he expects to receive in the face, she hits him in the wind and he finds himself knocked out.

But she had dealt otherwise with Archie; for a week

ago he had been specially detailed to proceed to Angus to hunt for that important rebel, Captain James Logie, who was believed to have made his way southward to his native parts.

At Fort Augustus it was felt that Flemington was exactly the right man to be entrusted with the business. He was familiar with the country he had to search, he was a man of infinite resource and infinite intelligence; and Cumberland meant to be pleasant in his harsh, ungraceful manner, when he gave him his commission in person, with a hint that he expected more from Mr. Flemington than he did from anybody else. He was to accompany Captain Callandar and his three men. The officer, having made a last sweep of Glen Esk, was to go on by Brechin to Forfar, where he would be joined by another and larger party of troops that was on its way down Glen Clova from Braemar, for Cumberland was drafting small forces into Angus by way of the Grampians, and the country was filling with them.

He had dealt drastically with Montrose. The rebellion in the town had been suppressed, and the neighbourhood put under military law. This bit of the east coast had played a part that was not forgotten by the little German general, and he was determined that the hornet's nest he had smoked out should not re-collect. Whilst James Logie was at large there could be no security.

Of all the rebels in Scotland, Logie was the man whom Cumberland was most desirous to get. The great nobles who had taken part in the rising were large quarry indeed, but this commoner who had worked so quietly in the eastern end of Angus, who had been on the Prince's staff, who had the experience of many campaigns at his back, whose ally was the notorious Ferrier, who had seized the harbour of Montrose under the very guns of a Government sloop of war, was as dangerous as any Highland chieftain, and the news that he had been allowed to get back to his own haunts made the Whig generals curse. Though he might be quiet for the moment, he would be ready to stir up the same mischief on the first recrudescence of Stuart energy. It was not known what had happened to Ferrier, for although he was a marked man and would be a rich haul for anybody who could deliver him up to Cumberland, he was considered a less important influence than James; and Government had scarcely estimated his valuable services to the Jacobites, which were every whit as great as those of his friend.

Lord Balnillo was a puzzle to the intelligence department. His name had gone in to headquarters as that of a strongly suspected rebel; he was James's brother; yet, while Archie had included him in the report he had entrusted to the beggar, he had been able to say little that was definite about him. The very definite information he had given about James and Ferrier, the details of his pursuit of the two men and his warning of the attack on the *Venture*, had mattered more to the authorities than the politics of the peaceable old judge, and Balnillo's subsequent conduct had been so little in accordance with that of his brother that he was felt to be a source of small danger. He had been no great power on the bench, where his character was so easy that prisoners were known to think themselves lucky in appearing before him. No one could quite account for his success in the law, and the mention of his name in the legal circles of Edinburgh raised nothing worse than a smile. He had taken no part in the rejoicing that followed James's feat at Montrose, but had taken the opportunity of leaving the neighbourhood, and during his long stay in Edinburgh he had frequented Whig houses and had been the satellite of a conspicuous Whig lady, one who had been received by Cumberland with some distinction, the grandmother of the man who had denounced Logie. The authorities decided to leave him alone.

When the hills were behind the riders and the levels of the country had sunk and widened out on either hand, they crossed the North Esk, which made a shallow curve by the village of Edzell. The bank rose on its western side, and the shade of the trees was delightful to the travellers, and particularly to the prisoner they carried with them. As the horses snuffed at the water they could hardly be urged through it, and Callandar and Archie dismounted on the farther shore and sat on a boulder whilst they drank. They watched them as they drew the draught up their long throats and raised their heads when satisfied, to stare, with dripping muzzles, at distant nothings, after the fashion of their kind. The prisoner's aching arms were unbound that he might drink too.

'Egad, I have pitied that poor devil these last miles,' said Archie, as the man knelt at the brink and extended his stiffened arms into a pool.

The other nodded. Theoretically he pitied him, but a rebel was a rebel.

'You have no bowels of compassion. They are not in your instructions, Callandar. They should be served out, like ammunition.'

Callandar turned his grave eyes on him.

'The idea displeases you?' said Archie.

'It would complicate our duty.'

He spoke like a humourless man, but one side of his mouth twitched downwards a little, and Flemington, who had the eye of a lynx for another man's face, decided that the mere accident of habit had prevented it from twitching up. He struck him as the most repressed person he had ever seen.

'There would not be enough at headquarters to go round,' observed Archie.

Callandar's mouth straightened, and, like the horses, he looked at nothing. Criticism was another thing not in his instructions.

'They have drunk well,' he said at last. 'An hour will bring us to the foot of Huntly Hill. We can halt and feed them at the top before we turn off towards Brechin. You know this country better than I do.'

'Wait a little,' said Archie. 'I am no rebel, and you may have mercy on me with a clear conscience.'

He had slipped his arm out of the sling and was resting it on his knee.

'You are in pain?' exclaimed Callandar, astonished.

Archie laughed.

'Why, man, do you think I ride for pleasure with the top half of a bone working east and the bottom half working west?'

'I thought—' began Callandar.

'You thought me churlish company, and maybe I have been so. But this ride has been no holiday for me.'

'I did not mean that. I would have said that I thought your wound was mended.'

'My flesh-wound is mended and so is my rib,' said Flemington, 'but there are two handsome splinters hob-nobbing above my elbow, and I can tell you that they dance to the tune of my horse's jog.'

Callandar's opinion of him rose. He had found him disappointing as a companion, but Archie had hid his pain, and he understood people who did that.

The Edzell villagers turned out to stare at them as they passed a short time later, when they took the road again. After the riders left its row of houses their way ran from the river-level through fields that had begun to oust the moor, rising to the crest of Huntly Hill, on the farther side of which the southern part of Angus spread its partial cultivation down to the Basin of Montrose. Archie's discomfort seemed to grow; he shifted his sling again and again, and Callandar could see his mouth set in a hard line. Now and then an impatient sound of pain broke from him. They rode on, silent, the long rise of the hill barring their road like a wall, and the stems of the fir-strip that crowned it beginning to turn to a dusky black against the sky, which was cooling off for evening. Flemington's horse was a slow walker, and he had begun to jog persistently. His rider, holding him back, had fallen behind. Callandar rode on, preoccupied, and when, roused from his thoughts, he turned his head, Archie waved him on, shouting that he would follow more slowly, for the troopers moved at a foot's pace because of their prisoner, and he stayed abreast of them.

As Callandar passed a green sea of invading bracken that had struggled on to the road his jaw dropped and he pulled up. Behind the feathering waves an individual was sitting in a wooden box on wheels, and four dogs, harnessed to the rude vehicle, were lying on the ground in their leathern traces. He noticed with astonishment that the man had lost the lower parts of his legs.

'You'll be Captain Callandar,' said Wattie, his twinkling eyes on the other's uniform; 'you're terrible late.'

'What do you want?' said the officer, amazed.

The beggar peered through the fern and saw the knot of riders and their prisoner coming along the road some little way behind.

'Whaur's yon lad Flemington?' he demanded.

'What do you want?' exclaimed Callandar again. 'If you are a beggar you have chosen a strange place to beg in.'

For answer Wattie pulled up his sliding panel and took out two sealed letters, holding them low in the shelter of the fern, as if the midges, dancing their evening dance above the bracken-tops, should not look upon them. Callandar saw that one of the letters bore his own name.

'Whisht,' said the beggar, thrusting them back quickly, 'come doon here an' hae a crack wi' me.'

As Callandar had been concerned exclusively with troops and fighting, he knew little about the channels of information working in the country, and it took him a moment to explain the situation to himself. He dismounted under the fixed glare of the yellow dog. He was a man to whom small obstacles were invisible when he had a purpose, and he almost trod on the animal, without noticing the suppressed hostility gathering about his heels. But, so long as his master's voice was friendly, the cur was still, for his unwavering mind answered to its every tone. Probably no spot in all Angus contained two such steadfast living creatures as did this green place by the bracken when Callandar and the yellow dog stood side by side.

The soldier tethered his horse and sat down on the moss. Wattie laid the letters before him; the second was addressed to Archie. Callandar broke the seal of the first and read it slowly through; then he sat silent, examining the signature, which was the same that Flemington had showed to the beggar on the day when he met him for the first time, months ago, by the mill of Balnillo.

He was directed to advance no farther towards Brechin, but to keep himself out of sight among the woods round Huntly Hill, and to watch the Muir of Pert, for it was known that the rebel, James Logie, was concealed somewhere between Brechin and the river. He was not upon the Balnillo estate, which, with Balnillo House, had been searched from end to end, but he was believed to be in the neighbourhood of the Muir.

'You know the contents of this?' asked Callandar, as he put away the paper inside the breast of his coat.

'Dod, a ken it'll be aboot Logie. He's a fell man, yon. Have ye na got Flemington wi' ye?'

Callandar looked upon his companion with disapproval. He had never seen him, never heard of him before, and he felt his manner and his way of speaking of his superiors to be an outrage upon discipline and order, which were two things very near his heart.

He did not reply.

'Whaur's Flemington?' demanded the beggar again.

'You make very free with Mr. Flemington's name.'

'Tuts!' exclaimed Wattie, ignoring the rebuke, 'a've got ma orders the same as yersel', an' a'm to gie yon thing to him an' to nae ither body. Foo will a dae that if a dinna ken whaur he is?'

His argument was indisputable.

'Mr. Flemington will be with me in a moment,' said Callandar stiffly. 'He is following.'

The sound of horses' feet was nearing them upon the road, and Callandar rose and beckoned to Archie to come on.

'Go to the top of the hill and halt until I join you,' he told the corporal as the men passed.

As Archie dismounted and saw who was behind the bracken, he recoiled. It was to him as if all that he most loathed in the past came to meet him in the beggar's face. Here, at the confines of the Lowland country, the same hateful influences were waiting to engulf him. His soul was weary within him.

He barely replied to Wattie's familiar greeting.

'Do you know this person?' inquired Callandar.

He assented.

'Ay, does he. Him and me's weel acquaint,' said Wattie, closing an eye. 'Hae, tak' yon.'

He held out the letter to Flemington.

The young man opened it slowly, turning his back to the cart, and his brows drew together as he read.

His destiny did not mean him to escape. Logie had been marked down, and the circle of his enemies was narrowing round him. Flemington was to go no farther, and he was to remain with Callandar to await another message that would be brought to their bivouac on Huntly Hill, before approaching nearer to Brechin.

He stood aside, the paper in his hand. Here was the turning-point; he was face to face with it at last. He could not take part in Logie's capture; on that he was completely, unalterably determined. What would be the end of it all for himself he could not think. Nothing was clear, nothing plain, but the settled strength of his determination. He looked into the mellowing light round him, and saw everything as though it were unreal; the only reality was that he had chosen his way. Heaven was pitiless, but it should not shake him. Far above him a solitary bird was winging its way into the spaces beyond the hills; the measured beat of its wings growing invisible as it grew smaller and smaller and was finally lost to sight. He watched it, fascinated, with the strange detachment of those whose senses and consciousness are numbed by some crisis. What was it carrying away, that tiny thing that was being swallowed by the vastness? His mind could only grasp the idea of distance . . . of space . . .

Callandar was at his elbow, and his voice broke on him as the voice of someone awakening him from sleep.

'These are my orders,' he was saying, as he held out his own letter; 'you know them, for I am informed here that they are the duplicate of yours.'

There was no escape. Callandar knew the exact contents of both papers. Archie might have kept his own orders to himself, and have given him to suppose that he was summoned to Forfar or Perth, and must leave him; but that was impossible. He must either join in hunting Logie, or leave the party on this side of Huntly Hill.

'We had better get on,' said Callandar.

They mounted, and as they did so, Wattie also got under way. His team was now reduced to four, for the terrier which had formerly run alone in the lead had died about the new year.

He took up his switch, and the yellow cur and his companions whirled him with a mighty tug on to the road. He had been waiting for some time in the bracken for the expected horseman, and as the dogs had enjoyed a long rest, they followed the horses at a steady trot. Callandar and Flemington trotted too, and the cart soon fell behind. Beyond the crest of Huntly Hill the Muir of Pert sloped eastwards towards the coast, its edges resting upon the Esk, but before the road began to ascend it forked in two, one part running upwards, and the other breaking away west towards Brechin.

'Callandar, I am going to leave you,' said Archie, pulling up his horse.

'To leave?' exclaimed the other blankly. 'In God's name, where are you going?'

'Here is the shortest way to Brechin, and I shall take it. I must find a surgeon to attend to this arm. There is no use for me to go on with you when I can hardly sit in my saddle for pain.'

'But your orders?' gasped Callandar.

'I will make that right. You must go on alone. Probably I shall join you in a few days, but that will depend on what instructions I get later. If you hear nothing from me you will understand that I am busy out of sight. My hands may be full – that is, if the surgeon leaves me with both of them. Good-bye, Callandar.'

He turned his horse and left him. The other opened his mouth to shout after him, ordering him to come back, but remembered that he had no authority to do so. Flemington was independent of him; he belonged to a different branch of the King's service, and although he had fought at Culloden he was under different orders. He had merely accompanied his party, and Callandar knew very well that, though his junior in years, he was a much more important person than himself. The nature of Archie's duties demanded that he should be given a free hand in his movements, and no doubt he knew what he was about. But had he been Callandar's subordinate, and had there been a surgeon round the nearest corner, his arm might have dropped from his shoulder before the officer would have permitted him to fall out of the little troop. Callandar had never in all his service seen a man receive definite orders only to disobey them openly.

He watched him go, petrified. His brain was a good one, but it worked slowly, and Archie's decision and departure had been as sudden as a thunderbolt. Also, there was contempt in his heart for his softness, and he was sorry.

Archie turned round and saw him still looking after him. He sent back a gibe to him.

'If you don't go on I will report you for neglect of duty!' he shouted, laughing.

TWENTY-ONE

Huntly Hill

CALLANDAR RODE up Huntly Hill. The rose-red of the blossoming briar that decks all Angus with its rubies glowed in the failing sunlight, and the scent of its leaf came in puffs from the wayside ditches; the blurred heads of the meadow-sweet were being turned into clouds of gold as the sun grew lower and the road climbed higher. In front the trees began to mantle Huntly Hill.

He had just begun the ascent at a foot's pace when he heard the whirr of the beggar's chariot-wheels behind him, then at his side, and he turned in his saddle and looked down on his pursuer's bald crown. Wattie had cast off his bonnet, and the light breeze springing up lifted the fringe of his grizzled hair.

'Whaur awa's Flemington?' he cried, as he came up.

The other answered by another question; his thoughts had come back to the red-haired prisoner at the top of the hill, and it struck him that the man in the cart might recognize him.

'What's your name?' he asked abruptly.

'Wattie Caird.'

'You belong to these parts?'

He nodded.

'Then come on; I have not done with you yet.'

'A'm asking ye whaur's Flemington?'

If Callandar had pleased himself he would have driven Wattie down the hill at the point of the sword, his persistence and his pestilent, unashamed curiosity were so distasteful to him. But he had a second use for him now. He was that uncommon thing, a disciplinarian with tact, and by virtue of the combination in himself he understood that the troopers in front of him, who had been looking forward eagerly to getting their heads once more under a roof that night, would be disgusted by the orders he was bringing. He had noticed the chanter sticking out from under Wattie's leathern bag, and he thought that a stirring tune or two might ease matters for them. He did not see his way to dispensing with him at present, so he tolerated his company.

'Mr. Flemington has a bad wound,' he answered. 'He has gone to Brechin to have it attended to.'

'Whaur did he get it?'

'At Culloden Moor.'

'They didna tell me onything aboot that.'

'Who tells you anything about Mr. Flemington? What do you know about him?'

'Heuch!' exclaimed Wattie, with contempt, 'it's mysel' that should tell them! A ken mair aboot Flemington than ony ither body – a ken fine what's brocht yon lad here. He's seeking Logie, like a'body else, but he kens fine he'll na get him – ay, does he!'

Callandar looked down from his tall horse upon the grotesque figure so close to the ground. He was furious at the creature's assumption of knowledge.

'You are a piper?' said he.

'The best in Scotland.'

'Then keep your breath for piping and let other people's business be,' he said sternly.

'Man, dinna fash. It's King Geordie's business and syne it's mine. Him and me's billies. Ay, he's awa', is he, Flemington?'

Callandar quickened his horse's pace; he was not going to endure this offensive talk. But Wattie urged on his dogs too, and followed hard on his heels.

All through the winter, whilst the fortunes of Scotland were deciding themselves in the North, he had been idle but for his piping and singing, and he had had little to do with the higher matters on which he had been engaged in the autumn, whilst the forces of the coming storm were seething south of the Grampians. He had not set eyes on Flemington since their parting by the farm on Rossie Moor, but many a night, lying among his dogs, he had thought of

Archie's voice calling to Logie as he tossed and babbled in his broken dreams.

He had long since drawn his conclusion and made up his mind that he admired Archie as a mighty clever fellow, but he was convinced that he was more astute than anybody supposed, and it gave him great delight to think that, probably, no one but himself had a notion of the part Flemington was playing. Wattie was well aware of his advancement, for his name was in everybody's mouth. He knew that he was on Cumberland's staff just as Logie was on the staff of the Prince, and he wagged his head as he thought how Archie must have enriched himself at the expense of both Whig and Jacobite. It was his opinion that, knowledge being marketable, it was time that somebody else should enrich himself too. He would have given a great deal to know whether Flemington, as a well-known man, had continued his traffic with the other side, and as he went up the hill beside the dark Whig officer he was turning the question over in his mind.

He had kept his suspicions jealously to himself. Whilst Flemington was far away in the North, and all men's eyes were looking across the Grampians, he knew that he could command no attention, and he had cursed because he believed his chance of profit to be lost. Archie had gone out of range, and he could not reach him; yet he kept his knowledge close, like a prudent man, in case the time should come when he might use it. And now Flemington had returned, and he had been sent out to meet him.

The way had grown steep, and as Callandar's horse began to stumble, the soldier swung himself off the tired beast and walked beside him, his hand on the mane.

Wattie was considering whether he should speak. If his information were believed, it would be especially valuable at this time, when the authorities were agog to catch Logie, and the reward for his services must be considerable if there was any justice in the world. They would never catch Logie, because Flemington was in league with him. Wattie knew what many knew – that the rebel was believed to be somewhere about the great Muir of Pert, now just in front of them, but so far as he could make out, the only person who was aware of how the wind set with Archie was himself.

What he had seen at the foot of Huntly Hill had astonished him till he had read its meaning by the light of his own suspicions. Though he had not been close enough to the two men to hear exactly what passed between them when they parted, he had seen them part. He had seen Callandar standing to look after the other as though uncertain how to act, and he had heard Archie's derisive shout. There was no sign of a quarrel between them, yet Callandar's face suggested they had disagreed; there was perplexity in it and underlying disapproval. He had seen his gesture of astonishment, and the way in which he had sat looking after Flemington at the cross-roads, reining back his horse, which would have followed its companion, was eloquent to the beggar. Callandar had not expected the young man to go.

Wattie did not know the nature of the orders he had brought, but he knew that they referred to Logie. He understood that those who received them were hastening to meet those who had despatched them, and would be with them that night; and this proved to him how important it was that the letters should be in the hand of the riders before they advanced farther on their way. He had been directed to wait on the northern side of Huntly Hill, and had been specially charged to deliver them before Callandar crossed it. He told himself that only a fool would fail to guess that they referred to this particular place. But the illuminating part to Wattie was the speech he had heard by the bracken: it was all that was needed to explain the officer's stormy looks.

'These are my orders,' Callandar had said, 'but you know them, for I am informed that they are the duplicate of yours.'

Archie had disobeyed them, and Wattie was sure that he had gone, because the risk of meeting Logie was too great to be run. Now was the time for him to speak.

He had no nicety, but he had shrewdness in plenty. He was sudden and persistent in his address, and divining the obstacles in Callandar's mind, he charged them like a bull.

'Flemington'll na let ye get Logie,' said he.

He made his announcement with so much emphasis that the man walking beside him was impressed in spite of his prejudices. He was annoyed too. He turned on him angrily.

'Once and for all, what do you mean by this infernal talk about Mr. Flemington?' he cried, stopping short. 'You will either speak out, or I will take it upon myself to make you. I have three men in the wood up yonder who will be very willing to help me. I believe you to be a meddlesome liar, and if I find that I am right you shall smart for it.'

But the beggar needed no urging, and he was not in the least afraid of Callandar.

'It's no me that's sweer to speak, it's yersel' that's sweer to listen,' said he, with some truth. 'Dod, a've tell't ye afore an' a'm telling ye again – *Flemington'll no let ye get him!* He's dancin' wi' George, but he's takin' the tune frae Chairlie. Heuch! dinna tell me! There's mony hae done the same afore an' 'll dae it yet!'

The officer was standing in the middle of the road, a picture of perplexity.

'It's no the oxter of him that gars him gang,' said Wattie, breaking into the broad smile of one who is successfully letting the light of reason into another's mind. 'It's no his airm. Maybe it gies him a pucklie twist, whiles, and maybe it doesna, but it's no that that gars the like o' him greet. *He wouldna come up Huntly Hill wi' you, for he ken't he was ower near Logie.* It's that, an' nae mair!'

Callandar began to think back. He had not heard one complaint from Archie since the day they rode out of Fort Augustus together, and he remembered his own astonishment at hearing he was in pain from his wound. It seemed only to have become painful in the last couple of hours.

'It is easy to make accusations,' he said grimly, 'but you will have to prove them. What proof have you?'

'Is it pruifs ye're needin'? Fegs, a dinna gang aboot wi' them in ma poke! A can tell ye ma pruifs fine, but maybe ye'll no listen.'

He made as though to drive on.

Callandar stepped in front of the dogs, and stood in his path.

'You will speak out before I take another step,' said he. 'I will have no shuffling. Come, out with what you know! I will stay here till I get it.'

TWENTY-TWO

Huntly Hill (continued)

CALLANDAR SAT a little apart from his men on the fringe of the firwood; on the other side of the clearing on which the party had bivouacked Wattie formed the centre of a group. It was past sunset, and the troop-horses, having been watered and fed, were picketed together. Callandar's own horse snatched at the straggling bramble-shoots behind a tree.

The officer sat on a log, his chin in his hand, pondering on the amazing story that the beggar had divulged. It was impossible to know what to make of it, but, in spite of himself, he was inclined to believe it. He had questioned and cross-questioned him, but he had been able to form no definite opinion. Wattie had described his meeting with Archie on the day of the taking of the ship; he had told him how he had accompanied him on his way, how he had been forced to ask shelter for him at the farm, how he had lain and listened in the darkness to his feverish wanderings and his appeals to Logie. If the beggar's tale had been true, there seemed to be no doubt that the intelligence officer whose services were so much valued by Cumberland, had taken money from the rebels, though it seemed that he had hesitated over the business. His conscience must have smitten him even in his dreams. 'I will say nothing, but I will tell you all!' he had cried to Logie. 'I shall know where you are, but they shall never know!' In his delirium, he had taken the beggar for the man whose fellow-conspirator he was proving himself to be, and when consciousness was fighting to return, and he had sense enough to know that he was not speaking to Logie, it was his companion's promise to deliver a message of reassurance that had given him peace and sleep. 'Tell him that he can trust me,' he had said. What puzzled Callandar was the same thing that had puzzled Wattie: why had these two men, linked together by a hidden understanding, fought? Perhaps Flemington had repented of the part he was playing, and had tried to cut himself adrift. 'Let me go!' he had exclaimed. It was all past Callandar's comprehension. At one moment he was inclined to look on Wattie as an understudy for the father of lies; at another, he asked himself how he could have had courage to invent such a calumny – how he had dared to choose a man for his victim who had reached the position that Archie had gained. But he realized that, had Wattie been inventing, he would hardly have invented the idea of a fight between Flemington and Captain Logie. That little incongruous touch seemed to Callandar's reasonable mind to support the truth of his companion's tongue.

And then there was Flemington's sudden departure. It did not look so strange since he had heard what the beggar had to say. He began to think of his own surprise at finding Archie in pain from a wound which seemed to have troubled him little, so far, and to suspect that his reliable wits had been stimulated to find a new use for his injured arm by the sight of Huntly Hill combined with the news in his pocket. His gorge rose at the thought that he had been riding all these days side by side with a very prince among traitors. His face hardened. His own duty was not plain to him, and that perturbed him so much that his habitual outward self-repression gave way. He could not sit still while he was driven by his perplexities. He sprang up, walking up and down between the trees. Ought he to send a man straight off to Brechin with a summary of the beggar's statement? He could not vouch for the truth of his information, and there was every chance of it being disregarded, and himself marked as the discoverer of a mare's nest. There was scarcely anything more repugnant to Callandar than the thought of himself in this character, and for that reason, if for no other, he inclined to the risk; for he had the overwhelmingly conscientious man's instinct for martyrdom.

His mind was made up. He took out his pocket-book and wrote what he had to say in the fewest and shortest words. Then he called the corporal, and, to his extreme

astonishment, ordered him to ride to Brechin. When the
man had saddled his horse, he gave him the slip of paper.
He had no means of sealing it, here in the fir-wood, but
the messenger was a trusted man, one to whom he would
have committed anything with absolute conviction. He was
sorry that he had to lose him, for he could not tell how long
he might be kept on the edge of the Muir, nor how much
country he would have to search with his tiny force; but
there was no help for it, and he trusted that the corporal
would be sent back to him before the morrow. He was the
only person to whom he could give the open letter. When
the soldier had mounted, Callandar accompanied him to
the confines of the wood, giving him instructions from the
map he carried.

Wattie sat on the ground beside his cart; his back was
against a little raised bank. Where his feet should have
been, the yellow dog was stretched, asleep. As Callandar
and his corporal disappeared among the trees, he began to
sing 'The Tod' in his rich voice, throwing an atmosphere
of dramatic slyness into the words that made his hearers
shout with delight at the end of each verse.

When he had finished the song, he was barely suffered
to take breath before being compelled to begin again; even
the prisoner, who lay resting, still bound, within sight of the
soldiers, listened, laughing into his red beard. But suddenly
he stopped, rising to his feet:

> A lang-leggit deevil wi' his hand upon the gate,
> An' aye the Guidwife cries to him—

Wattie's voice fell, cutting the line short, for a rush of
steps was bursting through the trees – was close on
them, dulled by the pine-needles underfoot – sweeping
over the stumps and the naked roots. The beggar stared,
clutching at the bank. His three companions sprang
up.

The wood rang with shots, and one of the soldiers rolled
over on his face, gasping as he tried to rise, struggling
and snatching at the ground with convulsed fingers. The
remaining two ran, one towards the prisoner, and one
towards the horses which were plunging against each other

in terror; the latter man dropped midway, with a bullet through his head.

The swiftness of the undreamed-of misfortune struck panic into Wattie, as he sat alone, helpless, incapable either of flight or of resistance. One of his dogs was caught by the leaden hail and lay fighting its life out a couple of paces from where he was left, a defenceless thing in this sudden storm of death. Two of the remaining three went rushing through the trees, yelping as the stampeding horses added their share to the danger and riot. These had torn up their heel-pegs, which, wrenched easily from a resistance made for the most part of moss and pine-needles, swung and whipped at the ends of the flying ropes behind the crazy animals as they dashed about. The surviving trooper had contrived to catch his own horse, and was riding for his life towards the road by which they had come from Edzell. The only quiet thing besides the beggar was the yellow cur who stood at his master's side, stiff and stubborn and ugly, the coarse hair rising on his back.

Wattie's panic grew as the drumming of hoofs increased and the horses dashed hither and thither. He was more afraid of them than of the ragged enemy that had descended on the wood. The dead troopers lay huddled, one on his face and the other on his side; the wounded dog's last struggles had ceased. Half a dozen men were pursuing the horses with outstretched arms, and Callandar's charger had broken loose with its comrades, and was thundering this way and that, snorting and leaping, with cocked ears and flying mane.

The beggar watched them with a horror which his dislike and fear of horses made agonizing, the menace of these irresponsible creatures, mad with excitement and terror, so heavy, so colossal when seen from his own helpless nearness to the earth that was shaking under their tread, paralysed him. His impotence enwrapped him, tragic, horrible, a nightmare woven of death's terrors; he could not escape; there was no shelter from the thrashing hoofs, the gleaming iron of the shoes. The cumbrous perspective of the great animals blocked out the sky with its bulk as their rocking bodies went by, plunging, slipping, recovering themselves within the cramped circle of the open space. He knew nothing of what was happening, nor did he see that the prisoner stood freed from his bonds. He knew James Logie by sight, and he knew Ferrier, but, though both were standing by the red-bearded man, he recognized neither. He had just enough wits left to understand that Callandar's bivouac had been attacked, but he recked of nothing but the thundering horses that were being chased to and fro as the circle of men closed in. He felt sick as it narrowed and he could only flatten himself, stupefied, against the bank. The last thing he saw was the yellow coat of his dog, as the beast cowered and snapped, keeping his post with desperate tenacity in the din.

The bank against which he crouched cut the clearing diagonally, and as the men pressed in nearer round the horses, Callandar's charger broke out of the circle followed by the two others. A cry from the direction in which they galloped, and the sound of frantic nearing hoofs, told that they had been headed back once more. The bank was high enough to hide Wattie from them, as they returned, but he could feel the earth shake with their approach, which rang in his ears like the roar of some dread, implacable fate. He could see nothing now, as he lay half-blind with fear, but he was aware that his dog had leaped upon the bank behind him, and he heard the well-known voice, hoarse and brutal with defiant agony, just above his head. All the qualities that have gone to make the dog the outcast of the East seemed to show in the cur's attitude as he raised himself, an insignificant, common beast, in the path of the great, noble, stampeding creatures. It was the curse of his curship that in this moment of his life, when he hurled all that was his in the world – his low-bred body – against the danger that swooped on his master, he should take on no nobility of aspect, nothing to picture forth the heart that smote against his panting ribs. Another moment and the charger had leaped at the bank, just above the spot where Skirling Wattie's grizzled head lay against the sod.

The cur sprang up against the overwhelming hulk, the smiting hoofs, the whirl of heel-ropes, and struck in mid-air by the horse's knee, was sent rolling down the slope. As he fell there was a thud of dislodged earth, and the charger, startled by the sudden apparition of the prostrate figure below him, slipped on the bank, stumbled, sprang, and checked by the flying rope, crashed forward, burying the beggar under his weight.

James and Ferrier ran forward as the animal struggled to its feet, unhurt; it tore past the men, who had broken their line as they watched the fall. The three horses made off between the trees, and Logie approached the beggar. He lay crushed and mangled, as quiet as the dead troopers on the ground.

There was no mistaking Wattie's rigid stillness, and as James and Ferrier, with the red-bearded man, approached him, they knew that he would never rise to blow his pipes nor to fill the air with his voice again. The yellow dog was stretched, panting, a couple of paces from the grotesque body, which had now, for the first time, taken on dignity. As Logie bent to examine him, and would have lifted him, the cur dragged himself up; one of his hind-legs was broken, but he crawled snarling to the beggar's side, and turned his maimed body to face the men who should dare to lay a hand on Wattie. The drops poured from his hanging tongue and his eye was alight with the dull flame of pain. He would have torn Logie to bits if he could, as he trailed himself up to shelter the dead man from his touch. He made a great effort to get upon his legs and his jaws closed within an inch of James's arm.

One of the men drew the pistol from his belt.

'Ay, shoot the brute,' said another.

James held up his hand.

'The man is dead,' said he, looking over his shoulder at his comrades.

'And you would be the same if yon dog could reach you,' rejoined Ferrier. 'Let me shoot him. He will only die lying here.'

'Let him be. His leg is broken, that is all.'

The cur made another attempt to get his teeth into Logie, and almost succeeded.

Ferrier raised his pistol again, but James thrust it back.

'The world needs a few such creatures as that in it,'

said he. 'Lord! Ferrier, what a heart there is in the poor brute!'

'Stand away from him, Logie, he is half mad.'

'We must get away from this place,' said James, unheeding, 'or that man who has ridden away will bring the whole country about our ears. It has been a narrow escape for you, Gourlay,' he said to the released prisoner. 'We must leave the old vagabond lying where he is.'

'There is no burying him with that devil left alive!' cried Ferrier. 'I promise you I will not venture to touch him.'

'My poor fellow,' said James, turning to the dog, 'it is of no use; you cannot save him. God help you for the truest friend that a man ever had!'

He pulled off his coat and approached him. The men stood round, looking on in amazement as he flung it over the yellow body. The dog yelled as Logie grasped and lifted him, holding him fast in his arms; but his jaws were muffled in the coat, and the pain of the broken limb was weakening his struggles.

Ferrier looked on with his hands on his hips. He admired the dog, but did not always understand James.

'You are going to hamper yourself with him now?' he exclaimed.

'Give me the piper's bonnet,' said the other. 'There! push it into the crook of my arm between the poor brute and me. It will make him go the easier. You will need to scatter now. Leave the piper where he is. A few inches of earth will do him no good. Ferrier, I am going. You and I will have to lie low for awhile after this.'

The cur had grown exhausted, and ceased to fight; he shivered and snuffled feebly at the Kilmarnock bonnet, the knob of which made a red spot against the shirt on James's broad breast. Ferrier and Gourlay glanced after him as he went off between the trees. But as they had no time to waste on the sight of his eccentricities, they disappeared in different directions.

Dusk was beginning to fall on the wood and on the dead beggar as he lay with his two silent comrades, looking towards the Grampians from the top of Huntly Hill.

TWENTY-THREE

The Muir of Pert

CALLANDAR WATCHED his corporal riding away from the confines of the wood. His eyes followed the horse as it disappeared into hollows and threaded its way among lumps of rock. He stood for some time looking out over the landscape, now growing cold with the loss of the sun, his mind full of Flemington. Then he turned back with a sigh to retrace his way. His original intention in bringing Wattie up the hill came back to him, and he remembered that he had yet to discover whether he could identify the red-bearded man. It was at this moment that the fusillade from his halting-place burst upon him. He stopped, listening, then ran forward into the wood, the map from which he had been directing the corporal clutched in his hand.

He had gone some distance with the soldier, so he only reached the place when the quick disaster was over to hear the hoof-beats of the escaping horses dying out as they galloped down Huntly Hill. The smoke of the firearms hung below the branches like a grey canopy, giving the unreality of a vision to the spectacle before him. He could not see the beggar's body, but the overturned cart was in full view, a ridiculous object, with its wooden wheels raised, as though in protest, to the sky. He looked in vain for a sign of his third man, and at the sight of the uniform upon the two dead figures lying on the ground he understood that he was alone. Of the three private soldiers who had followed him down Glen Esk there was not one left with him. Archie, the traitor, was gone, and only the red-bearded man remained. He could see him in the group that was watching James Logie as he captured the struggling dog.

Callandar ground his teeth; then he dropped on one knee and contemplated the sight from behind the great circle of roots and earth that a fallen tree had torn from the sod. Of all men living he was one of the last who might be called a coward, but neither was he one of those hot-heads who will plunge, to their own undoing and to that of other people, into needless disaster. He would have gone grimly into the hornet's nest before him, pistol in hand, leaving heaven to take care of the result, had the smallest advantage to his king and country been attainable thereby. His own death or capture would do no more than prevent him from carrying news of what had happened to headquarters, and he decided, with the promptness hidden behind his taciturn demeanour, that his nearest duty was to identify James Logie, if he were present. Callandar's duty was the only thing that he always saw quickly.

From his shelter he marked the two Jacobite officers, and, as he knew Ferrier very well from description, he soon made out the man he wanted. James was changed since the time when he had first come across Archie's path. His clothes were worn and stained, and the life of wandering and concealment that he had led since he parted from the Prince had set its mark on him. He had slept in as many strange places of late as had the dead beggar at his feet; anxious watching and lack of food and rest were levelling the outward man to something more primitive and haggard than the gallant-looking gentleman of the days before Culloden, yet there remained to him the atmosphere that could never be obliterated, the personality that he could never lose until the earth should lie on him. He was no better clothed than those who surrounded him, but his pre-eminence was plain. The watcher devoured him with his eyes as he turned from his comrades, carrying the dog.

As soon as he was out of sight, the rebels scattered quietly, and Callandar crouched lower, praying fortune to prevent anyone from passing his retreat. None approached him, and he was left with the three dead men in possession of the wood.

He rose and looked at his silent comrades. It would be useless to follow Logie, because, with so many of his companions dispersing at this moment about the fringes of the Muir of Pert, he could hardly hope to do so unobserved. There would be no chance of getting to close quarters with him, which was Callandar's chief desire, for the mere suspicion of a hostile presence would only make James shift his hiding-place before the gathering troops could draw their cordon round him. He abandoned the idea with regret, telling himself that he must make a great effort to get to Brechin and to return with a mounted force in time to take action in the morning. The success of his ambush and his ignorance that he had been watched would keep Logie quiet for the night.

He decided to take the only road that he knew, the one by which Flemington had left him. The upper one entangled itself in the Muir, and might lead him into some conclave of the enemy. He began to descend in the shadows of the coming darkness that was drawing itself like an insidious net over the spacious land. He had almost reached the road, when a moving object not far from him made him stop. A man was hurrying up the hill some little way to his right, treading swiftly along, and, though his head was turned from Callandar, and he was not near enough for him to distinguish his features, the sling across his shoulder told him that it was Flemington.

Callandar stood still, staring after him. Archie's boldness took away his breath. Here he was, returning on his tracks, and if he kept his direction, he would have to pass within a few hundred yards of the spot on which he knew that the companions he had left would be halted; Callandar had pointed out the place to him as they approached the hill together.

Archie took a wider sweep as he neared the wood, and the soldier, standing in the shadow of a rowan-tree, whose berries were already beginning to colour for autumn, saw that he was making for the Muir, and knew that the beggar was justified. One thing only could be bringing him back. He had come, as Wattie had predicted, to warn Logie.

He had spoken wisdom, that dead vagabond, lying silent for ever among the trees; he had assured him that Flemington would not suffer him to take Logie. He knew him, and he had laughed at the idea of his wounded arm turning him out of his road. 'It's no the like o' that that gars the like o' him greet,' he had said; and he was right. Callandar, watching the definite course of the figure through the dusk, was sure that he was taking the simplest line to a retreat whose exact position he knew. He turned and followed, running from cover to cover, his former errand abandoned. It was strange that, in spite of all, a vague gladness was in his heart, as he thought that Archie was not the soft creature that he had pretended to be. There were generous things in Callandar. Then his generous impulse turned back on him in bitterness, for it occurred to him that Archie had been aware of what lay waiting for them, and had saved himself from possible accident in time.

They went on till they reached the border of the Muir, Flemington going as unconcernedly as if he were walking in the streets of Brechin, though he kept wide of the spot on which he believed the riders to have disposed themselves for the night. There was no one who knew him in that part of the country, and he wore no uniform to make him conspicuous in the eyes of any chance passer in this lonely neighbourhood. As Callandar emerged from the straggling growth at the Muir's edge, he saw him still in front going through the deep thickness of the heather.

Callandar wished that he knew how far the Muir extended, and exactly what lay on its farther side. His map was thrust into his coat, but it was now far too dark for him to make use of it; the tall figure was only just visible, and he redoubled his pace, gaining a little on it. A small stationary light shone ahead, evidently the window of some muirland hovel. There is nothing so difficult to decide as the distance of a light at night, but he guessed that it was the goal towards which Archie was leading. He went forward, till the young man's voice hailing someone and the sound of knocking made him stop and throw himself down in the heather. He thought he heard a door shut. When all had been quiet for a minute he rose up, and, approaching the house, took up his stand not a dozen yards from the walls.

Perplexity came on him. He had been surprisingly successful in pursuing Flemington unnoticed as far as this hovel, but he had yet to find out who was inside it. Perhaps the person he had heard speaking was Logie, but equally perhaps not. There was no sound of voices within, though he heard movements; he dared not approach the uncurtained window to look in, for the person whose step he heard was evidently standing close to it. He would wait, listening for that person to move away, and then would try his luck. He had spent perhaps ten minutes thus occupied when, without a warning sound, the door opened and Archie stood on the threshold, as still as though he were made of marble. It was too dark for either man to see more than the other's blurred outline.

Flemington looked out into the night.

'Come in, Callandar!' he called. 'You are the very man I want!'

The soldier's astonishment was such that his feet seemed frozen to the ground. He did not stir.

'Come!' cried Archie. 'You have followed me so far that you surely will not turn back at the last step. I need you urgently, man. Come in!'

He held the door open.

Callandar entered, pushing past him, and found himself in a low, small room, wretchedly furnished, with another at the back opening out of it. Both were empty, and the light he had seen was standing on the table.

'There is no one here!' he exclaimed.

'No,' said Flemington.

'Where is the man you were speaking to?'

'He is gone. The ill-mannered rogue would not wait to receive you.'

'It was that rebel! It was Captain Logie!' cried Callandar.

'It was not Logie; you may take my word for that,' replied Archie. He sat down on the edge of the table and crossed his legs. 'Try again, Callandar,' he said lightly.

Callandar's lips were drawn into an even line, but they were shaking. The mortification of finding that Archie had been aware of his presence, had pursued his way unconcerned, knowing that he followed, had called him in as a man calls the serving-man he has left outside, was hot in him. No wonder his own concealment had seemed so easy.

'You have sent him to warn Logie – that is what you have done!' he cried. 'You are a scoundrel – I know that!'

He stepped up to him, and would have laid hold of his collar, but the sling stopped him.

'I have. Callandar, you are a genius.'

As the other stood before him, speechless, Flemington rose up.

'You have got to arrest me,' he said; 'that is why I called you in. I might have run out by the back of the house, like the man who is gone, who went with my message almost before the door was shut. Look! I have only one serviceable arm and no sword. I left it where I left my horse. And here is my pistol; I will lay it on the table, so you will have no trouble in taking me prisoner. You have not had your stalking for nothing, after all, you mighty hunter before the Lord!'

'You mean to give yourself up – you, who have taken so much care to save yourself?'

'I have meant to ever since I saw you under the rowan-tree watching me, flattened against the trunk like a squirrel. I would as soon be your prisoner as anyone else's – sooner, I think.'

'I cannot understand you!' exclaimed Callandar, taking possession of the weapon Archie had laid down.

'It is hard enough to understand oneself but I do at last,' said the other. 'Once I thought life easy, but mine has been mighty difficult lately. From here on it will be quite simple. And there will not be much more of it, I fancy.'

'You are right there,' said Callandar grimly.

'I can see straight before me now. I tell you life has grown simple.'

'You lied at the cross-roads.'

'I did. How you looked after me as I went! Well, I have done what I suppose no one has ever done before: I have threatened to report you for neglecting your duty.' He threw back his head and laughed. 'And I am obliged to tell you to arrest me now. O Callandar, who will correct your backslidings when there is an end of me?'

The other did not smile as he looked at Flemington's laughing eyes, soft and sparkling under the downward curve of his brows. Through his anger, the pity of it all was smiting him, though he was so little given to sentiment. Perhaps Archie's charm had told on him all the time they had been together, though he had never decided whether he liked him or not. And he looked so young when he laughed.

'What have you done?' he cried, pacing suddenly up and down the little room. 'You have run on destruction, Flemington; you have thrown your life away. Why have you done this – you?'

'If a thing is worthless, there is nothing to do but throw it away.'

Callandar watched him with pain in his eyes.

'What made you suspect me?' asked Archie. 'You can tell me anything now. There is only one end to this business. It will be the making of you.'

'Pshaw!' exclaimed the other, turning away.

'Why did you follow me?' continued Archie.

Callandar was silent.

'Tell me this,' he said at last: 'What makes you give yourself up now, without a struggle or a protest, when little more than two hours ago you ran from what you knew was to come, there, at the foot of the hill? Surely your friends would have spared *you!*'

'Now it is I who do not understand you,' said Archie.

His companion stood in front of him, searching his face.

'Flemington, are you lying? On your soul, are you lying?'

'Of what use are lies to me now?' exclaimed Archie impatiently. 'Truth is a great luxury; believe me, I enjoy it.'

'You knew nothing of what was waiting for us at the top of Huntly Hill?'

'Nothing, as I live,' said Archie.

'The beggar betrayed you,' said Callandar. 'When you were gone he told me that you were in Logie's pay – that you would warn him. He was right, Flemington.'

'I am not in Logie's pay – I never was,' broke in Archie.

'I did not know what to think,' the soldier went on; 'but I took him up Huntly Hill with me, and when we had unsaddled, and the men were lying under the trees, I sent the corporal to Brechin with the information. I went with him to the edge of the wood, and when I came back there was not a man left alive. Logie and Ferrier were there with a horde of their rebels. They had come to rescue the prisoner, and he was loose.'

'Then he *was* Ferrier's cousin!' exclaimed Flemington. 'We were right.'

'One of my men escaped,' continued Callandar, 'or I suppose so, for he was gone. The beggar and the other two were killed, and the horses had stampeded.'

'So Wattie is dead,' mused Flemington. 'Gad, what a voice has gone with him!'

'They did not see me, but I watched them; I saw him – Logie – he went off quickly, and he took one of the beggar's dogs with him, snarling and struggling, with his head smothered in his coat. Then I went down the hill, meaning to make for Brechin, and I saw you coming back. I knew what you were about, thanks to that beggar.'

Neither spoke for a minute. Archie was still sitting on the table. He had been looking on the ground, and he raised his eyes to his companion's face.

Something stirred in him, perhaps at the thought of how he stood with fate. He was not given to thinking about himself, but he might well do so now.

'Callandar,' he said, 'I dare say you don't like me—' Then he broke off, laughing. 'How absurd!' he exclaimed. 'Of course you hate me; it is only right you should. But perhaps you will understand – I think you will, if you will listen. I was thrown against Logie – no matter how – but, unknowing what he did, he put his safety in my hands. He did more. I had played upon his sympathy, and in the generosity of his heart he came to my help as one true man might do to another. I was not a true man, but he did not know that; he knew nothing of me but that I stood in need, and he believed I was as honest as himself. He thought I was with his own cause. That was what I wished him to believe – had almost told him.'

Callander listened, the lines of his long face set.

'I had watched him and hunted him,' continued Archie,

'and my information against him was already in the beggar's hands, on its way to its mark. I could not bring myself to do more against him then. What I did afterwards was done without mention of his name. You see, Callandar, I have been true to nobody.'

He paused, waiting for comment, but the other made none.

'After that I went to Edinburgh,' he continued, 'and he joined the Prince. Then I went north with Cumberland. I was freed from my difficulty until they sent me here to take him. The Duke gave me my orders himself, and I had to go. That ride with you was hell, Callandar, and when we met the beggar to-day I had to make my choice. That was the turning-point for me. I could not go on.'

'He said it was not your wound that turned you aside.'

'He was a shrewd rascal,' said Flemington. 'I wish I could tell how he knew so much about me.'

'It was your own tongue: once you spent the night in a barn together when you were lightheaded from a blow, and you spoke all night of Logie. You said enough to put him on your track. That is what he told me as we went up Huntly Hill.'

Archie shrugged his shoulders and rose up.

'Now, what are you going to do?' he said.

'I am going to take you to Brechin.'

'Come, then,' said Archie, 'we shall finish our journey together after all. It has been a hard day. I am glad it is over.'

They went out together. As Callandar drew the door to behind them Archie stood still.

'If I have dealt double with Logie, I will not do so with the king,' said he. 'This is the way out of my difficulty. Do you understand me, Callandar?'

The darkness hid the soldier's face.

Perhaps of all the people who had played their part in the tangle of destiny, character, circumstance, or whatsoever influences had brought Flemington to the point at which he stood, he was the one who understood him best.

TWENTY-FOUR

The Vanity of Men

THE LAST months had been a time of great anxiety to Lord Balnillo. In spite of his fine steering and though he had escaped from molestation, he was not comfortable as he saw the imprisonments and confiscations that were going on; and the precariousness of all that had been secure disturbed him and made him restless. He was unsettled, too, by his long stay in Edinburgh, and he hankered afresh after the town life in which he had spent so many of his years. His trees and parks interested him still, but he looked on them, wondering how long he would be allowed to keep them. He was lonely, and he missed James, whom he had not seen since long before Culloden, the star of whose destiny had led him out again into the world of chance.

He had the most upsetting scheme under consideration that a man of his age can entertain. At sixty-four it is few people who think seriously of changing their state, yet this was what David Balnillo had in mind; for he had found so many good reasons for offering his hand to Christian Flemington that he had decided at last to take that portentous step. The greatest of these was the effect that an alliance with the Whig lady would produce in the quarters from which he feared trouble. His estate would be pretty safe if Madam Flemington reigned over it.

It was pleasant to picture her magnificent presence at his table; her company would rid country life of its dulness, and on the visits to Edinburgh, which he was sure she would wish to make, the new Lady Balnillo would turn their lodging into a bright spot in society. He smoothed his silk stockings as he imagined the stir that his belated romance would make. He would be the hero of it, and its heroine, besides being a safeguard to his property, would be a credit to himself.

There were some obstacles to his plan, and one of them was Archie; but he believed that, with a little diplomacy, that particular difficulty might be overcome. He would attack that side of the business in a very straightforward manner. He would make Madam Flemington understand that he was large-minded enough to look upon the episode in which he had borne the part of victim in a reasonable yet airy spirit. In the game in which their political differences had brought them face to face the honours had been with the young man; he would admit that with a smile and with the respect that one noble enemy accords to another. He would assure her that bygones should be bygones, and that when he claimed Archie as his grandson-in-law, he would do so without one grudging backward glance at the circumstances in which they had first met. His magnanimity seemed to him an almost touching thing, and he played with the idea of his own apposite grace when, in some sly but genial moment, he would suggest that the portrait upstairs should be finished.

What had given the final touch to his determination was a message that James had contrived to send him, which removed the last scruple from his heart. His brother's danger had weighed upon David, and it was not only its convenience to himself at this juncture which made him receive it with relief. Logie was leaving the country for Holland, and the next tidings of him would come from there, should he be lucky enough to reach its shores alive.

Since the rescue of Gourlay the neighbourhood of the Muir of Pert – the last of his haunts in which Logie could trust himself – had become impossible for him, and he was now striving to get to a creek on the coast below Peterhead. It was some time since a roof had been over him, and the little cottage from which Flemington had despatched his urgent warning stood empty. Its inmate had been his unsuspected connection with the world since his time of wandering had begun; for though his fatal mistake in discovering this link in his chain of communication to Flemington had made him abjure its shelter, he had had no choice for some time between the Muir and any other place.

The western end of the county swarmed with troops. Montrose was subdued; the passes of the Grampians were watched; there remained only this barren tract west of the river; and the warning brought to him from a nameless source had implored him to abandon it before the soldiery, which his informant assured him was collecting to sweep it from end to end, should range itself on its borders.

Archie had withheld his name when he sent the dweller in the little hovel speeding into the night. He was certain that in making it known to James he would defeat his own ends, for Logie would scarcely be disposed to trust his good faith, and might well look on the message as a trick to drive him into some trap waiting for him between the Muir and the sea.

James did not give his brother any details of his projected flight; he merely bade him an indefinite good-bye. The game was up – even he was obliged to admit that – and Ferrier, whose ardent spirit had been one with his own since the beginning of all things, was already making for a fishing village, from which he hoped to be smuggled out upon the high seas. Nothing further could be gained in Angus for the Stuart cause. The friends had spent themselves since April in their endeavours to resuscitate the feeling in the country, but there was no more money to be raised, no more men to be collected. They told themselves that all they could do now was to wait in the hope of a day when their services might be needed again. That day would find them both ready, if they were above ground.

David knew that, had James been in Scotland, he would not have dared to think of bringing Christian Flemington to Balnillo.

He had a feeling of adventure when he started from his own door for Ardguys. The slight awe with which Christian still inspired him, even when she was most gracious, was beginning to foreshadow itself, and he knew that his bones would be mighty stiff on the morrow; there was no riding of the circuit now to keep him in practice in the saddle. But he was not going to give way to silly apprehensions, unsuited to his age and position; he would give himself every chance in the way of effect. The servant who rode after him carried a handsome riding-suit for his master to don at Forfar before making the last stage of his road. It grieved Balnillo to think how much of the elegance of his well-turned legs must be unrevealed by his high boots. He was a personable old gentleman, and his grey cob was worthy of carrying an eligible wooer. He reached Ardguys, and dismounted under its walls on the following afternoon.

He had sent no word in front of him. Christian rose when he was ushered into her presence, and laid down the book in her hand, surprised.

'You are as unexpected as an earthquake,' she exclaimed, as she saw who was her visitor.

'But not as unwelcome?' said David.

'Far from it. Sit down, my lord. I had begun to forget that civilization existed, and now I am reminded of it.'

He bowed, delighted.

A few messages and compliments, a letter or two despatched by hand, had been their only communications since the judge left Edinburgh, and his spirits rose as he found that she seemed really pleased to see him.

'And what has brought you?' asked Christian, settling herself with the luxurious deliberation of a cat into the large chair from which she had risen. 'Something good, certainly.'

'The simple desire to see you, ma'am. Could anything be better?'

It was an excellent opening; but he had never, even in his youth, been a man who ran full tilt upon anything. He had scarcely ever before made so direct a speech.

She smiled, amused. There had been plenty of time for thought in her solitude; but, though she had thought a good deal about him, she had not a suspicion of his errand. She saw people purely in relation to the uses she had for them, and, officially, she had pronounced him harmless to the party in whose interests she had kept him at her side. The circumstances were not those which further sentiment.

'I have spent this quiet time in remembering your kindnesses to me,' he began, inspired by her smile.

'You call it a quiet time?' she interrupted. 'I had not

looked on it in that way. Quiet for us, perhaps, but not for the country.'

'True, true,' said he, in the far away tone in which some people seek to let unprofitable subjects melt.

Now that the active part of the rebellion had become history, she had no hesitation in speaking out from her solid place on the winning side.

'This wretched struggle is over, and we may be plain with one another, Lord Balnillo,' she continued. 'You, at least, have had much to alarm you.'

'I have been a peaceful servant of law and order all my life,' said he, 'and as such I have conceived it my place to stand aloof. It has been my duty to restrain violence of all kinds.'

'But you have not restrained your belongings,' she observed boldly.

He was so much taken aback that he said nothing.

'Well, my lord, it is one of my regrets that I have never seen Captain Logie. At least you have to be proud of a gallant man,' she went on, with the same impulse that makes all humanity set a fallen child upon its legs.

But Balnillo had a genius for scrambling to his feet.

'My brother has left the country in safety,' he rejoined, with one of those random flashes of sharpness that had stood him in such good stead. His cunning was his guardian angel; for he did not know what she knew – namely, that Archie had left Fort Augustus in pursuit of James.

'Indeed?' she said, silenced.

She was terribly disappointed, but she hid her feelings in barefaced composure.

The judge drew his chair closer. Here was another opening, and his very nervousness pushed him towards it.

'Ma'am,' he began, clearing his throat, 'I shall not despair of presenting James to you. When the country is settled – if – in short—'

'I imagine that Captain Logie will hardly trust himself in Scotland either in my lifetime or in yours. We are old, you and I,' she added, the bitterness of her disappointment surging through her words.

She watched him to see whether this barbed truth pierced him; it pierced herself as she hurled it.

'Maybe,' said he; 'but age has not kept me from the business I have come upon. I have come to put a very particular matter before you.'

She was still unsuspicious, but she grew impatient. He had wearied her often in Edinburgh with tedious histories of himself, and she had endured them then for reasons of policy; but she felt no need of doing so here. It was borne in upon her, as it has been borne in upon many of us, that a person who is acceptable in town may be unendurable in the country. She had not thought of that as she welcomed him.

'Ma'am,' he went on, intent on nothing but his affair, 'I may surprise you – I trust I shall not offend you. At least you will approve the feelings of devotion, of respect, of admiration which have brought me here. I have an ancient name, I have sufficient means – I am not ill-looking, I believe—'

'Are you making me a proposal, my lord?'

She spoke with an accent of derision; the sting of it was sharp in her tone.

'There is no place for ridicule, ma'am. I see nothing unsuitable in my great regard for you.'

He spoke with real dignity.

She had not suspected him of having any, personally, and she had forgotten that an inherited stock of it was behind him. The rebuke astonished her so much that she scarcely knew what reply to make.

'As I said, I believe I am not ill-looking,' he repeated, with an air that lost him his advantage. 'I can offer you such a position as you have a right to expect.'

'You also offer me a brother-in-law whose destination may be the scaffold,' she said brutally; 'do not forget that.'

This was not to be denied, and for a moment he was put out. But it was on these occasions that he shone.

'Let us dismiss family matters from our minds and think only of ourselves,' said he; 'my brother is an outlaw, and as such is unacceptable to you, and your grandson has every reason to be ashamed to meet me. We can set these disadvantages, one against the other, and agree to ignore them.'

'I am not disposed to ignore Archie,' said she.

'Well, ma'am, neither am I. I hope I am a large-minded man – indeed, no one can sit on the bench for the time that I have sat on it and not realize the frailty of all creatures—'

'My lord—' began Christian.

But it is something to have learned continuance of speech professionally, and Balnillo was launched; also his own magnanimous attitude had taken his fancy.

'I will remember nothing against him,' said he. 'I will forget his treatment of my hospitality, and the discreditable uses to which he put my roof.'

'Sir!' broke in Christian.

'I will remember that, according to his lights, he was in the exercise of his duty. Whatsoever may be my opinion of the profession to which he was compelled, I will thrust it behind me with the things best forgotten.'

'That is enough, Lord Balnillo,' cried Madam Flemington, rising.

'Sit, madam, sit. Do not disturb yourself! Understand me, that I will allow every leniency. I will make every excuse! I will dwell, not on the fact that he was a spy, but on his enviable relationship to yourself.'

She stood in the middle of the room, threatening him with her eyes. Some people tremble when roused to the pitch of anger that she had reached; some gesticulate; Christian was still.

He had risen too.

'If you suppose that I could connect myself with a disloyal house you are much mistaken,' she said, controlling herself with an effort. 'I have no quarrel with your name, Lord Balnillo; it is old enough. My quarrel is with the treason in which it has been dipped. But I am very well content with my own. Since I have borne it, I have kept it clean from any taint of rebellion.'

'But I have been a peaceful man,' he protested. 'As I

told you, the law has been my profession. I have raised a hand against no one.'

'Do you think I do not know you?' exclaimed she. 'Do you suppose that my ears were shut in the winter, and that I heard nothing in all the months I spent in Edinburgh? What of that, Lord Balnillo?'

'You made no objection to me then, ma'am, I was made happy by being of service to you.'

She laughed scornfully.

'Let us be done with this,' she said. 'You have offered yourself to me and I refuse the offer. I will add my thanks.'

The last words were a masterpiece of insolent civility.

A gilt-framed glass hung on the wall, one of the possessions that she had brought with her from France. David suddenly caught sight of his own head reflected in it above the lace cravat for which he had paid so much; the spectacle gathered up his recollections and his present mortification, and fused them into one stab of hurt vanity.

'I see that you can make no further use of me,' he said.

'None.'

He walked out of the room. At the door he turned and bowed.

'If you will allow me, I will call for my horse myself,' said he.

He went out of the house and she stood where she was, thinking of what he had told her about his brother; she had set her heart upon Archie's success in taking Logie, and now the man had left the country and his chance was gone. The proposal to which she had just listened did not matter to her one way or the other, though he had offended her by the attitude he took up when making it. He was unimportant. It was of Archie that she thought as she watched the judge and his servant ride away between the ash-trees. They were crossing the Kilpie burn when her maid came in, bringing a letter. The writing on it was strange to Christian.

'Who has brought this?' she asked as she opened it.

'Just a callant,' replied the girl.

She read the letter, which was short. It was signed 'R.

Callandar, Captain,' and was written at Archie Flemington's request to tell her that he was under arrest at Brechin on a charge of conspiring with the king's enemies.

The writer added a sentence, unknown, as he explained, to Flemington.

'The matter is serious,' he wrote, 'the Duke of Cumberland is still in Edinburgh. It might be well if you could see him. Make no delay, as we await his orders.'

She stood, turning cold, her eyes fixed on the maid.

'Eh – losh, mem!' whimpered Mysie, approaching her with her hands raised.

Madam Flemington felt as though her brain refused to work. There seemed to be nothing to drive it forward. The world stood still. The walls, an imprisoning horror, shut her in from all movement, all action, when action was needed. She had never felt Ardguys to be so desperately far from the reach of humanity, herself so much cut off from it, as now. And yet she must act. Her nearest channel of communication was the judge, riding away.

'Fool!' she cried, seizing Mysie, 'run – run! Send the boy after Lord Balnillo. Tell him to run!'

The maid hesitated, staring at the pallor of her mistress's face.

'Eh, but, mem – sit you down!' she wailed.

Christian thrust her from her path as though she had been a piece of furniture, and swept into the hall. A barefooted youth was outside by the door. He stared at her, as Mysie had done. She took him by the shoulder.

'Run! Go instantly after those horses! That is Lord Balnillo!' she cried, pointing to the riders, who were mounting the rise beyond the burn. 'Tell him to return at once. Tell him he must come back!'

He shook off her grip and ran. He was a corner-boy from Brechin and he had a taste for sensation.

Madam Flemington went back into her room. Mysie followed her, whimpering still, and she pushed her outside and sank down in her large chair. She could not watch the window, for fear of going mad.

She sat still and steady until she heard the thud

of bare feet on the stone steps, and then she hurried out.

'He tell't me he wadna bide,' said the corner-boy breathlessly. 'He was vera well obliged to ye, he bad' me say, but he wadna bide.'

Christian left him and shut herself into the room, alone. Callandar's bald lines had overpowered her completely, leaving no place in her brain for anything else. But now she saw her message from Lord Balnillo's point of view, and anger and contempt flamed up again, even in the midst of her trouble.

'The vanity of men! Ah, God, the vanity of men!' she cried, throwing out her hands, as though to put the whole race of them from her.

TWENTY-FIVE

A Royal Duke

THE DUKE of Cumberland was at Holyrood House. He had come down from the North by way of Stirling, and having spent some days in Edinburgh, he was making his final arrangements to set out for England. He was returning in the enviable character of conquering hero, and he knew that a great reception awaited him in London, where every preparation was being made to do him honour; he was thinking of these things as he sat in one of the grim rooms of the ancient palace. There was not much luxury here; and looking across the table at which he sat and out of the window, he could see the dirty roofs of the Canongate – a very different prospect from the one that would soon meet his eyes. He was sick of Scotland.

Papers were littered on the table, and his secretary had just carried away a bundle with him. He was alone, because he expected a lady to whom he had promised an audience, but he was not awaiting her with the feelings that he generally brought to such occasions. Cumberland had received the visits of many women alone since leaving England, but his guests were younger than the one whose approach he could now hear in the anteroom outside. He drew his brows together, for he expected no profit and some annoyance from the interview.

He rose as she was ushered in and went to the open fireplace, where he stood awaiting her, drawn up to his full height, which was not great. The huge iron dogs behind him and the high mantelpiece above his head dwarfed him with their large lines. He was not an ill-looking young man, though his hair, pulled back and tied after the fashion of the day, showed off the receding contours that fell away from his temples, and made his blue eyes look more prominent than they were.

He moved forward clumsily as Christian curtsied.

'Come in, madam, come in. Be seated. I have a few minutes only to give you,' he said, pointing to a chair on the farther side of the table.

She sat down opposite to him.

'I had the honour of being presented to your Royal Highness last year,' she said.

'I remember you well, ma'am,' replied he shortly.

'It is in the hope of being remembered that I have come,' said she. 'It is to ask you, Sir, to remember the services of my house to yours.'

'I remember them, ma'am; I forget nothing.'

'I am asking you, in remembering, to forget one thing,' said she. 'I shall not waste your Royal Highness's time and mine in beating about bushes. I have travelled here from my home without resting, and it is not for me to delay now.'

He took up a pen that lay beside him, and put the quill between his teeth.

'Your Royal Highness knows why I have come,' continued she, her eyes falling from his own and fixing themselves on the pen in his mouth. He removed it with his fat hand, and tossed it aside.

'There is absolute proof against Flemington,' said he. 'He accuses himself. I presume you know that.'

'I do. This man – Captain Logie – has some strange attraction for him that I cannot understand, and did him some kindness that seems to have turned his head. His regard for him was a purely personal one. It was personal friendship that led him to – to the madness he has wrought. His hands are clean of conspiracy. I have come all this way to assure your Highness of that.'

'It is possible,' said Cumberland. 'The result is the same. We have lost the man whose existence above ground is a danger to the kingdom.'

'I have come to ask you to take that difference of motive into consideration,' she went on. 'Were the faintest shadow of conspiracy proved, I should not dare to approach you;

my request should not pass my lips. I have been in correspondence with him during the whole of the campaign,
and I know that he served the king loyally. I beg your
Highness to remember that now. I speak of his motive
because I know it.'

'You are fortunate, then,' he interrupted.

'Captain Callandar, to whom he gave himself up, wrote
me two letters at his request, one in which he announced
his arrest, and one which I received as I entered my coach
to leave my door. Archie knows what is before him,' she
added; 'he has no hope of life and no knowledge of my
action in coming to your Highness. But he wished me to
know the truth – that he had conspired with no one. He is
ready to suffer for what he has done, but he will not have
me ashamed of him. Look, Sir—'

She pushed the letter over to him.

'His motives may go hang, madam,' said Cumberland.

'Your Highness, if you have any regard for us who have
served you, read this!'

He rose and went back to the fireplace.

'There is no need, madam. I am not interested in the
correspondence of others.'

He was becoming impatient; he had spent enough time
on this lady. She was not young enough to give him
any desire to detain her. She was an uncommon-looking
woman, certainly, but at her age that fact could matter to
nobody. He wondered, casually, whether the old stories
about her and Charles Edward's father were true. Women
struck him only in one light.

'You will not read this, your Royal Highness?' said
Christian, with a little tremor of voice.

'No, ma'am. I may tell you that my decision has not
altered. The case is not one that admits of any question.'

'Your Highness,' said Christian, rising, 'I have never
made an abject appeal to anyone yet, and even now,
though I make it to the son of my king, I can hardly
bring myself to utter it. I deplore my – my boy's action
from the bottom of my soul. I sent him from me – I
parted from him nearly a year ago because of this man
Logie.'

He faced round upon her and put his hands behind his back.

'What!' he exclaimed, 'you knew of this? You have been keeping this affair secret between you?'

'He went to Montrose on the track of Logie in November,' said she; 'he was sent there to watch his movements before Prince Charles marched to England, and he did so well that he contrived to settle himself under Lord Balnillo's roof. In three days he returned to me. He had reported on Logie's movements – I know that – your Highness's agents can produce his report. But he returned to my house to tell me that, for some fool's reason, some private question of sentiment, he would follow Logie no longer. "I will not go manhunting after Logie" – those were his words.'

'Madam—' began Cumberland.

She put out her hand, and her gesture seemed to reverse their positions.

'I told him to go – I told him that I would sooner see him dead than that he should side with the Stuarts! He answered me that he could have no part with rebels, and that his act concerned Logie alone. Then he left me, and on his way to Brechin he received orders to go to the Government ship in Montrose Harbour. Then the ship was attacked and taken.'

'It was Flemington's friend, Logie, who was at the bottom of that business,' said Cumberland.

'He met Logie and they fought,' said Madam Flemington. 'I know none of the details, but I know that they fought. Then he went to Edinburgh.'

'It is time that we finished with this!' exclaimed Cumberland. 'No good is served by it.'

'I am near the end, your Highness,' said Christian, and then paused, unnerved by the too great suggestiveness of her words.

'These things are no concern of mine,' he observed in the pause; 'his movements do not matter. And I may tell you, ma'am, that my leisure is not unlimited.'

It was nearing the close of the afternoon, and the sun stood like a red ball over the mists of the Edinburgh smoke. Cumberland's business was over for the day, and he was looking forward to dining that evening with a carefully chosen handful of friends, male and female.

Her nerve was giving way against the stubborn detachment of the man. She felt herself helpless, and her force ineffective. Life was breaking up round her. The last man she had confronted had spurned her in the end – through a mistake, it was true – but the opportunity had been given him by her own loss of grip in the bewilderment of a crisis. This one was spurning her too. But she went on.

'He performed his work faithfully from that day forward, as your Royal Highness knew when you took him to the North. His services are better known to you, Sir, than to anyone else. He gave himself up to Captain Callandar as the last proof that he could take no part with the rebels. He threw away his life.'

'*That*, at least, is true,' said the Duke, with a sneer. He was becoming exasperated, and the emphasis which he put on the word 'that' brought the slow blood to her face. She looked at him as though she saw him across some mud-befouled stream. Even now her pride rose above the despair in her heart. He was not sensitive, but her expression stung him.

'I am accustomed to truth,' she replied.

He turned his back. There was a silence.

'I came to ask for Archie's life,' she said, in a toneless, steady voice, 'but I will go, asking nothing. Your Royal Highness has nothing to give that he or I would stoop to take at your hands.'

He stood doggedly, without turning, and he did not move until the sound of her sweeping skirts had died away in the anteroom. Then he went out, a short, stoutish figure passing along the dusty corridors of Holyrood, and entered a room from which came the ring of men's voices.

A party of officers in uniform got up as he came in. Some were playing cards. He went up to one of the players and took those he held from between his fingers.

'Give me your hand, Walden,' said he, 'and for God's sake get us a bottle of wine. Damn me, but I hate old women! They should have their tongues cut out.'

TWENTY-SIX

The Vanishing Bird

THE HOUSES of Brechin climb from the river up the slope, and a little camp was spread upon the crest of ground above them, looking down over the uneven pattern of walls, the rising smoke, and the woods that cradled the Esk. Such of Cumberland's soldiery as had collected in Angus was drawn together here, and as the country was settling down, the camp was increased by detachments of horse and foot that arrived daily from various directions. The Muir of Pert was bare, left to the company of the roe-deer and the birds, for James had been traced to the coast, and the hungry North Sea had swallowed his tracks.

The spot occupied by the tents of Callandar's troop was in the highest corner of the camp, the one farthest from the town, and the long northern light that lingered over the hill enveloped the camp sounds and sights in a still, greenish clearness. There would be a bare few hours of darkness.

Callandar was now in command of a small force consisting of a troop of his own regiment which had lately marched in, and two of his men stood sentry outside the tent in which Archie Flemington was sitting at an improvised table writing a letter.

He had been a close prisoner since his arrest on the Muir of Pert, and during the week that had elapsed, whilst correspondence about him and orders concerning him had gone to and fro between Brechin and Edinburgh, he had been exclusively under Callandar's charge. That arrangement was the one concession made on his behalf among the many that had been asked for by his friends. At his own request he was to remain Callandar's prisoner till the end, and it was to be Callandar's voice that would give the order for his release at sunrise to-morrow, and Callandar's troopers whose hands would set him free.

The two men had spent much time together. Though the officer's responsibility did not include the necessity of seeing much of his prisoner, he had chosen to spend nearly all his leisure in Archie's tent. They had drawn very near together, this incongruous pair, though the chasm that lay between their respective temperaments had not been bridged by words. They had sat together on many evenings, almost in silence, playing cards until one of them grew drowsy, or some officious cock crowed on the outskirts of the town. Of the incident which had brought them into their present relationship, they spoke not at all; but sometimes Archie had broken out into snatches of talk, and Callandar had listened, with his grim smile playing about his mouth, to his descriptions of the men and things amongst which his short life had thrown him. As he looked across at his companion, who sat, his eyes sparkling in the light of the lantern, his expression changing with the shades of humour that ran over his words, like shadows over growing corn, he would be brought up short against the thought of the terrible incongruity to come – death. He could not think of Archie and death. At times he would have given a great deal to pass on his responsibility to some other man, and to turn his back on the place that was to witness such a tragedy. In furthering Archie's wishes by his own application for custody of him he had given him a great proof of friendship – how great he was only to learn as the days went by. Would to God it were over – so he would say to himself each night as he left the tent. He had thought Archie soft when they parted at the cross-roads, and he had been sorry. There was no need for sorrow on that score; never had been. The sorrow to him now was that so gallant, so brilliant a creature was to be cut off from the life of the world, to go down into the darkness, leaving so many of its inhabitants half-hearted, half-spirited, half alive, to crawl on in an existence which only interested them inasmuch as it supplied their common needs.

His hostility against Logie ran above the level of the just antagonism that a man feels for his country's enemy, and

he questioned whether his life were worth the price that
Flemington was paying for it. The hurried words that Archie
had spoken about Logie as they left the hovel together had
told him little, and that little seemed to him inadequate to
explain the tremendous consequences that had followed.
What had Logie said or done that had power to turn
him out of his way? A man may meet many admirable
characters among his enemies without having his efforts
paralysed by the encounter. Flemington was not new to
his trade, and had been long enough in the secret service
to know its requirements. A certain unscrupulousness was
necessarily among them, yet why had his gorge only risen
against it now? Callandar could find no signs in him of
the overwrought sensibility that seemed to have prompted
his revolt against his task. Logie had placed his safety in
Archie's hands, and it was in order to end that safety that
the young man had gone out; he had laid the trap and the
quarry had fallen into it. What else had he expected? It
was not that Callandar could not understand the scruple;
what he could not understand was why a man of Archie's
occupation should suddenly be undone by it. Having
accepted his task, his duty had been plain. In theory, a
rebel, to Callandar was a rebel, no more, and Archie, by
his deed, had played a rebel's part; yet, in spite of that, the
duty he must carry out on the morrow was making his heart
sink within him. One thing about Archie stood out plain –
he was not going to shirk his duty to his king and yet take
Government money. Whatsoever his doings, the prisoner
who sat in the tent over yonder would be lying under the
earth to-morrow because he was prepared to pay the last
price for his scruple. No, he was not soft.

Callandar would have died sooner than let him escape,
yet his escape would have made him glad.

Callandar came across the camp and passed between
the two sentries into Flemington's tent. The young man
looked up from his writing.

'You are busy,' said the officer.

'I have nearly done. There seems so much to do at the
last,' he added.

The other sat down on the bed and looked at him, filled

with grief. The lantern stood by Archie's hand. His head was bent into the circle of light, and the yellow shine that fell upon it warmed his olive skin and brought out the brown shades in his brows and hair. The changing curves of his mouth were firm in the intensity of his occupation. He had so much expression as a rule that people seldom thought about his features but Callandar now noticed his long chin and the fine lines of his nostril.

His pen scratched on for a few minutes; then he laid it down and turned round.

'You have done me many kindnesses, Callandar,' said he, 'and now I am going to ask you for another – the greatest of all. It is everything to me that Captain Logie should get this letter. He is safe, I hope, over the water, but I do not know where. Will you take charge of it?'

'I will,' said the other – 'yes.'

The very name of Logie went against him.

'You will have to keep it some little time, I fear,' continued Archie, 'but when the country has settled down you will be able to reach him through Lord Balnillo. Promise me that, if you can compass it, he shall get this.'

'If it is to be done, I will do it.'

'From you, that is enough,' said Flemington, 'I shall rest quietly.'

He turned to his writing again.

Callandar sat still, looking round the tent vaguely for something to distract his heavy thoughts. A card lay on the ground and he picked it up. It was an ace, and the blank space of white round it was covered with drawing. His own consideration had procured pens and books – all that he could find to brighten the passing days for his prisoner. This was the result of some impulse that had taken Flemington's artistic fingers.

It was a sketch of one of the sentries outside the tent door. The figure was given in a few lines, dark against the light, and the outline of the man's homely features had gained some quality of suggestiveness and distinction by its passage through Archie's mind, and by the way he had placed the head against the clouded atmosphere made by the smoke rising from the camp. Through it, came a

touched-in vision of the horizon beyond the tents. He
looked at it, seeing something of its cleverness, and tossed
it aside.

When Archie had ended his letter, he read it through:

When this comes to your hands perhaps you will know
what has become of me [he had written] and you will
understand the truth. I ask you to believe me, if only
because these are the last words I shall ever write.
A man speaks the truth when it is a matter of hours
with him.

You know what brought me to Balnillo, but you do
not know what sent me from it. I went because I had
no courage to stay. I was sent to find out how deep you
were concerned in the Stuart cause and to watch your
doings. I followed you that night in the town, and my
wrist bears the mark you set on it still. That morning
I despatched my confirmation of the Government's
suspicions about you. Then I met you and we sat
by the Basin of Montrose. God knows I have never
forgotten the story you told me.

Logie, I went because I could not strike you again.
You had been struck too hard in the past, and I could
not do it. What I told you about myself was untrue, but
you believed it, and would have helped me. How could
I go on?

Then, as I stood between the devil and the deep sea,
my orders took me to the *Venture*, and we met again
on Inchbrayock. I had made sure you would be on the
hill. When I would have escaped from you, you held me
back, and as we struggled you knew me for what I was.

You know the rest as well as I do, and you know
where I was in the campaign that followed. Last of
all I was sent out with those who were to take you
on the Muir of Pert. I had no choice but to go – the
choice came at the cross-roads below Huntly Hill.
It was I who sent the warning to you from the little
house on the Muir. You had directed me there for a
different purpose. I sent no name with my message,
knowing that if I did you might suspect me of a trick

to entrap you again. That is all. There remained only the consequences, and I shall be face to face with them to-morrow.

There is one thing more to say. Do not let yourself suppose that I am paying for your life with mine. I might have escaped had I tried to do so – it was my fault that I did not try. I had had enough of untruth, and I could no longer take the king's money; I had served his cause ill, and I could only pay for it. I have known two true men in my life – you and the man who has promised that you shall receive this letter. If you will think of me without bitterness, remember that I should have been glad.

ARCHIBALD FLEMINGTON

He folded the paper and rose, holding it out to Callandar.

'I am contented,' said he; 'go now, Callandar. You look worn out. I believe this last night is trying you more than it tries me.'

IT WAS SOME little time after daybreak that Callandar stood again at the door of the tent under the kindling skies. Archie was waiting for him and he came out. The eyes of the sentries never left them as they went away together, followed by the small armed guard that was at Callandar's heels.

The two walked a little apart, and when they reached the outskirts of the camp they came to a field, an insignificant rough enclosure, in which half a dozen soldiers were gathered, waiting. At the sight of Callandar the sergeant who was in charge of them began to form them in a line some paces from the wall.

Callandar and Flemington stopped. The light had grown clear, and the smoke that was beginning to rise from the town thickened the air over the roofs that could be seen from where they stood. The daily needs and the daily avocations were beginning again for those below the hill, while they were ceasing for ever for him who stood above in the cool morning. In a few minutes the sun would get up; already there was a sign of his coming in the eastward sky.

The two men turned to each other; they had nothing

more to say. They had settled every detail of this last act of their short companionship, so that there should be no hesitation, no mistake, nothing to be a lengthening of agony for one, nor an evil memory for the other.

Archie held out his hand.

'When I look at you,' he said.

'Yes,' said Callandar.

'There are no words, Callandar. Words are nothing – but the last bit of my life has been the better for you.'

For once speech came quickly to the soldier.

'The rest of mine will be the better for you,' he answered. 'You said once that you were not a true man. You lied.'

Flemington was giving all to disprove the accusation of untruth, and it was one of the last things he was to hear.

So, with these rough words – more precious to him than any that could have been spoken – sounding in his ears, he walked away and stood before the wall. The men were lined in front of him.

His eyes roved for a moment over the slope of the country, the town roofs, the camp, then went to the distance. A solitary bird was crossing the sky, and his look followed it as it had followed the one he had seen when he made his choice at the foot of Huntly Hill. The first had flown away, a vanishing speck, towards the shadows gathering about the hills. This one was going into the sunrise. It was lost in the light . . .

'Fire!' said Callandar.

For Archie was looking at him with a smile.

TWENTY-SEVEN

Epilogue

JAMES LOGIE stood at the window of a house in a Dutch town. The pollarded beech, whose boughs were trimmed in a close screen before the walls, had shed its golden leaves and the canal waters were grey under a cloudy sky. The long room was rather dark, and was growing darker. By the chair that he had left lay a yellow cur.

He had been standing for some minutes reading a letter by the fading light, and his back was towards the man who had brought it. The latter stood watching him, stiff and tall, an object of suspicion to the dog.

As he came to the end, the hand that held the paper went down to James's side. The silence in the room was unbroken for a space. When he turned, Callandar saw his powerful shoulders against the dusk and the jealous shadows of the beech-tree's mutilated arms.

'I can never thank you enough for bringing me this,' said Logie. 'My debt to you is immeasurable.'

'I did it for him – not for you.'

Callandar spoke coldly, almost with antagonism

'I can understand that,' said James.

But something in his voice struck the other. Though he had moved as if to leave him, he stopped, and going over to the window, drew a playing-card from a pocket in his long coat.

'Look,' he said, holding out the ace scrawled with the picture of the sentry.

James took it, and as he looked at it, his crooked lip was set stiffly, lest it should tremble.

'It was in his tent when I went back there – afterwards,' said Callandar.

He took the card back, and put it in his pocket.

'Then it was you—' began James.

'He was my prisoner, sir.'

James walked away again and stood at the window. Callandar waited, silent.

'I must wish you a good-day, Captain Logie,' he said at last, 'I have to leave Holland to-night.'

James followed him down the staircase, and they parted at the outer door. Callandar went away along the street, and James came back slowly up the steep stairs, his hand on the railing of the carved banisters. He could scarcely see his way.

The yellow dog came to meet him when he entered his room, and as his master, still holding the letter, carried it again to the light, he followed. Half-way across the floor he turned to sniff at an old Kilmarnock bonnet that lay by the wainscot near the corner in which he slept.

He put his nose against it, and then looked at Logie. Trust was in his eyes and affection; but there was inquiry, too.

'My poor lad,' said James, 'we both remember.'

THE END

Notes

These notes draw on numerous sources. Among the works consulted most, and to which specific reference is made below, are the following:

William Ferguson, *Scotland 1689 to the Present* (Edinburgh: Oliver & Boyd, 1968); refs are to the pbk. ed., 1978.

James Holloway, *Patrons and Painters: Art in Scotland 1650–1760* (Edinburgh: Scottish National Portrait Gallery, 1989).

William Allen Illsley (ed.), *The Third Statistical Account of Scotland: The County of Angus* (Arbroath: Herald Press, 1977).

Violet Jacob, *The Lairds of Dun* (London: John Murray, 1931).

Bruce Lenman, *The Jacobite Risings in Britain 1689–1746* (London: Eyre Methuen, 1980).

Duncan Macmillan, *Painting in Scotland: The Golden Age* (Oxford: Phaidon Press, 1986).

Frank McLynn, *France and the Jacobite Rising of 1745* (Edinburgh: Edinburgh University Press, 1981).

Frank McLynn, *The Jacobites* (London: Routledge & Kegan Paul, 1985); refs are to pbk. ed., 1988.

Sir Charles Petrie, *The Jacobite Movement* (London: Eyre & Spottiswoode, 1959).

T.C. Smout, *A History of the Scottish People 1560–1830* (Glasgow: William Collins, 1969); refs. are to the pbk. ed., Fontana, 1979.

The New Statistical Account of Scotland vol. XI: Forfar and Kincardineshire (Edinburgh & London: William Blackwood and Sons, 1845).

title Flemington: The name of the central character and his family may have been suggested by the Castle of Flemington at Aberlemno in Angus, now a ruin but inhabited at the time the novel is set. According to the *Third Statistical Account*, the castle was a centre of Jacobite sympathy and was searched by government soldiers after the Forty-Five, but Jacobites sheltering there managed to escape.

p.279 *Ardguys*: A note pencilled in the poet Helen Cruickshank's copy of the novel suggests that the house is modelled on Baldovie, near Kirkton of Kingoldrum, some 3 miles from Kirriemuir. The nearby burn would thus probably be the Cromie.

the Sidlaws: Hills to the south of the Vale of Strathmore.

p.280 *while the approaching middle of the* [18th] century was bringing a marked improvement to country ministers as a class . . . 'Many ministers began to drop their primitive character of preachers and eager reprovers, and to adopt the *personae* of polite and unenthusiastic gentlemen, able to embellish God's word in an elegant address indicating to the poor the prime virtues of obedience and industry, and able to catch up the standard of Scottish culture to bear it proudly in the European Enlightenment' (Smout, p.214). It is also relevant, perhaps, that with the revival of patronage in 1712 ministers were more closely affiliated to the lairds and therefore shared their general outlook and aims (see Smout, p.216).

p.281 *the Court of James II of England at St Germain*: From 1689–1715 the deposed Stuart king, James II, his wife, Mary of Modena, and his successors, had residence at the château of St-Germain-en-Laye, outside Paris, as 'guests' of Louis XIV.

Mary Beatrice of Modena (1658–1718): was of Italian origin; her father was Alphonse IV, Duke of Modena. She was widowed when James II died in 1701.

p.282 *the young Chevalier de St. George*: The title was conferred by Louis XIV on James Francis Edward Stuart (1688–1766), recognised by true Jacobites as King James VIII of Scotland and III of England, later known by supporters of the House of Hanover as 'the Old Pretender'.

smallpox had carried off her son: This disease was quite common in the period, and carried off even members of royalty, including Princess Louise Mary Stuart, the fourth daughter of Mary of Modena, at St Germain in April 1712.

a rank Whig: Originally a nickname for an adherent of the National Covenant of 1638 and thus of Presbyterianism in the 17th century, the name Whig later came to apply to Presbyterians in general; and at the time the novel is set, to supporters of the government, and of the royal House of Hanover.

p.283 *She [Christian] was an Episcopalian*: This religous affiliation was typical of north-east Scotland at the time; Christian is atypical in having changed allegiance from the Stuarts to the House of Hanover.

himself and his community: Mr Duthie is a minister of the Established Church of Scotland.

like a young David: See Bible I.Sam.17. When no-one else would respond to the challenge of Goliath, the huge champion of the Philistines, David killed the giant with only his slingshot and some stones.

plunged deeper into the vernacular: In this post-Union period, there was growing pressure in Scotland to speak 'standard' English, although as Violet Jacob notes in *The Lairds of Dun* 'the language of educated Scotsmen was still the language of their forbears' (p.244), i.e., Scots.

p.284 *Venus goes stripped*: Venus, the Roman goddess of beauty and sensual love, is often depicted in art as a naked figure. The naked female figure also often denotes Truth. This links in with the novel's key engagement with questions of 'truth' and integrity.

The Pope of Rome: Mr Duthie is a Presbyterian minister at a time when the Established church in Scotland was particularly austere and repressive (during the period approximately 1690–1720).

p.285 *His skin and his dark eyes hinted at his mother's French blood*: It is notable that Archie is half-French. Besides reflecting the European, especially French, dimension of political conflict in this period (see Lenman, 1980), it emphasises his 'apartness' from the community and its narrow attitudes. Jacob was interested in 'outsider' figures of different kinds, as is suggested by her short fiction and some of her novels such as *The Interloper*. Archie's French blood may also suggest his passionate nature; as in some 19th-century Scottish and English fiction, many of Jacob's passionate figures have foreign blood. Violet Jacob herself lived in France for a short time as a child with her widowed mother, as an article by her, 'A Manor House in Brittany', in *Country Life*, 22 May 1920, pp.685–6, recounts.

Nemesis: The Greek goddess of vengeance; personification of divine retribution.

p.288 *a square stone mansion*: Almost certainly the prototype is the House of Dun, built between 1730 and 1742 for

David Erskine, on an estate owned by the family since 1375, some half a mile north of the Montrose Basin (a semi-natural circular piece of water).

Lord Balnillo: The estate of Balnillo is based on Dun; lands with the name of Balnillo were held by the Erskines in the past (see *The Lairds of Dun*, p.11).

David Logie: based on David Erskine, Lord Dun, 13th Laird (1672–1758).

his wife Margaret: The wife of the real-life David Erskine was Magdalene Riddell (d.1736). Her portrait, by Sir John de Medina, hangs in the house today, alongside that of her husband. David Erskine's portrait was painted by William Aikman (1682–1731).

p.289 *James Logie*: Based on Captain James Erskine (b.1671), elder brother of David Erskine, who became a soldier serving in the 2nd Battalion of the Royal Regiment of Foot, and was gazetted to its 2nd Battalion as Ensign to Captain Peter MacIlvain at Breda in 1694. His regiment was in the Netherlands at the beginning of the War of the Spanish Succession. He fought with Marlborough at Blenheim (i.e. for the English against the French), and for the Jacobite cause in 1715. He died in his 70s, where and when exactly is unknown. The name 'Logie' appears in Violet Jacob's ancestry (John of Logy, the 7th Laird, d.1591). Logie is also a name attached to several places in the locality of Dun, such as the parish of Logie Pert.

the Scots Brigade in Holland: The Scots Brigade had its origins in Dutch need of assistance against the Spanish Duke of Alva in the 1570s; three regiments of Scots were recruited and paid by the United Provinces, although swearing allegiance to the Scottish Crown. The Brigade tended to attract Whigs rather than Jacobites; indeed the Brigade had played a key role in the expulsion of James II. Like his prototype, James Logie is a soldier of Jacobite conviction; like James Erskine he is also presumably a professional mercenary soldier.

p.290 *an elder*: Senior figure in the Presbyterian church and in Church of Scotland congregation.

the Den of Balnillo: Again, suggested by 'the Den' to the west of the House of Dun.

p.291 *Basin of Montrose . . . River Esk*: Still known as such, the Basin is a semi-natural 2000 acre tidal basin into which the river South Esk flows. It is now a local nature reserve.

p.293 *his long chin*: Archie's appearance may have been suggested by the traditional Erskine family 'long chin', illustrated in family portraits at the House of Dun.

p.295 *wore his own hair*: i.e., rather than a wig; this is significant, suggesting Archie's naturalness.

an agreeable ready-made figure from a selection brought forward by a painter: Sir John de Medina (1659–1710), who painted David and James Erskine, came to Scotland to paint the family of Lord Leven, and 'some time either at the end of 1693 or the beginning of the following year Medina travelled north to paint the heads on his already completed bodies'; see James Holloway, *Patrons and Painters: Art in Scotland 1650–1760*, p.38. De Medina was born in Brussels of a Spanish father, but lived first in England, then in Scotland, where he remained for nearly 20 years. His oval portraits of the Erskine brothers hang in the House of Dun. *Van Dyck*: Sir Anthony van Dyck (1599–1641), b. Antwerp, the great Flemish artist, court painter of Charles I, known especially for his portraits.

p.297 *gean-trees*: Wild cherries. Compare Jacob's description of the House of Dun: 'Ancient gean trees in its eastern approach once held their twisted arms in fantastic angles against the winter skies till spring covered them with a sheet of white and they passed again through summer into the flaming red of their autumn leaf. But age and the gales have taken their glory now and left only a few battered trunks; and even the great beech trees are fast thinning in the storms of these later years' (*The Lairds of Dun*, p.3). There is also a poem, 'The Gean Trees', in Jacob's *Songs of Angus* (1915).

Montrose . . . like some Dutch town: The Third Statistical Account comments that Montrose has many houses 'with their gable ends to the street, the entrance being down a close. No doubt they reflect the influence of the architecture of the Low Countries with which Montrose had in its heyday as a port much intercourse' (p.477).

p.298 *whose acquaintance I had laid so many plots to compass*: Archie is a government spy. According to Frank McLynn, 'From the very first days of the small exiled court's existence at St Germain-en-Laye, espionage played an important part in the story of the Jacobites' (*The Jacobites*, p.171).

skirts . . . highlandman: A reference to the wearing of the plaid or kilt by male Highlanders.

p.301 *road . . . Brechin*: There is a modern road connecting Montrose with Brechin, a cathedral town in Angus of ancient origins (see also note to page 370).

p.302 *Skirlin' Wattie*: This character's name makes reference to the 'skirling' or shrill sound of the bagpipes he plays.

p.303 *the head of Falstaff, the shoulders of Hercules*: Sir John

Falstaff, Shakespeare's celebrated comic character (*Henry IV*, parts I and II, and *The Merry Wives of Windsor*), although a lusty and lying braggart, is nevertheless engaging. Hercules is the mythical Greek hero of fabulous strength.

Kilmarnock bonnet: A broad flat coloured woollen bonnet, the traditional headwear of the Scottish peasantry. This becomes an emblem of Wattie himself.

p.304 *The Tod*: A song called 'The Tod' (fox) appears in David Herd's collection *Ancient and Modern Scottish Songs* (1776), but the version here is very different and appears in Violet Jacob's own volume of poetry *Songs of Angus* (1915). The fact that 'tod' can suggest a sly, cunning, untrustworthy person is significant in this context.

p.305 *Logie Kirk*: This also appears in *Songs of Angus*. 'Logie Kirk' is probably the old church of Logie, close by the North Esk river in the parish of Logie Pert, near Dun.

p.306 *Auld Nick*: Old Nick, the devil.

p.308 *the curious mixture of awe and contempt accorded to charlatans and to those connected with the arts*: See also p.310, 'this womanish trade'. From the beginning of the novel, this is shown as a society hostile to the visual arts, which are criticised or sneered at by the minister, the soldier, and now the servants. Presbyterian Scotland is thought by many writers to have been especially antipathetic to creativity in all forms; in the early 18th century the influence of the Covenanters was still possibly felt, even in the Episcopalian north east. According to William Ferguson, 'They suppressed the "profane arts" . . . and their anti-art tradition took root' (p.100). Note, however, that music and dancing still flourish among the ordinary folk.

p.309 *to ride the circuit*: The circuit is the journey made by a judge in a particular district to administer justice (there were three circuits in Scotland). 'The Scottish judges travelled their circuits in the saddle and even when road-making had so far improved as to permit of wheel traffic, the custom went on, it being thought a part of judicial dignity to "ride the circuit" ' (*The Lairds of Dun*, p.246).

p.313 *Charles Edward Stuart*: (1720–1788), son of James Francis Edward Stuart, grandson of James II; popularly known as 'Bonnie Prince Charlie', or, to his enemies, as 'the Young Pretender'.

the glamour of a manner: 'glamour' here recalls the old Scots meaning of magic or enchantment.

he had extorted the wonder of an east-coast Scotsman by his comprehensive profanity: Suggests that his oaths were impressive, the implication being that east-coast Scotsmen were not easily shocked.

p.314 *the Pleiades, Taurus, Orion*: The Pleiades is the great cluster of stars in the constellation Taurus, particularly the seven larger ones, so called by the Greeks. Orion is the constellation pictured as a giant hunter with sword and belt, surrounded by his dogs and animals, named after the giant hunter of Greek mythology.

the North Port: The old north entrance or gateway to the town.

stairhead: The landing at the top of a flight of stairs, often that leading from one floor of a building to another.

p.315 *Glenfinnan*: the Stuart standard was raised at Glenfinnan, at the north end of Loch Shiel, on 19 August 1745, over an army of some 1300 clansmen.

Cope: Sir John Cope (?? –1760), the Government commander-in-chief in Scotland, defeated by the Jacobites at the battle of Prestonpans on 21 September 1745.

Lords Elcho, Balmerino, Kilmarnock, Pitsligo: David Wemyss, Lord Elcho (1721–1787), Commander of Prince Charles' Life Guards; Arthur Elphinstone, Lord Balmerino (1688–1746); William Boyd, 4th Earl of Kilmarnock (1704–1746); Alexander Forbes, Lord Pitsligo (1678–1762). Pitsligo remained in hiding for many years; Balmerino and Kilmarnock were beheaded after the Act of Attainder was passed in June 1746.

Lord George Murray: (1694–1760), Lieutenant-General of the Jacobite army.

p.316 *the landing of those French supplies*: At this point the French were still supporting the Stuart cause, although their ships had difficulty in bringing the aid needed. See Frank McLynn, *France and the Jacobite Rising of* 1745, Chapter V, especially pp.109–112.

p.317 *David Ferrier*: 'Ferrier was a merchant of Brechin, who owned the farm of Unthank in the neighbourhood', according to *The Lairds of Dun* (p.250); he was made Deputy-Governor of Brechin, and 'it is said that the Prince did this on the advice of James' (p.250), i.e. James Erskine, the model for James Logie.

Lord Ogilvie: David, Lord Ogilvy, titular Earl of Airlie (1725–1803), a Jacobite who fought with Prince Charles at Derby, Falkirk and Culloden.

the village of Edzell: Edzell is a parish in the north east of Angus, in which is situated the village, known for its castle. Beyond it lies Glen Esk.

The government sloop-of-war Venture: Modelled on a vessel

in reality called the *Hazard* which was, according to McLynn (1981), 'one of the very few maritime successes gained by the Prince's followers' (p.387). It was later renamed 'Le Prince Charles', for obvious reasons. For a full account of the events fictionally narrated here, see *The Lairds of Dun*, pp.249–257.

fishing village of Ferryden: Now more developed.

p.318–19 *the New Wynd . . . the Happy Land*: Real places in Montrose, the former still there in modern times. According to a review of *Flemington* in the *Montrose Standard and Angus and Mearns Register* 26 January 1912, p.12, 'There are local names and references that will strike strange chords in the hearts of the score of centenarians still surviving in Montrose, such, for example, as that famous residence in the New Wynd, so appropriately and satirically designated by our pious forefathers as "The Happy Land".'

p.323 *campaigning by the walls of Dantzig*: Probably with Field Marshall Lacy (see also note to page 338), who, commanding Russian troops in January 1734 in Danzig, besieged Stanislas, a contender for the Polish throne, on behalf of the claimant who later became Augustus III, after the death of Augustus II in 1733.

Inchbrayock Island: The name of a real place, from the Gaelic *Inchbraoch*; more commonly known today as Rossie Island. A church or chapel formerly stood on this piece of land, which was also the parish burial ground.

p.326 *'risp', or tirling pin*: A vertical serrated bar fixed on the door of a house, up and down which a ring is drawn with a grating noise, acting as a door-knocker or bell.

p.331 *the parks*: The enclosed grounds of the estate; 'parks' can also denote 'fields' or 'farmlands'.

p.335 *the unsuccessful rising of the '15*: The Jacobite rising of 1715 which was a failure. The Earl of Mar, John Erskine (who drew up original plans for the House of Dun) proved a vacillating and uncertain leader in Scotland, the Battle of Sheriffmuir was inconclusive, and the campaign in England was disastrous.

p.338 *Marshal Lacy . . . War of the Polish Succession*: (see also note to p.323) Peter Lacy (1678–1751), a Russian Field-Marshall. Born in Limerick, he had fought as an Irish Jacobite and in the French service, and entered the service of Czar Peter the Great of Russia around 1698/9. He commanded Russian troops in the War of the Polish Succession, already alluded to, which took place after the death of Augustus II in 1733. Augustus III was recognised in 1735–6.

bloody campaign against the Turks . . . and again in Finland:

The war of Russia and Austria against Turkey took place 1735–9; Russia acquired parts of Finland between 1721 and 1743.

p.339 *Holland with the Scots Brigade*: See note to page 289.
the Dutchmen can paint them too: An allusion to the Dutch skill at painting flowers and still-lifes.

p.340 *Diane . . . The Conte de Montdelys . . . Frenchman*: It is interesting that Diane is French; apart from again reflecting the Scottish-French connection which figures in the novel generally, this may also illustrate a 19th-century association between romance/passion and 'the foreign', especially the French. The setting of the love and marriage of James and Diane in Holland echoes Stevenson, who sets the love interest in *Catriona* in that country.

p.341 *I was a Protestant*: Somewhat unusual for a Jacobite.
a rich Spaniard: Spain controlled parts of the Netherlands (now roughly Belgium and Luxembourg) 1579 to 1713.
Breda a town in Noordbrabant province, south west Netherlands.

p.342 *Bergen-op-Zoom*: A town in Noordbrabant province, south west Netherlands. It was much fought over and came under the control of various powers from the 16th century onwards, including the French and Spanish.

p.350 *Muir of Pert*: Old name for a tract of land in the area of Dun.
Parental authority: See Smout: 'On such things it is always hard to generalise, but people later often referred with wonder to instances of domestic sternness in the early part of the century . . .' (p.269). Also: 'Marjorie Plant has produced a certain amount of evidence to show that child-rearing in the upper classes became less authoritarian in the course of the eighteenth century, but she believes it was still stricter in the first half of the century in Scotland than in England' (pp.92–3).
feu sacré: sacred fire (French).

p.357 *the Queen and her favourite, Lady Despard*: Lady Despard seems to be a fictional creation of Violet Jacob's; she may be based on such historical figures as the Duchess of Powis who was 'among the most faithful of the Queen's ladies, and was greatly in her confidence. Burnet describes her as "a zealous managing Papist" ' (Edwin and Marion Sharpe Grew *The English Court in Exile: James II at Saint-Germain* (London: Mills & Boon, 1911), p.270); she died, however, in 1691. Other possible models for this character are Lady Middleton and Lady Melfort, both Irish ladies at the Court of St Germain. Many Irish Jacobites did, in fact, flee to St

Germain for refuge after the fall of Limerick.

p.359 *Christian's affinity with savage creatures* . . .: This implies a view not unlike Stevenson's as suggested in, for instance, *Dr Jekyll and Mr Hyde*, of the closeness of the civilized and the 'savage'. The influence of Darwin may show here.

p.361 *Magdalen Chapel*: A burial place at the eastern end of the parish of Brechin.

p.363 *the tune of the East Neuk of Fife*: Popular Scottish dance tune named after the so-called 'East Neuk' of Fife; 'neuk' can mean either 'corner' or 'projecting point of land'.

p.364 *the passion for dancing*: Dancing in this period was denounced by the General Assembly of the Church of Scotland, along with sabbath-breaking and merriment at weddings and funerals (see Smout, p.214). In Scott's *The Heart of Midlothian*, Effie Deans defies her father and the Cameronian community by taking pleasure in dancing. In many modern Scottish novels dancing appears to suggest, amongst other things, the enduring nature of traditional culture; see, for instance, Catherine Carswell *Open the Door!* (1920), Lewis Grassic Gibbon, *Sunset Song* (1932), Jessie Kesson *Another Time, Another Place* (1983) among others.

p.370 *Brechin* . . . *its ancient round tower*: Brechin is one of the oldest towns and ecclesiastical centres in Scotland. The round tower stands at the south-west corner of the Cathedral; it is reputed to have been built in the late 10th-century, and is of Christian Irish origin.

p.371 *'Dinna bring yon brute near me!' cried Wattie*: Wattie's fear of the horse is ironically significant given the nature of his fate (see pp.480–2).

p.372 *Captain Hall*: According to *The Lairds of Dun*, the commander of the boat in the historical incident was one Captain Hill.

p.384 *Dial Hill*: A real place mentioned by Jacob also in *The Lairds of Dun*, p.253.

p.399 *a French frigate*: According to *The Lairds of Dun*, this was 'La Fère'.

p.401 *Leith*: The port serving Edinburgh.
       Aberbrothock: An old name for the town of Arbroath; 'Aber' means 'at the mouth of', while 'Brothock' is the name of the river which enters the sea at this place.

p.404 *Skirling Wattie* . . . *spirit of the national poetry of Scotland*: A figure akin to Wandering Willie in *Redgauntlet*, Madge Wildfire in *The Heart of Midlothian*, Edie Ochiltree in *The Antiquary*, and numerous other characters in Scott's novels.

p.411 *Monrummon Moor*: Montreathmont Moor on the modern map, referred to here by the common local name.

p.423 *Wattie Caird*: 'Caird' is a surname; it also means 'tinker, vagrant'.

p.424 *Forfar*: Small market town in Angus, south west of Brechin, and in the eighteenth century a royal burgh of considerable antiquity. It was the capital of the county of Angus, which was also known as Forfarshire.

the muir o' Rossie: Rossie Muir (or moor) is an area of land lying to the south west of Montrose Basin.

p.427 *he might have sung 'The Tod'*: This song would have had more relevance to the situation, or at least appealed more to Madam Flemington, herself a schemer.

p.427-8 *My love stood at the loanin' side*: This appears with the title 'The Jacobite Lass' in Jacob's *Songs of Angus* (1915).

p.430 *the Old Town of Edinburgh*: The area of the city stretching from the Castle down the Royal Mile to Holyrood Palace. Plans for the 'New Town' were already afoot in the first half of the 18th century, but building did not begin until later in the century.

the Nor' Loch: The North Loch, artificially created in 1460, was partly drained in 1763, and filled in, forming what is now Princes Street Gardens.

Lady Anne Maxwell . . . his kinswoman: This character does not seem to be based on any particular individual in Violet Jacob's own family history, but may draw on other 18th-century figures.

lands: Tenement buildings, often many storeys high.

p.431 *Lord Grange*: James Erskine, Lord Grange (1679-1754), a kinsman of David Erskine of Dun, secretly intrigued with Jacobites though professing loyalty to the Hanoverian dynasty.

p.432 *Lord John Drummond's troops*: Lord John Drummond (1715-47) was the brother of the Duke of Perth. He was sent by Louis XV to Scotland with his Scots Royal regiment and arrived on the east coast in early December 1745.

girls wore white roses: The white rose was a Jacobite emblem.

p.437 *Mrs Cockburn*: Possibly based on Alison Cockburn (1712?-1794), best known for the words of one version of the song 'The Flowers of the Forest'. Of the Rutherford family of Selkirkshire, she moved to Edinburgh and married an advocate, Patrick Cockburn. She was related to, and friendly with, Walter Scott, and counted other outstanding writers and thinkers among her circle. Described by Scott as having 'talents for conversation', she supported the Whig government in the 1745 Rebellion.

p.446 *Hyndford's Close*: The name of a narrow passage giving entrance to a tenement at 34 High Street (south side), in Edinburgh. In 1742 the home of the Earl of Selkirk was here.

p.451 *Culloden*: The Jacobites, led by Prince Charles Edward Stuart, were defeated disastrously in the Battle of Culloden at Drummossie Moor, on 16 April 1746, by government troops under the command of the Duke of Cumberland. According to Ferguson, 'Much more than Jacobitism died at Culloden. Thereafter the disintegration of the old Highland society, already advanced in some quarters, was accelerated' (p.154).

Cumberland's soldiers: William Augustus, Duke of Cumberland (1721–65), third son of King George II, commander of the army which defeated the Jacobites at Culloden.

the country smelt of blood: Atrocities were committed against many fleeing Jacobites and Highlanders after Culloden by both English and Scottish soldiers. There were also high-level reprisals, with many Jacobite leaders being executed. See Petrie, pp.392–401.

p.452 *Kingston's Horse*: Cavalry regiment.

John Campbell of Mamore: John Campbell, 4th Earl of Loudoun (1705–1782) supported George II in the Highlands, 1745–6. The Campbells as a clan were strong Whig supporters.

p.453 *Ruthven, in Badenoch*: Those at Ruthven included Lord George Murrary, the Duke of Perth and Lord John Drummond. See Petrie, pp.388–91.

p.455 *Highland army's retreat to Scotland*: The shift of focus here to Christian Flemington is accompanied by a jump back in time to before Culloden: having reached Derby in December 1745, with the intention of conquering England, Prince Charles, the Jacobite leaders and their Highland army turned back, doubting support from English Jacobites and the French.

the Battle of Falkirk: Having laid siege to Stirling Castle, a Jacobite army led by Prince Charles clashed with government troops under General Henry Hawley at Falkirk and defeated them.

the despatch of the Duke of Cumberland to the North: After the Battle of Falkirk, Cumberland went north to take over from Hawley.

p.458 *battle of Falkirk and the siege of Stirling Castle*: See note to p.455.

p.459 *Glen Esk . . . Loch Lee*: Glen Esk lies in the large northern Angus parish of Lochlee, which derives its name from a loch in its western end. The area is Highland in character, surrounded by the Grampian mountains and 'Braes of Angus'.

No place had a darker record: During the 1745 Glenesk was a Jacobite stronghold. The leading Jacobite Ferrier, based here, raised over 200 men in the surrounding glens; in response Cumberland sent a force of 300 men who were only just dissuaded from burning the Glen entirely. After Culloden, Government troops searched the area for Jacobite fugitives.

p.460   *Ligonier's regiment*: Jean-Louis Ligonier, British government Field Marshal (1680–1770), born in France, went to Dublin 1697; fought many battles, including Blenheim (1704) under Marlborough.

p.462   *Glen Clova from Braemar*: Glen Clova is another of the Angus glens. A pass leads over the hills from here to the town of Braemar in Deeside.

the little German general: Cumberland, as 'this fat young third son of George II' (David Daiches *Charles Edward Stuart: The Life and Times of Bonnie Prince Charlie* (first publ. London: Thames & Hudson, 1973; ref. here to pbk. ed., Pan, 1975, p.185)), came of the royal House of Hanover, and was thus of German origin.

p.464   *Huntly Hill*: Name of an actual hill, so-called because Alexander Gordon, Early of Huntly, won a battle here in the 15th century.

p.472   *King Geordie's business*: i.e., King George II (reigned 1727–1760).

p.475   *dancin' wi' George, but he's takin' the tune frae Chairlie*: i.e., appearing to act for King George II, but working for Prince Charles Edward Stuart.

p.480   *the beggar . . . his dislike and fear of horses*: Besides the obvious explanation for Wattie's fear, there is perhaps a symbolic dimension; the horse in Christian art is held to represent courage and generosity.

p.481   *the dog the outcast of the East*: Violet Jacob had lived in India from 1895 to about 1900, and knew that dogs there and in some other countries were often scavengers of the streets who struggled for survival, but were held in contempt.

p.489   *you mighty hunter before the Lord*: Nimrod was so called; see Genesis 10.9. The meaning seems to be 'a conqueror'.

p.494   *Peterhead*: Fishing port on the east coast of Scotland, north of Aberdeen.

p.497   *But you have not restrained your belongings*: Christian means Balnillo's family, i.e. James.

p.503   *the Duke of Cumberland*: See note to p.451.

Holyrood House: At one time residence of Scottish royalty, in Edinburgh; subsequently the official Scottish residence of British royalty. Cumberland did, in fact, stay here at this time.

sick of Scotland: On leaving his command in Scotland in July 1746, Cumberland expressed his feelings toward Scotland in a letter to the Duke of Newcastle:

> I am sorry to leave this country in the condition it is for all the good that we have done has been a bloodletting, which has only weakened the madness, but not at all used [it up] and I tremble for fear that this vile spot may still be the ruin of this island and of our family.

Quoted by Alexander Murdoch, *The People Above: Politics and Administration in Mid-Eighteenth Century Scotland* (Edinburgh: John Donald, 1980), p.35.

p.506 *the mists of the Edinburgh smoke*: Edinburgh became known in the eighteenth century as 'Auld Reekie' (Old Smoky).

p.507 *I hate old women*: According to Bruce Lenman in *The Jacobite Cause* (Glasgow: Richard Drew, 1986), 'Duncan Forbes of Culloden ... had earned the epithet of "old woman" from Cumberland for urging that royal brute to show clemency in his hour of victory ...' (p.116).

p.515 *pollarded beech*: Beech tree that has been cropped, had its top cut off. The image recalls that of the maimed beech-tree at Balnillo near the beginning of the novel. In the second edition of 1915 this has been changed to a lime-tree; perhaps Jacob wants to emphasise the different location of Holland at the end.

the ace scrawled with the picture of the sentry: The drawing has various kinds of significance. The playing card suggests the role of 'Chance'; the ace, of course, is usually a winning card, so that there is a sad irony here.

Glossary

THE FOLLOWING lists words mainly in Scots; most lexical items and forms that might be unfamiliar have been explained, even at risk of obviousness. The primary works consulted are:

Mairi Robinson (ed.), *The Concise Scots Dictionary* (Aberdeen: Aberdeen University Press, 1985). Reference to the edition of 1987; *The Scottish National Dictionary*, 10 vols, eds William Grant (1929–46) and David Murison (1946–76) (Edinburgh: The Scottish National Dictionary Association Ltd).

a in places denotes 'I'
a'body everybody
aboon, abune above
aboot about
ach exclamation expressing impatience, contempt, remonstrance etc.
ae a certain; the same
a'thing everything
aff off
afore before
agin against
aheid ahead
ahint behind
aichty eighty
aifter after
airly early
amang(st) among(st)
ane one
angert angered
anither another
'apple-ringie' southernwood

aucht aught, anything else
auld old
awa' away
aweel expression used to introduce a remark
awfae awful
ay(e) yes
aye all; always
bairn child
baith both
bannock a round flat cake usually made of oatmeal, barleymeal or peasemeal, baked on a griddle (iron plate for baking over fire)
bauld bold, brave
bawbee a coin
beddit bedded, put to bed
ben inside; in or towards the inner part of a house
besom term of contempt (esp. for a woman)

bide remain, stay, await

billy close friend, comrade

billies fellows, lads

bittie a little bit, bit of

bizzar loud-tongued person (see notes to 'The Fifty-Eight Wild Swans')

blethers talk, nonsense

boab bob, a shilling, i.e. money

boattle bottle

bocht bought

body person

bonnie fine, handsome

bothy (pl. bothies) living quarters of unmarried male farmworkers

brae bank, hillside

braw fine, splendid

braw bittie considerable amount

breeks trousers

breith breath

brig bridge

brither brother

brocht brought

broun brown

bubblyjock turkey-cock

burn stream

ca' pull, call

ca awa' keep going

ca'ed off removed

caird tinker, vagrant

callant fellow

cam' came

cankered ill-tempered

canna cannot

canny careful(ly); cautious(ly)

carle man, fellow

cattle can denote birds and beasts in general, as well as cows

causeys paved areas, streets

chanter double-reeded pipe on which

bagpipe melody is played

chapper knocker

claes clothes

clap close, slam

clortie dirty, muddy

close entry to a tenement; the passageway giving access to the common stair

clour blow

clout piece of doth, a rag

contentit contented

coont count

coorse rough; (of weather) foul, stormy

coortin' courting

corp corpse

coup (verb) to upset, overturn

couthy, couthier (more) agreeable; comfortable

cowp to fall over, capsize; upset, overturn

crack talk, converse, gossip

crater, cratur' creature

craw crow

cried in the kirk to have marriage banns proclaimed

cry on to call on (e.g. for help); summon

cuppie cup (of)

cutty disobedient, mischievous girl or woman

dae(in') do(ing)

daft crazy, insane

dairk dark

daur'd na, daurna dared not, dare not

dawmed damned

deave provoke, goad; annoy with noise or talk; perhaps also 'drive'

dee die

deef deaf

deevil devil

deid dead

deil devil

denner dinner, a meal

denty dainty

dicht wipe, rub clean

didna did not

dinna don't

disna does not

deuk duck

dirk small Highland dagger

div do

doag dog

dod an interjection, exclamation

doited foolish, silly

done exhausted, past it

doon down

doot lit. doubt; believe

doups buttocks

dram small drink of liquor

drappie little drop of

drooned drowned

drouth thirst

dune done, exhausted, past it

dunt knock, blow

dyke wall

eneuch enough

fa' fall

fair disgustit absolutely or simply disgusted

fairly demented quite mad

fairm farm

fash bother (oneself)

feared o' afraid of

feared for afraid for

fechtin' fighting

fegs emphatic exclamation: 'indeed!'

fell fierce, ruthless, remarkable; extremely, very

feuch! exclamation of disgust, pain or impatience

feyther father

fine very, well

fine an' pleased very pleased

fine an' glad very glad

fit foot

fleg, fleggit fright, frightened

folla follow

foo how

forbye besides, in addition

forrit forward (*get forrit* go forward)

fou full, drunk

fower four

fowk folk

frae from

freend(s) friend(s)

freish fresh

fufty-aicht fifty-eight

fule; fulishness fool; foolishness

fushionless lacking ability or vigour, spiritless

fut foot

gait way, manner

gang on wi' go on with

gar, gar'd make, made

gey an' rather, very

gie, gied give, gave

gloamin' twilight, dusk

goon gown

gowk fool, simpleton

grat cried, wept

greeting cry(ing)

grieve head workman on farm, overseer, farm bailiff

gude sakes for goodness sake

guid good

guidit guided

guidwife mistress of a house or place

haar cold mist or fog (esp. east coast sea fog)

hae exclamation; have

haena, ha'na have not

hairm harm

hakes hooks

hale whole

hame home

haste ye hurry

haud hold, keept

haud awa' keep away

haud yer whisht be quiet, hold your tongue

haund hand

haun'lt handled

havena have not

haver (ing) speak(ing) nonsense; talking in a foolish way

havers nonsense

heed, heid head

henches haunches

heuch exclamation, e.g. of impatience

hizzy hussy

hoose, hoosies (small) houses

hoots exclamation expressing dissent, impatience etc.

howkit dug

hurl move (on wheels)

hurley cart

huts! exclamation

ilka every

ill lad wicked, difficult, hostile fellow

impidence impudence

in-by in (e.g., *come inby* to come from outside to inside)

intill into

I'se first person emphatic present form

is she she is (indeed)

ither other (*ither body* anybody else)

iver ever

jalouse to suppose, suspect

jist just

kaipit met

keek glance, peep

ken/kent know, knew

kennel channel, street gutter

kerrage carriage

kirk church

kirkton town or village in which the parish church is situated

kirkyard churchyard

kyte stomach

lairn learn, teach

lairned taught

lands tenements

lane (e.g. *her lane*) alone

lang long

lauch laugh

leddy, Leddyship lady, Ladyship

lee, leein', leear lie, lying, liar

licht light

liket liked

limmer loose or disreputable woman; general term of abuse

loan part of farm ground, farm track

loanin' part of farm ground or roadway; milking place, common ground; grassy track

lookit looked

loon, loonie young lad, fellow

losh interjection

loss, lossin' lose, losing

loup leap, spring, hop about

lugs ears

ma my

mair more

maircy, maircies mercy, mercies

married upon married to

maun must

mauna must not

maun hae tae gang on have to, must go on

mebbe maybe

meenit minute

merriet married

micht might, may

michtna might not

michty me expression of surprise or exasperation

min man
mind (of) remember
mirk darkness, twilight
mischieve mischief
mither mother
mony many
morn, the tomorrow
morn's morn tomorrow
  morning
mou' mouth
muckle big, great; much
muir(land) moor(land)
murder't murdered
na no
nae not
naebody nobody
nae mair no more, no longer
naething nothing
nae use ava till no use
  at all to
nane none
narra narrow
near doon nearly down
needna need not
nicht night; *the nicht* tonight
niver never
noo, the now, just now
nor than
ony any
ony ither body anybody else
onything anything
oor our
oot out
oot-by out(side); away from
owre over
noo now
oxter armpit
pairish parish
pechin' puffing, wheezing
peewee lapwing
piece piece of food, snack,
  e.g., bread
pit put
pit aboot distressed, upset
pit by a bittie saved a
  little money

plaid woollen cloth (often
  tartan) worn as outer
  garment
poke bag, pouch
pollis police
poupit pulpit
poupit owre dropped over
pouthered powdered
pow head
presairv's preserve us
pridefu' snobbish, arrogant
pruifs proofs
pucklie a small amount, a
  little
puir poor
pushon poison
rashes rushes
recht right
reddit up cleared up,
  sorted out
reelin' playing or dancing
  reels
reid red
respec'it respected
richt right
rin run
roastit roast, roasted
roof-tree main beam or ridge
  of a house; figuratively,
  house or home
roogit pulled
roug pull, tug
sabbin' sobbing
saft soft
sair sore; hard, harsh
sang song
Sawbaths Sabbaths
saxteen sixteen
saxty sixty
scabbit scabbed
schule school
sconce screen
set suit, look becoming in
shaws stalks and leaves
shelt shelty, pony
shieling roughly-made

hut, hovel, small house

shoppie (small) shop

sic such

sic a deal such a lot, so much

sicht sight

siller silver; money

skailed dismissed, broken up, dispersed

skelloch shriek, scream, cry

skirlin' (making a) shrill sound

sma' small

smiddy, smithy blacksmith's

sodgers soldiers

soond sound

soucht sought, looked for

soutars shoemakers, cobblers

spate flood, sudden rise of water

speer, speir for ask about

speer(in) ask(ing)

stackyard rickyard

stairve starve

stane stone

stap stop

stock(s) chap(s), bloke(s)

stoot stout

(the) streen yesterday (evening); last night

stude stood

sune soon

suppie little drink of

swampit swamped

sweer unwilling, reluctant

sweit sweat

swiggit go with a swinging motion, rock, jog

syne directly after, next, afterwards; since; ago

tae to

tae ye for you

ta'en taken

ta'en up emotional, worked up (adjective)

tak take

tapsalteerie upside-down, topsy-turvy

tattie (lifting) (lifting, digging up) potatoes

tawpie giddy, careless young woman

tell't, tellt told

terrible terribly

thegither together

they folk those people

thocht thought

thole suffer, endure, tolerate

thraw throw

thrawn perverse, stubborn

ticht tight

till to, for

tither the other

tod fox

tolbooth town prison

toom empty

toon town

toots, no! exclamation (see Tuts!)

towmont two months

traivellin', traivelt travelling, travelled

treid tread

Tuts! interjection suggesting expostulation or disapproval; 'nonsense!'

twa two

tynt lost

unchancy dangerous, threatening

unkent unknown

vera' very

wa' wall

wad would

wadna would not

waefu' woeful

wag-at-the-wa' clock unencased pendulum clock

wantin' lacking, without

wantin' ye lacking, without you

warld world

warna were not

warst worst

wasna was not

wastit wasted

waur (nor) worse (than)

wean(s) child(ren)

weel well

weepies weebies, or common ragwort

weicht weight, amount

wha who

what ails ye at me? what objection have you to me?

what for no? why not?

whatlike what sort of

what way why

whaup curlew

whaur where

(a) wheen siller a bit of silver (money)

wheeps; e.g. gie ye yer wheeps give you a whipping

whiles sometimes

whisht be quiet! shut up!

whummled tumbled

whuskey whisky

whustlin' whistling

wi with

widdie widow

wifie woman

wiggie wig

win doon get down

win in get in

win up the stair get up, manage to climb the stairs

winna will not

wrang wrong

wrocht looked after

wull will, way

wull a be tae . . . ? should I?

wumman woman

wurk work

wynd narrow (often winding) street, lane

ye you

ye'll no can you won't be able to

yella yellow

yer your

yersel' yourself

yestreen yesterday

yon that or those (over there)

yowe ewe, female sheep

Other Books by Violet Jacob

The Baillie MacPhee (a poem), by Walter Douglas Campbell
and Violet Kennedy-Erskine (William Blackwood, Edinburgh and London, 1888), with illustrations by Violet
Kennedy-Erskine.

The Sheepstealers (William Heinemann, London, 1902),
a novel.

The Infant Moralist (verses), by Lady Helena Carnegie and
Mrs Arthur Jacob (R. Grant and Son, Edinburgh, and
R. Brimley Johnson, London, 1903), with illustrations
by Mrs Arthur Jacob.

The Interloper (William Heinemann, London, 1904), a
novel.

The Golden Heart and Other Fairy Stories (William Heinemann, London, 1904).

Verses (William Heinemann, London, 1905).

Irresolute Catherine (John Murray, London, 1908), a novel.

The History of Aythan Waring (William Heinemann,
London, 1908), a novel.

Stories Told by the Miller (John Murray, London, 1909),
for children.

The Fortune Hunters and Other Stories (John Murray,
London, 1910).

Flemington (John Murray, London, 1911), a novel.

Flemington was also published in the Association for Scottish
Literary Studies series in 1994

Songs of Angus (John Murray, London, 1915), poems.

More Songs of Angus and Others (Country Life/George
Newnes, London, and Charles Scribner's Sons, New
York, 1918), poems.

Bonnie Joann and Other Poems (John Murray, London,
1921).

Tales of My Own Country (John Murray, London, 1922).

Two New Poems: 'Rohallion' and 'The Little Dragon' (Porpoise Press, Edinburgh, 1924).

The Northern Lights and Other Poems (John Murray, London, 1927).

The Good Child's Year Book (Foulis, London, 1928), with illustrations by Violet Jacob.

The Lairds of Dun (John Murray, London, 1931), a history of the Erskine family.

The Scottish Poems of Violet Jacob (Oliver & Boyd, Edinburgh, 1944).

The Lum Hat and Other Stories: Last Tales of Violet Jacob, edited by Ronald Garden (Aberdeen University Press, Aberdeen, 1982).

Diaries and Letters from India 1895–1900, edited by Carol Anderson (Canongate, Edinburgh, 1990).

'Thievie', a story from *Tales of My Own Country* is reprinted in Moira Burgess (ed.), *The Other Voice: Scottish Women's Writing Since 1808* (Polygon, Edinburgh, 1987), pp.123–39.

There are also stories and articles in journals.